THE PRISONER'S THRONE

BY HOLLY BLACK

NOVELS OF ELFHAME

The Stolen Heir Duology

The Stolen Heir
The Prisoner's Throne

The Folk of the Air

The Cruel Prince
The Wicked King
The Queen of Nothing
How the King of Elfhame Learned to Hate Stories

The Darkest Part of the Forest

The Coldest Girl in Coldtown

THE PRISONER'S THRONE

A NOVEL OF ELFHAME

HOLLY BLACK

LITTLE, BROWN AND COMPANY

NEW YORK   BOSTON

Little, Brown and Company
Hachette Book Group
1290 Avenue of the Americas, New York, NY 10104
Visit us at LBYR.com

First Edition: March 2024
Simultaneously published in 2024 by Hot Key Books in the United Kingdom

Little, Brown and Company is a division of Hachette Book Group, Inc.
The Little, Brown name and logo are registered trademarks of Hachette Book Group, Inc.

The publisher is not responsible for websites (or their content) that are not owned by the publisher.

Little, Brown and Company books may be purchased in bulk for business, educational, or promotional use. For information, please contact your local bookseller or the Hachette Book Group Special Markets Department at special.markets@hbgusa.com.

Library of Congress Cataloging-in-Publication Data
Names: Black, Holly, author. | Black, Holly. Stolen heir
Title: The prisoner's throne : a novel of Elfhame / Holly Black.
Description: First edition. | New York : Little, Brown and Company, 2024. |
Series: The stolen heir ; 2 | Audience: Ages 14+ | Summary: "Prince Oak must find a way to stop a war between Elfhame and the north." —Provided by publisher.
Identifiers: LCCN 2023043868 | ISBN 9780316592710 (hardcover) |
ISBN 9780316592734 (ebook)
Subjects: CYAC: Fantasy. | Wars—Fiction. | Kings, queens, rulers, etc.—Fiction. | LCGFT: Fantasy fiction. | Novels.
Classification: LCC PZ7.B52878 Pr 2024 | DDC [E]— dc23
LC record available at https://lccn.loc.gov/2023043868

ISBNs: 978-0-316-59271-0 (hardcover), 978-0-316-59273-4 (ebook), 978-0-316-57588-1 (int'l), 978-0-316-56930-9 (B&N exclusive edition), 978-0-316-57888-2 (large print)

Printed in Indiana, USA

LSC-C

Printing 5, 2024

For Joanna Volpe, who is, as her last name
suggests, every bit the charming and tricksy fox

I MET the Love-Talker one eve in the glen,

He was handsomer than any of our handsome young men,

His eyes were blacker than the sloe, his voice sweeter far

Than the crooning of old Kevin's pipes beyond in Coolnagar.

I was bound for the milking with a heart fair and free—

My grief! my grief! that bitter hour drained the life from me;

I thought him human lover, though his lips on mine were cold,

And the breath of death blew keen on me within his hold.

I know not what way he came, no shadow fell behind,

But all the sighing rushes swayed beneath a faery wind

The thrush ceased its singing, a mist crept about,

We two clung together—with the world shut out.

—Ethna Carbery,
"The Love-Talker"

SIX WEEKS BEFORE
IMPRISONMENT

Oak jammed his hooves into velvet pants.

"Have I made you late?" Lady Elaine asked from the bed, her voice full of wicked satisfaction. She propped up her head with an elbow and gave a little laugh. "It won't be too much longer before you don't have to do anything at their beck and call."

"Yes," Oak said, distracted. "Only yours, right?"

She laughed again.

Doublet only half-buttoned, he tried desperately to remember the fastest route to the gardens. He'd *meant* to be punctual, but then the opportunity to finally see the scope of the treasonous plot he'd been pursuing had presented itself.

I promise I will introduce you to the rest of my associates, she'd told him, her fingers sliding beneath his shirt, untucking it. *You will be impressed with how close to the throne we can get....*

Cursing himself, the sky, and the concept of time in general, Oak raced out the door.

"Hurry, you scamp," one of the palace laundresses called after him. "It will look ill if they begin without you. And fix your hair!"

He tried to smooth down his curls as servants veered out of his way. In the palace of Elfhame, no matter how tall he grew, Oak was forever the mischievous, wild-haired boy who coaxed guards into playing conkers with horse chestnuts and stole honey cakes from the kitchens. Faerie caught its inhabitants in amber, so if they were not careful, a hundred years might pass in the lazy blink of an eye. And so, few noticed how much the prince had changed.

Not that he didn't resemble his younger self right then, pelting down another corridor, hooves clattering against stone. He dodged left to avoid running into a page with an armful of scrolls, wove right so as not to knock over a small table with an entire tea tray atop it, then almost slammed into Randalin, an elderly member of the Living Council.

By the time he made it to the gardens, Oak was out of breath. Panting, he took in the garlands of flowers and musicians, the courtiers and revelers. No High King or Queen yet. That meant he had a chance to make his way to the front with no one the wiser.

But before he could slip into the crowd, his mother, Oriana, grabbed hold of his sleeve. Her expression was stern, and since her skin was usually ghostly white, it was easy to see the flush of anger in her cheeks. It pinked them so they matched the rosy color of her eyes.

"Where have you been?" Her fingers went to Oak's doublet, fixing his buttons.

"I lost track of time," he admitted.

"Doing what?" She dusted off the velvet. Then she licked her finger and rubbed a smudge on Oak's nose.

He grinned at her fondly, letting her fuss. If she thought of him as barely more than a boy, then she wouldn't look more deeply into any trouble he made for himself. His gaze went to the crowd, looking for his guard. Tiernan was going to be angry when he understood Oak's plan in full. But flushing out a conspiracy would be worth it. And Lady Elaine had been *so close* to telling him the names of the other people involved.

"We'd better head toward the dais," he told Oriana, catching hold of her hand and giving it a squeeze.

She squeezed back, swift and punishingly hard. "You are heir to all of Elfhame," she said as though he might have missed that bit. "It's time to start behaving like someone who could rule. Never forget that you must inspire fear as well as love. Your sister hasn't."

Oak's gaze went to the crowd. He had three sisters, but he knew which one she meant.

He put out his arm, like a gallant knight, and his mother allowed herself to be mollified enough to take it. Oak kept his expression every bit as grave as she could wish. That was easily done, because as he took the first step, the High King and Queen came into view at the edge of the gardens.

His sister Jude was in a gown the color of deep red roses, with high slashes on the sides so that the dress wouldn't restrict her movements. She wore no blade at her waist, but her hair was done up in her familiar horns. Oak was almost certain she hid a small knife in one of them. She would have a few more sewn into her garment and strapped beneath her sleeves.

Despite being the High Queen of Elfhame, with an army at her disposal and dozens of Courts at her command, she still acted as though she'd have to handle every problem herself—and that each one would best be solved through murder.

Beside her, Cardan was in black velvet adorned with even blacker feathers that shone like they'd been dragged through an oil spill, the darkness of his clothes the better to show off the heavy rings shining on his fingers and the large pearl swinging from one of his ears. He winked at Oak, and Oak smiled in return despite his intention to remain serious.

As Oak made his way forward, the crowd parted for him.

His other two sisters were among the throng. Taryn, Jude's twin, had clasped her son tightly by the hand, attempting to distract him from the running around he had probably been doing a moment before. Beside her, Vivienne giggled with her partner, Heather. Vivi was pointing to Folk in the audience and whispering into Heather's ear. Despite being the only one of his three sisters who was a faerie, it was Vivi who liked living in Faerie the least. She did, however, still keep up on the gossip.

The High King and Queen moved to stand before their Court, bathed in the light of the setting sun. Jude beckoned to Oak, as they'd practiced. A hush came over the gardens. He glanced to both sides, at the winged pixies and watery nixies, clever hobs and sinister fetches, kelpies and trolls, redcaps stinking of dried blood, silkies and selkies, fauns and brags, lobs and shagfoals, hags and treefolk, knights and winged ladies in tattered dresses. All subjects of Elfhame. All *his* subjects, he supposed, since he was their prince.

Not a one of them afraid of Oak, no matter what his mother hoped.

Not a one afraid, no matter the blood on his hands. That he'd tricked them all so handily frightened even him.

He halted in front of Jude and Cardan and made a shallow bow.

"Let all here bear witness," Cardan began, his gold-rimmed eyes bright, his voice soft but carrying. "That Oak, son of Liriope and Dain of the Greenbriar line, is my heir, and should I pass from this world, he will rule in my place and with my blessing."

Jude bent down to take a circlet of gold from the pillow a goblin page held up to her. Not a crown, but not quite *not* one, either. "Let all here bear witness." Her voice was chilly. She had never been allowed to forget that she was mortal, back when she was a child in Faerie. Now that she was queen, she never let the Folk feel entirely safe around her. "Oak, son of Liriope and Dain of the Greenbriar line, raised by Oriana and Madoc, *my brother*, is my heir, and when I pass from the world, he shall rule in my place and with my blessing."

"Oak," Cardan said. "Will you accept this responsibility?"

No, Oak yearned to say. *There is no need. The both of you will rule forever.*

But he hadn't asked Oak if he *wanted* the responsibility, rather if he would accept it.

His sister had insisted he be formally named heir now that he was of an age when he could rule without a regent. He could have denied Jude, but he owed all his sisters so much that it felt impossible to deny them anything. If one of them asked for the sun, he'd better figure out how to pluck it from the sky without getting burned.

Of course, they'd never ask for that, or anything like it. They wanted him to be safe, and happy, and good. Wanted to give him the world, and yet keep it from hurting him.

Which was why it was imperative they never discovered what he was really up to.

"Yes," Oak said. Perhaps he should make some kind of speech, or do something that would make him seem more suitable to rule, but his mind had gone utterly blank. It must have been enough, though, because a moment later, he was asked to kneel. He felt the cold metal on his brow.

Then Jude's soft lips were against his cheek. "You'll be a great king when you're ready," she whispered.

Oak knew he owed his family a debt so large he would never be able to repay it. As cheers rose all around him, he closed his eyes and promised he would try.

Oak was a living, breathing mistake.

Seventeen years ago, the last High King, Eldred, took the beautiful, honey-tongued Liriope to his bed. Never known for fidelity, he had other lovers, including Oriana. The two might have become rivals, but instead became fast friends, who walked together through the royal gardens, dipped their feet into the Lake of Masks, and spun together through circle dances at revels.

Liriope had one son already, and few faeries are blessed twice with progeny, so she was surprised when she found herself with child again. And conflicted, because she'd had other lovers, too, and knew the father of the child was not Eldred, but his favorite son, Dain.

All his life, Prince Dain had planned to rule Elfhame after his father. He had prepared for it, creating what he called his Court of

Shadows, a group of spies and assassins that answered only to him. And he had sought to hasten his ascension to the throne, poisoning his father by incremental degrees to steal his vitality until he abdicated. So, when Liriope fell pregnant, Dain wasn't going to let his by-blow mess things up.

If Liriope bore Dain's child, and his father discovered it, Eldred might choose one of his other children for an heir. Better both mother and child should die, and Dain's future be assured.

Dain poisoned Liriope while Oak was still in the womb. Blusher mushrooms cause paralysis in small doses. In larger ones, the body slows its movements like a toy with a battery running down, slower and slower until it moves no more. Liriope died, and Oak would have died with her if Oriana hadn't carved him from her friend's body with a knife and her own soft hands.

That's how Oak came into the world, covered in poison and blood. Slashed across the thigh by a too-deep cut from Oriana's blade. Held desperately to her chest to smother his squalling.

No matter how loud he laughed or how merry he made, it would never drown that knowledge.

Oak knew what wanting the throne did to people.

He would never be like that.

After the ceremony, there was, of course, a banquet.

The royal family ate at a long table partially hidden from view beneath the branches of a weeping willow, not far from where the rest of the Court feasted. Oak sat at the right of Cardan, in the place of favor.

His sister Jude, at the opposite head of the table, slumped in her chair. In front of family, she was totally different from the way she was in front of the Folk: a performer offstage, still wearing her costume.

Oriana was put at Jude's right. Also a place of honor, although Oak wasn't sure either of them was particularly happy to have to make conversation with the other.

Oak had an abundance of sisters—Jude, Taryn, Vivi—all of them no more related to him than Oriana or the exiled grand general, Madoc, who had raised them. But they were still his family. The only two people at the entire table who were kin to him by blood were Cardan and the small child squirming in the chair to his right: Leander, Taryn's child with Locke, Oak's half brother.

An assortment of candles covered the table, and flowers had been tied to the hanging branches of the weeping willow, along with gleaming pieces of quartz. They made a beautiful bower. He would have probably appreciated it more had it been in anyone else's honor.

Oak realized he'd been so lost in his thoughts that he'd missed the beginning of a conversation.

"I didn't enjoy being a snake, and yet I appear to be doomed to be reminded of it for all eternity," Cardan was saying, black curls falling across his face. He held a three-pronged fork aloft, as though to emphasize his point. "The excess of songs hasn't helped, nor has their longevity. It's been what? Eight years? Nine? Truly, the celebratory air about the whole business has been excessive. You'd think I never did a more popular thing than sit in the dark on a throne and bite people who annoyed me. I could have always done that. I could do that now."

"Bite people?" echoed Jude from the other end of the table.

Cardan grinned at her. "Yes, if that's what they like." He snapped his teeth at the air as though to demonstrate.

"No one is interested in that," Jude said, shaking her head.

Taryn rolled her eyes at Heather, who smiled and took a sip of wine.

Cardan raised his brows. "I could *try*. A small bite. Just to see if someone would write a song about it."

"So," Oriana said, looking down the table at Oak. "You did very well up there. It made me imagine your coronation."

Vivi snorted delicately.

"I don't want to rule anything, no less Elfhame," Oak reminded her.

Jude kept her face carefully neutral through what appeared to be sheer force of will. "No need to worry. I don't plan on kicking the bucket anytime soon, and neither does Cardan."

Oak turned to the High King, who shrugged elegantly. "Seems hard on pointy boots, kicking buckets."

When Oak was Leander's age, Oriana hadn't wanted him to be king. But the years had made her more ambitious on his behalf. Perhaps she'd even begun to think that Jude had stolen his birthright instead of saved him from it.

He hoped not. It was one thing to flush out plots against the throne, but if he found out his mother was involved in one, he didn't know what he'd do.

Don't make me choose, he thought with a ferocity that unsettled him.

This was a problem that ought to solve itself. Jude was mortal. Mortals conceived children more easily than faeries. If she had a baby, it would supplant his claim to the throne.

Considering that, his gaze went to Leander.

Eight, and adorable, with his father's fox eyes. The same color as

Oak's, amber with a lot of yellow in it. Hair dark as Taryn's. Leander was almost the same age Oak had been when Madoc had schemed to get him the crown of Elfhame. When Oak looked at Leander, he saw the innocence that his sisters and mother must have been trying to protect. It gave him an ugly feeling, something that was anger and guilt and panic all mixed up together.

Leander noticed himself being studied and pulled on Oak's sleeve. "You look bored. Want to play a game?" he asked, harnessing the guile of a child eager to press someone into the service of amusement.

"After dinner," Oak told him with a glance at Oriana, who was already looking rather pained. "Your grandmother will be angry if we make a spectacle of ourselves at the table."

"*Cardan* plays with me," Leander said, obviously well prepared for this argument. "And he's the *High King*. He showed me how to make a bird with two forks and a spoon. Then our birds fought until one fell apart."

Cardan was spectacle incarnate and wouldn't care if Oriana scolded him. Oak could only smile, though. He had often been a child at a table of adults and remembered how dull it had been. He would have loved to fight with silverware birds. "What other games have you played with the king?"

That launched a distractingly long catalog of misbehavior, from tossing mushrooms into cups of wine on the other ends of tables to folding napkins into hats to making awful faces at each other. "And he tells me funny stories about my father, Locke," Leander concluded.

At that, Oak's smile stiffened. He barely remembered Locke. His clearest memories revolved around Locke's wedding to Taryn, and even those were mostly about how Heather had been turned into a cat and got really upset. It had been one of the moments that had made Oak realize that magic wasn't fun for everyone.

On that thought, he looked across the table at Heather, suddenly wanting to reassure himself she was okay. Her hair was in microbraids with strands of vibrant, synthetic pink woven through them. Her dark skin glowed with shimmering pink highlights on her cheeks. He tried to catch her eye, but she was too busy studying a tiny sprite attempting to steal a fig off the center of the table.

His gaze went to Taryn next. Locke's wife and murderer, tucking a lacy napkin into Leander's shirt. It would be no wonder if Heather was nervous to sit at this table. Oak's family was soaked in blood, the lot of them.

"How's Dad?" Jude asked abruptly, raising her eyebrows.

Vivi shrugged and nodded in Oak's direction. He'd been the one to see their father last. In fact, he'd spent a lot of time with their father over the past year.

"Keeping out of trouble," Oak said, hoping it stayed that way.

After dinner, the royal family rejoined the Court. Oak danced with Lady Elaine, who smiled her cat-who-swallowed-a-mouse-and-is-still-hungry smile and whispered in Oak's ear about how she was arranging a meeting in three days' time with some people who believed in "their cause."

"You're certain you can go through with this?" she asked him, breath hot against his neck. Her thick red hair hung down her back in a single wide braid, strands of rubies woven into the plaits. She wore a dress adorned with threads of gold, as though already auditioning to become his queen.

"I've never thought of Cardan as any relation of mine, but I have often resented what he took from me," Oak reassured her. And if he shuddered a little at her touch, she might imagine it was a shudder of passion. "I have been looking for just this opportunity."

And she, misunderstanding in just the way he hoped, smiled against his skin. "And Jude isn't your real sister."

At that, Oak smiled back but made no reply. He knew what she meant, but he could never have agreed.

She departed after the end of the dance, pressing a last kiss on his throat.

He *was* certain he could go through with this. Though it led inexorably to her death and he wasn't at all sure what that meant about him.

He'd done it before. When he glanced around the room, he couldn't help noticing the absence of those whom he'd already manipulated and then betrayed. Members of three conspiracies he'd undone in the past, tricking members into turning against one another—and him. They'd gone to the Tower of Forgetting or the chopping block for those crimes, never even knowing they'd fallen into his trap.

In this garden full of asps, he was a pitcher plant, beckoning them to a tumble. Sometimes there was a part of him that wanted to scream: *Look at me. See what I am. See what I've done.*

As though drawn by self-destructive thoughts, his bodyguard, Tiernan, approached with an accusatory look, brows drawn sharply together. He was dressed in banded leather armor with the crest of the royal family pinning a short cape across one shoulder. "You're making a scandal of yourself."

Conspiracies were often foolish things, wishful thinking combined with a paucity of interesting Court intrigues. Gossip and too much wine and too little sense. But he had a feeling this one was different. "She's arranging the meeting. It's almost over."

Tiernan cut his glance toward the throne and the High King lounging on it. "He knows."

"Knows what?" Oak had a sinking feeling in the pit of his stomach.

"Exactly? I'm not sure. But someone overheard something. The rumor is that you want to put a knife in his back."

Oak scoffed. "He's not going to believe that."

Tiernan gave Oak an incredulous look. "His own brothers betrayed him. He'd be a fool if he didn't."

Oak turned his attention to Cardan again, and this time the High King met his eyes. Cardan's eyebrows rose. There was a challenge in his gaze and the promise of lazy cruelty. *Game on.*

The prince turned away, frustrated. The last thing he wanted was for Cardan to think of him as an enemy. He ought to go to Jude. Try to explain.

Tomorrow, Oak told himself. When it would not spoil her evening. Or the day after next, when it would be too late for her to prevent him from meeting the conspirators, when he still might accomplish what he had hoped. When he learned who was behind the conspiracy. After that, he'd do his usual thing—pretend to panic. Tell the conspirators he wanted out. Give them reason to become afraid he was going to go to the High King and Queen with what he knew.

Attempting *his* murder was what he planned on their going down for, rather than treason. Because multiple attempts on Oak's life allowed him to retain his reputation for fecklessness. No one would guess that he deliberately brought down this conspiracy, leaving him free to do it again.

And Jude wouldn't guess he'd been putting himself in danger, not now and not those other times.

Unless, of course, he had to confess to all of it in order to convince Cardan he wasn't against him. A shudder went through him at the thought of how horrified Jude would be, how upset his whole family would get. His well-being was the thing they all used to justify their own sacrifices, their own losses. *At least Oak was happy, at least Oak had the childhood we didn't, at least Oak...*

Oak bit the inside of his cheek so hard he tasted blood. He needed to make sure his family never truly knew what he'd turned himself into. Once the traitors were caught, Cardan might forget about his suspicions. Maybe nothing needed to be said to anyone.

"Prince!" Oak's friend Vier pulled free from a knot of young courtiers to sling an arm over Oak's shoulder. "There you are. Come celebrate with us!"

Oak pushed his concerns aside with a forced laugh. It was his party, after all. And so he danced under the stars with the rest of the Court of Elfhame. Made merry. Played his part.

A pixie approached the prince, her skin grasshopper green, with wings to match. She brought two friends with her, and they twined their arms around his neck. Their mouths tasted of herbs and wine.

He moved from one partner to another in the moonlight, spinning beneath the stars. Laughing at nonsense.

A sluagh pressed herself to him, her lips stained black. He smiled down at her as they were swept up into another of the circle dances. Her mouth had the sweetness of bruised plums.

"Look at my face and I am someone," she whispered in his ear. "Look at my back and I am no one. What am I?"

"I don't know," Oak admitted, a shiver running between his shoulders.

"Your mirror, Highness," she said, her breath tickling the hairs on his neck.

And then she slipped away.

Hours later, Oak staggered back to the palace, his head hurting and dizziness making his steps uneven. In the mortal world, at seventeen, alcohol was illegal and, by consequence, something you hid. That night, however, he'd been expected to drink with every toast—blood-dark wines, fizzing green ones, and a sweet purple draught that tasted of violets.

Unable to discern whether he already had a hangover, or if something still worse was yet to come once he slept, Oak decided to try to find some aspirin. Vivi had handed a bag from Walgreens to Jude upon their arrival, one which he was almost certain contained painkillers.

He staggered toward the royal chambers.

"What are we doing here, exactly?" Tiernan asked, catching the prince's elbow when he stumbled.

"Looking for a remedy for what ails me," said Oak.

Tiernan, taciturn at the best of moments, only raised a brow.

Oak waved a hand at him. "You may keep your quips—spoken and unspoken—to yourself."

"Your Highness," Tiernan acknowledged, a judgment in and of itself.

The prince gestured toward the guard standing in front of the entrance to Jude and Cardan's rooms—an ogress with a single eye, leather armor, and short hair. "She can look after me from here."

Tiernan hesitated. But he would want to visit Hyacinthe, bored and angry and fomenting escape, as he'd been every night since being bridled. Tiernan didn't like leaving him too long alone for lots of reasons. "If you're sure . . ."

The ogress stood up straighter. "The High Queen is not in residence."

Oak shrugged. "That's okay." It was probably better for him to get the stuff when Jude wasn't there to laugh at the state of him. And while the ogress appeared not to like it, she didn't stop him from walking past her, pushing open one of the double doors, and going inside.

The chambers of the High King and Queen were hung with tapestries and brocades depicting magical forests hiding even more magical beasts, with most surfaces covered in unlit, fat pillar candles. Those would be for his sister, who couldn't see in the dark the way the Folk could.

Oak found the Walgreens bag tossed onto a painted table to one side of the bed. He dumped the contents onto the elaborately embroidered blanket thrown across a low couch.

There were, in fact, three bottles of store-brand ibuprofen. He opened one, stuck his thumb through the plastic seal, and fished out three gelcaps.

There was a castle alchemist he could go to who would give him a terrible-tasting potion if he was really hurting, but Oak didn't want to be prodded, nor make conversation while the cure was prepared. He tossed the pills back and dry-swallowed them.

Now what he needed was a lot of water and his bed.

Swaying a little, he started shoving the contents back into the bag. As he did, he noticed a packet of pills in a paper sleeve. Curious, he turned it over and then blinked down in surprise that it was a prescription. Birth control.

Jude was only twenty-six. Lots of twenty-six-year-olds didn't want kids yet. Or at all.

Of course, most of them didn't have to secure a dynasty.

Most weren't worried about cutting their little brother out of the line of succession, either. He hoped he wasn't the reason she was taking these. But even if he wasn't the only reason, he couldn't help thinking he was in the mix.

And on that dismal thought, he heard steps in the hall. Cardan's familiar drawling voice carried, although he couldn't make out the words.

Panicking, Oak shoved the rest of the drugstore stuff back into the bag, flung it onto the table, and then scrambled beneath. The door opened a moment later. Cardan's pointy boots clacked on the tiles, followed by Jude's soft tread.

As soon as Oak's belly hit the dusty floor, he realized how foolish he was being. Why hide, when neither Jude nor Cardan would have been angry to find him there? It was his own shame at invading his sister's privacy. Guilt and wine had combined to make him absurd. Yet he would be even more absurd if he emerged now, so he rested next to an abandoned slipper and hoped they left again before he sneezed.

His sister sat on one of the couches with a vast sigh.

"We cannot ransom him," Cardan said softly.

"I know that," Jude snapped. "I am the one who sent him into exile. I *know* that."

Were they speaking of his father? And ransom? Oak had been with them most of the night, and no mention had been made of this. But who else had she exiled that she would care enough to want to ransom? Then he remembered Jude's question at dinner. Perhaps she hadn't been asking after Madoc at all. Perhaps she'd been trying to determine whether any of them knew something.

Cardan sighed. "Let it be some comfort that we don't have what Lady Nore wants, even should we allow ourselves to be blackmailed."

Jude opened something out of the line of Oak's sight. He crawled a little to get a better angle and see the box of woven branches she had in her hand. Tangled in her fingers was a chain, strung with a glass orb. Inside it, something rolled restlessly. "The message speaks of Mellith's heart. Some ancient artifact? I think she looks for an excuse to hold him."

"If I didn't know better, I might think this is your brother's fault," Cardan said in a teasing tone, and Oak almost banged his head against the wood frame of the table in surprise at hearing himself referenced. "First, he wanted you to be nice to that little queen with the sharp teeth and the crazy eyes. Then he wanted you to forgive that former falcon his bodyguard likes for trying to murder me. It seems too great a coincidence that Hyacinthe came from Lady Nore, spent time with Madoc, and had no hand in his abduction."

Those words were laced with suspicion, although Cardan was smiling. His mistrust hardly mattered beside the danger their father was in, though.

"Oak got mixed up with the wrong people, that's all," Jude said wearily.

Cardan smiled, a curl of black hair falling in front of his face. "He's more like you than you want to see. Clever. *Ambitious*."

"If what's happening is anyone's fault, it's mine," Jude said with another sigh. "For not ordering Lady Nore's execution when I had the chance."

"All the obscene snake songs must have been greatly distracting," Cardan said lightly, moving on from the discussion of Oak. "Generosity of spirit is so uncharacteristic in you."

They were silent for a moment, and Oak saw his sister's face. There was something private there, and painful. He hadn't known, back then, how close she'd come to losing Cardan forever, and maybe losing herself, too.

Mind slowed by drink, Oak was still putting all this information together. Lady Nore, of the Court of Teeth, held Madoc. And Jude wasn't going to try to get him back. Oak wanted to crawl out from beneath the table and plead with her. *Jude, we can't leave him there. We can't let him die.*

"Rumor has it that Lady Nore is creating an army of stick and stone and snow creatures," Jude murmured.

Lady Nore was from the old Court of Teeth. After allying with Madoc and attempting to steal the crown of Elfhame, her entire Court had been disbanded. Their best warriors—including Tiernan's beloved, Hyacinthe—were turned into birds. Madoc had been sent into exile. And Lady Nore had been made to swear fealty to the daughter she tormented: Suren. The little queen with the sharp teeth that Cardan mentioned.

Oak felt a flush of an unfamiliar emotion at the thought of her.

Remembered running away to her woods and the rasp of her voice in the dark.

His sister went on. "Whether Lady Nore wishes to use them to attack us or the mortal world or just have them fight for her amusement, we ought to stop her. If we delay, she has time to build up her forces. But attacking her stronghold would mean my father's death. If we move against her, he dies."

"We can wait," Cardan said. "But not long."

Jude frowned. "If she steps from that Citadel, I will cut her throat from ear to ear."

Cardan drew a dramatic line across his throat and then slumped exaggeratedly over, eyes closed, mouth open. Playing dead.

Jude scowled. "You need not make fun."

"Have I ever told you how much you sound like Madoc when you talk about murder?" Cardan said, opening one eye. "Because you do."

Oak expected his sister to be angry, but she only laughed. "That must be what you like about me."

"That you're terrifying?" he asked, his drawl becoming exaggeratedly languorous, almost a purr. "I adore it."

She leaned against him, resting her head on his shoulder, and closed her eyes. The king's arms came around her, and she shivered once, as though letting something fall away.

Watching her, Oak turned his thoughts to what he knew would happen. He, the useless youngest child, the heir, would be protected from the information that his father was in peril.

Hyacinthe would be dragged away for questioning. Or execution.

Probably both, one following on the other. He might well deserve it, too. Oak knew, as his sister did not yet, that Madoc had spoken with the former falcon many times in recent months. If Hyacinthe *was* responsible, Oak would cut his throat himself.

But what would come after that? Nothing. No help for their father. Lady Nore bought herself time to build the army Jude described, but eventually Elfhame would move against her. When war came, no one would be spared.

He had to act quickly.

Mellith's heart. That's what Lady Nore wanted. He wasn't sure if he could get it, but even if he couldn't, that didn't mean there wasn't a way to stop her. Though he hadn't seen Suren in years, he knew where she was, and he doubted anyone else in the High Court did. They'd been friends once. Moreover, Lady Nore had sworn a vow to her. She had the power of command over her mother. One word from her could end this conflict before it started.

The thought of seeking Wren out filled him with an emotion he didn't want to inspect too closely, as drunk and upset as he already was. But he could plan instead how he would use the secret passageway to sneak out of his sister's room once she was asleep, how he would interrogate Hyacinthe as Tiernan packed up their things. How he would go to Mandrake Market and find out more about this ancient heart from Mother Marrow, who knew nearly everything about everything.

The conspiracy would wait. It wasn't as though they could make their move without a candidate for the throne standing by.

Oak would save their father. Maybe he could never fix his family, but he could try to make up for what he'd already cost them. He could try to measure up to them. If he went, if he persuaded Wren, if they succeeded, then Madoc would live and Jude wouldn't have to make another impossible choice.

They would have all forbidden him from going, of course. But before they had a chance, he was already gone.

CHAPTER 1

The cold of the prisons eats at Oak's bones, and the stink of iron scrapes his throat. The bridle presses against his cheeks, reminding him that he is shackled to an obedience that binds him more securely than any chains. But worst of all is the dread of what will happen next, a dread so great that he wishes it would just *happen* so he could stop dreading it.

On the morning after he was locked in his cell in the stone dungeons beneath the Ice Needle Citadel of the former Court of Teeth, a servant brought him a blanket lined in rabbit fur. A kindness he didn't know how to interpret. No matter how tightly he wraps it around himself, though, he is seldom warm.

Twice each day he is brought food. Water, often with a rime of ice on the surface. Soup, hot enough to make him comfortable for a scant hour or so. As the days stretch on, he fears that, rather than putting his torment off, as one puts a particularly delicious morsel to the side of one's plate to be saved for last, he has simply been forgotten.

Once, he thought he recognized Wren's shadow, observing him from a distance. He called to her, but she didn't answer. Maybe she'd never been there. The iron muddles his thoughts. Perhaps he only saw what he so desperately wanted to see.

She has not spoken with him since she sent him here. Not even to use the bridle to command him. Not even to gloat.

Sometimes he screams into the darkness, just to remind himself that he can.

These dungeons were built to swallow screams. No one comes.

Today, he screams himself hoarse and then slumps against a wall. He wishes he could tell himself a story, but he cannot convince himself that he is a brave prince suffering a setback on a daring quest, nor the tempestuous, star-crossed lover he has played at so many times in the past. Not even the loyal brother and son he meant to be when he set out from Elfhame.

Whatever he is, he's certainly no hero.

A guard stomps down the hall, driving Oak to his hooves. One of the falcons. Straun. The prince has overheard him at the gate before, complaining, not realizing his voice carries. He is ambitious, bored by the tediousness of guard duty, and eager to show off his skill in front of the new queen.

Wren, whose beauty Straun rhapsodizes over.

Oak hates Straun.

"You there," the falcon says, drawing close. "Be quiet before I quiet you."

Ah, Oak realizes. He's so bored that he wants to make something happen.

"I am merely trying to give this dungeon an authentic atmosphere," Oak says. "What's a place like this without the cries of the tormented?"

"Traitor's son, you think much of yourself, but you know nothing of torment," Straun says, kicking the iron bars with the heel of his boot, making them ring. "Soon, though. Soon, you'll learn. You should save your screams."

Traitor's son. Interesting. Not just bored, then, but resentful of Madoc.

Oak steps close enough to the bars that he can feel the heat of the iron. "Does Wren intend to punish me, then?"

Straun snorts. "Our queen has more important things to attend to than you. She's gone to the Stone Forest to wake the troll kings."

Oak stares at him, stunned.

The falcon grins. "Worry not, though. The storm hag is still here. Maybe *she'll* send for you. Her punishments are legendary." With that, he walks back toward the gate.

Oak sags to the cold floor, furious and despairing.

You have to break out. The thought strikes him forcefully. *You must find a way.*

Not easy, that. The iron bars burn. The lock is hard to pick, though he tried once with a fork. All he managed to do was snap off one of the tines and ensure that all subsequent food was sent only with spoons.

Not easy to escape. And besides, maybe, after everything, Wren still might visit him.

Oak wakes on the stone floor of his cell with his head ringing and his breath clouding in the air. He blinks in confusion, still half in dreams. He's seldom able to sleep deeply with so much iron around him, but that's not what woke him tonight.

A great cresting wave of magic washes over the Citadel, coursing from somewhere south, crashing down with unmistakable power. Then there is a tremble in the earth, as though something massive moved upon it.

It comes to him then that the Stone Forest is south of the Citadel. The trembling is not something moving upon the earth but something disgorged from it. *Wren did it.* She has released the troll kings from their bondage beneath the ground.

Broken an ancient curse, one so old that for Oak it seems woven into the fabric of the world, as implacable as the sea and sky.

He can almost hear the cracking sound of the rocks that imprisoned them. Fissures spider-webbing out from two directions at once, from both boulders. Waves of magical force flowing from those twinned centers, intense enough that nearby trees would split apart, sending the ice-crusted blue fruit to scatter on the snow.

He can almost see the two ancient troll kings, rising up from the earth, stretching for the first time in centuries. Tall as giants, shaking off all that had grown over them in their slumber. Dirt and grass, small trees, and rocks would all rain down from their shoulders.

Wren had done it.

And since that is supposed to be impossible, the prince has no idea what she might do next.

Since he's unlikely to be able to sleep again, Oak goes through the exercises the Ghost taught him long ago so that he could still practice while stuck in the mortal world.

Imagine you have a weapon. They had been in Vivi's second apartment, standing on a small metal balcony. Inside, Taryn and Vivi had been fussing over Leander, who was learning to crawl. The Ghost had asked about Oak's training and been uninterested in the excuse that he was eleven, had to go to school, and couldn't be swinging around a longsword in the common space of the lawn without neighbors getting worried.

Oh, come on! Oak laughed, thinking the spy was being silly.

The Ghost conjured the illusion of a blade out of thin air, its hilt decorated with ivy. His glamour was so good that Oak had to look closely to see that it wasn't real. *Your turn, prince.*

Oak had actually liked making his own sword. It was huge and black with a bright red hilt covered in demonish faces. It looked like the sword of someone in an anime he'd been watching, and he felt like a badass, holding it in his hands.

The sight of Oak's blade had made the Ghost smile, but he didn't laugh. Instead, he started moving through a series of exercises, urging Oak to follow. He told the prince he should call him by his nonspy name, Garrett, since they were friends.

You can do this, the Ghost—Garrett—told him. *When you have nothing else.*

Nothing else *to practice with,* he probably meant. Although right now, Oak has nothing else, full stop.

The exercises warm him just enough to be halfway comfortable when he wraps the blanket around his shoulders.

The prince has been imprisoned three weeks, according to the tallies he's made in the dust beneath the lone bench. Long enough to dwell on every mistake he has made on his ill-fated quest. Long enough to endlessly reconsider what he ought to have done in the swamp after the Thistlewitch turned to him and spoke in her raspy voice: *Didn't you know, prince of foxes, what you already had? What a fine jest, to look for Mellith's heart when she walks beside you.*

At the memory, Oak stands and paces the floor, his hooves clattering restlessly against the black stone. He should have told her the truth. Should have told her and accepted the consequences.

Instead, he convinced himself that keeping the secret of her origin protected her, but was that true? Or was it more true that he'd manipulated her, the way he manipulated everyone in his life? That was what he was good at, after all—tricks, games, insincerity.

His family must be in a panic right now. He trusts that Tiernan got Madoc to Elfhame safely, no matter what the redcap general wanted. But Jude would be furious with Tiernan for leaving Oak behind and even angrier with Madoc, if she guesses just how much of this is his fault.

Possibly Cardan would be relieved to be rid of Oak, but that wouldn't stop Jude from making a plan to get him back. Jude has been ruthless on Oak's behalf before, but this is the first time it's scared him. Wren is dangerous. She is not someone to cross. Neither of them are.

He recalls the press of Wren's sharp teeth against his shoulder. The nervous fumble of her kiss, the shine of her wet eyes, and how he repaid her reluctant trust with deception. Again and again in his mind, he sees the betrayal on her face when she realized what an enormous secret he'd kept.

It doesn't matter if you deserve to be in her prisons, he tells himself. *You still need to get out.*

Sitting in the dark, he listens to the guards play dice games. They have opened a jug of a particularly strong juniper liquor in celebration of Wren's accomplishment. Straun is the loudest and drunkest of the bunch, and the one losing the most coin.

Oak dozes off and wakes to the tread of soft footfalls. He surges to his hooves, moving as close to the iron bars as he dares.

A huldu woman comes into view, bearing a tray, her tail swishing behind her.

Disappointment is a pit in his stomach.

"Fernwaif," he says, and her eyes go to his. He can see the wariness in them.

"You remember my name," she says, as though it's some kind of trick. As though princes have the attention spans of gnats.

"Most certainly I do." He smiles, and after a moment, she visibly relaxes, her shoulders lowering.

He wouldn't have noted that reaction before. After all, smiles were *supposed* to reassure people. Just maybe not quite so much as his smiles did.

Maybe you can't help it. Maybe you do it without knowing. That's what Wren had said when he claimed he didn't use his honey-mouthed charm, his gancanagh ability, anymore. He'd stuck to the rules Oriana had given him. Sure, he knew the right things to say to make someone *like* him, but he'd told himself that wasn't the same as just giving himself over to the magic, not the same as enchanting them.

But sitting in the dark, he has reconsidered. What if the power leaches out of him like a miasma? Like a poison? Perhaps the seducing of conspirators he'd done wasn't his being clever or companionable; instead, he was using a power they couldn't fight against. What if he is a much worse person than he's supposed?

And as though to prove it, he presses his advantage, magical or not.

He smiles more broadly at Fernwaif. "You're far superior company to the guard who brought my food yesterday," he tells her with utter sincerity, thinking of a troll who wouldn't so much as meet his gaze. Who spilled half his water on the ground and then grinned at him, showing a set of cracked teeth.

Fernwaif snorts. "I don't know if that's much of a compliment."

It wasn't. "Shall I tell you instead that your hair is like spun gold, your eyes like sapphires?"

She giggles, and he can see her cheeks are pink as she pulls out the empty bowls near the slot at the bottom of the cell and replaces them with the new tray. "You best not."

"I can do better," he says. "And perhaps you might bring me a little gossip to cheer the chilly monotony of my days."

"You're very silly, Your Highness," she says after a moment, biting her bottom lip a little.

His gaze travels, evaluating the pockets of her dress for the weight of keys. Her blush deepens.

"I am," he agrees. "Silly enough to have gotten myself into this predicament. I wonder if you could take a message to Wr—to your new queen?"

She looks away. "I dare not," she says, and he knows he ought to leave it at that.

He remembers Oriana's warning to him when he was a child. *A power like the one you have is dangerous*, she said. *You can know what other people most want to hear. Say those things, and they will not only want to listen to you. They will come to want you above all other things. The love that a gancanagh inspires—some may pine away for desire of it. Others will carve the gancanagh to pieces to be sure no one else has it.*

He made a mistake when he first went to school in the mortal world. He felt alone at the mortal school, and so when he made a friend, he wanted to keep him. And he knew just how. It was easy; all he had to do was say the right things. He remembers the taste of the power on his tongue, supplying words he didn't even understand. Soccer and *Minecraft*, praise for the boy's drawings. Not lies, but nowhere near the truth, either. They had fun together, running around the playground, drenched in sweat, or playing video games in the boy's basement. They had fun together until he found that when they were apart, even for a few hours, the boy wouldn't speak. Wouldn't eat. Would just wait until he saw Oak again.

With that memory in his mind, Oak stumbles on, forcing his mouth into a smile he hopes looks real. "You see, I wish to let your queen know that I await her pleasure. I am hers to command, and I hope she will come and do just that."

"You don't want to be saved?" Fernwaif smiles. She's the one teasing him now. "Shall I inform my mistress that you are so tame she can let you out?"

"Tell her...," Oak says, keeping his astonishment at the news she's returned to the Citadel off his face through sheer force of will. "Tell her that I am wasted in all this gloom."

Fernwaif laughs, her eyes shining as though Oak is a romantic figure in a tale. "She asked me to come today," the huldu girl confides in a whisper.

That seems hopeful. The first hopeful thing he's heard in a while.

"Then I greatly desire your report of me to be a favorable one," he says, and makes a bow.

Her cheeks are still pink with pleasure when she leaves, departing with light steps. He can see the swish of her tail beneath her skirts.

Oak watches her go before bending down and inspecting his tray—a mushroom pie, a ramekin of jam, an entire steaming teapot with a cup, a glass of melted snow water. Nicer food than usual. And yet he finds he has little appetite for it.

All he can think of is Wren, whom he has every reason to fear and desires anyway. Who may be his enemy and a danger to everyone else he loves.

Oak kicks his hoof against the stone wall of his cage. Then he goes to pour himself a cup of the pine needle tea before it cools. The warmth of the pot on his hands limbers his fingers enough that, had he another fork, he would try that lock again.

That night, he wakes to the sight of a snake crawling down the wall, its black metal body jeweled and glittering. A forked emerald tongue tastes the air at regular intervals, like a metronome.

It startles him badly enough for him to back up against the bars, the iron hot against his shoulders. He has seen creatures like it before, forged by the great smiths of Faerie. Valuable and dangerous.

The paranoid thought comes to him that poison would be one straightforward way to solve the problem of his being held by an enemy of Elfhame. If he were dead, there'd be no reason to pay a ransom.

He doesn't think his sister would allow it, but there are those who might risk going around her. Grima Mog, the new grand general, would know *exactly* where to find the prince, having served the Court of Teeth herself. Grima Mog might look forward to the war it would start. And, of course, she answered to Cardan as much as Jude.

Not to mention there was always the *possibility* that Cardan convinced Jude that Oak was a danger to them both.

"Hello," he whispers warily to the snake.

It yawns widely enough for him to see silver fangs. The links of its body move, and a ring comes up from its throat, clanging to the floor. He leans down and lifts it. A gold ring with a deep blue stone, scuffed with wear. His ring, a present from his mother on his thirteenth birthday and left behind on his dresser because it no longer fit his finger. Proof that this creature was sent from Elfhame. Proof that he was supposed to trust it.

"Prinss," it says. "In three daysssss, you mussss be ready for ressssss-cue."

"Rescue?" Not here to poison him, then.

The snake just stares with its cold, glittering eyes.

Many nights, he hoped someone would come for him. Even though he wanted it to be Wren, there were plenty of times he imagined the Bomb blowing a hole in the wall and getting him out.

But now that it's a real possibility, he's surprised by how he feels.

"Give me longer," he says, no matter that it's ridiculous to negotiate with a metal snake and even more ridiculous to negotiate for his own imprisonment, just in order to get a chance to speak with someone who refuses to see him. "Two more weeks perhaps. A month."

If he could only *talk* to Wren, he could explain. Maybe she wouldn't forgive him, but if she saw he wasn't her enemy, that would be enough. Even convincing her that she didn't have to be an enemy to Elfhame would be something.

"Three daysssssss," it says again. Its enchantment is either too simple to decode his protests or it has been told to ignore them. "Be rehhhhdy."

Oak slides the ring onto his pinkie finger, watching the snake as it coils its way up the wall. Halfway to the ceiling, he realizes that just because it wasn't sent to poison him doesn't mean it wasn't sent to poison *someone*.

He jumps onto the bench and grabs for it, catching the end of its tail. With a tug, it comes off the wall, falling against his body and coiling around his forearm.

"Prinsssss," it hisses. As it opens its mouth to speak, he notes the tiny holes in the points of its silvery fangs.

When it does not strike, Oak pries the snake carefully from around his arm. Then, gripping the end of its tail firmly, he slams it down against the stone bench. Hears the cracking of its delicate mechanical parts. A gem flies off. So does a piece of metal. He whips it against the bench again.

A sound like the whistle of a teakettle comes from it, and its coils writhe. He brings its body down hard twice more, until it is broken and utterly still.

Oak feels relieved and awful at the same time. Perhaps it was no more alive than one of the ragwort steeds, but it had spoken. It had seemed alive.

He sinks to the floor. Inside the metal creature, he finds a glass vial, now cracked. The liquid inside is bloodred and clotted. Blusher mushroom. The one poison unlikely to harm him. Welcome proof that his sister doesn't want him dead. Maybe Cardan doesn't, either.

The snake is limp in his hands, the magic gone from it. He trembles to think of what could have happened had the creature been sent to visit Wren *before* finding him in the prisons. Or if his iron-addled mind had only realized the danger too late.

Three days.

He can no longer dawdle. No longer dread. No longer scheme. He has to act, and fast.

Oak listens for the changing of the guard. Once he hears Straun's voice, he bangs on the bars until the guard comes. It takes a long time, but not as long as it might have if Straun wasn't in a foul mood from a night of drinking and losing money at dice.

"Didn't I tell you to shut up?" the falcon roars.

"You're going to get me out of this cell," Oak says.

Straun pauses, then sneers, but there's a little wariness in it. "Have you run mad, princeling?"

Oak holds out his hand. A collection of gemstones rests in his scratched palm. He spent the better part of the night prying them out of the body of the snake. Each is worth ten times what Straun gambled away.

The falcon snorts in disgust but cannot disguise his interest. "You intend to bribe me?"

"Will it work?" Oak asks, walking to the edge of his cell. He's not sure if it's his magic urging him on or not.

Almost against his will, Straun steps closer. Good. The prince can smell the sharpness of the juniper liquor on his breath. Perhaps he is still a little drunk. Even better.

Oak reaches his right hand halfway through the bars, lifting it so the gems catch the faint edge of torchlight. He slides his other hand through, too, lower.

Straun smacks Oak's arm hard. His skin hits the iron bar on his cell, burning. The prince howls as the gems fall, most scattering across the corridor between the cells.

"Didn't think I was half so clever as you, did you?" Straun laughs as he gathers up the stones, not having promised a single thing.

"I did not," Oak admits.

Straun spits on the floor in front of the prince's cage. "No amount of gold or gems will save you. If my winter queen wants you to rot here, you're going to rot."

"*Your* winter queen?" Oak repeats, unable to stop himself.

The falcon looks a little shamefaced and turns to go back to his post. He's young, Oak realizes. Older than Oak, but not by so very much. Younger than Hyacinthe. It shouldn't be a surprise that Wren made such an impression on him.

It shouldn't bother Oak, shouldn't fill him with a ferocious jealousy.

What the prince needs to concentrate on is the key in his left hand. The one he grabbed from the loop at Straun's belt when the falcon smacked his right arm. Straun, who was, thankfully, *exactly* as clever as Oak had supposed him to be.

The key fits smoothly into the lock of Oak's cell. It turns so soundlessly it might as well have been greased.

Not that Straun is likely to come back to check on him, no matter how loud he bangs on the bars. The guard will be feeling smug. Well, let him.

The prince lifts a piece of cloth he's torn from his shirt and soaked in blusher mushroom liquid salvaged from the snake. Then he starts down the hall, his breath clouding in the cold air.

The Ghost taught him how to move stealthily, but he's never been very good at it. He blames his hooves, heavy and hard. They clack at the worst possible times. But he makes an effort, sliding them against the floor to minimize noise.

Straun is grumbling to another guard about how the others are cheats, refusing to play any more dice games. Oak waits until one leaves to bring back more refreshments and listens hard to the retreating steps of boots.

After he's sure there's only one guard there, he tries the gate. It's not even locked. He supposes there's no reason for it to be when there's only one prisoner, and he wears a bridle to keep him obedient.

Oak moves fast, jerking Straun backward and covering his nose and mouth with the cloth. The guard struggles, but inhaling blusher mushroom slows his movements. Oak presses him to the floor until he's unconscious.

From there, it's just a matter of arranging his body so that when the other guard returns, he might believe he's dozed off. It's hard for Oak to leave the guard's sword at his hip, but its absence would almost certainly give him away. He does, however, snatch up the cloak he finds hanging on a hook beside the door.

CHAPTER
2

O ak takes the stairs, careful now.

He has the surreal feeling of being in a video game. He played enough of them, sitting on Vivi's couch. Creeping through pixelated rooms that had more of the appearance of Madoc's stronghold where he grew up than anywhere they went in the mortal world. Leaning on Heather's shoulder, controller in his hands. Killing people. Hiding the bodies.

This is a stupid, ugly, violent game, Vivi said. *Life isn't like that.* And Jude, who was visiting, raised her eyebrows and said nothing.

He recalls following Wren through these icy halls. Killing people. Hiding the bodies.

There are more visitors to the Citadel now than there were then; ironically, that makes it easier to be overlooked. There are so many new faces, neighboring Folk arriving to discover the nature of the new lady and curry her favor. Well-dressed nisse and huldufólk courtiers gather in knots, passing gossip. Trolls size one another up, and a few selkies hang around at the edges, no doubt gathering news of a rising power to take back to the Undersea.

Oak cannot blend in, not in his worn and filthy clothes, not with the straps of Grimsen's bridle tight to his cheeks. He sticks to the shadows, putting up the hood of the cloak and moving with slow deliberation.

After growing up with servants in his father's stronghold in Faerie and then without any when he was in the mortal world, the prince is very aware of what it takes to keep a castle like this one running. As a small child, he was used to his dirty clothing disappearing from his floor and returning to his armoire, cleaned and hung. But after he and Vivi and Heather had to carry bags of laundry to the basement of their apartment building and feed quarters into a machine, along with detergent and fabric softener, he realized that *someone* must have been performing a related service for him in Faerie.

And someone is performing that service here in the Citadel, washing linens and uniforms. Oak heads in the direction of the kitchens, figuring the flames of the ovens are likely the same ones used to heat the tubs of water necessary to clean fabric. Real fire would be easier to keep confined to the stone basements and first floor of the Citadel.

Oak keeps his head down, although the servants barely spare him a glance. They rush through the halls. He's sure the household is vastly understaffed.

It takes him a tense twenty minutes of creeping about before a change in the humidity of the air and the scent of soap reveal the laundry area. He pushes open the door to the room gingerly and is relieved to find no servant currently doing the wash. Three steaming vats rest on the black rock floor. Dirty bedding, tablecloths, and uniforms soak inside them. Clean linens hang from ropes strung overhead.

Oak pulls off his own filthy garments, dropping them into the water before stepping in, too.

He feels a bit foolish as he wades into a vat, naked. Should he be discovered, he will doubtless have to play the silly, carefree prince, so vain that he escaped his prison for a bath. It would be a crowning achievement of embarrassment.

The soapy water is merely warm, but it feels deliciously hot after being so chilled for so long. He shudders with the pleasure of it, the muscles in his limbs relaxing. He dunks himself, submerging his head and scrubbing at his skin with his fingernails until he feels clean. He wants to stay there, to float in water as it grows ever more tepid. For a moment, he allows himself to do just that. To stare at the ceiling of the room, which is black stone, too, although above this level, the walls, floors, and ceilings are all of ice.

And Wren, somewhere inside them. If he could just speak to her, even for a moment...

Oak knows it's ridiculous, and yet he can't help feeling as though they have an *understanding* of each other, one that transcends this admittedly not-great moment. She will be angry when he talks with her, of course. He deserves her anger.

He has to tell her that he regrets what he did. He's not sure what happens after that.

Nor is he sure what it means about him that he finds hope in the fact that Wren has *kept* him. Fine, not everyone would see being thrown into a dungeon as a romantic gesture, but he's choosing to at least consider the possibility that she put him there because she wants something more from him.

Something beyond, say, skinning him and leaving his rotting corpse for ravens to pick over.

On that thought, he splashes his way out of the tub.

Among the drying uniforms, he finds one that seems as though it will fit him—certainly fit better than the bloodstained one he used to get into the palace weeks ago. It's damp, but not so much as to draw notice, and only slightly too tight across his chest. Still, dressed this way and with the hood of the cloak pulled forward to hide his face, he might be able to walk straight out the door of the Citadel, as though he were going on patrol.

It would serve her right for never coming to see him, not even to use the bridle and command him to stay put.

He's not sure how far he could get in the snow, but he still has three of the stones from the snake. He might be able to bribe someone to take him in their carriage. And even if he didn't want to risk that, he might well find his own horse in the stables, since Hyacinthe was the one who stole Damsel Fly and Hyacinthe is now Wren's second-in-command.

Either way, he'd be free. Free to not need rescuing. Free to attempt to talk his sister out of whatever homicidal plan she might foment against the Citadel. Free to return home and go back to performing feckless-ness, back to sharing the bed of anyone he thought might be planning a political coup, back to being an heir who never wants to inherit.

And never seeing Wren again.

Of course, he might not make it to Jude in time for her to know he was free, to stop whatever plans she set in motion. Whatever murders her people would commit in his name. And then, of course, there would be the question of what Wren did in retaliation.

Not that he knows how to stop either of them if he remains here. He's not sure *anyone* knows how to stop Jude. And Wren has the power of annihilation. She can break curses and tear spells to pieces with barely any effort. She took apart Lady Nore as though she were a stick creature and spread her insides over the snow.

Really, that memory alone should send the prince out of the Citadel as quickly as his legs could carry him.

He pulls the hood of the cloak down over his face and heads toward the Great Hall. Getting a glimpse of her feels more like a compulsion than a decision.

He can feel the gaze of courtiers drift toward him—covering one's face in a hood is unusual, at the very least. He keeps his own eyes unfocused and his shoulders back, though his every instinct screams to meet their looks. But he is dressed like a soldier, and a soldier would not turn.

It is harder to pass falcons and to know they might spot his hooves and wonder. But he is hardly the only one to have hooves in Faerie. And everyone who knows that the Prince of Elfhame is in the Citadel believes him to be locked up tight.

Which doesn't make him any less of a fool for coming into the throne room. When everything goes wrong, he will have no one to blame but himself.

Then he sees Wren, and longing shoots through him like a kick to the gut. He forgets about risk. Forgets about schemes.

Somewhere in the crowd, a musician plucks at a lute. Oak barely hears it.

The Queen of the Ice Citadel sits upon her throne, wearing a severe black dress that shows her bare pale blue shoulders. Her hair is a tumble of azure, some strands pulled back, a few pieces braided through with black branches. On her head is a crown of ice.

In the Court of Moths, Wren flinched away from the gazes of courtiers as she entered the revel on his arm, as though their very notice stung. She curled her body so that, small as she was, she appeared even smaller.

Now her shoulders are back. Her demeanor is that of someone who does not consider anyone in this room—not even Bogdana—a threat. He flashes on a memory of her younger self. A little girl with a crown sewn to her skin, her wrists leashed by chains that threaded between bones and flesh. No fear in her face. That child was terrifying, but no matter how she seemed, she was also terrified.

"The delegation of hags has come," snaps Bogdana. "Give me the remains of Mab's bones and restore my power so that I can lead them again."

The storm hag stands before the throne, in the place of the petitioner, although nothing about her suggests submission. She wears a long black shroud, tattered in places. Her fingers move expressively as she speaks, sweeping through the air like knives.

Behind her are two Folk. An old woman with the talons of some bird of prey instead of feet (or hooves) and a man shrouded in a cloak. Only his hand is visible, and that is covered in what seems to be a scaled, golden glove. Or perhaps his hand itself is scaled and golden.

Oak blinks. He knows the woman with the feet like a bird of prey. That's Mother Marrow, who operates out of Mandrake Market on the isle of Insmire. Mother Marrow, whom the prince went to at the very start of his quest, asking for guidance. She sent him to the Thistlewitch for answers about Mellith's heart. He tries to recall now, all these weeks later, whether she'd said anything that might have put him in Bogdana's path.

Knots of courtiers are scattered around the room, gossiping, making it hard to hear Wren's soft reply. Oak steps closer, his arm brushing against a nisse. She makes an expression of annoyance, and he shifts away.

"Have I not suffered long enough?" asks Bogdana.

"You would speak to me of suffering?" Nothing in Wren's expression is soft or yielding or shy. She is every bit the pitiless winter queen.

Bogdana frowns, perhaps a little unnerved. Oak feels somewhat unnerved himself. "Once I have them, my might will be restored—me, who was once first among hags. That's what I gave up to secure your future."

"Not *my* future." There is a hollowness to Wren's cheeks, Oak notices. She's thinner than she was, and her eyes shine with a feverish brightness.

Has she been ill? Is this because of the wound in her side when she was struck by an arrow?

"Do you not have Mellith's heart?" demands the storm hag. "Are you not her, reborn into the world through my magic?"

Wren does not reply immediately, letting the moment stretch out. Oak wonders if Bogdana has ever realized that the trade she made must have ruined her daughter's life, long before it led to her horrible death. From the Thistlewitch's tale, Mellith must have been *miserable* as Mab's heir. And since Wren has at least some of Mellith's memories in addition to her own, she has plenty of reasons to hate the storm hag.

Bogdana is playing a dangerous game.

"I have her heart, yes," says Wren slowly. "Along with part of a curse. But I am not a child, no less *your* child. Do not think you can so easily manipulate me."

The storm hag snorts. "You are a child still."

A muscle jumps in Wren's jaw. "I am your queen."

Bogdana does not contradict her this time. "You have need of my strength. And you have need of my companions if you hope to continue as you are."

Oak stiffens at those words, wondering at their meaning.

Wren stands, and courtiers turn their attention to her, their conversations growing hushed. Despite her youth and her small stature, she has vast power.

And yet, Oak notices that she sways a little before gripping the arm of her throne. Forcing herself upright.

Something is very wrong.

Bogdana made this request in front of a crowd rather than in private and named herself as Wren's maker. Called Wren a child. Threatened her sovereignty. Brought in two of her hag friends. These were desperate, aggressive moves. Wren must have been putting her off for some time. But also, the storm hag may have thought she was attacking in a moment of weakness.

First among the hags. He doesn't like the thought of Bogdana being more powerful than she already is.

"Queen Suren," says Mother Marrow, stepping forward with a bow. "I have traveled a long way to meet you—and to give you this." She opens her palm. A white walnut sits at the center of it.

Wren hesitates, no longer quite as remote as she seemed a moment before. Oak recalls the surprise and delight in her face when he bought her a mere hair ornament. She hasn't been given many presents since she was stolen from her mortal home. Mother Marrow was clever to bring her something.

"What does it do?" A smile twitches at the corners of Wren's mouth, despite everything.

Mother Marrow's smile goes a little crooked. "I have heard you've been traveling much of late and spending time in forest and fen. Crack the nut and say my little poem, and a cottage will appear. Bring the two halves together again with another verse, and it will return to its shell. Shall I demonstrate?"

"I think we need not conjure a whole building in the throne room," Wren says.

A few courtiers titter.

Mother Marrow does not seem discomfited in the least. She walks to Wren and deposits the white walnut in her hand. "Remember these words, then. To conjure it, say: *We are weary and wish to rest our bones. Broken shell, bring me a cottage of stones.*"

The nut in Wren's hand gives a little jump at the words but then is quiescent once more.

Mother Marrow continues speaking. "And to send it away: *As halves are made whole and these words resound, back into the walnut shell shall my cottage be bound.*"

"It is a kind gift. I've never seen anything like it." Wren's hands curl around it possessively, belying the lightness of her tone. He thinks of the shelter she made from willow branches back in her woods and imagines how well she would have liked to have something solid and safe to sleep in. A well-considered gift, indeed.

The man steps forward. "Though I do not like to be outdone, I have nothing so fine to give you. But Bogdana summoned me here to see if I can undo what—"

"That is enough," Wren says, her voice as harsh as Oak has ever heard it.

He frowns, wishing she'd have let the man finish. But it was interesting that for all the damning things she allowed Bogdana to say, whatever he wanted to undo was the one thing she didn't want her Court to hear.

"Child," Bogdana cautions her. "If my mistakes can be unmade, then let me unmake them."

"You spoke of power," Wren snaps. "And yet you suppose I will let you strip me of mine."

Bogdana begins to speak again, but as Wren descends from the throne, guards gather around her. She heads toward the double doors of the Great Hall, leaving the storm hag behind.

Wren sweeps past Oak without a look.

The prince follows her into the hall. Watches the guards accompany her to her tower and begin to ascend.

He follows, staying to the back, blending in with a knot of soldiers.

When they are almost to her rooms, he lets himself fall behind farther. Then he opens a random door and steps inside.

For a moment, he braces for a scream, but the room is—thankfully—empty. Clothing hangs in an open armoire. Pins and ribbons are scattered across a low table. One of the courtiers must be staying here, and Oak is very lucky not to be caught.

Of course, the longer he waits, the luckier he will have to be.

Still, he can hardly barge into Wren's rooms now. The guards would not have left yet. And there would certainly be servants—even with so few in the castle—attending her.

Oak paces back and forth, willing himself to be calm. His heart is racing. He is thinking of the Wren he saw, a Wren as distant as the coldest, farthest star in the sky. He cannot even focus on the room itself, which he should almost certainly hunt through to find a weapon or mask or something useful.

But instead he counts the minutes until he believes he can safely—
well, as safely as possible, given the inherent danger of this impulsive
plan—go to Wren's rooms. He finds no guard waiting in the hall—
unsurprising, given the narrowness of the tower, but excellent. No
voices come from inside.

What is surprising is that when he turns the knob, the door opens.

He steps into her rooms, expecting Wren's anger. But only silence
greets him.

A low couch sits along one wall, a tray with a teapot and cups on the
table in front of it. In a corner beside it, the ice crown rests on a pillow
atop a pillar. And across the room, a bed hung with curtains depicting
thorned vines and blue flowers.

He walks to it and sweeps the fabric aside.

Wren is sleeping, her pale cerulean hair spread out over the pillows. He recalls brushing it out when they were in the Court of Moths.
Recalls the wild tangle of it and the way she held herself very still while
his hands touched her.

Her eyes move restlessly under their lids, as though she doesn't even
feel safe in dreams. Her skin has a glassy quality, as though from sweat
or possibly ice.

What has she been doing to herself?

He takes a step closer, knowing he shouldn't. His hand reaches out,
as though he might graze his fingers over her cheek. As though to prove
to himself that she's real, and there, and alive.

He doesn't touch her, of course. He's not that much of a fool.

But as though she can sense him, Wren opens her eyes.

CHAPTER 3

Wren blinks up at Oak, and he gives her what he hopes is an apologetic grin. Her startled expression smooths out into puzzlement and some emotion he is less able to name. She reaches up, and he bends lower, going to one knee, so that she can brush her fingers over the nape of his neck. He shivers at her touch. Looking down into her dark green eyes, he tries to read her feelings in the minute shifts of her countenance. He thinks he sees a longing there to match his own.

Wren's lips part on a sigh.

"I want—" he begins.

"No," she tells him. "By the power of Grimsen's bridle, get on your knees and be silent."

Surprise makes him try to pull away, to stand, but he cannot. His teeth close on the words he now cannot say.

It's an awful feeling, his body turning against him. He was on one knee already, but his other leg bends without his deciding to move. As his calves strike the frozen floor, he understands, in a way that he never has before, Wren's horror of the bridle. Jude's need for control. He has never known this kind of helplessness.

Her mouth curves into a smile, but it isn't a nice one. "By Grimsen, I command you to do exactly as I say from here forward. You will stay on your knees until I say otherwise."

Oak should have left when he had the chance.

She rises from the bed and draws on a dressing gown. Walks over to where he kneels.

He looks at her slippered foot. Glances up at the rest of her. A strand of light blue hair has fallen across one scarred cheek. Her lips have a little pink at the inner edges, like the inside of a shell.

It is hard to imagine her as she was when they began their quest, a feral girl who seemed like the living embodiment of the woods. Wild and brave and kind. There is no shyness in her gaze now. No kindness, either.

He finds her fascinating. He's always found her fascinating, but he is not foolish enough to tell her that. Especially not in this moment, when he is afraid of her.

"You've gone to a lot of trouble to see me again, prince," Wren says. "I understand that you called for me in your cell."

He screamed for her. Screamed until his throat was hoarse. But even if he was allowed to speak, clarifying that would only compound his many, many mistakes.

She goes on. "How frustrating it must be not to have *everyone* eager to comply with your desires. How impatient you must have become."

Oak tries to push himself to his hooves.

She must note the impotent flex of his muscles. "How impatient you are even yet. Speak, if you wish."

"I came here to repent," he says, taking what he hopes will be a steadying breath. "I should never have kept what I knew from you. Certainly not something like that. No matter how I thought I was protecting you, no matter how desperate I was to help my father, it wasn't my place. I did you a grievous wrong, and I am sorry."

A long moment passes. Oak stares at her slipper, not sure he can bear to look into her face. "I am not your enemy, Wren. And if you throw me back into your dungeons, I won't have a chance to show you how remorseful I am, so please don't."

"A pretty speech." Wren walks to the head of her bed, where a long pull dangles from a hole bored into the ice wall. She gives it a hard tug. Somewhere far below, he can hear the faint ringing of a bell. Then the sound of boots on the stairs.

"I am already bridled," he says, feeling a little frantic. "You don't need to lock me away. I can't harm you unless you let me. I am entirely in your power. And when I did escape, I came directly to your side. Let me kneel at your feet in the throne room and gaze up adoringly at you."

Her green eyes are hard as jade. "And have you spending all your waking hours trying to think of some clever way to slither around my commands?"

"I have to occupy myself somehow," he says. "When I am between moments of gazing adoringly, of course."

The outer corner of her lip twitches, and he wonders if he almost made her smile.

The door opens, and Fernwaif comes in, a single guard behind her. Oak recognizes him as Bran, who occasionally sat at Madoc's dinner table when Oak was a child. He looks horrified at the sight of the prince on his knees, wearing the livery of a guard beneath a stolen cloak.

"How—" Bran begins, but Wren ignores him.

"Fernwaif," she says. "Go and have the guards responsible for the prisons brought here."

The huldu girl gives a small bob of her head and, with a wary glance at Oak, leaves the room. So much for her being on his side.

Wren's gaze goes to Bran. "How is it that no one saw him strolling through the Citadel? How is it that he was allowed to walk into my chambers with no one the wiser?"

The falcon steps up to Oak. The fury in his gaze is half humiliation.

"What traitor helped you escape?" Bran demands. "How long have you been planning to assassinate Queen Suren?"

The prince snorts. "Is *that* what I was trying to do? Then why, given everything I stole from that fool Straun and the laundry, didn't I bother to steal a weapon?"

Bran gives him a swift kick in the side.

Oak sucks in the sound of pain. "That's your clever riposte?"

Wren lifts a hand, and both of them look at her, falling silent.

"What shall I do with you, Prince of Elfhame?" Wren asks.

"If you mean for me to be your pet," he says, "there's no reason to return me to my pen. My leash is very secure, as you have shown. You have only to pull it taut."

"You think you know what it is to be under someone's control because I have given you a *single* command you were forced to obey," she says, heat in her voice. "I could give you a demonstration of what it feels like to own nothing of yourself. You are owed a punishment, after all. You've broken out of my prisons and come to my rooms without my permission. You've made a mockery of my guards."

A cold feeling settles in Oak's gut. The bridle is uncomfortable, its straps pulling tight against his cheeks, but not painful. At least not yet. He knows that it will continue to tighten and that if he wears it long enough, it will cut into his cheeks as it cut Wren's. If he wears it longer than that, longer than she did, it will eventually grow to be a part of him. Invisible to the world and impossible to remove.

That is why it was made. To make Wren eternally obedient to Lord Jarel and Lady Nore.

Wren hated that bridle.

"I grant you that I don't know what it feels like to be compelled to follow someone else's orders again and again," Oak says. "But I don't think you want to do that, not to anyone. Not even to me."

"You don't know me as well as you think, Greenbriar heir," she says. "I remember your stories, like the one about how you used a glamour against your mortal sister and made her strike herself. How would you like to feel as she felt?"

He confessed that when Wren won a secret from him in a game they played with three silver foxes, tossed in the dirt outside the war camp of the Court of Teeth. Another thing he maybe ought not to have done.

"I'll slap myself silly willingly, if you like," he offers. "No need for a command."

"What if, instead, I force you onto your hands and knees to make a bench for me to sit upon?" Wren inquires lightly, but her eyes are alight with fury and something else, something darker. She pads around his body, a prowling animal. "Or eat filth from the floor?"

Oak does not doubt that she saw Lord Jarel demand those things from people. He hopes that she was never asked to do those things herself.

"Beg to kiss the hem of my dress?"

He says nothing. Nothing he says could possibly help him.

"Crawl to me." Her eyes shine, fever bright.

Again, Oak's body moves without his permission. He finds himself writhing across the floor, his stomach against the carpet. He flushes with shame.

When he reaches her, he stares upward, rage in his eyes. He's humiliated, and she's barely begun. She was right when she said he didn't understand what it would feel like. He hadn't counted on the embarrassment, the fury at himself for not being able to resist the magic. He hadn't counted on the fear of what she would do next.

Oak cuts his gaze toward Bran, who has remained stiff and still, as though afraid to draw Wren's attention. The prince wonders how far she would go if he were not present.

How far she will go anyway.

Then the door opens.

Straun enters, along with a guard wearing battle-scraped armor and bearing a scar across the broadest part of his nose. He seems familiar, but Oak can't quite place him—he must have served with Madoc but not come to the house much. Straun looks as though he's fighting to move, and the scarred guard is looking as though he wants to murder Straun.

Straun steps forward, going to one knee. "Queen of winter, know that I only ever wished to serve—"

She holds up a hand, forestalling the groveling he seems to be working up to. "I have been tricked by the prince often enough to know how clever he can be. Now you will not be deceived again."

"I shall make a new oath to you," he declares. "That I will never—"

"Make no oaths you are not certain you can keep," she tells Straun, which is better advice than he deserves. Still, he looks chastened by it.

Oak pushes to his hooves, since she hadn't told him to stay there.
Wren barely spares him a glance.

"Bind my prisoner's wrists," she tells the scarred guard.

"As you command, Queen." His voice is gruff.

He walks to Oak, pulling his arms behind him sharply. Tying his
bonds uncomfortably tight. The prince's wrists are going to be sore by
the time he makes it back to his cell.

"We were discussing how best to discipline Prince Oak," she says.

Straun and the other guard look a lot happier at that thought. Oak
is certain that, after they were punished by the High Court for their
treason, it would be at least a little satisfying to see a prince of Elfhame
brought low. And that was before he gave them a reason to have a personal grudge.

Wren turns to him. "Perhaps I ought to have you sent to the Great
Hall tomorrow and command that you endure ten strikes of an ice
whip. Most barely get through five."

Bran looks worried. He might want Oak humiliated but perhaps
didn't expect to see Madoc's son's blood spilled. Or maybe he is concerned
that if they have to give back the prince, Elfhame will want him in one
piece. Straun seems thrilled by the prospect of some suffering, however.

Dread and humiliation coil in Oak's stomach. He has been such a fool.

"Why not whip me now?" he asks, a challenge in his voice.

"Spending a night dreading what will come in the morning is its
own punishment." She pauses. "Especially as you now know your own
hand can be turned against you."

Oak looks directly into her eyes. "Why are you keeping me at all,
Wren? Am I a hostage to be ransomed? A lover to be punished? A possession to be locked away?"

"That," she says, bitterness in her voice, "is what I am trying to figure out myself." She turns to the guards. "Take him back to his cell."

Bran reaches for him, and the prince struggles, pulling out of the guard's grasp.

"Oak," Wren says, pressing her fingers to his cheek. He goes still beneath her touch. "Go with Straun. Do not resist him. Do not trick him. Until you are confined again, you will follow these commands. And then you will stay in my prisons until you are sent for." She gives the prince a stern look and withdraws her hand. Turns to the soldiers. "Once Oak is in his cell, the three of you can go to Hyacinthe and explain how you allowed the prince to slip past you."

Hyacinthe. A reminder that the person in charge of the guards hates Oak more than the rest of them combined. As though he needed more miserable news.

"Will you send for me?" the prince asks, as though there's any room for bargaining. As though he has a choice. As though his body will not obey its own accord. "You said only *perhaps* you'd have me whipped."

Straun shoves him toward the door.

"Good night, Prince of Elfhame," Wren says as he is led from the room. He manages a single glance back. Her gaze locks with his, and he can feel the frisson of something between them. Something that might well be terrible, but that he wants more of all the same.

CHAPTER

4

The scarred-nose guard follows Straun and Oak down the stairs. Bran trails behind them. For a while, none of them speak.

"Let's take him to the interrogation room," the guard says, low-voiced. "Pay him back for the trouble we're going to be in. Find some information to make up for it."

Oak clears his throat loudly. "I'm a valuable possession. The queen won't thank you for breaking me."

One corner of the guard's mouth turns up. "Don't recognize me? But then, why would you? I'm just another of your father's people, just another one who fought and bled and nearly died to put you on the throne. All for you to throw it back in our faces."

I didn't want the throne. Oak bites the inside of his cheek to keep from shouting the words. That isn't going to help. Instead, he stares at the scarred man's face, at the dark eyes and auburn hair that hangs across his forehead. At the scar itself, which pulls his mouth up, as though his lip is perpetually curled.

"Valen," he prompts before Oak can recall his name. One of the generals who campaigned with Madoc for years. Not a friend, either. They vied against each other for the position of grand general, and Valen never forgave Madoc for winning. Madoc must have promised him something extraordinary to get Valen to betray the High King.

Oak could well believe that once coming to Madoc's side, Valen was unwilling to return to the military in Elfhame, tail between his legs. And now he is here, after spending perhaps *nine years* as a falcon. Oh, yes, Oak could well believe Valen despises him. Valen may actually hate him more than Hyacinthe does.

"I was a child," the prince says.

"A spoiled, disobedient boy. You still are. But that won't stop me from wringing every last drop of information out of you."

Straun hesitates, cutting his gaze toward Bran, still far enough back that he hasn't overheard their plan. "Aren't we going to get in more trouble? The prince said—"

"You take orders from a prisoner now?" Valen needles. "Perhaps you're still loyal to his father, despite being abandoned by him. Or the High Court? Maybe you think you made the wrong choice, not swearing fealty to that spoiled snake boy and his mortal concubine."

"That's not true!" Straun spits out, mightily offended. It's a fine piece of manipulation. Valen has made Straun feel as though he has to prove himself.

"Then let's go strap him down," Valen says with a crooked grin. Oak would be willing to bet that this is the soldier who took Straun's money playing dice.

"He's just goading you—" Oak manages to get out before he is shoved roughly forward. And, of course, he has been commanded not to resist.

"What's going on?" asks Bran, frowning at them.

"The boy has a smart mouth," Valen says, and Bran narrows his eyes in suspicion but doesn't ask any further questions.

Down they go, past the prisons. No matter how Oak tries to stop himself, his body moves like an automaton, like one of those stick soldiers Lady Nore created from Mab's bones. His heart thuds dully in his chest, his body alight with panic.

"Listen," he tries again. "Whatever you're thinking of doing to me—"

"Shut your mouth," snaps Valen, kicking the prince in the back of the leg.

"This isn't the right direction," Bran says, seeming to notice how far they've descended for the first time.

Oak hopes he will do something. Order them to stop. Tattle to Hyacinthe. It would be embarrassing to be saved by him, but the prince would far prefer that to whatever Valen is planning.

"We need information," the scarred guard says. "Something to give the queen so that we don't look like fools. You think you're not going to be demoted? Mocked? He got past all three of us."

Bran nods slowly. "I suppose there's something to that. And I am given to understand the interrogation rooms are well outfitted."

"You hardly need to strap me down. I will tell you how I stole the key, how I got into her tower, all of it." Oak can tell, though, how little they want to be convinced. "I—"

"Quiet." Straun shoves him hard enough for him to overbalance, arms behind his back as they are.

The prince hits the stone floor hard, smacking his head.

Valen laughs.

Oak pushes himself back up. A cut just above his left brow is bleeding, the blood dripping down over his eye. Since his hands are bound, he can't wipe it away. He flexes his wrists a little to test the bindings, but there is no give.

Fury chokes him.

A few more shoves and he's down the hall and into a room he's never seen before—one with manacles attached to a black stone table and instruments of interrogation in a glass-paned cabinet. Straun and Valen press Oak's back down onto the slab. They cut the bindings on his wrists, and for a moment, he's free.

Desperately, he tries to struggle, but he finds he cannot, not with the bridle's magic holding him down more firmly than they could. *Go with Straun. Do not resist him. Do not trick him.* The prince has to allow them to manacle his wrists and then his ankles.

He doesn't bother pretending he's not afraid. He's terrified.

"Hyacinthe has been dreaming of torturing me for years." The prince is unable to keep his voice from shaking a little. "I can't imagine what I know that would make him forgive you if you jump the line."

Bran squints in slight confusion as he parses the human phrase, looking more worried. "Maybe we should tell—"

Valen reaches for the small handheld crossbow on his hip.

"Bran!" Oak shouts in warning.

The falcon goes for his sword, unsheathing it in a single fluid movement. But the bolt from Valen's crossbow strikes him in the throat before he can so much as advance.

Go with Straun. Do not resist him. Do not trick him. Until you are confined again, you will follow these commands.

Now that he is confined, Oak can finally resist. He pulls against his bindings, writhing and kicking, shouting every filthy thing he can think of—but, of course, it's too late.

Bran drops heavily to the floor as two more bolts lodge in his chest.

This doesn't seem like a good move. It doesn't seem clever, and Oak doesn't like the idea that Valen may be desperate enough or paranoid enough to make decisions that don't make strategic sense. He's not an amateur. He must have really believed that Bran was about to betray him.

"Bar the door," Valen tells Straun.

Straun does it, stepping over Bran's body. He's breathing hard. If he'd been asked to choose sides, he might have chosen Bran's. But no one's asking him now.

"Well," says Valen, turning toward Oak. "Now you and I are finally going to have a conversation."

Oak cannot repress the shudder that goes through him at those words. He has been poisoned and stabbed many times over the course of his short life. Pain is transient, he tells himself. He has endured it before—broken bones and bled and survived. Pain is better than being dead.

He tells himself a lot of things.

"It seems rude for me to be lying down during it," Oak says, but his voice doesn't come out as calmly as he hoped.

"There are lots of ways to hurt us Folk," says Valen, ignoring the prince's words as he draws on a brown leather glove. "But cold iron is the worst. Burns through faerie flesh like a hot knife through lard."

"A grim topic to discuss, but if that's what you'd like to talk about, you are the host of this little get-together. . . ." Oak tries to sound light, unconcerned. He's heard Cardan speak just this way on many occasions, and it disarms his audience. Oak can only hope it works that way now.

Valen's hand comes down hard on the corner of his mouth. It's more a slap than a blow, but it still stings. He tastes blood where a tooth cuts into his lip.

Straun gives a guffaw. Maybe he feels torture will be a proper vengeance for Oak's making him look like a fool. But with Bran's body lying by the guard's feet, Straun *is* a fool if he thinks himself safe.

Still, the game that has always served Oak best is seeming feckless, and he needs to play that up. Be that spoiled boy Valen expects.

At least until he can come up with something better.

"Let's talk about what your sister will do," says Valen, surprising Oak by not bothering to ask a single question about his escape. "Where were you planning on meeting her forces once you escaped your cell and murdered the queen?"

Clever of him to assume guilt and only press for details. Clever, but wrong.

With the stick creatures scattered into pieces, the falcons are the entire force of Wren's military. That gives Valen room to rise in the ranks, since those ranks are thin, but it puts him in danger, too. Whatever Elfhame sends at the Citadel, he and his falcons will have to meet it.

That's what Valen wants above all else, Oak realizes. Power. He's been simmering with that desire for as long as he's been laboring under the curse. And being Wren's military leader would have appeased him a little. But she passed him over, and now he is hungrier than ever.

"Sorry to disappoint, but I have no way to communicate with my sister," Oak says. That was true enough since he smashed the snake.

"You can't expect me to believe you were going to—what—murder the queen and then run off through the snow, hoping for the best?" Valen sneers.

"I'm glad you don't think that, though Bran certainly did," Oak says, keeping his gaze off the corpse on the floor. "I never wanted to hurt Wren, no less *murder* her."

Straun frowns at the familiar form of address—Wren, rather than Queen Suren or the Winter Queen or whatever fanciful title he thinks best suits her.

Can Straun truly believe he has a chance with her? There does not seem to be much guile in him. She may like that, even if Oak thinks he's dull as a toad.

Valen studies the prince's face, perhaps seeing the jealousy in it. "And you didn't intend to run, either?"

Oak isn't certain how to answer that. He's not sure he can explain his intentions, even to himself. "I was considering it. Prison isn't very nice, and I like nice things."

Valen's mouth turns down in disgust. This is what he expects a prince of Elfhame to be—vain and fussy and unused to suffering of any kind. The more Oak leans into that role, the more he will be able to hide himself.

"Although," Oak says, "freezing isn't particularly nice, either."

"So you drugged Straun and broke out of the prisons," Valen says slowly, incredulously, "with no plan at all?"

Oak cannot shrug, as tied down as he is, but he makes a gesture to indicate his nonchalance. "Some of my best ideas come to me in the moment. And I did get a bath."

"He must know *something*," Straun says, worried that they are risking all this for nothing. Worried, no doubt, about the corpse that will be hard to dispose of without anyone noticing.

Valen turns toward Oak, pressing a finger into his cheek. "The prince knows his sister."

Oak sighs dramatically. "Jude has an army. She has assassins. She has control of the Courts of other rulers who are sworn to her. She holds all the cards and could deploy any of them. You want me to tell you that in a duel, she turns her front foot inward while lunging, giving you an opening? I don't think you'll ever get close enough to find that information useful."

Straun's eyes narrow in calculation. "She turns her front foot?"

Oak smiles up at him. "Never."

Valen lifts an iron knife from the cabinet and presses the point of it to the hollow of Oak's throat. It sizzles against his skin.

The prince bites back a cry as his whole body jerks with pain.

Straun flinches despite his previous eagerness. Then he sets his jaw and makes himself watch as the prince's skin blisters.

"*Ouch*," Oak says, enunciating the word slowly and deliberately in a whiny sort of voice, despite how much the hot iron against his throat burns.

Straun is startled into a snort of laughter. Valen pulls the knife back, furious.

It's easy to make someone look foolish if you're willing to play the fool.

"*Leave*," shouts Valen, waving at Straun. "Guard from the other side of the door. Alert me if someone is coming."

"But—" Straun begins.

"Better do as he says," Oak tells him, breathing hard because despite his performance, the press of the iron is agony. "Don't want to end up like Bran."

Straun's gaze flicks guiltily to the floor, then back to Valen. He goes out.

Oak watches him with mixed feelings. The prince has few moves, and none of them are good. He can keep at getting under Valen's skin, but it's likely to cost him his own. Now that Straun is out of the room, though, he could try a different tack. "Maybe I could give you something better than impressing Hyacinthe, but I'd need something in return."

Valen smiles, letting his knife hover over Oak's face. "Bogdana told me that you inherited your mother's twisting tongue."

It takes all the prince's concentration not to look at the blade directly. He forces himself to stare up into the falcon's eyes. "Bogdana doesn't like me. I doubt she likes you much, either. But you want Hyacinthe's position, and I know a great deal about him... his vulnerabilities, the ways he is likely to fail."

"Tell me this," Valen says, looming over him. "Where did you get the poison you used on Straun?"

Well, crap. That's a very good question. Oak thinks of the jeweled snake. Imagines how he will look if he tries to explain.

"I thought I didn't need to torture you to get you to tell me whatever I wanted to know?" Valen turns the knife so that the point hovers over Oak's eye. He glances at it and sees the edge of one of the straps of the bridle reflected in the blade. A reminder that Wren didn't sanction this interrogation, that she doesn't know about it. She wouldn't need to torture him to find out any of this. All she'd have to do, with the bridle on him, was ask. He could no more deny her than he could stop his own heart from beating.

Of course, whether she'd care if Valen hurt him was another matter. He liked to think that she would, at least for her pride. After all, ten lashes from an ice whip wouldn't seem like much of a punishment if someone else had already gouged out one of his eyes.

He'd rather not lose the eye, though. Still, all he has going for him is his charm, and that's a double-edged sword. "You asked me about my sister—and you're right. I do know her. I know she's likely to send someone to negotiate for my return. Whatever you think of me, I am valuable to Elfhame."

"She'd pay a ransom?" Valen licks his lips. Oak can see his desire, a hunger for glory and gold and all the things that were denied him.

"Oh yes," Oak agrees. "But it hardly matters if Wren won't agree to give me up. Whatever my sister offers now could have always been Wren's, along with the Citadel, as a reward for removing Lady Nore."

Valen's mouth twists into a harsh smile. "But you seem to have made Queen Suren angry enough to prefer your being brought low to her own rise."

That stung, being uncomfortably true. "You could make your own bargain with the High Queen."

The tip of the iron knife presses against Oak's cheek. It burns like a lit match against his skin. He jerks again, a puppet on a string.

"How about you answer the question about the poison, and then we can discuss what deals I am going to make."

Panic floods Oak. He's going to refuse to talk. And he's going to be tortured until he gives in and talks anyway. Once Hyacinthe learns about the snake, he will tell Wren, and she'll believe Oak is her enemy, no matter what he says in his defense. And whatever his sister's plan is, it's sure to become exponentially more lethal.

But with enough pain and enough time, anyone will say almost anything.

Perhaps, Oak thinks, perhaps he can get himself hurt so badly the questioning *can't* continue. It's a terrible plan, but no other idea presents itself. He can hardly smile at Valen as he did at Fernwaif and have that be enough to persuade him to let Oak leave the dungeon.

Unless . . .

It's been a long time since he used his *twisting tongue*, as Bogdana put it. His true gancanagh power. Let his mouth speak for him, let the words come without his will. Say all the right things in the right way at the right time.

It's terrifying, like letting go in a sword fight and allowing pure instinct to take over, not being entirely sure whose blood will wind up on his hands.

But whatever Valen is going to do next is more terrifying. If Oak can escape this room in one piece and without putting anyone he cares about in danger, he can figure out the rest from there.

Of course, part of the problem is that his power isn't one of pure persuasion. He can't just make someone do what he wants. He can only make himself into what they want and hope that is enough. Worse, he is never sure what that will be. Once he gives in, his mouth makes the words, and he is left with the consequences.

"*The trolls of the Stone Forest have blusher mushroom. It's not so very hard to come by. Forget the poison. Think of your future,*" Oak says, his voice sounding strange, even to his own ears. There's a rough hum underneath and a buzz on his lips, like the sting of electricity. It's been a long time since he has reached for this power, but it uncurls languorously at his command. *"You only want command of Lady Wren's army? You were meant for greater things."*

Valen's eyes dilate, the irises blowing wide. He scowls in confusion, shaking his head. "The trolls? That's where you got the poison."

Oak doesn't like how eager the enchantment feels, now that it's awakened. How easily it flows through him. He's felt trickles of this magic before, but not since he was a child has he let himself feel the full force of it. *"I am closer to the center of power than anyone at this Citadel,"* he says. *"Madoc is out of favor, and many in the High Court do not like our armies being led by Grima Mog. Many would prefer you—and isn't that really what you want?"*

"I have lost all chance of that." Valen's words aren't scornful, though. He sounds frightened by his own hopes. The iron knife dips low enough in his gloved hand that he seems in danger of burning his own thigh with the tip.

"You have lived as a falcon for nine years," Oak says, the words dragging against his tongue. *"You were strong enough not to stagger beneath that burden. You are free, and yet if you are not careful, you will be caught in a new net."*

Valen listens as though fascinated.

"You are headed toward a conflict with Elfhame, yet you have no army of stick and stone and no authority of command. But with me, things could change. Elfhame could reward you instead of targeting you. I could help. Unbind me, and I will give you what you have long deserved."

Valen backs himself against the wall, breathing hard, shaking his head. "What are you?" he asks with a tremor in his voice and an ocean of wanting in his eyes.

"What do you mean?" The words come out of Oak's mouth without the basilisk charm in them.

"You—what did you do to me?" Valen growls, a spark of hot anger in his gaze.

"I was just talking." Oak reaches desperately for the honey-tongued roughness to his voice. He's too panicked to find it. Too unused to using it.

"I am going to make you *suffer*," Valen promises.

Back to Oak's first, worse plan, then. He gives Valen his most careless, insouciant grin. "I almost had you, though. You were almost mine."

Valen slams his forehead into the prince's face. Oak's skull snaps back to knock against the slab to which he's been bound. Pain blooms between his eyes, and his head feels as though it rattles on his neck. Valen's fist connects next, and Oak counts it as a win that the third blow is hard enough to knock him unconscious.

CHAPTER 5

Oak is dreaming of a red fox that is also his half brother, Locke. They are in a forest at twilight, and things are moving in the shadows. Leaves rustle as though animals peer from between trees.

"You really screwed up this time," says the fox as he trots beside the prince.

"You're dead," Oak reminds him.

"Yes," agrees the fox who is also Locke. "And you're close to joining me."

"Is that why you've come?" Oak looks down at his muddy hooves. A leaf is stuck to the top of the one on his left.

The fox's black nose scents the air. Its tail is a wavering flame behind it. Its paws pad sure-footedly along a path that Oak cannot see. He wonders if he is being led somewhere that he doesn't want to go.

A breeze brings the scents of old, drying blood and weapon oil. It reminds Oak of the smell of Madoc's house, of home.

"I am a trickster, like you. I am here because it amuses me. When I am bored, I will go away."

"I'm not like you," Oak says.

He's *not* like Locke, even if they have the same power. Locke was Master of Revels, who spirited away his sister Taryn to his estate, where she drank wine and dressed in beautiful gowns and became sadder than he'd ever seen her.

Locke thought life was a story, and he was responsible for introducing the conflict. Oak had been nine when Taryn murdered Locke, with his tenth birthday soon after. He would like to say he hadn't known what she'd done, but he had. None of them tried to hide violence. By then, they were used to murder being an option that was *always* on the table.

At the time, though, he hadn't quite put together that Locke was his half brother.

Or quite how much Locke was a terrible person.

The fox's mouth opens, its pink tongue lolling out. It studies Oak with eyes that look alarmingly like his own. "Our mother died when I was just a child, but I still remember her. She had long red-gold hair, and she was always laughing. Everyone she met adored her."

Oak thought of Hyacinthe, whose father had loved Liriope too well and killed himself because of it. He thought of Dain, who had desired her and then murdered her.

"I am not like our mother, either," Oak says.

"You never met her," the fox tells him. "How do you know if you're like her or not?"

To that, Oak has no answer. He doesn't want to be like her. He wanted people to love him a normal amount.

But it was true that he wanted everyone to love him.

"You're going to die like her. And like me. Murdered by your own lover."

"I'm not dying," the prince snaps, but the fox scampers off, sliding between the trees. At first his bright coat gives him away, but then the leaves become scarlet and gold and withered brown. They fall in a great gust that seems to whirl around the prince. And in the shiver of the boughs, Oak hears laughter.

CHAPTER
6

Oak isn't sure how long he has lain on the cold stone tiles, dropping in and out of consciousness. He dreams of hunting snakes that glisten with gems as they whip through the night, of girls made of ice whose kisses cool his burns. Several times, he thinks he ought to crawl toward his blanket, but just contemplating the idea of moving hurts his head.

Whatever the prince thought of himself before, however skilled he claimed to be at evading traps and laughing in the face of danger, he isn't laughing now. He'd have been better off sitting in his cell and waiting. He'd have been better off if he ran out into the snow. He took a chance and lost, lost *spectacularly*, which is just about all he can say to his credit—at least it was spectacular.

It is the shift of shadows that causes him to realize someone is standing outside his cell. Feverishly, he looks up. For a moment, her face swims in front of him, and he thinks she must be part of another nightmare.

Bogdana.

The storm hag looms tall, her hair a wild mane around her head. She peers at him with black eyes that shine like chips of wet onyx.

"Prince Oak, our most honored guest. I was afraid you might have died in there," she says, kicking a tray beneath the door of his cell with her foot. On it rests a bowl of watery soup with scales floating on top, beside a carafe of sour-smelling wine. He has no doubt she selected the food personally.

"Well, hello," Oak says. "What an unexpected visit."

She smiles down in malicious glee. "You seem unwell. I thought a simple meal might be to your liking."

He pushes himself into a sitting position, ignoring how it makes his head pound. "How long was I out?" He isn't even sure how he got to the prisons. Had Straun been forced to carry him here, once Valen realized he wasn't going to wake anytime soon? Had Valen brought him back, in case he never woke?

"Somewhere you need to be, Prince of Elfhame?" Bogdana asks him.

"Of course not." Oak's hand goes to his chest. The burn by his throat is scabbed over. He can feel the wild beat of his heart beneath his palm. He couldn't have been unconscious long since Wren hadn't sent anyone to drag him before her Court for a whipping.

Bogdana's smile widens. "Good. Because I came to tell you that I will gut every servant you conscript, should you try to use one to escape your cell again."

"I didn't—" he begins.

She gives a harsh laugh, something that is half a snarl. "The huldu girl? You cannot truly expect me to believe you don't have her eating out of your hand. That you didn't put her under your spell?"

"You think Fernwaif helped me escape?" he snaps, incredulous.

"Feeling remorseful now, when it's too late?" The storm hag's lip curls. "You knew the risk when you used her."

"The girl did nothing." Fernwaif, who believed in romance, despite living in Lady Nore's Citadel. Who he hoped was still alive. "I got the key from Straun, and that's because he's a fool, not because I conscripted him."

Bogdana watches Oak's expression, drawing out the moment. "Suren interceded on Fernwaif's behalf. She's safe from me, for the moment."

Oak lets out a breath. "I shall be as unpleasant to the servants of the Citadel as you like hereafter. Now I hope our business is concluded."

Bogdana frowns down at him. "Our business won't be concluded until the Greenbriars have repaid their debt to me."

"With our lives, blah, blah, I know." Pain and despair have made the prince reckless.

The storm hag's eyes are bright with reflected light. Her nails tap against the iron of the bars as though contemplating shoving her hand inside and slashing him with them. "You desire something from Suren, don't you, prince? Perhaps it's that you aren't used to being rejected and it's not sitting well with you. Perhaps you see the greatness in her and want to ruin it. Perhaps you truly are drawn to her. Any which way, it will make the moment she bites out your throat all the sweeter."

Oak cannot help thinking of his dream and the fox walking beside him, prophesying his doom. Cannot help thinking of other things. "She's bitten me before, you know," he says with a grin. "It wasn't so bad."

Bogdana looks satisfyingly infuriated by the comment. "I am glad you're still locked up tight, little bait," she tells him, eyes flashing. "Were you less useful, I would flay your skin from your bones. I would hurt you in ways you cannot imagine." There is a hunger in her words that unnerves him.

"Someone beat you to that." Oak leans back onto the pillow of his own arm.

"You're still breathing," says the storm hag.

"If you were actually worried I was dead," he says, recalling the first thing she said to him when she came to his cell, "I must have looked pretty bad."

He may have been unconscious longer than he guessed. Is there still a day before Elfhame makes its move? Is it happening already? He really, really wishes the metal snake had been more specific about what Jude was planning. *Three dayssssss* was just not enough information.

"I don't need you to last long," Bogdana says. "It's the High King I want."

Oak snorts. "Good luck with that."

"You're my luck."

"I wonder what Wren thinks," he says, trying to hide his discomfiture. "You're using her every bit as much as Lord Jarel and Lady Nore ever did. And you've been planning on using her for a long time."

Lightning sparks along Bogdana's fingers. "My revenge is hers as well. Her crown and throne were stolen."

"She's got both a crown and a throne now, hasn't she?" Oak asks. "And it seems you're the one likely to cost her them, *again*."

The look the storm hag gives him could have boiled his blood. "For what Mab did, I will see the end of the Greenbriar reign," snaps Bogdana.

"You think you know Suren, but you do not. Her heart is that of my dead daughter. She was born to be the ruin of your kin."

"I know her well enough to call her *Wren*," he says, and watches the storm hag's eyes glisten with deeper malice. "And we don't always do the thing we were born for."

"Eat up, boy," Bogdana says, gesturing to the disgusting food she brought. "I'd hate to see you go to your slaughter hungry."

It's only hours later, when the footsteps of three guards wake him from another half sleep, that Oak realizes she may have meant those last words literally. His head still hurts enough that he thinks about just lying there and letting them do their worst, but then he decides that if he is going to die, at least he will do so standing.

He's up by the time they arrive. As they open the door to his cell, he uses the tip of his hoof to flip the bowl of soup into his hands. Then he slams it into the first guard's face.

The guard goes down. Oak kicks the second into the iron bars and, in a moment of hesitation from the third, grabs for the first guard's fallen sword.

Before he can get it, a club hits him in the stomach, knocking the air out of him.

He was faster, before the iron. Before his muscles got stiff. Before getting hit in the head several times by Valen. A few weeks ago, he would have had the sword.

They're crowded in the entrance of his cell; that's his main advantage. Only one can really come at him at a time, but all three have weapons drawn and Oak has only his hands and hooves. Even the bowl is lying on the ground, cracked in half.

But he refuses to be dragged back to the interrogation chamber. Panic fills him at the thought of Valen starting the torture over. At the strike of an ice whip. At Bogdana's nails peeling off his skin.

The second guard, the one who hit the bars, lunges at him with the sword. It's a small space, though, too small to get a real swing in, and the guard is slow as a consequence. Oak ducks and barrels into the first guard, who has managed to get onto his feet. The prince slams into him, and they both sprawl onto the cold stone tiles of the prison hall. Oak attempts to scramble up, only to be hit between the shoulder blades with the club by the third guard. He is knocked down again, falling heavily onto the second guard. He goes for a knife strapped to that one's belt. Drawing it, he rolls onto his back, ready to throw.

As he does, he feels a familiar shift in his mind. The shuttering of all other thoughts, the casting off of himself. There is a relief in letting go, allowing the future and past to drop away, to become someone without a hope or fear beyond this moment. Someone for whom there was only ever this fight and there will only ever be this fight.

It worries him, too, though, because every time it happens, he feels less and less in control of what he does when he's outside himself. How many times now has he found himself standing over a body with blood on his clothes, blood on his face and his sword and his hands—and no memory of what happened?

It makes him think of the gancanagh power, of all the warnings he doesn't seem able to heed anymore.

"*Oak!*" Hyacinthe shouts.

The prince lets his arm with the dagger in it sag. Somehow being yelled at by Hyacinthe brings him back to himself. Maybe it is just the familiarity of his scorn.

When he isn't hit again, he lets himself lie there, breathing hard. The other guard stands.

"She wants you to sit down to supper with her," Hyacinthe says. "I'm supposed to get you cleaned up."

"Wren?" Oak's sense of time is still very unclear. "I thought she was going to have me punished."

Hyacinthe raises both his eyebrows. "Yes, Wren. Who else?"

The prince looks at the guards, who glare at him resentfully. If he'd been thinking more clearly, he would have realized he had no cause to try to *murder* them. They weren't necessarily working for Valen or Bogdana, weren't necessarily leading him to his doom. He probably would have figured that out sooner had his head not hurt so much. Had Bogdana not come and threatened him.

"No one mentioned supper," Oak complains.

One of the guards, the one with the club, snorts. The other two wear scowls that remain unaltered.

Hyacinthe turns to all of them. "Find something else to do. I will escort the prince."

The guards depart, one spitting on the stone floor as he leaves.

"I warn you," Oak says. "If you are also planning on hitting me, it will have to be quite a blow to have any effect on the swelling and bruises already coming in."

"You might consider occasionally bowing to wisdom and keeping your tongue between your teeth," Hyacinthe says, reaching out a hand to pull Oak to his feet.

For a moment, the prince is certain he's going to open his mouth and say something Hyacinthe will not think is at all funny. Something that probably won't *be* at all funny.

"Unlikely, but we can both live in hope," Oak manages as he lets himself be levered up. He staggers a little and realizes that if he tries to catch himself, he will have to burn his hand on the iron bars. Dizziness washes over him. "If you intend to gloat, have at it."

Hyacinthe's mouth twists into a smile. "You're being paid, Prince of Elfhame. In exactly the coin you once demanded."

To that, Oak can make no refutation. He is staying upright by sheer force of will, taking deep breaths until he is sure he is going to stay that way.

"Well, come on," says Hyacinthe. "Unless you want me to carry you."

"Carry me? What a delightful offer. You can bear me in your arms like a maiden in a fairy tale."

Hyacinthe rolls his eyes. "I can throw you over my shoulder like a sack of grain."

"Then I suppose I shall walk," Oak says, hoping he can. He staggers after Hyacinthe, remembering how Hyacinthe was once his prisoner, feeling the poetic justice of the moment. "Are you going to bind my hands?"

"Do I need to?" Hyacinthe asks.

For a moment, Oak thinks he's referring to the bridle. But then the prince realizes Hyacinthe is simply offering him an opportunity to walk up the stairs without restraints. "Why are you—"

"A kinder captor than ever you were to me?" Hyacinthe supplies with a short laugh. "Maybe I am just a better person."

Oak doesn't bother to remind Hyacinthe of how he tried to *murder the High King* and, if Oak hadn't interceded, would have been executed or sent to the Tower of Forgetting. It doesn't matter. It is very possible that neither of them is a particularly nice person.

They move down the hall, past lit torches. Hyacinthe takes a long look at Oak and frowns. "You've got bruises, and it's too soon for them to have come from the fight I just saw. Those iron burns aren't fresh, either, and they're the wrong shape and angle to come from your prison bars. What happened?"

"I'm a miracle of self-destructiveness," Oak says.

Hyacinthe stops walking and folds his arms. The pose is so like one that Tiernan regularly makes that Oak is certain it's a copy, even if Hyacinthe isn't aware he's doing it.

Maybe that's what makes him talk, that familiar gesture. Or maybe it's that he's so tired and no small amount afraid. "You know a guy named Valen? Former general. Thick neck. More anger than sense?"

Hyacinthe's brow furrows, and he nods slowly.

"He wants your job," Oak says, and begins walking again.

Hyacinthe falls into step beside him. "I don't see what that has to do with you."

They come to the stairs and head up, out of the dungeons. The fading sunlight hits his face, hurting his eyes, but the only thing he feels is gratitude. He wasn't sure he'd ever see the sun again. "He may have told you something about a soldier named Bran deserting. He didn't. He's dead."

"Bran is—" Hyacinthe begins, and then lowers his voice to a whisper. "He's *dead*?"

"Don't look at me like that," Oak says quietly. "I didn't kill him."

Guards flank an entrance a few paces ahead, and by unspoken consensus, they both fall silent. Oak's shoulders tense as he passes them, but they do nothing to stop his progress through the halls. For the first time, as he steps into a high-ceilinged corridor, he is free to look around the Citadel without the danger of being caught. He catches the scent of melting wax and the sap of fir trees. Rose petals, too, he thinks. Without the persistent stink of the iron, his head hurts less.

Then the prince's gaze goes to one of the large, translucent walls of ice, and he stumbles.

As through a window, he can see the landscape beyond the Citadel and the troll kings moving across it. Although distant, they are far larger than the boulders in the Stone Forest, as if those massive boulders represented only the topmost portions of their bodies and the rest were buried beneath the earth. These trolls are larger than any giant Oak saw in the Court of Elfhame, or the Court of Moths, for that matter. He watches them lurch through the snow, dragging enormous chunks of ice, and mentally recalculates Wren's resources.

They are building a wall. A miles-wide defensive shield, encircling the Citadel.

In less than a month, between her own newfound power and her newfound allies, Wren has made the Court of Teeth more formidable and more forbidding than it ever was during Lord Jarel's reign. But when he thinks of her, he cannot help seeing the darkness beneath her eyes and the feverish shine of them. Cannot put aside the thought that something is wrong.

"Wren looks as though she's been unwell," Oak says. "Has she been sick?"

Hyacinthe frowns. "You can't really expect me to betray my queen by telling you her secrets."

Oak's smile is sharp-edged. "So there's a secret to tell."

Hyacinthe's frown deepens.

"I am a prisoner," Oak says. "Whether you have me in chains or no, I can't hurt her, and I wouldn't if I could. I warned you about Valen. About Bran. Surely, I have proved some measure of loyalty."

Hyacinthe huffs out a breath, his gaze going to the troll kings beyond the icy pane. "Loyalty? I think not, but I am going to tell you because you might be the one person who *can* help. Wren's power takes something terrible out of her."

"What do you mean?" Oak demands.

"It's eating away at her," Hyacinthe says. "And she's going to keep having to use it, again and again, so long as you're here."

Oak opens his mouth to demand further explanation, but at that moment, a knot of courtiers passes, all of them pale and cold-looking, their gazes sliding over Oak as though the very sight of him is an offense.

"You're going to the leftmost tower," Hyacinthe says.

Oak nods, trying not to be rattled by the hate in their eyes. The tower he's heading toward is, ironically, the same one he was caught in the day before. "Explain," he says.

"What she does—it's not just unbinding, it's *unmaking*. She became sick after what she did to Lady Nore and her stick army. *Harrowed.* And Bogdana was so insistent that Wren use it again to break the curse of the Stone Forest because she's going to need the trolls if Elf-hame moves against us. But she's formed of magic herself, and the more she unmakes, the more she is unmade."

Oak recalls the strain in Wren's face as she looked down from the dais in the Great Hall, the hollows beneath her cheekbones as she slept.

He assumed that Wren didn't visit the prisons because she didn't want to see him out of uninterest or anger. But she might not have come if she was sick. As much as she knows that looking weak in front of her newly formed Court is dangerous, it's possible she feels it is similarly risky to look weak in front of him.

And if she doesn't keep using her power...

No matter how dangerous the magic, Oak can too easily imagine Wren believing that if she doesn't use it, she won't be able to keep her throne. This was a land of huldufólk, nisser, and trolls, used to bowing only to strength and ferocity. They followed Lady Nore, but they were willing to hail Wren, her murderer, as their new queen.

She may be inclined to push herself past her limits to keep that support. To prove herself worthy. Has he not witnessed his sister doing just that?

You know what would really impress them? his mind supplies unhelpfully. *Daring to skewer the heir to Elfhame.*

"Tonight, at dinner," Hyacinthe says, "persuade her to let you go. And if you can't, then leave. Go. Actually *escape* this time, and take your political conflict with you."

Oak rolls his eyes at the assumption that getting out of the prisons was easy and he could have done it at any time. "You could advise her to *let* me go. Unless she doesn't trust you, either."

Hyacinthe hesitates, not taking the bait. "She would trust me less if she knew we were having this conversation. Perhaps wisely, I am not sure she trusts anyone. All the Folk in the Citadel have their own agendas."

"I am last on the list of those whose advice she'd heed," Oak says. "As you well know."

"You have a way of persuading people."

It's a barbed comment, but the prince grits his teeth and refuses to be offended. No matter how barbed, it's also the truth. "It would be far easier if I wasn't wearing this bridle."

Hyacinthe gives him a sideways look. "You'll manage." He must have heard the specifics of her command. *You will stay in my prisons until you are sent for.*

Oak sighs.

"And in the interim, stop picking fights," Hyacinthe says, making Oak want to pick a fight with *him*. "Is there no situation you're not compelled to make worse?"

Oak climbs the steps of the tower, thinking of the dinner ahead of him with Wren. The idea of sitting across from her at a table seems surreal, part of his hectic, fox-filled dreams.

They come to a wooden door with two locks on the outside. Hyacinthe moves past the prince to fit a key inside the first one and then the other.

One key. Two locks. Oak notes that. And none of it iron.

The room it opens onto is well appointed. Low couches are arranged on a rug looking so much softer than anything he's seen in weeks that he could sink down onto that and be happy. Blue flames burn in the grate of a fireplace. They seem hot, and yet when he puts a hand to the ice wall above the fire, there is none of the slickness that would indicate melting. Where the rug doesn't cover, the floor is inset with stone. If you didn't look carefully, you could suppose that you weren't in an ice palace at all.

"A far finer class of prison," Oak says, moving to lean against one of the posts of the bed. While he was moving, he wasn't dizzy, but now that he's stopped, he feels the immense need to be supported by something.

"Get dressed," Hyacinthe says, pointing to a set of clothes laid out on the bed. He holds the key in his palm pointedly, then places it on the mantel. "If you can't persuade her, it may interest you to know there's a shift in the guard at dawn. I left you a book on the table over there as well. It's mortal literature, and I understand you like that sort of thing."

Oak stares at the key as Hyacinthe leaves. Part of him wants to dismiss this as a trick, a way for the former falcon to prove the prince untrustworthy.

His gaze goes to the clothing left for him and then the mattress beneath, stuffed with goose down or perhaps duck feathers. He feels almost sick with the desire to lie down, to allow his throbbing temple to rest on a pillow.

He takes a deep breath and forces himself to pick up the book that Hyacinthe indicated—a hardback with a dust jacket that proclaims *Magic Tricks for Dummies*. He ruffles the pages, thinking of how he once made a coin disappear and reappear in front of Wren. Remembering his fingers brushing against her ear, her surprised laugh.

He should have let her leave that night. Let her take the damned bridle, get on the bus, and go, if that was what she wanted.

But no, he had to show off. Be clever. Manipulate everyone and everything, just the way he'd been taught. Just the way his father had manipulated him to come here.

With a sigh, he frowns down at the book again. There doesn't seem to be anything tucked inside. He isn't sure what it means then, except that Hyacinthe thinks he's a dummy. Just in case, he goes through the pages again, more slowly this time.

On 161, he finds an almost thoroughly dried stalk of ragwort.

Guards wait for him in the hall when he emerges from the room, dressed in the clothes he was given.

The doublet is of some silvery fabric that feels sturdy and stiff, as though there might be silver threads woven into the cloth. His shoulders are a little broader and his torso a little longer than the original owner, and it feels even more uncomfortably tight than the uniform. The pants are black as a starless sky and have to be pushed up a little because of the curve of his leg above his hooves.

He says nothing to the guards, and their faces are grim as they escort him to a high-ceilinged dining room where their new queen is waiting.

Wren stands at the head of a long table in a dress of some material that seems to be black and then silver, depending on the light. Her hair is pulled away from her pale blue face, and while she does not wear a crown, the ornaments in her hair suggest one.

She looks every bit a terrifying Queen of Faerie, beckoning him to some final supper of poisoned apples.

He bows.

Her gaze rests on him, as though trying to decide if the gesture is mockery or not. Or maybe she's only inspecting his bruises.

He's certainly noting how fragile she looks. *Harrowed.*

And something else. Something he ought to have noted in her

bedroom, when she'd given him orders, but he'd been too panicked to think about. There's a defensiveness in her posture, as though she's bracing for his anger. After having held him prisoner, she believes he *hates* her. She might still be angry with him, but she quite obviously expects him to be furious with her.

And every time he behaves as though he isn't, she thinks he's playing a trick.

"Hyacinthe told me you were reluctant to explain how you came to be hurt," Wren says.

Oak doesn't need to glance at the entrances to note the guards. He saw them upon his arrival. Not knowing their loyalties, he can hardly mention Valen, or even Straun, without stripping Hyacinthe of the element of surprise. Did she know that? Was this a play put on for their benefit? Or was this another test? "What would you say if I told you I grew so bored that I hit myself in the face?"

Her mouth becomes an even grimmer line. "No one would believe that lie, could you even tell it."

Oak's head dips forward, and he cannot keep the despair out of his voice. This is off to a bad start, and yet he truly does seem unable to keep himself from making it worse. "What lie *would* you believe?"

CHAPTER

7

Wren stiffens. He can see the careful way she is holding herself. Transforming her habit for shyness into remoteness. He is all admiration, except for the part where this new queen might decide he is nothing but a thorn to be excised from her side.

"Am I to advise you how best to deceive me?" she says, and he knows they are no longer just talking about his bruises.

Oak walks to the end of the table opposite her. A servant comes and pulls out the chair for him. Dizzily, he drops into the seat, well aware that it probably makes him seem sulky.

He has no idea what to say.

He thinks of the moment in the Court of Moths when he was told that Wren betrayed him, when it seemed certain that she had. Used him as he was familiar with being used. Kissed him to distract from her true purpose. He was furious with her, certainly, and with himself for being a fool. He was angry enough to let them take her away.

It was only later when he understood the details that a terrible panic set in. Because she *had* betrayed him, but she did it to free those she felt were unfairly imprisoned. And she did it with no strategic or personal benefit, putting herself in danger for Folk and mortals she barely knew. Just as she helped all those mortals who made bad bargains with the Folk back in her town.

He hadn't found out her reasons before he'd let them take her. He recalls the uncomfortable mix of anger and fear over what might be happening to her, the horror of not being certain he could save her from Queen Annet.

He wonders if this dinner is because Wren heard he was hurt and regrets that, if nothing else. She certainly felt betrayed. But betrayal didn't stop one from feeling other things. "I do have some experience with deception," he admits.

She frowns at that unexpected confession, taking her seat as well.

Another servant pours black wine into a goblet in front of him, one carved of ice. Oak lifts it, wondering if there's any way to tell if the liquid within is poisoned. Some he can identify by taste, but plenty have either no flavor or one subtle enough to be masked by something more aromatic.

He thinks of Oriana, patiently feeding him a little bit of poison along with goat milk and honey when he was an infant, making him sicker to make him better. He takes a tentative sip.

The wine is strong and tastes of something like currants.

He notes that Wren has not touched her glass.

I have to show her that I trust her, he tells himself, even though he's not entirely sure that he does. After all, she wouldn't be the first person he liked who tried to kill him. She wouldn't even be the first person he *loved* who tried to kill him.

He pushes the thought away. Lifting his wineglass in salute, he takes a deep draught. At that, Wren finally brings her goblet to her lips.

Oak tries not to show his relief. "I asked you once about whether you might like to be queen in earnest. It seems you changed your mind." He manages to keep his voice light, although he still isn't sure why he's sitting here and not at the other end of an ice whip.

"Have you changed yours?" she asks.

He smiles. "Ought I? Tell me, Your Majesty, what is it like, now that you sit on a throne and have so many demands on your time and resources? Do you like having courtiers at your beck and call?"

Her returning smile is tinged with bitterness. "You know well, prince, that sitting at the head of the table does not mean your guests will not fall to bickering over the portions on their plates, the seating arrangements, or the polish on the silver. Nor does it mean they will not scheme for your seat."

As though part of her speech, two huldufólk servants enter the room and set the first course before Oak and Wren.

Thin slivers of cold fish on a plate of ice with a scattering of cracked pink peppercorns. Elegant and cold.

"As your guest," Oak says, lifting his fork, "I have few complaints. And I am, in fact, at your beck and call."

"Few complaints?" she echoes, one pale blue brow rising. "The prisons were just to your liking?"

"I would prefer not to return to them," Oak admits. "But if I had to remain there to be here, then I have none at all."

A faint flush comes into Wren's cheeks, and she frowns again. "You asked me what I wanted with you." She peers down the table at him with her moss-green eyes. A soft green, he always thought, but they are hard now. "But all that matters is that I *do* want you. And I have you." Though that seems like a confession, she delivers the words like a threat.

"I thought you believed that there could be no love where one person was bound. Isn't that what you told Tiernan?"

"You need not love me," she tells him.

"What if I did? If I do?" Oak has proclaimed his love to people before, but that felt like play and this feels like pain. Maybe it's because she sees him, and no one else has. The illusion he wears is much easier to love than what's underneath.

Wren laughs. "What if? Do not play word games with me, Oak."

He feels a hot flush of shame, realizing that was exactly what he was doing. "You're right. Let me be plain. I do—"

"*No*," she says, cutting him off, her voice simmering with the magic of unmaking, sending one of the fruits on a footed tray to pulp and seeds, one of the platters to molten silver. It sears through the ice of the table to drip onto the floor in shining strings, cooling on the way down.

She looks as startled as he is, but she recovers quickly, pushing herself into a standing position. A strand of blue hair has come loose, falling over her face. "Do not think I will be flattered because you think me a better opponent and therefore set me a more careful romantic riddle to solve. I need no protestations of your feelings. Love can be lost, and I am done with losing."

He shivers, thinking of Lady Nore and Lord Jarel and how, though what was between them certainly was not love, it had something of love in it. He saw the former queens of the Court of Teeth immured inside the frozen walls of the Hall of Queens. That's what it was to want to possess another, being unwilling to let them go, even in death. To murder them when you decided it was time for them to be replaced, so that you could keep them still.

Oak hadn't thought Wren capable of wanting to possess someone that way, and he didn't want to believe it now.

But she may think—after throwing him in prison and leaving him there—they are enemies. That she made a choice in anger that cannot be taken back. That whatever else he says, he will always hate her.

And perhaps he would hate her, eventually. He blames himself for much, and is willing to endure much, but there's an end to his endurance.

"Perhaps you could remove the bridle, at least?" he asks. "You want me. You can have me. But will you kiss me even as I wear it? Feel the leather straps against your skin once more?"

A small shudder goes through her as she takes her seat again, and he knows he scored that point at least.

"What would you do to be freed from it?" she asks.

"Since you can use the bridle to make me do anything, it stands to reason that there ought to be nothing I wouldn't do to get it off," he says.

"But that's not the case." Her expression is canny, and he remembers how many bad bargains she has heard mortals make with the Folk.

He gives her a small, careful smile. "I would do *a lot*."

"Would you agree to stay here with me?" she asks. "Forever."

He thinks of his sisters, his mother and his father, his friends, and the idea of never seeing them again. Never being in the mortal world nor walking through the halls of Elfhame. He cannot imagine it. And yet, perhaps they could visit, perhaps in time he could persuade—

She must see the hesitation in his face. "I thought not."

"I didn't say no," he reminds her.

"I'll wager you were thinking of how you might bend the language in your favor. To promise something that sounded like what I asked for but had another meaning entirely."

He bites the inside of his cheek. That wasn't what he was thinking, but he would have eventually come around to it.

Oak stabs a piece of fish and eats it. It's peppery and has been splashed with vinegar. "What will you do when the High Court asks for me back?"

She gives him a mild look. "What makes you think they haven't already?"

He thinks of all the war meetings she was dragged to by a silver chain back in the Court of Teeth. She knows what a conflict with Elfhame means. "If you let me speak with my sister—" he begins.

"You would put in a good word?" There's a challenge in her voice.

Before, she played defensively. Her goal was to protect herself, but one cannot win that way.

I am done with losing.

He sees in Wren's face the desire to sweep the board.

He thinks of Bogdana, standing outside his cell, telling him that it is the High King she wants.

Was this all part of the storm hag's plan? His sister's lessons and his father's lessons come to him in a confusing rush, but they are all wrong for this.

"I could persuade Jude to give us a little longer to settle our differences. But I admit that it will be harder with this bridle on my face."

Wren takes another sip of her wine. "You can't stop what's coming."

"What if I promise to return if you let me go?" Oak asks.

She looks at him as though they are sharing an old joke. "Surely you don't expect me to fall for such a simple trick as that."

The prince thinks of the key on the mantel, of the possibility of escape. "I could have left."

"You wouldn't have gotten far." She sounds very sure.

Another course comes. This one is hot, so hot that the plate steams and the side of his ice wine goblet shines with melt. Deer hearts grilled over a fire, a sauce of red berries beneath them.

He wonders if Wren planned the progression of this meal. If not, someone in the kitchens has a truly grim sense of humor.

He doesn't lift his fork. He doesn't eat meat, but he's not sure he'd eat this even if he did.

She watches him. "You wish me to make you my advisor. To sit at my feet, tame and helpful. So advise me—I wish to be obeyed, even if I cannot be loved. I have few examples of queens that I might model myself after. Ought I rule like Queen Annet, who executes her lovers when she grows tired of them? Like your sister? I am told the High King himself called her method of diplomacy *the path of knives*. Or perhaps like Lady Nore, who used arbitrary and almost constant cruelty to keep her followers in line."

Oak sets his jaw. "I believe that you can be obeyed *and* loved. You don't need to rule like anyone other than yourself."

"Love, again?" Wren says, but the twist of her mouth softens. Some part of her must be frightened to be back in this Citadel, to be sovereign over those she was fighting mere weeks before, to have been ill, to have demands on her power. She doesn't behave as though she's afraid, though.

He looks across the table at the scars on her cheeks that came from wearing the bridle so long. At her moss-dark eyes. A feeling of helplessness sweeps over him. All his words tangle in his mouth, though he is used to having them come easily, tripping off his tongue.

He would tell her that he wants to stay with her, that he wants to be her friend again, wants to feel her teeth against his throat, but how can he possibly convince her of his sincerity? And even if she did believe him, what would it matter when his desires didn't keep her safe from his machinations?

"I never pretended to feelings that weren't real," he manages.

She watches him, her body tense, her eyes haunted. "Never? In the Court of Moths, would you really have endured my kiss if you didn't think you needed me on your quest?"

He snorts in surprise. "I would have *endured* it, yes. I would endure it again right now."

A slight rosiness comes into her cheeks. "That's not fair."

"This is nonsensical. Surely you could tell I liked it," he says. "I even liked it when you bit me. On the shoulder, remember? I might have a few tiny scars yet from the points of your teeth."

"Don't be ridiculous," she tells him, annoyed.

"Unfair," he says. "When I so love being ridiculous."

Servants come to collect their plates. The prince's food is untouched.

She looks down at her lap, turning enough away from him to hide her expression. "You cannot really expect me to believe you liked being bitten?"

He finds himself in the position he has so often put others, on his back foot. A hot flush creeps up his neck.

"Well?" she says.

He grins at her. "Didn't you mean for me to enjoy it a little?"

For a long moment, there's a silence between them.

The final course comes. Cold again, ice shaved into a pyramid of flakes, coated in a thin syrup as red as blood.

He eats it and tries not to shiver.

A few minutes later, Wren stands. "You will go back to the room in the tower, where I trust you will remain until I summon you again."

"To sprawl at your feet like a war prize?" he asks hopefully.

"That might amuse you enough to keep you from mischief." A small smile tugs at a corner of her mouth.

Oak pushes back his chair and walks to her, reaching for her hand. He is surprised when she lets him take it. Her fingers are cold in his.

She glances toward the guards. A red-haired falcon steps forward. Before Oak lets her hand go, though, he brings the back of it to his lips.

"My lady," he says, eyes closing for a moment when his mouth touches her skin. He feels as though he is attempting to cross a chasm on a bridge of razors. One misstep and he's going to be in a world of pain.

But Wren only makes a small frown, as though expecting to find mockery in his gaze. She takes back her hand, her face unreadable as the guards lead him to the door.

"I am not the person you believe me to be," she says in a rush.

He turns back to her, surprised.

"That girl you knew. Inside her was always this great rage, this emptiness. And now it's all I am." Wren looks wretched, her hands pressed together in front of her. Her eyes haunted.

Oak thinks of Mellith and her memories. Of her death and Wren's birth. Of the way she's watching him now.

"I don't believe that," he tells her.

She turns to one of the guards. "On the way to his rooms," she tells him, "make sure you pass the Great Hall."

One of the falcons nods, looking discomfited. The guards escort Oak out, marching him through the corridor. As they pass the throne room, they slow their steps enough for him to get a clear look inside.

Against the ice of the wall, as though a piece of decor, hangs Valen's body. For a moment, Oak wonders if this is Bogdana's handiwork, but the falcon is neither flayed nor displayed in the manner of the storm hag's other victims.

His throat is cut. A gruesome necklace of blood has dried along his collarbone. His clothing is stiff with it, as though starched. Oak can see the gape of flesh, cut cleanly with a sharp knife.

The prince glances back in the direction of where he had dinner with Wren.

When she noted his reluctance to name the person responsible for his bruises, she already knew. Hyacinthe must have conveyed Oak's words to her. She could have done this while the prince donned his clothes for their dinner.

It is not as if he hasn't seen murders before. In Elfhame, he saw plenty. His hands aren't clean. But looking at the dead falcon, displayed thus, he recognizes that, even without Mellith's memories, Wren saw things that were far more terrifying and cruel than anything he witnessed. And perhaps somewhere inside her, she is coming to learn that she can be all the things that once scared her.

CHAPTER

8

Oak was a child when Madoc was exiled to the mortal world, and yet, no matter what anyone said, he still knew it was his fault.

Without Oak, there would have been no war. No plan to steal the crown. No family at one another's throats.

At least your father wasn't executed for treason, Oriana told Oak when he complained about not being able to see him. Oak laughed, thinking she made a joke. When he realized that really could have happened, the idea of Madoc's dying while he watched, powerless to stop it, haunted his nightmares. Beheadings. Drownings. Burnings. Being buried alive. His sisters, grim-faced. Oriana, weeping.

Those bad dreams made not seeing Madoc even harder.

It's not a good idea right now, Oriana told him. *We don't want to seem as though we're not loyal to the crown.*

And so he lived with Vivi and Heather in the mortal world, went to the mortal school, and during library time, compulsively looked up new, horrible details of executions. Sometimes Jude or Taryn would visit him at the apartment. His mother came often. Occasionally, someone like Garrett or Van would show up and instruct him in bladework.

No one thought he had any real talent for it.

Oak's problem was that he thought of sword fighting as a game and didn't want to hurt anyone. Games were supposed to be fun. Then, after a lot of scolding, he understood sword fighting as a deadly game and still didn't want to hurt anyone.

Not everyone needs to be good at killing things, Taryn told him with a pointed look at Jude, who was dangling a toy over baby Leander's head as though he were a cat ready to swat at it.

Sometimes after his nightmares, Oak would sneak out and stand on the lawn of the apartment complex and look up at the stars. Missing his mother and father. Missing his old house and his old life. Then he would walk into the woods and practice with his sword, even though he didn't know what he was practicing for.

A few months in, Oriana finally took him to see Madoc. There was no objection or interference from Jude. Either she didn't know—which was unlikely—or she looked the other way, reluctant to forbid the visits but unable to officially allow them.

Be nice to your father, Oriana warned. As though Madoc was ill, rather than exiled and bored and angry. But if Oriana taught Oak one thing, it was how to pretend everything was fine without actually lying about it.

Oak felt shy as he stood in front of his father after all this time. Madoc had a ground-floor apartment in an old brick building by the waterfront. It wasn't quite like Vivi's, since it was furnished with ancient pieces from their home in Elfhame, but it was clearly a mortal space.

There was a refrigerator and an electric stove. Oak wondered if his father resented him.

Madoc seemed mostly concerned about Oak becoming soft.

"Those girls were always fussing over you," his father said. "Your mother, too."

Because he was born poisoned and was sickly as a baby, Oriana was constantly worried that Oak would overextend himself or that one of his sisters would be too rough with him. He hated her fretting. He was forever running off and swinging from trees or riding his pony in defiance of her edicts.

After months apart from his father, though, he felt ashamed of all the times he went along with her wishes.

"I'm not very good with a sword," he blurted out.

Madoc raised his brows. "How's that?"

Oak shrugged. He knew that Madoc never trained him the way he trained Jude and Taryn, certainly not the way he trained Jude. If he'd come inside with bruises the way she used to, Oriana would have been furious.

"Show me," Madoc said.

Which is how he found himself on the lawn of a cemetery, blade raised, as his father walked around him. Oak went through the exercises, one after the other. Madoc poked him with a mop handle when he was in the wrong position, but it wasn't often.

The redcap nodded. "Good, fine. You know what you're doing."

That part was true. Everyone had seen to that. "I have a hard time hitting people."

Madoc laughed in surprise. "Well, that is a problem."

Oak made a sour face. Back then, he didn't like being laughed at.

His father saw the expression and shook his head. "There's a trick to it," he said. "One that your sisters never quite learned."

"*My* sisters?" Oak asked, incredulous.

"You need to let go of the part of your mind that's holding you back," Madoc said moments before he attacked. The redcap's mop handle caught Oak in the side, knocking him into the grass. By the conditions of his exile, Madoc wasn't allowed to hold a weapon, so he improvised.

Oak looked up, the breath knocked out of him. But when Madoc swept the wooden stick toward him, he rolled to one side, blocking the blow.

"Good," his father said, and waited for him to get up before striking again.

They sparred like that, back and forth. Oak was used to fighting, although not with this great intensity.

Still, his father wore him down, hit by hit.

"All the skill in the world doesn't matter if you won't *strike me*," Madoc shouted finally. "Enough. Halt!"

Oak let his blade sag, relieved. Tired. "I told you."

But his father didn't look as though he was going to let things go. "You're blocking my blows instead of looking for openings."

Barely blocking, Oak thought, but nodded.

The redcap looked like he was going to gnash his teeth. "You need to get some fire in your belly."

Oak didn't reply. He'd heard Jude tell him something similar many times. If he didn't fight back, he could die. Elfhame wasn't a safe place. Maybe there were no safe places.

"You need to turn off the part of you that's *thinking*," Madoc said.

"Guilt. Shame. The desire to make people *like* you. Whatever is getting in your way, you need to excise it. Cut it out of your heart. From the time your sword leaves your sheath, put all that aside and strike!"

Oak bit his lip, not sure if that was possible. He liked being liked.

"Once your sword is out of your sheath, you aren't Oak anymore. And you stay that way until the fight is over." Madoc frowned. "And do you know how to tell the fight is over? All your enemies are dead. Understand?"

Oak nodded and *tried*. He willed himself to forget everything but the steps of the fight. Block, parry, strike.

He was quicker than Madoc. Sloppier, but faster. For a moment, he felt as though he was doing okay.

Then the redcap came at him hard. Oak responded with a flurry of parries. For a moment, he thought he saw an opportunity to get under his father's guard but flinched from it. His nightmares flashed in front of him. He parried instead, harder this time.

"Halt, child," said Madoc, stopping, frustration clear on his face. "You let two obvious openings pass."

Oak, who had seen only one, said nothing.

Madoc sighed. "Imagine splitting your mind into two parts: the general and the foot soldier. Once the general gives an order, the foot soldier doesn't need to think for himself. He just has to do what he's told."

"It's not that I'm *thinking* I don't want to hit you," Oak said. "I just don't."

His father nodded, frowning. Then his arm shot out, the flat of the mop handle knocking Oak into the dirt. For a moment, he couldn't get his breath.

"Get up," Madoc said.

As soon as he did, his father was on him again.

This time Madoc was serious, and for the first time, Oak was scared of what might happen. The hits came hard enough to bruise and too fast to be stopped.

He didn't want to hurt his father. He wasn't even sure that he could.

His father wasn't supposed to *really* hurt him.

As the blows came relentlessly, he could feel tears sting his eyes. "I want to stop," he said, the words coming out in a whine.

"Then fight back!" Madoc shouted.

"No!" Oak threw his sword to the ground. "I give up."

The mop handle caught him in the stomach. He went down hard, scuttled back, out of his father's range. Only barely, though.

"I don't want to do this!" he shouted. He could feel that his cheeks were wet.

Madoc came forward, closing the distance. "You want to die?"

"You're going to *kill* me?" Oak was incredulous. This was his *father*.

"Why not?" Madoc said. "If you don't defend yourself, *someone* is going to kill you. Better it be me."

That made no sense. But when the mop handle hit him in the side of the head, he started to believe it.

Oak looked at his sword, across the grass. Pushed himself to his hooves. Ran toward it. His cheek was throbbing. His stomach hurt.

He wasn't sure he'd ever been scared like this, not even when he was in the Great Hall with the serpent coming toward his mother.

When he turned back to Madoc, his vision was blurry with tears. Somehow that made things easier. To not have to really see what was happening. He could feel himself slipping into that state of not quite awareness. Like times that he was daydreaming on the walk to school and got there without remembering being on the route. Like when he gave over to his gancanagh magic and let it turn his words to honey.

Like those things, except he was angry enough to give himself a single order: *win*.

Like those things, except when he blinked, it was to find the point of his blade nearly at his father's throat, held back only by the half-splintered end of the mop handle. Madoc was bleeding from a slash on his arm, one Oak didn't recall causing.

"Good," said Madoc, breathing hard. "Again."

CHAPTER

9

When Oak returns to the bedroom in the tower, two servants are waiting for him. One has the head of an owl and long, gangly arms. The other has skin the color of moss and small moth wings.

"We are to ready you for bed," says one, indicating the dressing gown.

After weeks wearing the same rags, this is a lot. "Great. I can take it from here," he says.

"It is our duty to make sure you're properly cared for," says the other, ignoring Oak's objections and shoving his arms into the positions necessary for the removal of his doublet.

The prince submits, allowing them to strip him down and put him in the robe. It's a thick blue satin, lined in gold and warm enough that he doesn't entirely begrudge the change. It is strange to have spent weeks being treated as a prisoner, to now be treated as a prince. To be pampered and bullied just as he would be in Elfhame, not trusted to do basic tasks for himself.

He wonders if they do this to Wren. If she lets them.

He thinks of the rough silk of her hair slipping through his fingers.

All that matters is that I do *want you.*

As he sat for those long weeks in the prisons, he dreamed of her speaking words like those. But if she truly desired him only to be a handsome object with no will of his own, sprawled at her feet like a lazy hound, he would come to hate it. Eventually, he would hate her, too.

He goes to the mantel and takes the key. The metal is cold in the palm of his hand.

If she wants more from him, if she wants *him*, then she has to trust that if he leaves, he'll return.

Taking a deep breath, he walks to the bed. The dressing gown is warm but won't be once he hits the wind. He takes the thickest of the blankets and wraps it over his shoulders like a cloak. Then, ragwort stalk in one hand, he opens the door and peers out into the corridor.

No guard waits for him. He supposes Hyacinthe made sure of that.

As lightly as he can with his hooves, he goes to the stairs and begins to ascend. Up the spiraling structure, avoiding the landings until at last he comes to the top of the parapet. He steps out into the cold and looks out on the white landscape below.

As high up as he is, he can see beyond the trolls' massive—and as yet unfinished—wall. He squints as he spots what appears to be a flickering flame. And then another. A sound comes to him with the wind. Metallic and rhythmic, at first it sounds like sheeting rain. Then like the early rumblings of thunder.

Below him, behind the battlements, guards shout to one another. They must have spotted whatever it is that Oak is seeing. There's a confusion of footsteps.

But it isn't until the prince hears the distant blare of a horn that he finally identifies what he's been looking at. Soldiers marching toward the Citadel. The snake promised that in three days' time, someone would rescue him. What he didn't expect was that it would be the *entire army of Elfhame*.

Oak paces back and forth atop the cold parapet, panic making it impossible to focus. *Think*, he tells himself. *Think*.

He could use the ragwort steed and fly to them—assuming they would know it *was* him and not shoot him out of the sky. But once he got there, then what? They marched here for a war, and he wasn't foolish enough to believe they would merely turn around and go home once he was safe.

No, once he was safe, they would have no reason to hold back.

He grew up in a general's home, so he has a sense of what's likely to happen next. Grima Mog will send ahead riders to meet with Wren. They will demand to see him and offer terms of surrender. Wren will reject that and possibly unmake the messengers.

He needs to do something, but if he goes there with the bridle cutting into his cheeks, that will end all hope of peace.

Closing his eyes, Oak thinks through his options. They're all terrible, but the sheer mad audacity of one has a particular appeal.

Is there no situation you're not compelled to make worse?

The prince hopes that Hyacinthe isn't right.

He doesn't have a lot of time. Dropping the blanket, he heads down the steps, not bothering to care how loud his hooves are on the ice. Any guard that hears him has bigger problems.

Halfway down the spiral stairs, he almost crashes into a nisse with hair the green of celery and eyes so pale they are almost colorless. The faerie is carrying a tray with strips of raw venison arranged on a plate beside a bowl of stewed seaweed. Startled, the nisse takes a step back and loses his balance. The whole tray crashes down, plate cracking, seaweed splashing onto the steps.

The terror on the nisse's face makes it clear that the punishment for such a mishap in the old Court of Teeth would have been terrible. But when the nisse realizes who is standing in front of him, he becomes, if anything, more afraid.

"You're not supposed to be out of your rooms," the nisse says.

Oak notes the raw meat. "I suppose not."

The nisse starts to move away, stepping down a stair, looking behind him in a nervous way that suggests he will run. Before he can, Oak presses his hand over the nisse's mouth, pushing the faerie's back to the wall, even as he struggles against the prince's grip.

Oak needs an ally, a willing one.

Hating himself, the prince reaches for the honey-mouthed power that stretches languorously at his summons. He leans in to whisper in the nisse's ear. "I don't want to frighten you," he says, his voice sounding strange to his own ears. "And I don't intend to hurt you. When you came here, I'll wager it was because of a bad bargain."

That's how it was in Balekin's house. And he didn't think anyone would stay working for Lord Jarel and Lady Nore if they had any other option.

The nisse doesn't respond. But something in his expression and his stance makes Oak understand that the servant has been punished before, has been badly hurt, more than once. No wonder Oak scares him.

"What did you promise? I can help," Oak asks, pulling his hand away slowly. The burr is still in his voice.

The nisse relaxes some, tipping his head back against the wall. "Mortals found my family. I don't know what they thought we were, but they killed two of us and caught the third. I got away and came to the only place I knew could get back the lover that was taken—the Ice Needle Citadel. And I promised that if they were returned to me, I would loyally work in the Citadel until one of the royal family thought I had repaid my debt and dismissed me."

Oak lets out a groan. That's the sort of desperate, foolish bargain he associates with mortals, but mortals are not the only ones who grow desperate or who can be foolish. "Is that *exactly* what you promised?" Again, his voice has lost its honey-tongued power. He became too distracted to maintain it, too interested in what he wants to remember to say the right thing.

The nisse winces. "I will never forget."

Oak thinks about being a child and reckless about magic. He thinks about Valen and how furious he was after he realized Oak was enchanting him.

When he speaks, he can feel the air thicken. "I am one of the royal family. Not the one you meant, but you didn't specify, so I ought to be able to free you from your debt. But I need your help. I need someone to act as a messenger." Oak can feel the moments his words sink in, like a fish biting a worm, only to have a hook sink through its cheek.

He remembers the feeling of his body betraying him, the feeling of his limbs fighting against his will. There's none of that here. This is the opportunity the nisse has been looking for.

"We could both get in a lot of trouble," he says with a nervous glance down the stairs.

"We could," Oak says in his regular voice.

The nisse nods slowly, pushing off from the wall. "Tell me what you will have me do."

"First, I need something other than this to wear."

The nisse raises his eyebrows.

"Yes, yes, you find me to be vain," says Oak. "But I'm afraid I still need to discover wherever it is that they keep Lord Jarel's old clothes."

The nisse flinches. "You'd wear them?"

Probably the dressing gown Oak has on once belonged to Lord Jarel, as well as what Oak was given to put on for dinner. There hadn't been time to commission whole new outfits, nor had they fit right. And if they had been fetched for him, then he could fetch something else for himself. "Let's just take a look. What ought I call you?"

"Daggry, Your Highness."

"Lead on, Daggry," Oak says.

It's easier to move through the Citadel with a servant able to scout ahead and report which ways are clear. They make it to a storeroom, slipping inside before they are spotted.

"This is very near my bedchamber," says Daggry. "Should you wish to visit me there tonight."

Oak makes his mouth curve, though guilt chokes him. "I don't think either one of us will have much time for sleeping."

Oak thinks of his mother's warning: *Say those things, and they will not only want to listen to you. They will come to want you above all other things.*

"No," Daggry says. "I was not proposing sleep."

The narrow room is piled with trunks, stacked haphazardly one on the next. And packed in them, the prince finds clothes spread with dried lavender and picked over for gold and pearl ornaments. Strings hang loose from the places where buttons and trims were cut away. He wonders if Lady Nore sold the missing pieces before she discovered the value of the bones she stole from the tombs underneath Elfhame. Before Bogdana began whispering in her ear, urging her on the path that would bring Wren back to the storm hag.

He finds paper and ink, books and pen nibs attached to owl feathers. At the very bottom of the trunk, Oak digs up a few scattered weapons. Cheap, flat ones, a few pitted or scratched where gems were obviously removed from hilts. He lifts up a small dagger, keeping it mostly hidden in the palm of his hand.

"I am going to write a note," he says.

Daggry watches him with unnerving eagerness.

Taking out the paper, pens, and ink, Oak braces against one of the chests and scratches out two messages. The owl feather pen stains his fingers and makes him wish for a Sharpie. "Take the first of these to Hyacinthe," Oak says. "And the second one to the army that waits beyond the wall."

"The High Court's army?" the nisse says with a squeak in his voice.

Oak nods. "Go to the stables of the Citadel. There you will find my horse. Her name is Damsel Fly. Take her, and ride as fast as you are able. Once you come to the army, tell them you have a message from Prince Oak. Do not let them send you back with a message. Tell them it wouldn't be safe for you."

Daggry frowns, as though thinking things through. "And you will be grateful?"

"Very," Oak agrees.

"Enough to—" the nisse begins to say as he tucks away the notes.

"As a member of the royal family, I deem the time you have served a fair recompense for what you were given, and I dismiss you from service at the Citadel," Oak tells the nisse, frightened of the low burr in his own voice, like the purr of a cat. Frightened of the way the nisse gives him a look so full of gratitude and longing that it feels like a lash.

"I will do just as you've asked," says the nisse as he leaves, closing the door behind him.

For a moment, Oak just rubs at his face, not sure if he should be ashamed of what he's done, and if so, how ashamed. Forcibly, he thrusts that confusion of guilt aside. He has made his choices. Now he must live with them and hope they were the right ones.

The army of Elfhame is in danger because of him. Planning to hurt Wren because of him. Perhaps about to die because of him.

He strips off the dressing gown, pulling out a more regal outfit, grateful for Lord Jarel's height. The clothes are still a little short on him, a little tight across the chest.

You are such a beanstalk, he remembers Heather's mother saying. *I remember when I could pick you up.* He is surprised by how much that memory hurts, since Heather's mother is still alive and still kind and would let him sleep in her guest room anytime he wanted. Of course, that's predicated on his leaving this Citadel alive.

Sometimes, Oak thinks, it's not in his best interest to investigate his feelings too closely. In fact, right now, perhaps he ought not investigate his feelings at all.

Oak puts on a blue doublet, threaded with silver, then the matching pants. The hem rips a little as he puts his left hoof through one leg, but it's not immensely noticeable.

He hides the knife in the waistband, hoping he won't need it.

I can still fix things. That's what he tells himself over and over. He has a plan, and it might be mad and desperate and even a little presumptuous, but it can work.

Despite the cold, he discovers only two cloaks in the pile of clothes. He rejects the one lined in sealskin on the theory it may be from a selkie. That leaves him with the other, lined in fox fur, though he likes it little better.

Oak draws the hood over his face and heads to the Hall of Queens, where he asked Hyacinthe to meet. The room is echoing and empty; as he waits, he stares at the two women frozen inside the walls, former brides of Lord Jarel. Former queens of the Court of Teeth. Their cold, dead eyes seem to watch him back.

The prince paces the floor, but minutes pass and no one comes. His breath steams in the air as he listens for footsteps.

As dawn breaks, through the wavy ice he can see riders passing through the gap in the ice wall. They thunder toward the Citadel with banners streaming behind them, on faerie steeds whose hooves are light on the frozen crust of the snow.

His plan—wobbly from the start, he now has to admit—feels as though it is capsizing.

"Why are you still here?" a gruff voice asks.

For a long moment, relief robs the prince of breath. When he can compose his face, he turns toward Hyacinthe. "If I run from the Citadel wearing this bridle," he says, "no one in command will care what I say. They will believe I am in Wren's power. I will have even less sway over the army than I do, and that isn't much. With Grima Mog in charge of them, and orders already in place from my sister, they'll be looking forward to a fight."

"All they want is you," Hyacinthe says.

"Maybe, but once they have me, what's the next thing they will want? If I am safe, they have no reason *not* to attack. Help me help Wren. Remove the bridle."

Hyacinthe snorts. "I know the words of command well. I could use them to order you to leave the Citadel and surrender yourself to Grima Mog."

"If you send me away with the bridle on, no one will ever believe that we are not at war," Oak says.

Hyacinthe crosses his arms. "Am I supposed to believe you're on Wren's side in this conflict? That escaping is somehow all for her?"

Oak wishes he could say that. Wishes he even believed in clear sides with defined borders. He had to give those up when his father crossed swords with his sister. "Even if Wren can unmake the entire army of Elfhame, pull them apart as easily as she might pull the wings off butterflies, it will cost her. Hurt her. Make her sicker."

"You're their prince," Hyacinthe says with a sneer. "You look to save your own people."

"How about no one dies? Let's try for that!" Oak snaps, his voice loud enough to echo in the room.

Hyacinthe looks at the prince for a long moment. "Very well. I'll take off the bridle and let you try whatever it is you're planning, so long as you promise no harm will come to Wren—and you agree to do something for me."

No matter how much he wants to, Oak knows better than to give his word without hearing the conditions. He waits.

"You thought I was foolish for going after the High King," Hyacinthe says.

"I still do," Oak confirms.

Hyacinthe gives him a frustrated look. "I admit that I'm impulsive. When the curse started again, when I could feel myself becoming a falcon again—I thought if Cardan were dead, it would end the curse. I blamed him."

Oak bites his tongue. Hyacinthe has not yet come to the favor part.

"There's something I want to know, but I am not crafty enough to discover it. Nor am I so well connected." Hyacinthe looks as though he hates admitting this. "But you—you deceive as easily as you breathe and with as little thought."

"And you want..."

"Revenge. I thought it was impossible, but Madoc told me something different," Hyacinthe says. "You should care, you know? You owe her a blood debt as well."

Oak frowns. "Prince Dain killed Liriope, and he's dead himself. I know you want to punish someone—"

"No, he *ordered* her killed," Hyacinthe says. "But he wasn't the one to administer the poison. Not the one to sneak past my father as he guarded her. Not the one to leave you both for dead. That is the person I can still kill for my father's sake."

Oak assumed that Dain administered the poison. Slipped it into a drink. Poured it over her lips while she slept beside him. He never imagined that her murderer was still alive.

"So I find the person who gave her the poison. Or try, at least—and you remove the bridle," Oak says. "I agree."

"Bring me the hand of the person responsible for her death," Hyacinthe says.

"You want a *hand*?" Oak raises both brows.

"That hand, I do."

Oak doesn't have time to negotiate. "Fine."

Hyacinthe gives a strange smile, and Oak worries that he's made the wrong decision, but it's too late to question it.

"*In Grimsen's name,*" Hyacinthe begins, and Oak jams his hand into the pocket of the cloak for the knife he found. His skin is clammy despite the cold. He cannot be sure that Hyacinthe won't use the command to do something other than unbind him. If so, Oak is going to try to cut the falcon's throat before he finishes speaking.

Probably there wouldn't even be time. Oak's fingers twitch.

"*In Grimsen's name, let the bridle no longer bind you,*" Hyacinthe says.

Oak takes his blade to the strap, but it doesn't cut. He nicks his own cheek for the effort. A moment later, though, he has unhooked the bridle with shaking hands. He pulls it off his face, throwing it to the ground. He can feel the indentations where the straps pressed into his cheek. Not sunken so deeply to scar, but tight enough to mark.

"A monstrous object," Hyacinthe says as he bends to pick up the bridle. He wore it long enough to hate it, perhaps even more than Oak. "Now what?"

"We go to the Great Hall to meet the riders." Oak traces his fingers over his cheeks, the cold of them a relief. He doesn't like the idea that Hyacinthe has the bridle, but even if the prince could wrest it from him, he dreads so much as touching it.

Hyacinthe frowns. "And...?"

"Attempt to seem convincingly happy to be Wren's guest," Oak says. "Then figure out how to send the army of Elfhame on its way."

"That's what you're calling a plan?" Hyacinthe snorts. "We can't be seen together, so give me a head start. I don't want anyone to guess what I've done, in case it doesn't work."

"It would be a lot easier to get into the Great Hall with your help," Oak points out.

"I'm sure it would be," says Hyacinthe.

The falcon stalks off, leaving Oak to wait. To pace the Hall of Queens some more. Count off the minutes. Trace his fingers over his cheek to feel for any trace of the straps. There's something there, but light, like the creases left from a pillow in the morning. He hopes these marks will disappear soon. Finally, he can bear to bide his time no longer. He pushes back the hood of his cloak and, head held high, walks toward the Great Hall.

If there is one thing he has learned from Cardan, it is that royalty inspires awe and awe can be cultivated easily into menace. It is with that in mind that he strides toward the guards.

Startled, they raise their spears. Two falcons, neither of whom he recognizes.

Oak looks at them blandly. "Well," he says with an impatient wave of his hand. "Open the doors."

He watches them hesitate. After all, he's dressed well and clean. He doesn't have on the bridle. And they must all know he is no longer being held in the prisons. They must all know Wren killed the last guard who put a finger on him.

"The emissaries of Elfhame are inside, are they not?" he adds.

One of the falcons nods to the other. Together, they open the double doors.

Wren sits on her throne; Bogdana and Hyacinthe stand beside her—along with a trio of heavily armored falcons.

And standing before her are four Folk—all of whom Oak recognizes. Unarmored, the Ghost appears to be playing the part of an ambassador. He's dressed in finery, and the slightly human cast of his features makes him look far less threatening than he is.

An actual ambassador, Randalin, one of the Living Council, bites off his words at Oak's arrival. Known as the Minister of Keys, he is short, horned, and even more beautifully dressed than the Ghost. As far as Oak is aware, Randalin can't fight and, given the danger, Oak is surprised he came. Jude never much liked him, though, so he can certainly see why she allowed—and even perhaps encouraged—it.

Behind them are two soldiers. Oak knows Tiernan instantly, despite the helmet hiding his face. He assumes Hyacinthe knows him, too. At his side is Grima Mog, the grand general who replaced Oak's father. A redcap, like Madoc, and the former general of the Court of Teeth. No one knows the defenses of the Citadel better than she does, so no one would have an easier time breaching them.

As Oak strides in, everyone becomes more alert. Tiernan's hand goes automatically to the pommel of his sword in a foolish rejection of diplomacy.

"Hello," the prince says. "I see you all started without me."

Wren raises both her brows. *Good game*, he imagines her saying. *Point to you.* Possibly right before she tells her guards to pop off his head like a wine cork.

And then the Ghost stabs her in the back. And everyone cuts everyone else to pieces.

"Your Highness," says Garrett, as though he really is some stuffy ambassador who hasn't known Oak half his life. "After receiving your note, we expected you to be in attendance. We were growing concerned."

Wren gives the prince a sharp look at the mention of a note.

"Hard to choose the right outfit for such a momentous occasion,"

Oak says, hoping that the sheer absurdity of his plan will help sell it. "After all, it's not every day that one gets to announce one's engagement."

At that, all of them stare at him agog. Even Bogdana seems to have lost the power of speech. But that is nothing to the way Wren is looking at him. It is as though she could immolate him in the cold green flame of her eyes.

Heedless of the warning, he walks to her side. Taking her hand, he slides the ring—the ring he was sent in the belly of an enchanted metal snake—off his pinkie finger and onto hers in the stealthy way the Roach taught him. So that it might be possible to believe she'd been wearing it the whole time.

He smiles up at her. "She's accepted my ring. And so, I would be delighted to tell you that Wren and I are to be wed."

Oak keeps his gaze on Wren. She could deny him, but she remains silent. Hopefully she sees that in the face of their *engagement*, it will be possible to avoid a war. Or, since she holds all the cards, maybe she finds it amusing to let him reshuffle a little.

A wordless growl comes from deep in Bogdana's throat.

Hyacinthe gives Oak an accusatory look that seems to say, *I can't believe you talked me into helping you with such a stupid plan.*

This was the gamble. That Wren didn't want to fight. That she'd see the path to peace with Elfhame was through playing along with him.

"Quite a surprise," the Ghost says, voice dry. Hyacinthe's gaze drifts to him, and his expression stiffens, as though he recognizes the spy and understands the danger of his being here.

Tiernan's hand has yet to leave his sword hilt. Grima Mog's eyebrows are raised. She seems to be waiting for someone to tell her this is all a joke.

Oak goes on smiling, as though everyone has been expressing only their utmost delight.

Randalin clears his throat. "Let me be the first to offer my felicitations. Very wise to secure the succession."

Although the councilor's reasoning seems muddled, the prince is happy for any ally. Oak makes a shallow bow. "I can occasionally be wise."

Eyebrows raised, the Ghost moves his gaze from Wren to Oak. "Your family will be pleased to know you are well. The reports... let's say they suggested otherwise."

At that, Bogdana manages a toothy smile. "Your besotted princeling seems none the worse for wear. Accept our hospitality. We offer you rooms and repast. Stay the night, then take your army and toddle back to Elfhame. Perhaps send the king and queen for a little visit."

"I didn't realize you were empowered to offer us much of anything, storm hag." Grima Mog makes the words sound almost as though they were spoken in honest confusion. "Is it not Queen Suren alone who rules here?"

"For now," says the storm hag with an almost gracious nod toward Oak, as if she were indicating he would rule beside Wren rather than asserting her own power.

Wren motions toward a servant and then turns back to the Minister of Keys. "You must be tired after your travels, and cold. Perhaps a hot drink before you are led to your rooms."

"We would be honored to accept your accommodation," Randalin says, puffing himself up. He accompanied the army, so he must have thought there would be some kind of negotiation for him to lead. Maybe he convinced himself this would be an easy situation to resolve and is gratified to believe himself correct. "On the morrow, we must discuss your plans to return to Elfhame. The prince returning with his bride-to-be will be glad tidings indeed and a cause for much celebration. And of course, there will be a treaty to negotiate."

Oak winces. "A treaty. Of course." He cannot help but cut a glance in Wren's direction, trying to gauge her reaction.

The Ghost tilts his head as he regards Wren. "Are you certain about accepting the young prince's proposal? He can be something of a fool."

Her lips twitch.

Randalin draws in a shocked breath.

Oak gives the Ghost a speaking look. "The question is whether she will have me be *her* fool."

Wren smiles. "I'm certain."

Oak glances at her in surprise, unable to help himself. He attempts to smooth out his expression but is certain he's too late. Someone saw. Someone knows he isn't sure of her love.

"We have a great deal in common, after all," Wren affirms. "Especially a love of games."

She's good at them, too. Quick to pick up on his plan, to measure its worth, and play along. They've been working against each other for so long that he forgot how easy it was to work together.

"We can unravel the details of the treaty in Elfhame," Randalin says. "It will be easier with all parties present."

"I am not sure I'm ready to leave my Citadel," says Wren, and she glances at Oak. He can see her weighing the choice to let him return with them. Can see the calculation in her face as to whether this was his intention all along.

Two servants enter the room bearing a large wooden tray with steaming silver goblets atop it.

"Please, take one," Wren offers.

Do not try to poison them, he thinks, staring at her as though he can somehow speak through his gaze. *Garrett will switch cups with you, and you'll never guess it.*

The Ghost takes the hot drink. Oak lifts one, too, the metal warm in his hand. He catches scents of barley and caraway.

Randalin raises his glass. "To you, Lady Suren. And to you, Prince Oak. In the hopes you will reconsider and join us in returning to Elfhame. Your family will insist on it, prince. And I was meant to remind you, should I be so fortunate as to have an audience with *you*, Lady Suren, that you made vows to the High Court."

"If they mean to give me orders, let them come here and do so," Wren says. "But perhaps I can sweep aside a promise like I would a curse. Pull it apart like a cobweb."

The Folk stare, horrified by even the possibility that someone in Faerie could not be bound by her word. Oak never thought of the promises they made as *magic*, but he supposes they are a kind of binding.

"You ought not want things to start off on the wrong foot," Randalin warns, sounding as though he were reprimanding a student who gave a wrong answer. The councilor seems unaware of how quickly this conversation might devolve into violence.

Grima Mog cracks her knuckles. She is very aware.

"Randalin—" Oak begins.

Bogdana interrupts him. "The councilor is correct," she says. "Wren ought to be properly wed to the heir of Elfhame, with all the pomp and circumstance appropriate to such a union. Let us journey together to the Shifting Isles."

Wren gives the storm hag a sharp look but doesn't contradict her. Doesn't say she won't go. Instead, her fingers linger on the ring sitting loosely on her hand. She turns it anxiously.

Oak recalls Wren coming to the gardens of Elfhame years and years ago, where Jude had received her, along with Lord Jarel, Lady Nore, and Madoc. Recalls that one of them had proposed a truce, cemented with a marriage between him and Wren.

He was a little afraid of her, with her sharp teeth. He had yet to hit the growth spurt that came at thirteen and pulled his body like taffy; she almost certainly was taller than him. He didn't want to marry her—he didn't want to marry *anyone*—and was relieved when Jude refused.

But he saw the expression in Wren's face when Vivi referred to her as *creepy.* The sting of hurt, the flash of rage.

She is going to destroy Elfhame. It's what she was born to do. That's what Bogdana believes, what she wants. And maybe Wren wants it a little bit, too. Maybe Oak has made a horrifically large mistake.

But, no. Wren couldn't have known he would do anything like this. Still, whatever Bogdana favors is unlikely to be a good idea.

"We don't need to depart immediately," the prince hedges. "No doubt you will need time to get together your trousseau."

"Nonsense," says Bogdana. "I know a hag who will enchant Queen Suren three dresses, one for every day in Elfhame before her wedding. The first shall be the pale colors of morning, the second the bright colors of the afternoon, and the last spangled with the jewels of night."

"Three days won't be enough time," says Randalin, frowning.

"Now who is trying to delay?" the storm hag demands, as though the councilor has committed a grave offense. "Perhaps none of this is necessary. He could marry her now, with those gathered here as witnesses."

"*No*," says Wren firmly.

A shame, because Oak doesn't think it's such a bad idea. If they were married, then surely his sister couldn't attempt to burn the Citadel to the ground. Her troops would have to pull back while Oak could keep the ragwort stalk safely in his pocket and bide his time.

"We would not want to disrespect the High Court," Wren says. "We will return with you to Elfhame so long as you withdraw your army from this territory. Whatever preparations are necessary, we will manage."

The Ghost smiles enigmatically. "Excellent. Randalin, your ship is small and swift and well outfitted for traveling in comfort. We can use it to return to Elfhame ahead of the army. If you expect to be ready within a day or two, I will send the message right now."

"You may do so," Wren tells him.

"No, no need," Grima Mog interrupts them gruffly. "I am here to negotiate over battles, not withdrawals. I will return to my army and inform them that no blood will be shed upon the morrow, nor possibly at all." She says this as though they are to be deprived of a great treat. She's a redcap; she might actually believe that.

Her leaving is also almost certainly a test, to see if her departure will be allowed.

As she stomps out, the rest of them drink the contents of their steaming goblets. Randalin makes an officious and confusing speech that manages to be partially about his grievances over the discomforts he endured on the journey, his loyalty to the throne and to Oak, and his belief that alliances are very important. By the time he's done, he's behaving as though he negotiated the marriage himself.

After that, servants make ready to lead each of them to rooms.

The Ghost catches Wren's eye. "We hope that you will choose wisely when you select your retinue." He gives a pointed look in the direction of the storm hag.

A small smile pulls at the corner of Wren's mouth, making her sharp teeth evident. "Someone will have to remain here and watch over the Citadel."

After the Elfhame ambassadors and their guards depart, Wren puts a hand on Oak's arm, as though she needs to draw his attention. "What kind of game is this?" She lowers her voice, although Bogdana is watching them closely. Hyacinthe and the other guards are pretending they are not.

"The kind where no one loses so badly that they have to throw away all their cards," Oak says.

"You only delay the inevitable." She turns from him, her skirts whirling around her.

He wonders how she must have felt when the army of Elfhame arrived. She seems to have resigned herself to the battle with a certain hopelessness, as though she couldn't imagine a way out.

"Maybe I can keep delaying it." Daringly, he walks after her, stepping in front so that she's forced to look up at him. "Or maybe it isn't inevitable."

A few strands of light blue hair have fallen around her face, lessening the severity of the style. But nothing can alter the hardness in her expression. "Hyacinthe," she says.

He steps forward. "My lady."

"Take the prince back to his rooms. And this time, make sure he actually stays there." It's not an accusation, but it's close.

"Yes, my lady," Hyacinthe affirms, taking Oak by the arm and tugging him in the direction of the hall.

"And bring the bridle to my chambers immediately after," she says.

"Yes, my lady," Hyacinthe says again, his voice remarkably even.

The prince goes along willingly. At least until they enter the stairwell and Hyacinthe shoves him against the wall, hand to his throat.

"What exactly do you think you were doing?" Hyacinthe demands.

The prince holds his hands out in surrender. "It worked."

"I didn't expect you to . . . ," he starts, but cannot seem to finish the sentence. "I should have, of course. Do you think that traveling to Elfhame will help her use her power less?"

"Than fighting a war?" Oak asks. "I do."

"And whose fault is it that she's in this position in the first place?"

"Mine," Oak admits with a wince. "But not just mine. You were the one who put the idea of defeating Lady Nore in order to end his exile into my father's head. If Madoc had never come here, then none of this would have ever happened."

"You're blaming me for the former grand general's schemes. I ought to be flattered."

"My sister would have *executed* you for your part in those schemes," Oak tells Hyacinthe. "Had we not taken you that night, at best, you would have been locked in the Tower of Forgetting. But most likely she would have had your head. And then Tiernan's for good measure."

"Is that how you justify manipulating all the people around you like pieces on a chessboard?" Hyacinthe accuses. "That you're doing the best for them?"

"As opposed to you, who doesn't care how much Tiernan suffers for your sake? I suppose you think that makes you honest, rather than a coward." Oak isn't thinking about what he's saying anymore. He's too angry for that. "Or maybe you want to cause him pain. Maybe you're still furious with him for not following you into exile. Maybe making him miserable is your way of having revenge."

Hyacinthe's punch sends Oak staggering back. He can taste blood where a tooth caught on the inside of his mouth. *Is there no situation you're not compelled to make worse?*

"You have no right to *speak* of my feelings for Tiernan." Hyacinthe's voice is raw.

For a moment, in the hot flush of his anger, Oak wonders what would happen if he said all the right things now, instead of the wrong ones. It would serve Hyacinthe right to *have* to like him.

But it was so satisfying to do just the opposite.

"You've been wanting to hit me for a long time." Oak spits blood onto the ice steps. "Well, come on, then."

Hyacinthe punches him again, this time connecting with his jaw, knocking him against a wall.

When Oak looks up, it's as though he's seeing through a haze. *Oh, this was a bad idea.* There's a roaring in his ears.

He's afraid suddenly that he cannot hold back.

"Fight, you coward," Hyacinthe says, punching him in the stomach.

Oak's hand goes to his side, to the knife he concealed there, wrapped tight enough not to muss the line of the doublet. He doesn't remember deciding to draw it before it's in his hand, sharp and deadly.

Hyacinthe's eyes widen, and Oak is very afraid that he is about to lose time again.

He lets the blade drop.

They stare at each other.

Oak can feel the pulse of his blood, that part of him that's eager for a *real* fight, that wants to stop thinking, stop feeling, stop doing anything but make the cold calculations of combat. His awareness of himself flickers like a light, warning that it's about to cut out and welcome in the dark.

"Well," says a voice from behind the prince. "This is not at all what I expected to find when I went looking for both of you."

He whirls to see Tiernan standing there, sword drawn.

A flush creeps up Hyacinthe's neck. "You," he says.

"Me," says Tiernan.

"Be flattered." Oak wipes blood off his chin. "I think we were fighting over you."

Tiernan looks at Hyacinthe with frightening coldness. "Striking the heir to Elfhame is treason."

"Good thing I am already well known to be a traitor," Hyacinthe growls. "Allow me to remind you, however. This is my Citadel. I am in charge of the guard here. I am the one who enforces Wren's will."

Tiernan bristles. "And I am responsible for the prince's well-being, no matter where we are."

Hyacinthe sneers. "And yet you abandoned him."

Tiernan's jaw is tight with the force of his restraint. "I assume you have no objections to the prince finding his own way back to his rooms. We can handle what is between us without him."

Hyacinthe glares at Oak, perhaps thinking of Wren ordering him to make sure the prince didn't wind up wandering the Citadel again.

"I'll be good," Oak says, heading up the stairs before Hyacinthe decides to stop him.

When he glances back, Tiernan and Hyacinthe are still staring at each other with painful suspicion, in a standoff that he doesn't think either of them knows how to end.

Oak climbs two floors before he stops and listens. If he hears the clang of metal on metal, he's going back. He must have missed something, because Hyacinthe speaks as though replying to Tiernan.

"And where am I in this reckoning?" Hyacinthe asks.

"Three times I put aside my duty for you," Tiernan says, as angry as Oak has ever heard him. "And three times you spurned it. Once, when I went to you in the prisons before you were to be judged for following Madoc. Do you remember? I promised that were you sentenced to death, I would find a way to get you out, no matter the cost. Second, when I persuaded the prince, *my charge*, to use his power to mitigate the curse you wouldn't even have had if you had simply repented your betrayal of the crown. And let's not forget the third, when I pleaded for you to wear the bridle instead of being put to death for an attempted assassination. Do not ask me to do so again."

"I wronged you," Hyacinthe says. Oak shifts on the stairs so he can see just a bit of him—his shoulders are slumped. "You have put aside your duty more than I have put aside my anger. But I—"

"You will never be satisfied," Tiernan snaps. "Joining Madoc's falcons and turning on Elfhame, spitting on mercy, blaming Cardan and Oak and Oak's dead mother and everyone except your father.

"No vengeance will ever be enough, because you want to punish his murderer, but he *died by his own hand*. You refuse to hate him, so you hate everyone else, including yourself."

Tiernan didn't raise his voice, but Hyacinthe makes a sound as though struck.

"Including me," says Tiernan.

"Not you," Hyacinthe says.

"You didn't punish me for being like him, for guarding her son? You didn't hate me for that?"

"I believed I was doomed to lose you," Hyacinthe says, voice so soft that Oak can barely hear it.

For a long moment, they are quiet.

It seems unlikely they are going to break into violence. Oak should go up the rest of the stairs. He doesn't want to invade their privacy more than he already has. He needs to go slowly, though, so they don't hear his hooves.

"Joy is never guaranteed," Tiernan says, his voice gentle. "But you can wed yourself to pain. I suppose, at least in that, there is no chance of surprise."

Oak winces at those words. *Wed yourself to pain.*

"Why would you want me after all I have done?" Hyacinthe asks, anguished.

"Why does anyone want anyone else?" Tiernan answers. "We do not love because people deserve it—nor would I want to be loved because I was the *most deserving* of some list of candidates. I want to be loved for my worst self as well as my best. I want to be forgiven my flaws."

"I find it harder to forgive your virtues," Hyacinthe tells him, a smile in his voice.

And then Oak is up the stairs far enough to be unable to hear the rest. Which is good, because he hopes it involves a lot of kissing.

CHAPTER
11

When Oak was a child, he came down with fevers that laid him up for weeks. He would thrash in bed, sweating or shivering. Servants would come and press cold cloths to his brow or put him in baths stinking with herbs. Sometimes Oriana would sit with him, or one of his sisters would come and read.

Once, when he was five, he opened his eyes to see Madoc in the doorway, regarding him with an odd, evaluating expression on his face.

Am I going to die? he asked.

Madoc was startled out of whatever he was thinking, but there was still something grim in the set of his mouth. He walked to the bed and placed his large hand on Oak's brow, ignoring his small horns. *No, my boy*, he said seriously. *Your fate is to cheat death like the little scamp you are.*

And because Madoc could not lie, Oak was comforted and fell back to sleep. The fever must have broken that night, because when he woke, he was well again and ready for mischief.

This morning, Oak feels like a scamp who's cheated death again.

Waking to warmth and softness is such a delicious luxury that Oak's burns and bruises cannot dent the pleasure of it. There is a taste on his tongue that is somehow the flavor of sleep itself, as though he went so deep into the land of dreams that he brought some of it back with him.

He looks at his little finger, bare now, and smiles up at the ice ceiling.

There is a knock on the door, shaking him out of his thoughts. Before he realizes he's not wearing much in the way of clothes, Fernwaif bustles in with a tray and a pitcher. She's got on a brown homespun dress and an apron, her hair pulled back in a kerchief.

"Still abed?" she asks, plopping down the tray on his coverlets. It contains a teapot and cup, along with a plate of black bread, butter, and jam. "You're leaving with the tide."

The prince feels oddly self-conscious at sleeping late, although lounging around at all hours is part of the self-indulgent persona he's played for years. He's not sure why that role feels so suffocating this morning, but it does.

"We're leaving *today*?" He pushes his back against the headboard so he can sit upright.

Fernwaif gives a little laugh as she pours water into a bowl on a washing stand. "Will you miss us when you're in the High Court?"

Oak will not miss the endless boredom and despair of his prison cell, or the sound of cold wind howling through trees, but it occurs to him that while he's glad to be headed home, being with Wren there will be complicated in new ways. The High Court is a place full of intrigues and ambition. Once Oak returns, he will be at the swirling center of at least one conspiracy. He has no idea if it will even be *possible* to play the feckless, merry courtier while winning Wren's goodwill.

And he is even less sure that's who he wants to be.

"Fate may bring me again to these shores," Oak says.

"My sister and I will look forward to tales of the great feasts and dances," Fernwaif says, looking wistful. "And how you honored our lady."

Oak can only imagine what Wren might say if somehow she found herself having to actually exchange vows with him. *I pledge my troth to thee and promise to turn thy guts inside out if you deceive.* Oh yes, this is going well.

What was it that Hyacinthe said? *You deceive as easily as you breathe and with as little thought.* Oak very much hopes that's not true.

He doesn't hear the turn of the lock as Fernwaif leaves. He supposes there's no point in restricting his movements now, when they're planning on his leaving.

Rising, Oak splashes his face with the water from the washing stand, slicking back his hair. He manages to pull on Lord Jarel's pants before heavy footsteps on the stairs herald the appearance of five knights. To his surprise, they wear the livery of Elfhame—the crest of the Greenbriar line imprinted on their armor with its crown, tree, and grasping roots.

"Your Highness," one says, and Oak feels disoriented at the sound of his title, spoken without hostility. "Grima Mog sent us. Our commander wishes you to know that the boat awaits you and that we will accompany you on your return to the isles."

They have more appropriate garments for him, too—a green cloak embroidered in gold, heavy gloves, and a woolen tunic and trousers.

"Do you have anything here you wish us to pack?" one of the knights asks. She has eyes like those of a frog, gold-flecked and wide.

"I seem to have...misplaced my armor and my sword," Oak admits.

No one questions the strangeness of that. No one questions him at all. A knight with sharply pointed ears and moonlight-colored hair passes over his own curved blade—a cutlass—along with its sheath.

"We can find some armor for you among our company," the knight says.

"That's not necessary," Oak says, feeling very self-conscious. They are looking at him as though he has endured a terrible trial, even though they must know he's betrothed. "You really ought to keep your sword."

"Return it to me once you've found one better," says the knight, crossing to the door. "We will await you in the hall."

Quickly, the prince changes clothes. The fabric carries the scent of the air that blew across the line where it was hung to dry—sweetgrass and the salty tang of the ocean. Breathing it in fills him with homesickness.

Outside the Citadel, more soldiers of Elfhame wait, bundled up in heavily padded and fur-trimmed armor, their cloaks whipping behind them. They glare across the snow at the former falcons.

One of them holds Damsel Fly's reins. His horse's legs are wrapped against the snow, and a blanket hangs over her back. When the prince draws close, she frisks up to him, butting her head against his shoulder.

"Damsel!" Oak exclaims, stroking his hand over his horse's neck. "Was there a messenger from the Citadel with her?"

The soldier looks surprised to be asked for information. "Your Highness, I believe so. He rode into the camp yesterday. We recognized your steed."

"Where is that messenger now?" Valen became violent when Oak stopped actively using enchantment against him—but Valen *hated* Oak. Hopefully Daggry felt their transaction benefited them both. Hopefully Daggry was well on his way back to the lover he sacrificed so many years to save.

"I'm not sure—" the soldier begins.

From inside the stable comes the sounding of a horn, and he sees an open-topped carriage roll out, pulled by elk. It is all of black wood, looking as though it wasn't painted that way but scorched instead. The wheels are as tall as one of the soldiers standing beside it, the spokes slender as spun sugar. A groom perches on the back, all in white with a mask in the shape of a falcon, the leather twisting like branches over his eyebrows. A similarly masked driver—this one wearing the mask of a wren—sits in the front, urging the elk on with a whip.

They stop and open the door to the carriage, standing at attention.

Wren walks from the Citadel, unaccompanied by guards or ladies-in-waiting. Her gown is all black, and the toothlike, obsidian crown of the Court of Teeth rests on her head. Her feet are bare—perhaps to show that the cold cannot harm her or because she prefers it. After all, she went barefoot for many years in the woods.

She allows her groom to hand her into the carriage, where she sits, back straight. Her blue skin is the color of the clear sky. Her hair blows in a wild nimbus around her face, and her gown billows, making her seem elemental. One of the Folk of the Air.

Wren's gaze goes to him once, then darts away.

The rest of Wren's retinue assembles around her. Hyacinthe rides a large, shaggy deer, which seems as though it will be far better in picking its way through the snow than the delicate hooves of Oak's faerie horse.

Half a dozen falcons accompany him, wearing livery all of a shimmering gray. Bogdana rides a bear, which lumbers around, unnerving everyone.

Tiernan rides up to where Oak has mounted Damsel Fly. His jaw is tight with tension. "This doesn't feel right."

Randalin arrives a moment later, the Ghost beside him.

"Your betrothed really is remarkable," the Minister of Keys says. "Do you know she has two ancient troll kings swearing fealty to her?"

"I certainly do," Oak says.

"It would be better for everyone if we move now," says the Ghost.

"I suppose," Randalin says with a long-suffering sigh, somehow oblivious to the danger all around him. "We were in such a hurry to march here, and now we're in such a hurry to leave. I personally would be interested in sampling local dishes."

"The kitchens are somewhat understaffed," Oak says.

"I am going to check on the queen's party," the Ghost says, then rides off in that direction.

"When did the knights arrive?" Oak asks Tiernan, gesturing toward the Folk swarming around the castle.

"This morning. Courtesy of Grima Mog. To escort us to the boat," Tiernan says mildly since Randalin is beside them.

Oak nods, taking that in.

The horn blows again, and they begin to move.

It takes them more than an hour to arrive at the rough-hewn ice wall built by the troll kings. As they draw closer, Oak is awed by the sheer scale of it. It towers over them as they ride into the gap.

And then past the army of Elfhame.

Fires dot the landscape, burning where soldiers crowd around them for warmth. Several knights sit alone on makeshift stools, polishing weapons, while larger groups gather to drink barley tea and smoke pipes. Although a few call out cheerfully at the sight of Oak, he notes something ugly in their gaze when they see Wren's carriage.

A loud sound like a clang of metal on metal rings across the snow, and the group comes to an abrupt halt. Bogdana's bear growls. Wren's guards crowd around her carriage, hands on their weapons. She says something to them, low. The air is thick with the threat of violence.

Grima Mog and a group of armored soldiers walk toward the procession. Oak spurs Damsel Fly toward the grand general, his heart beating hard.

Do they mean to betray Wren? Make a captive of her? If they try, he'll invoke his authority as Cardan's heir. He will find out the extent of all his powers. He will do *something*.

"Greetings, Prince Oak," says Grima Mog. She wears a hat, clotted and black with blood. Armor covers the rest of her, and she has a massive, two-handed sword strapped to her back. She passes a scroll up into his hands. It's sealed with a ribbon and wax. "This explains to the High King and Queen that we will remain here until a treaty is signed."

The entire army, camped in the cold just beyond the wall, waiting and planning.

"Word will come soon," Oak promises.

Grima Mog gives a half smile, lower canine escaping her lip. "Waiting is dull business. You wouldn't want us to grow restless."

Then, taking a step back, Grima Mog gives a signal. Her people fall back. The soldiers of Elfhame who were part of Oak's procession begin to move again. The wheels of Wren's carriage roll forward. The bear plods on.

Oak is immensely relieved to leave the army behind.

Next, they draw close to the Stone Forest, the trees hanging heavy with their strange blue fruit. Wind whistles through branches, making an eerie tune.

The Ghost rides up to Oak, reining in his horse. "I wasn't sure how to interpret your note," the spy says quietly.

"I meant it quite literally," Oak returns.

He wrote it in haste, sitting on the floor of the storage room, with Daggry watching him. Certainly it could have been better, but he thought it was quite clear:

Things are not as they seem. Call off the battle. Send someone to the Citadel, and I will explain.

"Although I admit not to fully understanding how you accomplished what you did," the Ghost says, "I am impressed."

Oak frowns, not liking what the spy is implying. That Oak's offer of marriage is insincere, a lure. That the prince has set and sprung a trap. Oak doesn't want Wren cast in the role of their enemy, nor that of a mark.

"When one is charmed," the prince says, "it's easy to be charming."

"You worried your sisters," the Ghost counters.

Oak notes the plural. The spy has been close to Jude's twin, Taryn, for years, leaving *how close* as a matter of speculation among the family.

"They ought to recall what they were doing when they were my age," Oak says. Jude has been worrying the rest of them for years.

The spy gives a half smile. "Perhaps that's what stopped the High

Queen from hanging Tiernan up by his toes for going along with your plan instead of stopping you."

No wonder Tiernan was so stiff with Oak. He must have been interrogated, insulted. "Perhaps she remembered that if Tiernan had stopped me, that would have meant letting our father die."

The Ghost sighs, and neither of them speaks for the rest of the ride to the shore.

A ship made of pale wood is anchored out past the black stones and shallow waters of the beach. Long and slender, with both bow and stern tapered to points that curl like the stems of leaves, she is a proud ship. Two masts rise from her deck, and around their bases, Oak can see puddles of the white sails that will be hoisted to catch the wind. The name *Moonskimmer* is emblazoned along the side in carved letters.

And from the other direction, he sees the troll kings, stepping through the snow toward them. Their skin is the deep gray of granite, riddled with what appear to be cracks and fissures. Their faces look more sculpted than alive, even as their expressions shift. One has a beard, while the other's face is bare. Both wear old and tattered scale armor, marbled with tarnish. Both have circlets on their brows of rough, dark gold. One has a club made from most of a fir tree attached to a leather belt that must have been sewn from the whole hides of several bears.

Oak draws Damsel Fly up short. The others stop as well; even Wren's carriage skids to a halt, the elk pawing at the ground and shaking their heads as though wishing they could pull free from their harnesses.

Wren hops down fearlessly, her bare feet in the snow.

Alone, she walks toward them. Her dress furls around her as the wind whips at her hair.

Oak slides off his horse, sinking his nails into the palm of his hand. He wants to run after Wren even though he knows this would be a terrible moment to undermine her authority. Still, it's hard to watch her, small and alone, standing before these massive, ancient beings.

One begins to speak in an old tongue. Oak sort of learned it in the palace school, but only ever as a language used to read equally old books. No one spoke it conversationally. And it turned out his instructor's pronunciations were waaaaay off.

The prince is able to understand only the vaguest gist. They promise to watch over her lands until she returns. They agree to stay clear of the army but don't seem to like the idea. Oak isn't sure *how* Wren understands them—perhaps Mellith knew their speech—but she clearly does.

"We entrust these lands to you while we are away," she says. "And if I do not return, make war in my name."

Both troll kings sink to one knee and bow their heads to her. A deeper hush falls over the Folk standing witness. Even Randalin looks more awed than delighted.

Wren touches the hand of each king, and they rise at the press of her fingers.

Then she walks back, barefoot, to her carriage. Halfway there, she glances at Oak. He gives her a smile, a small one because he's still a bit stunned. She doesn't return it.

The procession moves on to the coastline. Oak rides alone and speaks to no one.

At the edge of the black rocks, where the waves crash, Tiernan dismounts. He says something to the Ghost, who signals to the ship with a waved hand. They cast off a rowboat to ferry the passengers aboard in groups.

"You should head over first, Your Highness," the Ghost says.

Oak hesitates, then shakes his head. "Let the queen's party go."

Tiernan sighs with annoyance at what he no doubt sees as Oak's objection to reasonable security. Oak is aware that it seems he's just being contrary, but he refuses to give them an opportunity to sail once he's aboard, leaving Wren to Elfhame's army.

The Ghost gestures toward Hyacinthe, indicating Wren's people should take precedence.

It's a strange feeling, after being in captivity for weeks, to realize that no one here has the authority to make him do anything. People have been thrusting power at Oak since the beginning of Cardan's rule, and he's been avoiding it for just as long. He wonders if, after being stripped of so many choices, he has finally grown a taste for it.

Hyacinthe hands Wren into the boat. Her masked driver stays with the coach, though the footman climbs down and joins her, taking a seat in the front. The rest of her soldiers remain on the rocks as the crewperson who rowed to shore casts off again.

Oak watches in puzzlement. Surely, she isn't going with that few attendants?

The storm hag dismounts from her bear. With a twist of her head, she transforms herself into a massive vulture. Giving a screech, she flies out to the ship, alighting atop the mast. And then, as if responding to some unseen signal, Wren's soldiers become falcons. They soar up into the sky, leaving the sound of feathered wings echoing all around Oak.

"What has she done?" Tiernan mutters.

Oh, no one in Elfhame is going to like this. Wren didn't just break the curse on the traitors; she turned it into a boon. She gave them the ability to turn into their cursed form *at will*.

The falcons fly to the ship, landing on the boom, where, one by one, they drop to the deck as Folk again.

Oak wonders if Hyacinthe can do that. He's in a boat, so perhaps not. She broke his curse before she discovered the extent of her power.

When the rowboat returns, Oak gets in with half the knights of Elfhame accompanying him. At the ship, sailors help him aboard, then bow low. The captain introduces himself—he is a wizened man with wild white hair and skin the color of rich clay.

"Welcome, Your Highness. We're all so glad the rescue was successful."

"I wasn't precisely saved," Oak says.

The captain glances in Wren's direction, a flicker of unease in his face. "Yes, we understand."

As the captain moves to greet the Minister of Keys, Oak admits to himself that went poorly.

Then there is a great deal of negotiation over accommodations and storage, most of which the prince ignores. As the billowing white sails marked with the sigil of Elfhame rise, and the ship steers out into the sea, his heart speeds with the thought of going home.

And with what he will find when he gets there.

He stopped a war—or at least *paused* one. And yet, he is aware that bringing Wren into the heart of Elfhame puts the people there—people he loves—at risk. At the same time, spiriting Wren from her stronghold and separating her from the largest part of her defenders put her in an equally vulnerable position.

Wren knows that. And so does Jude. He must be very careful to keep either of them from feeling they must act on that knowledge.

He understands—or at least thinks he does—why Wren went along with his plan. She used up a lot of her power freeing the troll kings from their curse, and an engagement with the army of Elfhame, an army that could continuously replenish soldiers from the lower Courts, would be nearly impossible to win. After all, that's what he'd been counting on when he put his ring on her finger.

And after some consideration, he believes he also understands why Bogdana wants them to go to Elfhame. She hates the Greenbriars, hates the High Court, and yet has long desired to see her daughter on the throne. If she was willing to trade a portion of her own power for Mellith to be Mab's heir, then as much as she desires revenge, she must also long for a do-over. If Wren marries Oak, she will be in line to be High Queen. That has to have some appeal.

And if not, Cardan will be in Bogdana's sights. She will have gotten closer to him than would be possible otherwise.

And Wren herself? He suspects she's venturing to the High Court because she wants the Court of Teeth made officially hers. But, of course, he hopes that some part of it has to do with him. He hopes that some part of her wants to see where this goes. The last time they were together in the Court of Elfhame, they'd been children. He hadn't been able to do much for her. Neither of them is a child now, and he can do better. He can show her he cares about her. And he can show her some fun.

Of course, Oak will have to keep his family from making things extra complicated. Jude will want to punish Wren for holding Oak captive. Cardan will probably still be a bit resentful if he thinks Oak is plotting against him. Cardan may even think Wren is part of a new plot.

And so Oak needs to show his loyalty to a lot of different people, keep Bogdana from hurting anyone, and get a treaty signed before a battle breaks out in the heart of Elfhame. Not to mention he has to do that while proving to Wren he isn't out for revenge—and that if she forgives him, he won't see it as a chance to hurt her.

Well, no time like the present to begin. Oak moves across the deck toward her. Two falcons step in his way.

"She is my betrothed," Oak says, as though there is merely some misunderstanding.

"You ought to be her *prisoner*," says one, low enough that he will not be overheard by the Elfhame contingent.

"Both those things can be true," Oak tells him.

Wren frowns at the guards and the prince both. "I will receive him. I wish to hear what he has to say."

Her guards step away, but not far enough to be out of earshot.

Oak smiles and attempts to find a tone to communicate his sincerity. "My lady, I wished to tell you how glad I was that you decided to accept my suit and return to Elfhame by my side. I hope you do not begrudge too greatly the manner in which the proposal was given."

"Should I?" she asks.

"You might consider it romantic," he suggests, but he knows what she really thinks—that this is a game. And should he claim otherwise, she will be insulted that he thinks her such a poor opponent as to fall for that.

And it is not as though there is *no* strategy behind his offer, but he feels more like a hopelessly besotted ninny than a master strategist. He'd marry her, and happily.

She gives him a chilly little smile. "However I might feel, I will keep my word."

Though you may not is heavily implied.

"We need not forever be at daggers drawn," he says, and hopes she will believe him. "To that end, I did hope that Bogdana would not be accompanying us, since she wants to murder the High King—and me. I think that could complicate our visit."

To his surprise, Wren glances up at the vulture in frustration. "Yes," she says. "I told her to stay behind, but apparently I wasn't clear enough. That's why she's hiding up there. If she came down, I could order her to go home."

"She can't hide from you forever," Oak says.

The corners of Wren's mouth twitch. "What do you think we will find when we arrive in Elfhame?"

An excellent question. "The High King and Queen will throw us some sort of party. But I suppose they may have a few concerns for me to allay first."

Her lip lifts, showing off sharp teeth. "A polite way of putting it. But you are ever charming."

"Am I?" he asks.

"Like a cat lazing in the sun. No one expects it to suddenly bite."

"I am not the one fond of biting," he says, and is gratified when she blushes, the pink coming up bright enough to show through the pale blue of her skin.

Not waiting to be dismissed, he takes that victory, makes a shallow bow, and departs, heading in the direction of Tiernan.

Her guards watch him go with angry looks. They probably blame him for Valen. Perhaps they blame him for all the things that Valen blamed him for. Might there really be some day that he and Wren were not at daggers drawn? He believed it enough to say it, but he was an eternal optimist.

"You've got a bruise on your face," Tiernan says.

Oak reaches up self-consciously and prods around until he finds it, to the left of his mouth. It joins the bump on his head and the burns from the iron knife hidden by his collar. He's a mess.

"How is my father?" he asks.

"Allowed back into Elfhame, just as he planned," Tiernan says. "Giving your sister lots of unsolicited advice."

Just because I'm bad doesn't mean the advice is. That's what Madoc told Wren, although Oak isn't so sure he agrees on that point. Still, his father must be doing well, to be behaving like himself. That is the main thing.

He lets out a sigh of relief, his gaze going to the horizon, to the waves. His mind wanders to the last time they crossed this water and how Loana tried to distract him with a kiss and then drag him down to the watery depths. That was the second time she tried to drown him.

Drown me once, shame on me . . . He decides he doesn't like the direction his thoughts are taking him. Nor does he like acknowledging that he has a particular sort of taste for paramours—the more dangerous, the better.

"Do you still love Hyacinthe?" the prince asks.

Tiernan looks at him in surprise. It isn't that they never talk about their feelings, but Oak supposes it isn't the second thing Tiernan expected him to ask about.

Or perhaps it isn't something that Tiernan is prepared to think too closely on, because he shrugs. When Oak does not retract the question, Tiernan shakes his head, as though at the impossibility of answering. Then, finally, he gives in and speaks. "In ballads, love is a disease, an affliction. You contract it as a mortal might contract one of their viruses.

Perhaps a touch of hands or a brush of lips, and then it is as though your whole body is fevered and fighting it. But there's no way to prevent it from running its course."

"That's a remarkably poetic and profoundly awful view of love," Oak says.

Tiernan looks back at the sea. "I was never in love before, so all I had were ballads to go by."

Oak is silent, thinking of all the times he thought himself to be in love. "Never?"

Tiernan gives a soft huff of breath. "I had lovers, but that's not the same thing."

Oak thinks about how to name what he feels about Wren. He does not wish to write her ridiculous poems as he did for so many of the people with whom he thought he was in love, except that he does wish to make her laugh. He does not want to give her enormous speeches or to make grand, empty gestures; he does not want to give her the *pantomime* of love. He is starting to suspect, however, that pantomime is all he knows.

"But...," Tiernan says, and hesitates again, running a hand through his short blackberry hair. "What I feel is not like the ballads."

"Not an affliction, then?" Oak raises an eyebrow. "No fever?"

Tiernan gives him an exasperated look—one with which the prince is very familiar. "It is more the feeling that there is a part of me I have left somewhere and I am always looking for."

"So he's like a missing phone?"

"Someone ought to pitch you into the sea," Tiernan says, but he has a small smile in the corner of his mouth. He doesn't seem like someone who would like being teased. His grimness is what often allows him to be mistaken for a knight, despite his training as a spy. But he does like it.

"I think he's rather desperately in love with you," Oak says. "I think that's why he was punching me in the mouth."

When Tiernan sighs and looks out at the sea, Oak follows his example and is silent.

CHAPTER
12

Three days, they are supposed to spend at sea. Three days before they land on the isles and Oak must face his family again.

As the prince drowses in a hammock with the stars far above him on the first night, he hears Randalin boasting loudly that of course he was willing to give up his private cabin to Wren, as a queen *needed* privacy for travel, and that he *hardly* minded the hardship. Of course, she *nearly* persuaded him not to *inconvenience* himself, which was quite *gracious* of her. And she *insisted* on keeping him there for several hours to eat, drink, and speak with her of the Shifting Isles and his own *loyalty* to the prince, whereupon she *praised him* greatly, one might even say *excessively*.

Oak is certain that her evening was stultifyingly dull and yet he can't help wishing he'd been there, to share a glance over the obsequious councilor's head, to watch her smother her smiles at his puffery. He craves her smiles. The shine of her eyes when she is trying to hold back laughter.

He is no longer locked in a cell, no longer barred from seeing her. He may go to the door of the room where she is resting and bang on it until she opens up. But somehow knowing that he can and being afraid he wouldn't be welcome make her seem even farther away.

And so he lies there, listening to Randalin going on and on about his own consequence. The councilor falls silent only after the Ghost throws a balled-up sock at him.

That reprieve lasts only the night.

Invigorated by the success of their mission and certain of his elevated status with Wren, Randalin spends much of the second day trying to talk everyone into a version of the story where he can take credit for brokering peace. Maybe even for arranging a marriage with Oak.

"Lady Suren just needed a little *guidance*. I really see the *potential* in her to be one of our great leaders, like a queen of old," he is saying to the captain of the ship as Oak passes.

The prince's gaze goes to Wren, standing at the prow. She wears a plain dress the color of bone, dotted with sea spray, its skirts fluttering around her. Her hair is blown back from her face, and she bites her lower lip as she contemplates the horizon, her eyes darker and more fathomless than the ocean.

Above them, the sky is a deep, bright blue, and the wind is good, filling the sails.

"I *told* Jude," Randalin goes on. "She proposed *violent* solutions, but you know *mortals*, and her in particular—no patience. I *never* supported her elevation. Neither kith nor kin to *us*."

Oak sets his jaw and reminds himself that nothing good will come of punching the councilor in his smug little horned face. Instead, the prince tries to concentrate on the feeling of the sun on his skin and the knowledge that things could have turned out much worse.

Later that afternoon, when Oak is summoned to Wren's cabin, he is particularly glad he didn't hit anyone.

The guard who leads him to her chambers isn't one the prince knows, but he's had enough experience of her falcons for just the uniform to put him on edge.

Wren sits on a chair of white wood, beside a marble-topped side table and a settee upholstered in scarlet. Small, round windows high on the walls illuminate the space. A bed was built in to a corner, wood frame keeping the cushions from shifting with the swells, a half-open curtain for privacy. When he enters, she makes a movement with her hand and her guard leaves.

Fancy, he thinks. *I should work out a signal like that with Tiernan.* Of course, he doubts Tiernan would leave if there was a gesture he could just ignore.

"May I sit?" Oak asks.

"Please," she says, her fingers anxiously turning the ring he gave her. "I summoned you to talk about the dissolution of our engagement."

His heart sinks, but he keeps his voice light. "So soon? Shall we turn the ship around?" He settles himself grimly on the settee.

She gives a little sigh. "Too soon, yes, I agree. But we will have to break it off eventually. I understand what you did at the Citadel. You managed to keep a battle from happening and bloodshed at bay with your lies, and you managed to remove yourself from my clutches. It was nicely done."

"I can't lie," he objects.

"You lived in the mortal world," Wren says. "But you never had a mortal mother. Mine would have called that a *lie of omission*. But name it a trick or a deception, name it whatever you will. What matters is that this betrothal cannot continue too long or we shall be wed and you, tied to me forever."

"A terrible fate?" Oak inquires.

She nods briskly, as though he's finally understanding the seriousness of the problem. "I suggest that you allow your family to persuade you to put off the ceremony for months. I will agree, of course. I can conclude my visit to Elfhame and return north. You will strongly suggest that your sister give me what was once the Court of Teeth to rule."

"Is that what you want?" he asks.

She looks down at her hands. "Once, I thought I might return to my mortal home, but I cannot imagine it now. How could they see me as that child, when I would frighten them, even without knowing the nature of my magic?"

"They don't have to see you as a child to care for you," he says.

"They would never love me as much as I want to be loved," she tells him with painful honesty. "I will do well in the north. I am well suited to it."

"Do you—" he begins, not sure how to ask this question. "Do you remember much of being Mellith?"

She starts to shake her head and then hesitates. "Some things."

"Do you remember Bogdana being your mother?"

"I do," she says, so softly he can barely hear it. "I remember believing she loved me. And I remember her giving me away."

"And the murder?" he asks.

"I was so happy to see her," she says, fingers going almost unconsciously to her throat. "I almost didn't notice the knife."

For a moment, the sadness of the story robs him of speech. His own mother, Oriana, is so fiercely protective of him that he cannot imagine being pushed out on his own, among people who hate him enough to arrange his death. And yet, he recalls sitting at the end of his bed and hearing Vivi explain how it was a miracle Jude was alive after the way their father carved her up. And from the time he learned that he had a first father, he knew that person tried to kill him.

Maybe he doesn't understand how she feels exactly, but he understands that familial love isn't guaranteed, and even when you have it, it doesn't always keep you safe.

Wren watches him with her fathomless eyes. "It seems as though it should change me, to have those memories, but I do not feel much changed." She pauses. "Do I seem different?"

He notes the careful way she's holding herself. Stiff, her back upright. She seems wary, yet underneath there's a hunger in her. A spark of desire she cannot mask, although whether it is for him or power, he cannot say.

"You seem more like yourself than ever before," he says.

He can see her considering that but not misliking his words. "So we are agreed. We delay the exchange of vows. Your sister will have a reason to send me back north with a kingdom of my own, and we will let her believe that her plan to separate us has worked. You can take up with any number of courtiers to drive the point home. Drown whatever lingering feelings you have for me in a new love, or ten." She says the last bit with some asperity.

He puts a hand to his chest. "Have you no feelings to drown?"

Wren looks down. "No," she says. "Nothing I have would I ever want to give away."

After a dinner of kelp and cockles, which the cook serves up in wooden bowls with no spoons, the captain invites them to sit on the deck and tell tales, as is his crew's tradition. Wren arrives with Hyacinthe by her side, settling some distance from the prince. When her gaze meets his, she tucks a long strand of hair behind her ear and gives him a hesitant smile. Her green eyes shine as one of the crew begins to speak.

She loves a story. He remembers that, remembers their evenings around the fire as they traveled north. Remembers her talking about Bex, her mortal sister, and their games of pretend. Remembers how she laughed when he retold some of his own antics.

The prince listens as crew members speak of far-off shores they've visited. One tells of an island with a queen who has the head and torso of a woman and the appendages of an enormous spider. Another, of a land so thick with magic that even the animals speak. A third, of their adventures with merfolk and how the captain wed a selkie without stealing its skin.

"We avoid talking politics," the captain qualifies with a puff on a long, thin pipe of carved bone.

In a lull, the storm hag clears her throat.

"I have a tale for you," says Bogdana. "Once, there was a girl with an enchanted matchbook. Whenever she lit one—"

"Is this a true story?" the Ghost interrupts.

"Time will tell," the storm hag answers, giving him a lethal look. "Now, as I was about to say—when this girl struck a match, a thing of her choosing was destroyed. This made all of those in power want her on their side, but she fought only for what she herself considered right."

Wren looks down at her hands, strands of hair falling to shield her face. Oak supposes there's going to be a lesson in this, one that no one will like.

"The more terrible the destruction, the more matches needed to be struck. And yet, each time the girl looked in the matchbook, there were at least a few new matches within. To have such vast power was a great burden for the girl, but she was ferocious and brave in addition to being wise, and shouldered her burden with grace."

Oak sees the way Hyacinthe is frowning at the storm hag, as though disagreeing with the idea that Wren's "matches" are so easily replaced. When Oak thinks of the translucency of her skin, the hollowness beneath her cheekbones, he worries. But he believes that Bogdana very much wants to believe this is how Wren's magic works.

"Then the girl met a boy with a shining brow and an easy laugh." The storm hag's eyes narrow, as though in warning of what is to come. "And she was struck low by love. Though she ought to fear nothing, she feared the boy would be parted from her. Not wisdom, nor ferocity, nor bravery saved her from her own tender heart."

Ah, so this isn't going to be about Wren's magic. This is going to be about him. Great.

"Now, our girl had many enemies, but none of those enemies could stand against her. With a single match, she caused castles to crumble. With a handful of matches, she burned whole armies to the ground. But in time the boy tired of that and persuaded her to put away her matchbook and fight no more. Instead, she would live with him in a cottage in the woods, where no one would know of her power. And though she ought to have known better, she was beguiled by him and did what he wished."

The ship goes quiet, the only sounds the slap of water against wood and the luff of the sails.

"For some time they lived in what passed for happiness, and if the girl felt as though there was something missing, if she felt as though to be loved he must look through her and not at her, she pretended that away."

Oak opens his mouth to object and at the last moment bites his tongue. He would only make himself seem like a fool, and a guilty one at that, to argue with a story.

"But in time, the girl was discovered by her enemies. They came for her together and caught her unawares, locked in an embrace with her beloved. Still, in her wisdom, she always kept her matchbook in a pocket of her dress. Under threat, she drew it out and struck the first match, and those who came for her fell back. The flames that consumed them consumed her cottage, too. Yet still more enemies came. Match after match was struck and fire raged all around her, but it was not enough. And so the girl struck all the remaining matches at once."

Oak glares at the storm hag, but she seems too swept up in her tale to even notice. Wren is plucking at a thread of her dress.

"The armies were defeated and the land scorched black. The girl went up in flames with them. And the boy burned to cinders before he could pull free from her arms."

A respectful silence follows her final words. Then the captain clears his throat and calls for one of his crewmen to take up a fiddle and play a merry tune.

As a few begin to clap along, Wren stands and moves toward her cabin.

Oak catches up at her door, before her guards seem to have realized his intention. "Wait," he says. "Can we speak?"

She tilts her head and regards him for a long moment. "Come in."

One of her guards—Oak realizes, abruptly, that it's Straun—clears his throat. "I can accompany you and make sure he doesn't—"

"There is no need," she says, cutting him off.

Straun attempts to keep the sting of her words from showing on his face. Oak almost feels sorry for him. Almost, except for the memory of his being party to the prince's torture.

Because of that, he gives Straun an enormous, irritating grin as he follows Wren across the threshold and into her room.

Inside, he finds the chamber much as it was before, except that a few dresses have been spread out on her bed and a tray with tea things rests on the marble table.

"Is that what your power is like?" Oak asks. "A book of matches."

Wren gives a soft laugh. "Is that truly why you've followed me? To ask that?"

He smiles. "It's hardly a surprise that a young man would want to spend time with his betrothed."

"Ah, so this is more playacting." She moves across the floor gracefully, the pitch and roll of the ship not causing her a single stumble. Finding her way to the upholstered settee, she takes a seat, indicating with a gesture that he should take the chair across from her. A reversal of their positions the last time he visited this room.

"I *do* wish to spend time with my betrothed," he says, going to sit.

She gives him a look of disdain, but her cheeks have a flush of pink on them. "My magic might be like the matches in the story, but I think it burns me, too. I just don't know how much yet."

He appreciates her admitting that to him. "She's going to want you to keep using it. If there's one thing I took away from her story, it's that."

"I do not plan on dancing to her tune," Wren says. "Not ever again."

His father has managed to manipulate him cannily, without Oak ever once agreeing to a single thing that Madoc proposed out loud. "And yet you haven't ordered her to go home."

"We're far from shore," Wren says with a sigh. "And she promised to be on her best behavior. Now, to be fair, since I told you about my magic, tell me about yours."

Oak raises his brows in surprise. "What do you want to know?"

"Persuade me of something," she says. "I want to understand how your power works. I want to know what it feels like."

"You want me to charm you?" This seems like a terrible idea. "That suggests a great deal more trust on your part than you've indicated you're willing to extend to me."

She leans back on her cushions. "I want to see if I can break the spell."

He thinks of all the matches set ablaze. "Won't it hurt you to do that?"

"It should be a small thing," she says. "And in return, you can obey an order."

"But I'm not wearing the bridle," he protests, hoping that she isn't going to ask him to put it on. He won't, and if it's a test, it's one he's going to fail.

"No," she says. "You're not."

Willingly following a command seems interesting and not *too* dangerous. But he doesn't know how to make his gancanagh magic tame. If he tells her what she most wants to hear and it is a distortion of the truth, what then? And if the words are ones he means, how will they ever seem true when they've first come from his mouth as persuasion?

"Are you doing it?" Her body is slightly hunched as though against some kind of attack.

"No, not yet," he says with a surprised laugh. "I have to actually *say* something."

"You just *did*," she protests, but she's laughing a little, too. Her eyes glitter with mischief. She was right when she said they both loved games. "Just do it. I'm getting nervous."

"I'm going to try to persuade you to pick up that teacup," he says, waving toward a clay vessel with a wide base and a little bit of liquid still at the bottom. It's resting on the marble-topped table, and with all the rocking the boat has done as it goes over swells, he's surprised it hasn't slid to the floor already.

"You're not supposed to tell me," she says, smiling. "Now you'll never manage it."

He finds himself filled with a strange glee at the challenge. At the idea he could share this with her and it could be fun instead of awful.

When he opens his mouth again, he allows the honey-tongued words to spill out.

"When you came to Elfhame as a child," he says, his voice going strange, "you never got to see the beauty of it. I will show you the silvery white trees of the Milkwood. We can splash in the Lake of Masks and see the reflections of those who have looked into it before us. I will take you to Mandrake Market, where you can buy eggs that will hatch pearls that shine like moonlight."

He can see that she's relaxed, sinking back onto the cushions, eyes half-closed as though in a daydream. And although he wouldn't choose those words, he does plan to take her to all those places.

"I look forward to introducing you to each of my sisters and reminding them that you helped our father. I will tell the story of how you single-handedly defeated Lady Nore and bravely took an arrow in the side." He's not sure what he expects from his magic, but it isn't this rush of words. Not a single thing he said is anything other than true. "And I will tell them the story of Mellith, and how wronged she was by Mab, how wronged you were and how much I want—"

Wren's eyes open, wet with unshed tears. She sits up. "How dare you say those things? How dare you throw everything I cannot have in my face?"

"I didn't—" he starts, and for a moment, he isn't sure if he's speaking as himself. If he's using his power or not.

"Get out," she growls, standing.

He holds up his hands in surrender. "Nothing I said was un—"

Wren hurls the teacup at him. It smashes against the floor, jagged bits of pottery flying. "Get out!"

He stares at the shards in horror, realizing what it means. *She picked up the cup. I persuaded her to pick up the cup.* This is the exact problem with being a love-talker. His power cares nothing for consequences.

"You told me you'd give me an order after I tried to persuade you." Oak takes a step toward the door, his heart beating painfully hard. "I shall obey."

When he passes Straun, the guard snorts, as though he believes Oak had his chance and blew it.

The prince stands on the deck for the better part of the night, staring numbly into the sea as dawn blushes on the horizon. He's still there when he hears a scream behind him.

At the cry, he whirls, hand already going to the blade at his hip—finding not the needle-thin rapier he's used to wielding but a borrowed cutlass. The curved blade rattles in its scabbard as he pulls it free—just as a thick black tentacle sprawls across the deck.

It wriggles toward the prince like some disembodied finger, dragging itself forward. Oak takes several steps back.

Another tentacle rises from the water to twine around the prow, ripping through one of the sails.

A troll sailor, interrupted from a game of Fidchell with an ogre, scrambles to his feet and up the rigging in horror. Shouts ring out.

"The Undersea! The Undersea is attacking!"

The ocean churns as seven sharks surface with merrows astride their backs. All the merrows are different shades of mottled green and wield jagged-looking spears. They are armored in pearlescent scales of shells and draped in woven ropes of seaweed. The expression in their cold, pale eyes makes it clear they have come to fight.

The captain blows on a crooked pipe. Sailors run to positions, beginning to haul out massive harpoons from hatches beneath the deck, each weapon heavy enough to take several of them to move.

The knights and falcons spread out, swords and bows to hand.

"Subjects of Elfhame," a merrow shouts. Like the others, he is clad in shells cut into discs that overlap one another to make a sort of scale armor, but his bare arms are encircled in bracelets of gold, and his hair is knotted into thick braids, decorated with the teeth of sea creatures. "Know the power of Cirien-Cròin, far greater than the line of Orlagh."

Oak steps toward the gunwale, but Tiernan grabs his shoulder and squeezes it hard. "Don't be a fool and draw their eye. Perhaps they won't recognize you."

Before Oak can argue, Randalin raises his voice. "Is that your name? The name of your monster?" He sounds somewhere between stern lecturer and on the verge of panic.

The merrow laughs. "The name of our master, who has gone courting. He sends us with a message."

"Deliver it, and go on your way," says Randalin, making a shooing motion toward the tentacle. "And get that thing off our deck."

Oak spots Wren, not sure when she left her chambers. He catches her gaze, remembering the warning she was given by the merrow she freed from the Court of Moths—that a war was coming for control of the Undersea. And Loana mentioned that Nicasia was having a contest for her hand and, with it, her crown. Then Loana tried to drown him, which overshadowed the warning. But he recalls it vividly now.

Wren widens her eyes, as though trying to tell him something. Probably that they're screwed. If she unmakes the tentacle, she might unmake the ship along with it.

At least this seems to have put their disastrous game out of her mind.

"You are the message," the merrow says. "You, at the bottom of the sea with crabs picking out your eyes."

Another tentacle rises from the waves, slithering up the side of the boat. Well, this is very, very bad.

Seven merrows and one monster. The thing with the tentacles doesn't seem to have any particular cleverness. As far as Oak can tell, it can't even see what it is grabbing for. If they can get rid of the merrows, there is a chance that without anyone commanding it to strike, the thing will go away. Of course, there is also a chance it may decide to rip the ship to teeny, tiny pieces.

"Queen Suren," the merrow says, spotting her. "You should have taken our offer and given us your prize. I see you lost your war. Here we find you in the hands of your enemy. Were you our ally, we would save you, but now you will die with the others. Unless..."

"Your Highness," Tiernan hisses at Oak. His sword is drawn and his jaw set. "Get below."

"And how will that help, exactly?" Oak demands. "Will waiting to drown make the experience better?"

"For once, just—" Tiernan begins.

But Oak has already come to a decision. "Hello there!" he says, striding toward the merrow. "Looking for a prize? What did you have in mind?"

From behind him, he thinks he hears Tiernan muttering about how strangling Oak himself may be a kindness. At least it would be a merciful death.

"Prince Oak of Elfhame," the merrow says with a scowl. As though he is finding this much too easy. "We're taking you to Cirien-Cròin."

"Wonderful plan!" says Oak. "Did you know that she chained me up? And now I'm supposed to marry her unless *someone* takes me away. Come aboard. Let's go."

Wren's expression has gone shuttered. She can't possibly believe he's serious, but that doesn't mean his words don't cut close to the bone.

"You can't mean to go with them," Randalin says, because Randalin is an idiot.

The merrow signals, and six of the sharks swim closer so that the merrows on their backs can climb onto the deck. One has a silver net in his hands. It gleams in the morning light.

Six. That's almost all of them.

"Take the queen, too," commands the merrow leader. "Leave the rest to Sablecoil."

Sablecoil. That must be the monster.

"You're not taking anyone," says one of the knights. "If you board the ship, we'll—"

"Oh, let them come," Oak interrupts with a speaking look. "Maybe they'll take her and allow the rest of us to go."

"Your Highness," says another knight, his voice respectful but slow, as though Oak is a greater fool than the councilor. "I very much doubt that's their plan. If it were, I would hand her over in a heartbeat."

The prince glances toward Wren, hoping she didn't hear. Randalin has caught hold of her hand and is attempting to drag her toward the stateroom near the helm of the ship, in what appears to be an act of actual valiance on his part.

"Perhaps we can come to some arrangement," the merrow commander says. "After all, who can speak of Cirien-Cròin's might if all who witness it are dead? We will take the prince and the queen, then Sablecoil will release you while we treat with one another."

That's a terrible deal. That's such a bad deal even Sablecoil would know better than to take it.

"Yes, yes!" Oak says cheerily. "I look forward to discussing this Cirien-Cròin's wooing of Nicasia. I might have some insights to share. My half-brother seduced her, you know."

A nearby sailor makes a startled noise. None of them would speak of her that way while they crossed her waters.

The merrow commander, still on his shark, smiles, showing thin teeth, like those of some deepwater fish. The six merrows on the deck

split up, four heading toward Wren and two toward the prince. They
don't expect Oak to be difficult to subdue, even if he resists.

As the merrows get closer, he feels a momentary spike of panic.

Most of the people on this boat don't expect him to be hard to subdue, either, or anything other than a fool. That's the reputation he's
painstakingly built. A reputation he's about to throw away.

He tries to push that out of his mind, to concentrate on sinking into
the moment. The merrows are perhaps five feet from him and seven feet
from Wren when he attacks.

He slashes the throat of the first, spraying the deck with thin, greenish blood. Twisting around, he sinks the edge of the cutlass into the second merrow's thigh, slicing open the vein. More blood. So much blood.
The deck is slippery with it.

Arrows fly. The massive harpoons fire.

Oak runs across the deck toward the four bearing down on Wren.
A pair of her falcons match blades with one merrow. A lone falcon flies
up in bird form and lands behind another, transforming in time to stab
a knife into his back. Wren herself has thrown a knife at one fleeing
across the deck. Oak gets there in time to dispatch the last by cleaving
his head clean from his shoulders.

There are a lot of screams.

From the top of the mast, Bogdana descends on black wings. Oak
glances toward Wren.

In that moment of inattention, he is knocked off his hooves by a sinuous
tentacle that wraps around his calf. He tries to pull free, but it yanks him
across the deck fast enough that his head slams against the wooden boards.

He kicks out with a hoof at the same time he stabs the blade of his cutlass deep into Sablecoil's rubbery flesh, pinning the tentacle to the deck. Writhing, it drops the prince. He stumbles to his hooves.

Tiernan hacks at the tentacle, trying to sever it from the body of the monster.

With a shudder, it rips free from the deck. The cutlass is still stuck in it when it wraps around Tiernan. Then it hauls him backward into the sea.

"Tiernan!" Oak runs to the gunwale of the ship, but Tiernan has disappeared beneath the waves.

"Where is he?" Hyacinthe shouts. There's black blood smeared across his face and a bow in his hand.

Before Oak can get any words out, Hyacinthe has dropped the bow and jumped off the side. The ocean swallows him whole.

No, no, no. Oak is wild with panic. He can swim, but certainly not well enough to haul both of them out.

All around him, there's fighting. The fleeing merrow is cut down. The Ghost slashes at another enormous tentacle, battling to save one of the fallen falcons. Three more tentacles curl around the prow. From everywhere, there are cries. From some places, screams.

Oak wants to scream, too. If Tiernan dies, it will be because of Oak.

This is why he never wanted a bodyguard. This is why he should never have been given one.

The prince loosens a rope from a cleat, wrapping one end around his waist and knotting it there. Once tied, the prince gives a hard tug to test whether it can bear his weight.

He looks into the waves. This close, he can see shapes moving in the deep.

He sucks in a breath and prepares to join them when a crack of lightning draws his attention back to the deck. Fog is rolling toward the ship, along with higher swells.

Bogdana has brought a storm.

Well, that seems completely unhelpful.

Taking another breath, Oak drops himself down, rappelling off the side of the boat. As his hoof hits the water, Hyacinthe surfaces, Tiernan limp in his arms. Oak reaches for him automatically, afraid it's too late.

"Highness," Hyacinthe says, relief in his voice. Tiernan's head lolls against his shoulder.

Waves splash Oak's face as he grabs hold of his bodyguard. The sky overhead has darkened. He hears a crack of thunder behind him and sees another bright streak of lightning reflecting in Hyacinthe's eyes.

Tiernan's body is heavy in his arms. He tries to find a way to hold him securely enough that he won't slip, tries to find a way to haul them all back up onto the deck.

He lifts himself upward, one-handed. He gets a few inches higher, but it's slow and he's not sure his strength will hold.

And then Garrett is there, peering down.

"Hold on," he calls. "Hold him."

Swells roll against the side of the ship. The Ghost is stronger than he seems, and yet Oak can see how hard it is to pull them up. As soon as he's over the gunwale, the prince rolls himself and Tiernan onto the deck. A sailor is already tossing another rope over the side to Hyacinthe.

Tiernan coughs up water, then lies still again.

When Oak looks up, he sees one of the tentacles slide across the deck toward Wren. The wind steals his cry of warning. He tries to rise to his hooves in time, but he is too slow and has no sword anyway. Hyacinthe, just making it over the side, shouts in horror.

Wren lifts her hand. As she does, the skin of Sablecoil peels back from the muscle, the tentacle going limp and shriveled. A horrible shuddering goes through the ship as all the tentacles detach at once. The boards creak.

The last of the merrows disappears beneath the waves, whatever last taunt he may have spoken dying on his lips.

The storm hag, in vulture form, makes a guttural sound as she flies. The wind rises higher, blowing all around them, as though she is conjuring a shield of rain and wind.

Wren stumbles, reaching for Oak's arm. He puts it around her waist, holding her upright.

"I killed it." Already, her skin has a waxy appearance.

He thinks about Bogdana's story. About how if Wren's power really works like matches, she keeps taking handfuls of them and setting them alight. "Killing is my thing," he tells her. "You should get your own thing."

Her lip quirks. Her gaze seems a little unfocused.

The wind lifts the sail, snapping ropes that were already frayed. The hull of the ship seems to rise above the slap of the waves.

Oak's gaze goes to Tiernan, still as stone, with Hyacinthe bent over him. To the blood washing the deck. To the wounded falcons and knights and sailors. Then to the purpling cast, not unlike a bruise, creeping over Wren's pale blue skin.

The ship rises higher. Abruptly, Oak realizes that it's *above the waves*. Bogdana has used her storm to make their ship fly.

If she devoured the remains of Mab's bones, perhaps she really did have a large portion of her old power back. And perhaps she really was first among hags.

Wren leans more heavily against him, the only warning before she collapses. He catches her in time to swing her up into his arms, her head lying against his chest. Her eyes remain open, but they are fever bright, and though she blinks up at him, he's not sure she sees him.

A few of her guards frown, but not even Straun tries to stop Oak from pushing the door of her room open with one hoof and carrying her inside.

Her sofa and the small table have been tipped over. The rug beneath them is wet, and shards of pottery are scattered over it—the remains of her teapot have joined her broken teacup.

Oak crosses the room and places Wren down gently on her coverlets, her long hair spreading over the pillow. Her deep green eyes are still glassy. He recalls what Hyacinthe said about her power. *The more she unmakes, the more she is unmade.*

A moment later, her hand comes up, running over his cheek. Her fingers push into his hair, then slip over his nape to his shoulder. He goes very still, afraid that if he moves, it will startle her into pulling back. She has never touched him this way, as though things could be easy between them.

"You must stop," she says, her voice little more than a whisper. Her expression is fond.

He frowns in puzzlement. Her hand has dipped down to his chest, and even as she speaks, she opens her palm over his heart. He has barely moved. "Stop what?"

"Being kind to me. I can't bear it."

He tenses.

She withdraws her hand, letting it fall to the coverlet. The blue stone in the ring he gave her glints up at him. "I'm not...I am not good at pretending. Not like you."

If she is speaking of her coldness toward him, she is far better than she believes. "We can stop. We can call a truce."

"For now," she says.

"Then today, my lady, speak freely," he tells her with what he hopes is a reassuring smile. "You can deny me tomorrow."

She looks up at him, her lashes falling low. She seems to be half in a dream. "Is it exhausting to be charming all the time? Or is it just the way you're made?"

His grin fades. He thinks of the magic leaching out of him. He can control his charm, sort of. More or less. And he can resist using it. He will.

"Have you ever wondered if *anyone* truly loved you?" she asks in that same fond, unfocused voice.

Her words are a kick to the stomach, the more because he can tell she doesn't mean to be cruel. And because he *hadn't* thought of it. He sometimes wondered if gancanagh blood meant Folk liked him a little better than they might have otherwise, but he was too vain to think of it affecting Oriana or his sisters.

Oriana, who loved his mother so well that she took Liriope's son and raised him as her own, risking her life to do so. Jude and Vivi, who sacrificed their own safety for him. Jude, who was still making sacrifices to ensure he would someday be the High King. If magic is the cause of that loyalty, instead of love, then he is a curse on the people around him.

A part of him must have suspected, because why else keep himself so apart? He told himself that it was because he wanted to repay them for all the sacrifices they made, told himself that he wanted to become as great as they were, but maybe it had always been this.

He feels sick.

And sicker still when his mouth curves unconsciously into a smile. It has become such an automatic reaction to pain, for him to mask it with a grin. Oak, laughing all the time. Pretending nothing hurts. A false face hiding a false heart.

He can't blame her for saying what she did. Probably someone should have said it to him much sooner. And how could he have ever supposed she would come to care for him? Who can love someone who is empty inside? Someone who steals love instead of earning it?

The prince recalls lying on the ground after drinking several cups of liquor laced with blusher mushroom, back in the troll village. That was the last time he felt Wren's hand on his flushed cheek, her skin cool enough to ground him in that moment, to keep him hanging on to consciousness.

I am poison, he told her then. And he didn't even know the half of it.

Oak sits with Wren until she falls asleep. Then he spreads a blanket over her and stands. Inside, the horror he felt when she spoke those words— *have you ever wondered if* anyone *truly loved you*—hasn't faded, but he can hide that. Easily. For the first time, he hates how easily. He hates that he can fold himself up so tightly in his own skin that there's nothing real about him on the outside.

He climbs the step. Standing on the deck, he looks at the ocean far below. It seems as though they're sailing through a sea of clouds.

Soldiers are attempting to repair the gunwale, shattered by tentacles. Others are trying to smooth out the raw, splintered bits of wood where spearpoints gouged the deck, a faint spatter of blood marring the light color of it.

The ship flies high enough for sailors and soldiers to trail their fingers through clouds and let the mist wet their skin. High enough for seabirds to soar beside them; a few even rest on the mast and rigging.

Bogdana stands at the helm. Her expression is strained, and when she sees him, her eyes narrow. Whatever she wishes to say to him, though, it seems she cannot move away from directing the storm that propels them in order to do it.

Scanning the ship, Oak spots Tiernan near the mast, beneath the netting running up to the base of the sail. His head is pillowed on a cloak, his blackberry hair still damp and stiff with salt. His eyes are shut, his skin gone very pale.

Hyacinthe sits beside him, long fall of dark hair over his face. When Oak squats nearby, Hyacinthe pushes it back to reveal his pained expression. He looks as though he is losing blood from some invisible wound.

"She woke up enough to speak with me," Oak tells him so at least he doesn't have Wren to worry about. "Told me some very unpleasant things about myself."

"He's breathing," says Hyacinthe, nodding toward Tiernan.

For a long moment, they watch the rise and fall of Tiernan's chest. Each inhalation comes with what seems like a lot of effort. As he watches, the prince doesn't trust that one breath will follow the next.

"His loyalty to me might cost him his life," Oak says.

To his surprise, Hyacinthe shakes his head. His hand goes to the other man's chest, coming to rest over his heart. "It was my lack of loyalty to him that was the problem." His voice is so soft that the prince isn't sure he heard the words correctly.

"You couldn't have—" Oak begins, but Hyacinthe cuts him off.

"I could have loved him better," Hyacinthe says. "And I could have better believed in his love."

"How could that have helped against a monster?" the prince asks. He's in the mood for an argument and beginning to hope that Hyacinthe might give him one.

"You don't think what I said is true?"

"Of course I do," Oak says. "You should better believe in his love— you should beg him for another chance. But that wouldn't have saved him from drowning. You jumping in after him *did* save him."

"And you being there to pull us back onto deck saved us both." Hyacinthe shoves his hair behind his ear and gives a shuddering sigh. His gaze snags on Tiernan as he shifts a little. "Perhaps I have had enough of vengeance. Perhaps I need not make things so hard." As Oak begins to stand, though, the former falcon looks up at him. "That doesn't mean I release you from your promise, prince."

Right. He'd promised to cut off someone's hand.

As afternoon moves toward night, Tiernan finally wakes. Once he understands what happened, he's furious with Oak and Hyacinthe both.

"You shouldn't have gone after me," he tells Hyacinthe, then turns to the prince. "And you *certainly* shouldn't have."

"I barely did anything," says Oak. "While it's possible that Hyacinthe battled a shark for you."

"I did *not*." For all Hyacinthe's talk of love, the evening finds him sullen.

Oak stands. "Well, I leave you two to that argument. Or some other argument."

The prince heads to the helm, where he finds the Ghost sitting alone, watching the sails billow. He has a staff beside him. Like Vivi, the Ghost had a human parent, and it's visible in the sandy brown of his hair, an unusual color in Faerie.

"There is a tale about hags to which you might hearken," Garrett says.

"Oh?" Oak is almost certain he's not going to like this.

The Ghost gazes past the prince, at the horizon, the bright blaze of the sun fading to embers. "It is said that a hag's power comes from the part of them that's missing. Each one has a cold stone or wisp of cloud or ever-burning flame where their hearts ought to be."

Oak thinks of Wren and her heart, the only part of her that was ever flesh, and doesn't think that can be true. "And?"

"They are as different from the rest of the Folk as mortals are from faeries. And you're bringing two of the most powerful of their kind to Elfhame." The Ghost gives him a long look. "I hope you know what you're doing."

"So do I," Oak says, sighing.

"You remind me of your father sometimes, though I doubt you would like to hear it."

"Madoc?" No one has ever said that to him before.

"You're very like Dain in some ways," says the Ghost.

Oak frowns. Being compared to Dain can be no good thing. "Ah yes, my father who tried to kill me."

"He did terrible things, brutal things, but he had the potential in him to be a great leader. To be a great king. Like you." Garrett's gaze is steady.

Oak snorts. "I am not planning on leading anyone."

The Ghost nods toward Wren. "If she's a queen and you marry her, then you'd be a king."

Oak stares at him in horror because he's right. And Oak didn't really consider that. Possibly because he still thinks it's unlikely that Wren will go through with it. Possibly also because Oak is a fool.

Across the ship, Hyacinthe is leading Tiernan toward a cabin. Hyacinthe, who hasn't really let Oak off the hook. "Since you knew Dain so well, can you tell me who really poisoned Liriope?"

The Ghost's brows rise. "I thought you believed *he* did?"

"Possibly there was someone else who helped him," Oak presses. "Someone who actually slipped the blusher mushroom into her cup."

Garrett looks genuinely uncomfortable. "He was a prince of Elfhame, and his father's heir. He had many servants. Plenty of help with whatever he attempted."

Oak doesn't like how many of those words also apply to him. "Have you heard there was someone else involved?"

Garrett is silent. Since he cannot lie, the prince assumes he has.

"Tell me," Oak says. "You owe me that."

The line of the Ghost's mouth is grim. "I owe many people many things. But I know this. Locke had the answer you seek. He knew the name of the poisoner, much good it did him."

"I am cleverer than Locke." But what Oak thinks of is his dream and the fox's laughter.

The Ghost stands and dusts off his hands on his pants. "That doesn't take much."

Oak can't tell if Garrett knows the name or only knows that Locke did. Taryn may have told him any secrets that Locke told her. "Does my sister know?"

"You should ask her," says the Ghost. "She's probably waiting for you on the shore."

The prince lifts his eyes and sees the Shifting Isles of Elfhame in the distance, breaking through the mist shrouding them.

The Tower of Forgetting rises like a black and forbidding obelisk from the cliffs of Insweal, and beyond it he can make out the green hill of the palace on Insmire, the blaze of the sunset making it look as though it caught fire.

CHAPTER

13

*O*nce upon a time, there was a woman who was so beautiful that none
could resist her.

That was how Oriana told the story of Liriope to Oak once he
crowned Cardan as the new High King. It sounded like a fairy tale. The
kind with princes and princesses that mortals told to one another. But
this fairy tale was about how Oak had been told a lie, and that lie was
the story of his life.

Oriana was and wasn't his mother. Madoc was and wasn't his father.

*Once upon a time, there was a woman who was so beautiful that none could
resist her. When she spoke, it seemed that the hearts of those who listened beat for
her alone. In time, she caught the eye of the king, who made her the first among
his consorts. But the king's son loved her, too, and wanted her for his own.*

Oak hadn't known what consorts were, and because it was Faerie and
sex didn't embarrass them, Oriana explained that a consort was someone
the king wanted to take to bed. And if they were boys like Val Moren, it

was for delight; if they were girls like herself, then it was for delight, but also might yield babies; and if the lover were of some other gender, that was for delight and the part about the babies could be a surprise.

"But you didn't have the king's baby," he said. "You only have me."

Oriana smiled and tickled him in the crook of his arm, making him shriek and pull away.

"Only you," she agreed. "And Liriope wasn't going to have the king's child, either. The baby in her belly was sired by his son, Prince Dain."

Once upon a time, there was a woman who was so beautiful that none could resist her. When she spoke, it seemed that the hearts of those who listened beat for her alone. In time, she caught the eye of the king, who made her the first among his consorts. But the king's son loved her, too, and wanted her for his own. When he got a child on her, however, he was afraid. Although the king favored his son, he had other sons and daughters. His favor might change if he knew that his son had taken the king's consort to bed. And so the prince slipped poison into the woman's cup and left her to die.

"I don't understand," said Oak.

"People can be greedy about love," Oriana said. "It's all right if you don't understand, my darling."

"But if he loved her, why did he kill her?" The story made Oak feel strange, as though his life didn't quite belong to him.

"Oh, my sweet boy," his mother told him. His second mother, the only mother he would ever know. "He loved power best, I'm afraid."

"If I love someone—" he started, but he didn't know where to go from there. *If I love someone, I won't kill them* was a poor vow. Besides, he loved lots of people. His sisters. His father. His mother. His other mother, though she was gone. He even loved the ponies in the stables and the hunting dogs his father told him weren't pets.

"When you love someone," Oriana told him, "be better than your father was."

Oak shuddered at the word *father*. He'd accepted that he had two mothers and that he might act like or look like Liriope because he inherited part of himself from her, but until that moment, he'd never thought of the villain of the story, the "king's favored son," as someone with whom he shared anything other than blood.

He looked down at his hooves. The Greenbriars were noted for their animal traits. Those must have come from Dain, along with his horns. Maybe along with things he couldn't see.

"I—"

"And be more careful than your mother. She had the power to know what was in anyone's heart and to say the words they most wanted to hear." She gave him a look.

He was silent, afraid. Sometimes he knew those words, too.

"You can't help what you are. You can't help being charming. But look into too many other hearts, and you may lose your way back to your own."

"I don't understand," he said again.

"You can become the embodiment of someone's—oh, you're so young, I don't know how to say this—you can make people see you the way they want to see you. This seems harmless, but it can be dangerous to become *everything* a person wants. The embodiment of all their desires. And more dangerous for you to twist yourself into shapes others choose for you."

He looked up at her, still confused.

"Oh, my darling, my sweet child. Not everyone needs to love you." She sighed.

But Oak liked everyone loving him. Oak liked it so much that he didn't understand why he would want it to be otherwise.

CHAPTER

14

Half the Court seems to have come out to watch the ship touch down in the water near Mandrake Market. When the hull drops with a splash, it sends salt spray high into the air. The sail luffs, and Oak hangs on to the rigging to keep from stumbling around the deck like a drunk.

He can guess that the onlookers have come, in part, to see the Crown Prince home and, in part, to get a look at the new northern queen, to decide if she and Oak might really be in love, to determine if this is meant to be a marriage, or an alliance, or the prelude to an assassination.

The Living Council stands near the back of the crowd in a knot. Baphen, the Minister of Stars, strokes a blue beard threaded with celestial ornaments. Beside him, Fala, the Grand Fool, dressed in purple motley, pulls a matching purple rose from his hair and chews on the petals, as though he has been waiting long enough for their landing to need a snack. Mikkel, the troll representative of the Unseelie Courts, looks intrigued by the flying ship, while insectile Nihuar, the representative of the Seelie Courts, blinks blankly. With her bug-like eyes, Oak has always found her to be eerily inscrutable.

Oak's family members aren't far off. Taryn's skirts blow around her from the last of the wind that propelled the ship. Her head is bent toward Oriana while Leander runs in circles, as restless as Oak was as a child, playing while dull, important things happened around him.

Sailors aboard the ship throw down the anchor. Small boats launch off the shore of Insmire to ferry the passengers home. A collection of vessels—none of the armada, but pleasure boats. One in the shape of a swan, two carved to appear like they are fishes, and a silvery skiff.

As Oak watches, Jude emerges from a carriage. Ten years into her reign, she doesn't bother waiting for a knight or page to hand her down as would be proper, but simply jumps out. She hasn't bothered with a gown today, either, but wears a pair of high boots, tight-fitting trousers, and a vestlike doublet over a shirt poufy enough that it may have been borrowed from Cardan. The only sign that she is the High Queen is the crown on her head—or perhaps the way the crowd quiets upon her arrival.

Cardan emerges from the carriage next, wearing all the finery she eschewed. He is in a black doublet as ink dark as his hair with lines of scarlet thorns along the sleeves and across the chest. As if the suggestion of prickliness isn't enough, his boots come to stiletto points. The smirk on his face manages to convey royal grandeur and boredom all at once.

Knights swarm around them, full of the alarm the king's and queen's expressions hide.

After the pleasure boats arrive at the ship, Hyacinthe goes below and emerges with Wren at his side. She has recovered enough to dress for the occasion in a gown of cloud gray, which sparkles when she moves. Her feet remain bare, but her hair has been braided high on her head, woven between the tines of the jagged onyx crown. And if she leans heavily on Hyacinthe, at least she is dressed and upright.

"I will go across first," Randalin informs the prince. "And you may proceed next, with the queen. I have taken the liberty of instructing your armsfolk to bring up the rear, with Bogdana. That is, of course, if you approve?" The question is clearly meant as a formality. The command was already issued, the procession set. The Minister of Keys may have been unusually quiet since the ship was attacked, but that hasn't cut down on his pompousness.

Once, Oak would have been amused rather than annoyed. He knows the councilor is harmless. Knows his annoyance is overreaction. "Go ahead," the prince says, trying to get back his equilibrium.

When the councilor heads off toward shore, Oak heaves a sigh and stalks toward Wren. Hyacinthe is whispering something in her ear while she shakes her head.

"If you're well enough—" Oak begins.

She cuts him off. "I am."

"Then, Your Majesty," says the prince, "will you take my arm?"

She looks up at him, as remote and impenetrable as the Citadel itself. Oak feels a little awed by her and then angry on her behalf. He hates that she must wear a mask, no matter how much it costs her, no matter what she's been through.

As you must.

She nods, placing her hand lightly atop his. "I shall be the politest of monsters."

For a moment, in the flash of her eyes, in the lifted corner of her mouth, and the glint of a sharp tooth, he sees the girl who quested with him. The one who was fierce and kind, resourceful and brave. But then she is gone again, submerged into cold stiffness. No longer looking like the girl he loved in the weeks leading up to this, but very like the one he loved as a child.

She's nervous, he thinks.

As Oak leads her ashore, toward the onlookers, he hears whispers. *Witch Queen. Hag Queen.*

Still, he is their prince. Their whispers fade as the crowd dutifully parts around him. Tiernan and Hyacinthe both follow, one on each side.

When Oak comes to his sister, he bows. Wren, seeming unsure of the etiquette, bobs in a shallow curtsy.

Despite how much magic it must have taken to destroy that monster in the sea, despite how sick she was after, she appears remarkably composed.

"Welcome home, Prince Oak," Jude says formally, and then her mouth twists into a wry smile. "And congratulations on the completion of your epic quest. Remind me to knight you when I get the chance."

Oak grins and bites his tongue. He is certain she will have much more to say to him later when they are alone.

"And you, Queen Suren of the former Court of Teeth," says Cardan in his silky voice. "You've changed quite a bit, but then you would have, I suppose. Felicitations on the murder of your mother."

Wren's body stiffens with surprise.

Oak desperately wants to stop Cardan from talking, but short of kicking him or throwing something at his head, he has no idea how.

"The Ice Needle Citadel is full of old nightmares," Wren says after a beat of silence. "I look forward to making new ones."

Cardan gives her a half smile of appreciation for that line. "We shall dine together at dusk tomorrow to celebrate your arrival. And betrothal, if the frantic messages we received from Grima Mog were accurate."

Oak's mind spins, trying to figure out if he should object to any part of this. "We are, indeed, betrothed," he confirms.

Jude looks over at him, studying his face. Then she turns to Wren. "So you're to be my new sister."

Wren flinches, as though her words are the opening move of some kind of cruel game. Oak wants to put his hand out, to touch her arm, to reassure her, except he knows better than to make Wren look as though she needs reassurance.

Besides, he's not entirely sure what his sister *did* intend with those words.

A moment later, the black vulture lands on the dirt beside them and transforms into Bogdana, dark feathers becoming her dress and hair.

All around, there is the rattle of swords coming free of sheaths.

"What an appropriate greeting, Your Majesties," says the storm hag. She does not bow. Nor does she curtsy. She doesn't even incline her head.

"Bogdana," Jude says, and there is something that is possibly admiration in her voice. "Your reputation precedes you."

"How pleasing," says the storm hag. "Especially since I saved your ship from certain destruction."

Jude looks toward the Ghost—then checks herself and turns to Randalin instead.

"It is even so, Your Majesty," the councilor affirms. "The Undersea launched an attack on us."

A ripple of surprise goes through the crowd.

Cardan raises his brows, looking skeptical. "The Undersea?"

"One of the contenders for Queen Nicasia's hand," Randalin clarifies.

The High King turns to Oak with an amused smirk. "Perhaps they were worried you might throw your hat into that ring."

"They wanted to send a message," Randalin goes on, as though arguing the case, "that the land ought to keep to itself and let the Undersea work out its ruler business on its own. If we act otherwise, we will have made a powerful new enemy."

"Their dim view of treaties gives me a dim view of them," says Cardan. "We will give Nicasia aid, as she once aided us, and as we swore to do."

It was the Undersea who'd rallied to Jude's side when Cardan had been enchanted into a serpent, while Madoc and his allies conspired to take crown and throne, and while Wren hid in Oak's room.

"We are grateful to you for your help," Jude tells Bogdana.

"I saved the ship, but Wren saved those on board," the storm hag says, curling her long fingers possessively on the girl's shoulder.

Wren tenses at the touch or the praise.

"And saved our father as well," Oak affirms, because he has to make his sister understand that Wren isn't their enemy. "I couldn't have gotten to Madoc without her, nor gotten him out—but I'm sure he told you as much."

"He told me many things," says Jude.

"I hope we will see him at the wedding," says Bogdana.

Jude raises her eyebrows and glances in the High King's direction. It's obvious they thought Oak being betrothed was a long way from an exchange of vows. "There are several celebrations that ought to precede—"

"Three days' time," Bogdana says. "No longer."

"Or?" Cardan asks, voice light. A dare.

"Enough," Wren hisses under her breath. She cannot quite call the storm hag to account in front of everyone, and Bogdana knows it, but past a certain point, she will have to do something.

The storm hag places both hands on Wren's shoulders. "Prince?"

They all look at him, all weighing his loyalty. And while he would marry Wren right then if it were only up to him, he can't help thinking that anything Bogdana is this eager for can't be good. Maybe she's guessed that Wren doesn't intend to ever go through with it.

"It would pain me to wait even three days," Oak says, lightly, deflecting. "But if we must, for the sake of propriety, better the thing is done right...."

"There are rituals to complete," Jude says. "And your family to gather." She is certainly stalling, as Wren hoped she would.

Cardan watches the interaction. Most particularly, he watches Oak. He suspects the prince of something. Oak has to get him alone. Has to explain.

"We have rooms ready at the palace—" Jude begins.

Wren shakes her head. "There is no need to trouble yourself for my sake. I can keep and quarter my own people." From a pocket in her shimmering gray dress, she takes out the white walnut.

Jude frowns.

Oak can well believe Wren doesn't want to be at the palace, to have them observe her every weakness. Still, to refuse the hospitality of the rulers of Elfhame makes a statement about her loyalties.

Cardan seems distracted by the walnut itself. "Oh, very well, I will be the one to ask the obvious question—*what have you there?*"

"If you will allow us a patch of grass, this is where myself and my people will stay," Wren says.

Jude glances toward Oak, and he shrugs.

"By all means," says the High Queen, gesturing toward the guard. "Clear a space."

A few of her knights disperse the crowd until there is an expanse of grass near the edge of the black rocks overlooking the water.

"Is this enough room?" Jude asks.

"Enough and more than enough," says Bogdana.

"We can be generous," says Cardan, clearly choosing his words to irritate the storm hag.

Wren takes a few steps away from them, then tosses the walnut against a patch of mossy earth, reciting the little verse under her breath. Cries of astonishment ring out around them as a pavilion the white of swan feathers, with golden feet like those of a crow, rises from the dirt.

It reminds him of one of the tents in the encampment of the Court of Teeth. He recalls seeing something very like it when he came to cut through the ropes that tied Wren to a post. Recalls listening for Madoc's voice among those of the other soldiers, half in longing and half in fear. He'd missed his father. He'd also been afraid of him.

The prince wonders if Wren is reminded of the encampment, too, not far from where they currently stand. Wonders if she hates being back here.

Mother Marrow was the one who gave her the magic walnut. Mother Marrow, who keeps a place at Mandrake Market. Who gave Oak the advice that sent him off to the Thistlewitch, who sent him straight to Bogdana, in turn. Passed him from hag to hag, perhaps with a specific plan in mind. A specific version of a shared future.

All his thoughts are disturbing.

"What a clever nut," says Cardan with a smile. "If you will not stay in the palace, then we have no recourse but to send you refreshments and hope to see you tomorrow." He gestures toward Oak. "I trust that you don't also have a cottage in your pocket. Your family is eager to spend some time with you."

"A moment," the prince says, turning to Wren.

It's almost impossible to say anything meaningful to her here, with many eyes on them both, but he can't leave without promising that he will see her. He needs her to know he's not abandoning her.

"Tomorrow afternoon?" he says. "I will come and find you."

She nods once, but her face seems braced for betrayal. He understands that. Here, he has power. If he was going to hurt her, this would be the time to do it. "I really do want to show you the isles. We could go to Mandrake Market. Swim in the Lake of Masks. Picnic on Insear, if you're feeling up to it."

"Perhaps," she says, and lets him take her hand. Even lets him press a kiss to her wrist.

He isn't sure what to make of the tremble in her fingers as he releases them.

And then Oak is herded toward the palace, with Tiernan behind him and Randalin complaining vociferously to the High King and Queen about the discomforts of the journey.

"*You* insisted on going north," Jude reminds the councilor.

As soon as they pass through the doors of the Palace of Elfhame, Oriana embraces Oak, hugging him tightly. "What were you thinking?" she asks, which is so exactly what he expects her to say that it makes him laugh.

"Where's Madoc?" he asks between being released by his mother and Taryn sweeping him into another hug.

"Probably waiting for us in the war room," Jude says.

Leander comes up to Oak, demanding to be swung around. He lifts the boy in his arms and whirls, rewarded with the child's laughter.

Cardan yawns. "I hate the war room."

Jude rolls her eyes. "He's probably arguing with Grima Mog's second-in-command."

"Well, if there's an actual *fight* to watch, that's different, obviously," Cardan says. "But if it's just pushing little wooden people around on maps, I will leave that to Leander."

At the mention of his name, Leander capers over. "I'm bored and you're bored," he says. "Play with me?" It's half request, half demand.

Cardan touches the top of the child's head, brushing back his dark coppery hair. "Not now, imp. We have many dull adult things to do."

Oak wonders if Cardan sees Locke in the boy. Wonders if he sees the child he and Jude do not—and will not anytime soon, it seems—have.

When she turns toward him, Oak holds up a hand to forestall whatever his sister is about to say. "May I speak with Cardan for a moment?"

The High King looks at him with narrowed eyes. "Your sister has precedence, and she would like some time with you."

At the thought of Jude's lecture and then the lectures of all the other family members who took precedence, Oak feels exhausted.

"I haven't been home in almost two months and am sticky with salt spray," he says. "I want to take a bath and put on my own clothes and sleep in my own bed before you all start yelling at me."

Jude snorts. "Pick two."

"What?"

"You heard me. You can sleep and then have a bath, but I am going to be there the moment you're done, not caring a bit about your being naked. You can bathe and put on fresh clothes, and see me before you sleep. Or you could sleep and change your garments, no bath, although I admit that's not my preference."

He gives her an exasperated look. She smiles back at him. In his mind, she has always been his sister first, but right at that moment it's impossible to forget that she's also the Queen of Elfhame.

"Fine," he says. "Bath and clothes. But I want coffee and not the mushroom kind."

"Your wish," she tells him, like the liar she is, "is my command."

"Explain this to me from the beginning," Jude says, sitting on a couch in his rooms. Her arms are crossed. On the table beside her is an assortment of pastries, a carafe of coffee, cream so fresh that it is still warm and golden, along with bowls of fruit. Servants keep coming with more food— oatcakes, honey cakes, roasted chestnuts, cheeses with crystals that crunch between his teeth, parsnip tarts glazed in honey and lavender—and he keeps eating it.

"After I left Court, I went to see Wren because I knew she could command Lady Nore," he begins, distracted by someone putting a cup of hot coffee into his hand. His hair is wet and his body relaxed from soaking in hot water. The abundance that he has taken for granted all his life surrounds him, familiar as his own bed.

"You mean *Suren?*" Jude demands. "The former child-queen of the Court of Teeth? Whom you call by a cute nickname."

He shrugs. *Wren* is not precisely a nickname, but he takes his sister's point. His use of it indicates familiarity.

"Tiernan says that you've known her for years." He can see in Jude's face that she believes he took a foolish risk recruiting Wren to his quest, that he trusts too easily, and that's why he often winds up with a knife in his back. It's what he wants her to believe about him, what he has carefully made her believe, and yet it still stings.

"I met her when she came to Elfhame with the Court of Teeth. We snuck off and played together. I told you back then that she needed help."

Jude's dark eyes are intent. She's listening to all the nuances of what he says, her mouth a hard line. "You snuck off with her during a *war?* When? Why?"

He shakes his head. "The night you and Vivi and Heather and Taryn were talking about serpents and curses and what to do about the bridle."

His sister leans forward. "You could have been killed. You could have been killed by *our father.*"

Oak takes an oatcake and begins tearing it apart. "I saw Wren once or twice over the years, although I wasn't sure what she thought of me. And then, this time..."

He sees the change in Jude's face, the slight tightening of the muscles of her shoulders. But she's still listening.

"I betrayed her," Oak says. "And I don't know if she'll forgive me."

"Well, she's wearing your ring on her finger," Jude says.

Oak takes one of the shredded pieces of oatcake and puts it into his mouth, tasting the lie he can't tell.

His sister sighs. "And she came here. That has to be worth something."

And she held me prisoner. But he isn't sure that Jude will be at all moved by that as proof of Wren's caring about him.

"So do you really intend to go through with this marriage? Is this real?"

"Yes," Oak says, because none of his concerns are about his own willingness.

Jude doesn't look happy. "Dad explained that she has a unique power."

Oak nods. "She can unmake things. Magic, mostly, but not exclusively."

"People?" Jude asks, although if Cardan can congratulate Wren on the death of Lady Nore, he clearly knows the answer, which means she knows, too.

Still, his sister wants to hear it from him. Maybe she just wants to make him admit it. He nods.

Jude raises a brow. "And that means what exactly?"

"Scattering our guts across the snow. Or whatever landscape she has to hand."

"Lovely," she says. "And are you going to tell me she's our ally? That we're safe from that power?"

He licks dry lips. No, he cannot say that. Nor does he want to confess that he's worried Wren will take herself apart without meaning to.

Jude sighs again. "I am going to choose to trust you, brother mine. For now. Don't make me regret it."

CHAPTER

15

Oak wakes in his familiar bedroom, among a familiar mess. Papers cover his dresser and desk. Books are piled in untidy stacks, shoved back into their shelves at odd angles. On his bedside table, a volume is open facedown, its spine cracked.

The prince has very poor book etiquette. It has been remarked on before by his tutors.

Tacked up on the wall is a collage of drawings and photographs and other artifacts from both worlds that Oak occupies. A bright orange ticket from a fair hangs beside a riddle on a piece of vellum found in the gullet of a fish. A napkin with the number of a boy he met at a movie theater written in ballpoint pen. A sticky note with three books he means to pick up from a library. A golden necklace in the shape of an acorn, given by his first mother to his second and then to him, attached with gum to the wall. A silver fox figurine with twine around its middle, twin to the one Wren has. A manga-style portrait of Oak done by

Heather in markers. A pencil sketch for a formal portrait of the family that hangs in one of the halls.

It all is just as it was when he left. Looking around makes him feel as though time telescoped, as though he stepped out for only a few hours. As though he couldn't have come back so changed.

Oak hears a sound from the sitting room outside his bedroom—part of the chambers that ought to be his alone. He comes fully awake, sliding out of bed, his hand going automatically to the dagger beneath his mattress.

That's right where he left it as well.

He creeps along the wall, careful with his hooves against the stone floor. He peers through the gap between door and frame.

Madoc is picking over the remainder of the food on the table.

With a sigh of disgust—at himself, his father, and his apparent paranoia—he stabs the dagger into the wall and grabs a robe. By the time he comes out, Madoc is sitting on a couch and drinking cold, leftover coffee from the night before. An eye patch covers a quarter of his face, and a twisted black cane rests against a side table. The reminders of his father's suffering in the Citadel temper Oak's rage toward him but don't rid him of it.

"You're alive," Madoc says with a grin.

"I might say much the same of you," Oak points out, sitting across from his father. He's in a dressing gown embroidered with a pattern of deer, half of them shot with arrows and bleeding red thread on the golden cloth. Everything in Elfhame feels surreal and sinister at the moment, and the dying deer on his robe aren't helping. "And before you make *any* point about *anything* I've done that you believe was risky, I suggest you recall you did something riskier and far more foolish."

"I am chastened," Madoc says, and then his mouth lifts in a grin. "But I did get what I wanted."

"She pardoned you?" Oak isn't entirely surprised. His father is here in the palace, after all.

The redcap shakes his head. "Your sister rescinded the exile. *For now*." He snorts, and Oak understands that's all Jude could do without looking as though he was getting some kind of special favor out of her. But it was enough.

"And you're done with scheming?" Oak asks him.

Madoc waves a hand in the air. "What would I need to scheme for when my children control everything I ever wanted for them?"

In other words, no, he's not done.

Oak sighs.

"So let's discuss your wedding. You know several factions here are enthusiastic about it."

Oak's eyebrows go up. People who want him out of the way?

"If you had a powerful queen, it would be more possible to support you against the current occupants of the thrones."

Oak should have known better. "Since I haven't made myself look as though I would make a competent ruler."

"Some Folk prefer incompetence. Their desire is for their rulers to have enough power to hold the throne and enough naivete to listen to those who put them there. And your queen exudes both."

"Oh?" Madoc holding forth about politics is comforting in its familiarity, but it bothers him that Madoc so quickly identified the factions at Court that were up for treachery. It worries Oak how Madoc might respond if Oak ever indicated he *was* interested in becoming

High King. He's concerned that the redcap might prize naivete in Oak as much as any conspirator.

"They will sidle up to your little queen tonight," his father goes on. "They will introduce themselves and curry her favor. They will attempt to ingratiate themselves with her people and compliment her person. And they will gauge just how much she hates the High King and Queen. I hope her vows were ironclad."

Oak can't help recalling the way she told Randalin she might be able to break her vows like she broke a curse. *Pull it apart like a cobweb.* He doesn't like thinking how intrigued his father would be by that information. "I better get dressed."

"I'll ring the servants," Madoc says, reaching for his cane and pushing himself to his feet.

"I can manage," Oak tells his father firmly.

"They ought to clear these platters and bring you some breakfast." His father is already moving toward the pull beside the door. As with so many things, it is not as though Oak *couldn't* stop him, but it would take so much effort that it doesn't seem worth doing.

Oak's family is used to thinking of him as someone who needs to be taken care of. And for all that Madoc knew that Oak was dangerous enough to spring him from the Ice Needle Citadel, he suspects Madoc would be surprised about the prince's machinations at Court.

Before a servant can be called in to give him help he neither wants nor needs, Oak goes back to his bedroom and hunts through his armoire for something to wear. As soon as he finishes with his father, he will steal a basket of food from the kitchens and go to Wren's clawfooted cottage, so there's no need for anything fussy. He chooses a plain woolen green jacket and dark pants that stop at the knee. He's going to tempt Wren to run wild in Elfhame. Leave their guards behind and politics behind, too. He's determined to make her laugh. A lot.

A fierce knock on the door brings him out of his bedroom. Despite having gorged the night before, and despite telling his father not to bother summoning more food, his stomach growls. Probably he has some meals to catch up on. Possibly he can take this food and not bother robbing the kitchens.

"Ah," Madoc says. "That would be your mother."

Oak gives the redcap a look of betrayal. There would have been no avoiding Oriana for long, but he could have managed a little longer. And his father could have warned him. "What about breakfast?"

"She'll have brought you something." He supposes they had some kind of prearranged signal when Madoc was done with Oak—the bell pull, a servant to run and alert her.

With a sigh, the prince opens the door, then moves to one side as his mother sweeps into the room. She has a tray in her hands. On it rests a teapot and some sandwiches.

"You're not going to marry that girl," Oriana says, fixing him with a glare. She sets down the tray sharply, ignoring the loud sound of it hitting the table.

"Careful," Oak warns.

Madoc rises, leaning heavily on his black cane. "Well, I will leave you two to catching up." His expression is mild, fond. He is not fleeing conflict. He loves conflict. But perhaps he doesn't want to be in the position of openly telling Oriana that her priorities do not match his own.

"Mom," Oak says.

She makes a face. She is dressed in a gown of white and rose, a frothy ruff at her throat and the ends of her sleeves. With her pink eyes and pale skin and petallike wings on her back, she sometimes looked like a flower to him—a snapdragon. "You sound like a mortal. Is it so hard to say in full?"

He sighs. *"Mother."*

She presents her cheek to be kissed, then presses the backs of his hands to her lips. "My beauty. My precious child."

He smiles automatically, but her words hurt. He never before doubted her love for him—she turned her life upside down, even marrying Madoc, for the sake of Oak's protection. But if that love was something forced on her, some enchantment, then it wasn't real and he would have to find a way to free her from the burden of it.

"You worried me when you left," she says. "I know you adore your father, but he wouldn't want you to risk your life for him."

Oak bites his tongue to keep from answering that. Not only was Madoc willing to let Oak risk his life, but he was counting on it. Perhaps Oak should be grateful, though. At least he was certain Madoc's feelings were real—he was far too manipulative to have been manipulated by magic. "Father looks well."

"Better than he was. Not resting enough, of course." She looks up at Oak, impatience in her face. Normally, she is rigid about etiquette, but he can tell she's not interested in small talk now. He's only surprised that she allowed Madoc and Jude to get at him first. Of course, by buttonholing him after they left, she had the advantage of being able to lecture him as long as she liked without the worry of being interrupted. "Questing I understand, even if I didn't like the thought of you in danger, but not this. Not offering this girl marriage when she has none of the qualities anyone might look for in a bride."

"So let me get this straight," Oak says. "You understand the part where I might have had to kill a lot of people, but you think I chose the wrong girl to kiss?"

Oriana gives him a sharp look, then pours him some tea.

He drinks. The tea is dark and fragrant and almost washes the taste of bitterness from his mouth.

"You were in her prisons. I have spoken with Tiernan many times since he returned. I asked him dozens of questions. I know you sent him away with Madoc to save them both. So tell me, are you marrying her because you care for her or because you want to save the world from her?"

Oak grimaces. "You didn't include saving her from the world as a possibility."

"Is that your reason?" Oriana inquires.

"I care for her," Oak says.

"As the Crown Prince, you have a responsibility to the throne. When you—"

"No." A thin tendril of worry uncurls inside him at the thought she, like Madoc, might grow too ambitious on his behalf. "There's no reason to believe I will outlive either Jude or Cardan. No reason for me ever to wear the crown."

"I admit that once I dreaded the possibility," Oriana says. "But you're older now. And you have a kind heart. That would be a great boon to Elfhame."

"Jude is doing just fine. And it's not like she doesn't have a kind heart."

Oriana gives him an incredulous look.

"Besides, Wren is a queen in her own right. If you want me to wear a crown, there you go. If I marry her, I get one by default." He takes one of the sandwiches and bites into it.

Oriana is not appeased. "This is nothing to take lightly. Your sister certainly doesn't. She sent her people to bring you back the moment she found that you'd gone after your father. And though she failed to get hold of you, her people brought back one of your traveling companions—a kelpie."

"Jack of the Lakes," Oak says, delighted until the rest of what Oriana is saying catches up with him. "Where is he? What did she do to him?"

Oriana gives a minute shrug. "What is it you were saying about your sister having a kind heart?"

He sighs. "Your point is made."

"Jack was hauled before us and made to tell us all he knew of your journey and its intention. He's still in the palace—a guest of the Court, not *exactly* a prisoner—but he described Suren as more animal than girl, rolling in mud. And I remember how she was as a child."

"*Tortured* is how she was as a child. Besides, how can he call anyone an animal when he turns into a literal horse?"

Oriana presses her lips together. "She is not for you," she says finally. "Feel as sorry for her as you like. Desire her if you must. But do not marry her. I will not have you stolen from us again."

Oak sighs. He owes his mother so much. But he does not owe her this. "You want to rule over me as though I were a child. But you also want me to be a ruler. You will have to trust me when I say that I know what I want."

"You have grown tired of far more fascinating girls," Oriana says with a wave of her hand. "A few boys, too, if Court rumors are true. Your Suren is dull, without grace or manners, and furthermore—"

"Enough!" Oak says, surprising both of them. "No, she is not going to become the Mistress of Revels and have all of Court eating out of her hand. She's quiet. She doesn't love crowds or people staring at her or having to find things to say to them. But I don't see what that has to do with my loving her."

For a moment, they just stare at each other. Then Oriana goes to his wardrobe and riffles through the clothes.

"You ought to change into the bronze. Here, this." She holds up a doublet shining with metallic thread. It is the brown of dried blood, and velvet leaves have been sewn on it as though they were blown in a great gust across its surface. Most of them are various shades of brown and gold, but a few green ones catch the eye with their brightness. "And per- haps the golden horn and hoof covers. Those are lovely in candlelight."

"What's wrong with what I'm wearing?" he asks. "I am going out for the rest of the afternoon, and tonight it's only dinner with the family and a girl you don't want me to impress."

Oriana gives him an incredulous look. "Dinner? Oh no, my darling. It's a *feast*."

CHAPTER

16

Of course, when Cardan invited Wren to dinner, he didn't mean dining together at a table. He meant attending a feast held in her honor. *Of course he did.*

Oak forgot how things worked, how people behaved. After being away from Elfhame for so long, he is being crammed back into a role he no longer remembers how to fit into.

Once he's dressed, scolded, and kissed by his mother, he manages to make it out the door. On his way to the kitchens, he runs into his nephew, who demands a game of hide-and-seek and chases after a palace cat when he's put off. Then, as the prince packs a basket, he endures being good-naturedly fussed over by several of the servants, including the cook who sent up little iced cakes. Finally, having obtained a pie, several cheeses, and a stoppered bottle of cider, he slips away, his cheeks stinging only a little from the pinching.

Still, the sky over Insmire is the blue of Wren's hair, and as he makes his way to her cottage, he cannot help feeling hopeful.

He is most of the way there when a girl darts from the trees.

"Oak," Wren says, sounding out of breath. She's clad in a simple brown dress with none of the grandeur of the clothes he's seen her in since she took over the Court of Teeth. It looks like something she threw on in haste.

"I love you," Oak says, because he needs to say it simply, so she can't find a way to see a lie in it. He's smiling because she came through the woods in a rush, looking for him. Because he feels ridiculously happy. "Come have a picnic with me."

For a moment, Wren looks utterly horrified. The prince's thoughts stagger to a stop. He feels a sharp pain in his chest and fights to keep the smile on his lips.

It's not as though he expected her to return the sentiment. He expected her to laugh and perhaps be a little flattered. Enjoy the thought of having a little power over him. He thought she *liked* him, even if she found him hard to forgive. He thought she *had* to like him some to *want* him.

"Well," he manages, hefting the basket with false lightness. "Luckily, there's still the picnic."

"You fall in love with the ease of someone slipping into a bath," she tells him. "And I imagine you extricate yourself with somewhat more drama, but no less ease."

Now that was more the sort of thing he was prepared to hear. "Then I urge you to ignore my outburst."

"I want you to call off the marriage," she says.

He sucks in a breath, stung. Truly, he didn't expect her to rub salt in so fresh a wound, although he supposes she gave him no reason to think she wouldn't. "That seems like an excessive response to a declaration of love."

Wren doesn't so much as smile. "Still, call it off."

"Call it off yourself," he snaps, feeling childish. "As I remember from the ship, we had a plan. If you wish to change it now, go right ahead."

She shakes her head. Her hands are clenched into fists at her sides. "No, it must be you. Come on, it's not as though a marriage is what you want, not really, right? No matter how you say you feel. It was a clever thing to do—a clever thing to say. You've always been clever. Be clever now."

"And break things off with you? Cleverly?" He sounds brittle, resentful.

She actually looks hurt by his tone. Somehow that makes him angrier than anything else. "I should never have come here," she tells him.

"You can go," he reminds her.

"You don't understand." She wears a pained expression. "And I can't explain."

"Then it seems we are at an impasse." He folds his arms.

She glances down at her hands, which are gripping each other tightly, fingers threaded together. When she looks back up into his eyes, she seems sorrowful.

"I shall see you at the feast," he says, attempting to regain his dignity.

Then he turns and stomps off toward the woods, before he can say more things he will regret. Before she takes the chance to hurt him worse. He feels petty, petulant, and ridiculous.

Rubbing the heel of his hand over one eye, he doesn't look back.

Striding toward Mandrake Market with a picnic basket in his hand, Oak feels a perfect fool.

Several people bow low when he passes, as though sharing the same path is a singular honor. He wonders if he would feel less awkward if he had grown up entirely on the isles and wasn't used to being treated as nothing special in the mortal world.

He gloried in it when he was younger. Loved how all the children here wanted to play with him, how everyone had smiles for him.

And yet you knew it was false. That was part of what drew you to Wren—she had your measure from the first.

But though she had his measure, he wasn't sure he had hers. Mother Marrow was summoned north by Bogdana. Mother Marrow gave Wren the gift of that cottage where she and her people spent the night.

Mother Marrow knew *something* of their plans.

Mandrake Market, on the tip of Insmoor, used to be open only on misty mornings, but it's grown into a more permanent fixture. There, one can find everything from leather masquerade masks to charms for the bottoms of shoes, swirling tinctures of everapple, potion-makers, and even poisons.

Oak passes maple sugar in the shape of strange animals, a lace-maker weaving skulls and bones into her patterns. A shopkeeper sets out trays of acorn cups full to their tiny brims with blood-dark wine. Another offers to tell fortunes from the pattern of spit on a page of fresh parchment. A goblin grills fresh oysters over an outdoor fire. The midday sun stains everything gold.

Like the growth of the market, stalls and tents have given way to more permanent structures. Mother Marrow's house is a sturdy stone cottage with none of the fancifulness of walls shingled in candy. Out

front, an herb garden grows wild, vines tied so they weave over the top
of a diamond-paned window.

Steeling himself, he raps on the wooden planks of her door.

There is a shuffling from the other side, and then it opens, squeak-
ing on dry hinges. Mother Marrow appears in the doorway, standing
on clawed feet, like those of a bird of prey. Her hair is gray as stone, and
she wears a long necklace of rocks carved with archaic symbols on them,
ones that puzzle the eye if you look too long.

"Prince," she says, blinking up at him. "You look far too fine for a
visit to poor Mother Marrow."

"Could any grandeur be great enough to properly honor you?" he
asks with a grin.

She huffs, but he can tell she's a little pleased. "Come in, then. And
tell me of your adventure."

Oak moves past her into her cottage. There is a low fire in the
grate and several stumps before it, along with a wooden chair. Another
threadbare chair sits off to one side with knitting equipment piled in
a basket at its feet. The yarn seems freshly spun, yet not carded well
enough to remove all the bits of thistle. On the wall, a large, painted
curio cabinet contains an array of things that don't reward observing
too closely. Tiny skeletons covered in a thin layer of dust. Viscous fluids
half-dried in ancient bottles. Beetle wings, shining like gems. A bowl
of nuts, a few shaking and one hazelnut rolling back and forth. Beyond
the cabinet, the prince can see a passageway into a back room, perhaps
a bedroom.

She urges him to sit in the wooden chair by the fire, the back carved
in the shape of an owl.

"Tea?" she offers.

Oak nods, to be polite, although he feels as though he's been swimming in tea since his homecoming.

Mother Marrow tops off a pot from the kettle hanging over the fire and pours him a cup. It's a blend of some kind, carrying the scent of kelp in it, and anise.

"This is very kind," he says, because the Folk do not like to have their efforts dismissed with mere thanks and take hospitality very seriously.

She grins, and he notes a cracked tooth. She picks up her own cup, which she has freshened, using it to warm her hands. "I see the advice I gave you was useful. Your father has returned. And you have won yourself a prize."

He nods, feeling as though he's on unsteady ground. If she's referring to Wren, it seems dismissive to call her a prize, as though she were an object, but he can't think what else she could be talking about. Perhaps Mother Marrow has a reason to appear not to care too much for Wren. "Leaving me to seek your guidance again."

She raises her eyebrows. "On what subject, prince?"

"I saw you in the Ice Citadel," he says.

She stiffens. "What of it?"

He sighs. "I want to know why Bogdana brought you there. What she hoped you were going to do."

Silence stretches out for a long moment between them. In it, he hears the boiling of the water and the clack of the nuts as they move in her cabinet.

"Did you know I have a daughter?" she asks finally.

Oak shakes his head, although now that she mentions it, he does remember something about her having a child. Perhaps someone referred to the daughter before, although the context eludes him.

"I tried to trick the High King into marrying her."

Oh, right. That was the context. Mother Marrow gave Cardan a cape that, when worn, makes him immune to most blows. It's said to be woven of spider silk and nightmares, and although Oak has no idea how that could be done, he doesn't doubt the truth of it. "So you have some interest in your line ruling."

"I have some interest in my *kind* ruling," she corrects him. "I would have liked to see my daughter with a crown on her head. She's very beautiful and quite clever with her fingers. But I will be glad to see any hag daughter on the throne."

"I don't intend to be High King," he informs her.

At that, she smiles, takes a sip of her tea, and says nothing.

"Wren?" he prompts. "The Citadel? Bogdana's request?"

Her smile widens. "We hags were the first of the Folk, before those of the air alighted and claimed dominion, before those of the Undersea first surfaced from the deep. We, like the trolls and the giants, come from the earth's bones. And we have the old magic. But we do not rule. Perhaps our power makes other Folk nervous. Little wonder that the storm hag was tempted by Mab's offer, though in the end the cost was high."

"And now she bears a grudge against my family," he says.

Mother Marrow snorts, as though at the delicacy of his phrasing. "So she does."

"Do you?" he asks.

"Have I not been a loyal subject?" she asks him. "Have I not served the High King and his mortal queen well? Have I not served you, prince, to the best of my poor abilities?"

"I don't know," he says. "Have you?"

She stands—acting offended to cover that she does not—and perhaps dares not—answer. "I think it's time you go. I am sure you are wanted at the palace."

He sets down his untouched cup of tea and rises from the chair. She's intimidating, but he's taller than her and royal. He hopes he seems more formidable than he feels. "If Bogdana has a plan to move against Jude and Cardan, and you're a part of it, the punishment will not be worth whatever reward you've been promised."

"Is that so? Rumors abound about *your* loyalties, prince, and the company *you* keep."

"I am loyal to the throne," he says. "And to my sister, the queen."

"What about the king?" asks Mother Marrow, her eyes like flint.

Oak's gaze doesn't waver. "So long as he doesn't cross Jude, I am his to command."

She scowls. "What about the girl? What loyalties do you owe her? Would you give her your heart?"

An ominous question, given what he knows of Mellith's history.

He hesitates, wanting to give a real answer. He is drawn to Wren. He is consumed by thoughts of her. The rough silk of her voice. Her shy smile. Her unflinching gaze. The memory of fine, wispy strands of her hair under his hands, the nearness of her skin, her indrawn breath. Memory of the way she sparred with him across that long table in the Citadel—the familiarity of it, so like many of his own family meals. But the sting of his confession and her rejection is fresh. "I would give her whatever she wanted of me."

Mother Marrow raises her brows, looking amused. Then her smile dims. "Poor Suren."

Oak puts a hand to his heart. "I think I'm offended."

She gives a little laugh. "Not that, foolish boy. It's that she should have been one of the greatest of hags, an inheritor of her mother's vast power. A maker of storms in her own right, a creator of magical objects so glorious that the walnut I gave her would be a mere trinket. But instead, her power has been turned inside out. She can only absorb magic, break curses. But the one curse she cannot break is the one on herself. Her magic is warped. Every time she uses it, it hurts her."

Oak thinks of the story Bogdana told, of a girl whose magic burned like matches, and considers that Bogdana's own magic doesn't work in that way. The storm hag was exhausted, perhaps, after she made the ship fly, but not sick. When Cardan brought a whole island from the bottom of the sea, he didn't faint afterward. "And that's what Bogdana brought you north to try to fix?"

She hesitates.

"Shall I ask one of the Council to come and inspect what potions and powders you keep in your cabinet?"

She only laughs. "Would you really do such a thing to an old lady such as myself, to whom you already owe a debt? What bad manners that would be!"

He gives her an irritated look, but she's right. He does owe her a debt. And he is one of the Folk, brought up in Faerie enough to almost believe that bad manners outweigh murder in a list of crimes. Besides, half the Council probably buys from her. "Can you undo Wren's curse?"

"No," she says, relenting. "As far as I know, it cannot be undone. When the power of Mellith's death was used to curse Mab, Mellith's heart became the locus for that curse. How can you fill something that devours everything you put into it? Perhaps you can answer that. I can't. Now go back to the palace, prince, and leave Mother Marrow to her ruminations."

He's probably late for the banquet already. "If you see Bogdana," he says, "be sure to give her my regards."

"Oh," says Mother Marrow. "You can give her those yourself soon enough."

By the time he arrives in the brugh, the hall beneath the hill is full of Folk. He is, as he predicted, late.

"Your Highness," Tiernan says, falling into step behind him.

"I hope you rested," Oak says, attempting to seem as though he hasn't just been dumped, as though he hasn't a care in the world.

"No need." Tiernan speaks in a clipped fashion, and he's frowning, but since he's so often frowning, the prince can't tell if it indicates more disapproval than usual. "Where were you this afternoon?"

"I took a quick trip to Mandrake Market," Oak says.

"You might have fetched me," Tiernan suggests.

"I might have," Oak agrees amiably. "But I thought you might be the worse for wear after almost drowning—or perhaps otherwise occupied."

Tiernan's frown deepens. "I was neither."

"I *hoped* you might be otherwise occupied." Oak glances around the hall. Cardan lounges on his throne on the dais, a goblet hanging off his fingers as though it may spill at any moment. *Cardan.* Oak has to speak with him, but he can't do it here, in front of everyone, in front of Folk who may be part of the conspiracy the prince needs to disavow.

Jude stands close to Oriana, who is gesturing with her hands as she speaks. He doesn't spot any of the other members of his family, although that doesn't mean they're not here. It's quite a crowd.

"Hyacinthe is a traitor thrice over," Tiernan says. "So you can cease speaking of him."

Oak raises a single eyebrow, a trick he is almost sure he stole from Cardan. "I don't recall mentioning Hyacinthe at all."

Not unexpectedly, that irritates Tiernan even more. "He betrayed you, helped imprison you. And struck you. He attempted to kill the High King. You ought to dismiss me from your service for how I feel about him, not inquire about it as though it were perfectly normal."

"But if I don't inquire, how will I know enough to dismiss you from my service?" Oak grins, feeling a bit lighter. Tiernan said *feel*, not *felt*. Maybe Oak's romance is doomed, but that doesn't mean someone else's can't succeed.

Tiernan gives him a look.

Oak laughs. "If anyone wants to torture you, all they need to do is make you talk about your feelings."

Tiernan's mouth twists. "On the ship, we...," he begins, and then seems to think better about the direction of that statement. "He saved me. And he spoke to me as though we could...but I was too angry to listen."

"Ah," Oak says. Before he can go further, Lady Elaine moves toward him in the crowd. "Ah, shit."

Her ancestry is half from river creatures and half from aerial ones. A pair of small, pale wings hangs from her back, translucent and veined in the manner of dragonfly wings. They shimmer like stained glass. On her brow, she wears a circlet of ivy and flowers, and her gown is of the same stuff. She is very beautiful, and Oak very much wishes she would go away.

"I will tell your family that you've arrived," Tiernan says, and melts into the crowd.

Lady Elaine cups Oak's cheek in one delicate, long-fingered hand. Through sheer force of will, he neither steps back nor flinches. It bothers him, though, how hard it is to steel himself to her touch. He's never been like that before. He's never found it hard to sink into this role of besotted fool.

Maybe it's harder now that he actually *is* a besotted fool.

"You've been hurt," she says. "A duel?"

He snorts at that but grins to cover it. "Several."

"Bruised plums are the sweetest," she says.

His smile comes more easily now. He is remembering himself. Oak of the Greenbriar line. A courtier, a little irresponsible, a lot impulsive. Bait for every conspirator. But it chafes worse than before to pretend to ineptitude. It bothers him that had he not pretended for so long, it was possible his sister would have entrusted him with the mission he had to steal.

It bothers him that he's pretended so long he's not sure he knows how to be anything else.

"You are a wit," he tells Lady Elaine.

And she, oblivious to any tension, smiles. "I have heard a rumor that you are being promised in marriage to some creature from the north. Your sister wishes to make an alliance with a hag's daughter. To placate the shy folk."

Oak is surprised by that story, which manages to be almost wholly accurate and yet totally wrong, but he reminds himself that this is Court, where all gossip is prized, and though faeries cannot lie, tales can still grow in the telling.

"That's not quite—" he begins.

She places a hand on her heart. Her wings seem to quiver. "What a relief. I would hate for you to have to give up the delights of Court, forever sentenced to a cold bed in a desolate land. You have already been away so long! Come to my rooms tonight, and I will remind you why you wouldn't want to leave us. I can be gentle with your cuts and scrapes."

It comes to Oak that he doesn't want gentle. He isn't sure how he feels about that, although he doesn't want Lady Elaine, either. "Not tonight."

"When the moon is at its zenith," she says. "In the gardens."

"I can't—" he begins.

"You wished to meet my friends. I can arrange something. And afterward, we can be alone."

"Your friends," Oak says slowly. Her fellow conspirators. He had hoped their plans had fallen apart, given how many rumors were flying around. "Some of them seem to be speaking very freely. I've had my loyalty questioned."

It is on that statement that Wren enters the brugh.

She wears a new gown, one that looks like nothing that could have come from Lady Nore's wardrobe. It is all of white, like a cocoon of spider silk, clinging to Wren's body in such a way that the tint of her blue skin shows through. The fabric wraps around her upper arms and widens at the wrists and the skirts, where it falls in tatters nearly to the floor.

Woven into the wild nimbus of her hair are skeins of the same pale spider silk. And on her head rests a crown, not the black obsidian one of the former Court of Teeth, but a crown of icicles, each an impossibly thin spiral.

Hyacinthe stands at her side, unsmiling, in a uniform all of black.

Oak has seen his sister reinvent herself in the eyes of the Court. If Cardan leads with his cruel, cold charm, Jude's power comes from the promise that if anyone crosses her, she simply cuts their throat. It is a brutal reputation, but would she, as a human, have been afforded respect for anything gentler?

And if he didn't wonder how much that myth cost Jude, how much she disappeared into it, well, he wonders now. He hasn't been the only one playing a role. Maybe none of his family has quite been seeing one another clearly.

Wren's gaze sweeps the room, and there's relief in her face when she finds him. He grins before he remembers her rejection. But not before she gives him a minute grin in return, her gaze going to the woman at his side.

"Is that her?" Lady Elaine asks, and Oak realizes how close to him she stands. How her fingers close possessively on his arm.

The prince forces himself not to take a step back, not to pull free of her grip. It won't help, and besides, what reason does he have to worry over sparing Wren's feelings? She doesn't want him. "I must excuse myself."

"Tonight, then," Lady Elaine says, even though he never agreed. "And perhaps every night thereafter."

As she departs, he is aware he has no one to blame but himself that she ignored his words. Oak is the one who makes himself appear empty-headed and easily manipulated. He is the one who falls into bed with anyone he thinks may help him discover who is betraying Elfhame. And, to be fair, with plenty of others to help forget how many of the Folk are dead because of him.

Even those he cared for, he hid from.

Maybe that's why Wren can't love him. Maybe that is why it seems so believable that he may have enchanted everyone in his life into caring for him. After all, how can anyone love him when no one really knows him?

CHAPTER

17

The crowd ought to be familiar, but the noise of the gathered Folk is loud and strange in his ears. He tries to shake it off and hurry. His mother will be annoyed he's late again, and not even Jude and Cardan are going to sit down to a feast in his honor without him, which means it can't officially begin until he gets to the table.

And yet, he keeps getting distracted by his surroundings. By hearing his father's name on certain lips. Hearing his own on others. Listening to knots of courtiers speculate about Wren, calling her the Winter Queen, the Hag Queen, the Night Queen.

The prince notes Randalin, the little horned man drinking from an enormous, carved wooden mug, chatting with Baphen, whose curling beard sparkles with a new selection of ornaments.

Oak passes tables with wines of different colors—gold and green and violet. Val Moren, the former Seneschal, and one of the few mortals in Elfhame, is standing beside one, laughing to himself and turning in circles as though playing the childish game of seeing how dizzy he can become.

"Prince," he calls out. "Will you fall with me?"

"Not tonight, I hope," Oak answers, but the question echoes eerily in his mind.

He passes a table with roasted pigeons, looking entirely too pigeon-y for Oak's comfort. Several leek and mushroom tarts rest beside them, as well as a pile of crab apples being set upon by sprites.

His friend Vier spots him and raises a flagon. "A toast to you," he cries, walking over to sling an arm over Oak's shoulders. "I understand you've won yourself a northern princess."

"*Won* is definitely overstating the case," Oak says, sliding out from his friend's arm. "But I ought to go to her."

"Yes, don't leave her waiting!"

The prince wades back into the crowd. He sees a flash of metal and spins, looking for a blade, but it is just a knight wearing a single sleeve of her armor over a frothy gown. Near her are several ladies of the Court with enormous, cloudlike clusters of baby's breath for wigs. He passes faeries in mossy capelets and dresses that end in branches. Elegant gentlemen in embroidered robes and doublets of birch bark. One green-skinned girl with gills has a train on her gown long enough to catch occasionally on roots as she passes. As he's looking, Oak realizes it isn't a train at all but the spill of her hair.

By the time he makes it to the High Table, he sees Wren standing before his sister and Cardan. He really should have gotten here sooner.

Wren catches his gaze as he approaches. Though her expression does not alter, he thinks he sees relief in her eyes.

Jude watches them both, calculating. Still, after two months away

THE PRISONER'S THRONE 223

and a long rest to clear his head, what he notices most is how young Jude looks. She *is* young, but he can see a difference between her and Taryn. Perhaps it is only that Taryn has been to the mortal world more recently and has caught up to her years. Or that having a young child is tiring, and she doesn't look older so much as exhausted.

A moment later, he wonders if it was only the fancy of the moment that made him think that. But another part of him wonders if Jude is quite as mortal as she once was.

He bows to his sister and to Cardan.

"Wren was just telling us of her powers," says Jude, voice hard. "And we asked for the return of the bridle *you* borrowed."

He's missed something and not something good. Did she refuse them?

"I have sent one of my soldiers for it," Wren tells him, as though in answer to the question he did not ask.

Perhaps they are only annoyed at the reminder of how many traitors to Elfhame serve in the Court of Teeth. If so, they must be doubly annoyed when a falcon swoops into the room, becoming a man as he lands. Straun.

Oak's former prison guard gives him a smug look as he holds out the bridle to Wren.

The prince can still conjure the feeling of the straps against his skin. Can still remember the helplessness he felt when she commanded him to crawl. How Straun watched him, how he laughed.

Wren takes it from the soldier, letting it lie across her palm. "It's a cursed thing."

"Like all Grimsen's creations," Jude says.

"I don't want it," Wren says. "But I won't give it to you, either."

Cardan raises his brows. "A bold statement to make to your rulers in the heart of their Court. So what do you propose?"

In her hands, the leather shreds and shrivels. The magic departs from it like a thunderclap. The buckles fall to the dirt floor.

Jude takes a step toward her. Everyone in the brugh is looking at them now. The sound the destruction made drew their attention as surely as a shout.

"You unmade it," says Jude, staring at the remains.

"Since I have cheated you out of one gift, I will give you another. There's a geas on the High Queen, one that would be easy enough for me to remove." Wren's smile is sharp-toothed. Oak isn't sure what the nature of the geas is, but he is sure from the spark of panic in Jude's face that she doesn't want it gone.

The offer hangs in the air for a long moment.

"So many secrets, wife," Cardan says mildly.

The look Jude gives him in return could have peeled paint.

"Not only the geas, but half a curse," Wren tells his sister. "It winds around you but cannot quite tighten its grip. Gnaws at you."

The shock on Jude's face is obvious. "But he never finished speaking—"

Cardan holds up a hand to stop her. All teasing is gone from his voice. "What curse?"

Oak supposes the High King may well take a curse seriously, since he was once cursed into a giant, poisonous serpent.

"It happened a long time ago. When we went to the palace school," Oak's sister says.

"Who cursed you?" asks Cardan.

"Valerian," Jude spits out. "Right before he died."

"Right before you killed him, you mean," Cardan says, his dark eyes glittering with something that looks a lot like fury. Although whether it is toward Jude or this long-dead person, Oak isn't certain.

"No," Jude says, not seeming in the least afraid. "I'd already killed him. He just didn't know it yet."

"I can remove that and leave the geas alone," Wren says. "You see, I can be quite helpful."

"One supposes so," says the High King, his thoughts clearly on the curse and this Valerian. "A useful alliance."

Oak supposes that means Wren is still pretending she's willing to marry him.

Wren reaches her hand into the air, extending her fingers toward Jude and making a motion as though gripping something tightly. Then her hand fists.

His sister gasps. She touches her breastbone, and her head tips forward so that her face is hidden.

The High Queen's knight, Fand, unsheathes her blade, the glint of the steel reflecting candlelight. All around, guards' hands go to their hilts.

"Jude?" Oak whispers, taking a step toward her. "Wren, what did you—"

"If you've hurt her—" Cardan begins, his gaze on his wife.

"I removed the curse," Wren says, her voice even.

"I'm fine," Jude grates out, hand still pressing against her chest. She moves to a chair—not the one at the head of the table, not her own—and sits. "Wren has given me quite a gift. I will have to think long and hard about what to give her in return."

There's a threat in those words. And looking around, Oak realizes the reason for it.

It isn't just that Wren took apart the bridle without permission and the curse without warning, nor that she exposed something that Jude may have wanted to stay hidden, but she made the High King and Queen look weak before their Court. It's true they weren't up on the dais for all to see, but enough courtiers were listening and watching for rumors to spread.

The High King and Queen were helpless in the face of Wren's magic.

That Wren did them a service and put them in her debt.

She did to Jude what Bogdana had done to her in the Citadel—and did it more successfully.

But to what purpose?

"You bring an element of chaos to a party, don't you?" Cardan says, his tone light, but his gaze fierce. He lifts a goblet from the table. "We obviously have many things to discuss regarding the future. But for now, we share a meal. Let us toast, to love."

The High King's voice has a ringing quality that enjoins people to pay attention. Nearby, many glasses are raised. Someone presses a silver-chased goblet into the prince's hand. Wren is given one by a servant, already filled to the brim with a dark wine.

"Love," Cardan goes on. "That force that compels us to be sometimes better and often worse. That power by which we can all be bound. That which we ought to fear and yet most desire. That which unites us this evening—and shall unite the both of you soon enough."

Oak glances at Wren. Her face is like stone. She is clutching her own goblet so tightly that her knuckles are white.

There is a half smile on Cardan's face, and when his gaze goes to Oak, he gives a small extra tip of his goblet. One that may be a challenge.

I do not want your throne, Oak wishes he could just say aloud and not care if anyone hears, not care if it makes the moment awkward. But the conspirators will reveal themselves just after midnight, and it's worth waiting a single day.

The Ghost, standing near Randalin, raises his own glass in Oak's direction. Not far from them, standing by Taryn and Leander, Oriana does not toast and, in fact, appears to be contemplating pouring her wine onto the dirt.

Well, this is going great.

He turns toward Wren and realizes how pale she's grown.

He thinks of her feverish gaze aboard the ship and how he had to carry her to her bed. If she passes out now, all her work—the way she forced herself upright to walk on the shore, this exchange with his sister—will be undone. The Court will see her as weak. He hates to admit it, but his family may see her that way, too.

But she can't be well. She was weak from breaking the troll kings' curse before they left. Then she took apart that monster, and now this. He thinks of Mother Marrow's words, about how Wren's own hag power—a power of creation—has been turned inside out.

"I would have a moment with my betrothed," Oak says, reaching a hand toward her. "A dance, perhaps."

Wren looks at him with wild eyes. He's put her in a difficult position. She can't very well turn him down, and yet she is probably wondering how much longer she can stay upright.

"We're soon to eat," his mother objects, having come closer without his noticing.

Oak makes a gesture of carelessness. "It's a banquet, and now that the toast is made, we're not needed here to sample every dish."

Before anyone else can weigh in, he puts his arm around Wren's waist and escorts her to the floor.

"Perhaps," Oak says, when they've gone a few steps, "we continue on to a corner and sit for a moment."

"I will dance," she says, as though meeting his challenge. Not what he intended, but it was so ill-done that it may as well have been.

Cursing himself, he takes one of her hands in his. Her fingers are cool, her grasp on him tightening. He can feel her force herself to relax.

He guides her through the steps he taught her, back in the Court of Moths. The dance isn't quite appropriate for the music, but it hardly matters. She barely remembers the steps, and he barely cares. Her skin has that same pale, waxy look it had aboard the ship. The same bruises around her mouth and eyes.

He presses her to him so no one can see.

"I will be well enough in a moment," she says as he turns with her in his arms. She missteps, and he catches her, holding her upright.

"Let's sit in some dark corner," he says. "Take a moment to rest."

"No," she tells him, although he's holding her whole weight now. "I see the way they look at me already."

"Who?" Oak asks.

"Your family," she says. "They hate me. They want me gone."

He wants to contradict her, but he forces himself to consider what she's saying. As he does, he moves through the dance, one hand at her waist, another against her back, holding her feet above the ground, pressing her body to his. So long as she doesn't pass out entirely, so long as her head doesn't loll, they will seem like they're moving together.

There's some truth to Wren's fears. His mother would spit at Wren's feet if she could find a way to do it that would reconcile with her rigid sense of etiquette. And while Jude seems conflicted, she would murder Wren herself if she thought Wren's death would shield people she cares about. Jude wouldn't need to dislike her to do it.

"My family believes they must protect me," he says, the words sour in his mouth.

"From me?" she asks, her face no longer looking so pale and bruised. She manages to even seem a little amused.

"From the cruel, terrible world," he says.

Her lip turns up at the corner. Her gaze rests on him. "They don't know what you're capable of, then?"

He takes a deep breath, trying to find his way to the answer. "They love me," he says, knowing that's not enough.

"How many people does your sister Jude believe you've killed?" Wren asks.

There was the bodyguard who turned on him. There was no hiding that. And that duel he was in with Violet's other lover. *Two.* Jude could have guessed some of the others, but he doesn't think she did.

Of course, he didn't want her to guess. So why did it bother him so much? And how many people *had* he killed? Two dozen? More?

"Your father?" Wren asks into his silence.

"He knows more," Oak says, a betrayal in and of itself.

That is the problem with being Madoc's son. The redcap understands people, and he understands his children best of all. When he isn't consumed by rage, he is horribly insightful.

He sees in Oak what no one else has. He sees the desperate and impossible desire to repay all that he owes his family. Has Madoc used that to manipulate Oak? Oh, most definitely. Many times over.

He smiles at Wren. "*You* know what I am capable of."

"A terrifying thought," she says, but doesn't sound displeased. "I should have understood better—what you did for your father and why. I wanted it to be simple. But my sis—Bex—" A choking fit stops her speech.

"Perhaps you might like a glass of something. Watered wine?"

She smiles tremulously in return. "A goblet of only water, if that will cause no one offense. What I drank during the toast seems to have gone to my head."

They both know that isn't the reason she feels faint, but he carries on the pretext. "Of course. Will you—"

"I can stand now," she says.

He maneuvers them close to a chair, then sets her on her feet. If nothing else, she can hold on to the chair back. He remembers how weak he felt after leaving her dungeons. Something to lean against helped.

Then, leaving her reluctantly, he heads toward the nearest table where drinks have been set. Food is still being brought out from the kitchens, though at the High Table, most everyone is seated. As he pours water into a glass, he notes that a few courtiers have crowded around Wren and seem intent on charming her. He watches her give a smile that is perfectly polite, watches her eyes narrow, watches her listen.

He cannot help but think of Madoc's words. *They will sidle up to your little queen tonight. They will introduce themselves and curry her favor. They will attempt to ingratiate themselves with her people and compliment her person. And they will gauge just how much she hates the High King and Queen.*

"Prince," the Ghost says, hand on Oak's shoulder, making him startle. "I need to speak with you a moment."

Oak raises his eyebrows. "I haven't asked Taryn about Liriope yet, if it's about that."

Garrett does not meet his gaze. "Other things have taken up my attention as well. I overheard something, and I have been following the path of it, but I want to warn you not to go wandering out alone. Keep Tiernan by your side. No assignations. No heroics. No—"

The Ghost bites off the words as Jack of the Lakes approaches, the kelpie looking relieved and as unamused as he did when he swore his allegiance to Oak.

"Forgive the interruption," says the kelpie. "Or don't. I don't care. I have need of the prince."

"You presume much," the Ghost says.

"I often do," says Jack silkily.

Probably the kelpie doesn't know he's baiting a master assassin. Probably.

"I have heard your warning," Oak tells the Ghost.

The Ghost sighs. "I will have more information for you tomorrow, although perhaps not what you will want to hear." With that, he walks off into the crowd.

The prince looks over at Wren. She's speaking to another courtier, her hand heavy on the back of the chair.

Oak drags his attention to the kelpie. "I think I can guess the purpose of this conversation. Yes, I will help. Now, I must get back to my betrothed."

Jack snorts. "I haven't come to complain. Your sister terrorized me only a little."

"Then what is it you want?"

"I saw a most interesting meeting last night," Jack says. "Bogdana and a man with golden skin. He was carrying a large trunk. He opened it to show her the contents, then shut it again and took it away."

Oak remembers the hag with the golden skin from the Citadel. He was the one who didn't give Wren a present. "And you have no idea what was inside?"

"No, indeed, prince. Nor did he seem the sort who would take kindly to being followed by one such as myself."

"I appreciate your telling me," says Oak. "And it's good to see you."

Jack grins. "I share that sentiment, yet I would be away from this place if you put in a good word with your sister for my release."

At that, Oak laughs. "So you wish to complain after all?"

"I would not wish to turn your good nature ill," says Jack, looking around him uncomfortably. "Nor would I wish that ill nature directed at me. But I am not well suited to your home."

"I'll talk to my sister," Oak promises.

On his way back to Wren, he spots Taryn speaking with Garrett. Oak's gaze picks out Madoc in the crowd, leaning heavily on his cane. Leander is telling a story, and the redcap is listening with what seems rapt attention to his grandchild.

It occurs to him how strange a family they all are. Madoc, who murdered Jude and Taryn's parents—and yet somehow, they consider him their father. Madoc, who almost killed Jude in a duel. Who might have used Oak to get to the throne and then ruled through him.

And Oriana, who was cold to his sisters, even to Vivi. Who didn't trust Jude enough to leave Oak alone with her when they were young, but asked her to lay down her life to protect him just the same.

And Vivi, Taryn, and Jude, each different, but all of them clever and determined and brave. Then there is Oak, still trying to figure out where he fits in.

As the prince approaches Wren, he clears his throat.

"Your water," he says when he's close, his voice loud enough that the courtiers surrounding her make their excuses. He offers her the goblet of water, which she drinks thirstily.

"I was waylaid," he says by way of apology.

"As was I," she tells him. "We should go back to your family's table."

He hates that she's right but offers her his arm.

She takes it, leaning on him with some force. "When you said you loved me..." It begins as a question, but one she cannot seem to complete.

"Alas that I cannot lie," he tells her as he guides her through the hall, the smile easy on his lips now. "I hope you will try to find the humor in my feelings. I shall endeavor to do so myself."

"But... don't you want revenge?" she asks, her voice even softer than before.

He glances at her swiftly and takes a moment to decide how to answer. "A little," he admits finally. "I wouldn't mind if there was some dramatic reversal where you pined while I remained aloof."

Wren laughs at that, a startled sort of sound. "You are the least aloof person I know."

He makes a face. "Alas once again, my dreams crushed."

She stops smiling. "Oak, please. I've made a mistake. I've made several and I need..."

He stops. "What do you need?"

For a moment, it seems as though she will answer. Then she shakes her head.

Just then, the musicians cease playing their instruments. The rest of the courtiers begin to move toward the banquet tables.

Oak guides Wren back to her chair. Predictably enough, the leaf place card with her name on it is set across the table from him, in the place of honor, beside Cardan. His own seat is two down from Jude, next to Leander. A snub.

He's almost sure that's not where his chair was before he took off.

A servant comes with pies in the shape of trout.

"You'll like this," Taryn says to him and Leander both. "There's a coin inside one of the dishes, and if you find it, you'll receive a boon."

The High King is speaking to Wren, perhaps telling her about the coin as well. Oak can see the effort she's making not to shrink in on herself.

Slabs of mushroom, grilled and shiny with a sweet sauce, are brought out. Then stewed pears alongside platters of cheese. Seed cakes. Sweet, fresh cream. Broad beans, still in their pods. More fanciful pies arrive. They're shaped like stags and falcons, swords and wreaths—each with a different filling. Partridge stewed in spices. Blackberries and hazelnuts, pickled sloes, mallow fruit.

When he looks over at Wren again, he can see that she is covering her mouth as she eats, as though to hide the sharpness of her teeth.

There is a sound at the entrance, a clatter of armor as guards leap to attention. The storm hag has arrived, hours late, wearing a tattered black dress that hangs off her like a shroud and a smile full of menace.

Bogdana thrusts her hand into the pie in the shape of a stag. Her hand is stained red with the juice of sloes as she pulls it out, her fingers gripping a coin. "I shall have my boon, king. I want Wren and your heir married tomorrow."

"You requested three days," Cardan reminds her. "To which we gave no answer."

"And three days it will be," says Bogdana. "Yesterday was the first, and tomorrow will be the third."

Oak sits up straighter. He glances across the table, waiting for Wren to stop this. Waiting for her to say she doesn't want to marry him.

Her gaze meets his, and there is something like pleading in it. As though she wants to both break his heart publicly and have some guarantee he won't hold it against her.

"Go ahead," he mouths.

But she remains silent.

A glance passes between Jude and Cardan. Then Jude stands and raises her glass, turning to Oak. "Tonight, we feast in the hall in celebration of your betrothal. Tomorrow, we will have a hunt in the afternoon, then dance on Insear. At the end of the night, I will ask your bride a question about you. Should she get it wrong, you will delay your marriage for seven days. Should she answer rightly, we will marry you both on the spot, if such is still your desire."

Bogdana scowls and opens her mouth to speak.

"I agree to those conditions," Wren says softly before the storm hag can answer for her.

"So do I," Oak says, although no one asked him. Still, this is all a performance. "Provided that I am the one who comes up with the question for my betrothed."

Wren looks panicked. His mother looks as though she'd like to stab him with her fork. Jude's expression is impossible to read, so rigidly does she keep her features set.

Oak smiles and keeps smiling.

He doesn't think she'll contradict him in public. Not when Bogdana drew so much attention to them.

"So be it, brother," his sister says, sitting back in her chair. "The choice will be yours."

CHAPTER

18

S hortly after that, Wren rises and makes her excuses.

On her way out, she stops by Oak whispers in his ear. "Meet me in the gardens at midnight."

He nods with a slight shiver. She's already moving away from the table, fingers resting briefly on his shoulder as she goes. The storm hag spots her leaving, rises, and follows, menace in her movement.

That's two assignations for Oak. The moon's zenith tonight is about an hour past midnight, so they're a little too close together for him to feel easy about moving between them. And yet, he's helpless to do anything but agree to see Wren. When they were alone on the floor of the brugh, he felt as though they were friends again. And something was obviously wrong. Wren said she made mistakes—could that have to do with allowing Bogdana to accompany her? The storm hag wants them to marry—and soon—but he isn't sure why Wren doesn't tell her that isn't going to happen. Is it because Wren's power is at such a low ebb that she's afraid she will lose if she has to fight?

He can postpone the betrothal easily enough. Pose her a question to which she doesn't know the answer—or pose it in such a way that it's possible for her to pretend to guess wrong.

Who is my favorite sister?

What's my favorite color?

Can you ever forgive me?

Okay, maybe not that last one.

Out of the corner of his eye, he notices that Tiernan has walked up to Hyacinthe. Both of them stood near the High Table throughout dinner; Hyacinthe didn't follow Wren out. Instead, he had remained behind, looking uncertain.

"I want you," the prince hears Tiernan say. Oak feels some chagrin at overhearing that, but he is also surprised at the starkness of the admission. It sounds almost like an accusation.

"And what are you going to do about it?" Hyacinthe asks.

Tiernan snorts. "Pine, I suppose."

"Aren't you tired of that?" Hyacinthe could have said the words like a tease, but instead he sounds exhausted. A man offering a truce after a long battle.

"What else is there?" Tiernan's voice is harsh.

"What if I said you could have me? Have me and keep me."

"I could never compete with your rage toward Elfhame," Tiernan says.

"Eavesdropping, prince?" asks the Ghost, taking the seat on the other side of Leander.

Oak turns toward him guiltily. He would really like to have heard what Hyacinthe said next.

"I am behaving just as you wished," Oak says. "No going off on my own. No heroics. Even a little spy work."

Garrett rolls his eyes. "It's been a mere handful of hours—barely that. Manage to last the night, and I will actually be impressed."

Since Oak didn't plan on lasting the night without sneaking out, he says nothing.

"Show me the trick," Leander says to the Ghost, interrupting them.

"Which trick?" Garrett's smile is indulgent. It's surprising to see the shift in his behavior. But then he's known Leander since the child was born. Garrett and Taryn became close before the Battle of the Serpent, possibly even before Locke's death. Vivi and Heather—and Oak himself—have long believed they're lovers, but after Taryn's disastrous first marriage, Taryn hadn't admitted it out loud.

"The one with the coins."

Oak grins. He knows a few of those. The Roach taught them to him when he was only a little older than Leander.

Garrett reaches into his pocket and comes out with a silver coin. Before he can demonstrate, though, Madoc walks up, leaning heavily on his twisted black cane.

"My lads," the redcap says, putting a hand on Leander's head. The boy turns to smile up at him.

The Ghost sets the coin before Leander. "Why don't you practice and show me what you learned," he instructs, then rises.

"But . . . ," the boy protests, a whine coming into his voice.

"I will show you the trick again tomorrow." With a sharp look at Madoc, he leaves the table.

Oak frowns. He had no idea how uncomfortable the Ghost was around Madoc, but of course the redcap was in exile for years. Oak never saw them together before. Leander picks up the coin but does nothing more with it.

"So you're really going through with this marriage?" Madoc asks the prince.

"We'll all find out the answer to that tomorrow." And Oak will look more like the fickle and flighty courtier than ever when he asks Wren a question she can't answer and postpones their engagement.

The redcap raises his eyebrows. "And have you asked yourself why the storm hag is in favor of your union?"

Truly, his father takes him for a fool. "If you know, perhaps you ought to tell me."

Madoc looks in the direction where the Ghost went. "Hopefully, your sister's spies will turn up something. There are worse things, though, than to learn how to rule in the harsh north."

Oak doesn't argue with him. He's tired of arguing with his father.

When Madoc wanders off, though, he shows Leander all the coin tricks he knows. He runs the silver disc over his knuckles, makes it disappear behind the child's ear, makes it reappear in his glass of nectar.

"Did it seem to you that Garrett doesn't like your grandfather?" Oak says, handing back the coin.

Leander tries to roll the disc over his knuckles, but it slides off and onto the floor. He jumps down to scrounge for it. "He knows his name," the boy says.

For a moment, Oak isn't sure he heard right. "His name?"

"Garrett's secret name," Leander says.

"How do you know that?" Oak must have spoken too harshly, because Leander looks startled. The prince gentles his voice. "No, no one's in trouble. I was just surprised."

"I heard Mom and him talking," Leander says.

"Is the Ghost his secret name?" Oak asks, just to be sure.

Leander shakes his head. "That's just his code name."

Oak nods and shows Leander the trick again, his mind running in circles. There was absolutely no reason for Garrett to give his true name to Madoc.

But then the Ghost's words from the ship come back to the prince: *Locke had the answer you seek. He knew the name of the poisoner, much good it did him.*

Had Locke told Taryn during their disastrous marriage? Had she told Madoc? But no—surely the Ghost wouldn't have forgiven that. Maybe Locke gave Madoc the name directly—but why?

Oak looks across the table at Taryn, deep in conversation with Jude. How it happened didn't matter. What mattered was what it meant.

They knew Garrett was the one who murdered his mother. Who fed her blusher mushroom. He feels hot and cold all over, rage making him tremble.

Did they think he didn't deserve this answer? That he was too much a child?

Or did they not tell him because they didn't think there was anything wrong with what Garrett had done?

At midnight, the gardens are full of night-blooming plants, limned in moonlight. Wren's blue skin is the same color as the petals of a flower, and as she enters the clearing, she seems as remote as a star in the sky.

He is still reeling from what he has learned. From the idea that someone he knows—someone he likes—tried to kill him. From the betrayal of his family.

"You wanted to see me?" he asks Wren, and wonders if, in the state he's in, he should have come at all.

"I did," she says with a sly smile. "I do."

He remembers what it was like to be a child with her. He is half-tempted to propose a game. He wonders if he can get her to run wild through the grass with him.

"It was wrong to lock you away in my prisons," she says.

That's so unexpected that he laughs.

She makes a face. "Very well, I concede that's obvious."

"I am not sitting in judgment of you," he says. Not with all the blood on his hands. "Does this mean you forgive me?"

She raises an eyebrow but doesn't deny it.

"Shall I say instead that there's peace between us at last?"

At that, he does get a smile. "Peace?"

"Not even that?" Oak puts a hand to his chest, as if wounded. Under his fingers, he can feel the thrum of his heart.

"I am not a peaceful person," she says. "And neither are you."

He loves that she knows he's not peaceful. Loves that she doesn't think him kind. He doesn't know how, but from the first she seemed to recognize something in him that no one else does—that inner kernel of hardness, of coldness.

He never convinced her that he was a hero. He perhaps half-convinced her he was a fool, but never for long. She saw through his playacting and his smiles. Heard the riddles and schemes his charmed tongue tried to obscure.

And so, when she kissed him, it felt as though *he* was being kissed. Perhaps for the first time.

And he loves the way she's watching him now, as though he fascinates her. As though she's drawn to him. As though he's got a chance.

Even if she doesn't want to marry him. Even if she doesn't love him. Wren draws in a deep breath. "It's beautiful here."

Oak looks around the gardens, full of flowers. Golden evening primrose, carpets of night phlox with tiny white buds, pale moonflowers, the purple night-scented stock, and the large silvery flowers of the cereus. He cups one. "Did you know this is called Queen of the Night?"

Wren shakes her head, smiling. "I dreamed about this place sometimes."

He thinks about her comment that she would make new nightmares and is silent. When she looks at him, there is something vulnerable in her face, though her voice is sharp with sudden anger.

"You could have kept me here, in Elfhame, but you let your sister send me away." Wren turns her gaze to the flower, speaking to it instead of him. "You gave me the first safe place—the *only* safe place I had after I was stolen from my unfamily—and then you took it from me."

He wants to object and insist that he *helped* her. He interceded with his sister. He hid her from the Court of Teeth. But though he did those things, he didn't keep doing them. He helped a little, and then having done so, assumed he did enough.

"It never occurred to me that you didn't have a home to go back to." He didn't understand. He didn't ask.

"You were bored with me," she accuses, but there isn't much heat in her voice. He can tell that she believes it and that she has believed it for a long time. Maybe she doesn't even condemn him for it.

"I would have hidden you in my rooms forever if I thought that's what you wanted," he vows. "I thought about you a lot ever since. Which you must know, since I showed up in your forest a few years later."

She clearly wants to object.

"Whereupon you sent *me* away," he concludes, and watches her expression change to one of exasperation.

"You think I did that because I didn't like you?"

He gives her a steady look.

"I did it to help you! If you stayed in the forest with me, the best thing that could ever have happened was that your family came and dragged you back to Elfhame. I'd lose you again, and you'd gain nothing."

"So you thought—" he starts, but she cuts him off.

"And the worst thing, the more likely thing, was that one of the enemies you were telling me about would find you. And then you'd be dead."

Her logic is alarmingly sound, although he doesn't like to admit it. He must have seemed very dramatic, showing up in her woods like that. Very dramatic and very, very, *very* foolish. The typical spoiled, naive royal. "And you couldn't tell me that?"

"*What if you didn't listen?*" she shouts. There's a desperation in her voice that's out of step with the conversation they're having.

"I'm listening," he says, puzzled.

"It's not safe," she says. "Not then and not now."

"I know that," he tells her.

"*I'm* not safe," she says. "You can't trust me. I—"

"I don't need safe," he says, and leans down, putting his hands in her hair. She doesn't move, looking up at him with lips that are slightly parted, as though she can't quite believe what he's doing.

Then he kisses her. Kisses her like he's wanted to for days and weeks and what feels like forever.

It isn't a careful kiss. He can feel her teeth against his tongue, her dry lips. He can feel the sharp edges of her nails as they dig into his neck. He shivers with sensation. He doesn't want careful any more than he wants safe.

He wants *her*.

Wren pulls him down, lower, until they are kneeling in the gardens. Oak feels dizzy with desire. All around them, the petals of night-blooming flowers have opened, and their thick perfume scents the air.

"Do you want—?" he starts, but she is already pushing up her dress.

"I want," she says. "That's my problem. I want and I want and I want."

"What do you want?" he asks, voice soft.

"*Everything.* Charm me. Rip me open. Ruin me. Go too far."

He shudders at her words, shaking his head against them.

She goes on, whispering against his skin. "You cannot understand. I am a chasm that will never be full. I am hunger. I am need. I cannot be sated. If you try, I will swallow you up. I will take all of you and want more. I will use you. I will drain you until you are nothing more than a husk."

"Use me, then," he whispers, mouth on her throat.

Then her lips are against his, and there is no more talking for a long time.

Wren is lying against him, her head pillowed against his shoulder, when the shifting branches alert him.

"Someone's coming," Oak says, grabbing for his trousers and also his knife.

Wren springs to her feet, pulling on her gown, trying to make herself look less like she's been rolling around in the dirt.

For a moment, their gazes meet, and they both grin helplessly. There's something so silly about this moment, scrambling to get dressed before they're caught. Neither of them can pretend to anything but merriment.

"Your Highness," says Lady Elaine, taking in the situation with a frown as she steps into the clearing. "I see you had a surfeit of trysts planned for this evening."

Her words wipe the smile from Oak's face. He was supposed to meet her, and he didn't pay attention to the zenith of the moon. Didn't pay attention to anything but Wren. Didn't care about conspirators or schemes or even his family's lies.

After years of bending his whole self to be a lure for the worst of Elfhame, he simply *forgot* to be that person.

"Moonrise, sunrise, dawn, dusk, zeniths," he says as flippantly as he can manage. If anything can make this moment worse, it would be his acting as though he feels *caught*. "Regrettably, I can be imprecise about imprecise times. My apologies. I hope you didn't wait long."

Wren looks between Lady Elaine and Oak, no doubt coming to her own conclusions.

"You're the girl from the Court of Teeth," Lady Elaine says, the gossamer of her wings apparent in the moonlight.

"I am the queen of what was once the Court of Teeth." Wren's expression is stony, and despite her dress gaping open in the back and the leaves tangled in her hair, she looks quite fearsome. "Betrothed to the Prince of Elfhame. And you are?"

Lady Elaine looks as astonished as if she bit into a pear and found it full of ants. She walks to Oak and puts her arm around his. "I am Elaine. *Lady* Elaine, a courtier from the Court of Moss in the west and an old friend of the prince's. Isn't that right?"

"Despite my being a trial to her," agrees Oak, avoiding giving any real confirmation.

Wren offers up a chilly smile. "I will go back to the feast, I think. Might you do up the back of my dress?"

Lady Elaine gives her a scathing look.

"Of course." Oak has to hide his smile at that as he walks behind Wren and does up the laces of her gown.

As she makes ready to go, she looks back at Lady Elaine. "I hope he will give you half the delight he's given me."

Oak has to swallow a laugh.

As Wren leaves, Lady Elaine turns to Oak, hands on her hips. "Prince," she says, sterner than any instructor in the palace school.

He is so tired of being treated as though he is a fool, as though he is in need of—what did Randalin say about Wren—a *little guidance*. Maybe he is a fool, but he is a fool of a different sort.

"There was little I could do," he protests with a shrug, choosing his words carefully. "She is my betrothed, after all. It's not the easiest thing to get rid of someone."

Lady Elaine's mouth relaxes a little, although she's not going to let him out of this that easily. "You expect me to believe you wanted to be rid of her?"

Well, it would be *convenient* if she thought that. "I mean her no insult," Oak says, deliberately misunderstanding. "But you were going to introduce me to your friends—and, well, I haven't seen you in a long while."

"Perhaps it's time you explained this betrothal," she says.

"Not here." It's too strange to stand in the place he was with Wren and attempt to deceive Lady Elaine about her. "Where was it you were going to take me?"

"We were to meet at the edge of the Crooked Forest," she tells him, walking with him as he makes his way down one of the paths. "But they will be long gone. This is dangerous, Oak. They are putting themselves at great risk for your benefit."

He notes that she didn't say *for your sake*, although he's sure that's how she wants him to take her words. "Wren is powerful," Oak says, hating himself. "And would be useful."

"That point has been made to me before," Lady Elaine says bitterly, and to his surprise. "That you were clever to make this alliance, and having the storm hag with her puts us all in a better position."

For a moment, he is tempted to explain that Bogdana is never going to be on the side of anyone with his bloodline, but what would be the point? Let her believe anything that will have her accepting Wren and taking him to the rest of the conspirators.

"She will make you unhappy," Lady Elaine tells him.

"Not all alliances are happy ones," he says, and takes one of her hands in his.

"But you," she says, putting her hand to his cheek. "You, who have little experience of sacrifice. Who have always seemed filled with such joy. How will you bear it when that joy is dimmed?"

He laughs outright at her words and then has to think fast to cover up the reason. "See? I can yet be merry. And I shall be merry still, even if wed."

"Perhaps this plan asks too much of all of us," Lady Elaine says, and he understands. *Her plan*, to be by his side, at the very least a sort of ruling consort, would be in shambles were he to marry Wren. If she cannot have that role, then she doesn't want to risk her neck.

He turns toward her, and a kind of desperation rises in him. If she gives this up, then the conspirators scurry away—rats back into their holes—and he learns nothing.

Oak can fix this. He can use his honey-tongued words on her. He can feel them, sitting on his lips, ready to fall. If he says the right things, if he draws her into his arms, then she will believe in their plan once more. He will be able to convince her that Wren means nothing, that it will be her counsel he heeds once he is on the throne. He can even persuade her to take him to the conspirators, if perhaps not tonight.

But if he does nothing, then she gives up treason. Maybe the plan falls apart, becomes idle discontented conversation and nothing more. Then she will not be shut up in a tower, or cursed into a dove, or executed in a bloody spectacle.

He gives her hand a squeeze. Gives her one last sad smile. Maybe this can be over and everyone can live. "Perhaps you're right," he says. "Sadness just doesn't suit me."

CHAPTER

19

Oak wakes with dread in his heart. As he lingers over a coffee-like substance that is made from roasted dandelions and picks at a plate of acorn cakes, his mind spins. His thoughts fly between Wren in his arms, her eyes bright and teeth sharp, kissing him as though they could crawl into each other's skin—then Lady Elaine and the capsizing of his plans—then circling back to what he learned about the Ghost.

Who gave Oak's mother poison.

Who gave Oak's mother poison so that Oak would die.

How could the Ghost *look* at Oak when, if not for Oriana, if not for *sheer luck*, he could have been the prince's murderer?

It galls Oak to think of Taryn and Jude watching him be trained, letting the Ghost clap him on the shoulder or reposition his arm to swing a sword.

Somehow, it's Taryn's betrayal that strikes Oak the most sharply. Jude has always been constrained by position and politics while Madoc has been constrained by his nature. Oak thought of Taryn as the kind-hearted one, the one who wanted a gentler world.

Maybe she just wanted an easier one.

Oak kicks one hoof against the low table, sending the coffeepot and the tray it was sitting on crashing to the floor, crockery smashing, cakes going everywhere. He kicks it again, splintering a wooden leg and causing the whole thing to collapse.

If his mother came in, she would frown, call him childish or petulant. Summon servants to clean up. Ignore any reason he may have for his anger.

That's what his family does. Ignores everything uncomfortable. Talks around betrayals and murders. Papers over bloodstains and duels. Brushes all the bones under the rug.

Since he was old enough to really understand why he had to be the one to put the Blood Crown on Cardan's head or live with Vivi and Heather in the mortal world, away from his parents, Oak wasn't able to think of his sisters without being aware of the debt he owed them. The sacrifices they made for him. Everything he could never repay. So it is entirely new for him to think of them and be absolutely *furious*.

Then his thoughts slide back to Wren. To her expression of horror when he told her he loved her. To her warning of the night before, after he kissed her, while she dug her nails into his nape.

He was playing fast and loose back in the Ice Needle Citadel, determined to win her over despite the danger. And then he came up with a desperate plan to avoid a conflict when it was clear that Elfhame considered Wren a dangerous enemy.

When she agreed to come home with him, he thought it might *help* to be away from the Citadel. Wren was focused on survival for so long—and whatever else you may say about the isles, they are full of wine and song and other lazy indulgences.

But ever since they arrived, she's been different. Of course, he could just as easily say that she's been different ever since he confessed his love.

You've always been clever, she told him when she asked him to break things off. *Be clever now.*

Does she think that if she is the one to dump him, Elfhame will take her crown for breaking his heart?

And yet, he can't shed the feeling there is a greater wrongness she was trying to communicate. Could someone be leveraging something against her in order to stop their marriage? Was it one of her retinue? One of his family? He didn't think it could be Bogdana, who was so vocal in support of their union.

Or perhaps it *was* the storm hag—maybe Bogdana threatened Wren if she strayed from that path? And yet, if that was the case, why not tell Oak outright?

A knock comes on the door. A moment later, it opens and Tatterfell enters. She frowns at him, her inkdrop eyes taking in the wreckage of the table.

"Leave it," he tells her. "And leave off lecturing me about it, too."

She presses her thin lips together. She's been a servant in Madoc's household, paying off some debt, and then moved to the castle with Jude, possibly as a spy for their father. He's never much liked her. She's impatient and prone to pinching.

"The hunt is today," she says. "And then that farce on Insear right after. There are tents for you to change in, but we still need to select what garb to send over."

"I don't need your help with that," he tells her. Her words *that farce on Insear* echo in his head.

The little faerie looks up at him with her shining black eyes. "You ought to clothe yourself as though you expect to exchange vows, even if there's little chance of that."

He frowns at Tatterfell. "Why do you think so?"

She snorts, going to his wardrobe and taking down a tunic of deep burgundy cloth embroidered with golden leaves and pants of a deep brown. "Oh, it's not my place to speculate on the plans of my betters."

"And yet," Oak says.

"And yet, were I Jude," Tatterfell says, pulling out riding clothes of mouse gray, "I might want to marry you to the new queen of the Undersea. It would be a better alliance, and if you *don't* marry her, the alliance goes to someone else."

The prince thinks of the contest he was told of for Nicasia's hand. The one that Cirien-Cròin was attempting to prevent with the attack. "Cardan courted her, didn't he?"

Tatterfell is quiet for a moment. "Another good reason for your sister to marry you to her. Besides, I hear she threw over the High King for Locke. You look something like him."

Oak scowls as she urges him out of his nightshirt. "Jude doesn't usually expect much from me."

"Oh, I don't know," Tatterfell says. "I hear you're widely considered to be a rake."

Oak wants to object, but he has to consider that maybe Jude *does* think a marriage of Oak to Nicasia would be possible and useful. Maybe it *did* seem like a good solution to Cardan, who's heard rumors of Oak's treachery.

And if Jude wanted him to compete to be King of the Undersea, would that lead Jude to move against Wren? Would Jude push her to break off the betrothal while pretending to allow it? Push Wren to hide her interference from Oak—and have enough power to back up any threat.

Well, given the secrets she's already kept, if that is what she's doing, he'd never know about it?

Dressed in mouse gray, with Tatterfell taking his evening clothes on to Insear, Oak heads to the stables. From there, he will ride out to the Milkwood, where he intends to determine the actual reason Wren wants Oak in particular to break off their betrothal.

As he heads toward Damsel Fly, he finds Jack of the Lakes waiting for him. The kelpie is in his person form, dressed all in brown and black, bits of seaweed hanging out of his breast pockets. A rough-beaten gold hoop hangs from one ear.

"Hullo," Jack says, brushing the hair back from his eyes.

"My apologies," Oak says, resting one hand on the needle of a sword he insisted on strapping to his belt. "I haven't yet managed to speak with my sister on your behalf."

He shrugs. "My obligation to you is greater than yours to me, prince. I've come to dismiss some of it, if I can."

"Observe another clandestine meeting?" Oak asks.

"I am a steed. Get on my back, and we'll ride to the hunt together."

Oak frowns, considering. Jack is capricious and a gossip. But the vow he once gave Oak was sincere, and at the moment, Oak is feeling short on allies. Someone he can even *mostly* trust seems a boon. "Concerned about something?"

"I mislike this place," Jack says.

"Viper nest," Oak agrees.

"It seems quite the trick to tell the friendly snakes from the other ones."

"Ah," Oak says. "They're all friendly snakes until they bite you."

"Perhaps you'll have no need of me today," the kelpie tells him. "But if you do, I will be there."

Oak nods. Jack's concern makes his own worries all the more real. He reaches for a saddle. "You really don't mind?"

"So long as there's no bit between my teeth," Jack says, transforming shape on the last word. Where once there was a boy, there is a sharp-toothed black horse. The sheen on his coat is murky green, and his mane ripples like water.

Oak swings up on his back and rides out. Tiernan is waiting for him outside the palace stables on a white steed of his own. He takes one look at Jack and raises both his brows. "Have you run mad, trusting him again?"

Oak thinks of what he promised Hyacinthe in the Citadel—the hand of the person responsible for Liriope's death. And the prince considers Tiernan, whose happiness he will rob if he gives that to Hyacinthe—even supposing he could. He considers how awful it would be and all the consequences that would follow.

"Oh, don't worry," Oak says. "I'm not sure I trust anyone anymore. Not even myself."

They arrive at the Milkwood, riding beneath pale, silvery boughs covered with bleached leaves. There, the gentry of the Court are assembling in their riding garb. Cardan sits atop a black steed with flowers braided into its mane. He himself is wearing a doublet with a high collar and a crisscrossing pattern sewn into the dark fabric. Aside from shining buttons in the shape of beetles, he looks positively staid.

Taryn is all in lilac—a jacket with long tulip sleeves, breeches, and boots—and astride a dappled pony. The Ghost is beside her in dark gray, and somehow seems more knight, clad in her livery, than partner.

Oak feels a spike of rage at the sight of him. Rage that he swallows. For now.

Beside the High King, Jude is mounted on a riding toad, wearing a dress the color of unskimmed cream with billowing sleeves. Over that, a thin vest, embroidered with gold, laces over her chest. Calf-high brown boots dig into the stirrups. No crown sits on her head, and her hair is pulled simply back.

He tries to judge from her expression, from her body language, if she is working against him. If she has gone around his back and threatened Wren. But Jude is a consummate liar. There's no way he can tell, and asking would be worse than useless. All that would happen is that she'd know Wren gave something away.

On that thought, he notes Cardan watching him. He cannot, in this moment, bring himself to explain his true role in this or the other conspiracies. He cannot bring himself to be vulnerable in front of either of them. And if he begins to tell the story, Lady Elaine will face the very fate she would have if she hadn't renounced her treachery the night before. She will certainly be interrogated.

He thinks of the cold stone slab and Valen standing over him and shudders.

He wishes he could trust his sister as he once did. He wishes that he could be sure she trusted him.

The prince turns away, his gaze going to the servants loading baskets and blankets onto ponies for the picnic the courtiers will have once the hunt grows dull.

"We cannot possibly catch the silver stag," says a man in a hat with a plume sticking out of it and a longbow. He rides a chestnut steed with dainty hooves. "Nor anything much with two mortals among us. They will frighten off the beasts with their noise."

He means for Jude to hear, and she has. She gives him a lethal smile. "Well," she says, "there are always birds in the trees to hunt. Even a few falcons."

The reference to Wren's soldiers is not missed. Some of the gathered Folk appear uncomfortable. Others seem eager.

"Or we could draw lots to play the fox," she continues with a grin. "That's a fine sport, and one I've played before."

She's *been* the fox, but they don't know that. The man with the plumed hat looks nervous. "A ride through the Milkwood is its own delight."

"I could not agree more," she tells him.

Randalin blows a horn, calling for them to all assemble.

Oak spots Lady Elaine, whispering something to Lady Asha, Cardan's mother. When she notices him, she turns away without meeting his gaze.

The attention of the crowd shifts, and voices still. He turns to see Wren and Bogdana ride in, not on steeds, but on creatures enchanted from sticks and twigs and brambles. They move like horses but remind Oak of ragwort ponies in their uncanniness.

Unconsciously, he leans back, urging Jack away. Their presence bothers Oak, not just because he fought creatures like them, not just because they were Lady Nore's beasts and conjured from Mab's bones, but because he was aboard the *Moonskimmer* and did not see them there.

Another secret.

Wren is in a dress of pale gold. A chain veil is on her head, set with shimmering aquamarines. It contains her hair and falls down over her cheeks and chin, almost to her waist. She holds the reins of a bridle made from a thin chain that wraps around the horse's mouth. Though she looks majestic and even bridal, she frowns at her hands, shoulders hunched. She looks haunted.

By contrast, Bogdana is in another dark shroud, tattered in places and flying behind her in the breeze. Her expression is the picture of satisfaction.

Their arrival is greeted with murmurs of admiration. Courtiers ooh and aah over the bramble beasts, running hands over twiggy flanks.

He may not get answers out of his sister, but that doesn't mean he can't get answers. Pressing his knee gently against the kelpie's flank, he guides him toward Wren.

"Is that...?" Wren frowns.

"Jack of the Lakes," Oak says, patting the kelpie's neck. "A merry wight."

Wren's lip lifts in something that could have become a smile but doesn't stay long enough.

"Tonight I must ask you a question," Oak says. "What if it's impossible to respond to what I ask incorrectly?"

"You would bind me to marriage unwilling?" Nothing in her tone acknowledges the night before, their tangled limbs and ragged breaths. Her eloquent, whispered wants.

He feels guilty that he's not telling her the truth—he won't make her do anything she doesn't wish. But he needs to know if something is actually wrong.

"Am I supposed to declare that I was swept away first by one whim and then another?" he asks, blithe as ever. If her shield is coldness, his is mirth.

"Would they not believe it? Besides, you could tell the Court we had an argument." Wren glances over her shoulder, as though afraid someone can hear her. "I would be more than willing to have one right now. A *spectacular* fight."

He raises his brows. "And what might this argument be about?"

"Lady Elaine, perhaps," Wren offers. "Your fickle nature. I could tell you about it, loudly."

He winces. "I needed information from her."

"And did you get it?" Her brows draw together.

"I am not what I pretend to be here at Court. I would have thought you knew that."

"Don't be such a fool," she snaps. "It doesn't matter what I believe, only that..."

"Yes?" He waits for her to finish the statement.

But she only shakes her head, smothering a cough. Bogdana glances back at them.

For a long moment, they ride in silence.

"I suppose you're going to tell me that argument was enough," Oak says finally. There's definitely something strange about this conversation. "Jack could spread around a few details, given his penchant for gossip."

The kelpie makes a horselike whinny and tosses his mane, objecting.

"And I suppose you're also going to tell me that last night means nothing," Oak goes on.

Wren stiffens. "What does it matter? Despite your declaration of love, can you really say you want to marry me?"

"And if I do?" he asks.

"That doesn't matter, either," she says, her voice the snap of a lash.

He takes a breath. "Tonight—"

"Tonight is too late," she says, anguished. "It may already be too late." With that, she pulls at the lead on her twig-and-branch steed, wheeling away from him.

He watches after her, certain that someone is manipulating or threatening her. Obviously, she can't tell him directly or she would have done so. But how can anyone constrain her, as powerful as she is?

He sees Taryn steer her horse to Wren's side, hears his sister tell her how well she likes what Wren is wearing. Watches Bogdana guide her bramble steed toward Randalin. He doesn't have the wit to be afraid of her and begins merrily chatting away.

Some of the courtiers have ridden fast, in search of game, but many more have ambled along on their mounts, deep in conversation. A few have parasols of flowers or feathers or even cobwebs.

Oak rides alongside them, deep in thought, until a horn blares, signaling the beginning of the picnic.

He swings down from Jack's back and follows the others to the campsite. Servants have set up an array of differently patterned blankets and baskets, along with parasols and even musicians. If the presence of mortals or the lot of them trooping around hasn't frightened off the silver stag, a few sets of murder ballads surely will.

There are duck hand pies, stoppered carafes of wine, blackberry tarts beside piles of roasted chestnuts, and bread so light and airy that cold butter spread across it would tear it like tissue.

Oriana walks to Oak, holding out a cup of red clover tea. "I barely spoke with you last night," she says.

"We sat at the same table, Mother," the prince reminds Oriana.

She puts her arm through his. She is so much smaller that it seems impossible she ever tossed him in her arms. "Have you come up with your question for the girl?"

He shakes his head.

"Ask her your fondest memory," she urges slyly. "Or perhaps your deepest secret."

"They're clever questions," Oak says. "They seem difficult, but she might well be able to guess both. Not a bad suggestion."

His mother frowns, and he takes perverse delight in having turned her words against her. But at least he's certain that if she's so obvious in urging him to walk away, she isn't engaged in a secret manipulation of Wren. "Hoping I will seek Nicasia's hand instead?" he asks, thinking of Tatterfell's theory.

Oriana's eyes go wide. "Of course not. That would be madness."

"You don't think my sister wants—"

"No," his mother says. "She wouldn't. You would never survive down there."

If Jude *does* plan on his marrying Nicasia, she hasn't started the process of suborning Oriana. And while, being the High Queen, she could do whatever she wants, you'd think she'd have brought it up once, at least.

He reminds himself that he can't be sure, though. Right now, he can't be sure of anything.

Taryn has stuck by Wren. They are speaking together, standing beside the Ghost's horse. For a moment, he thinks of going over there and dumping his red clover tea over his sister's head.

Hyacinthe walks toward Oak, signaling with raised brows.

The prince kisses his mother's cheek. "See? After considering the Undersea, nothing seems so bad." Then he leaves her and goes to where Hyacinthe is scowling at him.

"I heard you last night," Hyacinthe says, low-voiced.

That could mean a lot of things. "And?"

"*With your nephew*," he says.

Oak winces. He should have realized that if he could eavesdrop on Tiernan and Hyacinthe, it was equally possible for him to be eavesdropped upon.

"Were you going to deliver what I asked of you?" Hyacinthe asks. "Or are you the coward who lets your mother's murderer walk free?"

Oak has been asking himself about the closer betrayals, but eventually he would have to answer that question. "I thought you'd had enough of revenge."

"I am not speaking of myself," Hyacinthe reminds him. "And I told you that I did not release you from your vow."

Choosing the worst possible moment, the Ghost moves toward them, a skin of wine and two carved wooden cups in his hand. *Right*, because he was going to give Oak an update on whatever it was he was seeking to find out the night before.

"Send him away," Hyacinthe says.

"He knows something," Oak objects.

"Send him away or I will stab him through," hisses Hyacinthe under his breath.

"A cup of mead, prince?" offers the Ghost, pouring one for Oak and then one for himself. He glances at Hyacinthe. "I am afraid I only brought the two, but if you bring yours, I will pour."

Oak's cheeks feel hot, and there is a roaring in his ears the way there is when he gives in to instinct and fights without mercy. He takes the cup of honey wine and drinks it. It's too sweet and cloying in his mouth.

The Ghost takes his in a gulp, then winces. "Not good wine, but wine nonetheless. Now, if you will walk with me."

"I am afraid I can't talk right now," the prince tells Garrett.

The Ghost must hear something in his voice. Looking puzzled, he says, "Come find me when you're ready, but it must be soon. I will ride a little ways north so that we will be alone. When we're done, we will speak with your sister."

"You're gripping your sword," Hyacinthe tells Oak in a low voice as the spy departs.

Oak glances down at his hand, surprised to find it curled around the hilt of his blade. Surprised to find it shaking a little.

"I have to go after him," the prince says. "Someone's manipulating Wren."

"Manipulating? Who? How?" Hyacinthe asks.

"I don't know."

Hyacinthe glances in the direction that the Ghost went. Courtiers are still sitting on blankets, so there's no chance of the hunt starting up again immediately. Oak needs to find out what information the spy has.

Garrett already disappeared into the Milkwood, somehow slipping between the white trunks.

With a glance toward Wren and a reminder that he needs to keep his temper, Oak remounts the kelpie and heads in the direction the Ghost went. His head is swimming. He's got to keep himself under control. Surely whatever it is that the spy knows will help Oak understand the constraints on Wren and who put them there.

He rides a little farther and looks down at his hand, which has started to tremble. He still has the sensation of being underwater. And with it, he feels a rush of something entirely too familiar.

Blusher mushroom. He's been poisoned.

He thinks of the honey wine, sweet enough to hide the flavor. Honey wine, given into his hand by the Ghost.

The prince laughs out loud. Of all the things the Ghost knows about murder, apparently he doesn't know that this is the one poison to which Oak is immune. If the spy hadn't decided to go with the symmetry of finishing the job the way he'd begun it, Oak might really be dead.

The prince draws his sword.

Oh, he's going to *murder* the spy. The Ghost thinks he knows what Oak can do, but he isn't aware of his other lessons, from Madoc. Garrett doesn't know what Oak has become under his father's tutelage. Doesn't know how many people he's already slain.

The prince urges Jack north through the brambles, past the columns of pale trees. Finally, he comes upon a clearing. The kelpie stops short. For a moment, Oak doesn't understand what he's looking at.

There, in a tangle of vines, lies a body.

Oak slides down from the kelpie's back to draw closer. The man's mouth is stained purple. His eyes are open, staring up at the late after-noon sky as though lost in contemplation of the clouds.

"Garrett?" Oak says, leaning down to shake him.

The Ghost does not move. He does not even blink.

The prince's fingers close on his shoulder. The spy's body is hard beneath his hand, more like fossilized wood than flesh.

Dead. The man who murdered his mother. The spy who had trained him to move quietly, to wait. Who bounced Leander on his shoulders. Taryn's lover. Jude's friend.

Dead. Impossibly dead.

Which means that Garrett didn't poison Oak. He shared his poisoned wine, all unknowing.

Could *Hyacinthe* have done this? He might have thought dosing the Ghost with what killed Liriope to be fitting—a symmetry of a different kind. And if he knew that Oak wouldn't die from it, he wouldn't be kind enough to stop him from drinking a portion of the blusher mushroom. He wouldn't care if Oak suffered a little.

But if it *wasn't* Hyacinthe, then it came down to the question of what the Ghost had learned. What he wanted to tell Oak. What they needed to go to Jude with. What couldn't wait.

CHAPTER
20

Guards and courtiers thunder up all around Oak. Did he cry out? Did Jack? The kelpie is standing beside the prince now, but he doesn't remember when Jack stopped being a horse. The noise and confusion mirror Oak's thoughts. People are shouting at one another, making Oak dizzy.

Or maybe that's the blusher mushroom still slowing his blood.

Jack is insisting they found the Ghost like this and someone is saying *how horrifying* and a lot of other meaningless words that blend together in Oak's mind.

Taryn is screaming, a high keening sound. She's on her knees beside the spy, shaking him. When she looks up at Oak, her gaze is so full of grief and accusation that he has to look away.

I hated him, Oak thinks. But he's not even sure that's true. He never knew Liriope, and he knew Garrett. *I should have hated him. I wanted to hate him.*

He didn't kill him, though.

He didn't kill him, but he might have. He could have. Could he have?

Jude moves to Taryn's side, one hand going to her twin's shoulders. Fingers pressing reassuringly.

The Roach leans down to check the body, and when one of the guards tries to stop him, it's Cardan who tells them to let him be. Oak didn't even realize the Roach was *at* the hunt.

Taryn lies down beside Garrett's corpse, her hair shrouding his face. One of her tears has pooled in the corner of his eye, wetting his lash.

Cardan kneels beside her, his hand going to Garrett's chest. Taryn looks up at him.

"What are you doing?" She doesn't sound happy, but they've never really gotten along.

"Blusher mushroom slows the body," he says, his gaze flickering to the Roach, who almost certainly taught him that. "But it slows it *slowly*."

"Do you mean he's not dead?" she asks.

"Is there something to be done?" Jude asks at almost the same time.

"Not in the way you mean," says Cardan, answering his wife's question and not Taryn's. He turns to Randalin and the crowd, then waves his beringed hand exaggeratedly. "Disperse. Go on."

Courtiers step away, heading to their horses, a buzz of rumors in the air. The Minister of Keys remains, glowering, standing beside Oriana. A few more Folk seem to believe this order doesn't apply to them. The Roach stays, too, but he's practically family.

Oak forces himself to scoot back, bracing against the trunk of a tree. For him, it was not much blusher mushroom, but he still feels the numbness tingling through his fingers and toes. Right now, he isn't certain whether he would fall back down if he tried to stand.

Wren crosses to his side. Bogdana stands at the edge of the clearing, half hidden by shadows.

"You're going to have to move as well," Cardan tells Taryn.

"What are you going to do to him?" she asks, shielding his body as though to protect it from the High King.

Cardan raises his eyebrows. "Let's just see if it works."

"Taryn," Jude says, reaching for her sister's hand and pulling her to her feet. "There isn't time."

Cardan closes his gold-rimmed eyes and, for all his extravagance, right then he looks like one of the paintings of the High Kings of old, somehow moved into the realm of myth.

All around them, wildflowers sprout, uncurling from buds. Trees shiver, sending down pale leaves. Brambles coil into unlikely shapes. There is a buzz of bees in the air, and then from the earth, roots rise, turning into the sturdy trunk of a tree around Garrett's body.

Taryn makes a sharp sound. The Roach lets out a breath, awe in his eyes. Oak feels it, too.

Bark wraps around Garrett and branches unfold, budding with leaves and fragrant blossoms the lilac of Taryn's clothing. A tree, unlike all that grow in the Milkwood, rises from the ground, shrouding the Ghost's body. Its limbs reach toward the sky, petals raining down around them.

Where Garrett stood, there is only the tree.

The High King opens his eyes, letting out a ragged breath. The courtiers that remained have taken several steps back. They are slack-jawed in surprise, perhaps having forgotten his command of the land beneath their feet.

"Will that—" Jude begins, her eyes shining.

"I thought that if the poison makes every part of him slow, then I could turn him into something that could live like that," says Cardan with a shudder. "But I don't know that it will save him."

"Will he be like this forever?" Taryn asks, her voice cracking a little. "Alive but imprisoned? Dying but not dead?"

"I don't *know*," Cardan says again, in a raw way that makes Oak think of being trapped in the royal bedchamber and overhearing him and Jude together. It's Cardan's real voice, the one he uses when he's not performing.

Taryn runs her hand over the rough bark, her tears coming on a sob. "He is still lost to me. He is still gone. And who knows if he's suffering?"

Oak feels Wren's hand in his, her fingers cool. "Come," she says, and at her tug, he finally rises. He's a little unsteady on his hooves, and she narrows her eyes at him. She's seen him poisoned before.

"We will discover who did this," Jude is telling her twin, voice firm. "We will punish them, I promise you that."

"Don't we know already?" Taryn says through tears, her voice breaking on the words. Her gaze goes to Wren. "I saw her by his horse."

"Wren had nothing to do with this," Oak snaps, squeezing Wren's fingers. "What possible motive could she have?"

"Queen Suren wants to destroy Elfhame," one of the remaining courtiers interjects. "Just as her mother did."

Jude does not speak, but Oak can tell she isn't unmoved by the argument that Wren may have had a hand in this. And to make it worse, Wren denies none of it. She says nothing. She just listens to their accusations.

Deny it, he wants to tell her. But what if she can't?

Just then, a cry fills the air. A vulture circles once to land heavily on Wren's shoulder. The storm hag.

"Prince?" Tiernan asks Oak, eyeing the vulture with misgiving.

"We should quit this place," says Randalin. "Our milling about cannot do anything in the way of helping."

The Bomb glares at everyone. "What did he eat or drink? We should isolate the poison."

"It was in the mead," Oak says.

The Bomb turns toward him, white hair a nimbus around her heart-shaped face. "How do you know that?"

The prince doesn't want to say this part out loud, not in front of even a small crowd, but he can't see a way out, either. "I drank some."

There is a ripple of shock through the remaining courtiers.

"Your Highness!" Randalin protests.

"And yet you're standing," says a pixie. "How is it that you're standing?"

"He must only have had the barest sip," Jude lies. "Brother, perhaps it's time to come away and rest."

Perhaps it would be better if they got out of the Milkwood. He's feeling somewhat unsteady on his feet. He's feeling somewhat unsteady, period.

"Do you think I'm responsible?" Wren whispers, her hand still in his.

No, of course not, Oak wants to say, but he isn't sure he can make his mouth spit out those words.

Did she poison the Ghost? Would she have done it for Hyacinthe's sake, if he asked her to help? Had he found out a secret so great she would protect it, even if it cost a life?

"I will believe whatever you tell me," Oak says. "Nor will I look for deceit in your words."

She watches the shifts of his expression, almost certainly looking for deceit in *his* words.

The vulture shifts, watching him with bead-black eyes. Bogdana's eyes, filled with rage.

"I'm sorry," Wren says. He sees the hag's talons sink into her shoulder hard enough to pierce flesh. A trickle of blood runs down her dress. But Wren's expression doesn't change.

He's sure she feels the pain. This is what she must have been like back in the Court of Teeth. This is how she endures all that she does. But he doesn't understand why she allows Bogdana to hurt her this way. She has the authority and power now.

Something is very, very wrong.

"You need to tell me what's going on," he says, keeping his voice low. "I can fix it. I can help."

"I'm not the one who needs saving." Wren lets go of his hand.

"It was *her*," insists Taryn. "Her or that witch she has with her or the traitorous knight who tried to kill Cardan. I want the knight arrested. I want the girl arrested. I want the witch in a cage."

Randalin blinks several times in surprise. "Well," he says to Wren. "Aren't you going to say anything? Tell them you didn't do it."

But again, she is silent.

The Minister of Keys sputters a bit as he tries to digest this. "My dear girl, you must speak."

Cardan turns toward Wren. "I'd appreciate it if you went with my knights," he says. "We have questions for you. Tiernan, show us your loyalty and accompany her. I am personally charging you with not letting her out of your sight."

Tiernan looks in Oak's direction in alarm.

Wren closes her eyes, as though her doom has come upon her. "As you command."

"Your Majesty," Tiernan begins, frowning. "I can't leave my charge—"

"Go," Oak says. "Don't let her out of your sight, as the High King said." He understands why Tiernan is concerned, however. Sending him away may mean that Cardan doesn't want Oak to have anyone to fight at his side when the High King questions him.

Randalin clears his throat. "If I may, I suggest we move to Insear. The tents are already set up and guards sent ahead. We will not be so out in the open."

"Why not?" says Cardan. "A perfect place for a party *or* an execution. Tiernan, take Queen Suren to her tent and wait with her there until I call on her. Keep everyone else out."

The vulture on her shoulder jumps into the sky, beating black wings, but Wren makes no protest.

Oak wonders if he could stop them. He doesn't think so. Not without a lot of death.

"Let me go with her," Oak says.

Jude turns toward him, raising her brows. "She didn't deny it. She isn't denying it now. You're staying with us."

"Furthermore," proclaims Cardan to the rest of his knights, "I want the rest of you to find Hyacinthe and bring him to *my* tent on Insear."

"Why not suspect me?" Oak demands, voice rising.

Taryn gives a little laugh, at odds with the tears staining her cheeks. "That's ridiculous."

"Is it? I found his body," the prince insists. "And I have a motive, after all."

"Explain," Cardan says, mouth a grim line.

Jude seems to sense what's coming. There are too many people around, guards, courtiers, Randalin, and Baphen. "Whatever Oak has to tell us, he can tell us in private."

"Then by all means," says Cardan, "let's depart."

But Oak doesn't want to be quiet. Maybe it's the blusher mushroom in his blood, maybe it's the sheer frustration of the moment. "He murdered my first mother. He's the reason she died, and you both—you all—hid it from me."

A hush goes through the courtiers like a gust of wind.

Oak feels the delirious abandon of breaking the rules. In a family of deceivers, telling the truth—out loud, where anyone could hear it—was a massive transgression. "You allowed me to treat him like a friend, and all the while you knew we were spitting on my mother's memory."

A drawn-out silence follows his last word. Oriana has a white-fingered hand pressing against her mouth. She didn't know, either.

Finally, Cardan speaks. "You make a very good point. You had an excellent reason to try to kill him. But did you?"

"I urge you all," interrupts Randalin, "if for no other reason than discretion, let us repair to the tents at Insear. We will have some nettle tea and calm ourselves. As the High Queen says, this is not a conversation to be had in public."

Jude nods. This may be the first time Randalin and Jude ever agreed on anything.

"If my family had their way," says Oak, "this isn't a conversation we'd have at all."

Then, from across the Milkwood, there's a scream.

Moments later, a knight steps into the clearing, looking as though she's run all the way there. "We found another body."

Most of the remaining knot of courtiers begin to move in the direction of the scream, and Oak goes along, though he still feels unsteady. They know he's poisoned, at least. If he falls down, no one will have many questions.

"Whose?" Jude demands.

They don't have to go far, though, and he sees the body before she gets her answer.

Lady Elaine, lying in a heap, one of her small wings half crushed when she fell from the horse that is nuzzling the end of her skirts. Lady Elaine, her cheek stained with mud. Her eyes open. Her lips purple.

Oak shakes his head, taking a step back. Hand coming up to cover his mouth. Two people poisoned—*three* people, counting himself. Because of the conspiracy?

Cardan is watching him with an unreadable expression. "Your friend?"

The Roach moves to Oak, puts one green clawed hand against the middle of his back. "Let's go ahead to Insear, as the Minister of Keys said. You're upset. Death's upsetting."

Oak gives him a wary look, and the goblin holds up his hands in surrender, his black eyes sympathetic. "I had no part in Liriope's murder nor these," the Roach says. "But I can't claim I've never done anything wrong."

Oak nods slowly. He can't claim that, either.

He mounts up again on Jack, who has obligingly become a horse again. The goblin rides a fat, spotted pony, low to the ground. Behind him, someone is saying that the festivities can't possibly go on as planned.

Oak thinks of Elaine, lying in the dirt. Elaine, who was dangerously ambitious and foolish. Had she told the rest of the conspirators that she was quitting and received this in answer?

His mind turns to Wren, with the vulture's talons digging into her skin. Her blank expression. He keeps trying to understand why Wren endures it without crying out or striking back.

Does it have something to do with Garrett and Elaine being poisoned?

Oak was a fool to bring Wren here. When he gets to the tents on Insear, he's going to find hers. Then he is going to get them both off the isles and out of this vipers' nest. Away from Bogdana. Away from his family. Maybe they could live in the woods outside her mortal family's home. She'd said, back when they were questing, that she'd like to visit her sister. What was her name? Bex. They could eat scavenged berries and look up at the stars.

Or maybe Wren wants to go back north, to the Citadel. That's fine, too.

"How long have you known?" the goblin asks.

For a moment, Oak isn't sure what he means. "About what Garrett did? Not long." Above them, the black bees of the Milkwood buzz, carrying nectar to their queen. Late afternoon sunlight turns the pale trees gold. He sets his jaw. "Someone should have told me."

"Someone clearly did," says the Roach.

Leander, he supposes, which hardly counts. And *Hyacinthe,* although he didn't know the whole of it. Oak doesn't want to blame either of them out loud, not to someone who will carry the tale to his sister. He understands what the Roach is doing, getting him alone like this, understands it well enough to avoid the trap. He shrugs.

"Did you poison him?" the Roach asks.

"I thought Garrett poisoned *me,*" the prince says, shaking his head.

"Never," says the goblin. "He regretted what he did to Liriope. Tried to make it up to Locke by giving him his true name. But Locke's not the person to trust with that sort of thing."

Oak wonders if Garrett tried to make it up to him, too, in ways he never saw. Teaching him the sword, volunteering to go north when the prince was in trouble, going to Oak with information before taking it to Jude. He didn't like having a reason to be anything but angry, but that didn't mean it wasn't true.

"There was something he needed to tell me," Oak says. "Not about any of that. Something else."

"Once you're delivered to Insear, I'll check out his part of the lair. If he had any sense, he wrote it down."

At the edge of the Milkwood, they pass the Lake of Masks. Oak's gaze goes to the water. You never see your own face, always the face of someone else, someone from the past or future. Today he sees a blond pixie laughing as she splashes someone else—a man in black with salt-white hair. Recognizing neither of them, he turns away.

At the coastline, several boats await them, pale, narrow boats with high prows and sterns curving upward so that they look like crescent moons floating on their backs—all crewed by armored guards. As the sun dips beneath the ocean on the horizon, Oak looks across to Insear, outfitted with tents for the festivities to come, then to the sparkling lights of Mandrake Market, and beyond, to the Tower of Forgetting, stark black against the red-and-gold sky.

He and the Roach get into one of the boats, and Jack, having shifted into his bipedal form, gets in after them. A guard Oak doesn't recognize nods to them and then puts up the sail. A few moments later, they are speeding across the short stretch of sea.

"Your Majesty," says the guard. "There are tents for your refreshment. Yours is marked with your father's sign."

The prince nods, distracted.

The Roach stays in the boat. "I'll find out what the Ghost knew, if I can," he says gruffly. "You stay out of trouble."

Oak couldn't count how many times someone said that to him. He isn't sure he ever listened.

On Insear, there is a small forest of pavilions and other elaborate tents. He looks among them for Wren's, listening in vain for the sound of her voice or Tiernan's. He doesn't hear either of them, and he doesn't see Madoc's moon-and-dagger crest marking a tent for him, either.

Everything feels wrong. He can see individual threads but not make out the larger web, and there isn't much time.

It may already be too late. Wasn't that what Wren said?

Surely, she couldn't have been referring to the poison.

I'm not the one who needs saving.

He pushes the thought from his mind. No, she couldn't have been speaking about that. She couldn't have a hand in murdering Lady Elaine and probably killing Garrett, too, for all that turning him into a tree might help.

As Oak and Jack walk on, the prince spots a tent with the flap open and Tatterfell within. But it isn't Madoc's crest that's stamped on the outside. The prince frowns at the mark until he understands what he's looking at. *Dain's crest.* But people don't generally refer to Oak as Dain's son, even though at this point it's well known where his Greenbriar blood comes from. If she sees this, Oriana is going to have a fit.

Oak puzzles over who arranged things this way. Not his sister. Nor Cardan, unless this is some kind of backhanded way of reminding Oak of his place. But it seems a little too backhanded. Cardan is subtle but not *confusingly* subtle.

He steps inside. The tent is furnished with rugs covering the rock and patches of grass. He spots a table is crowded with bottles of water and wine and the pressings of fruit. Candles burn to chase away shadows. Tatterfell looks up from spreading his change of clothes out on a low couch.

"You're early," the imp says. "And who's this?"

Jack comes forward to take Tatterfell's hand and bow deeply over it. "His steed and sometimes companion, Jack of the Lakes. It is my honor, lovely lady. Perhaps we shall dance together this evening."

The little faerie blushes, looking very unlike her usual grouchy self.

Oak looks at the burgundy doublet, chosen hours earlier. He can still feel the disorientation of the blusher mushroom coursing through his system, but his movements are less stiff and more sure.

"You must dress for the festivities," she says.

He opens his mouth to tell her that they're probably not going to happen, then remembers her calling tonight a farce. Did she know something? Did she have a part in this?

He needs to think straight, but it's so hard with blusher mushroom still addling his mind. Almost certainly, Tatterfell was not planning any assassinations. But he wonders if the poisonings had to do with stopping the ceremony.

That theory didn't withstand much scrutiny, though. If they wanted it stopped, and had some power over Wren, couldn't they pressure her to end it? Whoever *they* were.

As his mind runs in circles, he strips off his hunting clothes and puts on the new, more formal ones. In moments, Tatterfell is dusting him off and polishing away any mud on his hooves. As though he really is going to his wedding.

The flap of the tent opens, and two knights step inside.

"The High King and Queen request your presence in their tent before the revel begins," one says.

"Is Wren there?" he asks.

The knight who spoke shakes his head. He looks to be at least part redcap. The other knight has more elven features and dark eyes. He seems twitchy.

"Tell them I will be along presently," Oak says.

"I'm afraid we're to escort you—*now*."

That explains the twitchiness, then. "And if I don't comply?"

"We must yet bring you to them," the elven knight says, looking unhappy about it.

"Well, then," Oak says, walking to them. He could, perhaps, use his charm to talk the knights out of it, but that seems hardly worth it. Jude would only send more soldiers, and these two would get in undeniable trouble.

The prince carefully does not look in the direction of Jack. Since the kelpie wasn't mentioned, he doesn't have to go and will be the safer for it.

Lightning slices across the sky, followed by a crack of thunder. No rain has started yet, though the air is thick with it. The wind is picking up, too, whipping the skirts of the tents. Oak wonders if Bogdana has something to do with this. Certainly, she is in a bad enough mood.

He thinks of Wren again, of the talons biting into her skin. Of her words in the gardens. *I'm not safe. You can't trust me.*

There is little for him to do but walk across Insear behind the knights, past where garlands of ferns and wisteria and toadstools have been slung from trees, and musicians are tuning their fiddles, while a few courtiers, arriving unfashionably early, are selecting drinks from a large table, loaded with bottles of all shapes and sizes and colors.

One of the knights pushes aside the flap of a heavy cream-and-gold tent.

Inside, two thrones sit, although neither is occupied. Jude and Cardan stand with Taryn and Madoc. Cardan has changed into clothes of white and gold while Madoc is in deep red, as though they were opposing suits in a deck of cards. Taryn still wears her hunting clothes, her eyes red and swollen, as though she hasn't stopped crying until just before this moment. Oriana sits in a corner, entertaining Leander. Oak thinks of his own childhood and how she pulled him away from so many dangerous conversations, hiding them in the back, distracting him with a toy or a sweet.

It was a kindness, he knew. But it made him vulnerable as well.

Three members of the Living Council are in attendance. Fala, the fool; Randalin; and Nihuar, representative of the Seelie Courts. All three of them look grim. Hyacinthe is there, too, sitting on a chair, stony-faced and defiant. Oak can sense the panic he is trying to hide.

Ringed around the tent are guards, none of whom Oak knows. All of whom wear the expressions of people expecting an execution.

"Oak," Jude says. "Good. Are you ready to talk?"

"Where's Wren?" he asks.

"What an excellent question," she says. "I thought perhaps you knew."

They stare at each other.

"She's gone?" he asks.

"And Tiernan with her." Jude nods. "You can see why we have a lot to discuss. Did you arrange her freedom?"

Oak takes a deep breath. There are so many things he should have told her over the years. To tell her now is going to feel like peeling off his own skin. "You may have heard some things about me and the company I was keeping before I went north with Wren. Lady Elaine, for example. My reasons were not what you might suppose. I'm not—"

Outside, there's a crash and a howl of wind.

"What's that?" Taryn demands.

Cardan narrows his eyes. "A storm," he says.

"Brother," Jude says. "Why did you bring her here? What did she promise you?"

Oak remembers being caught in the rain and thunder of Bogdana's power, remembers his ragwort steed being torn out from beneath him. This portends disaster.

"When we were on our quest, I tricked Wren," Oak says. "I kept back information that wasn't mine to keep." He cannot help hearing the echo of his own complaint in those words. His family hid things from him the same way he hid things from her.

"And?" Jude frowns.

Oak tries to find the right words. "And she was angry, so she threw me in prison. Which seems extreme, but I was handling it. And then you...overreacted."

"Overreacted?" Jude echoes, clearly incensed.

"I was handling it!" Oak repeats, louder.

There's movement out of the corner of his eye, and then two bolts fly across the tent toward Jude. Oak hits the floor, pulling his sword from its sheath.

Cardan whips up his cloak in front of Jude—the cloak made by Mother Marrow, the one that was enchanted to turn the blades of weapons. The arrows fall to the ground as though they've struck a wall instead of cloth.

A moment later, the High King staggers back, bleeding. A knife juts out from his chest. Falling to his knees, he covers the wound with his hands, as though the blood seeping through his fingers is an embarrassment.

Randalin steps back, smug and satisfied. It's his dagger in the High King's chest.

"Put down your weapons," a soldier shouts unsteadily, taking a step forward. For a moment, Oak isn't sure whose side they're on. Then he sees the way they're standing. Seven soldiers moving closer to the Minister of Keys, two of them the knights who came to Oak's tent.

Finally, the unfamiliarity of them makes horrible sense. This is a trap.

This is the conspiracy he hoped Lady Elaine would reveal. Had Oak not missed their meeting in the gardens, had he not been so willing to believe that it was over when Lady Elaine herself gave it up, had he not departed on the quest to save his father in the first place, perhaps he could have discovered this. Discovered it and foiled it.

Oak recalls the councilor extolling the wisdom of his betrothal to Wren, recalls his pushing the royal family to come immediately to Insear after the hunt. Remembers how Randalin maneuvered a conference alone with Bogdana and Wren.

The Minister of Keys was laying the groundwork while acting so pompous and irritating that he couldn't be taken seriously. And Oak fell for it. Oak underestimated Randalin in the most foolish way possible— by falling for the same trick he played on others.

Jude eases Cardan to the ground and kneels beside him, sword in her hand. "I will cut your throat," she promises Randalin.

"Stabbity stab, knife wife," says Fala, with feeling. "Traitor's blood is hot, but it still spills."

Taryn has a dagger out. Madoc, dangerous enough with just his claw-tipped hands, has moved into a fighting stance. Oak rises and moves to his side.

"You should have listened to me," Randalin tells Jude from the safe distance he has put between them, behind one of his soldiers. "Mortals are not meant to sit on our thrones. And Cardan, the least of the Greenbriar princes, pathetic. But all that will be remedied. We will have a new king and queen in your place. You see, none of your own knights are here to save you. Nor can they cross to this isle while the storm rages. And it will rage until you're dead."

Oak blinks. "You made a deal with Bogdana. That's what the Ghost was getting proof of, that's the thing he thought I wouldn't like."

Because of Wren. That's *why* the Ghost thought Oak wouldn't like it.

"You should be grateful," Randalin tells the prince. "I persuaded Bogdana to spare you, though you are of the Greenbriar line and her enemy. Because of me, you will sit on the throne with a powerful faerie queen by your side."

"Wren would never...," Oak begins, but he's not sure how to finish. Would she agree to the murder of his family? Did she want to be the High Queen?

You can't trust me.

I'm not the one who needs saving.

Randalin laughs. "She didn't object. And neither did you, as I recall. Didn't you tell Lady Elaine of your resentment of the High King? Didn't you encourage her plot to get you on the throne?"

Oak's stomach hurts, hearing those words. Knowing a storm is raging outside because of someone he brought here. Seeing Cardan's body lying in a pool of red, no longer conscious and maybe no longer alive. Thinking of the Ghost's open, staring eyes. Seeing the way Oak's sisters are looking at him now and how his mother is looking away.

"*You* poisoned Garrett," Oak says.

Randalin laughs. "I gave him the wine. He didn't have to drink it. But he got too close to uncovering our plans."

"And Elaine?" he asks.

"What could I do?" Randalin says. "She wanted out." And pouring her wine from the same urn as the spy's convinced him it was safe to drink.

Expressing the desire to get out was how Oak planned on getting Elaine and her friends to turn on him. The same way he'd defeated other conspiracies—courting an attempted murder and exposing them for that instead of as traitors. But she hadn't known it would doom her. He should have given her a warning.

And now his family thinks he was part of this. He can see it in their faces. And worse, in bringing Wren here, maybe he was.

Maybe this *is* what Wren wanted when she agreed to come to Elfhame. Revenge on him. Revenge on the High King and Queen, who stripped her of her kingdom and sent her away with no help and no hope. The crown that Mellith was promised.

Wren, whom he believed he loved. Whom he believed he *knew*.

He sees now that she learned the lessons of betrayal, learned them down to the marrow of her bones.

There is no apology Oak can give that could be believed, no way to explain. Not anymore.

Oak feels something snap inside him. He draws his sword.

"Don't be foolish," Randalin says with a frown. "This is all for *you*."

There is a familiar roaring in Oak's ears, and this time he gives in to it eagerly. His limbs move, but he feels as if he's watching himself from far away.

He stabs into the stomach of the guard nearest to him, cutting up under his breastplate. The man screams. The thought that these soldiers believed he was on their side, believed he would be their High King, makes him even angrier. He turns, stabbing out. Someone else is screaming, someone he knows, urging him to stop. He doesn't even slow. Instead, he knocks a bolt aside as two more guards crowd around him. He pulls a dagger from one of their sheaths and uses it to stab the other while he parries a blow.

Oak can feel his consciousness slipping away, falling deeper into the trance of the fight. And it is such a relief to let go, the way he does when he allows the right words to fall from his tongue in the right order.

The last thing the prince feels before his awareness slides entirely away is a knife in his back. The last thing he sees is his sword biting through the throat of an enemy.

He finds himself with his blade pressed against Jude's. "Stop it," she shouts.

He staggers back, letting the sword fall from his hands. There's blood on her face, a fine spatter. Did he strike her?

"Oak," she says, not yelling anymore, which is when he realizes she's scared. He never wanted her to be scared of him.

"I'm not going to hurt you," he says. Which is true. Or at least he believes it's probably true. His hands have started shaking, but that's normal. That happens a lot, after.

Does she still think he's a traitor?

Jude whirls toward Madoc. *"What did you do to him?"*

The redcap looks baffled, his gaze on Oak speculative. "Me?"

Oak scans the room, the adrenaline of battle still running through his veins. The guards are dead. All of them, and messily. Randalin too. Oak isn't the only one holding a bloody sword, either. Hyacinthe has one as well, standing near Nihuar as though they had very recently been back-to-back. Fala is bleeding. The Roach and the Bomb are beside each other, having appeared from the shadows, the Bomb's fingers curled around a curved, nasty-looking knife. Even Cardan, using the throne to prop himself upright, has a dagger in his hand with red on the blade, although his other hand, holding his chest, is stained scarlet, too.

Cardan's not dead. The relief almost makes Oak sag to his knees, except that Cardan is still bleeding and pale.

"What did you turn Oak into?" Jude demands of Madoc. "What did you do to my brother?"

"He's good with a sword," the redcap tells her. "What can I say?"

"I am losing patience almost as fast as I am losing blood," says Cardan. "Just because your brother killed Randalin, it doesn't mean we should forget he was at the center of this conspiracy—and that he is at the center of whatever Bogdana and Wren are planning. I suggest that we lock Oak up where he won't be so tempting to traitors."

The prince spots Oriana, her arms still protectively around Leander, holding him turned toward her skirts so he can't see the slaughtered bodies. She's wearing an anguished expression. The prince feels the overwhelming urge to go to her, to bury his face in her neck as he might have done as a child. To see if she would push him away.

You wanted them to know you, his mind supplies unhelpfully.

Wren once described what she was afraid of, if she revealed herself to her family. How she imagined their rejecting her once they saw her true face. Oak sympathized, but until this moment he didn't understand the horror of having all the people who loved you best in the world look at you as though you were a stranger.

Charm them. The thought is not just unhelpful but wrong. And yet the temptation yawns in front of him. *Make them look at you as they once did. Fix this before it is broken forever.*

A shudder goes through him. "It's not Dad's fault or anyone else's that I'm good at killing," he makes himself say, meeting Jude's gaze. "I chose this. And don't you dare tell me that I shouldn't have. Not after what you've done to yourself."

Clearly, Jude was about to say something very much like that, because she chokes off the words. "You were supposed to—"

"What? Not make the same choices the rest of you did?"

"To have a childhood," she shouts at him. "To let us protect you."

"Ah," says Cardan. "But he had loftier ambitions."

Madoc's gaze is impassive. Does *he* believe Oak to be a traitor? And if so, does he applaud the ambition or scorn the failure?

"I think it's time to get off this isle." Cardan's trying to sound casual, but he's unable to hide that he's in pain.

The rain is still battering the tent. Taryn walks to the flap and looks outside. She shakes her head. "I am not sure we can get through the storm. The councilor was right about that, if nothing else."

Jude turns to Hyacinthe. "And what was your role in all this?"

"As though I would give any confidences to you," Hyacinthe says.

"Kill him," orders Cardan.

"Hyacinthe fought on your side," protests Oak.

Cardan gives an exhausted sigh and waves one lace-cuffed hand. "Very well, truss up Hyacinthe. Find the girl and the hag and kill *them*, at least. And I want the prince locked up until we sort this out. Lock up Tiernan, too, if he ever comes back."

I'm sorry, Wren said before she left him in the Milkwood.

She warned him not to trust her, and then she betrayed him. She conspired with Randalin and Bogdana. She allowed Oak to delude himself into believing that someone was controlling her, when she had all the power.

It was clever, to keep him chasing shadows.

That had been the part of the puzzle he wasn't able to solve—what any of them could have over her, who could unmake them all. The answer should have been obvious, only he didn't want to believe it. They had *nothing* over her.

A mystery with a void at its center.

"Shoot her on sight," Jude says, as though it's going to be that simple.

"Shoot her? She'll unmake the arrows," Oak says.

Jude raises her brows. "*All* the arrows?"

"Poison?" his sister asks.

The prince sighs. "Maybe." If he wasn't so busy drinking all the poison in sight, he might know.

"We'll find her weakness," his sister assures him. "And we will bring her down."

"No," says Oak.

"Another protestation of her innocence? Or yours?" asks Cardan in a silky voice, sounding like the boy Taryn and Jude used to hate, the one who Hyacinthe wouldn't believe was any different from Dain. The one who ripped the wings off pixies' backs and made his sister cry.

"I make no defense of myself," Oak says, leaning down to pick up his sword from the floor. "This is my fault. And my responsibility."

"What are you doing?" Jude asks.

"I am going to be the one to end this," Oak says. "And you will have to kill me to stop me."

"I'm going with you," Hyacinthe tells him. "For Tiernan."

The prince nods. Hyacinthe crosses the floor to stand against the prince's back. As one, they move toward the door, blades bared.

Jude doesn't order anyone to block their way. Doesn't confront Oak herself. But in her eyes, he can tell she believes that her little brother— the one she loves and would do anything to protect—is already dead.

CHAPTER
21

Oak and Hyacinthe plunge into a storm of terrifying ferocity. The fog is so thick the prince can't even see the shore of Insmire, and the waves have become towering things, beating against the shoreline, biting off rocks and sand.

Bogdana has sealed off Insear from aid, keeping Elfhame's military and all else who would help them at bay. And now the storm hag waits with Wren for some signal that the royal family is dead.

There's a problem with their plan, though. Oak *hasn't* married Wren. Perhaps Randalin thought no one would find the Ghost's or Elaine's body—or that no one would care. Must have believed the evening's festivities wouldn't turn into an inquest. But since things didn't happen that way, the murder of the High King and Queen wouldn't automatically give Wren the throne. She still needed him.

As he walks along the beach, soaking wet, Oak is shaking so hard it's difficult for him to tell what's from the chill and what is from rage.

He's become the fool he's spent so long pretending to be. If he hadn't fallen in love, then no one would be in danger. If he didn't believe in Wren, promise to be on her side, make every excuse for her, then Randalin's schemes would have come to nothing.

He loves her still, more's the pity.

No matter, though. He owes his family his loyalty, no matter their secrets. Owes Elfhame itself. Whether or not he likes being the prince, he accepted the role with all its benefits and obligations. He cannot be the one to put his people in danger. And whatever Wren once felt for him, he cannot believe she could do all this unless that was gone. He ruined it, and he wasn't able to fix it. Some broken things stay broken.

The prince runs through the storm, the cold cutting through his thin courtier's clothes. "Come on," he calls to Hyacinthe over the rumble of thunder, making a sweeping gesture with his arm to indicate a tent he wants them to duck into.

Marked with the sigil of a courtier from the Court of Rowan, it's empty. Oak wipes some of the water off his face.

"Now what?" Hyacinthe asks.

"We find Wren and Bogdana. Can you guess where they might go? Surely you overheard something these past few days." As the adrenaline of the fight ebbs away, Oak realizes there's a raw line of pain down his back where he dimly recalls being stabbed. There may also be a shallow slash at his neck. It stings.

"And if we find them," Hyacinthe hedges. "Then what?"

"We stop them," Oak says, pushing away pain, pushing away the thought of what stopping them will really entail. "They can't be too far. Bogdana needs to be close enough to control this storm."

"I owe Wren a debt," says Hyacinthe. "I swore myself to her."

"She has Tiernan," Oak reminds him.

The man looks away. "They'll be on Insmoor."

"Insmoor?" Oak echoes. The smallest isle, besides the one they're standing on. The location of Mandrake Market and not much else.

"Bogdana turned the cottage back into a walnut before the hunt and tucked it away in her pocket. Told us we might have to meet her on Insmoor."

So the rest of her falcons would be there with them. That makes things more complicated, but Oak won't mind a chance to face Straun. And it isn't like Wren could unmake Oak unless she wants to unmake her plans for ruling as well.

"I know how we can get to Insmoor," the prince says.

Hyacinthe meets his gaze for a long moment, seeming to understand his scheme. "You cannot be serious."

"Never more so," Oak says, and plunges back out into the storm.

Oak's teeth are chattering by the time he comes to the tent marked with Dain's crest. Tatterfell and Jack are inside, huddled far from the flaps, which keep blowing apart, letting the cold rain inside.

"Jack, I'm afraid I need your help again," Oak tells him.

"At your service, my prince," Jack says, bowing his head. "I promised to be of use to you, and I shall."

"After this, your debt to me will be more than paid. You will owe me nothing. Perhaps you will even be the one with a favor to call in."

"I should enjoy that," Jack says with a sly smile.

"I want you to take me under the waves to the shore. Do you have a way to keep me breathing while we go?"

Jack looks at him with wide eyes. "Alas, I am no help to you there. My kind do not much worry over the lives of our riders."

Hyacinthe gives Oak an incredulous look. "No, you delight in their deaths and then devour them. Can you control yourself with the prince on your back?"

That wasn't something Oak worried over before, but he doesn't like the flash of delight that passes across Jack of the Lakes' face at the mention of devouring.

"I can keep my teeth from the prince's sweet flesh, but if you want to come along, there's no telling what I might do to you," Jack says.

"I'm coming," Hyacinthe says. "They've got Tiernan."

Oak hoped he would. He's not sure he can do this alone. "No snacking on Hyacinthe."

"Not even a small bite?" Jack asks petulantly. "You are making it hard to be merry, Your Highness."

"Nonetheless," Oak says.

"What fool thing is it that you intend to do in this storm?" Tatterfell asks, poking the prince in the gut. "And are you bleeding?"

"Maybe," he says, touching a finger to his neck. It hurts, but his back hurts worse.

"Take off your shirt," the little faerie commands, blinking up at him.

"There isn't time," he tells her. "But if you have some bindings, I'll use them for my sword. I seem to have dropped the sheath somewhere."

Tatterfell rolls her ink-drop eyes.

"I will swim as swiftly as I am able," Jack says. "But it might not be swiftly enough."

"You can surface partway there," Oak suggests. "Let us catch a breath, then go on."

Jack considers that for a long moment, as though it is not much in his nature. But after a moment, he nods. Hyacinthe frowns and keeps frowning.

Tatterfell binds up the sword and belts it to Oak's waist with torn strips of his old clothes. She sews up the wound on his back as well, threatening to press her finger into the gouge if he moves.

"You're ruthless," he tells her.

She smiles as though he's delivered an extremely charming compliment.

Then, bracing against the wind and rain, Oak, Jack, and Hyacinthe make their way to the shore.

At the beach, Jack transforms into a sharp-toothed horse. He lowers himself to his knees and waits for them to lash themselves to him. Oak wraps a rope scavenged from the tent around the kelpie's chest and then around Hyacinthe, tying him tightly to Jack's back. Then he straps himself on, looping the rope a final time around their middles so they are bound to one another.

When Oak looks at the crashing waves, he begins to doubt the wisdom of his plan. He can barely make out the lights of Insmoor in the storm. Can he really hold his breath for as long as Jack is going to believe he needs?

But there's no going back. Nothing even to go back to, so he tries to inhale deeply and exhale slowly. Open up his lungs as much as he can.

Jack gallops toward the waves. The icy water splashes against Oak's legs. He grips the rope and takes one last breath as Jack plunges them all into the sea.

The cold of the ocean stabs the prince's chest. For a moment, it almost forces the breath from his lungs, but he manages to keep himself from gasping. Opens his eyes in the dark water. Feels the increasing, panicked pressure of Hyacinthe's grip on his shoulder.

Jack swims swiftly through the water. After a minute, it's clear it isn't fast enough. Oak's lungs burn; he feels lightheaded.

Jack needs to surface. He needs to do it now. *Now.* The prince presses his knees hard against the kelpie's chest.

Hyacinthe's hold on Oak's shoulder goes slack, his fingers drifting away. Oak concentrates on the pain of the rope cutting into his hand. Tries to stay alert. Tries not to breathe. Tries not to breathe. Tries not to breathe.

Then he can't hold on anymore, and water comes rushing in.

They surface abruptly, leaving Oak choking and coughing. He can hear Hyacinthe hacking behind him. A swell comes along and slaps him in the face, sending seawater down his throat, making him cough worse.

Jack's head is above the waves, his mane plastered to his neck. Some kind of membrane has closed over his eyes, causing them to appear pearlescent. A glance toward the shore reassures Oak they are more than halfway to Insmoor. He can't even catch his breath, though, no less hold it again. His chest hurts and he's still coughing and waves keep crashing over him.

"Oak," Hyacinthe manages to wheeze. "This was a bad plan."

"If we die, he's going to eat you first," Oak gets out. "So you better live."

Too soon, the kelpie begins to descend, slowly enough for Oak to suck in a breath, at least. It's a shallow one, and he is almost certain he can't hold it until the shore. His lungs are burning already.

This is the only way across, he reminds himself, closing his eyes.

Jack surfaces once more, just long enough for Oak to gulp down another breath. Then they race for the shore, only to hit the crashing waves there.

The kelpie is hurled forward, thrown against the sandy bottom. Oak and Hyacinthe are dragged along. A sharp rock scrapes against Oak's leg. He wriggles against the rope, but it is pulled tight.

Somehow Jack fights his way higher onto the beach. Another wave knocks against his flank, and he staggers, then transforms into a boy. The rope slackens. Oak slips down onto the sand. Hyacinthe falls, too, and the prince realizes he's not conscious. Blood is seeping from a cut above his brow where he may have struck a rock.

Oak puts his shoulder under Hyacinthe's arm and attempts to haul him away from the shoreline. Before he can get clear, a stray wave trips the prince, and he falls to his knees. He throws his body over Hyacinthe's to keep him from being sucked back into the sea.

A moment later, Oak is up and dragging Hyacinthe behind him. Jack grabs Hyacinthe's other arm, and together they pull the man up onto soft grass before collapsing beside him.

Oak starts coughing again, while Jack manages to turn Hyacinthe onto his side. The kelpie slaps him on the back, and he vomits up seawater.

"How—?" Hyacinthe manages, opening his eyes.

Jack makes a prim face. "You both get soggy rather fast."

Above their heads the sky is a clear and steady blue, the clouds pale and puffy as lambs. It is only when Oak looks back at Insear that he sees the storm, a thick fog surrounding the isle, crackling with lightning and a sheet of rain that blurs everything beyond it.

After a few minutes of lying on the grass, convincing himself that he's still alive, Oak pushes himself to his hooves. "I know this place. I am going to scout around and see if I can find them."

"What are we supposed to do?" Hyacinthe asks, although he looks too half-drowned to do much of anything.

"Wait here," says Oak. "I'll tell you if I find Tiernan."

Hyacinthe nods in what seems a lot like relief.

Insmoor is called the Isle of Stone because of how rock-covered and wild it becomes away from Mandrake Market. This is where treefolk wander among thick vines of ivy, their bark-covered bodies slow as sap. Birds cry from the trees. It is a good place for Wren and Bogdana to hide. Few soldiers and fewer courtiers are likely to stumble over them in this place. But Oak has lived in Elfhame much of his life, and he knows the paths. His hooves are soft on the moss and swift over the stone. He's quiet as he moves through the shadows.

Some distance off, he sees falcons roosting on trees. He must be getting close. Sticking to shadows, he hopes he won't be spotted.

A few steps more, he halts in surprise. Wren sits on a boulder, legs drawn up to her chest, arms encircling them. Her nails are digging into the skin of her calves, and her expression is anguished, as if, though she planned the royal family's doom, she isn't *enjoying* it. It's nice, he supposes, that betraying him isn't fun.

His honey-mouthed charm comes easily this time, the burr in his tone just right. "Wren," he says softly. "I was looking for you."

She looks up, startled. Her headpiece is gone; her hair loose down her back. "I thought you were—"

"On Insear, waiting for our wedding?"

Her expression turns puzzled for a moment, then clears. She slides down off the rock and takes a step toward him, as though in a trance.

He can't make himself hate her, even now.

But he can make himself kill her.

"We can exchange our vows right here," he says.

"We can?" There's a strange wistfulness in her voice. But why wouldn't there be? She needs to marry him if she intends to be the High Queen of Elfhame. He's promising her exactly what she wants. That's how his power works, after all.

He brings his hand to the side of her face, and she rubs her cheek against his palm as though she were a cat. The rough silk of her hair slides over his fingers. It is agony to touch her like this.

His sword is at his belt, still tied in its makeshift sheath. All he needs to do is slide it out and stab it through her ancient heart.

"Close your eyes," he says.

She looks up at him with a bleakness that makes him catch his breath. Then she closes them.

Oak's hand drops to the hilt of his needle blade. Curls around the cold, wet pommel. Draws.

He looks down at the shining steel, bright enough to see Wren's face reflected in it.

He can't help thinking of the Ghost's words when they were aboard the *Moonskimmer*, flying above the sea. *You're very like Dain in some ways.*

Nor can he forget that he once thought, *If I love someone, I won't kill them*, a vow too obvious to need to be made aloud.

Oak doesn't want to be like his father.

He wishes his hand was still trembling, but it is remarkably steady.

You've always been clever. Be clever now. That's what Wren told him when she urged him to break off their betrothal. She needs their marriage if she intends to rule once Cardan and his sister are dead. And yet, if he'd ended the betrothal when she asked him to, there would be no way to accomplish that.

You can't trust me.

Why warn him? To send him in circles? To set him to one puzzle so he didn't notice another? That was a complicated and risky plan, while merely expecting him to do his duty and marry her the way he'd said he would was a shockingly simple plan, one with a high chance of success.

Oak remembers Wren standing in the Milkwood over the body of the Ghost. Taryn accused her of poisoning him. Why not deny it? Why make everyone suspicious of her? Randalin admitted to having done it, and he'd urged her to declare her innocence. And the storm hag sank her talons into Wren's skin. All that it bought was a good excuse for the royal family to ask more questions.

I'm not the one who needs saving.

That had seemed the most damning statement, when bolts started flying on Insear. But if it wasn't a taunt about the murder of his family that Randalin was planning, then someone else needed saving. Not Oak, who was a necessary cog. The Ghost? Lady Elaine?

He recalls something else, from the banquet. *I should have understood better—what you did for your father and why. I wanted it to be simple. But my sis—Bex—*

Wren didn't finish speaking because of a coughing fit. Which could have been because she made herself sick using her magic. Or it could have been that she was trying to say something she made a vow not to say.

My sister. Bex.

I'm not the one who needs saving.

Maybe Oak has this all wrong. Maybe she's not his enemy. Maybe she's been given an impossible choice.

Wren loves her mortal family. She loves them so much she slept in the dirt near their house just to be close. Loves them so much that there might be nothing she wouldn't do to save her mother or father or sister. No one she wouldn't sacrifice, including herself.

He knows what love like that feels like.

Oak had wondered why Lady Nore and Lord Jarel left Wren's mortal family alive, given what he knew of their cruelty. Wouldn't it have been more to their taste to remove any chance at Wren's happiness? To butcher her family members one by one in front of her and drink her tears?

But now he sees what use they could have been. How could Wren ever rebel when there was always something else to lose? A hatchet that never fell. A threat to be delivered over and over again.

How pleased Bogdana must have been to find Bex still alive and usable.

Wren opens her eyes and looks up at him. "At least it will be you," she says. "But you better hurry up. Waiting is the worst part."

"You're not my enemy," he says. "You were never my enemy."

"Yet you're standing there with a bare blade," Wren reminds him.

Fair point. "I just figured it out. She has your sister, doesn't she?"

Wren opens her mouth, then closes it. But the relief in her expression is answer enough.

"And you can't tell me," he guesses. "Bogdana made you vow all sorts of things to make sure you couldn't give away her game. Made you vow to go through with the marriage, so the only way out was if I refused you. Hid Bex away, so you couldn't simply unmake everyone and free her. Left word with someone to do away with Bex if the storm hag turns up dead. All you could do was try to stall. And try to warn me."

All she could do was hope he was clever enough.

And perhaps, if he wasn't, she hoped that at least he would stop her from having to do the worst of what Bogdana commanded. Even if the only way to stop her was with a blade.

She, who never wanted to trust him again, having to do exactly that.

Wren's eyes are wet as she blinks, her lashes black and spiky. She reaches into a pocket of her dress and takes out the white walnut. "Tiernan is trapped in the cottage. Take it. This is all I can offer you." Her fingers brush the palm of his hand. "I am not your enemy, but if you can't help me, the next time we meet, I might be."

It's not a threat. He understands now. She's telling him what she fears.

The prince practically runs into Jack and Hyacinthe as they're coming off the beach. The kelpie yelps and glares at him accusatorily.

"I have Tiernan," Oak says, out of breath.

Hyacinthe raises both eyebrows and looks at the prince as though he must have fallen on his head, hard.

"No, not with me," he says. "He's in my pocket."

Inside of the cottage must have been how they brought the bramble horses without their being on the ship. And any other sinister supplies they may have needed. Arms and armor, certainly. And there was no reason for Wren to have even known.

"And your queen? Is she . . . ?" Jack makes a throat-slashing motion.

"Bogdana has her mortal sister," Oak says. "She's being blackmailed."

"Has her where?" Hyacinthe asks. "And when is a single thing you are saying going to start making sense?"

The first is the important question. And Oak thinks he may have the answer.

As Oak approaches Mandrake Market, he has a startlingly good view of the storm lashing Insear. The lanes are empty. Merchants huddle in their homes, probably hoping the waves don't rise too high, that lightning doesn't strike too close. Hyacinthe follows the prince, carrying the walnut in his pocket, while Jack brings up the rear.

Together, they come to Mother Marrow's cottage, the thatch roof overgrown with moss. Oak stands in front of the door while the other two go around the back. Looking inside, he can see her sitting on a stump before a fire, poking at a bucket hanging over the flames.

Oak pounds on the hag's front door. Mother Marrow frowns and goes back to her fire. He bangs his fist again. This time she stands. Scowling, she waddles to the door on her bird talons.

"Prince." She squints. "Aren't you supposed to be at a party?"

"May I come in?"

She steps back so he can make his way into the room. "Quite a storm we're having."

Mother Marrow closes the door behind him and bolts it. He goes to the window, looking across at Insear while his fingers undo the latch. He can see nothing but rain and fog and hopes fervently that his family is no worse than he left them.

"You're holding Wren's sister for Bogdana, aren't you?" he asks, turning and walking toward the back of her cottage. "Your friend with the gold skin picked her up, but you're the one with the place here, so you're the one who's keeping her, right?"

Her eyebrows rise. "Beware, Prince of Elfhame, what you accuse Mother Marrow of doing. You want to keep her as your friend, don't you?"

"I'd rather discover her treachery," he says, pushing open the door to a back room.

"How dare you?" she says as he enters her bedroom. A canopied bed rests against one wall, bedsheets smoothed out over it. A few bones lie in a corner, old and dry. There's a little desk with a skull resting on top of several tomes. A cup of tea sits beside her bed, old enough that a dead moth floats atop the liquid.

Ignoring her, he pushes past to open one of the two other doors. It's a bathing chamber, with a large wooden tub in the middle of the room and a pump beside it. A drain rests off to one side. And a large trunk, like the one Jack described.

He flips it open. Empty.

Mother Marrow presses her lips together. "You are making a mistake, boy. Whatever you think I have, is it worth the curse I will put on you?"

As angry as he is, he doesn't hesitate. "Have you not already betrayed me once, when you knew exactly where Mellith's heart was and sent me on a fool's errand anyway? I am Prince Oak of the Greenbriar line, kin to the High Queen and King, heir to Elfhame. Perhaps you should be afraid."

Surprise flashes across her features. She stands in the hall, staring after him as he opens the final door. Another bed, this one piled with pillows in sloppy needlepoint, as though done by a child. Shelves on the wall, with books on them, a few that look as ancient as the tomes piled up in Mother Marrow's room, a few that are newer and less dusty. There are even a few paperbacks that obviously came from the mortal world. This must be the daughter's room.

But no Bex.

"Where is she?" he demands.

"Come," Mother Marrow says. "Sit. You're shivering. Some tea will cure that."

Oak feels as though his blood is boiling. If he is shivering, it is not from cold. "We don't have time for this."

Nonetheless, she busies herself, fussing with the bucket over her fire. Something floats in the water that might be kelp. The hag dunks the wooden ladle and dishes up two servings of tea into ceramic mugs. His has a screaming face on it.

Mother Marrow sips at her tea. Oak's nerves spark like live wires underneath his skin. Randalin is dead, and whatever signal he planned to give Bogdana that he murdered the royal family will never come. Eventually, Bogdana will realize that and execute the next stage of her plan. Wren will be helpless to stop her. She may have to help her. And he must find Bex before that happens.

The room is as it was before—stumps and a wooden chair before the fire and a threadbare chair off to one side. The same painted curio cabinet with its collection of beetle wings, potions, and poisons. The same nuts rattling in the bowl. The passageway to the rest of the empty cottage.

"What can you possibly offer Mother Marrow in exchange for what you seek?" the hag asks mildly.

Oak considers hags unfathomable beings, different from other Folk. Creators of objects, casters of curses. Part witch, part god. Solitary by nature, according to his instructors. But he heard the story of Bogdana and Mellith. And he remembers Mother Marrow's desire for Cardan to wed her child.

Maybe not always so solitary. Maybe not entirely strange.

"I want to save Wren," he says.

"A little bird," she says. "Caught in a storm."

Oak gives her a steady look. "You have a daughter. One you wanted to marry to the High King. You told me about her."

Mother Marrow gives a small grunt. "That was some time ago."

"Not so much time, I will wager, that you've forgotten the insult of the courtly Folk thinking that a hag's daughter wasn't fit for a throne."

There's a growl in her voice. "You best be careful if you expect to get something from me. And you best not try honey-mouthing me, either. I enjoy sweet words, but I will enjoy eating your tongue even more."

He inclines his head in acknowledgment. "What is it you want in exchange for Bex?"

She snorts. "You found no girl. What if none is here?"

"Give me three guesses," he says, though he is far from certain he can succeed at this. "Three guesses to where you put her, and if I'm right, you give her to me."

"And if you fail?" Her eyes glitter. He knows she is intrigued.

"Then I will return here at the new moon and serve for a year and a day. I will wash your floors. I will scour your cauldron and trim your toenails. So long as it harms no one, I will do whatever you ask as a servant in your household."

He can feel the air shift around him, feel the rightness of these words. He isn't using his charm in the usual way, but he allows himself to feel the contortions that power urges on him, the way it wants him to reshape himself for Mother Marrow. The gancanagh part of him knows that she will believe herself to be more wily than he, that her pride will urge her to take the bet.

"*Whatever* I ask of you, Prince of Elfhame?" Her grin is wide and delighted at the anticipation of his humiliation.

"So long as I guess wrong three times," he says.

"Then guess away," she says. "For all you know, I've turned her into the lid on a pot."

"I would feel very stupid if I didn't guess that first, then," Oak says.

Mother Marrow looks extremely pleased. "Wrong."

Two guesses. He's good at games, but it's hard to think when it feels as though there's no time left, when he can hear the storm in the background and the rattling of the...

He thinks of the white walnut cottage and Tiernan. And he recalls who gave Wren that gift. Getting to his feet, Oak walks to the cabinet. "She's trapped in one of the nuts."

Rage washes across Mother Marrow's face briefly, only to be replaced by a smile. "Very good, prince," she says. "Now tell me which one."

There has to be a half dozen in the bowl. "I guessed correctly," Oak protests. "I got the answer."

"Did you?" she says. "That would be like saying I turned her into a flower and not being sure if it was a rose or a tulip. Choose. If you're wrong, you lose."

He opens the cabinet, takes out the bowl, then goes to her kitchen for a knife.

"What are you doing?" she shouts. "Stop that!"

He selects a filbert and jams the point of the blade into the seam. It bursts open, scattering an array of dresses around the room, each in a different diaphanous color. They drift gently to the floor.

"Put that one down," she says as he reaches for a hazelnut. "Immediately."

"Will you give me the girl?" Oak demands. "Because I don't need you to get her out now. I will open every one of these and destroy them in the process."

"Foolish boy!" Mother Marrow says, then intones:

> Be trapped inside with no escape
> Your fate is cast in acorn shape
> In the shadows, you'll dwell and wait

The world seems to grow larger and smaller at the same time. Darkness rushes up and over him. He does, in fact, feel quite foolish. And very disoriented.

Inside of the nut are curved walls, polished to a high mahogany-like shine. The floor is covered in straw. Thin light seems to emanate from everywhere and nowhere at once.

He hears a sharp gasp from behind him. His hand goes automatically to his sword as he turns, and he has to force himself not to draw it from the rag sheath.

A mortal girl stands among baskets and barrels and jars, against the curved wall of her prison. In the dim glow, her skin is the pale brown of early fall leaves, and she wears a white puffer coat, which swallows her up. Her arms are crossed over each other as though she's holding herself for comfort or warmth or to keep herself from coming apart.

"Don't scream," Oak says, holding up his hands to show that they're empty.

"Who are you, and why are you here?" the girl asks.

Oak takes a breath and tries to think of what he ought to say. He doesn't want to frighten her, but he can see from the way she's looking at his hooves and horns that it's possible that ship has already sailed. "I'd like to believe that we're going to be friends," he says. "If you tell me who you are, I will do the same."

The mortal girl hesitates. "There was a witch, and she brought me here to see my sister. But I haven't seen her yet. The witch says she's in trouble."

"A witch . . . ," he echoes. He wonders how aware the girl has been of the passage of time. "You're Wren's sister, Bex?"

"Bex, yes." A small smile pulls at her mouth. "You know Wren?"

"Since we were quite young," he says, and Bex relaxes a little. "Do you know what she is? What I am?"

"Faeries." *Monsters*, her expression says. "I keep rowan on me at all times. And iron."

When Oak was a child, living in the mortal world with his oldest sister, Vivi, he was super excited to show her girlfriend, Heather, magic. He took his glamour off and was crushed when she looked at him in horror, as though he wasn't the same little boy she took to the park or tickled. He thought of the news as a surprise present, but it turned out to be a jump scare.

He didn't realize then how vulnerable a mortal in Faerie can be. He should have, though, living with two mortal sisters. He should have, but he didn't.

"That's good," he says, thinking of the burn of the iron bars in the Citadel. "Rowan to break spells, and iron to burn us."

"Your turn," Bex says. "Who are you?"

"Oak," he says.

"The prince," Bex says flatly, all the friendliness gone from her voice. He nods.

She takes two steps forward and spits at his feet. "The witch told me about you," Bex says. "That you steal hearts, and you were going to steal my sister's. That if I ever saw you, I ought to run."

Used to people liking him, or at least used to having to court dislike, Oak is a little stunned. "I would never—" he begins, but she's already moving across the room, flattening herself against the curved wall as though he's going to come after her.

There's a sound in the distance, loud and sharp. The walls shake.

"What's that?" she demands, stumbling.

"My friends," Oak says. "I hope."

Bright light flashes, and the prison tilts to one side. Bex is thrown against him, and then they're both on the floor of Mother Marrow's cottage.

Hyacinthe has a crossbow pointed at Mother Marrow. The window Oak unlatched is open, and Jack is inside. The kelpie stoops down to lift an acorn, unbroken.

Mother Marrow glowers. "A bad-mannered lot," she grouses.

"You found her!" says Jack. "And what a toothsome morsel—I mean *mortal*."

Bex jumps up and pulls an antique-looking wrench from her back pocket—that must be the iron to which she was referring. She appears to be considering hitting the kelpie over the head with it.

In two strides, Oak is across the room. He claps his hand against the girl's mouth hard enough for her teeth to press against his palm.

"Listen to me," he says, feeling like a bully almost certainly because he was behaving like one. "I am not going to hurt Wren. Or you. But I don't have time to fight you, nor do I have time to chase you if you run."

She struggles against him, kicking.

He leans down and whispers in her ear, "I am here for Wren's sake, and I am going to take you to her. And if you try to get away again, remember this—the easiest way to make you behave would be to make you love me, and you don't want that."

She must really not, because she goes slack in his arms.

He takes his hand from her mouth, and she pulls away but doesn't scream. Instead, she studies him, breathing hard.

"I should have known something was wrong when you knew my name," Bex says. "Wren would have never told you that. She says that if you know my name, it would give you power over me."

He gives a surprised laugh. "I wish," he says, then winces. He should have found a better way to phrase that, one that didn't make him sound quite so much like an actual monster. But there is little for him to do but forge on. "You need someone's full name, their true name. Mortals don't have those. Not in the way that we do."

Bex's gaze shifts to the door of the cottage and then back, calculation in her eyes.

"Wren is in trouble," he says. "Some people are using your safety to make her do what they want. Which is going to mean killing a lot of my people."

"And you want to use me to stop her," Bex accuses.

That's a harsh way of putting it, but true. "Yes," he says. "I don't want my own sisters hurt. I don't want anyone hurt. Not Wren and not you."

"And you'll take me to her?" Bex asks.

He nods.

"Then I'll go with you," she says. "For now."

Oak turns his gaze to Mother Marrow. "I am going to grant you this, for whatever I owe you. Should I survive, I will not tell the High King and Queen that you took Bogdana's part against them. But now my debt is dismissed."

"And if she wins, what then?" Mother Marrow says.

"Then I will be dead," Oak tells her. "And you are more than welcome to spit on the moss and rocks where my body fell."

It is at that moment that the front door cracks in two. The smell of ozone and burning wood fills the air. The storm hag stands there as though summoned by the speaking of her name.

Lightning crackles between her hands. Her eyes are wild. "You!" cries Bogdana as she spots Bex beside the prince.

"Take the mortal to Wren," Oak shouts to Jack and Hyacinthe, drawing his sword. "Go!"

Then he rushes at the storm hag.

Electricity hits his blade, scorching his fingers. Despite the pain, he manages to swing, slashing through her cloak.

Out of the corner of his eye, Oak sees Jack lift Bex and push her feet through the window. From the other side, Hyacinthe grabs hold of her.

Bogdana reaches for Oak with her daggerlike fingers. "I am going to enjoy stripping the skin from your flesh."

He swings, blocking her grab. Then he ducks to her left. She takes another step toward him.

By now, Hyacinthe and Jack are out of sight, Bex with them.

A move occurs to Oak—a risky move, but one that might work. One that might get him to Wren faster than anything else. "What if I surrender?" he asks.

He can see her slight hesitation. "Surrender?"

"I'll sheathe my sword and go with you willingly." He shrugs, lowering his blade a fraction. "If you promise to bring me straight to Wren with no tricks."

"No tricks?" she echoes. "That's a fine thing coming from you."

"I want to see her," he says, hoping he seems convincing. "I want to hear from her lips what she's done and what she wants. And you don't want to leave her alone too long."

Bogdana regards him with a sly expression. "Very well, prince." She reaches out and runs her long claws over his cheek so lightly that they only scrape his bruises. "If I can't have the sister, then you'll be my prize. And I'll have you well-seasoned by the time I end you."

CHAPTER
23

Bogdana has one clawed hand around his wrist as she tugs him toward the water and the storm.

"I thought we were going back to Wren," he says.

"Ah, did you think she was still here on Insmoor? No, I brought her to Insear. We were there together when Mother Marrow signaled me."

He should have suspected Mother Marrow had a way to let Bogdana know her hostage was being released and regrets his generosity with her. All he is likely to get in the way of gratitude is a curse. "On Insear?" he says, staying with the part that matters. If Wren and Bogdana made it to Insear, what did that mean for his family?

"Come," Bogdana says, stepping off the edge of the rocks. A swirling wind catches and lifts her, as it caught and lifted the ship. The storm hag's robes billow. She gives a sharp tug on Oak's wrist. He follows her, his hooves walking on what seems like nothing but knots and eddies of air.

The fog parts, and droplets of rain do not fall in their path as the wind carries them over the sea.

Minutes later, they drop onto the black rocks of Insear. Oak slips and nearly falls, attempting to find his footing.

And in front of him, he sees Wren and Jude.

They are squared off, his sister holding a sword in one hand, her eyes shining. Most of her brown hair has come out of its braids and hangs loose and wet around her face. Her cheeks are pink with cold, and the bottom of her dress is raggedly cut away, as though she wants to be sure it won't trip her.

Wren wears the clothes she wore at the hunt, the same clothes she wore on Insmoor. They hang on her, as though there is even less of her now, as though more of her has been eaten away. Her cheekbones are sharper, the hollows beneath them more pronounced. Her expression is as bleak as the rain-streaked sky. As bleak as when she was going to let him stab her.

Behind his sister are four other Folk. The Roach, a dagger in one hand and a fresh wound on his brow. Two archers—knights that Oak recognizes, holding longbows. And a courtier, dressed in velvet and lace, hair and beard in braids, hands gripping a hammer. They are all soaked to the bone.

On Wren's side are more than a dozen of her soldiers—armored, swords at their belts and bows in their hands.

"*Jude*," Oak says, but she doesn't even seem to hear him.

As he watches, Wren lunges toward Jude, grabbing for her unsheathed blade. Wren's blood smears over the bare steel where the edge catches her palm. But before the sword can bite more deeply, before Jude can wrench it from her grip, the metal begins to melt. It pools on the ground, hissing where it hits water, cooling into jagged metal shapes. Unmade.

Jude takes a step back, dropping the hilt as though it bit her.

"Nice trick." Her voice isn't quite steady.

"I see you have things well in hand, daughter," Bogdana calls to Wren. "I have the prince. Now, where is the High King?"

"Shoot them," Jude snaps, ignoring Bogdana's words and instead focusing on the falcons transforming into soldiers. "Shoot *all* our enemies."

Arrows fly, soaring through the air in a beautiful and deadly arc.

Before they can fall, Wren raises a hand. She makes a small motion, as though brushing away a gnat. The arrows break and scatter like twigs caught in a harsh wind.

Jude has pulled two daggers from her bodice, both of them curved and sharp as razors.

Oak steps away from Bogdana, hand on the pommel of his own sword. "Stop!" he shouts.

The storm hag sneers. "Don't be foolish, boy; you're surrounded."

Several of the falcons have notched their own bows, and though Oak believes Wren doesn't want more death, if they fire, he isn't at all sure she'd stop her own archers' arrows from striking. It would be a drain on her power, and her falcons would take it much amiss.

"I have your sister," he calls, because that's the important thing. That's what she needs to know. "I have Bex."

Wren turns, her eyes wide, hair plastered to her neck. Lips parted, he can see her sharp teeth.

"He's stolen her from us," Bogdana shouts. "Believe nothing he says. He would use her to fetter you, child."

Jude looks across at them, eyebrows raised. "Blackmail, brother? Impressive."

"That's not—" he starts.

"You have some decisions to make," Jude tells him. "The falcons follow your lady. But perhaps she wants your head on a pike as much as the storm hag does. Give her an inch, and she might take your life."

Bogdana answers before Oak can. "Ah, Queen of Elfhame, you see how useless your weapons are. You're married to the faithless child of a faithless line. Your crown was secured with my daughter's blood."

"My crown was secured with a lot of people's blood." Jude turns to her archers. "Ready another volley."

"You cannot so easily hurt us with sharp sticks," Wren says, but her gaze keeps drifting to Oak. She must be aware that this is his family and he has hers.

Wren's magic harrowed her before they got to Elfhame. She sagged in Oak's arms just the day before. She cannot stop arrows endlessly. He's not sure what she can do.

"Randalin is dead," the prince tells the storm hag. "He conspired against Elfhame. He poisoned the Ghost. He planned this coup long before he tried to involve you in it. There is no reason to let him drag you down, too."

"Don't let him manipulate you," Bogdana says, as though it's Wren he's trying to convince. "He's using you just as Randalin hoped to— Randalin, who wanted to help put Prince Oak on the throne. See how the councilor was rewarded for his loyalty? And this is the person you would trust not to use your sister against you?"

Once Bex was safe, Oak thought Wren would be free of Bogdana's control. And she is, but that doesn't mean she's free. *He* has Bex. *He* can control Wren the way Bogdana did. He could make her crawl to him as assuredly as if strips of the bridle were digging into her skin.

He doesn't know how to convince her that's not what he intends to do. "You care for your sister. And I, mine. Let's end this. Tell Bogdana to stop the storm. Tell your falcons to stand down. This can be over."

Bogdana sneers. "He gave the mortal to Jack of the Lakes. Jack's likely drowned her by now."

Wren's eyes widen. "You didn't."

"He's bringing her to you," Oak says, realizing how bad it sounds. Not only that, but he isn't sure it's possible for Jack to bring Bex here, if he even guesses where they are. Oak nearly drowned, getting across.

"You believe that, girl?" snaps Bogdana. "They would have delighted if one of their arrows had pierced your heart. Let's find the High King and cut his throat. Your falcons can watch the prince."

Oak may be able to draw and strike before Bogdana can stop him, but if Wren tells her archers to fire, he'll be dead. He has no magical cloak to hide behind.

Jude shifts her stance. "Anyone who goes toward that tent, kill them," she orders her remaining Folk. "And you, little queen, better not interfere. If Oak has your sister, I assume you want her back in one piece."

"That's not helping, Jude," he says.

"I forgot," she says. "We're not on the same side."

"You're hiding the High King from me?" Bogdana asks. "He must be the coward everyone says, letting you fight his battles."

Oak sees rage flash across Jude's face, watches her swallow it. "I don't mind fighting."

Cardan *isn't* a coward, though. Hurt though he was, he picked up a weapon when Randalin's knights turned on them. How badly wounded must he be not to be here now—not to even have given Jude his cloak. Cardan was bleeding when Oak left—but he was conscious. He was giving orders.

"So before this battle happens and we all have to pick sides, I have a question." Jude's gaze sharpens. She's stalling, Oak realizes but has no idea what she can gain from it. "If you wanted the throne for Wren so badly, why not let her marry him? She was supposed to marry Prince Oak this very evening, isn't that so? Wouldn't that have given her a straight path to the throne? After she became High Queen, all she'd have to do is what she intended all those years ago—bite out his throat."

Perhaps Jude just meant to remind him not to trust Wren.

"As though *you* would ever let Prince Oak come to his throne," Bogdana sneers.

"Generally speaking, one doesn't have to *let* one's heir do the inheriting," says Jude. "Of course, perhaps you're acting now because you had no choice. Maybe Randalin moved ahead without consulting you. You meant for the marriage to happen, but he set the thing in motion before you managed it."

Bogdana's lip curls. "Do you think I care about the treason of one of your ministers? Your courtly intrigues are of little consequence. No, with Wren by my side, I can return Insear to the bottom of the sea. I can sink all the isles."

It would destroy Wren to do that. The magic would unmake *her* along with the land.

"We can all die together," Oak says. "In one grand, glorious final act of stupidity fit for a ballad."

Wren's hands tremble, and she presses them together to conceal it. He notices how purple her lips have gone. The way her skin looks pale and mottled, such that even the blue color of it cannot hide that something is wrong.

Unmaking the sword and the arrows must have cost her—and he was uncertain if that was all she'd done since the hunt.

"I was the first of the hags," Bogdana returns, her voice like the crash of waves. "The most powerful of the witches. My voice is the howl of the wind, my hair the lashing rain, my nails the hot strike of lightning that rends flesh from bone. When I gave Mab a portion of my power, it came with a price. I wanted my child to have a place among the Courtly Folk, to sit on a throne and wear a crown. But that's not what happened." Bogdana pauses. "I was tricked by a queen once. I will not be tricked again."

"Mab is gone," Oak says, trying to reason with her. Hoping that he can find the real words, the *true* words, ones that will be persuasive because they are right. "You're still here. And you have Wren again. You're the one with everything to lose now and nothing to—"

"Quiet, boy!" Bogdana says. "Do not try your power on me."

"It lets me know what you want." He glances at Wren. "I don't need to charm you to tell you this isn't the way to get it."

Bogdana laughs. "And if Wren wants her throne? Will you stand aside as she plans to take it? Will you help? Let your sister die to prove this love you claim to have for her?" She turns to Jude. "And you? Bluff all you want, but you have only four Folk behind you—half of them probably contemplating turning on you. And a brother whose loyalty is in question.

"Surely your people do not want to face three times as many soldiers, all of whom can shoot at will while you return no volley. I would greatly reward boldness. Should one of them kill the King of Elfhame—"

"What if I give you Oak's head instead of Cardan's?" Jude asks suddenly.

The prince turns toward his sister. She can't really mean that. But Jude's eyes are cold, and the knife in her hand is very sharp.

"And why would I accept such a poor offer?" asks the storm hag. "We had him for months. We could have executed him anytime we wanted. I could have killed him on Insmoor less than an hour ago. Besides, wasn't it you who reminded me how much easier to establish Wren as the new High Queen if she marries your heir?"

"If Oak were dead, that would thin the Greenbriar line by half," says Jude. "Mere chance might do the rest. Cardan was hurt—he might not survive the night. I schemed my way to the throne, despite being mortal. Make me your ally instead of him. I am the better bet. I know Elfhame politics, and I am mercenary enough to make practical choices."

He knows she's not serious about her offer. But that doesn't mean she's not serious about wanting to kill him.

How foolish Oak has been, making himself seem like Cardan's enemy. How can he prove to Jude now, here, that he has always been on her side? That he never plotted with Randalin. That he was trying to catch the conspirators so that something like this could never happen.

But how could Jude ever guess what Oak was planning to do when she has no idea what he's already done?

"Oak wouldn't fight you," Wren says.

Bogdana's eyes glitter. "Oh, I think he will. What if I make the prince this bargain—win, and I will let Wren keep you as a pet. I will let you live. I'll even let you marry her, if she so desires."

"That's very generous," he says. "Since Wren can already marry whomsoever she wants."

"Not if you're dead," says Bogdana.

"You want me to fight my own sister?" he asks, voice unsteady.

"I very much do." Bogdana's lips pull into a grim, awful smile. "High Queen, I will not merely accept the prince's head, struck off by one of your soldiers. Just as I was tricked into murdering my own kin, it will be justice to see you kill yours. But I will spare the one of you who kills the other. Let the High Queen abdicate her throne, and I won't chase her. She may return to the mortal world and live out the brief span of her days."

"And Cardan?" Jude asks.

The storm hag laughs. "How about this? Take him, and I'll give you a head start."

"Done," Jude says. "So long as you'll let me take my people, too."

"If you win," Bogdana says. "If you run."

"Don't do this," Wren whispers.

Oak takes a step forward, his head spinning. He ignores the way Wren is looking at him, as though he is a lamb come straight to the slaughter, too stupid to run.

As he walks closer to his sister, an arrow hits the ground beside him from Jude's camp. A warning shot.

He really hopes that was a warning shot and not a miss.

"Prince Oak," says Jude. "You're making some very dangerous decisions lately."

He takes a deep breath. "I understand why you'd think I was planning to betray—"

"Answer me on the field," Jude says, cutting him off. "Ready for our duel?"

Wren steps forward. The rain has plastered her long, wild hair to her throat and chest. "Oak, wait."

Bogdana grabs her arm. "Leave them to sort out their own family affair."

Wren wrenches free. "I warned you. You can't keep me your thrall. Not without Bex."

"You think not?" says the storm hag. "Child, I will have my revenge, and you are too weak to stop me. We both know that. Just as we know that the falcons will listen to me once you collapse. And you will—you overextended yourself when you broke the curse on the troll kings and again on the ship, and you've used your power twice today already. There's not enough of you left to face me. There's barely enough of you to remain standing."

Jude is adjusting her dress, slicing it so that she can tie the sides of the skirt into makeshift pants. What is her game?

Had they not been isolated on Insear, the army of Elfhame would have easily cut down Bogdana and Wren and her falcons. But so long as Bogdana's storm keeps them isolated, so long as Wren stops arrows, Jude won't be able to keep them from Cardan's tent forever.

Jude will never abdicate, though. She will never run, not even if Cardan is dead.

Of course, if Cardan *is* dead, Jude might well blame Oak.

He wants to see hesitation in his sister's face, but her expression reminds him of Madoc's before a battle.

Someone is going to kill you. Better it be me.

Oak thinks about being a child, spoiled and vain, making trouble. It shames him to think of smashing things in Vivi's apartment, crying for his mother, when they took him there for his protection. It shames him more to think of ensorcelling his sister and the delight he felt at the red sting of her cheek after she slapped herself. He knew it hurt and, later, felt guilty about it.

But he didn't understand Jude's pride and how he shamed her. How that was the far worse crime.

Jude attributes most of her worst impulses to their father, sparing
Oak's provocation. Sparing Oriana, too, who never made room in her
heart for a little mortal girl who lost her mother.

Still, that anger and resentment have to be in her somewhere. Waiting for this moment.

"I heard that Madoc offered the High King a duel," says Bogdana.
"But he was too much a coward to accept."

"My father should have asked me," Jude says, unbothered by the
insult to her beloved.

"I don't want to fight with you," Oak warns.

"Of course you do," Jude says. "Van, bring me my favorite sword
since Wren ruined the other one. I left it where I changed clothes."

The prince looks over to see the Roach, his mouth grim, walk
toward the tent. A few moments later, he returns with a sword wrapped
in heavy black cloth.

"I wasn't part of Randalin's conspiracy," Oak tries again.

But Jude only gives her brother a grim smile. "Well, then, what a
wonderful opportunity for you to prove your loyalty and die for the
High King."

The Roach unwraps a blade, but Oak can barely pay attention.
Panic has taken hold of him. He cannot fight her. And if he does, he
absolutely cannot lose control.

"There are twin swords," Jude says. "Heartseeker and Heartsworn.
Heartsworn can cut through anything. It once cut through an otherwise invulnerable serpent's head and broke a curse. You can see why I'd
like it."

"That hardly seems fair," Oak says, his eye on the sword at last.
It's finely crafted, as beautiful as one might expect one made in a great

smith's forge to be. And then he understands. He lets out his breath in a rush.

Jude moves into an easy stance. She's good. She's always been good. "What makes you think I am interested in fairness?"

"Fine," says Oak. "But you won't find me an easy opponent."

"Yes, I saw you inside. That was impressive," says his sister. "As was your cleverness. Apologies for not noticing what I should have long before."

"Apology accepted," says Oak with a nod.

Jude rushes at the prince. Oak parries, circling. "Cardan's okay, then?" he asks as quietly as he is able.

"He'll have an impressive scar," she returns, voice low. "I mean, not as impressive as several of mine, obviously."

Oak lets out a breath. "Obviously."

"But what he's really doing is getting the courtiers and servants off Insear," Jude goes on softly. "Through the Undersea. His ex-girlfriend is still queen there. He's leading them through the deep."

Oak glances toward the tents. The ones that Jude threatened to murder anyone who went near. The ones that are empty.

"Swordplay is a dance, they say." Jude raises her voice as she slashes her blade through the air. "One, two, three. One, two, three."

"You're terrible at dancing," Oak says, forcing himself to stay in the moment. He will not lose himself in the fight. He will not let himself go.

She grins and moves in, nearly tripping him.

"Wren was being blackmailed," he tells her, dodging a blow almost a moment too late, distracted by trying to think of what he can say to make her understand. "The thing with her sister."

"I am not sure you know your enemies from your allies."

"*I* do," Oak says. "And the falcons follow her."

"Tell me that you're sure of her," Jude says. "Really sure."

Oak thrusts, parries. Their swords clang together. If Jude really were fighting with Heartsworn, it would have sliced his blade in half. But Oak recognized the sword the Roach brought—it was Nightfell, forged by her mortal father.

As soon as Jude lifted it, Oak understood her game at last.

With as few soldiers as they had, she knew they had to get close to their enemy. Knew they needed the edge of surprise.

"I'm sure," says Oak.

"Okay." Jude presses her attack, forcing Oak back, closer and closer to the storm hag. "This dance I'm good at. One. Two. *Three.*"

Together they turn. Oak presses the tip of his sword to one side of Bogdana's throat. Jude's goes to the other.

The falcons turn their weapons toward Oak and Jude. Pull back bowstrings. On the other side, Elfhame's knights are ready to return a volley of arrows. If anyone fires, as close as they are to Bogdana, the storm hag is likely to be hit. But that doesn't mean they won't be hit, too.

"He tells me we can trust you," Jude says to Wren.

"Hold," Wren tells the falcons, her voice shaking a little. He can see in her face that she, despite everything, expected to find one of their blades to her throat. "Lower your weapons, and the High Court will do the same."

"Get away from her!" a voice comes from one of the tents, and Bex steps into view. She's soaked through and shivering, and when she sees them, her eyes go wide. "Wren?"

Horror clouds Wren's expression as Bex steps out of the shelter of the canvas into the rain. One hand goes to cover her mouth automatically, to hide her sharp teeth. Wren never wanted her family to look at her and see a monster.

Oak notes her swaying a little with nothing nearby to grasp to keep her upright. Wren has been drinking up far too much magic. She must feel as though she is fraying at the edges. She may *be* fraying at the edges.

"Bex," Wren says so quietly that he doubts the girl can hear the words over the storm.

The mortal takes a step toward her.

"She's actually here," Wren says, sounding awed. "She's okay."

"Oh no," says Bogdana. "That girl isn't your kin. You're my child. Mine. And you, boy—"

Lightning arcs down out of the sky, toward Oak. He steps back, lifting his sword automatically, as though he could block it like a blow. For a moment, everything around him goes white. And then he sees Wren lunge in front of him, her hair wild and wind-tossed around her head, electricity flashing inside her as though fireflies are trapped beneath her skin.

She caught the bolt.

Her lips curve, and she gives an odd, uncharacteristic laugh.

Bogdana's lips pull back in a hiss of astonishment. But she's accomplished this—Oak no longer has his sword to her throat, and even Jude has taken a step back.

The storm hag shakes her head. "You *imprisoned* the prince. You threw him into your dungeon. He tricked you. You *can't* trust him."

Wren slumps to her knees, as though her legs collapsed beneath her.

"This is done," Oak warns Bogdana. "You're done."

"Do not think to choose him over me," Bogdana snaps, ignoring him. "Your sister is a game piece. He'll use that mortal girl to manipulate you to do exactly what he wants, rather than use her, as I did, to help you take what is yours. And she is in more danger from him than she could ever be from me."

Wren's hands still spark with the aftereffects of the bolt. "You keep telling me that others will do to me what you have already done. I know what it is to want something so much that you would rather have the shadow of it than nothing, even if that means you will never have the real thing. And love is not that.

"You could have trusted me to choose my allies. Could have trusted how I would decide to use my powers. But no, you had to bring my unsis—my *sister* here and show her all the things I was afraid she would see. Show her the *me* that I was afraid for her to know. And if she spurns me, I am certain you will glory in it, the proof that I have no one but you."

Wren looks across the mud at Bex. "Prince Oak will make sure you get home."

"But—" the girl begins.

"You can trust him," Wren says.

"No, child," Bogdana snaps. Thunder rumbles. Dust devils begin to swirl around her, sucking up sand. "We have come too far. It's too late. They will never forgive you. He will never forgive you."

Oak shakes his head. "There is nothing to forgive. Wren tried to warn me. She would have given up her life to keep from being your pawn."

Bogdana remains focused on Wren. "Do you really think you're a match for my power? You caught one bolt of lightning, and you're already coming apart."

The falcons move toward their queen, turning their weapons on the storm hag for the first time.

Wren gives a wan smile. "I was never meant to survive. If we went through with this battle and the one that would inevitably come next, if you forced me to annihilate all the magic thrown at us, there would be nothing left of me. The magic that knits me together would have been eaten away."

"No—" Bogdana begins, but she can't say the rest. Can't, because it would have been a lie.

"You're right about one thing, though. It's too late." Wren opens her arms, as though to embrace the night. As she does, it seems that the whole storm—the spiraling wind, the lightning—recognizes her as its center.

Oak realizes what she's doing, but he has no idea how to stop her. And he understands now the despair that others have felt at the sight of him throwing himself at something, not caring for the consequences. "Wren, please, no!"

She takes the storm into herself, drinking down the rain that pelts her, letting it be absorbed into her skin. Wind whips her hair, then stills. Dark clouds dissipate, blowing away on her breath until they are no more.

The pale moon shines down on Elfhame again. The wind is still. The waves crash no more against the shores.

With the last of her might, Bogdana sweeps her hand at Wren.

A bolt of lightning cracks through the sky to strike her in the chest.

Wren staggers back, bending over with the pain of it. And when she looks up, her eyes are alight.

She glows with power. Her body rises into the air, hair floating around her. Her eyes open wide. Hovering in the sky, she's lit from within. Her body is radiant, so bright that Oak can see the woven sticks where bones ought to be, the stones of her eyes, the jagged pieces of shell used to make her teeth. And her black heart, dense with raw power.

He can feel it like a gravitational force, pulling him toward her. And he can feel when it stops.

CHAPTER

24

Wren collapses, her skin bruised and pale, her hair plastered across her face. Her eyes closed. The stillness of her is too profound for sleep.

Oak cannot seem to do anything but look at her. He cannot move. He cannot think.

Bex kneels beside Wren, pressing on her chest, counting under her breath. "Come on," she mutters between compressions.

Bogdana leans down to place her overlong fingers on Wren's cheek. Without her power, she looks old. Even her long nails look brittle. "Get away from her, human girl."

"I'm trying to save my sister," Bex snaps.

Jude stands behind the mortal. "Is she breathing?"

"*You destroyed her,*" Oak snarls at Bogdana, holding his sword pommel so hard that he feels the edge of the hilt dig into his hand. "You had a chance to undo what you did, to save your only daughter. No one tricked you this time. You did the very thing you knew would kill her."

"She betrayed me," Bogdana says, but there is a hitch in her voice.

"You cared nothing for her," Oak shouts. "You terrorized her so that she would come into a power that you could use. You let those monsters in the Court of Teeth hurt her. And now she's dead."

The hag narrows her eyes. "And you, boy? Are you so much better? You're the one who brought her here. What would you do to save her?"

"Anything!" he shouts.

"No!" Jude says, nearly as quickly, putting her body between his and the storm hag's. "No, he would not." She takes Oak by the shoulders and shakes him. "You can't just keep throwing yourself at things as though you don't matter."

"She matters more," he says.

"It's possible that Wren can be woken," says Bogdana.

"Deceive me in this, and I will bury you, so do I vow," Oak says.

"Her heart is stopped," says Bogdana. "But hag children don't need beating hearts. Just magical ones."

Oak recalls the Ghost giving him a warning when they were aboard the ship. *It is said that a hag's power comes from the part of them that's missing. Each one has a cold stone or wisp of cloud or ever-burning flame where their hearts ought to be.*

He'd dismissed it as a piece of superstition. Even Faerie found hags and their powers troubling enough to make up legends about them. And the Ghost had clearly been worried over Oak's plan to marry one.

The prince lowers himself back to the ground. He kneels in the wet sand on the other side of where Bex is working. She scowls at him as she counts. He puts his hand on Wren's chest. Desperately hoping the storm hag is right. But he feels not a single thrum of a pulse nor the movement of breath in her lungs. What he does feel is magic. There's a deep well of it, curled up inside her body.

Pulling back his hand, he doesn't know what to think.

Mother Marrow told him that Wren's magic was turned inside out. A power meant to be used for creation, warped until all it could do was destroy, annihilate, and unmake. Twisted on itself, a snake eating its own tail. But perhaps taking apart the storm and being struck twice by lightning was more than even her magic could devour. Maybe some of it spilled over.

Though she set all her matches alight and burned up with them, maybe something new could emerge from the ashes.

How many girls like Wren can there be, made from sticks and imbued with a cursed heart? She's made of magic, more than any of them.

"What will wake her?" he demands.

"That I do not know," Bogdana says, not meeting his eyes.

Jude raises both brows. "Helpful."

Oak remembers the story Oriana told him long ago about his mother. *Once upon a time, there was a woman who was so beautiful that none could resist her. When she spoke, it seemed that the hearts of those who listened beat for her alone.*

But how could he persuade someone who might not even be able to hear him?

"Wren," Oak says, letting the burr come into his voice. "Open your eyes. Please."

Nothing happens. Oak tries again, letting loose the full force of his honey-tongued charm. The nearby Folk watch him with a new, strange intensity. The air seems to ripple with power. Bex sucks in a breath, leaning toward him.

"Come back to me," he says.

But Wren is silent and still.

Oak lets go of his power, cursing himself. He glances up helplessly at Jude, who looks back at him and shakes her head. "I'm sorry." It is a very human thing for her to say.

He lets his head fall forward until his forehead is touching Wren's.

Gathering her in his arms, he studies the hollowness of her cheeks and the thinness of her skin. Presses a finger to the edge of her mouth.

Oak thought his magic was just finding what people wanted to hear and saying it in the way they wanted, but since he's let himself really use the power, he discovered that he can use it to find truth. And for once, he needs to tell her the truth. "I thought love was a fascination, or a desire to be around someone, or wanting to make them happy. I believed it just happened, like a slap to the face, and left the way the sting from such a blow fades. That's why it was easy for me to believe it could be false or manipulated or influenced by magic.

"Until I met you, I didn't understand to feel loved, one has to feel known. And that, outside of my family, I had never really loved because I hadn't bothered to know the other person. But I know you. And you have to come back to me, Wren, because no one gets us but us. You know why you're not a monster, but I might be. I know why throwing me in your dungeon meant there was still something between us. We are messes and we are messed up and I don't want to go through this world without the one person I can't hide from and who can't hide from me.

"Come back," he says again, tears burning the back of his throat. "You want and you want and you want, remember? Well, wake up and take what you want."

He presses his mouth against her forehead.

And startles when he hears her draw in a breath. Her eyes open, and for a moment, she stares up at him.

"Wren?" Bex says, and smacks Oak on the shoulder. "What did you do?" Then she pulls the prince into her arms and hugs him hard.

Jude is staring, hand to her mouth.

Bogdana stays back, glowering, perhaps hoping that no one noticed she rent her garments with her nails as she watched and waited.

"I'm cold," Wren whispers, and alarm rings through him like the sounding of a bell. She could walk barefoot through the snow and not have it hurt her. He never heard her complain of even the most frigid temperatures.

Oak stands, lifting Wren in his arms. She feels too light, but he is reassured by her breath ghosting across his skin, the rise and fall of her chest.

He still cannot, however, hear the beat of her heart.

With the storm stopped, it seems that all of Elfhame has forded the distance between Insear and Insmire. There are boats aplenty, and soldiers. Grima Mog's second-in-command is barking orders.

Bex scavenges a blanket from one of the tents, and Oak manages to bundle Wren in it. Then he carries her to a boat and commandeers it to take him back across so he can bring her to the palace. The journey is a blur of panic, of frantic questions, plodding steps. Finally, he carries her into his rooms. By then, her body is shivering, and he tries not to let terror leak into his voice as he speaks to her softly, explaining where they are and how she will be safe.

He puts Wren in his bed, then pushes it close by the fire and piles blankets on top of her. It seems to make no difference to her shuddering.

Herbalists and bonesetters come and go. *Like a banshee*, one of them says. *Like a sluagh*, says another. *Like nothing I've ever seen before*, says a third.

Wren's skin has become dry and oddly dull. Even her hair looks faded. It seems as though she is sinking so deeply into herself that he cannot follow.

Oak sits with her throughout that night and all through the next day, refusing to budge as people come in and out. Oriana tries to prize him from Wren's side to eat something, but he won't leave.

Bex comes and goes. That afternoon, she sits for a while, holding her sister's hand and crying as though she were already gone.

Tiernan brings them both hard cheese, fennel tea, and some bread. He also brings news of Bogdana, who is being held in the prisons of Hollow Hall, soon to be moved into the Tower of Forgetting.

Bex makes up a bed for herself on the floor out of scavenged cushions. Oak gives her one of his robes, all of gold and spider silk, to wear.

As night comes on, Wren seems like a husk of herself. When he touches her arm, it feels papery under his fingers. A wasp's nest instead of flesh. He draws his hand back and tries to convince himself of something other than the worst.

"She's not getting better, is she?" the mortal girl says.

"I don't know," Oak says, the words hard to get out, so close to being a lie.

Bex frowns. "I think I met your, uh, father. He was telling me about the Court of Teeth."

Well, he should know all about that place, Oak thinks but doesn't say.

"I guess I can see why Wren thought she couldn't come back to my family, and it wasn't because—I don't know, not because she didn't want to see us."

"She was willing to do a lot for your sake," Oak says, thinking of all the ways Wren must have struggled to free them from Bogdana's trap, how despair must have closed in around her when she realized she was going to have to choose between an agonizing death for her sister and the deaths of many others.

"I just wish—" Bex says. "I wish I'd talked to her when I first saw her sneaking into the house. I wish I'd followed her. I wish I'd done more, done *something*."

Over the past few days, Oak has been making a comprehensive and damning list of all the better choices he could have made. He's wondering whether he ought to admit them out loud when Bex screams.

He rockets to his feet, not sure what she's seeing.

And then he does. Inside of the husk of Wren, something is moving. Shifting beneath her skin.

"What is that?" Bex says, scuttling back until she hits the wall.

Oak shakes his head. The dullness of Wren's skin suddenly makes him think of the shed casings that spiders leave behind. He reaches out an unsteady hand—

Wren moves again, and this time, the papery flesh tears. Skin emerges, vibrant blue. Her body cracks open like a chrysalis.

Bex makes an alarmed sound from the floor.

From within, a new Wren emerges. Her skin the same cerulean blue, her eyes the same soft green. Even her teeth are the same, sharp as ever when she parts her lips to take a breath of air. But on her back are two feathered wings, light blue gray at the tips, with darker feathers closer to her body, and when they unfurl, they are large enough to canopy him, Bex, and Wren.

She stands, naked and reborn, looking around the room with the sharp gaze of a goddess, deciding whom to bless and whom to smite.

Her eyes settle on the prince.

"You have wings," he says, awestruck and foolish. He sounds as though he took a hard blow to the head. That isn't far from how he feels.

Astonished joy has robbed him of all cleverness.

"Wren?" Bex whispers.

Wren's attention swings to her, and he can see the mortal girl flinch a little under the weight of it.

"You don't have to be afraid," Wren says, although she looks positively terrifying right then. Even Oak is a little frightened of her.

Bex draws in a breath and pushes herself off the floor. Picking up a fallen blanket, she hands it to her sister, then gives Oak a pointed look. "You should probably stop staring at her like you never saw a naked girl with wings before."

Oak blinks and turns away, shamefaced. "Right," he says, heading for the door. "I'll leave you both."

He looks back once, but all he sees are feathers.

In the hall, a guard comes immediately to attention.

"Your Highness," he says. "Tiernan went to rest a few hours ago. Shall I send for him?"

"No need," says Oak. "Let him be."

The prince moves through the palace like a stunned sleepwalker, desperately happy that Wren is alive. So happy that when he finds Madoc in the game room, he can't contain his smile.

His father stands from behind a chess table. "You look pleased. Does that mean—"

Time—never particularly well calculated by the Folk—has blurred at the edges. He's not sure how long he's been in that room. "Awake. Alive."

"Come sit," Madoc says. "You can finish Val Moren's game."

Oak slips into the chair and frowns at the table. "What happened?"

In front of Madoc are several captured pawns, a bishop, and a knight. On Oak's side, only a single pawn.

"He wandered off when he realized he was going to lose," says the redcap.

Oak blinks at the game, too exhausted to have any move in mind, no less a good move.

"Your mother isn't particularly happy with me right now," Madoc says. "Your sisters, either."

"Because of me?" It was perhaps inevitable, but he felt guilty to hasten it along.

Madoc shakes his head. "Maybe they're right."

That's alarming. "Everything okay, Dad?"

Unlike Oriana, Madoc smiles at his use of the human term. *Dad.* Perhaps he likes it better because when Jude and Taryn used it, it meant they cared about him in a way he might not have thought they ever would.

"That mortal girl being around made me think."

It has to be strange for him to be back in Elfhame, and yet no longer the grand general. To be back in his old house, without his kids there. And to be away from Insear when the rest of them were in danger. "About my sisters?"

"About their mother," Madoc says.

Oak is surprised. Madoc doesn't usually speak of his mortal wife, Eva. Possibly because he murdered her.

"Oh?"

"It's not easy for mortals to live in this place. It's not easy for us to live in their world, either, but it's easier. I shouldn't have left her so much alone. I shouldn't have forgotten that she could lie, or that she thought of her life as brief, and would risk much for happiness."

Oak nods, sensing there's more, and advances his pawn out of the range of being taken by another.

"And I shouldn't have told myself that cultivating a killing instinct I couldn't control had no chance of bringing me tragedy. I shouldn't have been so eager to teach the same to you."

Oak thinks of the fear he'd felt when his father struck him to the ground all those years ago, of the hard kernel of shame he carried at that terror and his own softness, at how his sisters and mother protected him. "No," Oak says. "Probably not."

Madoc grins. "And yet, there are few things I would change. For without all my mistakes, I would not have the family I do." He moves his queen, sweeping across the board to rest in a place that doesn't seem imminently threatening.

Since Madoc would almost certainly have the crown if not for one of Eva's mortal daughters, that was quite an admission.

Oak moves his knight to take one of his father's undefended bishops. "I'm glad you're home. Try not to get banished again."

Madoc shifts his castle. "Checkmate," he says with a grin, leaning back in his chair.

On his way back to his rooms, Oak stops at Tiernan's. He taps lightly enough that if Tiernan is really asleep, the sound won't rouse him.

"Yes?" comes a voice. Hyacinthe.

Oak opens the door.

Tiernan and Hyacinthe are in bed together. Tiernan's hair is rumpled, and Hyacinthe is looking quite pleased with himself.

Oak smirks and comes to sit at the foot. "This won't take long."

Hyacinthe shifts so he's leaning against the headboard. His chest is bare. Tiernan shifts up, too, keeping a blanket over himself.

"Tiernan, I am formally dismissing you from my service," Oak says.

"Why? What did I do?" Tiernan leans forward, not worrying about the blanket anymore.

"Protected me," Oak says with great sincerity. "Including from myself. For many years."

Hyacinthe's looks outraged. "Is this because of me?"

"Not entirely," says Oak.

"That's not fair," Hyacinthe says. "I fought back-to-back with you. I got you out of Mother Marrow's. I practically got you out of the Citadel. I even let you persuade me to be half-drowned by Jack of the Lakes. You can't still think I would betray you."

"I don't," Oak says.

Tiernan frowns in confusion. "Why *are* you sending me away?"

"Guarding a member of the royal family isn't a position one is supposed to quit," Oak says. "But you should. I have been throwing myself at things and not caring what happens. I didn't see how destructive it was until Wren did it."

"You need someone—"

"I did need you when I was a child," Oak says. "Although I wouldn't admit it. You kept me safe, and trying not to put you in danger made me a little more cautious—although not nearly cautious enough—but more, you were my friend. Now both of us need to make decisions about our future, and those might not follow the same paths."

Tiernan takes a deep breath, letting those words sink in.

Hyacinthe gapes a little. Of all the things he has resented Oak for, what he seemed to feel most keenly was the fear that Tiernan was being taken from him. The idea that Oak might not actually want that clearly never occurred to him.

"I hope you'll always be my friend, but we can't *really* be friends if you're obliged to throw away your life for my bad decisions."

"I'll always be your friend," Tiernan says staunchly.

"Good," Oak says, standing up. "And now I will get out of here so Hyacinthe doesn't have a new reason to be angry with me and you can both—eventually—sleep."

The prince heads for the door. One of them throws a pillow at his back on his way out.

At the door to his rooms, Oak knocks. When neither Wren nor Bex answers, he goes in.

It takes him a few turns through the sitting area, the bedroom, and the library to realize she's not there. He calls her name and then, feeling foolish, sits on the edge of the bed.

A sheet of paper rests on his pillow, one ripped out of an old school notebook. On it in an unsteady hand is a letter addressed to him.

Oak,

    I have always been your opposite, shy and wild where you are all courtly charm. And yet you are the one who pulled me out of my forest and forced me to stop denying all the parts of me I tried to hide.

    Including the part of me that wanted you.

    I could tell you how easy it was to believe that I was monstrous in your eyes and that the only thing I could have of you was what I took. But that hardly matters. I knew it was wrong, and I did it anyway. I exchanged the certainty of possession for what I most wanted—your friendship and your love.

    I am going with Bex to visit my family and then return to the north. If I can no longer only take things apart, then it's time to learn how to create. It would be cruel to hold you to a promise made in duress, a marriage proposal given to prevent bloodshed. And crueler still to make you bid me a polite farewell, when I have already taken so much from you.

Wren

The prince crumples the paper in his hands. Didn't he make her an entire speech about how she taught him about love? About knowing and being known. After that, how could she—

Oh, right. He made that speech while she was *unconscious.*

He slumps down in a chair.

When Jude sends for him, he has spent the better part of the afternoon staring out a window miserably. Still, she's the High Queen and also his sister, so he makes himself somewhat presentable and goes to the royal chambers.

Cardan is lying on the bed, bandaged and sulking, in a magnificent dressing gown. "I hate being unwell," he says.

"You're not *sick*," Jude tells him. "You are recovering from being stabbed—or rather, throwing yourself on a knife."

"You would have done the same for me," he says airily.

"I would not," Jude snaps.

"Liar," Cardan says fondly.

Jude takes a deep breath and turns to Oak. "If you really want, you have our formal permission, as your sovereigns, to abdicate your position as our heir."

Oak raises his brows, waiting for the caveat. He's been telling her he didn't want the throne for as long as he can remember having a reason to say the words. For years, she acted as though he'd eventually come around. "Why?"

"You're a grown person. A *man*, even if I'd like to think of you as forever a boy. You've got to determine your own fate. Make your own choices. And I have to let you."

"Thank you," he forces out. It's not a polite thing to say among the Folk, but Jude ought to hear it. Those words absolve him of no debt.

He's let her down and possibly made her proud of him, too. His family cares about him in ways that are far too complex and layered for it to come from enchantment, and that is a profound relief.

"For listening to you? Don't worry. I won't make it a habit." Walking to him, she puts her arms around him, bumping her chin against his chest. "You're so annoyingly tall. I used to be able to carry you on my shoulders."

"I could carry *you*," Oak offers.

"You used to kick me with your hooves," she tells him. "I wouldn't mind a chance for revenge."

"I bet." He laughs. "Is Taryn still angry?"

"She's sad," Jude says. "And feels guilty. Like this is the universe punishing her for what she did to Locke."

If that were true, so many of them deserved greater punishment.

"I didn't want—I don't *think* I wanted Garrett dead."

"He isn't dead," Jude says matter-of-factly. "He's a tree."

He supposes it must be some comfort, to be able to visit and speak with him, even if he can't speak in return. And perhaps someday the enchantment could be broken when the danger was past. Perhaps even the hope of that was something.

"And you had every reason to be mad. We did keep secrets from you," Jude goes on. "Bad ones. Small ones. I should have told you what the Ghost had done. I should have told you when Madoc was captured. And—you should have told me some things, too."

"A lot of things," Oak agrees.

"We'll do better," Jude says, knocking her shoulder into his arm.

"We'll do better," he agrees.

"Speaking of which, I would speak with Oak for a moment," Cardan says. "Alone."

Jude looks surprised but then shrugs. "I'll be outside, yelling at people."

"Try not to enjoy it too greatly," says Cardan as she goes out.

For a moment, they are silent. Cardan pushes himself up off the bed. Messy black curls fall over his eyes, and he ties the belt of his deep blue dressing gown more tightly.

"I am sure she doesn't want you getting up," Oak says, but he offers his arm. Cardan is, after all, the High King.

And if he slipped, Jude would like that even less.

Cardan leans heavily on the prince. He points toward one of the low brocade couches. "Help me get over there."

They move slowly. Cardan winces under his breath and occasionally gives an exaggerated groan. When he finally makes it, he lounges against one of the corners, propped up with pillows. "Pour me a goblet of wine, won't you?"

Oak rolls his eyes.

Cardan leans forward. "Or I could get it myself."

Outmaneuvered, Oak holds his hands up in surrender. He goes to a silver tray that holds cut crystal carafes and chooses one half-full of plum-dark liquor. He pours it into a goblet and passes that over.

"I think you know what this is about," Cardan says, taking a long slug.

Oak sits. "Lady Elaine? Randalin? The conspiracy? I can explain."

Cardan waves his words away. "You have done enough and more than enough *explaining*. I think it is my turn to speak."

"Your Majesty," Oak acknowledges.

Cardan meets his gaze. "For someone who cannot outright lie, you twist the truth so far that I am surprised it doesn't cry out in agony."

Oak doesn't even bother denying that.

"Which makes perfect sense, given your father...and your sister. But you've even managed to deceive her. Which she doesn't like admitting—doesn't like, period, really."

Again, Oak says nothing.

"When did you start, with the conspiracies?"

"I don't want—" Oak begins.

"The throne?" Cardan finishes for him. "Obviously not. Nor have you waffled on that point. And if your sisters and your parents imagined you'd change your mind, that's for their own mad reasons. It's the only thing on which you have remained steadfast for more than a handful of years. And, I will have you know, I thought the same thing when I was a prince."

Oak can't help recalling the part he had in taking that choice away from Cardan.

"No, I don't suspect you of wanting to be High King," Cardan says, and then smiles a wicked, little smile. "Nor did I believe you wanted me dead for some other reason. I never thought that."

Oak opens his mouth and closes it. *Isn't* that what this is about? *Wasn't* that what Cardan believed? He overheard the High King tell Jude as much, back in their rooms in the palace, before he left to try to save Madoc. "I am not sure I understand."

"When your first bodyguard tried to kill you, I ought to have asked more questions. Certainly after one or two of your lovers died. But I thought what everyone else thought—that you were too trusting and easily manipulated as a result. That you chose your friends poorly and your lovers even more poorly. But you chose both carefully and well, didn't you?"

Oak gets up and pours himself a glass of wine. He suspects he is going to need it. "I overheard you," he says. "In your rooms, with Jude. I overheard you talking about Madoc."

"Yes," Cardan says. "Belatedly, that became obvious."

If I didn't know better, I might think this is your brother's fault. Oak tries to remember the exact words the High King chose. *He's more like you than you want to see.* "You didn't trust me."

"Having spent a great deal of time playing the fool myself," Cardan says, "I recognized your game. Not at first, but long before Jude. She didn't want to believe me, and I am never going to tire of crowing about being right."

"So you didn't think I was really allied with Randalin?"

Cardan smiles. "No," he says. "But I wasn't certain which of your allies were actually on your side. And I was rather hoping you'd let us lock you up and protect you."

"You could have given me some sort of hint!" Oak says.

Cardan raises a single brow.

Oak shakes his head. "Yes, well, *fine*. I could have done the same. And *fine*, you were losing blood."

Cardan makes a gesture as though tossing off Oak's words. "I have little experience of dispensing brotherly wisdom, but I know a great deal about mistakes. And about hiding behind a mask." He salutes with his wineglass. "Some might say that I still do, but they would be wrong. To those I love, I am myself. Too much myself sometimes."

Oak laughs. "Jude wouldn't say that."

Cardan takes a deep swallow of plum-dark wine, looking pleased with himself. "She *would*, but she'd be lying. But, most important"—he raises a single finger—"*I* knew what you were up to before she did." Then a second. "And if you decide you want to risk your life, perhaps you could also risk a little personal discomfort and let your family in on your plans."

Oak lets out a long sigh. "I will take that under advisement."

"Please do," says Cardan. "And there is one more thing."

Oak takes an even bigger slug of his wine.

"You may recall that Jude gave you permission to abdicate? Well, that's all well and good, but you can't do it immediately. We'll need several months more of your being our heir."

"Months?" Oak echoes, completely puzzled.

The High King shrugs. "More or less. Maybe a little longer. Just to make the Court feel as though there's some kind of backup plan if something happens while we're away."

"Away?" After so many surprises, Oak seems unable to do more than repeat the things Cardan tells him. "You want me to stay the heir while you two go off somewhere? And *then* I can step down, be de-princed, whatever?"

"Exactly that," says Cardan.

"Like on a vacation?"

Cardan snorts.

"I don't understand," Oak says. "Where are you going?"

"A diplomatic mission," says Cardan, leaning back on the cushions. "After that last little rescue, Nicasia has demanded we honor our treaty, meet her suitors, and witness the contest for her hand and crown. And so Jude and I are headed to the Undersea, where we will go to a lot of parties and try very hard not to die."

CHAPTER
25

Oak steps onto the crust of ice, his breath clouding in the air.

He is dressed in thick furs, his hands wrapped in wool and then in leather, even his hooves wrapped, and yet he can still feel the chill of this place. He shivers, thinks of Wren, and shivers again.

The Stone Forest is different from what he remembers, lush instead of menacing. He is not pulled toward it now, nor does he feel pursued by it. As he passes, he attempts to see the troll kings, but the landscape has swallowed them up. All he can see is the wall they built.

When he approaches it, he finds that a great ice gate—newly built— stands open. He passes through. As he does, some falcons fly into the air from the top, probably to announce his arrival.

Beyond, he expects to see the same Citadel that he invaded with Wren, the one in which he was imprisoned, but a new structure has taken its place. A castle all of obsidian instead of ice. The rock shines as though it were made of black glass.

If anything, it looks more forbidding and impossible than what was there before. Certainly more pointy.

Hag Queen. He thinks of those whispered words and is more aware than ever why Folk are afraid of this kind of power.

Oak trods past copses made entirely from ice, animals sculpted from snow peering out from their branches. It makes him think, eerily, of the forest in which he found Wren. As though she has re-created parts of it from memory.

She made all of this with her magic. The magic that should have always been her inheritance.

The doors to the new castle are high and narrow, without a knocker nor any handles. He pushes, expecting resistance, but the door swings open at the touch of his gloved hand.

The black hall beyond is empty but for a fireplace large enough to cook a horse, crackling with real flames. No servants greet him. His hooves echo against the stone.

He finds her in the third room, a library, only a portion of it stocked with books, but clearly built for the acquisition of more.

She is in a long dressing gown of a deep blue color. Her hair is down and falls over her shoulders. Her feet are bare. She sits on a long, low couch, novel in hand, wings spread. At the sight of her, he feels a longing so sharp that it is almost pain.

Wren sits up.

"I didn't expect you," she says, which is not encouraging.

He thinks of visiting her in the forest when they were young and how she sent him away for his own good. Perhaps wisely. But he isn't about to be sent away easily again.

She goes to one of her shelves and returns the book, sliding it back into place.

"I know what you think," Oak says. "That you're not whom I should want."

She ducks her head, a faint flush on her cheeks.

"It's true you inspire no safe daydream of love," he tells her.

"A nightmare, then?" she asks with a small, self-deprecating laugh.

"The kind of love that comes when two people see each other clearly," he says, walking to her. "Even if they're scared to believe that's possible. I adore you. I want to play games with you. I want to tell you all the truths I have to give. And if you really think you're a monster, then let's be monsters together."

Wren stares at him. "And if I send you away even after this speech? If I don't want you?"

He hesitates. "Then I'll go," he says. "And adore you from afar. And compose ballads about you or something."

"You could *make* me love you," she says.

"You?" Oak snorts. "I doubt it. You're not interested in my telling you what you want to hear. I think you might actually prefer me at my least charming."

"What if I am too much? If I need too much?" she asks, her voice very low.

He takes a deep breath, his smile gone. "I'm not good. I'm not kind. Maybe I am not even safe. But whatever you want from me, I will give you."

For a moment, they stare at each other. He can see the tension in her body. But her eyes are clear and bright and open. She nods, a slow smile growing on her lips. "I want you to stay."

"Good," he says, sitting on the couch beside her. "Because it's very cold out there, and it was a long walk."

She lets her head fall against his shoulder with a sigh, lets him put his arm around her and pull her into an embrace.

"So," she says, her lips against his throat. "If everything had gone well that night on Insear, what would you have asked me? A riddle?"

"Something like that," he says.

"Tell me," she insists, and he can feel the press of her teeth, the softness of her mouth.

"It's a tricky one," he says. "Are you sure?"

"I'm good at riddles," she says.

"What I would have asked you—if somehow I wasn't trying to manipulate the situation so that you could wriggle out of it—is this: Would you consider actually marrying me?"

She looks up at him, obviously surprised and a little suspicious. "Really?"

He presses a kiss to her hair. "If you did, I would be willing to make the ultimate sacrifice to prove the sincerity of my feelings."

"What's that?" she asks, peering up at him.

"Become a king of some place instead of running away from all royal responsibility."

She laughs. "You wouldn't rather sit by my throne on a leash?"

"That does seem easier," he admits. "I would make an excellent consort."

"Then I'll have to marry you, Prince Oak of the Greenbriar line," Wren says, with a sharp-toothed smile. "Just to make you suffer."

ACKNOWLEDGMENTS

I am grateful to all those who helped me along on the journey to the novel you have in your hands, particularly Cassandra Clare, Leigh Bardugo, and Joshua Lewis, who helped me plot this the first time (surrounded by cats), Kelly Link, Sarah Rees Brennan, and Robin Wasserman, who helped me replot and reconsider my plot (though with fewer cats). Also to Steve Berman, who gave me notes and encouragement throughout and who has been critiquing my books since before *Tithe*.

Thank you to the many people who gave me a kind word or a bit of necessary advice, and who I am going to kick myself for not including right here.

A massive thank-you to everyone at Little, Brown Books for Young Readers for returning to Elfhame with me. Thanks especially to my amazing editor, Alvina Ling, and to Ruqayyah Daud, who provided invaluable insight. Thank you to Crystal Castro for dealing with all my delays. Thank you as well to Marisa Finkelstein, Kimberly Stella, Emilie Polster, Savannah Kennelly, Bill Grace, Karina Granda, Cassie Malmo, Megan Tingley, Jackie Engel, Shawn Foster, Danielle Cantarella, and Victoria Stapleton, among others.

In the UK, thank you to Hot Key Books, particularly Jane Harris, Emma Matthewson, and Amber Ivatt.

Thank you to my publishers and editors all over the world—those who I have had the pleasure of meeting in the past year and those I have not. And thank you to Heather Baror for keeping everyone on the same page.

Thank you to Joanna Volpe, Jordan Hill, and Lindsay Howard, who read versions of this book as well and kept me feeling as though I was on the right track. And thank you to everyone at New Leaf Literary for making hard things easier.

Thank you to Kathleen Jennings, for the wonderful and evocative illustrations.

And thank you, always and forever, to Theo and Sebastian Black, for keeping my heart safe.

THE
STOLEN
HEIR

BY HOLLY BLACK

THE FOLK OF THE AIR

OTHER

THE STOLEN HEIR

A NOVEL OF ELFHAME

HOLLY BLACK

LITTLE, BROWN AND COMPANY

NEW YORK BOSTON

Copyright © 2023 by Holly Black
Map and illustrations by Kathleen Jennings

Cover art copyright © 2023 by Sean Freeman. Cover design by Karina Granda.
Cover copyright © 2023 by Hachette Book Group, Inc.
Interior design by Karina Granda.

Little, Brown and Company
Hachette Book Group
1290 Avenue of the Americas, New York, NY 10104
Visit us at LBYR.com

First Edition: January 2023

Little, Brown and Company is a division of Hachette Book Group, Inc.
The Little, Brown name and logo are trademarks of Hachette Book Group, Inc.

The publisher is not responsible for websites (or their content) that are not owned by the publisher.

Little, Brown and Company books may be purchased in bulk for business, educational, or promotional use. For information, please contact your local bookseller or the Hachette Book Group Special Markets Department at special.markets@hbgusa.com.

Library of Congress Cataloging-in-Publication Data
Names: Black, Holly, author.
Title: The stolen heir / Holly Black.
Description: First edition. | New York : Little, Brown and Company, 2023. |
Series: The stolen heir | Audience: Ages 14+. | Summary: "The changeling queen Suren must venture
back into the Court of Teeth with the help of the Prince of Faerie, Oak." —Provided by publisher.
Identifiers: LCCN 2022037583 | ISBN 9780316592703 (hardcover) |
ISBN 9780316422260 (ebook)
Subjects: CYAC: Fantasy. | LCGFT: Fantasy fiction. | Novels.
Classification: LCC PZ7.B52878 St 2023 | DDC [Fic]—dc23
LC record available at https://lccn.loc.gov/2022037583

ISBNs: 978-0-316-59270-3 (hardcover), 978-0-316-42226-0 (ebook), 978-0-316-54330-9 (int'l),
978-0-316-54351-4 (Walmart exclusive edition), 978-0-316-51904-5 (B&N exclusive edition)

Printed in the United States of America

LSC-C

Printing 1, 2022

*For Robin Wasserman, who has the
curse (and blessing) of True Sight*

One evening, too, by the nursery fire,
We snuggled close and sat round so still,
When suddenly as the wind blew higher,
Something scratched on the window-sill,
A pinched brown face peered in — I shivered;
No one listened or seemed to see;
The arms of it waved and the wings of it quivered,
Whoo — I knew it had come for me!
Some are as bad as bad can be!
All night long they danced in the rain,
Round and round in a dripping chain,
Threw their caps at the window-pane,
Tried to make me scream and shout
And fling the bedclothes all about:
I meant to stay in bed that night,
And if only you had left a light
They would never have got me out!

—Charlotte Mew,
"The Changeling"

PROLOGUE

A passerby discovered a toddler sitting on the chilly concrete of an alley, playing with the wrapper of a cat-food container. By the time she was brought to the hospital, her limbs were blue with cold. She was a wizened little thing, too thin, made of sticks.

She knew only one word, her name. Wren.

As she grew, her skin retained a slight bluish cast, resembling skimmed milk. Her foster parents bundled her up in jackets and coats and mittens and gloves, but unlike her sister, she was never cold. Her lip color changed like a mood ring, staying bluish and purple even in summer, turning pink only when close to a fire. And she could play in the snow for hours, constructing elaborate tunnels and mock-fighting with icicles, coming inside only when called.

Although she appeared bony and anemic, she was strong. By the time she was eight, she could lift bags of groceries that her adoptive mother struggled with.

By the time she was nine, she was gone.

As a child, Wren read lots of fairy tales. That's why, when the monsters came, she knew it was because she had been wicked.

They snuck in through her window, pushing up the jamb and slashing the screen so silently that she slept on, curled around her favorite stuffed fox. She woke only when she felt claws touch her ankle.

Before she could get out the first scream, fingers covered her mouth. Before she could get out the first kick, her legs were pinned.

"I am going to let you go," said a harsh voice with an unfamiliar accent. "But if you wake anyone in this house, you will most assuredly be sorry for it."

That was like a fairy tale, too, which made Wren wary of breaking the rules. She stayed utterly quiet and still, even when they released her, although her heart beat so hard and fast that it seemed possible it would be loud enough to summon her mother.

A selfish part of her wished it would, wished that her mother would come and turn on a light and banish the monsters. That wouldn't be breaking the rules, would it, if it was only the thundering of her heart that did the waking?

"Sit up," commanded one of the monsters.

Obediently, Wren did. But her trembling fingers buried her stuffed fox in the blankets.

Looking at the three creatures flanking her bed made her shiver uncontrollably. Two were tall, elegant beings with skin the gray of stone. The first, a woman with a fall of pale hair caught in a crown of jagged obsidian, wearing a gown of some silvery material that wafted around her. She was beautiful, but the cruel set of her mouth warned Wren not to trust her. The man was matched to the woman as though they were pieces on a chessboard, wearing a black crown and clothes of the same silvery material.

Beside them was a huge, looming creature, spindly, with mushroom-pale skin and a head full of wild black hair. But what was most notable were her long, clawlike fingers.

"You're our daughter," one of the gray-faced monsters said.

"You belong to us," rasped the other. "We made you."

She knew about *birth parents*, which her sister had, nice people who came to visit and looked like her, and who sometimes brought over grandparents or doughnuts or presents.

She had wished for birth parents of her own, but she had never thought that her wish could conjure a nightmare like this.

"Well," said the woman in the crown. "Have you nothing to say? Are you too in awe of our majesty?"

The claw-fingered creature gave an impolite little snort.

"That must be it," said the man. "How grateful you will be to be taken away from all of this, changeling child. Get up. Make haste."

"Where are we going?" Wren asked. Fear made her sink her fingers into her bedsheets, as though she could hang on to her life before this moment if she just gripped hard enough.

"To Faerie, where you will be a queen," the woman said, a snarl in her voice where there ought to have been cajoling. "Have you never dreamed of someone coming to you and telling you that you were no mortal child, but one made of magic? Have you never dreamed about being taken from your pathetic little life to one of vast greatness?"

Wren couldn't deny that she had. She nodded. Tears burned in the back of her throat. That's what she had done wrong. That was the wickedness in her heart that had been discovered. "I'll stop," she whispered.

"What?" asked the man.

"If I promise never to make wishes like that again, can I stay?" she asked, voice shaking. "Please?"

The woman's hand came against Wren's cheek in a slap so hard that it sounded like a crack of thunder. Her cheek hurt, and though tears pricked her eyes, she was too shocked and angry for them to fall. No one had ever hit her before.

"You are Suren," said the man. "And we are your makers. Your sire and dam. I am Lord Jarel and she, Lady Nore. This one accompanying us is Bogdana, the storm hag. Now that you know your true name, let me show you your true face."

Lord Jarel reached out to her, making a ripping motion. And there, underneath, was her monster self, reflected in the mirror over her dresser—her skimmed milk skin giving way to pale blue flesh, the same color as buried veins. When she parted her lips, she saw shark-sharp teeth. Only her eyes were the same mossy green, large and staring back at her in horror.

My name isn't Suren, she wanted to say. *And this is a trick. That's not me.* But even as she thought the words, she heard how similar Suren was to her own name. Su*ren*. Ren. Wren. A child's shortening.

Changeling child.

"Stand," said the huge, looming creature with nails as long as knives. *Bogdana.* "You do not belong in this place."

Wren listened to the noises of the house, the hum of the heater, the distant scrape of the nails of the family dog as it pawed at the floor restlessly in sleep, running through dreams. She tried to memorize every sound. Her gaze blurry with tears, she committed her room to memory, from the book titles on her shelves to the glassy eyes of her dolls.

She snuck one last pet of her fox's synthetic fur and pressed him down, deeper under the covers. If he stayed there, he'd be safe. Shuddering, she slid out of the bed.

"Please," she said again.

A cruel smile twisted up the corner of Lord Jarel's face. "The mortals no longer want you."

Wren shook her head, because that couldn't be true. Her mother and father *loved* her. Her mother cut the crusts off her sandwiches and kissed her on the tip of her nose to make her giggle. Her father cuddled up with her to watch movies and then carried her to bed when she fell asleep on the couch. She knew they loved her. And yet the certainty with which Lord Jarel spoke plucked at her terror.

"If they admit that they wish for you to remain with them," said Lady Nore, her voice soft for the first time, "then you may stay."

Wren padded into the hall, her heart frantic, rushing into her parents' room as if she'd had a nightmare. The noise of her shuffling feet and her ragged breaths woke them. Her father sat up and then startled, putting an arm up protectively over her mother, who looked at Wren and screamed.

"Don't be scared," she said, moving to the side of the bed and crushing the blankets in her small fists. "It's me, Wren. They did something to me."

"Get away, monster!" her father barked. He sounded frightening enough to send her scuttling back against the dresser. She'd never heard him shout like that, certainly never at her.

Tears tracked down her cheeks. "It's *me*," she said again, her voice breaking. "Your daughter. You love me."

The room looked exactly as it always had. Pale beige walls. Queen-size bed with brown dog fur dirtying their white duvet. A towel lying beside the hamper, as though someone had thrown and missed. The scent of the furnace, and the petroleum smell of some cream used to remove makeup. But it was the distorted-mirror nightmare version, in which all those things had become horrible.

Below them, the dog barked, sounding a desperate warning.

"What are you waiting for? Get that thing out of here," her father growled, looking toward Lady Nore and Lord Jarel as though he was seeing something other than them, some human authority.

Wren's sister came into the hall, rubbing her eyes, clearly awakened by the screaming. Surely Rebecca would help, Rebecca who made sure no one bullied her at school, who took her to the fair even though no one else's little sister was allowed. But at the sight of Wren, Rebecca jumped onto the bed with a horrified yelp and wrapped her arms around her mother.

"Rebecca," Wren whispered, but her sister only dug her face deeper into their mother's nightgown.

"Mom," Wren pleaded, tears choking her voice, but her mother wouldn't look at her. Wren's shoulders shook with sobs.

"*This* is our daughter," her father said, holding Rebecca close, as though Wren had been trying to trick him.

Rebecca, who'd been adopted, too. Who ought to have been exactly as much theirs as Wren.

Wren crawled to the bed, crying so hard that she could barely get any words out. *Please let me stay. I'll be good. I am sorry, sorry, sorry for whatever I did, but you can't let them take me. Mommy. Mommy. Mommy, I love you, please, Mommy.*

Her father tried to push her back with his foot, pressing it against her neck. But she reached for him anyway, her voice rising to a shriek.

When her little fingers touched his calf, he kicked her in the shoulder, sending her to the floor. But she only crawled back, weeping and pleading, keening with misery.

"Enough," rasped Bogdana. She yanked Wren against her, running one of her long nails over Wren's cheek with something like gentleness. "Come, child. I will carry you."

"No," Wren said, her fingers winding themselves in the sheets. "No. No. No."

"It is not meet for the humans to have touched you in violence, you who are ours," said Lord Jarel.

"Ours to hurt," Lady Nore agreed. "Ours to punish. Never theirs."

"Shall they die for the offense?" Lord Jarel asked, and the room went quiet, except for the sound of Wren sobbing.

"Should we kill them, Suren?" he asked again, louder. "Let their pet dog in and enchant it so that it turns on them and bites out their throats?"

At that, Wren's crying abated in astonishment and outrage. "No!" she shouted. She felt beyond the ability to control herself.

"Then hear this and cease weeping," Lord Jarel told her. "You will come with us willingly, or I will slay everyone on that bed. First the child, then the others."

Rebecca gave a little frightened sob. Wren's human parents watched her with fresh horror.

"I'll go," Wren said finally, a sob still in her voice, one she couldn't stop. "Since no one loves me, I'll go."

The storm hag lifted her up, and they were away.

Wren was discovered in the flashing lights of a patrol car two years later, walking along the side of the highway. The soles of her shoes were as worn as if she'd danced through them, her clothing was stiff with sea salt, and scars marred the skin of her wrists and cheeks.

When the officer tried to ask her what had happened, she either wouldn't or couldn't answer. She snarled at anyone who came too close, hid beneath the cot in the room they brought her into, and refused to give a name or an address as to where her home had been to the lady they brought with them.

Their smiles hurt. Everything hurt.

When they turned their backs, she was gone.

CHAPTER

1

The slant of the moon tells me that it's half past ten when my un-sister comes out the back door. She's in her second year of college and keeps odd hours. As I watch from the shadows, she sets down an empty cereal bowl on the top step of the splintery and sagging deck. Then she glugs milk into it from a carton. Spills a little. Squatting, she frowns out toward the tree line.

For an impossible moment, it's as though she's looking at me.

I draw deeper into the dark.

The scent of pine needles is heavy in the air, mingling with leaf mold and the moss I crush between my bare toes. The breeze carries the smell of the sticky, rotten, sugary dregs still clinging to bottles in the recycling bin; the putrid something at the bottom of the empty garbage can; the chemical sweetness of the perfume my unsister is wearing.

I watch her hungrily.

Bex leaves the milk for a neighborhood cat, but I like to pretend it's me she's leaving it for. Her forgotten sister.

She stands there for a few minutes while moths flit above her head and mosquitoes buzz. Only when she goes back inside do I slink closer to the house, peering through the window to watch my unmother knit in front of the television. Watching my unfather in the breakfast nook with his laptop, answering email. He puts a hand to his eyes, as though tired.

In the Court of Teeth, I was punished if I called the humans who raised me my mother and father. *Humans are animals*, Lord Jarel would say, the admonishment coming with a breathtakingly hard blow. *Filthy animals. You share no blood with them.*

I taught myself to call them unmother and unfather, hoping to avoid Lord Jarel's wrath. I keep the habit to remind myself of what they were to me, and what they will never be again. Remind myself that there is nowhere that I belong and no one to whom I belong.

The hair on the back of my neck prickles. When I look around, I note an owl on a high branch, observing me with a swivel of its head. No, not an owl.

I pick up a rock, hurling it at the creature.

It shifts into the shape of a hob and takes off into the sky with a screech, beating feathered wings. It circles twice and then glides off toward the moon.

The local Folk are no friends to me. I've seen to that.

Another reason I am no one, of nowhere.

Resisting the temptation to linger longer near the backyard where I once played, I head for the branches of a hawthorn at the edge of town. I stick to the dimness of shadowed woodland, my bare feet finding their way through the night. At the entrance to the graveyard, I stop.

Huge and covered in the white blooms of early spring, the hawthorn towers over headstones and other grave markers. Desperate locals, teenagers especially, come here and tie wishes to the branches.

I heard the stories as a kid. It's called the Devil's Tree. Come back three times, make three wishes, and the devil was supposed to appear. He'd give you what you asked for and take what he wanted in return.

It's not a devil, though. Now that I have lived among the Folk, I know the creature that fulfills those bargains is a glaistig, a faerie with goat feet and a taste for human blood.

I climb into a cradle of branches and wait, petals falling around me with the sway of the tree limbs. I lean my cheek against the rough bark, listening to the susurration of leaves. In the cemetery that surrounds the hawthorn, the nearby graves are more than a hundred years old. These stones have weathered thin and bone pale. No one visits them anymore, making this a perfect spot for desperate people to come and not be seen.

A few stars wink down at me through the canopy of flowers. In the Court of Teeth, there was a nisse who made charts of the sky, looking for the most propitious dates for torture and murder and betrayal.

I stare up, but whatever riddle is in the stars, I can't read it. My education in Faerie was poor, my human education, inconsistent.

The glaistig arrives a little after midnight, clopping along. She is dressed in a long burgundy coat that stops at the knees, designed to highlight her goat feet. Her bark-brown hair is pulled up and back into a tight braid.

Beside her flies a sprite with grasshopper-green skin and wings to match. It's only a bit larger than a hummingbird, buzzing through the air restlessly.

The glaistig turns to the winged faerie. "The Prince of Elfhame? How interesting to have royalty so close by..."

My heart thuds dully at *prince*.

"Spoiled, they say," the sprite chirps. "And wild. Far too irresponsible for a throne."

That doesn't sound like the boy I knew, but in the four years since I saw him last, he would have been inducted into all the pleasures of the High Court, would have been served up a surfeit of every imaginable debauched delight. Sycophants and toadies would be so busy vying for his attention that, these days, I wouldn't be allowed close enough to kiss the hem of his cloak.

The sprite departs, darting up and away, thankfully not weaving through the branches of the tree where I crouch. I settle in to observe.

Three people come that night to make wishes. One, a sandy-haired young man I went to fourth grade with, the year before I was taken. His fingers tremble as he ties his scrap of paper to the branch with a bit of twine. The second, an elderly woman with a stooped back. She keeps wiping at her wet eyes, and her note is tearstained by the time she affixes it with a twist tie. The third is a freckled man, broad-shouldered, a baseball cap pulled low enough to hide most of his face.

This is the freckled man's third trip, and at his arrival, the glaistig steps out of the shadows. The man gives a moan of fear. He didn't expect this to be real. They seldom do. They embarrass themselves with their reactions, their terror, the sounds they make.

The glaistig makes him tell her what he wants, even though he's written it three separate times on three separate notes. I don't think she ever bothers to read the wishes.

I do. This man needs money because of some bad business deal. If he doesn't get it, he will lose his house, and then his wife will leave him. He whispers this to the glaistig, fidgeting with his wedding ring as he does so. In return, she gives him her terms—every night for seven months and seven days, he must bring her a cube of fresh human flesh. He may cut it from himself, or from another, whichever he prefers.

He agrees eagerly, desperately, foolishly, and lets her tie an ensorcelled piece of leather around his wrist.

"This was crafted from my own skin," she tells him. "It will let me find you, no matter how you try to hide from me. No mortal-made knife can cut it, and should you fail to do as you have promised, it will tighten until it slices through the veins of your arm."

For the first time, I see panic on his face, the sort that he ought to have felt all along. Too late, and part of him knows it. But he denies it a moment later, the knowledge surfacing and being shoved back down.

Some things seem too terrible to seem possible. Soon he may learn that the worst thing he can imagine is only the beginning of what they are willing to do to him. I recall that realization and hope I can spare him it.

Then the glaistig tells the freckled man to gather leaves. For each one in his pile, he'll get a crisp twenty-dollar bill in its place. He'll have three days to spend the money before it disappears.

In the note he attached to the tree, he wrote that he needed $40,000. That's *two thousand* leaves. The man scrambles to get together a big enough pile, searching desperately through the well-manicured graveyard. He collects some from the stretch of woods along the border and rips handfuls from a few trees with low-hanging branches. Staring at what he assembles, I think of the game they have at fairs, where you guess the number of jelly beans in a jar.

I wasn't good at that game, and I worry he isn't, either.

The glaistig glamours the leaves into money with a bored wave of her hand. Then he's busy stuffing the bills into his pockets. He races after a few the wind takes and whips toward the road.

This seems to amuse the glaistig, but she's wise enough not to hang around to laugh. Better he not realize how thoroughly he's been had. She disappears into the night, drawing her magic to shroud her.

When the man has filled his pockets, he shoves more bills into his shirt, where they settle against his stomach, forming an artificial paunch. As he walks out of the graveyard, I let myself drop silently out of the tree.

I follow him for several blocks, until I see my chance to speed up and grab hold of his wrist. At the sight of me, he screams.

Screams, just like my unmother and unfather.

I flinch at the sound, but the reaction shouldn't surprise me. I know what I look like.

My skin, the pale blue of a corpse. My dress, streaked with moss and mud. My teeth, built for ease of ripping flesh from bone. My ears are pointed, too, hidden beneath matted, dirty blue hair, only slightly darker than my skin. I am no pixie with pretty moth wings. No member of the Gentry, whose beauty makes mortals foolish with desire. Not even a glaistig, who barely needed a glamour if her skirts were long enough.

He tries to pull away, but I am very strong. My sharp teeth make short work of the glaistig's string and her spell. I've never learned to glamour myself well, but in the Court of Teeth I grew skilled at breaking curses. I'd had enough put on me for it to be necessary.

I press a note into the freckled man's hands. The paper is his own, with his wish written on one side. *Take your family and run*, I wrote with one of Bex's Sharpies. *Before you hurt them. And you will.*

He stares after me as I race off, as though I am the monster.

I have seen this particular bargain play out before. Everyone starts out telling themselves that they will pay with their own skin. But seven months and seven days is a long time, and a cube of flesh is a lot to cut from your own body every night. The pain is intense, worse with each new injury. Soon it's easy to justify slicing a bit from those around you. After all, didn't you do this for their sake? From there, things go downhill fast.

I shudder, remembering my own unfamily looking at me in horror and disgust. People who I believed would always love me. It took me the better part of a year to discover that Lord Jarel had *enchanted* their love away, that his spells were the reason he was so certain they wouldn't want me.

Even now, I do not know if the enchantment is still on them.

Nor do I know whether Lord Jarel amplified and exploited their actual horror at the sight of me or created that feeling entirely out of magic.

It is my revenge on Faerie to unravel the glaistig's spells, to undo every curse I discover. Free anyone who is ensnared. It doesn't matter if the man appreciates what I've done. My satisfaction comes at the glaistig's frustration at another human slipping from her net.

I cannot help them all. I cannot prevent them from taking what she offers and paying her price. And the glaistig is hardly the only faerie offering bargains. But I try.

By the time I return to my childhood home, my unfamily has all gone to bed.

I lift the latch and creep through the house. My eyes see well enough in the dark for me to move through the unlit rooms. I go to the couch and press my unmother's half-finished sweater to my cheek, feeling the softness of the wool, breathing in the familiar scent of her. Think of her voice, singing to me as she sat at the end of my bed.

Twinkle, twinkle, little star.

I open the garbage and pick out the remains of their dinner. Bits of gristly steak and gobs of mashed potatoes clump together with scattered pieces of what must have been a salad. It's all mixed in with crumpled-up tissues, plastic wrap, and vegetable peels. I make a dessert of a plum that's mushy on one end and the little bit of jam at the bottom of a jar in the recycling bin.

I gobble the food, trying to imagine that I am sitting at the table with them. Trying to imagine myself as their daughter again, and not what's left of her.

A cuckoo trying to fit back into the egg.

Other humans sensed the wrongness in me as soon as I set foot in the mortal world. That was right after the Battle of the Serpent, when the Court of Teeth had been disbanded and Lady Nore fled. With nowhere else to go, I came here. That first night back, I was discovered by a handful of children in a park who picked up sticks to drive me off. When one of the bigger ones jabbed me, I ran at him, sinking my sharp teeth into the meat of his arm. I opened up his flesh as though he were a tin can.

I do not know what I would do to my unfamily if they pushed me away again. I am no safe thing now. A child no more, but a fully grown monster, like the ones that came for me.

Still, I am tempted to try to break the spell, to reveal myself to them. I am always tempted. But when I think of speaking with my unfamily, I think of the storm hag. Twice, she found me in the woods outside the human town, and twice she hung the strung-up and skinned body of a mortal over my camp. One who she claimed knew too much about the Folk. I don't want to give her a reason to choose one of my unfamily as her next victim.

Upstairs, a door opens and I freeze. I fold up my legs, circling my arms around my knees, trying to make myself as small as possible. A few minutes later, I hear a toilet flush and let myself breathe normally again.

I shouldn't come. I don't always—some nights, I manage to stay far away, eating moss and bugs and drinking from dirty streams. Going through the dumpsters behind restaurants. Breaking spells so that I can believe I'm not like the rest of them.

But I am lured back, again and again. Sometimes I wash the dishes in the sink or move wet clothes to the dryer, like a brownie. Sometimes I steal knives. When I am at my angriest, I rip a few of their things into tiny shreds. Sometimes I doze behind the couch until they all leave for work or school and I can crawl out again. Search through the rooms for scraps of myself, report cards and yarn crafts. Family photos that include a human version of me with my pale hair and pointy chin, my big, hungry eyes. Evidence that my memories are real. In one box marked *Rebecca*, I found my old stuffed fox and wonder how they explained away an entire room of my belongings.

Rebecca goes by Bex now, a new name for her fresh start in college. Despite her probably telling everyone who asks that she's an only child, she's in nearly every good memory I have of being a kid. Bex drinking cocoa in front of the television, squishing marshmallows until her fingers were sticky. Bex and I kicking each other's legs in the car until Mom yelled at us to stop. Bex sitting in her closet, playing action figures with me, holding up Batman to kiss Iron Man and saying: *Let's get them married, and then they can get some cats and live happily ever after.* Imagining myself scrubbed out of those memories makes me grind my teeth and feel even more like a ghost.

Had I grown up in the mortal world, I might be in school with Bex. Or traveling, taking odd jobs, discovering new things. That Wren would take her place in the world for granted, but I can no longer imagine my way into her skin.

Sometimes I sit up on the roof, watching the bats twirl in the moonlight. Or I watch my unfamily sleep, reaching my hand daringly close to my unmother's hair. But tonight, I only eat.

When I am done with the scavenged meal, I go to the sink and stick my head underneath the tap, guzzling the sweet, clear water. After I have my fill, I wipe my mouth with the back of my hand and slip out onto the deck. At the top step, I drink the milk my unsister put out. A bug has fallen in and spins on the surface. I drink that, too.

I am about to slink back into the woods when a long shadow comes from the side yard, its fingers like branches.

Heart racing, I pad down the steps and slide beneath the porch. I make it just moments before Bogdana lopes around the corner of the house. She is every bit as tall and terrifying as I remember her being that first night, and worse, because now I know of what she is capable.

My breath catches. I have to bite down hard on the inside of my cheek to keep quiet and still.

I watch Bogdana drag one of her nails across the sagging aluminum siding. Her fingers are as long as flower stalks, her limbs as spindly as sticks of birch. Weed-like strands of black straight hair hang over her mushroom-pale face, half-hiding tiny eyes that gleam with malice.

She peers in through the glass panes of a window. How easy to push up a sash, to creep in and slit the throats of my unfamily as they sleep, then flense the skins from their bodies.

My fault. If I had been able to stay away, she wouldn't have scented my spoor here. Wouldn't have come. *My fault.*

And now I have two choices. I can stay where I am and listen to them die. Or I can lead her from the house. It's no choice at all, except for the fear that has been my constant companion since I was stolen from the mortal world. Terror seared deep in my marrow.

Deeper than my desire to be safe, though, I want my unfamily to *live.* Even if I no longer belong with them, I need to save them. Were they gone, the last shred of what I was would be gone with them, and I would be set adrift.

Taking a deep, shuddery breath, I kick out from underneath the porch. I run for the road, away from the cover of woods, where she would easily gain on me. I am heedless in my steps across the lawn, ignoring the snapping of twigs beneath my bare feet. The crack of each one carries through the night air.

I do not look back, but I know that Bogdana must have heard me. She must have turned, nostrils flaring, scenting the breeze. Movement draws the eye of the predator. The instinct to chase.

I wince against the headlights of the cars as I hit the sidewalk.

Leaves are tangled into the muddy clots of my hair. My dress—once white—is now a dull and stained color, like the gown one would expect to adorn a ghost. I do not know if my eyes shine like an animal's. I suspect they might.

The storm hag sweeps after me, swift as a crow and certain as doom.

I pump my legs faster.

Sharp bits of gravel and glass dig into my feet. I wince and stumble a little, imagining I can feel the breath of the hag. Terror gives me the strength to shoot forward.

Now that I have drawn her off, I must lose her somehow. If she becomes distracted for even a moment, I can slip away and hide. I got very good at hiding, back at the Court of Teeth.

I turn into an alley. There's a gap in the chain-link fence at the end, small enough for me to wriggle through. I run for it, feet sliding in muck and trash. I hit the fence and press my body into the opening, metal scratching my skin, the stink of iron heavy in the air.

As I race on, I hear the shake of the fence as it's being climbed.

"Stop, you little fool!" the storm hag shouts after me.

Panic steals my thoughts. Bogdana is too fast, too sure. She's been killing mortals and faeries alike since long before I was born. If she summons lightning, I'm as good as dead.

Instinct makes me want to go to my part of the woods. To burrow in the cave-like dome I've woven from willow branches. Lie on my floor of smooth river stones, pressed down into the mud after a rainstorm until they made a surface flat enough to sleep on. Cocoon myself in my three blankets, despite them being moth-eaten, stained, and singed by fire along a corner.

There, I have a carving knife. It is only as long as one of her fingers, but sharp. Better than either of the other little blades I have on my person.

I dart sideways, toward an apartment complex, running through the pools of light. I cut across streets, through the playground, the creak of swing chains loud in my ears.

I have more skill at unraveling enchantments than making them, but since her last visit I warded around my lair so that a dread comes upon anyone who gets too close. Mortals stay away from the place, and even the Folk become uneasy when they come near.

I have little hope that will chase her off, but I have little hope at all.

Bogdana was the one person that Lord Jarel and Lady Nore feared. A hag who could bring on storms, who had lived for countless scores of years, who knew more of magic than most beings alive. I saw her slash open and devour humans in the Court of Teeth and gut a faerie with those long fingers over a perceived insult. I saw lightning flash at her annoyance. It was Bogdana who helped Lord Jarel and Lady Nore with their scheme to conceive a child and hide me away among mortals, and many times she had been witness to my torment in the Court of Teeth.

Lord Jarel and Lady Nore never let me forget that I belonged to them, despite my title as queen. Lord Jarel delighted in leashing me and dragging me around like an animal. Lady Nore punished me ferociously for any imagined slight, until I became a snarling beast, clawing and biting, barely aware of anything but pain.

Once, Lady Nore threw me out into the howling wasteland of snow and barred the castle doors against me.

If being a queen doesn't suit you, worthless child, then find your own fortune, she said.

I walked for days. There was nothing to eat but ice, and I could hear nothing but the cold wind blowing around me. When I wept, the tears froze on my cheeks. But I kept on going, hoping against hope that I might find someone to help me or some way to escape. On the seventh day, I discovered I had only gone in a great circle.

It was Bogdana who wrapped me in a cloak and carried me inside after I collapsed in the snow.

The hag carried me to my room, with its walls of ice, and set me down on the skins of my bed. She touched my brow with fingers twice as long as fingers ought to be. Looked down at me with her black eyes, shook her head of wild, storm-tossed hair. "You will not always be so small or so frightened," she told me. "You are a queen."

The way the hag said those words made me raise my head. She made the title sound as though it was something of which I ought to be proud.

When the Court of Teeth ventured south, to war with Elfhame, Bogdana did not come with us. I thought to never see her again and was sorry for it. If there was one of them who might have looked out for me, it was her.

Somehow that makes it worse that she's the one at my heels, the one hunting me through the streets.

When I hear the hag's footfalls draw close, I grit my teeth and try for a burst of speed. My lungs are already aching, my muscles sore.

Perhaps, I try to tell myself, perhaps I can reason with her. Perhaps she is chasing me only because I ran.

I make the mistake of glancing back and lose the rhythm of my stride. I falter as the hag reaches out a long hand toward me, her knife-sharp nails ready to slice.

No, I don't think I can reason with her.

There is only one thing left to do, and so I do it, whirling around. I snap my teeth in the air, recalling sinking them into flesh. Remembering how good it felt to hurt someone who scared me.

I am not stronger than Bogdana. I am neither faster nor more cunning. But it's possible I am more desperate. I want to live.

The hag draws up short. At my expression, she takes a step toward me, and I hiss. There is something in her face, glittering in her black eyes, that I do not understand. It looks triumphant. I reach for one of the little blades beneath my dress, wishing again for the carving knife.

The one I pull out is folded, and I fumble trying to open it.

I hear the clop of a pair of hooves, and I think that somehow it is the glaistig, come to watch me be taken. Come to gloat. She must have been the one to alert Bogdana to what I was doing; she must be the reason this is happening.

But it is not the glaistig who emerges from the darkness of the woods. A young man with goat feet and horns, wearing a shirt of golden scale mail and holding a thin-bladed rapier, steps into the pool of light near a building. His face is expressionless, like someone in a dream.

I note the curls of his tawny blond hair tucked behind his pointed ears, the garnet-colored cloak tossed over wide shoulders, the scar along one side of his throat, a circlet at his brow. He moves as though he expects the world to bend to his will.

Above us, clouds are gathering. He points his sword toward Bogdana.

Then his gaze flickers to me. "You've led us on a merry chase." His amber eyes are bright, like those of a fox, but there is nothing warm in them.

I could have told him not to look away from Bogdana. The hag sees the opening and goes for him, nails poised to rip open his chest.

Another sword stops her before he needs to parry. This one is held in the gloved hand of a knight. He wears armor of sculpted brown leather banded with wide strips of a silvery metal. His blackberry hair is cropped short, and his dark eyes are wary.

"Storm hag," he says.

"Out of my way, lapdog," she tells the knight. "Or I will call down lightning to strike you where you stand."

"You may command the sky," the horned man in the golden scale mail returns. "But, alas, we are here on the ground. Leave, or my friend will run you through before you summon so much as a drizzle."

Bogdana narrows her eyes and turns toward me. "I will come for you again, child," she says. "And when I do, you best not run."

Then she moves into the shadows. As soon as she does, I try to dash to one side of him, intent on escape.

The horned man seizes hold of my arm. He's stronger than I expect him to be.

"Lady Suren," he says.

I growl deep in my throat and catch him with my nails, raking them down his cheek. Mine are nowhere near as long or sharp as Bogdana's, but he still bleeds.

He makes a hiss of pain but doesn't let go. Instead, he wrenches my wrists behind my back and holds them tight, no matter how I snarl or kick. Worse, the light hits his face at a different angle and I finally recognize whose skin is under my fingernails.

Prince Oak, heir to Elfhame. Son of the traitorous Grand General and brother to the mortal High Queen. Oak, to whom I was once promised in marriage. Who had once been my friend, although he doesn't seem to remember it.

What was it the pixie had said about him? *Spoiled, irresponsible*, and *wild*. I believe it. Despite his gleaming armor, he is so poorly trained in swordplay that he didn't even attempt to block my blow.

But after that thought comes another one: I have *struck* the Prince of Elfhame.

Oh, I am in trouble now.

"Things will be much easier if you do exactly as we tell you from this moment forward, daughter of traitors," the dark-eyed knight in the leather armor informs me. He has a long nose and the look of someone more comfortable saluting than smiling.

I open my mouth to ask what they want with me, but my voice is rough with disuse. The words come out garbled, the sounds not the ones I intended.

"What's the matter with her?" he asks, frowning at me as though I am some sort of insect.

"Living wild, I suppose," says the prince. "Away from people."

"Didn't she at least talk to herself?" the knight asks, raising his eyebrows.

I growl again.

Oak brings his fingers to the side of his face and draws them back with a wince. He has three long slashes there, bleeding sluggishly.

When his gaze returns to me, there's something in his expression that reminds me of his father, Madoc, who was never so happy as when he went to war.

"I told you that nothing good ever came out of the Court of Teeth," says the knight, shaking his head. Then he takes a rope and ties it around my wrists, looping it through the middle to make it secure. He doesn't pierce my skin like Lord Jarel used to, leashing me by stabbing a needle threaded with a silver chain between the bones of my arms. I am not yet in pain.

But I do not doubt that I will be.

CHAPTER

2

As I trudge through the woods, I think about how I will escape. I have no illusions that I won't be punished. I *struck the prince*. And if they knew about the curses I've been unraveling, they'd be even more furious.

"Next time you'll remember not to drop your guard," the knight says, observing the wounds on Oak's cheek.

"My vanity took the worst of the blow," he says.

"Worried about your pretty face?" the knight asks.

"There *is* too little beauty in the world," says the prince airily. "But that is not my area of greatest conceit."

It can't be coincidence that they turned up clad in armor and prepared to fight at nearly the same time Bogdana started poking around my unfamily's home. They were all looking for me, and whatever the reason, it cannot be one I will like.

I breathe in the familiar scent of wet bark and kicked-up leaf mold. The ferns are silvery in the moonlight, the woods full of shifting shadows.

I wriggle my wrists experimentally. Unfortunately, I am tied well. Flexing my fingers, I try to slip one underneath the binding, but the knots are even too tight for that.

The knight snorts. "Not sure this is the luckiest start to a quest. If the hob hadn't spotted your little queen here, that hag might be wearing her skin for a coat."

The owl-faced hob. I grimace, not certain whether I ought to be grateful. I have no idea what they mean to do to me.

"Isn't that the very definition of luck—to have arrived in time?" Oak throws a mischief-filled glance in my direction, as though at some feral animal he wonders if it would be fun to tame.

I think of him in the High Court, as I was about to be sentenced for my crimes as queen of the traitorous Court of Teeth. I was eleven, and he'd just turned nine. I was bound then, as now. I think of him at thirteen, when he met me in the woods and I sent him away.

At seventeen, he has grown tall, towering over me, lithe and finely muscled. His hair catches the moonlight, warm gold threaded with platinum, bangs parting around small goat horns, eyes of shocking amber, and a constellation of freckles across his nose. He has a trickster's mouth and the swagger of someone used to people doing what he wanted.

Faerie beauty is different from mortal beauty. It's elemental, extravagant. There are creatures in Faerie of such surpassing comeliness that they're painful to look at. Ones that possess a loveliness so great that mortals weep at the sight of them or become transfixed, haunted by the desire to see them even once more. Maybe even die on the spot.

Ugliness in Faerie can be equally extravagant. There are those among the Folk so hideous that all living things shrink back in horror. And yet others have a grotesquerie so exaggerated, so voluptuous, that it comes all the way around to beauty.

It isn't that mortals can't be pretty—many of them are—but their beauty doesn't make you feel pummeled by it. I feel a little pummeled by Oak's beauty.

If I look at him too long, I want to take a bite out of him.

I turn my gaze to my muddy feet, scratched and sore, then Oak's hooves. I recall from a stolen school science book that hooves are made from the same stuff that makes up fingernails. Keratin. Above them, a dusting of fur the same color as his hair disappears into a pant cuff hitting just below his knees, revealing the odd curve of his lower legs. Slim-fitting trousers cover his thighs.

I shiver with the force of keeping myself from thrashing against my bindings.

"Are you cold?" he asks, offering his cloak. It's embroidered velvet, with a pattern of acorns, leaves, and branches. It's beautifully stitched and looks wildly out of place this far from Elfhame.

This is a pantomime I am familiar with. The performance of gallantry while keeping me in restraints, as though the chill in the air is what I am most worried about. But I suppose this is how princes are expected to behave. Noblesse oblige and all that.

Since my hands are tied, I am not sure how he expects me to put it on. When I say nothing, he drapes it over my shoulders, then ties it at my throat. I let him, even though I am used to the cold. Better to have something than not, and it's soft.

Also, it hangs over my hands, shielding them from view. Which means that if I *do* manage to get my wrists loose from the knots, no one will know until it's too late.

That's twice he's been foolish.

I try to concentrate on escape and on not allowing hopelessness to sweep over me. Were my hands free, I would still need to get away. But if I did, I think I could prevent them from tracking me. The knight may have been taught how to follow a trail, but I have had years of experience obscuring mine.

Oak's skills—if he has any outside of being a lordling—are unknown to me. It's possible that despite all his big talk and his pedigree, the prince has brought the knight along to make sure he doesn't trip and impale himself on his own fancy sword.

If they leave me alone for a moment, I can bring my arms down and step backward through the circle of them, bringing my bound hands to the front of my body. Then I'd chew through the rope.

I cannot think of any reason they will give me that chance. Still, under cover of Oak's cloak, I fidget with my bindings, trying to stretch them as far as I am able.

When we depart the woods, we step onto an unfamiliar street. The houses are farther apart than in my unfamily's neighborhood and more run-down, their lawns overgrown. In the distance, a dog is barking.

Then I am guided onto a dirt road. At the very end is a deserted house with boarded-up windows and grass so tall a mower might choke on it. Outside stand two bone-white faerie steeds, the gentle curve of their necks longer than those of mortal horses.

"There?" I ask. The word comes out clearly enunciated, even if my voice still sounds rough.

"Too filthy for Your Highness?" the knight asks, raising his brows at me as though I am unaware of the dirt on my dress and mud on my feet. As though I don't know I am no longer a queen, that I do not remember Oak's sister disbanding my Court.

I hunch my shoulders. I'm used to word games like this one, where there is no right answer and every wrong answer leads to punishment. I keep my mouth shut, my gaze going to the scratches on the prince's cheek. I have made enough mistakes already.

"Ignore Tiernan. It's not so awful inside," Oak says, giving me a courtier's smile, the kind that's supposed to convince you it's okay to relax your guard. I tense up even further. I have learned to be afraid of smiles like that. He continues, with a wave of one hand. "And then we can explain the necessity for our being so wretchedly impolite."

Impolite. That was one way to refer to tying me up.

The knight—*Tiernan*—opens the door by leaning his shoulder against it. We go inside, Oak behind me so there's no hope of running. The warped wooden floorboards groan beneath the tread of his hooves.

The house has obviously been empty for a long time. Graffiti sprawls across floral wallpaper, and a cabinet under the sink has been ripped out, probably to get at any copper pipes. Tiernan guides me toward a cracked plastic table that's in a corner of the kitchen along with a few scuffed-looking chairs.

In one is a soldier with a wing where an arm ought to be, light brown skin, a long fall of mahogany hair, and eyes the startling purple of monkshood. I do not know him, but I think I know the curse. Oak's sister, the High Queen, had the unrepentant soldiers who followed Madoc turned into falcons after the Battle of the Serpent. They were cursed so that if they wanted to return to their true forms, they couldn't hunt for a year and a day, eating only what they were given. I do not know what it means that he seems *half*-cursed now. If I squint, I can see the trailing threads of magic around him, winding and coiling like roots trying to regrow.

No easy spell to unmake.

And against his mouth, I see the thin leather straps and golden fastenings of a bridle. A shudder of recognition goes through me. I know *that*, too.

Created by the great smith Grimsen, and given to my parents.

Lord Jarel placed that bridle on me long ago, when my will was an inconvenience to be cleared away like a cobweb. Seeing the bridle brings back all the panic and dread and helplessness I'd felt as the straps slowly sank into my skin.

Later, he'd tried to use it to trap the High King and Queen. He failed and it fell into their hands, but I am horrified that Oak would have made a prisoner wear it, casually, as though it were nothing.

"Tiernan *captured* him outside your mother's Citadel. We needed to know her plans, and he's been immensely helpful. Unfortunately, he's also immensely dangerous." Oak is speaking, but it's hard to see anything but the bridle. "She has a motley crew of vassals. And she has stolen something—"

"More than one something," says the bridled former falcon.

Tiernan kicks the leg of the falcon's chair, but the falcon only smiles up at him. They can make that bridled soldier do anything, say anything. He is trapped inside himself far more securely than he could be bound by any rope. I admire his defiance, however useless.

"Vassals?" I echo the prince's statement, my voice scratchy.

"She has reclaimed the Citadel of the Court of Teeth and, since that Court is no more, has made a new one," Oak says, raising his brows.

"And she has an old magic. She can *create* things. From what we understand, mostly creatures from twigs and wood, but also parts of the dead."

"How?" I ask, horrified.

"Does it matter?" Tiernan says. "*You* were supposed to keep her under control."

I hope he can see the hate in my eyes. Just because the High Queen forced Lady Nore to swear fealty to me after the battle, just because I *could* command her, didn't mean I'd had the first idea of what to actually do.

"She was a kid, Tiernan," Oak says, surprising me. "As was I."

A few embers glow in the fireplace. Tiernan huffs and moves to kneel beside it. He adds logs from a pile, along with balled-up pages he rips from an already-torn cookbook. The edge of a page catches, and flames blaze up. "You'd be a fool to trust the former queen of the Court of Teeth."

"Are you so sure you know our allies from our enemies?" Oak takes out a long stick from the pile of wood, thin enough to be kindling. He holds it in the fire until the end sparks. Then he uses it to light the wicks of candles set around the room. Soon warm pools of light flicker, making the shadows shift.

Tiernan's gaze strays to the bridled soldier. It rests there a long moment before he turns to me. "Hungry, little queen?"

"Don't call me that," I rasp.

"Grouchy, are we?" Tiernan asks. "How would you like this poor servant to address you?"

"Wren," I say, ignoring the taunt.

Oak watches the interaction with half-lidded eyes. I cannot guess at his thoughts. "And do you desire repast?"

I shake my head. The knight raises his eyebrows skeptically. After a moment, he turns away and takes out a kettle, already blackened by fire, and fills it from the tap in the bathroom sink. Then he hangs it on a prop stick they must have rigged up. No electricity, but the house still has running water.

For the first time in a very long while, I think about a shower. About how my hair felt when it was combed and detangled, my scalp spared from the itch of drying mud.

Oak walks to where I am sitting, my tied wrists forcing my shoulders back.

"Lady Wren," he says, amber eyes like those of a fox meeting mine directly. "If I undo your bindings, may I rely upon you to neither attempt escape nor attack one of us for the duration of our time in this house?"

I nod once.

The prince gives me a quick, conspiratorial grin. My mouth betrays me into returning the smile. It makes me recall how charming he was, even as a child.

I wonder if somehow I have misread this situation, if somehow we could be on the same side.

Oak takes a knife from a wrist guard hidden beneath his white linen shirt and applies it to the rope behind me.

"Don't cut it," the knight warns. "Or we'll have to get new rope, and we may have to restrain her again."

I tense, expecting Oak to be angry at being told what to do. As royalty, it is out of order for him to be directed by someone of lower status, but the prince only shakes his head. "Worry no more. I'm only using the point of my blade to help me pry apart your too-clever knots."

I study Tiernan in the half light of the fire. It is hard to gauge age among the Folk, but he looks to be only a little older than Oak. His blackberry hair is mussed; one of his pointed ears has a single piercing through it, a silver hoop.

I bring my hands to my lap, rubbing my fingers over the indentations the rope left in my skin. Had I not been straining so hard against the bindings, they wouldn't be half so deep.

Oak puts the knife away and then says with great formality, "My lady, Elfhame requires your assistance."

Tiernan looks up from the fire but does not speak.

I don't know how to reply. I am unused to attention and find myself flustered to be the focus of his. "I have already sworn fealty to your sister," I manage to croak out. I wouldn't be alive if I hadn't. "I am hers to command."

He frowns. "Let me try to explain. Months before the Battle of the Serpent, Lady Nore managed to cause an explosion underneath the castle."

I glance over at the former falcon, wondering if he was part of it. Wondering if I should remember him. Some of my memories of that time are terribly vivid, while others are blotted out like ink running over paper.

"At the time, it was thought to be an attack on Elfhame's spies and a coincidence that Queen Mab's resting place was disturbed." Oak pauses, watching me as though he's trying to determine if I am following along. "Most faerie bodies break down into roots and flowers, but Mab's did not. Her remains, from her ribs to her finger bones, were imbued with a power that kept them from crumbling—a power to bring things to life. That's what Lady Nore stole, and that's what she's drawing her new power from."

The prince gestures toward the bridled soldier. "Lady Nore has attempted to recruit more Folk to her cause. For those who were cursed to be falcons, if they come to her Citadel, she offers to feed them from her own hand for the year and a day during which they are forbidden from hunting. And when they return to their original form, she demands their loyalty. Between them, her own Folk who remained loyal to her, and the monsters she's making, her plans for revenge on Elfhame seem well under way."

I look at the prisoner. The High Queen granted clemency to any soldier who repudiated what they'd done and swore fealty to her. Anyone who repented. But he'd refused.

I recall standing before the High Queen myself the night Oak spoke on my behalf. *Remember when you said we couldn't help her. We can help her now.* Pity in his voice.

I'd bragged to the High Queen that I knew all Lady Nore and Lord Jarel's secrets, hoping to be useful, thinking that since they spoke in front of me heedlessly, treating me as a dumb animal instead of a little girl, they'd kept nothing back. Still, they'd never spoken of this. "I can't recall any mention of Mab's bones."

Oak gives me a long look. "You lived in the Ice Needle Citadel for more than a year, so you must know its layout, *and* you can command Lady Nore. You're her greatest vulnerability. No matter her other plans, she has good reason to want to eliminate you."

I shudder at that thought because it should have occurred to me before now. I remember Bogdana's long nails, the panic of her chasing me through the streets.

"We need you to stop her," Oak says. "And you need our help to fend off whomever she sends to kill you."

I hate that he's right.

"Did you make Lady Nore promise you anything before she left Elf-hame?" Tiernan asks hopefully.

I shake my head, looking away in shame. As soon as she was able, Lady Nore slipped off. I never had a chance to tell her anything. And when I realized she was gone, what I felt had been mostly relief.

I think of the words she swore before the High Queen, when Jude demanded she give me her vow: *I, Lady Nore, of the Court of Teeth, vow to follow Suren and obey her commands.* Nothing about not sticking a dagger in my back, unfortunately. Nothing about not sending a storm hag after me.

Tiernan frowns, as though my failing to give Lady Nore any orders has confirmed his suspicion that I am untrustworthy. He turns to Oak. "You know the grudge Lady Nore bears against Madoc, justified or not. Who knows what slights *this one* won't forget."

"Let's not discuss my father right at the moment," Oak returns.

Madoc, the traitor who marched on Elfhame with the Court of Teeth. Before that, the Grand General who was responsible for the slaughter of most of the royal family. And Oak's foster father.

Madoc had sought to put Oak on the throne, where he could rule through him. Though the crown would have rested on Oak's head, all the power would have belonged to the redcap. At least until Lord Jarel and Lady Nore tricked Madoc and took over.

I know how precarious it is to be a queen without power, controlled and thoroughly debased. That could have been Oak's fate. But if the prince bears his father any ill will, it doesn't show on his face.

Tiernan leans forward to take the metal kettle off the prop stick with a poker, setting it gingerly on a folded-up towel. It steams steadily.

Then he takes out several foam containers of instant ramen from a kitchen cabinet, along with an already-opened box of mint tea. Noticing me looking, he nods toward Oak. "The prince introduced me to this delicacy of the mortal world. Bollockses up your magic for a while—all that salt—but I can't deny it is addictive."

The smell makes me recall the satisfaction of something burn-your-mouth hot, something straight from an oven instead of congealed in a garbage bin.

I don't take one of the noodle cups, but when Oak hands me a mug of tea, I accept that. I stare into the depths and see silt at the bottom. *Sugar*, he would tell me if I asked, and at least some of it would be, but I can't be sure the rest isn't a drug of some kind, or a poison.

They do not want me dead, I try to tell myself. *They need me.*

And I need them, too, if I want to live. If Lady Nore is hunting me, if Bogdana is helping her, the prince and his companion are my only hope of staying out of reach.

"So, what would you have me to do?" I am proud to get the whole sentence out without my voice cracking.

"Go north with me," Oak says, sitting on the plastic chair beside mine. "Command Lady Nore to tie a big bow around herself and make a present to Elfhame. We'll steal back Mab's bones and end the threat to—"

"With *you*?" I stare at him, sure I have misunderstood. Princes stay in palaces, enjoying revels and debauchery and the like. Their necks are too valuable to risk.

"And my brave friend Tiernan." Oak inclines his head toward Tiernan, who rolls his eyes. "Together, the four of us—counting Hyacinthe—will take back the Citadel and end the threat to Elfhame."

Hyacinthe. So that's the cursed soldier's name.

"And when we complete our quest, you can ask a boon of me, and if it is within my power and not too terrible, I will grant it." I wonder at the prince's motive. Perhaps ambition. If he delivers Lady Nore, he could ask a boon of his own from the High King and cement his position as heir, effectively cutting any future children out of the line of succession.

I can imagine a prince might do a lot for an unwavering path to the throne. One that by some accounts should have been his in the first place.

And yet, I cannot help thinking of the sprite saying he would be unsuitable as a ruler. Too spoiled. Too wild.

Of course, since she's a companion of the glaistig and the glaistig is awful, perhaps what she thinks shouldn't matter.

Tiernan takes out a wooden scroll case carved with a pattern of vines. It contains a map, which he unfurls on the table. Oak weighs down the edges with teacups, spoons, and a brick that might have been thrown through one of the windows. "First we must go a ways south," the prince says. "To a hag who will give us a piece of information that I hope will help us trick Lady Nore. Then we head north and east, over water, into the Howling Pass, through the Forest of Stone, to her stronghold."

"A small group is nimble," Tiernan says. "Easier to hide. Even if I think crossing through the Stone Forest is a fool's notion."

Oak traces the route up the coast with a finger and gives us a roguish grin. "I am the fool with that notion."

Neither seems inclined to tell me more about the hag, or the trickery she is supposed to inspire.

I stare at the path, and at its destination. The Ice Needle Citadel. I suppose it is still there, gleaming in the sun as though made of spun sugar. Hot glass.

The Stone Forest *is* dangerous. The trolls living there belong to no Court, recognize no authority but their own, and the trees seem to move of their own accord. But everything is dangerous now.

My gaze goes to Hyacinthe, noting his bird wing and the bridle sinking into his cheeks. If Oak leaves it on him long enough, it will become part of him, invisible and unable to be removed. He will forever be in the prince's thrall.

The last time I wore it, Lady Nore and Lord Jarel's plan to move against the High Court was the only reason they cut the bridle's straps from my skin, leaving the scars that still run along my cheekbones. Leaving me with the knowledge of what they would do to me if I disobeyed them.

Then they marched me before the High Queen and suggested that I be united in marriage with her brother and heir, Prince Oak.

It is hard to explain the savagery of hope.

I thought she might agree. At least two of Oak's sisters were mortal, and while I knew it was foolish, I couldn't help thinking that being mortal meant they would be kind. Maybe an alliance would suit everyone, and then I would have escaped the Court of Teeth. I kept my face as blank as possible. If Lady Nore and Lord Jarel thought the idea pleased me, they would have found a way to turn it to torment.

Oak was lounging on a cushion beside his sister's feet. No one seemed to expect him to act with any kind of formal decorum. At the mention of marriage, he looked up at me and flinched.

His eldest sister's lip curled slightly, as though she found the thought of me even coming near him repulsive. *Oak shouldn't have anything to do with these people or their creepy daughter*, she said.

In that moment, I hated him for being so precious to them, for being cosseted and treated as though he was deserving of protection when I had none.

Maybe I still hate him a little. But he was kind when we were children. It's possible there's a part of him that's still kind.

Oak could always remove the bridle from Hyacinthe. As he might, if he decides he wants to put it on *me*. If I am Lady Nore's greatest vulnerability, then he might well consider me a weapon too valuable to chance letting slip away.

It is too great a risk to think of a prince as so kind that he wouldn't.

But even if he wouldn't use the bridle to control me, or invoke his sister's authority, I still have to go north and face Lady Nore. If I don't, she will send the storm hag again or some other monster, and they will end me. Oak and Tiernan are my best chance at surviving for long enough to stop her, and they are my only chance at getting close enough to command her.

"Yes," I say, as though there was ever a choice. My voice doesn't break this time. "I'll go with you."

After all, Lady Nore ripped away everything I cared about. It will give me no small pleasure to do the same to her.

But that doesn't mean that I don't know that, no matter how courteously they behave, I am as much a prisoner as the winged soldier. I can command Lady Nore, but the Prince of Elfhame has the authority to command me.

CHAPTER

3

The night after Madoc, Lady Nore, and Lord Jarel failed to arrange our marriage, Oak snuck to the edge of where Madoc's traitorous army and the Court of Teeth had made camp. There, he found me staked to a post like a goat.

He was perhaps nine, and I, ten. I snarled at him. I remember that.

I thought he was looking for his father and that he was a fool. Madoc seemed the sort to roast him over a fire, consume his flesh, and call it love. By then, I had become familiar with love of that kind.

He looked upset at the sight of me. He ought to have been taught better than to let his emotions show on his face. Instead, he assumed that others would *care* about his feelings, so he didn't bother to hide them.

I wondered what would happen if, when he got close enough, I pinned him to the ground. If I beat him to death with a rock, I might be rewarded by Lord Jarel and Lady Nore, but it seemed equally likely that I would be punished.

And I didn't want to hurt him. He was the first child I'd met since coming to Faerie. I was curious.

"I have food with me," he said, coming closer and taking a bundle out of a pack he wore over one shoulder. "In case you're hungry."

I was always hungry. Here in the camp, I mostly filled my belly by eating moss and sometimes dirt.

He unwrapped an embroidered napkin on the ground—one made of spider silk finer than anything I wore—to reveal roasted chicken and plums. Then he moved away. Allowing me space to feed, as though he were the frightening one.

I glanced at the nearby tents and the woods, at the banked fire a few feet away, embers still glowing. There were voices, but distant ones, and I knew from long experience that while Lord Jarel and Lady Nore were out, no one would check on me, even if I screamed.

My stomach growled. I wanted to snatch the food, though his kindness was jarring and made me wonder what he'd want in return for it. I was used to tricks, to games.

I stared at him, noting the sturdiness of his body, solid in a way that spoke of having enough to eat and running outside. At the alienness of the little goat horns cutting through his soft bronze-and-gold curls and the strange amber of his eyes. At the ease with which he sat, faun legs crossed, hooved feet tipped in covers of beaten gold.

A woolen cloak of deep green was clasped at his throat, long enough to sit on. Underneath, he wore a brown tunic with golden buttons and knee-length trousers, stopping just above where his goat legs curved. I could not think of a single thing I had that he could want.

"It's not poisoned," he said, as though that was my worry.

Temptation won out. I grabbed a wing, tearing at the flesh. I ate it down to the bone, which I cracked so I could get at the marrow. He watched in fascination.

"My sisters were telling fairy tales," Oak said. "They fell asleep, but I didn't."

That explained *nothing* about his reasons for coming here, but his words gave me a strange, sharp pain in my chest. After a moment, I recognized it as envy. For having sisters. For having stories.

"Do you talk?" he asked, and I realized how long I'd been silent. I had been a shy child in the mortal world, and in Faerie nothing good had ever come from my speaking.

"Not much," I admitted, and when he smiled, I smiled back.

"Do you want to play a game?" He shuffled closer, eyes bright. Reaching into his pocket, he produced some little metal figures. Three silver foxes resting in the middle of his callused palm. Inset chips of peridot sparkled in their eyes.

I stared at him in confusion. Had he really come all this way to sit in the dirt and show me his toys? Maybe he hadn't seen another kid in a while, either.

I picked up one of the foxes to examine it. The detail work was very fine. "How do we play?"

"You throw them." He formed a cage of his hands with the foxes inside, shook it up, and then tossed them into the grass. "If they land standing, you get ten points. If they land on their backs, you get five points. If they land on their side, no points."

His landed: two lying on their sides, and one on its back.

I reached out eagerly. I wanted to hold those foxes, feel them fall from my fingers.

When they did and two landed on their backs, I gasped in delight.

Over and over, we played the game. We made tally marks in the dirt.

For a while, there was only the joy of escaping from where I was and who I was. But then I remembered that as little as he might want from me, there was plenty I needed.

"Let's play for stakes," I proposed.

He looked intrigued. "What will you bet?"

I was not so foolish as to ask for anything much that first time. "If you lose, you tell me a secret. Any secret. And I will do the same for you."

We played, and I lost.

He leaned in, close enough for me to smell the sage and rosemary his clothes had been wrapped with before he wore them, close enough to bite out a chunk of flesh from his throat.

"I grew up in the mortal lands," I said.

"I've been there." He seemed amused to discover we had something in common. "And eaten pizza."

It was hard to imagine a prince of Faerie journeying to the human world for anything but a sinister reason, but eating pizza didn't seem that sinister.

We played again, and this time he lost. His smile dimmed, and he dropped his voice to a whisper. "This is a *real secret*. You can't tell any-one. When I was little, I glamoured my mortal sister. I made her hit herself, a lot of times, over and over, and I laughed while she did. It was awful of me, and I never told her that I regretted it. I am afraid of making her remember. She might get really mad."

I wondered which sister he'd glamoured. I hoped not the one who sat on a throne now, his life in her hands.

His words stood as a reminder, though, that no matter how soft he seemed or how young, he was as capable of cruelty as the rest. But cruel or not, his help could still be won. My gaze went to the stake to which I was bound. "This time, if my score is better, you cut the rope and free me. If *your* score is better, you can . . . ask me to do something, anything, and I will."

A desperate bargain for me, but hope had made me reckless.

He frowned. "If I free you," he said, "what happens then?"

He must have wondered if I had been tied here because I was *dangerous*. Maybe he wondered if, once free, I would run at him and hurt him. I supposed he was not so stupid after all. But if he wanted me to swear myself into his service, I could not.

All Courts pledge fealty to their ruler and that ruler pledges fealty to the High Court. When High King Cardan came to power, because I was hidden, and Queen of the Court of Teeth, my failure to give him an oath of loyalty was the reason Lady Nore and Lord Jarel were able to betray him. They would kill me on the spot if I pledged myself to anyone, because I would have become useless to them.

"We can go to the palace, and you can show me your other games," I told him. I would hide there for as long as I could, perhaps long enough to get away from Lady Nore and Lord Jarel.

He nodded. "You toss first."

I cupped the foxes in my hand and whispered to them softly. "Please."

They fell, one on its back, one standing, and one on its side. A total of fifteen points. Good, but not great.

Oak picked them up, shook, and tossed. They all fell on their feet. Thirty points.

He laughed and clapped his hands. "Now you have to do whatever I want!"

I thought of what he'd made his sister do for his amusement and shuddered. At that moment the secret he'd told me seemed less a confession and more a warning.

"Well?" I growled.

Oak frowned, clearly trying to think of something. Then his brow cleared, and I dreaded what was to come next.

"Sing a song," he said with a wicked smile.

I glanced over at the camp in panic. "They'll hear," I protested.

He shook his head, still grinning. "You can sing quietly. And we've been talking all this time. It doesn't have to be any louder than that."

My mind went blank. Only perhaps a year before, my unsister and I were dancing around the house to songs from movies with brave princesses, but at that moment I could think of none of their words. All I could recall were bloodthirsty ballads from the Court of Teeth. But when I opened my mouth, the tune was from a song my unmother had sung when she was putting me to bed. And the lyrics were a mishmash of the two.

"*Sing a song of sixpence,*" I sang as softly as I could. "*Pocket full of snakes. If they take my head off, that'll cure my aches.*"

Oak laughed as though my song was actually funny and not just some weird, grim doggerel. But however poorly done, my debt was paid, which meant I had another chance to win my freedom.

I grabbed up the foxes to play again before he could change the stakes.

Mine landed with one standing, two on their sides. Five measly, stupid, useless points. Nearly impossible to win with. I wanted to kick the figurines into the dirt, to throw them at Oak. I would owe him twice over and still have nothing. I could feel the old burn of tears behind my eyes, the taste of salt in my mouth. I was an unlucky child, ill-fated and—

On Oak's toss, the foxes all landed on their sides for zero points.

I caught my breath and stared at him. I won. *I won.*

He didn't seem disappointed to have to pay the forfeit. He got up with a grin and took out a knife from a sheath I hadn't noticed, hidden in the sleeve of his shirt. The blade was small and leaf-shaped, its handle chased in gold, its edge sharp.

It barely parted the strands of the heavy rope, though, each one taking minutes of sawing to slice through. I had tried my own teeth on them before, with little success, but I hadn't realized how tough they really were.

"There's some kind of enchantment on this," he said, frustrated.

"Cut faster," I said, and received an annoyed look.

My fingers vibrated with the tension of waiting. Before he was a quarter of the way through, the thunder of horses and the rattle of a carriage made me realize that my win had come too late. Lady Nore and Lord Jarel were returning to camp. And they would check to make certain I was where they'd left me. Oak began to hack at the rope frantically, but I knew escape was impossible.

"Go," I told him, disappointment bitter in my mouth.

He caught hold of my hand, pressing one of the silver foxes into my palm. "I'll come back tomorrow," he said. "I promise."

I sucked in my breath at that casually given vow. Faeries couldn't break their promises, so I had no choice but to believe him.

The next night the entire Court of Teeth was preparing for what Lord Jarel had announced with great smugness was to be a celebratory feast. The mortal High Queen had agreed to accept the bridle, along with their offer of a truce. I had been given a dress and told not to get it dirty, so I stood rather than sat on the ground.

I worried that Oak wouldn't get there in time to keep me from being carted off to the feast. I was dreaming up ways to beseech him at the castle when he emerged from the woods. He dragged a sword behind him, too long to wear at his side. It made me recall that he'd jumped in front of his mother when the serpent king darted toward her, a prince from a fairy tale facing down a dragon. He might have been soft and cherished, but he could be brave.

Oak winked at me, and I wondered if he was brave because he didn't understand the danger he was in.

I glanced at the camp, then at him, widening my eyes in warning. But he came to my side anyway, drew the sword, and started to saw away at my bindings.

"The sword's name is Nightfell," he whispered. "It belongs to Jude."

His sister. The High Queen. It was such a different way to be royal, to have a family that you would consider by their relationship to you before their title. Whose weapon you wouldn't be afraid to steal.

The blade was sharp and must have been well made, since it sliced through the enchanted rope much faster than the little knife.

"Her human father was a blacksmith," he went on. "He forged the sword before she was born."

"Where is he now?" I wondered if she had her own unfamily somewhere.

"Madoc killed him." Oak's tone made it sound as though he was aware that was *bad*, but not *so bad* that his sister would bear a grudge. I don't know what I ought to have expected; Oak might make an exception for his sisters, might have enjoyed the pizza, but that didn't mean he thought much of mortal lives.

My gaze went in the direction of the main camp, where Madoc's tent would be. Inside, he'd be preparing for the banquet. Preparing to trick Jude, his foster daughter, whose sword this was and whose father he'd slain. Oak seemed to be laboring under the illusion that Madoc cared about him enough that Oak would be safe if he got caught, but I doubted that was the case.

The last strand of rope parted, and I was free, although it still braceleted my leg.

"They'll be traveling to the banquet," I whispered. "They might spot us."

He took my hand and pulled me toward the woods. "Then we better go fast. Come on, we can hide in my room."

Together, we ran through the mossy forest, past white trees with red leaves and streams holding pale-eyed nixies that watched us as we went by.

This felt a little bit like one of Lady Nore and Lord Jarel's games. Sometimes they would act in a way that suggested affection, then behave as though they had never felt anything but disgust. Leave out something I desperately desired—food, a key to a room in the Citadel where I might hide, a storybook to hide with—and then punish me for taking it.

But I ran anyway. And clutched his fingers as though he could drag me into a world where other kinds of games were possible. Hope lit my heart.

We slowed at certain points when we spotted another one of the Folk. This far from the camp of the Court of Teeth, the soldiers we were avoiding belonged to Elfhame. That did little to reassure me, though. No harm would come to Oak at their hands, but they might well lock me up in their dungeons or take me to their Tower of Forgetting.

At the palace, we passed our first set of guards. They bowed to Oak, and if they were surprised to see him with another child trailing a piece of dirty rope, they kept it to themselves. The palace of Elfhame was a grassy hill, set with windows. Inside, there were stone walls, occasionally covered in plaster or packed earth. Nothing like the cold, carved ice chambers of the Citadel. We climbed one flight of stairs, and then another, when a knight stepped out in front of us.

She was dressed all in green, with armor cleverly shaped into leaves. Celery-colored hair was pulled back from an angular, insect-like face.

"Prince," said the knight. "Your lady mother seeks you. She wanted to be sure you were safe."

Oak nodded stiffly. "You may tell her I've returned."

"And where ought I say you were . . . ?" The knight eyed me and then the stolen sword. I feared I saw a flash of recognition in her eyes.

"Tell her that I'm well," the prince said, seeming to deliberately misunderstand her.

"But by what name ought I call—" the knight began, attempting to interrogate him and be deferential to his position all at once.

Oak seemed to have come to the end of his patience.

"Call us whatever you like!" he interrupted her to say. Then he grabbed my hand again, and we hurried up the stairs and into his room, where we slammed the door. We collapsed against it.

He was grinning, and looking at him, I had the strangest urge to laugh.

The room was large and painted a bright white. A round window let in light from the lamps outside. I heard strains of music, probably from the banquet, which was sure to start soon. A bed sat along one wall, topped with a velvet coverlet. A painting hung above it, of deer eating apples in a forest.

"This is your room?" I asked. Nothing about it spoke of him, except for a few paperback books on a small table and playing cards scattered beside an armchair.

He nodded but seemed a bit cautious about it. "I've only just gotten back to the isles. I was staying in the mortal world with one of my sisters. Like I told you last night."

That wasn't exactly what he'd said. I had thought he'd *visited* the place, not that he'd lived there and definitely not so recently.

I looked out the window. He had a view over the woods and to the sea beyond, the dark water rippling in the moonlight. "Are you going back?" I asked.

"I guess." He knelt and opened a dresser drawer to reveal a few games and some toy bricks. "We couldn't bring much with us."

I supposed he wouldn't be sure of anything, what with the unlikeli-hood of his sister keeping her crown, with so many forces conspiring against her.

"You have Uno," I said, picking up the card game and staring at it as though it was the relic of some fallen city.

He grinned, delighted at my recognizing it. "And Nine Men's Morris, Sorry!, and Monopoly, but that takes *forever*."

"I've played some of those." I felt shy now that we were in the palace, his territory. I wondered how long he would let me stay.

"You pick one," he said. "I am going to see what I can swipe from the kitchens. The cooks ought to have plenty to spare, considering how much food they made for tonight."

After he left, I reverently took the Sorry! game out of its box, slid-ing my fingers over the plastic pieces. I thought about playing with my unfamily one night when Rebecca sent me to Start three times in a row and teased me about it, back before I learned how much there really was to lose. I'd cried, and my unfather had told Rebecca that it was as important to be a good winner as a good loser.

I wanted Oak to give me an opportunity to be a good winner.

When he returned, it was with a whole pie and a pitcher of cream. He'd forgotten spoons and plates and cups, so we had to scoop handfuls of blueberry filling and crust into our mouths and drink from the jug. We stained our fingers and then the edges of the game cards.

So lost in the joy of that moment, I didn't think of danger until the latch of the door turned. I was barely able to roll underneath Oak's bed, putting my sticky, stained fingers over my mouth, before Oriana came into the room.

I tried to remain as still as possible. Madoc's wife had camped with us when we were in the north and would know me instantly if she saw me.

For a moment, I even considered throwing myself on her mercy. I might have made a useful hostage. If Oriana turned me over to the High Queen, she might not be cruel. Certainly, I had heard no rumors of her being awful in that way.

But if there were to be a truce, then I would be handed back to Lord Jarel and Lady Nore. The High Queen would want to give them all the easy things they asked for so that she'd have half a chance at denying them the hard ones.

Moreover, I wasn't entirely sure whose side Oriana was on.

"Where were you?" she asked Oak, voice sharp. "Is this what Vivi and that Heather girl let you get up to in the mortal world? Running off without telling anyone?"

"Go away," Oak said.

"The guards said you had someone with you. And there's a rumor that monster child from the Court of Teeth is missing."

He gave her a bored look.

"You are not to go near her alone."

"I am the prince," he said. "I can do whatever I like."

Oriana looked momentarily surprised, then hurt. "I left Madoc's side for you."

"So what?" He didn't appear at all sorry. "I don't have to listen to you or do what you say. And I don't have to tell you anything."

I expected her to slap him or call the guards to do it for her, but then I realized the guards would follow the prince's commands over those of Lady Oriana. He was the one his sisters loved and they had all the power now.

But I could not have predicted how his mother went to him and touched his forehead, fingers pushing back his dark gold hair from his horns. "I know," she said. "I cannot hope for one side to win, either. I used to wish that Madoc never went looking for those girls, and now all I wish is that we could be together again as we once were."

Despite what he'd told her, Oak leaned his head against her hand and closed his eyes. In that moment, I understood how little I knew about any of them. But I recognized love, and I envied the brush of her hands through his hair.

She sighed. "Stay in your room tonight, if not because I ask you, then because the banquet will be dull and your sister cannot handle one more distraction."

With a kiss upon his brow, she left.

The closing of the door recalled me to the precariousness of my position. I needed to find a way to persuade Oak to keep me in the palace. A reason for him to stand up to his mother and sisters in my behalf. I was certain I knew the mortal games better than he did, even if he'd been in the mortal world more recently, and moreover, I knew how to cheat at them. I could count the number of blueberry stains, could shuffle so that the first few cards most benefited me. Rebecca used to do that all the time.

"Let's play Go Fish," I said.

He appeared relieved that I didn't ask him questions about his mother, like why he was upset with her or why she'd been kind despite it. I wondered again if he'd been looking for Madoc when he found me the night before.

I began to shuffle the cards and talked as I did so he wouldn't notice my hands. "What else was there in the kitchens?"

He frowned a little, and it made me nervous until I realized he was just concentrating. "Pheasant," he said. "Acorn cakes. Oh, and I think I have Ring Pops somewhere here, from trick-or-treating. I went as myself."

There was something horrifying about that, but some part of me wished I could have done it, too.

I dealt to him from the bottom of the deck and to myself from the top, where I'd been careful to put plenty of matches. He won once anyway. But I won twice.

He let me hide under his bed that day, and the next, after I learned that there hadn't ever been a chance at peace, that the Court of Teeth had lost the war, and that Lord Jarel, my father, was dead.

That was the first time in over a year that I slept through the night and deep into the afternoon without waking.

I will always be grateful for that, even after guards dragged me out of his room three days later in chains. Even after the High Queen sent me away from Elfhame, and Oak said not a single word to stop her.

CHAPTER
4

Behind the abandoned house, two faerie horses chew on dandelions as they wait for their riders. Slight as deer, with a soft halo of light surrounding their bodies, they glide between the trees like ghosts.

Oak goes to the first. Her coat a soft gray, her mane braided into something that looks like netting, and which is hung with gold beads. Tooled leather saddlebags rest against her flanks. She nuzzles into his hand.

"Have you ridden before?" he asks me, and I return him the look he deserves.

In the Court of Teeth, I was instructed on almost none of the things that a child of royalty ought to know. I was barely taught to use my own magic, leaving me as I am, with weak spells, poor etiquette, and no familiarity with faerie horses.

"No? And yet you would look so well with your hair whipping behind you," Oak says. "Wild as the Folk of old."

I feel the tightening coils of embarrassment in my gut. Although he may intend it as mockery, I am pleased as much as shamed by his words.

Tiernan has his hand on Hyacinthe's back, guiding him across the grass. An odd way of touching a prisoner. "You can't help trying to charm every snake you come upon, no matter how cold-blooded or vicious. Let that one be."

I want to bare my teeth, but I feel it will only justify Tiernan's words.

"I think you're giving me the advice you ought to have given yourself years ago," Oak returns without real annoyance, and I can see from Tiernan's expression that arrow struck true. The knight's eyes narrow.

Oak rubs a hand over his face and, in that moment, looks exhausted. I blink, and his features shift to mildly amused. I am left to wonder if I imagined the whole thing. "Making pleasant conversation with one's traveling companions leads to less miserable travel, I find."

"Oh, do you?" says Tiernan in a parody of the prince's drawl. "Well, then, by all means—carry on."

"Oh, I *shall*," Oak returns. Now they're both obviously annoyed with each other, although I have no idea why.

"What's your horse's name?" I ask in the long silence that follows. My voice rasps only a little.

Oak strokes fingers over the velvet nap of her flank, visibly pushing off his mood. "My sister Taryn called her Damsel Fly when we were young, and it stuck. I'll hand you up."

"Isn't that sweet?" Hyacinthe says, the first words I've heard him speak. "Riding your sister's horse into battle. Have you anything of your own, prince? Or just girls' castoffs and scraps?"

"Get up," Tiernan tells Hyacinthe gruffly. "Mount."

"As you command," the cursed soldier says. "You do delight in giving orders, don't you?"

"To you, I do," Tiernan returns, heaving himself up behind the prisoner. A moment later he seems to realize what he's said, and his cheeks pink. I don't think Hyacinthe can see him, but I can.

"He calls his horse Rags," Oak goes on as though neither of the others spoke, although ignoring them must take some effort.

Tiernan sees me glance in his direction and gives me a look that reminds me that, were it up to him, he'd have me bound and gagged and dragged along behind them.

"I need to get my things," I tell them. "From my camp."

Oak and Tiernan share a look. "Of course," Oak says after whatever silent communication passed between them. "Lead the way, Lady Wren."

Then the prince clasps his fingers together to make a step so I can hop up onto the horse. I do, scrambling to throw my leg over. He swings up in front of me, and I do not know where to put my hands.

"Hold on," Oak urges, and I have no choice but to dig my nails into the flesh of his hip bones, just below the scale mail, and try not to fall off. The warmth of his skin is scalding through the thin cloth he's wearing beneath the gold plates, and embarrassment pulls that heat to my cheeks. The faerie horse is supernaturally fleet of foot, moving so fast that it feels a little like flying. I try to speak into Oak's ear, to give him directions, but I feel as though half the things I say are swept into the wind.

As we get close to my woven willow hut, the horse slows to a trot. A shiver goes through the prince as he hits the spell I wove to protect this place. He turns with a swift accusatory look and then reaches into the air and swipes it away as easily as if it were cobwebs.

Does he think I meant to use it to escape? To harm him? When he stops, I slide down with relief, my legs wobbly. Usually, this would be the hour when I slept, and I am more exhausted than usual as I stagger to my little home.

I feel Oak's gaze on me, evaluating. I cannot help but see this place through his eyes. The den of an animal.

I grit my teeth and crawl inside. There, I scrounge around for an old backpack scavenged from a dumpster. Into this, I shove items, without being sure what I might need. The least-stained of my three blankets. A spoon from my unparents' kitchen drawers. A plastic bag with seven licorice jelly beans in it. A bruised apple I was saving. A scarf, the ends unfinished, which my unmother was still knitting when I stole it.

Oak walks through a pattern of mushroom rings nearby, studying my packing from a distance.

"Have you been living here since last we spoke?" he asks, and I try not to read too much into the question. His expression isn't disgusted or anything like that, but it is too carefully neutral for me to believe he isn't hiding what he thinks.

Four years ago, it was easier to disguise how far I'd fallen. "More or less," I tell him.

"Alone?" he asks.

Not entirely. I'd made a human friend at twelve. I'd met her rooting through trash behind a bookstore, looking for paperbacks with their covers stripped off. She'd painted my toenails a bright glittering blue, but one day I saw her talking to my sister and hid from her.

And then Bogdana showed up a few months later, hanging a human pelt over my camp and warning me not to reveal any of our secrets. I stayed away from mortals for a year after that.

But there'd been a boy I saved from the glaistig when I was fourteen and he, seventeen. We'd sit together by a pond a few miles from here, and I would carefully avoid telling him anything I thought the storm hag wouldn't like. I think he was half-sure that he'd conjured me with his vape pen, an imaginary girlfriend. He liked to start fires, and I liked to watch. Eventually, he decided that since I wasn't real, it didn't matter what he did to me.

Then I demonstrated that I was very real, and so were my teeth.

The storm hag came again after that, with another pelt, and another warning about mortals, but by then I hardly needed it.

There was a silver-haired banshee I visited sometimes. As one of the sluagh, the other local faeries avoided her, but we would sit together for hours while she wept.

But when I thought of telling Oak any of that, I realized it would make my life sound worse, instead of better. "More or less," I say again.

I pick up things and then put them down, wishing to keep them with me but knowing they won't all fit. A chipped mug. A single earring hanging from a branch. A heavy textbook of poetry from seventh grade, with *REBECCA* written in thick Sharpie on the side. The butcher knife from the family kitchen, which Tiernan eyes skeptically.

I stick with the two little knives I have on my person.

There is one last thing I take, swiping it fast, so neither of them sees. A tiny silver fox with peridot eyes.

"The Court of Moths is a savage place, risky even for a prince of Elfhame," Tiernan informs Oak from where he sits on a log, cutting bark from a branch with a wicked little blade. I sense this is not the first time they've had this conversation. "Sure, they're your sister's vassals, but they're violent as vultures. Queen Annet eats her lovers when she tires of them."

Hyacinthe kneels at the trickle of a nearby stream to drink. With only one hand to support himself and not a second to make a cup with, he puts his mouth directly into the water and gulps what he can. At Tiernan's words, he lifts his face. Alert, perhaps, to an angle for escape.

"We only need to speak with the Thistlewitch," Oak reminds him. "Queen Annet can grant us a way to navigate her swamps and find the hag. The Court of Moths is only half a day's ride, down and east, toward the sea. We won't dally. We can't afford to."

"The Thistlewitch," Tiernan echoes. "She's seen two queens dead in the Court of Termites. Rumor is, she had a hand in engineering it. Who knows what her game is now."

"She was alive during Mab's reign," Oak says.

"She was *old* during Mab's reign," Tiernan supplies, as though that makes his point for him. "She's dangerous."

"The Thistlewitch's dowsing rod can find anything." There is a deep anxiety under the surface of this conversation. I am too well acquainted with the feeling not to recognize it. Is he more afraid than he's letting on, a prince on his first quest, riding his sister's pretty horse?

"And then what?" Tiernan says. "That's a tricky gambit you're considering."

Oak heaves a heavy sigh and does not answer, leaving me to wonder about his motives all over again. Leaving me to wonder what part of his plan he has elided, that he needs a hag to find something for him.

Tiernan returns to whittling and doesn't issue any further warnings.

I wonder how hard it is to keep Oak out of trouble, and if Tiernan does it out of friendship or loyalty to Elfhame. If Oak is the sunlight filtering through trees in the woods, all shifting gold and shadow, then Tiernan seems like those same woods in winter, the branches barren and cold.

As I move to rise, I notice something white is tucked into the edge of my hut, pushed into the weave of the woods. A wadded-up piece of paper, unmarked by dirt. As they speak, I manage to smooth it out beneath one of my filthy blankets so I can read what's written there.

You cannot outrun fate.

I recognize Bogdana's spidery handwriting. I hate the thought of her intruding on the place where I feel most safe, and the note itself makes me angry. A taunt, to make it clear that she hasn't given up hunting me. A taunt, like giving me a head start in a game she is sure to win.

I crumple the note and shove it into my backpack, settling it beside the little silver fox.

"Got everything?" Oak asks, and I straighten up guiltily, slinging my bag across one shoulder.

A gust of wind makes my threadbare dress blow around me, its hem dirtier than ever.

"If you thought we went fast before—" the prince begins to say, his smile full of mischief. Reluctantly, I walk to the horse and resign myself to getting on her back again.

That's when arrows fly out of the dark.

One hits the trunk of a nearby maple tree, just above my head. Another strikes the flank of the knight's horse, causing her to let out a horrible whinny. Through my panic, I note the rough, uneven wood of the shafts, the way they are fletched with crow feathers.

"Stick creatures!" the winged soldier shouts.

Tiernan gives him a look of banked fury, as though this is somehow his fault. "Ride!"

Oak reaches for my hand, pulling me up onto Damsel so that I am seated in front, my back against his metal-covered chest. I grab for the knots of the horse's mane, and then we're racing through the night, the horse thundering beneath us, arrows hissing through the air at our heels.

The stick creatures come into view, beasts of branches and twigs— some shaped like enormous wolves, others like spiders, and one with three snapping heads, like nothing I have seen before. A few in vaguely human shapes, armed with bows. All of them crawling with moss and vine, with stones tucked into packed earth at their centers. But the worst part is that among those pieces of wood and fen, I see what appear to be waxy mortal fingers, strips of skin, and empty mortal eyes.

Terror breaks over me like a wave.

I throw a panicked glance back at the wounded horse riding after us, carrying Tiernan and Hyacinthe. Blood stains her flank, and her steps are stumbling, uneven. Though she is moving fast, the wicker creatures are swifter.

Oak must know it, because he pulls on the reins and Damsel wheels around, back toward our attackers. "Can you get behind me?" he says.

"No!" I shout. I am having a hard enough time hanging on, pressing my thighs against the horse's flanks as firmly as I can and clinging to its neck, my fingers tangled in its mane.

His arm encircles my waist, pressing me to him. "Then crouch down as low as you're able," he warns. With his other hand, he pulls a small crossbow from a saddlebag and notches a bolt with his teeth.

He fires, missing spectacularly. The bolt strikes the dirt between

Tiernan and the wicker men's deer. There isn't time to reload, and the prince doesn't try, just takes a sharp, expectant breath.

My heart sinks, desperately wishing for some talent other than curse breaking. Had I the storm hag's power, I could call down lightning and singe them to cinders. Had I better control of my own magic, perhaps I could hide us behind an illusion.

Then the bolt Oak shot explodes into blue shimmering fire, and I realize he didn't miss after all. Burning stick men fall from the backs of their stick mounts, and one of the spidery creatures darts off, aflame, into the woods.

Tiernan's horse has nearly caught up to ours when we gallop away. I feel Oak tense behind me and I turn, but he shakes his head, so I concentrate on holding on.

It was one thing to have Lady Nore's power described, but seeing the stick creatures with their bits of flesh made me all too aware of how easy it would be to harvest human parts from cities like she might take rocks from quarries, and carve armies from forests. Elfhame should worry. The mortal world should fear. This is worse than I imagined.

The horses break free of the woods, and we find ourselves on suburban roads, then crossing a highway. It's late enough that there's little traffic. Tiernan's glamour settles over us, not quite a disguise but a piece of misdirection. The mortals still observe something out of the corner of their eyes, just not us. A white stag, perhaps. Or a large dog. Something they expect and that fits into the world they can explain. The magic makes my shoulders itch.

We ride on for what feels like hours.

"Oak?" the knight calls as we come to a crossroads. His gaze goes to me. "When was the prince hit?"

I realize that the weight on my back has grown heavier, as though Oak slumped forward. His hand is still around me, but his grip on the reins has loosened. When I shift in the saddle, I see that his eyes are shut, lashes dusting his cheeks, limbs gone slack.

"I didn't know—" I begin.

"You *fool*," mutters Tiernan.

I try to turn in the saddle and grab for the prince's body so it doesn't fall. He slumps against me, large and warm in my arms, his armor making him heavier than I am sure I can manage. I dig in my fingers and hope I can hold him, although it is all too easy to imagine the prince's body dropped in the dirt.

"Halt," Tiernan says, slowing his horse. Damsel slows, too, keeping pace with the knight's mount.

"Get down," he tells Hyacinthe, then pokes him in the back.

The winged soldier slides off the horse with the sort of ease that suggests he's ridden many times before.

"So this is who you follow?" he asks sullenly, with a glare in the prince's direction.

Tiernan dismounts. "So you're suggesting I throw in my lot with those *things*?"

Hyacinthe subsides, but he studies me as though he wonders if I might be on his side. I am not, and I hope my look tells him so.

Tiernan strides to Damsel. He reaches up, taking Oak's weight in his arms and easing the prince onto the leaf-covered earth.

I slip off the saddle gracelessly, hitting the ground hard and staggering to one knee.

A bit of blood shows that one of the arrows struck Oak just above the shoulder blade. It was stopped by the scales of his golden armor, though; only the very tip punctured his flesh.

It must have been poisoned.

"Is he...?" I can see the rise and fall of his chest. He's not dead, but the poison could still be working its way through his system. He might be dying.

I don't want to think of that. Don't want to think that were he not behind me, I would have been the one struck.

Tiernan checks Oak's pulse. Then he leans down and sniffs, as though trying to identify the scent. Takes a bit of blood on his finger and touches it to his tongue. "Deathsweet. That stuff can make you sleep for hundreds of years if you get enough in your system."

"There can't have been more than a little bit on the arrow," I say, wanting him to tell me that couldn't possibly have been enough.

Tiernan ignores me, though, and rummages in a bag at his belt. He takes out an herb, which he crushes under the prince's nose and then presses onto his tongue. Oak has enough consciousness to jerk his head away when the knight's fingers go into his mouth.

"Will that fix him?" I ask.

"We can hope," Tiernan says, wiping his hand on his trousers. "We ought to find a place to shelter for the night. Among mortals, where Lady Nore's stick things are unlikely to look."

I give a quick nod.

"It shouldn't be too long a walk." He lifts the prince, draping Oak back over his steed. Then we proceed, with Tiernan leading Damsel Fly. Hyacinthe walks behind him, and I am left to lead the knight's mount.

The bloodstain on her flank has grown, and her limp is noticeable. So, too, is the piece of an arrow still embedded in her side. "Was she poisoned, too?"

He gives a curt nod. "Not enough to bring this tough girl down yet, though."

I reach into my backpack and take out the bruised apple I brought. I bite pieces off for both horses, who snuffle gently into my hands.

I stroke the hair over Rags's nose. She doesn't seem to be in too much pain from the arrow, so I choose to believe she'll be okay.

"Maybe it would be better if he did sleep for a hundred years," Tiernan says, although he seems to be talking more to himself. "Lady Nore is going to be hunting us as surely as we're hunting her. Asleep is better than dead."

"Why *is* Oak really doing this?" I ask.

The knight gives me a hard look. "Doing what?"

"This task is *beneath* him." I don't know how else to say it. In the Court of Teeth, Lady Nore made me understand that *she* might pierce my skin to make a leash of silver mesh run through it, might cause me agony so great that my thoughts shrunk to those of an animal, but any disrespect of me by a *commoner* was punished by death. Being royal mattered.

Surely, even at her worst, the High Queen cannot value the prince less than Lady Nore valued me. Jude ought to have sent a dozen knights rather than her own brother, with only a single guard to protect him.

"Maybe there's a lady he wants to impress with his heroics," the knight says.

"His sister, I imagine," I say.

He laughs at that. "Or Lady Violet, with lips of carmine and a crown of living butterflies in her hair, according to a poem written about her. Oak spent three days in her bed before a jealous lover appeared, waving around a dagger and making an ugly scene. There was a Lady Sibi, too, who will declare dramatically to anyone likely to listen that Oak made her mad with passion and then, once he tired of her, splintered her heart into shards.

"Actually, now that I think on it, he'd be well served not to impress Sibi more than he already has. But there's any of the other two dozen beauties of Elfhame, all of whom are very willing to be awed by his heroics."

I bite the inside of my cheek. "That's a ridiculous reason."

"Some people are ridiculous," says Tiernan with a glance back at the sullen Hyacinthe in the bridle, trudging along. "Especially when it comes to love."

Not a flattering assessment of Oak, but he is currently slung over the back of a horse. He also, possibly, saved the knight's life. And mine.

"Is that what you truly believe?" I ask.

"What? That there's a girl? Of that, I'm certain. There always is. But I'm equally certain that bravery shouldn't be beneath a prince," Tiernan tells me.

There are rumors that Cardan never wanted the throne, that he will hand it over to Oak willingly at some vague future time. But when I think of High King Cardan with his black curls and cruel mouth, the way he behaves—silly and dangersome all at once—I don't believe he would relinquish power. He might, however, trick Oak into going on a quest he wouldn't return from. Build him up with stories of honor and valiant deeds. "If the High King and Queen let him go without no more protection than you, someone wants him dead."

Tiernan's eyebrows raise. "You've got a suspicious mind."

"Says the lover of a traitor." I hadn't been certain I was right, but then I saw Tiernan glance at Hyacinthe when he spoke of love, and recalled what Oak said to him before about trust.

It's satisfying when I see the blow land.

Tiernan gapes at me, stunned, as though it never occurred to him that just because my voice is scratchy with disuse, just because I seem more beast than girl, it doesn't mean I haven't been paying attention.

Hyacinthe gives a hollow laugh.

"You think the High King is making a move against Oak through me?" asks the knight.

I shrug. "I think that even if you want to take every risk for the prince, there's only one of you. And I think it's odd for the royal family to allow a prince to gamble on glory with his life."

The knight looks away and does not respond.

We walk on for the better part of a mile before Oak makes a low moan and tries to sit up. *"Jude,"* he mutters. *"Jude, we can't just let him die."*

"You're all right," Tiernan says, putting a hand on his shoulder. "We lost them."

The prince opens his tawny fox eyes and looks around. When he sees me, he slumps back down, as though relieved that I am still here.

Near dawn we come to a windswept beach.

"Wait here with the prince," Tiernan tells me as we close on a jetty of black stone. "Hyacinthe, your commands stand. My enemies are yours. Defend her if necessary."

The prisoner gives a thin-lipped smile. "It's not I who has forgotten all I vowed."

I cannot see Tiernan's face, so I cannot tell if Hyacinthe's bitterness bothers him.

The air is thick with salt. I lick it off my top lip and watch as Tiernan leads his wounded horse onto the sand. Rags's hoof touches the edge of a wave. At the brush of sea-foam, she tosses her mane and gives a whinnying sound that causes the hair to stand up along my arms.

Hyacinthe turns to me. The crash of the surf makes it impossible for him to be heard by Tiernan, but he lowers his voice anyway. "There are things I could tell you, were I not bridled. Free me, and I'll help you."

I say nothing. I pity him, bridled as he is, but that doesn't make him my ally.

"Please," he says. "I would not live like this. When I was caught, Oak removed the curse, but he didn't have the power to keep it from creeping back. First my arm, then I know not what. It is worse than being a falcon entire, to lose oneself again slowly."

"Let me be clear. I *hate* Lady Nore," I say, a snarl in my voice, because I don't want to listen to him. I don't want to sympathize with him more than I do already. "And if you're loyal to her, I hate you, too."

"I followed Madoc," Hyacinthe says. "And now I am his son's prisoner. Because I was more constant, not less. More loyal than my lover, who became twisted around the finger of another and forswore me. Lady Nore promised to remove the curse on any falcon who would join her, but I never gave her any oath. You can trust me, lady. Unlike the others, I will not play you false."

Across the beach, Tiernan's horse charges into the black water, heedless of the swells breaking over her.

More loyal than my lover, who became twisted around the finger of another.

"Is Rags *drowning*?" I ask.

Hyacinthe shakes his head. "The sea folk will take her back to Elfhame, and she will be made well there."

I let out my breath. My gaze goes to Oak, his cheek pillowed on Damsel's flank. His armor glinting in the moonlight. The flutter of his lashes. The calluses on his hands. "Removing the bridle will neither halt nor hasten your curse," I remind Hyacinthe.

"Do not fall under Prince Oak's spell," he warns as the knight climbs up the rocks to us. "He's not what he seems."

Several questions are on the tip of my tongue, but there is no time to ask them. As Tiernan draws close, I look out at the sea. Rags has disappeared. I can't see so much as her head above the waves.

"We're down to one steed," Tiernan informs us.

We don't have a place to rest, either. I study the shadowy space beneath the boardwalk. We could curl up there on the cool, soft sand without being bothered. Just the thought of it makes me freshly aware of how exhausted I am.

The knight points up toward the road. "There's a motel that way. I saw the sign from the shoreline."

He takes the reins of Oak's horse and leads her up the hill. I follow, ahead of the winged soldier. I note how stiff they are with each other, how carefully they keep separate, as magnets must keep a safe distance or be slammed together by their very nature.

We walk, fading stars overhead, brine in the air. I wonder if the hum of traffic or the smell of iron bothers them. I am used to it. So long as we remain here, I am on solid ground. Once we get to the Court of

Moths, we will be far enough into Faerie for things to grow slippery and uncertain.

At the thought, I kick a desiccated fast-food drink cup, sending it spinning along the gutter.

A few blocks and we come to a motel with scrubby weeds pushing through the cracks of the parking lot. A few run-down cars are parked near the one-level stucco building. A sign overhead promised vacancies, cable, and little else.

The prince attempts to sit up again.

"Just stay where you are," says Tiernan. "We'll be back with the keys."

"I'm fine," Oak says, sliding off the horse and immediately collapsing onto the asphalt.

"*Fine?*" the knight echoes, eyebrows raised.

"I couldn't say it if it wasn't true," says the prince, and manages to stagger to his feet. He leans heavily on a nearby car.

"Hyacinthe," Tiernan says, pointing. "Do not let him fall again. Wren, you're with me."

"I could only dream of letting so important a personage drop," Hyacinthe sneers. "Or I would never dream. Or something."

"Flying is what you ought to dream of, falcon," Oak says, with enough heat that I wonder if he overheard part of our conversation.

Hyacinthe flinches.

"Wren," Tiernan says again, beckoning toward the motel.

"I'm bad at glamours," I warn him.

"Then we won't bother with one."

The reception area stinks of stale cigarettes despite the NO SMOKING sign over the door. Behind the desk is an exhausted-looking woman playing a game on her phone.

She glances up at us, and her eyes go wide. Her mouth opens to scream.

"You see totally normal people here for totally normal reasons," Tiernan tells her, and as I watch, her features smooth out into a glassy-eyed calm. "We want two rooms, right next to each other."

I think of how my unparents were glamoured and hate this, even though he's not asking her to do anything awful. Yet.

"Sure," says the woman. "Not too many tourists this time of year; you'll have most places to yourselves."

The knight nods vaguely as the woman shoves a blank motel key into the machine.

She says something about how she still needs a card for incidentals, but a few words later, she's forgotten all about that. Tiernan pays with bills that don't have the suspiciously crisp look of glamoured leaves. I cut him a strange glance and pocket a matchbook.

Outside, our remaining horse stands on a patch of scrubby grass, glowing softly, eating a dandelion. No one seems inclined to tie Damsel up.

Oak sits on the bumper of a car, looking a bit better. Hyacinthe leans against a dirty stucco wall.

"That money," I ask. "Was it real?"

"Oh, yes," the prince confirms. "My sister would be wroth with us otherwise."

"Wroth." I echo the archaic word, although I know what it means. Pissed off.

"*Super* wroth," he says with a grin.

To faeries, mortals are usually either irrelevant or entertainment.

But I suppose his sister can be relegated to neither. Many of the Folk must hate her for that.

Tiernan leads us to our rooms—131 and 132. He opens the first and ushers us all inside. There are two twin beds, with scratchy-looking coverlets. A television sits on the wall over a saggy desk that's been bolted to the floor, causing the carpet to be stained with small circles of rust around the screws. The heater is on, and the air smells vaguely of burning dust.

Hyacinthe stands beside the door, wing closed tight to his back. His gaze follows me, possibly to avoid resting on the knight.

Oak crawls onto the nearest bed but doesn't shut his eyes. He smiles up at the ceiling instead. "We learned something of her capabilities."

"And you want me to tell you that was worth you being poisoned?" the knight demands.

"I'm always being poisoned. Alas, that it wasn't blusher mushroom," the prince says nonsensically.

Tiernan nods his chin at me. "That girl thinks you're a fool for even being here."

I scowl, because that's not what I meant.

"Ah, Lady Wren," Oak says, a lazy smile on his mouth. Marigold hair brushing his forehead, half-hiding his horns. "You wound me."

I doubt I hurt his feelings. His cheeks are still slashed from my nails, though. Three lines of dried blood, pink around the edges. Nothing he says is a lie, but all his words are riddles.

Tiernan kneels and starts to unbuckle the sides of Oak's armor. "Give me a hand, will you?"

I squat on the other side of the prince, worried I am going to do something wrong. Oak's gaze slants to me as, with fumbling fingers, I try to work off the scale mail where it has stuck to his wound. He makes a soft huff of pain, and I can see the way his lips are white at the edges, from being pressed together as he bites back whatever other sounds he wants to make.

Underneath, his stained linen shirt is pushed up over the flat plane of his stomach, the dip of his hip bones. His sweat carries the scent of crushed grass, but mostly he smells like blood. He watches me, lashes low over his eyes.

Without his golden armor, he almost looks like the boy I remember.

Tiernan gets up, gathering towels.

"How did Lady Nore know you were coming for me?" I ask, trying to distance myself from the strange intimacy of the moment, from the heat and nearness of his body.

If she'd sent both Bogdana and stick creatures, she must suddenly want me very much, after ignoring me for eight years.

Oak tries to sit up higher on the pillows and winces, a hectic flush on his cheeks. "She's likely to have realized that asking you to come with me would be the clever thing to do," he says. "Or she could have had spies that saw the direction in which we were headed when we left Elfhame."

Tiernan nods toward Hyacinthe from the bathroom, where he's soaking cloth under steaming water from the tap. "Spies like him, I imagine."

I frown at the bridled former falcon.

"There's not a lot of work for birds out there," Hyacinthe says, putting up his hand in defense. "And I didn't spy on *you*."

Tiernan brings over the towels, picking one up as though he intends to wash the prince's wound. Before he can, Oak takes and presses it to his own shoulder, closing his eyes against the pain. The water trickles down his back to stain the sheets pink.

"We're within a few days' ride of the Court of Moths, but we're down to one horse," Tiernan says.

"I'll bargain for another," Oak tells us distractedly. I am not sure he realizes that in the mortal world, horses are not something you can just pick up at a local farmers' market.

When the prince begins to bind up his wound, Tiernan nods in my direction. "Come," he says, ushering me out of the room. "Let's leave him to dream of all the things he will do tomorrow."

"Like issue a royal decree that you won't mock me when I've been poisoned," says Oak.

"Keep dreaming," Tiernan tells him.

I glance back at Hyacinthe, since it doesn't seem to me that the knight is wrapped around the prince's finger. If anything, they seem like friends who've known each other a long time. But the former falcon is picking his fingernails with a dagger and ignoring all of us.

Tiernan uses his second key to open the way to a nearly identical space. Two beds, one television. Rust stains where the bolts have sat in contact with the rug. A polyester coverlet that looks as though spilled water might bead up on top of it.

There, the knight loops rope around my ankle, tying me to the bed with enough slack that I can lie down, even roll over. I hiss at him as he does it, pulling against the bonds.

"He might trust you," says Tiernan. "But I trust no one from the Court of Teeth."

Then he speaks a few words over the knot, a bit of enchantment that

I am almost certain I can break, what with all the practice I've had at unraveling the glaistig's spells.

"Sleep tight," he tells me, and goes out, closing the door hard after him. He's left his pack behind, and I bet he's planning on returning and sleeping here, where he can keep an eye on me. And where he can avoid whatever he's feeling about Hyacinthe.

Spitefully, I get up and throw the bolt lock, letting the rope pull taut.

Dawn has lengthened into day, and all around the motel, the mortal world is coming awake. A car engine fires to life. Two people argue near a vending machine. A slammed door sounds from the room next to mine. I peer out the window, imagining slipping away into the morning and disappearing. Imagining the look on Tiernan's face when he returns to find me gone.

But I would be foolish to try to face the storm hag or Lady Nore on my own. I would have been felled by the same poison that struck the prince, except without armor, the bolt would have sunk deeper into my flesh. And no one would have been there to give me an antidote or carry me on a horse.

Still, I don't want to be dragged along like an animal, worrying about being put on a leash.

If I cannot have respect, if I cannot be treated as their equal, then at least I want Oak to see that I have as much right as he does to this quest, more reasons to hate Lady Nore, and the power to stop her.

But it's hard to think of how I will manage to convince them of that when my ankle is tied to the leg of the bed, and my thoughts are woolly with exhaustion. Taking one of the blankets from my bag, I scrabble into the dusty space between mattress and floor, curling up there. The awareness of the slats over me and the familiar, forest smell of my blanket is comforting.

Pillowing my head on my arms, I try to settle in. It ought to be hard to fall asleep in this unfamiliar place, filled with strange sounds. My thighs hurt from the ride, and my feet are sore from walking. But as warm, buttery sunlight flows into the room like yolk from a cracked egg, my eyes drift closed. I do not even dream.

When I wake, the sky is dark. I crawl out from underneath the bed, hunger gnawing my belly.

Tiernan must have been in and then gone without my noticing, because the bolt lock is undone, his pack missing. I make quick work of his stupid enchanted knot, then go into the bathroom and fill the plastic cup I find there with water. I guzzle it, refill it, and drink again.

As I look up, I catch sight of my own reflection and take an automatic step back. Unglamoured, my skin is the pale blue-gray of hydrangea blooms, smeared with dirt along one cheek and across my nose. My hair is so woven with leaves and twigs and mud that it would be almost impossible to know that underneath it is an even darker blue. I have the same pointy chin I had when I thought I was mortal. A thin face, with large eyes, and an expression of startlement, as though I expect someone else when I look in the mirror.

At least my eyes could pass for human. They're green, deep and dark.

I smile a little to see the awfulness of my sharp teeth. A mouth full of knives. They make even the Folk flinch.

My gaze goes to the tub, thinking about what I must seem like to Oak, now that we're both grown. Turn the faucet and let the hot water run over my hand. As dirt washes off, I see that the skin underneath is a warmer, lighter blue.

But I am no Court lady with lips of carmine and butterflies in my hair. I am scrawny, like a stick bug.

I put the stopper in the tub and let it fill. Then slowly I lower myself in. The heat is almost more than I can bear. Still, I scrub at my skin with my jagged nails. In minutes the water is so filthy that I have to let it drain out. Then I do it again. Sinking my fingers into my hair, I try to pick apart the tangles. It's painful, and slathering it with the contents of the tiny bottle of conditioner does little to help. I am still not totally clean when I get out of the water, despite the fine layer of grit remaining behind in the tub.

Now that I've washed, my dress looks dirtier than ever, worn as thin as tissue in places, and discolored by both sun and mud. There's nothing else, so I pick it up and run it under the tap of the sink, scrubbing at it gently with soap and hoping it doesn't tear. Then I drape it over the shower-curtain rod and aim the hair dryer onto it. It's still damp when I take it down.

I start stepping into it when I see a shadow move outside the window.

I drop to the floor, but not before I recognize the long fingers. As I crawl naked underneath the bed, I hear the sound of nails scratching against glass. I brace for Bogdana to shatter the window or kick in the door.

Nothing happens.

I draw in a breath. Then another.

Minutes later, there's a knock. I don't move.

Oak's insistent voice comes from the other side. "Wren, open up."

"No," I shout, crawling out from underneath the bed and scrambling into my clothes.

I hear shuffling and a thud, and then something metal slides down the gap between door and jamb. It opens.

"I thought you were..." I start to explain, but I am not sure he's paying attention. He's put away what he was using to jimmy the door and is gathering back up a cardboard drink holder of coffees and a large paper bag.

When he looks up, he freezes for a moment, an unreadable expression on his face. Then he averts his gaze, turning it toward something just over my shoulder.

I glance down, at the way the damp cloth of my dress has stuck to my body, and flinch. My breasts are visible, even my nipples. Could he think I did this for his attention? Shame heats my cheeks, crawls down my neck.

Walking past me, he sets down the sack on the bed. His golden curls are only slightly mussed, his fresh linen shirt white and unwrinkled, as though he'd never been poisoned, or shot, or fallen off a horse. He certainly hadn't cleaned his clothes in the sink. And his mouth is twisted in an expression of insufferable amusement.

I wrap myself in the coverlet from the bed.

"I wasn't sure what you liked." Oak proceeds to take out a mango, three green apples, a handful of dried figs, a bag of crackers in the shapes of goldfish, frozen pizza bites, and four foil-wrapped hot dogs. He does all this without looking at me. "They seem like meat, but they're not."

I am hungry enough to accept one of his weird vegan hot dogs. "You don't eat meat? Your father must hate that."

He shrugs, but there's something in his face that tells me it's been discussed before. "More for him."

Then I am distracted by eating. I gobble three out of the four hot dogs so quickly that when I stop, I see Oak has his hand curved protectively over the remaining one. I pick up a fig and try to take smaller bites.

Leaving the remainder of the food on the mattress, he goes to the door. "Tiernan told me I should be grateful for your unwillingness to drop me on my head, however tempted you were," he says. "They'll sing ballads to your restraint."

"And why would you think I was tempted?" There's a growl in my voice I can't seem to get out.

"Many are. It must be something about my face." He smiles, and I think of the jealous lover with the knife.

"Maybe you keep dragging them on quests," I say.

He laughs. "This isn't how I thought to see you again."

"I imagine you thought you'd *never* see me again," I say, to remind myself of the many, many differences between our positions in life.

His grin slides off his mouth. "That did seem to be what you wanted."

I wish it didn't bother me that he isn't smiling anymore, but it does.

The door opens. Tiernan is on the other side, glowering at us. "Let's get moving. We've got a lot of ground to cover."

Outside, I see that we have acquired a new horse, black as ink and smelling of seawater. Oak's faerie steed shies away from it, blowing panicked breaths from flared nostrils.

The new mount catches my eye hungrily, and I realize what I'm looking at. The creature is one of the solitary Folk, a devourer of flesh. A kelpie.

CHAPTER 5

Get on up," Tiernan says impatiently, nodding toward the kelpie. The thing doesn't even have a saddle, no less reins. I look longingly at Damsel and wonder if the knight is forcing me onto a carnivorous monster out of sheer dislike.

But Oak goes to it willingly enough, patting its flank absently. Then he swings onto the kelpie's back and reaches down a hand to me. He is wearing his golden armor again, the boy who'd been my friend disappearing into a man I don't know.

The knight heaves me up behind the prince. As my hands go to Oak's waist, I am aware of the warmth of his skin even through the scale armor, of his body pressed against my thighs, and while the cloak he loaned me covers the thinness of my gown, it cannot protect me from that.

"Hope you're feeling rested after all that deathsweet," Tiernan tells Oak. "Because you're mutilating our timetable."

Oak gives him a look that makes me suspect the prince will finally call him to account for his familiarity. But if so, this is not the moment.

I wonder how hard it is for the kelpie not to run directly into a pond and drown us both. But, as one of the solitary fey, he has very likely made vows of obedience to Elfhame, and I can only hope those hold. I barely have time to wrap my arms around the prince's waist and try not to fall. Then we're off, thundering through the late afternoon without cease.

Through the sap-smeared woods of the Pine Barrens, crossing highways filled with the bright headlights of cars, we ride. My hair whips behind me, and when Oak glances back, I have to look away. Circlet at his brow, sword at his belt, in his shining mail, he looks like a knight from a child's imaginings, out of a storybook.

Break of day comes in pinks and golds, and the sun is high above us when we come to a stop. My thighs are sorer than before from rubbing against the kelpie's flanks, and even my bones feel tired. My hair is knotted worse than ever.

We make camp in a forest, quiet and deep. The distant hiss of traffic tells me that mortal roads are near, but if I don't listen too closely, I could mistake that for the sounds of a stream. Oak unpacks and unrolls blankets while Tiernan starts a fire. Hyacinthe watches, as if daring to be asked to help.

I slip away and return with handfuls of persimmons, two dryad's saddle mushrooms as large as helmets, wild garlic, and spicebush twigs. Even Tiernan pronounces himself impressed by my finds, although I think he's annoyed that Oak allowed me to wander off.

The prince ignores him and rigs up a way to cook the mushrooms. They've brought cheese and good black bread, and while we eat, Oak tells us stories of the Court. Ridiculous parties held by the High King. Pranks Oak has personally played and been punished for. No mention of his lovers, but he recounts a tragicomic romance involving a phooka, a pixie, and one of the king's counselors that was still playing out when he left.

Even Tiernan seemed different in the firelight. When he poured tea for Hyacinthe, he added honey without being asked, as though he'd made it that way many times before. And when he handed it over and their fingers met, I recognized in his face the sharp pain of longing, the unwillingness to ask for what you knew you would be denied. He hid it quickly, but not quickly enough.

"Will you tell me what this hag in the Court of Moths is supposed to find for us?" I ask when the stories come to an end.

I want the answer, but more than that, I want to know if they trust me enough to give me one.

Tiernan looks in Oak's direction, but the prince is looking directly at me, clear-eyed. "The limits of Lady Nore's power, I hope. The This-tlewitch lived during the time of Mab, and there was a curse on Mab's bones, if I understand right."

"So not an object?" I ask, thinking of their conversation in the woods.

Oak shrugs. "That depends on what she tells us."

I mull over his answer as I bed down in some of the prince's blankets. They are perfumed with the scents of Elfhame, and I pull my own muddy covering close to my nose to blot out the smell.

That afternoon there is another long, exhausting ride, with only a brief break for food. By the time we stop, I feel ready to fall off the kelpie's back and not care if it starts nibbling on me.

Nearby a wide, brackish river froths, bubbling around rock. Tall, slender saw palmettos make lonely islands of rubble and root. On a steep slope, a single wall of a five-story concrete building stands. It looks like a castle cut out of construction paper, flat instead of three-dimensional.

"The entrance to the Court of Moths is supposed to be here somewhere," Tiernan says.

I slide off the kelpie and lie down in the weeds while Oak and Tiernan debate where to find the entrance to the brugh. I breathe in the fine mist from the water, the scents of loam and clotted river grass.

When I open my eyes, a young man is standing where the kelpie was. Brown hair the color of mud in a riverbed and eyes the murky green of stagnant water. I startle, scuttling away, and reach into my pack for a knife.

"Greetings," he says expansively, bowing. "You must wish to know the name of the one who carried you on his back, who so stalwartly aided a young prince in his time of need, before the beginning of his true reign—"

"Sure," I say, interrupting him.

"Jack of the Lakes," he says with a menacing grin. "A merry wight. And whom do I have the honor of addressing?" He looks at me.

"Wren," I say, and immediately wish I hadn't. It's not my true name, but all names have some power.

"You have an unusual voice," he says. "Raspy. Quite fetching, really."

"I damaged my vocal cords a long time ago," I inform him. "Screaming."

Oak steps between us, and I am grateful for the reprieve. "What a fine gentleman you make, Jack."

Jack turns to the prince, his sinister smile dropping back into place. "Oak and Wren. Wren and Oak. Delightful! Named for woodland creatures, but neither of you so simple." He glances at Tiernan and Hyacinthe. "Not nearly as simple as these two."

"That's enough," Tiernan says.

Jack's gaze stays on Oak. "Will you caper for the pleasure of the Queen of Moths? For she is a grim ruler, and her favor hard to win. Not that you need to concern yourself with impressing anyone, Your Highness."

I get a cold feeling at his words.

"I don't mind a caper," Oak says.

"That's enough impertinence," says Tiernan, inserting himself into the conversation. He stands with his shoulders back and his arms folded, the picture of the officer in Madoc's army that he must have once been. "You had the privilege of carrying the prince a ways, and that's that. Whatever we see fit to give you in recompense, be it a coin or a kick in the teeth, you'll take it and be grateful."

Jack of the Lakes sniffs, offended.

Hyacinthe's eyes glitter with anger, as though he feels the knight spoke directly to him.

"Nonsense," Oak tells Jack. "Your hooves were swift and sure. Come with us to the Court, rest your feet, and take some refreshment." He claps his hand on Tiernan's shoulder. "We're the ones with reason to be grateful, isn't that so?"

The knight pointedly ignores him, clearly not experiencing the awe of Prince Oak that he expects of Jack of the Lakes.

"This way," the prince says, and ushers us along the bank. I follow, trying not to slide on the wet mud.

"Decide for yourself how well they repay gratitude," says Hyacinthe to the kelpie, touching the leather strap of the bridle he wears. "And do not give them cause for too much of it."

Tiernan rolls his eyes.

There's solid concrete blocking our path, with the river on one side and a hill covered in poisonous manchineel trees on the other. The remains of the old building have no door, only large windows that show an even more forbidding and swampy landscape beyond. And yet I can feel the stillness in the air, the crackling presence of magic. Oak stops, frowning. I am sure he can feel it, too.

The prince presses his hand against the concrete, like he's trying to find the source.

Jack of the Lakes is wading in the water, looking eager to drag someone down into its depths.

Hyacinthe moves to stand nearby, his free hand clenching as though missing something. I wonder what weapon he used when he was a soldier. "I bet you think you're all great friends now."

I lower my voice to a rasp, remembering our conversation by the sea. "I am not under anyone's spell."

His gaze goes to the prince, standing on a windowsill, and then back to me. "He seems like an open book, but that's the game he plays. He keeps plenty of secrets. For instance, did you know he received a message from Lady Nore?"

"A message?" I echo.

He smiles, satisfied he has rattled me.

Before I can press him for details, Oak turns to us with a grin that calls for an answer. "Come look."

A meadow of flowers flows impossibly from the other side of the window. There is no river there, no scrub grass or mud. Just endless blooms, and among them scattered bones, as white as petals.

He hops into the meadow, hooves sinking beneath the flowers, and then reaches up for me.

Do not fall under his spell.

I remind myself that I knew Oak when we were children, that we have the same enemies. That he has no reason to play me false. Still, thinking of Hyacinthe's words, I shake my head at Oak's offer of help and climb down myself.

"It's beautiful, no?" he asks, a little smile on his face. A light in his fox eyes.

It is, of course. All of Faerie is beautiful like this, with carnage hidden just beneath. "I am sure the Queen of Moths will be delighted that the Crown Prince thinks so."

"You're in a prickly mood," he tells me.

As though I am not all-over briars at all times.

We walk through a landscape with no sun or moon above us until we come to a patch of earth with a deep pit half-hidden by swirling fog. There cut into the dirt are steps spiraling down into darkness.

"The Court of Moths," says Jack of the Lakes softly.

As I glance back at the field, the bones bother me: signs of death strewn among a carpet of flowers. I wish we had not come here. I have a dread that feels like premonition.

I notice that Oak has his hand on his sword as he begins his descent.

We follow, Tiernan behind the prince, then me and Jack, with Hyacinthe bringing up the rear, bridle tight against his cheeks. I hold my knife against my belly, inhale the rich scent of earth, and remember all the times I broke curses, all the tricks I played on the Folk.

We step into a long hall of packed dirt, with pale roots forming a latticework along the ceiling. Occasional glowing crystals light our way. I find myself growing more uncomfortable the deeper we go into the hill. I feel the weight of the earth above me, as though the passageway could collapse, burying us all. I bite my lip and keep going.

Finally, we step into a high-ceilinged cavern, its walls shining with mica.

There stands a green-skinned troll woman, with piercings through her cheeks and two sets of black horns protruding from her head. Sabers hang on either side of her hips. She wears armor of leather, carefully worked so that it seems as though there are a dozen screaming mouths on her chest plate.

At the sight of us, she scowls. "I guard the passage to the Court of Moths. Declare your name and your purpose in coming here. Then I will very likely kill you."

The expression on Tiernan's face hardens. "Do you not know your own sovereign? This is Prince Oak, heir to Elfhame."

The troll's gaze goes to Oak, looking as though she could eat him in three bites. Finally, she makes a reluctant, shallow bow. "You do us honor."

The prince, for his part, appears genuinely pleased to meet her and not the least bit afraid, bespeaking either great arrogance or foolishness, or both. "The honor is ours," he says, looking ready to kiss her hand if she offered it to him. I cannot imagine being so certain of one's welcome.

Just imagining it makes my stomach hurt.

"We seek the Thistlewitch, who dwells in Queen Annet's lands. We understand that without permission to see her, supplicants become lost in her swamp for a hundred years," Oak says.

The troll tilts her head, as if still evaluating his deliciousness. "Some don't make it back at all."

The prince nods, as though she's confirming his suspicions. "Alas, we don't have time for either of those options."

The troll smiles a little despite herself, at the silliness of his words. "And your companions?"

"Sir Tiernan," says the knight, pointing to himself. "Jack of the Lakes. Lady Wren. Our prisoner, Hyacinthe."

The troll's gaze glides over Hyacinthe and Jack to rest on me for an uncomfortably long moment. My lip curls in automatic response, to reveal the points of my teeth.

Far from looking discomfited, the troll woman gives me a nod, as though appreciative of their sharpness and my mistrust.

"Queen Annet will wish to greet you personally," the troll says, kicking the wall behind her three times. "She is fain to fete you in her hall and all that sort of thing. I've summoned a servant to bring you to some rooms. There, you may refresh yourselves and dress for the evening's revel. We will even lock up your prisoner for the night."

"There's no need for that," Oak says.

The troll grins. "And yet we will do it."

Hyacinthe glances in Tiernan's direction, perhaps looking to his former lover to speak in his behalf. I feel all around me the closing of a trap, and yet I do not think I am the one who is meant to be caught.

"We would be delighted to enjoy the hospitality of the Court of Moths," Oak says. If he hopes to get what he came for, it would be impossible for him to say anything else.

The troll guard's smile grows impossibly wide. "Good. You may follow Dvort."

I note her gaze and turn, startled to see that one of the Folk has crept in behind us. His skin and beard are the same color as the roots winding down from the ceiling, his eyes a bloodshot pink. His ears are long, like those of a rabbit, and his clothes appear to be covered in a layer of moss, heavier on his shoulders. He does not speak, only bows, then turns and shuffles down the passageway.

Hyacinthe bumps my shoulder with his. "Before they take me, let me prove what I've said and give you at least this much information. The prince's mother was a gancanagh. A *love-talker*. Honey-mouths, we used to call them back at Court."

I give a quick shake of my head, dreading what he will say next.

"You've not heard of them? A love-talker is able to quicken such desire in mortals that they die of it. The Folk might not find the passion lethal, but we still feel it. Oak's first mother charmed the High King Eldred *and* his son Dain into her bed. Oak's half brother is said to have made both Jude and her twin, Taryn, his lovers and stolen Cardan's former betrothed from his side. What do you suppose the prince is able—"

Hyacinthe bites off his last words because we have stopped in front of four doors, all of them of stone with spiraling metal hinges.

But I can't help finishing the sentence for him, the way I fear it would have gone. *What do you suppose the prince is able to do to someone like you?* A shudder goes through me, a recognition of a desire that I would have preferred to deny.

Was that how he made everyone feel? No wonder there was always a girl. No wonder Hyacinthe believes Tiernan is wrapped around his finger.

Dvort bows again, gesturing toward the rooms, then gives Hyacinthe a shove to keep moving into one of three branching passageways.

"He stays with us," Oak says.

"You heard *His Majesty*." Despite the sneer in his voice when he speaks of Oak, Hyacinthe obviously doesn't want to be taken. He attempts to move around the page, toward the prince. But the silent page blocks his way.

Oak's hand goes to the hilt of a blade.

"Enough," Tiernan says, grabbing the prince's arm. "They want you to break hospitality. Stop it. It shouldn't hurt Hyacinthe to cool his heels in the queen's prison for one night. I'll accompany him and make sure he's comfortable enough."

"Unseelie is as Unseelie does," says Jack of the Lakes with some relish.

I watch them go, panic rising as our party is cleft in two. When I am ushered into my room, I only feel worse.

It is a grim chamber, its walls carved of stone and earth. There is a rough bed in one corner, heaped with blankets and opulent cushions, and hung with tapestries. Each curtain depicts hunted creatures bleeding out in forests of colorful foliage, their bodies full of arrows.

There's a jug of water and a washbasin on a stand, and a few hooks on the wall. I take a turn about the room, looking for spy holes, secret passageways, and hidden dangers.

The place makes my skin itch. Though it is warm here, and nothing is ice, it reminds me entirely too much of the Court of Teeth. I want to be away.

I sit on the bed, counting to one hundred, hoping that the panicky feeling will pass.

Just as I get to number eighty-eight, Oak opens the door. "I've arranged for you to see the royal seamstress."

My gaze alights on the hollow of his throat just above his collar. I try to avoid his eyes.

Love-talker.

"I don't want to go." All I want is to curl up in a corner until we can leave.

He looks incredulous. "You can hardly attend the revel like that."

Shame heats my cheeks, looking at him in all his finery.

It's not fair. I am cleaner than I've been in weeks. It's true that there are holes in my dress, the hem is ragged, and there are places where the fabric has worn thin enough to tear. Still, it's *mine*.

"If you think I will embarrass you, leave me to this room," I growl, hoping he agrees.

"If you go as you are, it will appear as though Elfhame does not value you, and that's perilous in the Court of Moths," he says.

I scowl, unwilling to be reasonable.

The prince sighs, pushing hair out of his fox eyes. "If you remain in this room, Tiernan must stay to watch over you, and he has a hankering to drink the sweet wines and hear the songs of the Court of Moths. Now, up. You can put your old dress back on tomorrow."

Humiliated, I rise and follow him.

Someone sings an eerie little song on the other side of the seamstress's door, and I feel the pull of magic, thick clots of it. Whatever is inside has power.

I shoot Oak a look of warning, but he knocks anyway.

The song stops.

"Who calls at Habetrot's chamber?" comes a whispery voice.

Oak raises his eyebrows at me, as though he intends me to answer.

Fine, if that's what he wants. "Suren, whose garb has been deemed inadequate by an obnoxious prince, despite the fact I've seen people go *naked* to revels."

Rather than be insulted, Oak laughs delightedly.

The door opens to reveal a woman with frog-green skin, a wide lower lip, and wild eyebrows. Dressed in a black garment large enough to swallow up her body, she's bent so far over that her fingers nearly touch the ground.

She looks at me and blinks wet black eyes. "Come, come," she calls.

"I'll leave you to it," says Oak with a departing bow.

I bite my lip against snarling and follow the faerie into a tunnel that's so low-ceilinged that I have to stoop.

When we emerge, it is into a chamber filled with bolts of cloth resting on shelves that go up high enough to be shrouded in darkness. What light there is comes from candles set in sconces around the room, covered in globes of cloudy glass.

"You know what they say about me?" Habetrot whispers. "That instead of sewing garments, I pluck them out of dreams. Raiments such as I create have never been seen before, or since. So, what do you dream of?"

I frown down at my tattered dress in confusion.

"Forest girl, is that what you were? One of the solitary fey brought to Court?"

I nod, because that's true enough, in a way.

"Perhaps you want something of bark and furs?" she asks, walking around me, squinting a little as though seeing some vision of what she will put me in.

"If that's appropriate," I say, unsure.

She grabs hold of my arm, encircling it with her fingers to measure. "Surely you would not insult me with such a lack of extravagance?"

I am at a loss. Even if she could see into my dreams, she would find no garment of the sort she would have me imagine. "I don't know what I want." The words come out a whisper, too true by half.

"Destruction and ruin," she says with a clack of her tongue. "I can practically smell it on you."

I shake my head, but I can't help thinking of the satisfaction I felt wrecking the glaistig's spells. Sometimes it feels as though there's a knot inside me, and were it to come apart, whatever emerged would be all teeth.

Habetrot regards me with her bead-black eyes, unsmiling. Then starts searching among her bolts of cloth.

Once, the thing I am wearing was a sundress, with fluttery sleeves. A diaphanous white gown that flowed around me when I spun. I found it in a shop late one night. I'd stripped off the clothes given to me in the Court of Teeth, left them behind, and put that on instead.

I liked the dress so much that I wove myself a crown of hellebores and danced through the night streets. I stared at myself in puddles, convinced that so long as I didn't smile, I might even be pretty. I know it doesn't look like that anymore, but I can no longer picture myself in anything else.

I wish Oak could have seen the dress as it was, even though it hasn't looked that way in a long time.

A few minutes later, Habetrot comes over with a fabric in a soft, deep gray that seems to shift in her hands between brown and blue when she turns it in the light. My fingers stray to the cloth, petting the nap of the velvet. It is as soft as the cloak that the prince draped over my shoulders.

"Yes, yes," she says. "This will do. Arms out like a bird. There."

As I stand there, letting her drape me in fabric, my gaze goes to her collections of buttons and fiber and cloth. To the spindle resting in one corner and the shimmer of the thread in it, bright as starlight.

"You," Habetrot says, poking me in the side. "Shoulders back. Don't crouch like an animal."

I do what she tells me but bare my teeth at her. She bares her teeth in return. They are blunt, blackened along the gums.

"I have dressed queens and knights, giants and hags. I will dress you, too, and give that for which you were too afraid to ask."

I don't see how that is possible, but I do not argue. I think instead of the way we came. I counted the passages, and I am almost certain I know the way back to the fog-shrouded hole in the ground. I go over them again and again to fix them in my memory in case I have to run. In case we all have to run.

When she has my measurements and perhaps my measure, she goes to her table and begins to rip and stitch, leaving me to awkwardly wander the room, peering at ribbons, some of which seem to be made of woven hair, others of toad skin. I pocket a pair of sharp-looking scissors with a handle in the shape of a swan. They are lighter than my knives and much easier to conceal.

I cannot deny that though I have avoided the Folk, I am fascinated by them. Despite them being deceivers, and dangerous.

My gaze alights on a button the exact shining golden bronze of Oak's hair. Then another the purple of Hyacinthe's eyes.

I think of him in the dungeons. Hyacinthe, half-cursed, wearing that awful bridle, so desperate that he would seek help even from me.

"Come and try this on," says Habetrot, surprising me out of my thoughts.

"But it's only been a few moments," I say, puzzled.

"Magic," she reminds me with a flourish, then ushers me behind a screen. "And give me that dress you're wearing. I want to burn it."

I pull the worn fabric over my head, letting it fall to the floor between us and fixing her with a look that dares her to wrest it from me. I feel as vulnerable as a selkie taking off her skin.

Habetrot pushes the soft blue-purple-gray garment into my hands. I put it on carefully, feeling the slide of the lining smooth against my skin, feeling the comforting weight of fabric.

It is a gown, but one such as I have never seen before. It is composed mostly of the cloth she showed me, but there are strips of other material running through it, some diaphanous and others satiny, some patterned in butterfly wings, some felted wool. Dangling threads hang from torn edges, and a few pieces of thin fabric have been wadded up to give them a new texture. The swirling patchwork she has created is at once tattered and beautiful.

As I look at it, I am not sure what to think. It is mockery that makes her dress me thus, in rags and scraps, no matter how deftly put together?

But perhaps that's what she thought would best suit me. Perhaps it is Oak who is the fool, who caught a wolf and thought that by putting it in a gown and speaking to it as though it were a girl, it would become one.

At least the hem of the skirt doesn't drag impractically on the floor. I can still run in it as I howl at the moon.

"Come out, come out," she says.

I step from behind the screen, taking a sharp breath as I do so, dreading seeing myself in the mirror and feeling the burn of further humiliation.

The little seamstress pushes me toward a polished bronze thing that looks like a shield. My reflection stares back at me.

I am taller than I remembered. My hair is a wild tangle despite my attempts at finger-combing and washing it back at the motel. I never got out all the knots. My clavicle shows at the top of the collar, and I know I am too thin. But the dress clings to my chest and waist, skirt flaring over my hips. The tattered edges give it a haunting elegance, as though I am wrapped in the shadows of dusk. I look the picture of a mysterious courtier, rather than someone who sleeps in dirt.

Habetrot drops boots beside me, and I realize how long I've been standing there, staring at myself. A different kind of shame heats my cheeks.

I twist my hands in the skirt. The dress even has pockets.

"I knew I kept these," she says, indicating the footwear. "If he's half as taken with you as you are with yourself, I imagine he'll be well pleased."

"Who?" I demand sharply, but she only shrugs and presses a bone comb into my hand.

"Fix your hair," she says, then shrugs again. "Or make it wilder. You look lovely either way."

"What will you want for all this?" I ask, thinking of all the faerie bargains I've overheard, and of how much I like the dress I am wearing, how I could use the boots. I understand the temptation felt by every fool in a forest.

Her bead-black eyes study me, then she shakes her head. "I serve Queen Annet, and she bade me gift whatever the prince of the High Court asked, were it within the scope of my talents."

Of course someone must have told Oak where Habetrot's chambers were and assured him that she could do what he asked. So it is not Habetrot I owe, but Oak. And he owes Queen Annet in turn. My heart sinks. Debt is not easily dismissed in Faerie.

And the Court of Moths are showing off what good hosts they are.

"The gown is the most gorgeous thing I've ever seen," I say to her, as I can pay her no other way without insult. It has been a long time since I have been given a gift, barbed though it may be. "It does feel as though it might come from a dream."

That makes Habetrot's cheeks pink. "Good. Maybe you will come back and tell me how the Prince of Sunlight liked the Queen of Night."

Embarrassed, I step out into the hall, wondering how she could believe that a dress—no matter how beautiful—could make me into an object of desire. Wondering if everyone at the revel would think that I was dangling after Oak and laugh behind their hands.

I stomp back through the hall to my room and swing open the door, only to find Oak lounging in one of the chairs, his long limbs spread out in shameless comfort. A flower crown of myrtle rests just above his horns. With it, he wears a new shirt of white linen and scarlet trousers embroidered with vines. Even his hooves appear polished.

He looks every bit the handsome faerie prince, beloved by everyone and everything. Rabbits probably eat from his hands. Blue jays try to feed him worms meant for their own children.

He smiles, as though not surprised to see me in a beautiful gown. In fact, his gaze passes over it quickly, to rest with an odd intensity on my face. "Striking," he says, although I do not see how he could have possibly given it enough attention to know.

I feel both shy and resentful.

The Prince of Sunlight.

I do not bother telling him what he looks like. I am sure he already knows.

He brushes one hand through his golden curls. "We have an audience with Annet. Hopefully we can persuade her to send us to the Thistlewitch swiftly. Until then, we have been invited to roam her halls and eat from her banquet tables."

I sit on a stool, pull on my new boots, and then tie up the laces. "Why do you think she took Hyacinthe?"

Oak rubs a hand over his face. "I believe she wanted to show she could. I hope there's no more to it than that."

I take the comb from a pocket of my new dress and then hesitate. If I begin to untangle my nimbus of snarls, he will see how badly my hair is matted and be reminded of where he found me.

He stands.

Good. He will leave, and then I will be able to wrangle my hair alone.

But instead he steps behind me and takes the comb from my hands. "Let me do that," he says, taking strands of my hair in his fingers. "It's the color of primroses."

My shoulders tense. I am unused to people touching me. "You don't need to—" I start.

"It's no trouble," he says. "I had three older sisters brushing and braiding mine, no matter how I howled. I had to learn to do theirs, in self-defense. And my mother..."

His fingers are clever. He holds each lock at the base, slowly teasing out the knots at the very ends and then working backward to the scalp. Under his hands, it becomes smooth ribbons. If I had done this, I would have yanked half of it out in frustration.

"Your mother...," I echo, prompting him to continue in a voice that shakes only a little.

He begins to braid, sweeping my hair up so that thick plaits become something like his circlet, wrapping around my head.

"When we were in the mortal world, away from her servants, she needed help arranging it." His voice is soft.

This, along with the slightly painful pull against my scalp, the brush of his fingertips against my neck as he separates a section, the slight frown of concentration on his face, is overwhelming. I am not accustomed to someone being this close.

When I look up, his smile is all invitation.

We are no longer children, playing games and hiding beneath his bed, but I feel as though this is a different kind of game, one where I do not understand the rules.

With a shiver, I take up the mirror from the dresser. In this hair and with this dress, I look pretty. The kind of pretty that allows monsters to deceive people into forests, into dances where they will find their doom.

CHAPTER
6

A knock on the door announces a knight with hair the color of rotten vegetation and eyes like onyx, who introduces herself as Lupine. She tells us that she is to lead us to the revel happening in the great hall of the palace. When she speaks, I see that the inside of her mouth is as black as her eyes. "The Queen of Moths awaits you."

She appears to be one of the sluagh, the half-dead Folk. Banshees, who are said to be the souls of those who died in grief. Fetches, which mirror the faces of the dying and announce their doom. If the Gentry are proof that faeries can live forever, and be forever young, then the sluagh are proof they might even live on after that. I find them both disconcerting and fascinating in equal measure.

Tiernan and Jack have made themselves presentable. The kelpie slicked back his dark hair and affixed a flower just below the collar of his shirt. Tiernan wears a doublet he must have hunted up from one of his bags, brown velvet and slightly wrinkled, more that of a soldier than a courtier. He frowned when he saw Oak emerge from my room with me.

"Lead on," Oak tells Lupine, and with a shallow bow, she sets off, leaving us to trail behind.

The tunnels of the Court of Moths carry the scents of fresh-turned earth and seawater. As the southernmost Court on the coast, it is perhaps not surprising that we pass through sea caves, their walls studded with the sharp remains of barnacles. There is a wet, crashing sound, and for a moment I imagine the ocean rushing in and drowning us all. But it recedes, and I realize the waves must be far enough off not to be a danger.

A little farther and we come to an underground grove. The air is suffocatingly humid. We pass floss-silk trees, their thick gray trunks covered in thorns bigger than two of my fingers together. From them hang what appear to be woolen nests of white seedpods. A few wriggle as I study them, as though something more than seeds is trapped inside, trying to be born.

The next room has a still pool dipping down into unknown depths, with night-dark water. Jack of the Lakes goes toward it, dabbling his hand. Tiernan tugs sharply on the back of his doublet. "You don't want to go swimming in there, kelpie."

"Do you think there's an enchantment on it?" Jack asks, fascinated, squatting to look at his reflection.

"I think it's where the sea folk come in," says the knight grimly. "Swim too far, and you will find yourself in the Undersea, where they have little love for lake dwellers."

I kick my skirt ahead of me. My fingers dig deep into my pockets, running over what I stuffed into them. The sharp scissors I stole from

Habetrot, the matchbook, the fox figurine, a single licorice jelly bean. I hate the idea of my things remaining in the room and being pawed over by inquisitive servants, inventoried for the queen.

Three more turns, and then I hear strains of music. We pass a smattering of guards, one that smacks their lips at me.

"Did they let you see Hyacinthe?" I ask Tiernan, matching my step to his. I do not like the thought of the former falcon being confined when he was already desperate to be free. And I am worried over Queen Annet's plans, no less her whims.

Tiernan seems surprised I have spoken to him voluntarily. "He's well enough."

I study the knight. His expression is stiff, his broad shoulders set. A thin dusting of stubble darkens his jaw. His short black hair appears unbrushed. I wonder how long he remained in the prisons and how quickly he had to dress because of it.

"What do you think Queen Annet will do with him?" I ask.

Tiernan frowns. "Nothing much. The prince has promised—" He bites off the end of the sentence.

I give him a swift, sideways look. "Did you really trick Hyacinthe into being captured?"

He turns toward me sharply. "He told you that?"

"Why shouldn't he? Would you have used the bridle to keep him from speaking had you known what he would say?" I keep my voice low, but something in my tone makes Jack of the Lakes glance my way, a small smile at the edge of his mouth.

"Of course I wouldn't!" Tiernan snaps. "And I am not the one with command of him anyway."

That seems like splitting hairs, since Oak must have told Hyacinthe to obey the knight. He's issued plenty of orders in my hearing. Still, I hate the reminder that the prince is the one who owns the bridle. I want to like him. I want to believe that he's nothing like Madoc.

Up ahead, Lupine is telling Oak something about the crystalline structures, how there are rooms of ruby and sapphire near the prisons. She points toward an arched doorway, beyond which I can see steps down. The prince bends to say something in return, and her face changes, her eyes going a little glassy.

Love-talker.

"Is that where he's being held?" I ask, angling my head in the direction that Lupine indicated.

Tiernan nods. "You think I am terrible, is that it? Hyacinthe's father was a sworn knight of Lady Liriope—Oak's birth mother. When she was poisoned, he killed himself out of shame at having failed her.

"Hyacinthe swore to avenge his father. When Madoc proved to him that Prince Dain was responsible, he declared that he would be loyal thereafter to the general who caused his death. And Hyacinthe was fantastically loyal."

"That's why he chose to be punished rather than repent?" I ask.

Tiernan made a motion of uncertainty. "Hyacinthe had heard awful things of the new High King—that he pulled the wings off of Folk who wouldn't bow to him, that sort of stuff. And Cardan was the brother of Prince Dain. So yes, his loyalty to Madoc was some of it, but not all. He can't let go of his desire for revenge, even if he's no longer sure whom he blames."

"Is that why he's wearing the bridle?" I ask.

He frowns. "There was an incident. This punishment was better than the others."

This is the most Tiernan has ever spoken to me, and even now, I suspect he is mostly talking to himself.

Still, if he expects me to believe he bridled Hyacinthe for Hyacinthe's own sake, I will find that hard to do. In the Court of Teeth, everything terrible that happened to me was supposed to be for my benefit. They probably could have found a way to slit my throat and call it a gift.

We pause at the edge of the great hall.

"Allow me to escort you in?" Oak asks me, offering his arm.

Lupine sighs.

Awkwardly, I place my hand over his, as I see others doing. The pressure of his skin against my palm feels shockingly intimate. I note the three gold rings on his fingers. I note that his nails are clean. Mine are jagged in places or bitten.

I am unfamiliar with Faerie Courts in times of peace, and yet I do not think it is just that which makes me sense the pull toward violence that is in the air. Faeries spin in intersecting circle dances. Some are in garments of silk and velvet, leaping along with those in gowns of stitched leaves or bark, others in bare skin. Among the petals, grasses, silks, and embroidered fabrics are human clothes—t-shirts, leather jackets, tulle skirts. One of the ogres wears a silver-sequined gown over their leather trousers.

Giants move slowly enough for the crowd to part around them, a few goblins dance, a troll sinks her teeth into what appears to be a stag's liver, a redcap adjusts his gore-soaked hat, pixies flit up into the tangled roots of the domed ceiling, and nixies toss their still-wet hair as they cavort. I note a trio of hobs playing a game of chestnuts in a corner, perhaps to decide what will happen to a sprite that one of them is holding in a birdcage, her feet stuck in honey.

As we enter, Folk turn toward us. They do not look at me in horror, as they did in the Court of Teeth, where I was often paraded before them while I tried to bite my captors and pulled at my chains. I see curiosity in the gazes that follow me, not entirely unmixed with admiration—though that part is doubtless either for the gown or the prince on my arm.

The air is thick with the sweetness of flowers and overripe fruit, making me feel dizzy when it fills my lungs. Small faeries buzz through it like living dust motes.

Long, low tables are heaped with food—grapes as black as ink rest beside golden apples, cakes dusted with sugar and rose petals rise in towers, and pomegranates spill their red seeds onto the tablecloth—pale silk that trails its fringe onto the packed dirt of the floor. Silver goblets stand near carafes of wines—one as green as grass, another the purple of violets, and a third the pale yellow of buttercups.

Fiddlers and pipers spread out across the brugh play songs that ought to have been discordant, but instead the notes come together in a wild and delirious noise. It makes my blood sing.

There are performers nearby, jugglers who toss golden balls into the air that turn silver before being caught. A horned acrobat steps into a flower-covered hoop and arches her back while twisting her body, making it spin. A few Folk gasp in delight. The Gentry flash their haughty, superior smiles.

For me, who has been so much alone, it feels like drowning in a deluge of sights and sounds and smells.

I make a fist of the hand that is not touching Oak, sinking my ragged nails into the pad of my thumb to keep my expression neutral. The pain works, clearing my head.

Do not scream, I tell myself. *Do not bite anyone. Do not cry.*

The guide indicates a slightly raised dais, where the Unseelie queen sits on a throne of mangrove, roots of it spread out so that they seem like the tentacles of some enormous octopus. Queen Annet wears a gown that is half leather armor and half dramatic extravagance, making her look ready to rise and fight upon a stage. Her hair falls loose in a cascade of black curls, caught in a crown of magenta bougainvillea. Her stomach is round and heavy with child. One of her clawed hands spreads across her belly protectively.

I have learned many things in the woods. I could tell you the flight patterns of crows, how to collect water droplets off leaves after a storm. I could tell you how to unravel the spells of the half dozen Folk who seek to bind mortals into unfair bargains. But I have learned nothing of politics. And yet, I have an awful feeling that every move Queen Annet has made since we arrived was pure calculation.

At Oak's approach, Queen Annet rises and sinks into a curtsy.

"Please do not trouble yourself," he says too late. He makes a bow of his own, clearly much surprised to find her pregnant. Faeries do not reproduce easily or often, and rumor was that Queen Annet had spent decades longing in vain for a child.

I make a curtsy, too, lowering my head. I am not sure the exact etiquette relative to our stations, but I hope that if I go low enough and stay there long enough, it will serve.

"Your kindness in giving us rest and refreshment is more than we would have asked," Oak says, a phrase that could have come only from someone who has been tutored in courtesy, since he sounds polite, but underneath that, a lot is left unsaid.

"And how may we accommodate you further?" asks Queen Annet

while settling herself back in her throne with the help of a goblin attendant.

"I have heard that the Thistlewitch makes her home deep in a cypress swamp in your lands. We know that those who seek her there do so at their peril. We ask for a clear path to her, if you can grant us one."

"And for what purpose do you seek her?" The queen's gaze brooks little in the way of evasion.

"It is said she can find all lost things," says Oak. "Maybe even see into the future. But we wish to know about the past."

Queen Annet smiles in a way that makes me worried. "I do not seek to anger the High Court by misplacing their prince. I could give you a marking to write on your shoes that would lead you straight through the swamp."

Oak opens his mouth, looking ready to thank her and be off on our way.

"And yet," Queen Annet says. "Let us consider your traveling companions. A kelpie, your bodyguard, and a fallen queen." Her gaze goes to me. "Do not think I do not know you, Suren, daughter of ice."

My gaze meets hers, quick and hostile, before I can make myself otherwise.

"And Hyacinthe," Oak says. "Whose return I would appreciate."

"Your prisoner?" Queen Annet raises her eyebrows. "We will secure him for the time being so that you need not play jailer in my house."

"It is no hardship," Oak says. "Whatever else you think of me, I know my duty to a captured foe, especially considering that my father is more than a little responsible for his being cursed. I ought to be the one to look after him."

Queen Annet smiles. "Sometimes duty can be a hardship. As long as everyone is well behaved, I will return him anon. Headed north, then, are you?"

"I am." The prince looks wary.

"The High Court won't help your father, will they?" the queen goes on, studying Oak.

He doesn't answer, and she nods as though his silence is answer enough.

"So you're left to save Madoc yourself." The queen draws forward on her throne. "Does that sister of yours even know you've embarked on this quest?"

Jude, we can't just let him die. That was what Oak said when he was delirious and half-unconscious.

That's why he seems tired and anxious, why he's the one putting himself in danger with only a single knight at his side. Why he and Tiernan evaded so many of my questions. Because Lady Nore took his foster father prisoner. And since Madoc was a traitor, banished from Elfhame, no one else is willing to lift a finger to get him back.

"What a dutiful boy you are," says Queen Annet when he doesn't answer.

The tilt of his mouth goes sharp-edged.

My heart beats double time. If he hid this from me, he did it for a reason. Maybe it was only that he thought I had cause not to like Madoc, since he was allied with the Court of Teeth. Or maybe he knew that we would be at cross purposes when we arrived at the Citadel, me wishing to bring Lady Nore down, and him looking to negotiate.

"The High Court might not thank me for aiding you," Queen Annet says. "Might even punish me for my part in your plan. It seems you've brought trouble to my household, Oak of Elfhame. This is poor repayment for our generosity."

And now, after realizing the game Oak has been playing with me, I understand the game Queen Annet has been playing with him.

Faerie rules around hospitality are extremely specific. For example, invoking parlay is how Madoc got the High Court to allow him, Lord Jarel, and Lady Nore to walk right into Elfhame without anyone touching a hair on his head, even though he had an enemy army camped right at the edge of one of the islands.

But once he lifted a sword and broke the rules of hospitality, well, all bets were off.

The Court of Moths declared themselves to be our hosts, so they were obligated to take care of us. Unless we were bad guests. Then they'd be free to do whatever they liked.

But what could Annet want from him? A boon for her unborn child? The bridle? The head of the heir to Elfhame?

"If my sister bears anyone a grudge for this," Oak says, "it will be me and me alone."

Queen Annet considers this. "Give me your hand," she says finally.

He does, turning it palm up. She cuts the tip of her finger with a knife taken from a strap at her wrist, then writes a symbol on his skin. "Trace that onto your shoes, and you will find your way through the swamp."

The ease with which she has given us what we want makes it clear to me she anticipates getting something from us later. Something we would not give her now, if she asked for it.

"We are all gratitude." Oak inclines his head toward her. This seems like a cue to curtsy again.

"I take very seriously my obligations as a host," Queen Annet warns, then gives Oak a small, strange smile. "You may depart in the morning. For tonight, make merry in my halls. You will need a little warmth where you are going."

Somewhere nearby, a new group of musicians starts up, playing an eerie tune.

As we make our way from the dais, Tiernan puts his hand on Oak's arm. "I don't like this."

I push my way into the crowd. My thoughts are a tangle. I recall Hyacinthe referring to Lady Nore communicating with Oak. She would have had to if she wanted him to know she had his father. And whatever else he intended, whatever he told me, Oak wants to secure his father's freedom far more than he wants to stop Lady Nore. Were I his sister, I wouldn't send him north, not when his goals might not match her own.

His goals almost certainly don't match mine.

"Elfhame requires your assistance." I repeat his words back to him with a sneer.

He doesn't look half as guilty as he ought. "I should have explained, about Madoc."

"I wonder why you decided against it," I say in a tone that indicates just the opposite.

He meets my gaze with all the arrogance of royalty. "Everything I *did* tell you was true."

"Yes, you deceive the way all the Gentry do. With your tricks and omissions. It's not as though you have the option of lying."

Out of the corner of my eye, I note that Tiernan has backed away from our argument. He is moving in the direction of the banquet table and the wine.

Oak sighs, and finally I hear something like chagrin creep into his voice. "Wren, you have plenty of reasons not to trust me right now, but I do intend to stop Lady Nore. And I believe we can. Though I plan on bringing back Madoc, we will still have done a deed no one can deny was of service to Elfhame. Whatever trouble I will be in, you'll be a hero."

I am not sure anyone has considered me that, not even the people I've saved. "And if I decide to part ways? Are you going to tie my hands and drag me along with you?"

He looks at me with trickster eyes beneath arched golden brows. "Not unless you scratch me again."

"Why do you *want* to help him?" I ask. Madoc had been willing to use Oak as a path to power, at the least.

"He's my father," he says, as though that should be enough.

"I am going north for the sole purpose of destroying my parent, and you've never seemed to think I would so much as hesitate," I remind him.

"Madoc is not the father of my blood," he says. "He's the person who raised me. He's my *dad*. And yes, fine, he's complicated. He always craved conquest. Not even power, really, but the fight itself. Maybe because he was a redcap, or maybe it's just how he was, but it's like a compulsion."

I am not sure it makes it better, to think of it as a compulsion.

"Strategy was dinner-table conversation. It was game play. It was everything. From the minute he met my mother and learned who sired me, learned that I could be the heir to Elfhame, he couldn't help scheming.

"After he got exiled to the mortal world, stuck with that geas that kept him from picking up a weapon, he was completely at a loss. Started working shifts at a slaughterhouse just for the smell of blood. Trained me in the combat he was barred from. Got involved in playing politics with the neighbors in his apartment building. Had them all at each other's throats inside of a month. Last I heard, one of the old ladies stabbed a young guy in the neck with a pen."

Oak shakes his head, but it's clear he loves Madoc, even knowing he's a monster. "It's his nature. I can't deny that he brought an army to Elfhame's shores. He's the reason Folk were killed. He made himself an enemy of the High Court. He would have *murdered* Cardan if he'd had a chance. And so, no matter how much my sister loves our dad, she can't ask her sworn subjects to help him. It would look terrible, to ask Folk to risk their lives for his when he put them in danger. But someone has to do it or he's going to die."

Now I am paying attention to what he doesn't say. "Did she *tell* you she wanted to help him?"

"No," he admits slowly.

"And does she want *you* to help him?"

He's caught and knows it. "Jude didn't know what I was planning, but if I were to guess how she's feeling right now—I'd go with enraged. But Madoc would have come for us if we were the ones that were trapped."

I've seen the High Queen angry, and no matter how she loves him, I am not sure she will forgive choosing their father over her. When she punishes the prince, though Oak believes otherwise, she will very probably punish those who helped him, too.

But when he reaches for my hand, I take it and feel the nervous, awful pleasure of his fingers threading through mine. "Trust me, Wren," he says. "Help me."

Love-talker.

Schemer.

My gaze goes to the scratches on his cheek, still raw-looking. My doing, for which he has not rebuked me. However secretive his nature, however foolish his reasons for loving his father, I like that he does. "I'll come with you," I say. "For now."

"I'm glad." The prince looks out at the hall, at the Gentry of the Court of Moths, at the dances and the revelry. Then he gives me his quicksilver smile, the kind that makes me feel as though we are friends conspiring together. "Since you're in a benevolent mood, perhaps you'll also dance with me."

My surprise must be evident. *"Why?"*

He grins. "To celebrate you continuing with this quest. Because we're at a party. So that Queen Annet believes we've got nothing to hide."

"Do we have something to hide?" I ask.

He smiles wider, giving me a tug toward the revelers. "Always."

I hesitate, but there is a part of me that wants to be convinced. "I don't know how."

"I have been trained in all the arts of the courtier," he says. "Let me show you."

I allow him to lead me into the crowd. Instead of going into one of the circle dances, though, he steers me to one side of them, so that we have room to practice. Turns me in his arms and shows me a movement, waiting for me to mirror it.

"Do you ever think about what it would be like to be a queen again?" he whispers against my cheek as we practice the steps.

I pull away to glare at him.

He holds up his hands in surrender. "It wasn't meant to be a trick question."

"You're the one that's going to rule," I remind him.

"No," he says, watching the other dancers. "I don't think I will."

I suppose he's been avoiding the throne for most of his life. I think of cowering beneath the bed in his room during the Battle of the Serpent and shove the memory from my mind. I don't want to think about *back then*. Just as I do not want to think about how, despite Hyacinthe's warnings, I am ready to eat out of the prince's hand as tamely as a dove.

It's too easy. I'm hungry for kindness. Hungry for attention. I want and want and want.

"We ought to eat something," I say. "We have a long journey ahead of us."

Although he must know it is an excuse, he releases me from his arms.

We wend through the crowd to a banquet table laden with delicacies. Oak takes a tart filled with golden faerie fruit and cuts it in half, giving a portion to me. Though I was the one who suggested food, I realize how hungry I am only after taking the first bite. Self-consciously, I pour a glass of water from the pitcher set out to mix with the wine and gulp that down.

Oak pours himself wine, undiluted.

"Will you tell me how you came to be living..." He stops, as if trying to find the words. "As you were."

I remember the care I'd given that he not know. How could I explain the way time seemed to slip from my fingers, the way I became incrementally more detached, more unable to reach out a hand to take anything I wanted? I will not allow him to pity me any more than he does.

"You could have come to see me," he says. "If you needed something."

I laugh at that. *You?*

He frowns down at me with his amber eyes. "Why not?"

The enormity of the reasons catches in my mouth. He's a prince of Elfhame, and I am the disgraced child of traitors. He befriends everyone, from the troll guard at the entrance to all those Tiernan mentioned back in the High Court, while I have spent years alone in the woods. But most of all, because he could have asked his sister to allow me to stay on the Shifting Isles and didn't.

"Perhaps I wanted to save that favor you still owe me," I say.

He laughs at that. Oak liking me is as silly as the sun liking a storm, but that doesn't stop my desire for it.

Me, with my sharp teeth and chilly skin. It's absurd. It's grotesque.

And yet, the way he looks at me, it almost seems possible. I imagine that's his plan. He wants me to be charmed by him so that I will stay by his side and do what he asks of me. No doubt he believes that a little attention and a few smiles will be all it requires of him. He expects me to be as malleable as one of the ladies of the Court.

So much of me wants to give in and pretend with him that it makes me hot with rage.

If he wants to charm me, the least I can do is make it cost him. I won't settle for smiles and a dance. I am going to call his bluff. I am going to prove to myself—prove to us both—that his flirtation isn't sincere. I lean toward him, expecting him to unconsciously move away. To be repulsed. But he only watches me curiously.

As I draw closer, his eyes widen a little.

"Wren," he whispers. I am not sure if it's a warning or not. I hate that I don't know.

At every moment, I expect him to flinch or pull back as I put one hand on his shoulder, then go up on my toes, and kiss him.

This is ridiculous. Kissing him is profane. It gives me all the horrible satisfaction of smashing a crystal goblet.

It's quick. Just the press of my dry mouth against his lips. A brief sense of softness, the warmth of breath, and then I pull away, my heart thrumming with fear, with the expectation that he will be disgusted.

With the certainty that I have well and truly punished him for trying to flirt with me.

The angry, feral part of me feels so close to the surface that I can almost scent its blood-clotted fur. I want to lick the scratches I made.

He doesn't look alarmed, though. He's studying my face, as though he's trying to work something out.

After a moment, his eyes close, pale lashes against his cheek, and he dips forward to press his mouth to mine again. He goes slower, one of his hands cupping my head. A shivery feeling courses down my spine, a flush coming up on my skin.

When he draws back, he is not wearing his usual complicated smile. Instead, he looks as though someone just slapped him. I wonder if a kiss from me is like being clawed on the cheek.

Did he force himself to go through with it? For the sake of keeping me on this quest? For the sake of his father and his plans?

I thought to punish him, but all I have succeeded in doing is punishing myself.

I take a breath and let it out slowly. My gaze slides from his, and I spot Tiernan, coming toward us. I am not certain how much he saw, but I do not want to hear anything he might have to say just now. "Your pardon," I tell Oak. "But I've had enough dancing. I think I will take my leave."

The corner of his mouth quirks. "You know where to find me if you change your mind."

I hate the way those words make my skin flush.

I head into the crowd, hoping he will lose sight of me. Cursing myself for being foolish. Cursing him for addling my thoughts.

As my eyes slide across the dancers, I know I must talk to Hyacinthe.

As long as everyone is well behaved, I will return him anon. That was what Queen Annet said, but it was possible we had already failed at being well behaved. That coming here against the wishes of the High Queen might be excuse enough to keep him locked away.

Imprisoned as he is, though, I can go and speak with him *right now* with no one the wiser. He can give me his warning in full, can tell me everything he knows.

I scoop up a handful of roasted chestnuts and eat them slowly, dropping peels onto the floor as I move toward an exit. A cat-faced faerie tears at a piece of raw meat on a silver platter. A two-headed ogre drinks from a goblet that looks, pinched between his fingers, small enough to belong to a doll.

I aim a look in Oak's direction. He's being pulled into one of the dances by a laughing girl with golden hair and deer antlers. I imagine he will swiftly forget our kiss in her arms. And if the thought makes my stomach hurt, that only makes me think of getting to Hyacinthe again.

A mortal man leaps up onto a table near me, hair in thin locs. He has an expressive face and a rangy vulnerability that draws the eye. Pushing his glasses up higher onto his nose, he begins to play a fiddle.

The song he sings is of lost places and homes so far away that they are no longer home. He sings of love so intense it is indistinguishable from hate, and chains that are like riddles of old, no longer holding him, and yet unbroken.

Automatically, I look for ensorcellment, but there is none. He seems here of his own volition, although I dread to think how mistaken he may be in his audience. Still, Queen Annet says she is a fair host. So long as he keeps to the baroque rules of Faerie, he might find himself back in his bed in the morning, his pockets full of gold.

Of course, no one will tell him the rules, so he won't know if he breaks one.

Turning away at that thought, I move the rest of the way through the crowd as fast as I can.

CHAPTER

7

I pass bored guards, who throw hungry looks in my direction. They do not follow me, though, either because they are forbidden from leaving their post or because I look too stringy to make much of a meal.

Once they are out of sight, I begin to run. I veer through the three turns to where Lupine spoke of the gem-encrusted rooms near the prisons so fast that I nearly trip.

My thoughts are racing as fast as my feet. I kissed two people before Oak. There was the boy who liked fires and, later, one of the treefolk. Neither of those kisses felt quite as doomed as the one I shared with the prince, and they had been doomed enough.

This is the problem with living by instinct. I don't *think*.

The lower level has a damp, mineral smell. I hear guards ahead, so I creep carefully to the bend in the corridor and peer around it. The enormous, copper-banded door they guard is almost certainly to the prisons, as it is carved with the words *Let Suffering Ennoble*. One is a knight with hair the color of red roses. She seems to be losing a game of dice to a snickering, large-eared bauchan. Both wear armor. She has a long sword at her hip, while his is curved and strapped to his back.

I am used to sliding into and out of a forest without being observed, but I have little experience in the sort of fast-talking trickery that might get me past guards. I draw myself up, though, and hope that my tongue does not betray me.

Then I feel a tap on the shoulder. Spinning, swallowing a scream, I come face-to-face with Jack of the Lakes.

"I can guess what you're about," he says, looking maliciously pleased, like someone who has ferreted out a delicious bit of gossip. "You intend to free Hyacinthe."

"I just want to ask him some questions," I say.

"So you don't want to break him out of the prisons?" His green eyes are sly.

I'd like to deny that, but I cannot. Like all the Folk, my tongue seizes up when I start to lie, and unlike Oak, no clever deception comes easily to my lips. Just because I want to, though, it doesn't mean I will.

"Oooooooh," says Jack, correctly interpreting my silence for a confession. "Is he your lover? Is this a *ballad* we're in?"

"A murder ballad maybe," I growl.

"No doubt, by the end," he says. "I wonder who will survive to compose it."

"Have you come to gloat?" I ask, frustrated. "To stop me?" I am not sure how powerful a kelpie is out of the water and in the shape of a man.

"To surprise you," he says. "Aren't surprises wonderful?"

I grind my teeth but say nothing for a long moment. I may not be

able to charm him with honey-mouthed words, but I understand resentment. "It must gall you, the way Tiernan talked to you."

Jack might be a merry wight, but I bet he's also a petty one.

"Maybe it wouldn't bother you so much to see him looking foolish in front of the prince? And if their prisoner was gone, the one noble
knight who checked on him last would look very foolish indeed."

I don't plan on freeing Hyacinthe. I don't even think I can. Still,
Jack doesn't need to know that. I am only playing into what he thinks
about me.

He considers my words, a smile growing on his mouth. "What if
I were to make a loud noise? Perhaps the guards would abandon their
posts to follow. What would you give me to make the attempt?"

"What do you want?" I ask, digging in my pockets. I take out the
swan-shaped scissors I stole from Habetrot. "These are pretty."

"Put them away," he scoffs. "It would be an insult to be stabbed by
them."

"Then do not court that fate," I growl softly, rummaging a bit more,
past Bogdana's note and the motel matchbook. I couldn't fit much in the
pockets of my dress, and it is not as though I had much in the first place.
But then my fingers close on the silver fox with the peridot eyes.

I take it out and hold it on my palm, reluctant to show it to him.

"What's this?" he asks.

I open my hand. "One of only three. A game piece of the Gentry."
I am proud of my answer, which is both true and yet missing the most
important detail. I am learning how to speak like them.

"You didn't steal it?" he asks, perhaps thinking of how disheveled I
was when he first met me.

"It's mine," I tell him. "No one would dispute that."

He plucks it up between two fingers. "Very well. Now it shall be mine, I suppose, since you have nothing finer. And in return I will lead the guards on a merry chase."

I clench my hand to force myself not to snatch the little fox back. He sees the gesture and smiles. I can tell he likes the trinket better now that he knows I didn't want to give it to him.

"On my signal," he says. "Hide!"

"Wait," I caution, but he is already moving.

The hall is lit with orbs that glow a sickly green, giving the stone walls a mossy cast. The orbs are spaced far enough apart that it is possible for me to push myself into a bend of the corridor and be concealed by darkness, so long as no one looks too closely.

I hold my breath. I hear the pelting of hoofbeats, then a great and foolish whooping accompanied by shouts.

"That's my sword!" the rose-haired knight yells, and then I see Jack of the Lakes streak by, running hell-for-leather in his horse form, laughing and gripping a bright silver sword in his teeth.

The knight comes into view. "When I catch you, I am going to turn you inside out, like a toad!" she shouts as she gives chase. The bauchan follows at her heels, his blade drawn.

When they are far enough, I slip out of the dark.

I head swiftly to the copper-banded door to the prisons. The rocks around the door are studded with crystals that gleam bright against the dull gray stone.

I turn the latch and walk inside. All the rooms are like chambers of a cave, with massive stalagmites and stalactites functioning as bars. It appears not unlike looking at rows and rows of mouths with rows and rows of awful teeth.

Figures move in some of the cells, shifting to blink at me from the gloom within.

A clawed hand darts out, grabbing for my arm. I jump out of its reach, jerking the cloth of my dress from its grip. I step on, shuddering.

Most of the chambers are empty, but in one I see a merrow. The floor of his cell is wet, but not enough for him to be comfortable. His scales have grown dull and dry. He watches me with eyes that are pale all the way through, the pupils barely discernible from the irises or scleras.

There is a scuffing sound from the other side, and I see a girl tossing a piece of rock into the air and catching it. For a moment, I think I am looking at a glamour, but a moment later I realize that she's actually human.

She looks as though she might be around my age, with hair the color of straw. There's a bruise on her cheek. "Can I have some water? Will you tell me how much longer I have to be here?" Her voice trembles.

I follow her gaze to the wooden tub in the corner of the room, a copper ladle hanging off one side, its body streaked with verdigris. She pushes a ceramic bowl toward the bars and looks up at me plaintively.

"Is a man with a single wing for an arm here?" I ask.

The human comes eagerly to her feet. "You're not one of the guards."

I dip the ladle into the tub and haul up some water, then pour it into her bowl. Across the way, the merrow makes a low moan. I dip the ladle again and splash him.

"The winged guy?" the human whispers. "He's down there." She points toward the end of the corridor. "See? I can be helpful. Let me out, and I could be of service to you."

It is tragic that she has only me to beseech. Does she not see my predator's teeth? How afraid must she already be for me to seem like a possible ally?

I splash the merrow again. With a sigh, he sinks down to the floor, gills flexing.

I need to see Hyacinthe, but looking at the girl, I cannot stop myself from thinking of Bex, my unsister. Imagining her in a place like this, with no one to help her and no way out.

"How did you come to be here?" I ask, knowing that more information is only going to make it harder to walk away.

"My boyfriend," she says. "He was *taken*. I met a creature, and he told me I could win Dario back if I threatened to dig down into their—" She stops, possibly at the remembrance that I *am* one of them.

I nod, though, and that seems enough to get her speaking again. "I got a shovel and came out to the haunted hill, where everyone says weird things happen."

While she talks, I evaluate the stalagmites and stalactites of her prison. Perhaps one could be cracked if someone very strong swung something very heavy at it, but since these prisons must have been constructed to hold even ogres, there's no way I would be able to do it.

"Then I was grabbed. And these *things* said they were going to bring me before their queen, and she would punish me. They started naming what they thought she might order done. All their suggestions were like something out of the *Saw* movies." She gives a weird giggle, one that tells me she's fighting off hysteria. "You've got no idea what I'm talking about, right?"

Living in the mortal world as I did, I have some idea, but there's no point in telling her that. Better get her mind away from what could happen. "Wait here."

She scrubs a hand over her face. "You have to help me."

I find Hyacinthe's cell at the end of the corridor. He's sitting on the floor, on a carpet of hay. Beside him is a tray of oranges and sweetmeats, along with a bowl of wine set down so that he might lap from it like a dog. He looks up at me in surprise, his amethyst eyes wide. I am surprised, too, because he is no longer bridled.

"Where is it?" I blurt out, terrified that it is in the possession of Queen Annet.

"The bridle?" He rubs his cheek against his wing. I see a few fresh feathers at his throat. The curse is spreading slowly, but it is spreading. "The prince was afraid of it falling into the hands of the Court of Moths, so he had Tiernan remove it."

"Oak has it?" I ask, wondering if that was the real reason he ordered it taken off. Wondering what he was planning on doing with it.

Hyacinthe nods. "I suppose." Then he sighs. "All I know is that I don't have to wear it, at least until we depart the Court of Moths. Are we leaving? Is that why you're here?"

I shake my head. "Has Queen Annet asked anything of you?"

He takes two steps closer to the bars. "I think she wishes to delay Oak long enough to determine if there's a profit in returning him to the High Court, but that's only from what I overheard the guards saying."

"You think his sister wants him back?"

Hyacinthe shrugs. "Trussing him up and handing him over could bring Queen Annet some reward if Jude does, but it would not do to *cross* her if she and the High King turn out to support his mission. Discovering what they want takes time, hence the delay."

I nod, calculating. "If Elfhame wants to stop us..."

If the High Court makes a captive out of the prince, from love or anger, then who will stop Lady Nore? Will I be held as well? And if not, then how long before Bogdana finds me?

"I don't know," he says in answer to one or all the questions I do not ask.

I lower my voice even further. "Tell me about the prince's powers as a gancanagh? And what Lady Nore sent in her message? You're not constrained by the bridle."

"Free me," he says, eyes intent. "Free me, and I will tell you all I know."

Of course. Why else try to interest me in the information he had? Not for my benefit. He wanted to escape.

I ought to focus on my own survival. This isn't what I came to the prisons for. Helping Hyacinthe will only make it certain that I wear the bridle myself.

And yet, I do not know how I can turn and walk away from him, leaving him in a cage. Neither Oak nor Tiernan were cruel to him when he was their prisoner, and still I was horrified. The Court of Moths could be so much worse.

Oak would never forgive me, though.

Unless...he never found out that I was the one who helped Hyacinthe escape. No one saw me come in here, save for Jack of the Lakes. And Jack can hardly tell anyone, since he had a part in it.

Perhaps I could keep this secret, as Oak kept secrets from me.

"Promise you will tell no one—especially not Lady Nore—anything of Oak, or me, or Tiernan that would put us in danger or expose our plans." I try to convince myself that this plan might be to the prince's advantage and that he would benefit if Queen Annet's schemes were at least partially thwarted. After all, if Hyacinthe goes missing from her prisons after she insisted on keeping him, she can hardly call herself a good host.

If Oak finds out, he will not see my actions in that light. He'll believe that I kissed him to divert his attention from the way I was stabbing him in the back. He'll believe that everything Tiernan ever said about me was true.

But if I do nothing, then Queen Annet is likely to keep Hyacinthe, in the hopes she can detain Oak or lure him to return to her Court. I cannot stand the idea of anyone being kept as I was, locked away and helpless.

"Help me escape and I will tell no one—especially not Lady Nore—anything of you, or Oak, or Tiernan that would put you in any danger or expose your plans," Hyacinthe vows prettily and in full.

The gravity of this moment settles heavily on my shoulders.

"So how do I get you out?" I ask, trying to focus on that and not the dread I suddenly feel at taking fate in my own hand, mine and Hyacinthe's. I study the stalagmites instead, looking for a seam. "These jaws must *open* somehow, but I can't see the way."

Hyacinthe puts his fingers through the gap in the teethlike bars and gestures toward the ceiling. "There's something up there, written in the stone. One of the guards looked up when he spoke, like he was reading. He shuffled his feet, too, as though there's a particular place to stand."

"You didn't *hear* what he said?" I ask, incredulous.

He shakes his head. "That must be part of the enchantment. I saw his mouth move, but there was no sound."

I squint up and spot a few scratchy, thin lines of writing. I take two steps back, and am able to make it out. It is no password to open the teethlike bars, however. It's a riddle. And as I look, I note a different one above each of the cells.

I suppose that if each chamber requires a different word or phrase to open or close, it'd be useful to have a reminder, especially with new guards coming in all the time. Not everyone's memory is keen, and there's a risk that should a word be forgotten, the cell would cease to work forevermore.

"*Daughter of the sun,*" I read. "*Yet made for night, fire causes her to weep, and if she dies before her time, cut off her head and she may be reborn.*"

"A riddle," Hyacinthe groans.

I nod, thinking of the Folk's love of games. Of how Habetrot had called Oak the *Prince of Sunlight.* Of the word puzzles my unfamily would play—Scrabble, Bananagrams. Of the poems I memorized from Bex's schoolbooks and recited to squirrels.

I try to clear my head. "The moon?" Nothing happens. As I look down, I notice there's a circle etched into the floor, just a little beyond where I stand. I step into it and speak again. "Moon."

This time, the jaws creak, but instead of opening, the cell shrinks, as though biting down on its prisoner.

Hyacinthe bangs on the toothlike stone bars, panicked. "How is the moon *beheaded*?"

"It thins to a sliver," I say, horrified at what I'd nearly done. "But it comes back. And it could be seen as the daughter of the sun—I mean, reflected light and all that."

No number of explanations for why I thought my answer was right can change that it almost got him crushed. Even now that the movement ceased, I am still left afraid that it will snap closed, grinding him to pieces.

"Be careful!" he hisses.

"Give me your answer, then," I growl.

He is silent at that.

I think more. Perhaps a *rose*? I have a vague recollection of being with my unmother at one of her friends' houses, playing in the backyard while the friend trimmed her rosebushes. There had been something about cutting off the flower heads so there would be more blooms the following year. And daughter of the sun—well, plants liked sun, right? And they didn't like fire. And, well, people thought of roses as romantic, so maybe they were made for night because people romance one another mostly at night?

That last seems like a stretch, but I can think of nothing better.

"I have something," I say, my lack of confidence clear in my voice.

He gives me a wary look, then heaves a sigh. "Go ahead," he tells me.

I move to the spot and take a deep breath. "A rose."

The teeth grind lower, the ceiling dropping so fast that Hyacinthe sprawls on the floor to avoid getting hit. I hear a sound that might be laughter from the merrow's cell, but the winged soldier is deathly silent.

"Are you hurt?" I ask.

"Not yet," he says carefully. "But I don't think there's room for the cell to close farther without cracking me like a nut."

It was different to lie in wait for the glaistig and rip apart her spells, knowing I was the one in danger. To sneak through mortal houses or even run from hags. But to think that because of a mistake of mine, a life could be snuffed out like a—

Daughter of the sun. Made for night. Cut off her head and she's reborn.

"Candle," I blurt out.

The stone cavern shifts with a groaning sound, and the bars spring apart like a mouth, like some enormous carnivorous flower. We stare at each other, Hyacinthe moving from terror to laughter. He springs to his feet and spins me around in one arm, then presses a kiss to the top of my head. "You delightful, amazing girl! You did it."

"We still have to get past the guards," I remind him, uncomfortable with the praise.

"*You* freed me from the prison. *I* will free us from the hill," he says with an intensity that I think might be pride.

"But first," I say, "tell what you know about Oak. All of it, this time."

He makes a face. "On the way."

I shake my head. "Now."

"What is it he's supposed to tell you?" the human girl asks from her cell, and Hyacinthe gives me an exasperated look.

"Not here," he says, widening his eyes to suggest the reason should be obvious: *The girl can hear us. So can the merrow.*

"We're going to get them out, too, so it doesn't matter," I say. After all, it wasn't as though I could be in *more* trouble if I were discovered.

He stares at me, wide-eyed. "That would be unwise."

"My name is Gwen," the girl calls. "Please. I promise I won't tell anyone what I overheard. I'll do whatever you want if you take me with you."

I look up at the writing over the door to her cell. Another riddle. *It gorges, yet lacks a maw. Well-fed, it grows swift and strong. Give it a draught, though, and you give it death.*

No mouth, but eats...

"Wren, did you hear me?" Hyacinthe demands.

"They're witnesses," I tell him. "Leaving witnesses behind would also be *unwise*."

"Then give me your knife," he says, frowning. "I'll take care of them."

Gwen has come to the edge of the stalagmites. "Wait," she says, her voice edged with desperation. "I can help you. There's lots of stuff I can do."

Like navigate the human world. I don't want to hurt his pride to say it, but she might be able to hide him in places the Folk are unlikely to look. Together, they can escape more easily than either of them could alone.

"The knife," Hyacinthe says, putting out his hand as though he really expects me to give him one and let him do it.

I turn, frowning. "You still haven't told me anything useful about the prince."

"Very well," he says. "When Lady Nore took Madoc, she sent a message to the High Court, asking for something in return for the old general's freedom. I don't know what she wanted, only that the king and queen refused her."

I nod. Oak spoke to me of desiring Lady Nore's defeat, though an exchange of messages suggests he might be willing to appease her instead. For a moment, I wonder if it is *me* that she wants. But if so, he hardly needs to go to the Thistlewitch. He knows exactly where I am. And the High Court would give me up immediately.

"What about being a gancanagh?" I ask.

Hyacinthe huffs out a frustrated sigh, clearly wishing to be away from here. "I will tell you what I know as quickly as I am able. He inherited some of Liriope's power, and she was able to kindle strong emotions in the people who got close to her, feelings of loyalty and desire and adoration. I am not certain how much of it was conscious and how much of it was just a tide all around her, sweeping people who got too close onto the shoals. Oak will use you until you're all used up. He will manipulate you until you don't know what's real and what isn't."

I remember what Tiernan said about Hyacinthe's father.

"Forget this quest. You will never know what the prince is thinking behind his smiles," Hyacinthe says. "You are a coin to be spent, and he is a royal, used to throwing around gold."

My gaze goes to the riddle above Gwen's door again, which suddenly seems easier to solve than any of my other problems.

What eats but doesn't drink? My gaze drifts to the water, to the verdigris. Then to gorging. To hungry mouths.

Mouths like the one that the bars represent, ready to devour Gwen if I get the answer wrong. The cell that Hyacinthe was in gave me three tries, but I note that the ceiling of Gwen's is lower. I might have only two guesses before she's crushed.

And since the guards may come in at any moment, it's possible I have less time than that.

I am terrified of coming up with the wrong answer and yet equally worried we will be caught. Both thoughts are distracting, creating a loop of nerves.

Give it a draught and you give it death.

I think of splashing the merrow with water. I think of the sea.

I think of the answer to the other door, a candle. It gorges, and giving it a drink would put out its flame. Could both riddles have the same answer? Could all the cells be opened the same way?

I open my mouth to speak, but caution stops me. *Well-fed, it grows swift and strong.* Candles do not grow. I almost spoke the wrong word again.

No, not a candle, but something like one. A candle might not grow, but its flame could.

"Fire," I whisper, and Gwen's cell opens, disgorging her.

She stumbles out, looking around the room as though this might be a trick. She studies Hyacinthe warily, perhaps worried he might use a knife on her after all.

"You're going to take her with you," I inform him. "Instead of me."

He looks at me as if I have lost my mind. "And why would I do that?"

"Because I am asking you to, and I got you out of prison," I say, fixing him with what I hope is a firm look.

He is not intimidated by me, however. "Nowhere in your price was helping a foolish mortal."

Panic churns in my gut. "What if I take the curse off you?"

"Impossible," he says. "Even Oak couldn't permanently remove it, and he is from the High Court."

The prince hasn't had the practice I have in removing curses, though. And perhaps he hadn't *wanted* it completely gone.

"But if I could . . . ," I ask in my rough voice.

Grudgingly he nods.

I turn to Gwen and show her my teeth, pleased when she flinches. "You solve the riddle to release the merrow. Do not get it wrong."

Then I reach for Hyacinthe's wing.

I feel the feathers in my hands, the softness and lightness of the bones underneath. And I sense the curse reknitting itself inside Hyacinthe, as though it were a living thing.

I reach into the magic and am surprised by the stickiness of the threads. It's like tugging at a spiderweb. The harder I pull, the more the curse seems to attach itself to me, trying to transform me, too. I feel the draw of the enchantment, the shimmer and burn of it, tugging at something inside me.

"What are you doing?" Hyacinthe asks. His wing pulls free of my fingers.

I open my eyes, only then realizing I'd closed them. "Did it hurt?"

"No—I don't know," he says. "It felt like you were touching—under my skin."

I take a breath and return to the work of pulling apart the curse. But each time I attempt to break it, the strands of the spell slip through my fingers. And each time I am drawn further in, until I feel as though I am choking on feathers. Until I am drowning. The knot inside me, at the center of my magic, is coming undone.

"Stop," Hyacinthe says, shaking my shoulder. "Enough."

I find myself on the ground with him kneeling beside me. I can't seem to get my breath back.

The glaistig's spells were simple compared with this webbing of enchantment. I grit my teeth. I might be good enough among the solitary fey of the mortal world, but it was sheer arrogance to think that meant I could unstitch the magic of the High Court.

A few feet away, I see Gwen and the merrow looking over at me. He blinks, his nictating membrane following a moment later.

"We puzzled out the riddle together," Hyacinthe says with a frown at Gwen. "Now let's go."

"But—" I start.

"I'll take her," he says. "The mortal girl. I will get her out of here, and that creature, too. Just get up."

I ought to do that. But his words seem to come from far away as I reach for the magic again, and this time when it tries to draw me into it, I pull it into me instead. I let it drag me under. I take the whole curse in a rush.

Everything stops. No air is in my lungs. There is a pain in my chest, as though my heart cannot beat. As though something inside me is cracking. As though I am going to come apart.

I concentrate on the curse. On wrestling that sticky, grasping enchantment and quashing it down until it is a solid thing, heavy and cold. And then I press it further, into nothing.

When I open my eyes, my ragged nails are digging into the skin of Hyacinthe's arm. His *arm*, which is no longer feathered, no longer a wing. He is on his knees, still. I am trembling all over, so light-headed that I can barely remember where I am.

"You did it. You broke the curse. My lady, I swear fealty to you." His words take a moment to sink in, and when they do, horror sweeps over me. "To you and you alone. I was wrong to doubt."

"No," I manage to choke out.

I do not want that responsibility. I have seen what power does to people. And I have seen how those who pledge loyalty come to resent those oaths and wish for the destruction of the one who holds them. I was never less free than when I ruled.

"I am your servant forevermore," he says, heedless, pressing his dry lips to the back of my hand. His dark brown hair falls forward in a curtain, brushing my arm like silk. "Obedient to your command."

I shake my head, but the vow is made. And I'm too tired to even be able to explain why that worries me. My mind feels too adrift.

I look up at the three prisoners I freed and am suddenly, acutely aware of how much trouble I made. I didn't realize how much I have changed from that terrified girl, forever looking for a place to hide in the Court of Teeth. Breaking spells on mortals has made me rebellious.

And for a moment, I am viciously glad. It doesn't feel good exactly, to be in danger, but it does feel good to be the cause of events rather than being swept along into them.

"Take off your shoes," I tell the girl, my voice rasping worse than ever.

She looks down at her sneakers. "What for?"

I give her a commanding look, and she toes them off.

I push myself up, trying to remember my half a plan. Hyacinthe grabs my arm as I sway, and my pride urges me to snap at him, but I am too grateful.

"So that your steps will be quiet," I explain. "You three can fit behind the water trough. It's dark, and if you crouch down, you won't be seen."

Hyacinthe pauses. "And you?"

I shake my head. "I said I wasn't coming. I'll keep the guards busy. Can you find your way out from here?"

He nods, briefly. He's a soldier, hopefully trained for situations not totally unlike this. Then he frowns. "If you stay behind, you will be in great danger," he tells me.

"I'm not going," I say.

"He won't forgive you for this."

If Oak discovers what I've done, Hyacinthe is probably right. But I still have to face Lady Nore or she will hunt me down. Nothing about this changes that.

"You swore to me," I remind him, although his words echo my fears. "Moments ago. What I ask is for you to get yourself and Gwen out of the Court of Moths alive. And get the merrow to the sea cave. It's on the way."

"Send me north, to Lady Nore, then," Hyacinthe tells me, almost whispering. "Should you make it there, at least you'll have an ally."

"And that is why you ought not dramatically vow to obey someone," I say, a growl in my voice. "They seldom ask for what you hope they will."

"I know about faeries and bargains," Gwen says to me, foolishly. "You're going to ask something from me, too, right?"

I look her over. I hadn't planned on asking for anything, but that was unwise. She probably has little on her, but her clothes and sneakers would allow me to pass into the mortal world more easily, if I had to do so. And there are other things. "Do you have a phone?"

Gwen appears surprised. "I thought you would ask for a year of my life, or a cherished memory, or my voice."

What would I do with any of that? "Would you prefer to give me a year of your life?"

"I guess not." Gwen reaches into her pocket and pulls out her phone, along with a plug-in charger she detaches from a key chain. "There's no reception here."

"When you and Hyacinthe get to safety, let me know," I say, taking it. The metal-and-glass object is light in my hand. I haven't held one in a long time.

"I was going to call my boyfriend," she tells me. "Once, he picked up, and I could hear their music in the background. If he calls—"

"I'll tell him to get out," I say. "Now hide, and when they come in, you leave."

Hyacinthe gives me a speaking look as he guides the mortal toward the darkness.

It is the merrow that takes my hand. "Lady of the land," he says, voice even raspier than mine, skin chilly. "The only gift I have to give you is knowledge. There is a war coming in the waves. The Queen of the Undersea has grown weak, and her child is weaker. When there comes blood in the water, the land would be well served to stay away. Cirien-Cròin is coming."

Then he lurches toward the water barrel.

And at his warning, I walk to the copper-banded door and turn the knob. I still feel wobbly and breathless, as though I have cast off a long fever. No breaking of a curse ever felt like this before, and it frightens me.

But the bauchan and the rose-haired knight on the other side scare me even more. At the sight of me, she reaches for her sword, which I note she retrieved. I hope that means that Jack of the Lakes dropped it and not that he was caught.

"How did you—" the bauchan begins.

I cut them off with the firmest voice I can summon. "The cursed soldier—the prince's prisoner—he's not in his cell!" Which is true enough, since I let him out.

"That doesn't explain what *you're* doing where you're not supposed to be," the rose-haired knight says.

"When I came, there was no one guarding the entrance," I say, letting that accusation hang in the air.

The rose-haired knight strides past me impatiently, a blush coloring her cheeks. She stalks to the end of the prison where Hyacinthe ought to be. I follow, carefully keeping my gaze from the shadows.

"Well?" I say, hand on my hip.

The panic in their eyes tells me that Queen Annet has earned her reputation for brutality honestly.

"*The girl*," the rose-haired knight says, realizing the human is gone, too.

"And the *spy* from the Undersea." The bauchan speaks a word to open the merrow's cell, then walks around it. Letting all the prisoners out has confused their suppositions about what happened, at least.

"You saw nothing?" the rose-haired knight asks.

"What was there to see?" I return. "What did *you* see, to leave your post?"

The bauchan gives the knight a look, seeming to will her to silence. Neither of them speaks for a long moment. Finally, the knight says, "Tell no one of this. We will catch the prisoners. They must never make it out of the Court of Moths."

I nod slowly, as though I am considering her words. I lift my chin as I have seen the Gentry do, as Lady Nore did. No one would have believed the part I am playing were I in my rags, with my wild hair, but I see the guards believe me now. Perhaps I could come to like this dress for more than its beauty.

"I must rejoin the prince," I say. "I will keep this from him as long as I can, but if you don't find Hyacinthe before we depart for the Thistle-witch at dawn, there will be no hiding that he's gone."

Heart thundering, I walk out into the hall. Then I retrace my steps to the revel, pressing my hands to my chest to still their trembling.

I head to a table and pour myself a long draught of green wine. It smells like crushed grass and goes straight to my head, drowning out the sour taste of adrenaline.

I spot Oak, a wine bottle in one hand and the cat-headed lady I saw before in his arms. She reaches up to pet his golden curls with her claws as they dance. Then there is a change of partners, and a crone moves into the cat lady's place.

The prince takes her withered hand and kisses it. When she leans in to kiss his throat, he only laughs. Then sweeps her away into the steps of the gavotte, his inebriated smile never dipping or faltering.

Until the ogre dancing with the cat-headed lady abruptly pulls her out of the spinning circle. He pushes her roughly through the throng toward a second ogre.

Oak stops dancing, leaving his partner as he strides across the floor to them.

I follow more slowly, unable to make the crowd part for me as he did.

By the time I get anywhere close, the cat-headed lady is standing behind Oak, hissing like a snake.

"Give her over," says one of the ogres. "She's a little thief, and I'll have it out of her hide."

"A thief? Purloining hearts, perhaps," says Oak, making the cat lady smile. She wears a gown of the palest pink silk with panniers on either side and earrings of crystals hanging from her furred ears. She looks too wealthy to need to steal anything.

"You think because you've got that good royal blood in you, you're better than us," says the ogre, pressing one long fingernail against the prince's shoulder. "Maybe you are. Only way to be sure is to have a taste."

There's a drunken wobble to Oak's movements as he pushes off the ogre's hand and obvious contempt in his voice. "The difference in flavor would be too subtle for your palate."

The cat-headed lady presses a handkerchief to her mouth and steps delicately away, not sticking around to witness the consequences of Oak's gallant defense of her.

"I doubt it will be much trouble to bleed you and find out," one ogre says, causing the other to laugh and close in. "Shall we put it to a test?"

At that, the prince edges back a little, but the second ogre is directly behind him. "That would be a mistake."

The last thing Oak ought to do is show them he's afraid. The scent of weakness is headier than blood.

Unless he *wants* to be hit.

Should he be drawn into a fight, he would violate guest etiquette. But if one of the ogres struck first—then it would be the host who had made the misstep. Judging by the size of the ogres, though, a single blow might knock the prince's head off his shoulders.

Not only are they large, but they look trained for violence. Oak wasn't even able to block my hand when I scratched his face.

I must have made some impulsive, jerky movement, because the prince's gaze goes to me. One of the ogres turns in my direction and chuckles.

"Well, well," he says. "She looks delicious. Is she yours? Since you defended a thief, perhaps we ought to show you what it feels like to be stolen from."

Oak's voice hardens. "You're witless enough not to know the difference between eating a rock and a sweetmeat until your teeth crack, but know this—she is not to be touched."

"What did you say?" asks his companion with a grunt.

Oak's eyebrows go up. "Banter isn't your strong suit, is it? I was attempting to indicate that your friend here was a fool, a muttonhead, a clodpate, an asshat, an oaf—"

The ogre punches him, massive fist connecting with Oak's cheekbone hard enough to make him stagger. The ogre hits him again, blood spattering from his mouth.

An odd gleam comes into the prince's eye.

Another blow lands.

Why doesn't he hit back? Even if Oak wanted them to strike first, they've done it. He would be well within his rights to fight. "Queen Annet will punish you for attacking the Crown Prince!" I shout, hoping the ogre will come to his senses before Oak gets hurt worse.

At my words, the other ogre clamps down on his friend's shoulder, restraining him from a third blow. "The boy's had enough."

"Have I?" Oak asks, wiping his mouth with the back of his hand. His smile grows, showing red teeth.

I turn to him in utter disbelief.

Oak stands up straighter, ignoring the bruise blooming beneath one eye, pushing away the hair hanging in his face. He looks a little dazed.

"Hit me again," the prince says, daring them.

The two ogres share a look. The companion seems nervous. The other makes a fist.

"Come on." Oak's smile does not seem to belong to him. It's not the one he turned on the dancers. Not the one he turned on me. It's full of menace, his eyes shining like a blade. *Hit me.*

"Stop it!" I scream, so loud that several more people turn toward me. "Stop!"

Oak appears chagrined, as though he were the only one I was yelling at. "Your pardon," he says.

They allow him to stumble over to me. Whether he's punch-drunk or just plain drunk, I cannot tell.

"You're hurt," I say, foolishly.

"I lost you in the crowd," Oak says. There's a bruise purpling at the corner of his mouth, and a few specks of blood mixed with his freckles.

The same mouth that I kissed.

I nod, too stunned to do more. My heart is still racing.

"Shall we put our dance practice to some purpose?" he asks.

"Dance?" I ask, my voice coming out a little high.

His gaze goes to the circles of leaping and cavorting Folk. I wonder if he is in shock.

I have just come from betraying him. I feel rather shocked myself.

I put my hand in his as if mesmerized. There is only the warmth of his fingers against my chilly skin. His amber fox eyes, pupils wide and dark. His teeth catch his lip, as though he's nervous. I reach up and touch his cheek. Blood and freckles.

He's shaking a little. I guess if I'd done what he did, I'd still be shaking, too.

"Your Highness," comes a voice.

I drop his hand. The rose-haired knight has pushed her way through the crowd, three more heavily armored soldiers behind her. Their expressions are grim.

My stomach drops.

The knight bows. "Your Highness, I am Revindra, part of Queen Annet's guard. And I bring news that your—that one of your companions broke into our prison and released Lady Nore's spy as well as one of Queen Annet's mortals and a merrow from the Undersea."

I say nothing. There's nothing for me to say.

"What evidence do you have?" Oak asks with a quick glance in my direction.

"A confession from a kelpie that he gave her aid. She paid him with this." Revindra opens her palm to show the silver fox with the peridot eyes.

His jaw tightens. "Wren?"

I don't know how to answer for what I did.

Oak takes the playing piece, an abstracted expression coming over his face. "I thought never to see this again."

"We're here to take Suren," Revindra goes on. "And we will take it ill if you attempt to prevent us."

The gaze that Oak slants toward me is as cold as the one he bestowed on the ogres.

"Oh," he says. "I wouldn't dream of stopping you."

CHAPTER

8

A t fourteen, I learned to make tea out of crushed spruce needles along with bee balm flowers, boiled over a fire.

"Would you like a cup, Mr. Fox?" I asked my stuffed animal solicitously, as though we were very fancy.

He didn't want any. Since stealing Mr. Fox back from my unparents' boxes, I'd cuddled up with him every night, and his fur had become dingy from sleeping on moss and dirt.

Worse, there were a few times I'd left him behind when I went to sit underneath windows at Bex's school or the local community college, repeating probably useless poems and snatches of history to myself, or doing sums by tracing the numbers in the earth. One night when I returned, I found he'd been attacked by a squirrel looking for material to nest in and most of his insides had been pulled out.

Since then, I'd stayed at my camp, reading him a novel about an impoverished governess I'd taken from the library when I'd picked up

Foraging in the American Southeast. There was a lot about convalescing and chilblains, so I figured it might make him feel better.

Mr. Fox looked uncomfortably like the skins Bogdana hung up to dry after her kills.

"We'll get you some new guts, Mr. Fox," I promised him. "Feathers, maybe."

As I flopped down, my gaze tracked a bird in the tree above us. I'd gotten fast and vicious in the wild. I could catch it easily enough, but it would be hard to be sure the feathers were clean and parasite-free. Maybe I should consider ripping apart one of my unfamily's pillows instead.

Out in the woods, I'd often think of the games Rebecca and I used to play. Like once, when we were pretending to be fairy-tale princesses. We carted out props—a rusty axe that had probably never been taken from the garage before, two paper crowns I'd made from glitter and cut-up newspaper, and an apple, only slightly bruised, but shiny with wax.

"First, I am going to be a woodsman and you are going to plead for your life," Rebecca told me. "I'll be sympathetic, because you're so pretty and sad, so I'll kill a deer instead."

So we played that out, and Rebecca hacked at weeds with the axe.

"Now I'll be the evil queen," I'd volunteered. "And you can pretend to give me—"

"*I'm* the evil queen," Rebecca insisted. "And the prince. And the woodsman."

"That's not fair," I whined. Rebecca could be so bossy sometimes. "You get to do everything, and all I get to do is cry and sleep."

"You get to eat the apple," Rebecca pointed out. "And wear a crown.

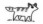

Besides, you *said* that you wanted to be the princess. That's what princesses do."

Bite the bad apple. Sleep.

Cry.

A rustling sound made my head come up.

"Suren?" a shout came through the woods. No one should have
been calling me. No one should have even known my name.

"Stay here, Mr. Fox," I said, tucking him into my dwelling. Then I
crept toward the voice.

Only to see Oak, the heir to Elfhame, standing in a clearing. All my
memories of him were of a merry young boy. But he'd become tall and
rawboned, in the manner of children who have grown suddenly, and
too fast. When he moved, it was with coltish uncertainty, as though not
used to his body. He would be thirteen. And he had no reason to be in
my woods.

I crouched in a patch of ferns. "What do you want?"

He turned toward my voice. "Suren?" he called again. "Is that you?"

Oak wore a blue vest with silver frogging in place of buttons.
Beneath was a fine linen shirt. His hooves had silver caps that matched
two silver hoops at the very top of one pointed ear. Butter-blond hair
threaded with dark gold blew around his face.

I glanced down at myself. My feet were bare and dark with filth. I
couldn't remember how long it had been since I washed my dress. A
bloodstain marred the cloth near my waist, from where I'd snagged my
arm on a thorn. Grass stains on the skirt, near my knees. I recalled him
finding me staked to a post, tied like an animal outside the camp of the
Court of Teeth. I could not bear more of his pity.

"It's me," I called. "Now go away."

"But I've only just found you. And I want to talk." He sounded as though he meant it. As though he considered us friends, even after all this time.

"What will you give me if I do, Prince of Elfhame?"

He flinched at the title. "The pleasure of my company?"

"Why?" Though it was not a friendly question, I was honestly puzzled.

He was a long time in answering. "Because you're the only person I know who was ever a royal, like me."

"Not like you," I called.

"You ran away," he said. "I want to run away."

I shifted into a more comfortable position. It wasn't that I'd run. I hadn't had anywhere else but here to go. My fingers plucked at a piece of grass. He had everything, didn't he? "Why?" I asked again.

"Because I am tired of people trying to assassinate me."

"I would have thought they'd prefer you on the throne to your sister." Killing him didn't seem as though it would accomplish anything useful to anyone. He was replaceable. If Jude wanted another heir, she could have a baby. She was human; she could probably have a lot of babies.

He pressed the toe of his hoof into the dirt, digging restlessly at the edge of a root. "Well, some people want to protect Cardan because they believe that Jude means to murder him and think my not being around would discourage it. Others believe that eliminating me is a good first step to eliminating her."

"That doesn't make any sense," I said.

"Can't you just come out so we can talk?" The prince turned, frowning, looking for me in the trees and shrubs.

"You don't need to see me for that," I told him.

"Fine." He sat among the leaves and moss, balancing his cheek on a bent knee. "Someone tried to kill me. Again. Poison. Again. Someone else tried to recruit me into a scheme where we would kill my sister and Cardan, so I could rule in their place. When I told them no, *they* tried to kill me. With a knife, that time."

"A poisoned knife?"

He laughed. "No, just a regular one. But it hurt."

I sucked in a breath. When he said there had been attempts, I assumed that meant they'd been prevented in some way, not that he merely *hadn't died.*

He went on. "So I am going to run away from Faerie. Like you."

That's not how I'd thought of myself, as a runaway. I was someone with nowhere to go. Waiting until I was older. Or less afraid. Or more powerful. "The Prince of Elfhame can't up and *disappear.*"

"They'd probably be happier if he did," he told me. "I'm the reason my father is in exile. The reason my mother married him in the first place. My one sister and her girlfriend had to take care of me when I was little, even though they were barely more than kids themselves. My other sister almost got killed lots of times to keep me safe. Things will be easier without me around. They'll see that."

"They *won't,*" I told him, trying to ignore the intense surge of envy that came with knowing he would be missed.

"Let me stay in your woods with you," he said with a huff of breath.

I imagined it. Having him share tea with me and Mr. Fox. I could show him the places to pick the sweetest blackberries. We would eat burdock and red clover and parasol mushrooms. At night we would lie on our backs and whisper together. He would tell me about the constellations, about theories of magic, and the plots of television shows he'd seen while in the mortal world. I would tell him all the secret thoughts of my heart.

For a moment, it seemed possible.

But eventually they would come for him, the way that Lady Nore and Lord Jarel came for me. If he was lucky, it would be his sister's guards dragging him back to Elfhame. If he wasn't, it would be a knife in the dark from one of his enemies.

He did not belong here, sleeping in dirt. Scrabbling out an existence at the very edges of things.

"No," I made myself tell him. "Go home."

I could see the hurt in his face. The honest confusion that came with unexpected pain.

"Why?" he asked, sounding so lost that I wanted to snatch back my words.

"When you found me tied to that stake, I thought about hurting you," I told him, hating myself. "You are not my friend."

I do not want you here. Those are the words I ought to have said, but couldn't, because they would be a lie.

"Ah," he said. "Well."

I let out a breath. "You can stay the night," I blurted out, unable to resist that temptation. "Tomorrow, you go home. If you don't, I'll use the last favor you owe me from our game to force you."

"What if I go and come back again?" he asked, trying to mask his hurt.

"You won't." When he got home, his sisters and his mother would be waiting. They would have worried when they couldn't find him. They'd make him promise never to do anything like that again. "You have too much honor."

He didn't answer.

"Stay where you are a moment," I told him, and crept off through the grass.

I had him there with me for one night, after all. And while I didn't think he was *my* friend, it didn't mean I couldn't be his. I brought him a cup of tea, hot and fresh. Set it down on a nearby rock, with leaves beside it for a plate, piled with blackberries.

"Would you like a cup of tea, prince?" I asked him. "It's over here."

"Sure," he said, walking toward my voice.

When he found it, he sat down on the stone, settling the tea on his leg and holding the blackberries in the palm of one hand. "Are you drinking with me?"

"I am," I said.

He nodded, and this time he didn't ask me to come out.

"Will you tell me about the constellations?" I asked him.

"I thought you didn't like me," he said.

"I can pretend," I told him. "For one night."

And so he described the constellations overhead, telling me a story about a child of the Gentry who believed he'd stumbled onto a prophecy that promised him great success, only to find that his star chart was upside down.

I told him the plot of a mortal movie I'd watched years ago, and he laughed at the funny parts. When he lay down in a pile of rushes and closed his eyes, I crept up to him and carefully covered him in dry leaves so that he would be warm.

When I woke up in the afternoon, he was already gone.

CHAPTER
9

I am dragged through the halls and brought not to the prisons, as I supposed I would be, but to the bedroom where I readied myself for the revel. My bag is still on the hook where I left it, the comb Oak used still on the dresser. Revindra, the rose-haired knight, pushes me inside hard enough that I hit the floor with my shoulder. Then she kicks me in the stomach, twice.

I curl around the pain, gasping. I reach into the folds of my dress, hand closing over the scissors I stole from Habetrot's rooms.

Here is what I learned in the Court of Teeth. It seemed, in the beginning, that fighting back would only bring me further pain. That's the lesson they wanted me taught, but soon I realized I would be hurt anyway. Better to hurt someone else when I had a chance. Better to make them hesitate, to know it would cost them something.

Revindra is wearing armor, so when I go for her, I slash where she is most unprotected—her face.

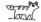

The sharp edge slices her cheek, down over the corner of her lips. Her eyes go wide, and she pulls away from me with a wild shout. Her hand goes to her mouth, wiping and staring at her fingers as though it were impossible for the wetness she's feeling to be her own blood. Another knight grabs my throat, holding me in place while a third slams my wrist on the ground until I let go of the scissors with a cry of pain.

It would be an insult to be stabbed by them, I recall Jack of the Lakes saying. I hope he's right.

When Revindra kicks me in the back of the head, I don't bother trying to muffle my anguished moan. In the Court of Teeth, they liked to hear me scream, cry out, and howl. Enjoyed seeing bruises, blood, bone. I've embarrassed Revindra, twice over. Of course she's angry. There is no profit in giving her anything but what she wants.

At least until she gives me another opening.

"Whatever your punishment is, I will ask to be the one to administer it, little worm," she tells me. "And I will do so with lingering thoroughness."

I hiss from the floor, scuttling back when she comes toward me again.

"See you very soon." Then she goes out, the other knights with her.

I crawl to the bed and curl up on it miserably.

I should have kept my temper, and I know it. If it gives me satisfaction to cause pain, that means only that I am more akin to Lady Nore and Lord Jarel than I like to suppose.

Seeking distraction from the agony in my wrist and my side, seeking a reason not to think about Oak's expression when he took his old gaming piece or to gauge the likelihood I will be executed in one of the ways that so horrified Gwen, I reach into my pocket for her phone. The glass isn't cracked. It lights up as my fingers travel over it, but there is no message from Hyacinthe. As I stare at the glowing screen, I think of my home number, the one my unparents made me repeat over and over back when Bex was Rebecca and I was their child.

We are far enough underground that the signal is very faint. A single little bar, occasionally two when I tilt it at an uncertain angle. I punch in the number. I do not expect it to ring.

"Hello." My unmother's voice is staticky, as though farther away than ever. I shouldn't have done this. I have to try to be emotionless when they come to hurt me again, and my unmother's voice makes me feel too much. It would be better to disconnect from everything, to float free from my body, to be nothing in an endless night of nothing.

But I want to hear her in case I never have a chance again.

"Mom?" I say so softly that I imagine she doesn't hear me, the connection being as bad as it is.

"Who's this?" she asks, voice sharp, as though she suspects me of playing a joke on her.

I don't speak, feeling sick. Of course this must seem like a wrong number or a prank. In her mind, she has no other daughter. I stay on the line another moment, though, tears burning the back of my eyes, the taste of them in my throat. I count her breaths.

When she doesn't hang up, I put the phone on the bed, speaker on. Lie down beside it.

Her voice quavers a little. "Are you still there?"

"Yes," I whisper.

"Wren?" she asks.

I hang up, too afraid to know what she might say next. I would rather hold her saying my name to my heart.

I press the palm of my hand to the cold stone of the wall to ground myself, to try to remember how not to feel again.

I don't know how long I lie there, but long enough to doze off and wake, disoriented. Fear crawls into my belly, clawed and terrible. My thoughts have to push through a fog of it.

And yet they come. I am afflicted with the memory of kissing Oak. Whenever I recall what I did, I wince with embarrassment. What must he think of me, to have thrown myself at him? And why kiss me in return, except to keep me docile?

Then comes the memory of Hyacinthe urging me to come with him, warning me I wouldn't be safe.

And again and again, I hear my unmother saying my name.

When the grind of the stone and the creaking of the hinges comes, I feel like a cornered animal, eager to strike. I shove the phone back into my pocket and stand, brushing myself off.

It's the rose-haired knight, Revindra. "You're to come and be questioned."

I say nothing, but when she reaches out to grab my arm, I hiss in warning.

"Move," she tells me, shoving my shoulder. "And remember how much pleasure it will give me if you disobey."

I walk into the hall, where two more knights are waiting. They march me to an audience chamber where Queen Annet sits on a throne covered in powdery white moths, each one fluttering its wings a little, giving the whole thing the effect of a moving carpet. She is dressed in simpler black than she was when I saw her last, but Oak is in the same clothes, as though he hasn't slept. His hands are clasped behind him. Tiernan stands at his side, his face like stone.

I realize how used to seeing Oak's easy smile I am, now that he no longer wears it. A bruise rests beneath one of his eyes.

I think of him staggering back from the ogre's blow, blood on his teeth, looking as though he was waiting for another hit.

"You stole from me." Annet's eyes seem to glint with barely concealed rage. I imagine that losing a mortal and a merrow was embarrassing enough, not to mention losing Hyacinthe, whom she had practically bullied Oak into letting her keep. She must especially mislike being humiliated in front of the heir to the High Court, even if I have given her an excuse to delay him a little longer. Still, she cannot make any legitimate claim that *he* was a party to what I did.

At least I don't think she can.

If Revindra is angry with me, Annet's rage will be far greater and much more deadly.

"Do you deny it?" the queen continues, looking at me with the expression of a hunting hawk ready to plunge toward a rat.

I glance at Oak, who is watching me with a feverish intensity. "I can't," I manage. I am trembling. I bite the inside of my cheek to ground myself in pain that I cause. This feels entirely too familiar, to wait for punishment from a capricious ruler.

"So," the Unseelie queen says. "It seems you conspire with the enemies of Elfhame."

I will not let her put that on me. "No."

"Then tell me this: Can you swear to being loyal to the prince in all ways?"

I open my mouth to speak, but no words come out. My gaze goes to Oak again. I feel a trap closing in. "No one could swear to that."

"Ahhh," says Annet. "Interesting."

There has to be an answer that won't implicate me further. "The prince doesn't need Hyacinthe, when he has me."

"It seems *I* have you," Queen Annet says, making Oak look at her sideways.

"Won't he go immediately to Lady Nore and tell her everything we plan?" asks Oak, speaking for the first time. I startle at the sound of his voice.

I shake my head. "He swore an oath to me."

Queen Annet looks at the prince. "Right under your nose, not only does your lady love take him from you, but uses him to build her own little army."

My cheeks heat. Everything I say just makes what I've done sound worse. Much, much worse. "It was wrong to lock Hyacinthe up like that."

"Who are you to tell your betters what is right or wrong?" demands Queen Annet. "You, traitorous child, daughter of a traitorous mother, ought to be grateful you were not turned into a fish and eaten after your betrayal of the High Court."

I bite my lip, my sharp teeth worrying the skin. I taste my own blood.

"Is that really why you did it?" Oak asks, looking at me with a strange ferocity.

I nod once, and his expression grows remote. I wonder how much he hates that I was called his lady love.

"Jack of the Lakes says that you were to escape with Hyacinthe," the queen goes on. "He was very eager to tell us all about it. Yet you're still here. Did something go wrong with your plan, or have you remained to commit further betrayal?"

I hope Jack of the Lakes' pond dries up.

"That's not true," I say.

"Oh?" says Annet. "*Didn't* you mean to escape, too?"

"No," I say. "Never."

She leans forward on her throne of moths. "And why is that?"

I look at Oak. "Because I have my own reasons to go on this quest."

Queen Annet snorts. "Brave little traitor."

"How did you persuade Jack to help you?" Oak asks, voice soft. "Did he truly do it for the game piece? I would have paid him more silver than that to tell me what you intended."

"For his pride," I say.

Oak nods. "All my mistakes are coming home to me."

"And the mortal girl?" asks Queen Annet. "Why interfere with her fate? Why the merrow?"

"He was dying without water. And Gwen was only trying to save her lover." I may be in the wrong by the rules of Faerie, but when it comes to Gwen, at least, I am right by any other measure.

"Mortals are liars," the Unseelie queen says with a snort.

"That doesn't mean everything they say is a lie," I return. My voice shakes, but I force myself to keep speaking. "Do you have a boy here, a musician, who has not returned to the mortal world in days, and yet through enchantment believes far less time has passed?"

"And if I have?" Queen Annet says, as close to an admission as I am likely to get. "Liar or no, you will take her place. You have wronged the Court of Moths, and we will have it out of your skin."

I shiver all over, unable to stop myself.

Oak's gaze goes to the Unseelie queen, his jaw set. Still, when he speaks, his voice is light. "I'm afraid you can't have her."

"Oh, can't I?" asks Queen Annet in the tone of someone who has murdered most of her past lovers and is prepared to murder again if provoked.

His grin broadens, that charming smile, with which he could coax ducks to bring their own eggs to him for his breakfast. With which he could make delicate negotiations over a prisoner seem like nothing more than a game. "As annoyed as you may be over the loss of Hyacinthe, it is I who will be inconvenienced by it. Wren may have stolen him from your prisons, but he was still *my* prisoner. Not to say that you weren't a wronged party." He shrugs apologetically. "But surely we could get you another mortal or merrow, if not something better."

Honey-mouthed. I think of how he'd spoken to that ogre in the brugh, how he could have used this tone on him but didn't. It appears to work on the Unseelie queen. She looks mollified, her mouth losing some of its angry stiffness.

It's a frightening power to have a voice like that.

She smiles. "Let us have a contest. If you win, I return her *and* the kelpie. If you fail, I keep them both, and *you* as well, until such time as Elfhame ransoms you."

"What sort of contest?" he asks, intrigued.

"I present you with a choice," she tells him. "We can play a game of chance in which we have equal odds. Or you can duel my chosen champion and bet on your own skill."

A strange gleam comes into his fox eyes. "I choose the duel."

"And I shall fight in your stead," Tiernan says.

Queen Annet opens her mouth to object, but Oak speaks first. "No. I'll do it. That's what she wants."

I take a half step toward him. She must have heard of his poor performance the night before. He's still got the bruise as evidence. "A duel isn't a contest," I say, cautioning. "It's not a game."

"Of course it is," Oak replies, and I am reminded once again that he is used to being the beloved prince, for whom everything is easy. I don't think he realizes this won't be the polite sort of duel they fought in Elfhame, with plenty of time for crying off and lots of deference given. No one here will feign being overcome. "To first blood?"

"Hardly." Queen Annet laughs, proving all I feared. "We are Unseelie. We want a bit more fun than that."

"To the *death*, then?" he asks, sounding as though the idea is ridiculous.

"Your sister would have my head if you lost yours," says Queen Annet. "But I think we can agree that you shall duel until one of you cries off. What weapon will you have?"

The prince's hand goes to his side, where his needle of a sword rests. He puts his hand on the ornate hilt. "Rapier."

"A pretty little thing," she says, as though he proposed dueling with a hairpin.

"Are you certain it's a fight you want?" Oak asks, giving Queen Annet a searching look. "We could play a different sort of game of skill—a riddle contest, a kissing contest? My father used to tell me that once begun, a battle was a living thing and no one could control it."

Tiernan presses his mouth into a thin line.

"Shall we set this duel for tomorrow at dusk?" Queen Annet inquires. "That gives us both time to reconsider."

He shakes his head, quelling her attempt at a delay. "Your pardon, but we are in a hurry to see the Thistlewitch, now more than ever. I'd like to have this fight and be on my way."

At that, some of Queen Annet's courtiers smile behind their hands, although she does not.

"So sure of winning?" she asks.

He grins, as though in on the joke despite it being at his expense. "Whatever the outcome, I would hasten it."

She regards him as one would a fool. "You will not even take the time to don your armor?"

"Tiernan will bring it here," he says, nodding toward the knight. "Putting it on won't take long."

Queen Annet stands and motions to her knight. "Then let us not detain you longer—Revindra, fetch Noglan and tell him to bring the slenderest and smallest sword he owns. Since the prince is in haste, we must make do with what he can find."

Tiernan bends toward me. He lowers his voice so that only I can hear. "You should have left with Hyacinthe."

I look down at my feet, at the boots that the Court of Moths gave me for the prince's sake. If I were to reach up to my head, I know I would be able to feel the braid he wove into my hair. If he dies, it will be my fault.

It is not long before the hall is filled with spectators. Watching the heir to Elfhame bleed will be a rare treat.

As Tiernan helps Oak into his scale-mail shirt, the crowd parts for an ogre I instantly recognize. The one that punched Oak twice the night before. He's grinning, walking into the room with insufferable swagger. He looms over the spectators in his leather-and-steel chest plate, his heavy pants tucked into boots. His arms are bare. His lower canines press into his top lip. *This* must be Noglan.

He bows to his queen. Then he sees me.

"Hello, morsel," he says.

I dig my fingers into my palm.

His gaze goes to the prince. "I guess I didn't hit you hard enough last time. I can remedy that."

Queen Annet claps her hands. "Clear some space for our duel."

Her courtiers arrange themselves in a wide circle around an empty patch of packed earth.

"You don't have to do this," I whisper to Oak. "Leave me. Leave Jack."

He gives me a sidelong look. His face is grave. "I can't."

Right. He needs me for his quest to save his father. Enough to make himself kiss me. Enough to bleed to keep me.

Oak strides to a place opposite where the ogre has chosen to stand. The ogre jests with a few folks in the eager, bloodthirsty crowd—I can tell because they laugh, but I am too far to hear what he says.

I think of Oak's father, who I saw in war councils. Mostly, his eyes went past me, as though I were like one of the hunting hounds that might lounge under a table, hoping to have bones tossed to them. But there was a night when he saw me sitting in a cold corner, worrying at my restraints. He knelt down and gave me the cup of hot spiced wine he had been drinking, and when he rose, he touched the back of my head with his large, warm hand.

I'd like to tell Oak that Madoc isn't worth his love, but I don't know if I can.

The cat-headed lady pushes herself to the front and offers Oak her favor, a gauzy handkerchief. He accepts it with a bow, letting her tie it around his arm.

Queen Annet holds a white moth on her open palm.

"If he's hurt…," Tiernan tells me, not bothering to finish the threat.

"When the moth takes flight, the duel shall begin," the queen says.

Oak nods and draws his blade.

I am struck by the contrast of his gleaming golden mail, the sharpness of his rapier, the hard planes of his body with the softness of his mouth and amber eyes. He scrapes one hoofed foot on the packed earth of the floor, moving into a fighting stance, turning to show his side to his opponent.

"I borrowed a toothpick," Noglan the ogre calls, holding up a sword that looks small in his hand but is far larger than what the prince wields. Despite Oak's height, the ogre is at least a foot taller and three times as wide. Muscles cord his bare arms as though rocks are packed beneath his skin.

At that moment, I see something waver in the prince's eyes. Perhaps he finally realizes the danger he's in.

The moth flutters upward.

Oak's expression changes, neither smiling nor grim. He looks blank, empty of emotion. I wonder if that's how he appears when he's scared.

The ogre strides across the circle, holding his thin sword like a bat. "Don't be shy, boy," he says. "Let's see what you've got." Then he swings his blade toward Oak's head.

The prince is fast, ducking to the side and thrusting the point of his rapier into the ogre's shoulder. When Oak pulls it free, Noglan roars. A dribble of blood trickles over the ogre's bicep.

The crowd sucks in a collective breath. I am stunned. Was that a lucky shot?

But I cannot continue to believe that when Oak spins to slash across the ogre's belly, just below his chest plate. The prince's movements are precise, controlled. He's faster than anyone I've seen fight.

There's a gleam of wet pink flesh. Then Noglan crashes to the floor, knocking other faeries out of his way. There are screams from the spectators, along with astonished gasps.

The prince steps to the other side of the circle. "Don't get up," he warns, a tremor in his voice. "We can be done with this. Cry off."

But Noglan pushes himself to his feet, snorting in pain. There is a bloodstain growing on his pants, but he ignores it. "I am going to eviscerate—"

"Don't," the prince says.

The ogre runs at Oak, slashing with his sword. The prince turns the slim rapier so that it slides straight up the blade, the sharp point sinking into the ogre's neck.

Noglan's hand goes to his throat, blood pooling between his fingers. I can see when the light goes out of his eyes, like a torch thrown into the sea. He slumps to the floor. The crowd roars, disbelief on their faces. The scent of death hangs heavily in the air.

Oak wipes his bloody blade against his glove and sheaths it again.

Queen Annet would have heard the story of Oak not defending himself against Noglan. She'd come to the same conclusion that I had, that there was no fight in him. That there was nothing sinister hidden behind Oak's easy smile. That he was the coddled prince of Faerie he seemed, spoiled by his sisters, doted on by his mother, kept in the dark regarding his father's schemes.

I had supposed he might not even know *how* to use his sword. He'd acted the fool, that his enemies might believe he was one.

How could I have forgotten that he'd been weaned on strategy and deception? He was a child when murders over the throne began, and yet not so young that he didn't remember. How had I not considered that his father and sister would have been his tutors in the blade? Or that if he was a favorite target of assassins, he might have had reason to learn to defend himself?

Queen Annet's expression is grim. She expected this match to go her way, with Noglan knocking around the prince, her honor restored, and us imprisoned long enough for her to get a message from her contacts at the High Court.

Tiernan turns a fierce look on me and shakes his head. "I hope you're pleased with what you wrought."

I am not sure what he means. Oak is clearly unharmed.

Seeing my expression, his only grows angrier. "Oak was never taught to fight any way but to kill. He doesn't know any elegant parries. He cannot show off. All he can do is deal death. And once he starts, he doesn't stop. I'm not sure he can."

A shiver goes through me. I remember the way his face went blank and the awfulness of his expression when he saw Noglan spread out on the ground, as though surprised by what he had done.

"Long, I wished for a child." Queen Annet's gaze goes to me again, then back to Oak. The shock seems to be wearing off, leaving her seeing that she must speak. "Now that one comes, I hope mine will do as much for me as you do for your sire. It pleases me to see a Greenbriar with some teeth."

I assume that last is a dig at the High King, well known for leaving the fighting to his wife.

"Now, Lady Suren, I promised to return you to the prince, but I don't recall promising you'd be alive when I handed you over." Then the Unseelie queen smiles without amusement. "I understand you like riddles, having solved so many in my prisons. So let us have one more contest of skill. Answer, or suffer the riddle's fate and leave Prince Oak with only your corpse: *Tell a lie and I will behead you. Tell me the truth and I will drown you. What is the answer that will save you?*"

"Queen Annet, I caution you. She is no longer yours to toy with," Oak says.

But her smile does not dim. She waits, and I am without any choice but to play her cruel little game.

Despite my mind having gone blank.

I take a shuddery breath. Queen Annet posited that there was a solution to the riddle, but it's an either-or situation. Either drowning or beheading. Either lying or truth. Two very bad outcomes.

But if the truth results in drowning and a lie results in beheading, then I have to find a way to use one of those against her.

I am tired and hurting. My thoughts are in knots. Is this one of those chicken-or-egg questions, a trap to seal my doom? If I were to choose drowning and it's the *truth*, then she'd have to do it. Which means beheading is the fate of a liar. So...

"I must say, 'You will behead me,' " I tell her. Because if she does it, then I am a truth-teller and she ought to have drowned me. There's no way to execute me properly.

I let out a sigh of relief—since there *is* an answer, whatever she might have wanted to do, she must now let me go.

Queen Annet gives a tight smile. "Oak, take your traitor with the blessings of the Court of Moths." As he takes a step toward me, she continues. "You may think that Elfhame will look ill on my attempts to keep you here, but I promise you that your sister would like it far less well to find I'd let you leave with Lady Suren, only to discover she sliced open your throat."

Oak winces.

Annet notes his reaction. "Exactly." Then she turns away with a swirl of her long black skirts, one hand on her gravid belly.

"Come," the prince commands me. A muscle in his jaw twitches, as though he's clenching his teeth too hard.

It would be safer if I hated him. Since I cannot, perhaps it is good that he now hates me.

They release Jack of the Lakes outside of the hill. His face is bruised. He slinks toward us, swallowing any witty comments. He goes to his knees before Oak, reminding me uncomfortably of Hyacinthe when he swore to me.

Jack says nothing, only bowing so low that his forehead touches Oak's hoof. The prince is still clad in his armor. The golden mail glitters, making him seem both royal and remote.

"I am yours to punish," says the kelpie.

Oak reaches out a hand and cups it lightly over Jack's head, as though offering a benediction.

"My debt to you is paid, and yours to me," Oak says. "We will owe each other nothing going forward, save friendship."

I wonder at his kindness. How can he mean it when he is so angry with me?

Jack of the Lakes rises. "For the sake of your friendship, prince, I would carry you to the ends of the earth."

Tiernan snorts. "Since Hyacinthe spirited off Damsel Fly, maybe you should take him up on his offer."

"It is tempting," Oak says, a half smile on his face. "And yet, I think we will make our own way from here."

I study the tops of my boots, avoiding eye contact with absolutely everyone.

"If you change your mind, you have only to call on me," says the kelpie. "Wheresoever you are, I will come."

Then Jack transforms into a horse, all mossy black and sharp-toothed. As he rides off into the waning afternoon, despite everything, I am sorry to see him go.

CHAPTER

10

Clouds of mosquitoes and gnats blow through the hot, wet air of the marsh where the Thistlewitch lives. My boots sink into the gluey mud. The trees are draped heavily in creeper and poisonous trumpet vine, swaths of it blocking the path. In the brown water, things move.

"Sit," Oak says when we come to a stump. This is the first time he's spoken to me since we left Queen Annet's Court. From his pack, he takes out a brush and a pot of shimmering gold paint. "Stick out a foot."

Tiernan walks ahead, scoping the area.

The prince marks the bottom of my one boot, then the other, with the symbol we were given. His fingers hold my calves firmly in place. A treacherous heat creeps into my cheeks.

"I know you're angry with me...," I begin.

"Am I?" he asks, looking up at me as though there is a bitter taste in his mouth. "Maybe I'm glad that you gave me an opportunity to be my worst self."

I am still sitting on the stump, pondering that, when Tiernan returns and yanks a twist of hair from my head.

I hiss, coming to my feet, teeth bared, hand going for a knife that I no longer have.

"You know how the bridle works as well as anyone," Tiernan says, low, so that Oak, busy drawing symbols on the bottoms of his hooves, does not seem to hear. He holds three pale blue strands of my hair in his hand. "Do not betray us again."

A chill goes through me at those words. The great smith Grimsen forged that bridle, and like all his creations, it has a corrupt secret. There is another way than wearing it to be controlled—wrapped hair, and a few words—that was how Lady Nore and Lord Jarel had hoped to trick the High Queen into binding herself along with the serpent king.

The strands of my hair between Tiernan's fingers are a reminder that even if they don't put it on me, I am not safe from it. I should be grateful that I am not wearing it already.

"Were it up to me," he says, "I'd have left you behind and taken my chances against Lady Nore."

"It's not too late," I say.

"Don't tempt me," the knight growls back. "If not for you, Hyacinthe would still be with us."

Even though I know he has reason to be cross with me, I am suddenly angry, too. Hyacinthe, with his half-broken curse, reminded me too much of myself, of my desire to have someone free me, whether I was deserving of it or not. "No one in chains could ever truly love you."

He glares. "Do you expect me to believe you know *anything* about love?"

The truth of that hits like a blow.

I turn away and tromp along through the muck and rotted vegetation, the song of frogs loud in my ears, reminding me that the sharpness of the knight's tongue already cost Oak the loyalty of Jack of the Lakes. He throws his words around like knives. Recklessly. Heedlessly.

Whatever the opposite of being honey-tongued might be.

A slithering snake catches my eye, its body as black as the serpent the High King became. Out in the water, something that is perhaps the head of a crocodile, if not more monstrous, breaks the surface. The creature's skin has become green with vegetation.

I trust that the others see it, too, although they do not slow their step.

The air is overwarm and close, and I am exhausted from the events of the night before. My ribs hurt where they met Revindra's boot. But I bite the inside of my cheek and keep going.

We walk for a long time before we come to a clearing where a few mismatched and rusty human chairs sit. A few steps farther and we see a shriveled and ancient faerie squatting beside a fire. Over it is a spit, and threaded on the metal rod is a skinned rat. The Thistlewitch turns it slowly, making the meager fat sizzle.

The braided weeds and briars of her hair fall around her, serving as a cape. Large black eyes peer out from the tangle. She wears a gown of drab cloth and bark. When she moves, I see her feet are bare. Rings shine on several of her toes.

"Travelers," she rasps. "I see you have made your way through my swamp. What is it that you seek?"

Oak steps forward and bows. "Honored lady, finder of lost things, we have come to ask you to use your power in our behalf." From his pack, he pulls a bottle of honey wine, along with a bag of powdery white doughnuts and a jar of chili oil, and sets them down on the earth in front of her. "We've brought gifts."

The Thistlewitch looks us over. I do not think she is particularly impressed. When her gaze falls on me, her expression changes to one of outright suspicion.

Oak's glance goes to me, frowning in puzzlement. "This is Wren."

She spits into the fire. "Nix. Naught. Nothing. That's what you are. *Nix Naught Nothing.*" Then she indicates the gifts with a wave of her hand. "What will you have of me that you think to buy my favor so cheaply?"

Oak clears his throat, no doubt not liking how this is going so far. "We want to know about Mab's bones and Mellith's heart. And we want to find something."

Mellith's heart? I think of Hyacinthe's warnings and the unseen message from Lady Nore. Is this the ransom she asked for in exchange for Madoc? I have heard nothing of it before.

As I look at the prince's face, soft mouth and hard eyes, I wonder how important playing the part of the feckless courtier might be, if to show competence would be to endanger his sister?

Wonder how many people he's killed.

"Ahhhhh," says the Thistlewitch. "Now, there's a story."

"Mab's bones were stolen from the catacombs under the palace of Elfhame," the prince says. "Along with the reliquary containing them."

The Thistlewitch's ink-drop eyes watch him. "And you want them back? That's what you mean to ask me to find for you?"

"I know where the bones are." Beneath Oak's calm is a grim resignation, writ in the furrow of his brow, the slant of his mouth. He means to get his father back, whatever the cost. "But not how Lady Nore can use them for what she has. And not why Mellith's heart matters. Baphen, the Court Astrologer, told me some of the story. When I asked Mother Marrow for more, she sent me to you."

The Thistlewitch shuffles to one of the chairs, her body hidden by the cape of her hair and all the briars and vines in it. I wonder, had I stayed in the woods long enough, if I might have found my hair turned into such a garment. "Come sit by my fire, and I will tell you a tale."

We drag over a few more chairs and seat ourselves. In the light of the flames, the Thistlewitch looks more ancient than ever, and far less human.

"Mab was born when the world was young," she says. "In those days, we Folk were not so diminished as we are now, when there is so much iron. Our giants were as tall as mountains, our trolls like trees. And hags like myself held the power to bring all manner of things into being.

"Once a century, there is a convocation of hags, where we, the witches and enchanters, the smiths and makers, come together to hone our craft. It is not for outsiders, but Mab dared enter. She besought us all for what she wanted, the power to *create*. Not a mere glamour or little workings, but the great magic that we alone possessed. Most turned her away, but there was one who did not.

"That hag gave unto her the power to create from nothing. And in return, she was to take the hag's daughter and raise the witch child as her heir.

"At first, Mab did as she was bid. She took for herself the title of the Oak Queen, united the smaller Seelie Courts under her banner, and began bestowing sentience on living things. Trees would lift their roots at her beckoning. Grass would scurry around, confusing her enemies.

Faeries that had never existed before grew from her hands. And she raised three of the Shifting Isles of Elfhame from the sea."

Oak frowns at the dirt. "Has the High King inherited some of her power? Is that why he can—"

"Patience, boy," says the Thistlewitch. "Prince or not, I will tell you in full or not at all."

The prince puts on an imp's grin of apology. "If I seem eager, it is only because the tale is so compelling and the teller so skilled."

At this, she smiles, showing a cracked tooth. "Flatterer."

Tiernan looks amused. He has his elbow propped on the arm of his chair and rests his head on his hand. When he isn't concentrating on keeping his guard up, he looks like another person entirely. Someone who isn't as old as he wants the people around him to believe, someone vulnerable. Someone who might have feelings that are deeper and more desperate than he lets on.

The Thistlewitch clears her throat and begins to speak again. "Mab called the child Mellith, which means 'mother's curse.' Not an auspicious beginning. And yet, it was only when her own daughter was born that she began to think of ways to weasel out of the bargain."

"Clovis," Oak says. "Who ruled before my grandfather, Eldred."

The Thistlewitch inclines her head. "Indeed. In the end, it was a simple trick. Mab boasted again and again that she had discovered a means for Clovis to rule until the rumors finally found their way to the hag. Enraged, she swore to kill Clovis. And so, the hag crept up on where the child slept in the night and fell upon the girl she found there, only to discover that she had murdered her own daughter. Mab had bested her."

I shudder. The poor kid. Both kids, really. After all, if the hag had been a bit more clever, the other girl could have just as easily died. Just because a pawn is better treated doesn't make it safer on the board.

The Thistlewitch goes on. "But the hag was able to put a final enchantment on her daughter's heart as it beat its last, for her daughter was a hag, too, and magic sang through her blood. The hag imbued the heart with the power of annihilation, of destruction, of unmaking. And she cursed Mab, so that piece of her child would be forever tied to the queen's power. She would have to keep the heart by her side for her magic to work. And should she not, its power would unmake all that Mab created.

"It is said that Mab put a curse on the hag, too, although that part of the story is vague. Perhaps she did; perhaps she didn't. We are not easy to curse."

The Thistlewitch shrugs and pokes the rat with a stick. "As for Mab, you know the rest. She made an alliance with one of the solitary fey and founded the Greenbriar line. A trickle of her power passed down to her grandson, Eldred, granting him fecundity when so much of Faerie is barren, and to the current High King, Cardan, who pulled a fourth isle from the deep. But a large amount of Mab's power stayed trapped with her remains, confined to that reliquary."

Oak frowns. "So Lady Nore needs this thing. The heart."

The Thistlewitch picks off a piece of rat and puts it into her mouth, chews. "I suppose."

"What can she do *without* it?" Tiernan says.

"Mab's bones can be ground to powder, and that powder used to do great and mighty spells," says the Thistlewitch. "But when the bones are used up, that will be the end of their power, and without Mellith's heart, all that's done will eventually unravel...."

She lets the moment dramatically linger, but Oak, rebuked once, does not hurry her on.

"Of course," the Thistlewitch intones, "that unraveling could take a long time."

"So Lady Nore doesn't need Mellith's heart?" I ask.

The witch fixes me with a look. "The power of those bones is great. Elfhame shouldn't have been so careless with them. But they would be far more useful accompanied by the heart. And no one is quite sure what the heart can do alone. It has great power, too, power that is the opposite of Mab's—and if it could be extracted, then your Lady Nore could style herself as both Oak Queen and Yew Queen."

A horrifying thought. Lady Nore would desire power of annihilation above all else. And if she could have *both*, she'd be more dangerous than Mab herself. Lady Nore would unmake everyone who had ever wronged her, including the High Court. Including me. "Is that really possible?"

"How should I know?" asks the Thistlewitch. "Open the wine."

Oak takes out a knife, using it to pry off the foil, then sticks the point of the blade into the cork and turns. "Have you a glass?"

I half-expect her to swig from the neck of the bottle, but instead, she gets to her feet and trundles off. When she returns, she's carrying four dirty jars, a chipped platter, and a basket with two melons in it, one green and the other brown.

Oak pours while the Thistlewitch removes the rat from the spit and sets it out on the platter. She begins cutting up the melon.

"Mellith's heart was supposed to be buried with Mab's bones beneath the castle of Elfhame," the prince says. "But it isn't there. Can you tell me where it is?"

When the hag is done arranging things to her liking, she pushes the platter toward us and picks up her jar of wine. She takes a long slug, then smacks her lips together. "You want me to discover its location with my dowsing rod? You want me to send eggshells spinning down the river and tell you your fate? But what then?"

Tiernan pulls a leg off the rat and chews on it delicately, while Oak helps himself to a slice of melon. I eat one of the doughnuts.

"I see you there, unnatural creature," the Thistlewitch informs me.

I narrow my eyes at her. She's probably angry I took a doughnut.

"Then I will use Lady Nore's desire for it to get my father back. What else?" Oak asks.

The Thistlewitch grins her wicked grin. She eats the tail of the rat, crunching on the bones. "Surely you know the answer, Prince of Elfhame. You seize the power. You have some of Mab's blood in you. Steal her remains and find Mellith's heart, and perhaps you can be Oak King and Yew King as well."

His sister would forgive him then, certainly. He wouldn't just return a hero. He would return a god.

After we eat, the Thistlewitch rises and dusts the bits of burned fur and powdered sugar off her skirts. "Come," she says to the prince. "And I will give you the answer you came here for."

Tiernan begins to rise as well, but she motions for him to sit.

"Prince Oak is the seeker," she says. "He will receive the knowledge, but he must also pay my price."

"I will pay it in his stead," Tiernan declares. "Whatever it is."

Oak shakes his head. "You will not. You've done enough."

"What is the point of bringing me along to protect you if you won't let me risk myself in your place?" Tiernan asks, some of his frustration over the fight in the Court of Moths obviously bleeding into his feelings now. "And do not give me some silly answer about companionship."

"If I get lost in the swamp and never return, I give you leave to be very cross with me," Oak says.

Tiernan's jaw twitches with the force of holding back a response.

"So, what will you have?" Oak asks the Thistlewitch.

She grins, her black eyes shining. "Ahhhhh, so many things I could ask for. A bit of your luck, perhaps? Or the dream you hold most dear? But I have read your future in the eggshells, and what I will have is this—your agreement that when you become king, you will give me the very first thing I request."

I think of the story the Thistlewitch told and the perils of bargaining with hags.

"Done," Oak says. "It hardly matters, since I will never be king."

The Thistlewitch smiles her private smile, and the hair stands up all along my arms. Then she beckons to Oak.

I watch them go, his hooves sinking into the mud, his hand out to support her, should she need it. She does not, scampering over the terrain with great spryness.

I take another doughnut and do not look in Tiernan's direction. I know he's still furious over Hyacinthe, and as mad as probably he is with Oak right now, I don't want to tempt him to snarl at me.

We sit in silence. I watch the crocodile creature rise in the water again and realize it must have followed us. It is larger than I supposed earlier and watches me with a single algae-green eye. I wonder if it was waiting for us to get turned around in the swamp and what might have happened if we had.

After long minutes, they return. The Thistlewitch carries a gnarled dowsing rod in her hand, swinging at her side. Oak's expression is haunted.

"Mellith's heart is not in a place Lady Nore is likely to find it," Oak says when he draws close enough for us to hear him. "Nor should we waste our time looking for something we can't get. Let's depart."

"You weren't really going to give it to her, were you?" I ask.

He does not meet my eyes. "My plans require keeping it out of her reach. Nothing more."

"But—" Tiernan begins.

Oak cuts off whatever he was about to say with a look.

Mellith's heart must have been what Lady Nore demanded in exchange for Madoc in the correspondence Hyacinthe was talking about. And if Oak was even considering turning it over, then I have every reason to be glad it's impossible to get. But I also have to remember that, as much as he wants to take Lady Nore down, she has something over him. In a moment of crisis, he might choose her side over mine.

At the edge of the swamp, the hob-faced owl is waiting for us, perched on the stringy roots of a mangrove tree. Nearby is a patch of ragwort, its flowers blooming caution-tape yellow.

Oak turns toward me, a grim set to his mouth. "You're not going to continue on with us, Wren."

He can't mean it. The prince fought and killed an ogre to keep me with them.

Tiernan turns to him, evidently surprised as well.

"But you need me," I say, ashamed of how plaintive I sound.

The prince shakes his head. "Not enough for the risk of bringing you. I don't plan on dueling my way up the coast."

"She's the only one who can control Lady Nore," says Tiernan grudgingly. "Without her, this is a fool's errand."

"*We don't need her!*" Oak shouts, the first time I have really seen his emotions out of his control. "And I don't want her."

The words hurt, the more because he cannot lie.

"Please." My arms wrap around myself. "I didn't try to run away with Hyacinthe. This is my quest, too."

Oak lets out a long breath, and I realize he looks even more exhausted than I am. The bruise under his eye from the punches he took has darkened, the purple yellowing at the edges, spreading over the lid. He pushes a stray lock of hair back from his face. "I hope you don't intend to continue to help us the way you did in the Court of Moths."

"I helped the *prisoners*," I tell him. "Even if it inconvenienced you."

For a long moment, we just stare at each other. I feel as though I've been running, my heart is beating so hard.

"We head straight north from here," he says, turning away. "There's a faerie market near the human city of Portland, in Maine. I've visited it before; it's not far from the Shifting Isles. Tiernan will buy a boat, and we'll gather other supplies to make the crossing into Lady Nore's lands."

Tiernan nods. "A good place to set off from. Especially if we need to lose anyone following us in the crowds."

"Good," says the prince. "At Undry Market, we can decide Wren's fate."

"But—" I start.

"It's four days of travel up the coast to get there," he says. "We pass through the territory of the Court of Termites, the Court of Cicadas, and half a dozen other Courts. Plenty of time for you to convince me of the mistake I am making."

He strides off to the patch of ragwort, taking a stalk of the plant and enchanting it into a fringed skeletal beast. When he has two, he gestures for us to mount. "We can cover a lot more distance in the sky."

"I hate these things," Tiernan complains, throwing a leg over the back of one.

The owl-faced hob alights on the prince's arm, and he whispers to it for a moment before it takes to wing again. Off on some secret mission.

I climb onto the ragwort steed behind Oak, putting my hands around his waist, feeling shame at being dismissed, along with anger. No matter how fast Oak's swordplay or how loyal Tiernan or how clever they might be, there are still only two of them. The prince will realize it makes more sense to bring me along.

As we rise into the air, I find myself as unnerved by ragwort horses as Tiernan is. They seem alive now, and though they are not an illusion, they are not quite what they seem, either. They will become ragwort stalks again and fall to earth, with no more awareness of what they were than any other plucked weed. Half-living things, like the creatures Lady Nore enchanted.

I try not to grip Oak too tightly as we fly. Despite the strangeness of the creature whose back I am on, my heart thrills in the air. The dark sky, dotted with stars, mirrors the lights of the human world below.

We glide through the night, a few of my braids coming loose and undone. Tiernan may distrust the ragwort steeds, but he and Oak sit astride them with immense ease. In the moonlight the prince's features are more fey, his cheekbones sharper, his ears more pointed.

We make camp beside a stream in a wood redolent of pine resin, on a carpet of needles. Oak coaxes the taciturn Tiernan into telling stories of jousts. I am surprised to find that some of them are funny and that Tiernan himself, when all attention is on him, seems almost shy.

Parts of the water are deep enough to bathe in, and Oak does, stripping off his armor and scrubbing himself with the sand of the bank while Tiernan boils up some of the pine needles for tea.

I try not to look, but out of the corner of my eye, I see pale skin, wet hair, and a scarred chest.

When it is my turn, I wash my hot face primly and decline to remove my dress.

We fly through another day and night. At the next camp, we eat more cheese and bread and sleep under the stars of a meadow. I find duck eggs, and Tiernan fries them with wild onions. Oak talks some about the mortal world and his first year there, when he used magic in foolish ways and nearly got himself and his sister into a lot of trouble.

The third night, we camp in an abandoned building. The air has grown chill, and we make a fire of cardboard and a few planks of wood.

Oak stretches out beside it, arching his back like a preening cat. "Wren, tell us something about your life, if you will."

Tiernan shakes his head, as though he thinks I won't do it.

His expression decides me. I stumble over the words in the beginning, but I give them the tale of the glaistig and her victims. In part, I suppose, to be contrary. To see if they will fault me for helping mortals and cheating one of the Folk out of her due. But they listen and even laugh at the times I get the better of her. When I am done talking, I feel strangely lighter.

Across the fire, the prince watches me, reflected flames flickering in his unreadable eyes.

Forgive me, I think. *Let me come with you.*

The following afternoon, Tiernan dons Oak's golden scale mail and sets off on his own, to set a false trail. We have a meeting place not far from the Undry Market, and I realize that I will have only one more night to persuade them to allow me to stay.

As we fly, I try to put together my arguments. I consider speaking them into Oak's ear as he can hardly escape me, but the wind would snatch my words. A faint drizzle dampens our clothes and chills our skin.

As the sun begins to set, I see a darkness that is not night coming on. Clouds form in the distance, billowing upward and barreling outward, turning the sky a sickly greenish gray. Inside, I can see the flicker of lightning. They seem to reach into the stratosphere, the top of the clouds in a shape like an anvil.

And beneath it, wind whirls, tornadoes forming.

I give a cry, which is whipped away. Oak wheels the ragwort horse downward as the air around us becomes thick. We plunge into the fog of clouds, their wet, heavy mist sinking into my lungs. The steed shivers beneath us. And then, without warning, the ragwort horse dips sharply, then drops.

We plummet through the sky, the speed of our descent shoving the scream back into my mouth. All I can do is hang on to the solid mass of Oak's body and wrap my arms around him as tightly as they will go. Thunder booms in my ears.

We plunge into a sheet of rain. It knocks us around, slicking our fingers and hair, making holding on difficult with everything so slippery. Coward that I am, I close my eyes and press my face into the prince's back.

"Wren," he shouts, a warning. I look up just before we hit the ground.

I am thrown off into mud, my breath knocked out of me. The ragwort steed crumbles away to the dried stalk of a plant under my bruised palms.

Everything hurts, but with a dull sort of pain that doesn't get worse when I move. Nothing seems broken.

Standing shakily, I reach out a hand to help Oak up. He takes it, levering himself to his feet. His golden hair is dark with rain, his lashes spiky with it. His clothes are soaked through. His scraped knee is bleeding sluggishly.

He touches my cheek lightly with his fingers. "You—I thought—"

I stare up into his eyes, puzzled by his expression.

"Are you hurt?" he asks.

I shake my head.

The prince turns away from me abruptly. "We need to get to the meeting spot," he says. "It can't be far."

"We need to find shelter." I have to shout to be heard. Above us, lightning cuts through the sky, striking into the woods just beyond us. Thunder cracks, and I see a dim thread of smoke curl upward from the site of the hit before the rain douses the fire. "We can find Tiernan when the storm lets up."

"At least let's walk in that direction," Oak says, lifting his pack and throwing it over one shoulder. Ducking his head against the storm, he walks deeper into the woods, using the trees for cover. He doesn't look back to see if I follow.

We go on like that for a while before I see a promising area to stop.

"There." I point at an area with several large rocks, not far from where the soil dips down into a ravine. There are two trees, less than six feet apart, with branches reaching toward one another. "We can make a lean-to."

He gives an exhausted sigh. "I suppose you are the expert. Tell me what I need to do."

"We find two huge sticks," I say, measuring with my hands. "Basically, as long as you are tall. They have to extend past the branches."

I discover one a few yards away that seems as though it could be partially rotted, but I drag it back anyway. Oak has caused another to bend helpfully, through some magic. I begin to tear the skirt of my dress into strips, trying not to think of how much I liked it. "Tie with this," I say, going to work on the other end.

Once they're in place, I use smaller sticks as ribs, stacking them to make a roof and then piling that with moss and leaves.

It is far from waterproof, but it's something. He's shivering by the time we crawl inside. Outside, the wind howls and thunder booms. I drag in a large log and start stripping away the bark to get at the drier wood within.

Seeing the slowness of my progress, he reaches into his boot and takes out a knife, then hands it over. "Don't make me regret giving you this."

"She wanted to delay you," I say softly, aware that he probably doesn't want to hear my justification.

"Queen Annet?" he asks. "I know."

"And you think she almost managed it because of me?" I ask. The insides of the log are drier, and I arrange the pieces I chip off on the stones in a pyramid shape, trying to keep the worst of the water off them.

He pushes wet hair out of his eyes, which are that strange fox color. Like gold that has been cut with copper. "I think you could have told me what you intended to do."

I give him a look of utter disbelief.

"Hyacinthe told you something about me, didn't he?" Oak asks.

I shiver, despite not being affected by the cold. "He said that you had a kind of magic where you could *make* people like you."

Oak makes an exasperated sound. "Is that what you believe?"

"That you inherited an uncanny ability to put people at ease, to convince them to go along with your desires? Should I not?"

His eyebrows go up. For a moment, he's quiet. All around us the rain falls. The thunder seems to have moved off. "My first mother, Liriope, died before I was born. After she was poisoned—at Prince Dain's orders—Oriana cut open her belly to save me. People do say that Liriope was a gancanagh, and her love-talking was how she caught the eye of the High King and his son, but it's not as though that power was much use to her. She paid for that charm with her life."

At my silence, he answers the question I did not ask. "Blusher mushroom. You remain conscious the whole time as your body slows and then stops. I was born with it in my veins, if you can call being torn out of your dead mother a birth."

"And Liriope and Prince Dain—"

"Were my dam and sire," he agrees. I knew that he was some part of the Greenbriar line, but I hadn't known the details. With that horrifying legacy, I suppose I can understand how Madoc would seem an admirable father, how he would adore the mother who rescued and raised him. "Whatever power I have of Liriope's, I don't use it."

"Are you sure?" I ask. "Maybe you can't help it. Maybe you do it without knowing."

He gives me a slow smile, as though I've just confessed to something. "I suppose you want to believe I charmed you into kissing me?"

I turn away, shame heating my face. "I could have done it to distract you."

"So long as you know that *you* did it," he says.

I frown at the mud, wondering how far he would have gone had I not pulled away. Would he have taken me to bed, loathing in his heart? Could I even tell? "You also—"

The sound of footsteps stops me. Tiernan stands in front of our lean-to, blinking at us in the downpour. "You're alive."

The knight staggers into the shelter, collapsing onto the ground. His cloak is singed.

"What happened?" Oak asks, checking his arm. I can see where the skin is red, but no worse.

"Lightning, very close to where I was waiting." Tiernan shivers. "That storm isn't natural."

"No," agrees Oak.

I think on Bogdana's final words. *I will come for you again. And when I do, you best not run.*

"If we make it to the market tomorrow and get our ship," Tiernan tells Oak, "we can seek the Undersea's aid to take us through the Labrador Sea swiftly and without incident."

"The merrow told me—" I begin, and then stop, because both of them are staring at me.

"Go on," Oak says.

I try to recall his exact words, but I cannot. "That there's trouble in

the sea, with the queen and her daughter. And warned me about someone, a name I didn't know."

Oak frowns, glancing at Tiernan. "So perhaps we take our chances
and do not seek the Undersea's aid."

"I am not sure I trust Wren's informant," Tiernan says. "Either way,
once we land, we ought to be able to travel from there on foot. The Citadel is perhaps thirty miles inland."

"Lady Nore will have those stick creatures patrolling everywhere
but the Stone Forest," Oak says.

The knight shakes his head. "Going through those woods is a *bad
plan*. It's cursed, and the troll king is mad."

"That's why no one will look for us there," says Oak, as though this
was part of an ongoing game in which he'd made an excellent move.

The knight makes a gesture of exasperation. "Fine. We go through
the Stone Forest. And when we're all about to die, I look forward to
your apology."

Oak stands. "As I have not yet sealed our doom, I am going for supplies. It's hard to imagine I could feel any colder or wetter, and I saw the
outskirts of a mortal town while we were in the air."

"Maybe the gale-force winds will clear your head," says the knight,
wrapping his wet cloak more tightly around himself and appearing not
even to consider volunteering to go along.

Oak makes an elaborate bow, then turns to me. "He's unlikely
to make you any promises like Hyacinthe did, but if you get that fire
going, he just might."

"Unfair," Tiernan growls.

Oak laughs as he tromps off through the wet forest.

I clear off some space on the ground to make a fire, piling up the dry bits of wood I stripped out of the center of the log. I fish in my pockets until I find the matchbook I took from the motel. I strike one against the strip of phosphorus, hoping it isn't too wet to work. When it flares to life, I cup my hand over it and try to set the small, dry pieces aflame.

Tiernan observes all this with a small frown.

"You're friends," I say, looking in the direction the prince went. "You and him."

He watches as the fire catches, smoke curling. "I suppose we are."

"But you're his guard, too, aren't you?" I am not sure if he's going to be offended by the question, or by my talking to him in general, but I am curious and tired of not knowing things.

Tiernan reaches out a hand to test the heat of the flames. "There were three before me. Two got killed protecting him. The third turned on him for a bribe. That's how Oak got the scar on his throat. At fourteen, he decided he didn't want any more guards. But his sister sent me anyway.

"First, he dragged me along to absurd parties, like he was going to embarrass me out of the job. Then I think he tried to bore me out of it by not going anywhere at all for weeks at a time. But I stayed. I was proud of being chosen for the position. And I thought he was nothing more than spoiled."

"That's what he wanted you to think," I say, having recently fallen for the same trick.

He nods to me in acknowledgment. "I didn't know that then, though. I just turned twenty myself and was more foolish than I like to remember. But it hardly matters, because a year later things went sideways. A mortal tried to stab Oak. I grabbed the guy, but he was meant to be a distraction. To my shame, it worked. A half dozen redcaps and goblins flooded the alley from the other direction, all well-armed. I told the prince to run.

"He stayed and fought like nothing I've ever seen before. Swift. Efficient. Brutal. He still wound up stabbed twice in the stomach and once in the thigh before the battle was over. I had failed him, and I knew it.

"He could have gotten rid of me after that, easily. All he would have had to do was tell anyone the truth of what happened that night. But he didn't. Got healing ointment in Mandrake Market so they wouldn't guess. I don't know when he would say I was his friend, but he was mine after that."

I look into the fire, thinking of Oak coming to see me in the woods, a year before he met Tiernan. I wonder if that was after his own guard turned on him and tried to cut his throat. Had I come out of hiding I might have noticed the newness of the scar.

Tiernan shakes his head. "Of course, that was before I realized *why* he hadn't wanted a guard. He'd taken up a new hobby. Decided to become a lure for the ambitious, anyone who might want to take a shot at the royal family. Did everything he could to make sure those shots were aimed at him."

I remember Oak coming to my woods. *Someone tried to kill me. Again. Poison. Again.* He'd been upset about the assassination attempts. Why would he court more of them? "Do they know?"

Tiernan doesn't bother asking whom I mean. "Certainly not. I wish the royal family would figure it out, though. It's exhausting to watch someone try to be a ship that rocks will break against."

I recall Oak's refusal to let Tiernan champion him in the Court of Moths, Oak's insistence that he be the one to take on the debt with the Thistlewitch. When I first met them, I thought Tiernan might grow tired of protecting Oak; now I see how hard he has to fight for an opportunity.

"Hyacinthe camped with the Court of Teeth during the war," Tier-nan says, and I glance at him through my lashes, evaluating the mean-ing of his subject change. "He told me a little about it. Not a nice place to be a child."

I frown at my hands, but I can't just ignore his words. "Not a nice place to be anything."

"What do you suppose they were planning for you?"

I draw my legs up and shrug.

"Marry the prince and then kill him, is that right?" He doesn't sound accusatory, only interested.

"I don't think they meant either of us to live long."

To that, he doesn't reply.

I stare into the fire, watch the flames crackle.

I sit there for a while, feeding bits of the log to the blaze, watching them catch, embers blowing up into the sky like lightning bugs.

Then I get up, feeling restless. Living in the woods as long as I have, I ought to be gathering things. Perhaps there isn't much I can do to make up for freeing the prisoners, but I can build up our shelter at least.

"I'll gather some more wood," I say. "And see if I can find anything worth foraging."

"Remember that I have three strands of your hair," the knight says, but there's no real threat in his voice.

I roll my eyes.

Tiernan gives me a strange look as I walk off, gathering his wet cloak around himself.

As the night envelops me, I scent the air, drinking in the unfamil-iar forest. I don't go far before I stumble on a patch of lemony wood sorrel and bullbrier. I gather some, tucking it into the pockets of my new dress. Pockets! Having them now, I cannot believe I went so long without them.

Idly, I pull the human's phone out. The screen is entirely black and will not wake. The battery has run down, and there's no way for me to charge it unless we stay in another mortal dwelling.

I tuck the phone away. Perhaps this is better, not having it work. It allows me to imagine that Hyacinthe and Gwen are safe, that my unmother was happy to hear from me. That perhaps she even called the number back.

Wandering farther into the woods, I discover a tree of loquats and pick them by the handful, eating as I go and filling my bag. I walk on, hoping to find chanterelles.

There's a rustling. I look up, expecting to see Tiernan.

But it is Bogdana who stands between the trees, her long fingers wrapped in the nearby branches. The storm hag looks down on me with her shining black eyes and smiles with her sharp, cracked teeth.

There is a rushing in my ears, and for a moment, I can hear only the thundering of my blood.

I take a branch from the floor of the woods and heft it like a bat.

Into that moment, she speaks. "Enough foolishness, child. I've come to talk."

I wonder how she found me. Was there a spy in Queen Annet's Court? Was it the Thistlewitch herself, out of courtesy toward another ancient power?

"What do you want?" I growl, feeling like a beast again despite the finery I've been dressed in. "Have you come to kill me for my lady mother? Tell me, then, how am I to die?"

The hag raises her eyebrows. "Well, well, look who's all grown up and throwing accusations around."

I make myself breathe. The branch is heavy and wet in my hand.

"I have come to fetch you," Bogdana says. "There is little profit in fighting me, child. It is time to separate your allies from your enemies."

I take a step back, thinking to put some distance between us. "And *you* are my ally?"

"I could be," the storm hag says. "Surely you'd prefer that to making me your opponent."

I take another step, and she grabs for me, nails slashing through the air.

I slam the branch against her shoulder as hard as I am able. Then I run. Through the night, between the trees, my boots sliding in the mud, thorned bushes tearing at my skin and branches catching on my clothes.

I slip, putting my foot wrong in a puddle. I crash down onto my hands and knees. Then I am up and running.

The solid weight of her comes down on my back.

We crash together, rolling on the carpet of wet leaves and pine needles, rocks digging into my bruises. Her nails digging into my skin.

The storm hag grabs my chin in her long fingers, pressing the back of my head against the forest floor. "It ought to sicken you to travel with the Prince of Elfhame." Her face is very close to mine, her breath hot. "Oak, whom you might have forced to cower at your side. To have to take orders from him is an affront. And yet, if he does disgust you, you have done well hiding it."

I struggle, kicking. Trying to pull away. Her nails scratch my throat, leaving a trail of burning lines on my flesh.

"But maybe he doesn't disgust you," Bogdana says, peering into my eyes like she sees something more there than her reflection. "They say that he can talk flowers into opening their petals at night, as though his face were that of the sun. He'll steal your heart."

"I doubt he would have the least interest in anything like that," I tell her, flinching away from her fingers.

This time she lets me go, grabbing one of my braids instead. She hauls me to my feet, using it like a leash.

I reach into my pockets and find the knife that Oak lent me to strip the log and pull it from its sheath.

The hag's eyes flare with anger at the sight of me with a weapon pointed at her. "The prince is your *enemy*."

"I don't believe you," I shout, slashing through the braid she's holding me by. Then I take off through the woods again.

And again, she gives chase.

"Halt," she calls to me, but I don't even slow. We crash through the brush. I have lost track, but I think I am headed in the direction of the lean-to. I hope I am headed toward the mortal town.

"Halt," she calls. "Hear me out, and when I am done, you may choose to stay or go."

Twice before she has nearly had me. I slow my step and turn, knife still gripped in my palm. "And no harm will come to me or my companions by your hand?"

She gives a wicked smile. "Not this day."

I nod but still make sure to leave plenty of space between us.

"You'd be well served to listen, child," she says. "Before it's too late."

"I'm listening," I say.

The hag's smile grows. "I'll wager your prince never told you the bargain Lady Nore offered. That she would trade Madoc to the prince in exchange for the very thing he is bringing north. A foolish girl. *You.*"

I shake my head. That can't be true.

No, Lady Nore must have asked for Mellith's heart. That was why he went to the Thistlewitch to find it. What use would Lady Nore have for me, who could command her? But then I recall Oak's words in the abandoned human house: *You're her greatest vulnerability. No matter her other plans, she has good reason to want to eliminate you.*

If Lady Nore wants me, she wants me dead.

And hadn't I wondered if it was me she asked for, when I was in the prisons with Hyacinthe? Suspected and then dismissed the idea. I hadn't wanted to believe it.

But the more I think on it, the more that I realize Oak never *said* that Lady Nore had asked for Mellith's heart. Only that he hoped to use her need for it against her. That he planned to trick her.

If it were *me* that Lady Nore wanted, I can see why he would have hidden so much of his plan. Why he was willing to risk his own neck to keep me out of Queen Annet's hands. Maybe even why he'd gone looking for Mellith's heart, if he thought that was something he could give to Lady Nore instead.

He must have wavered between wanting to save his father and knowing that turning me over to Lady Nore was monstrous.

At Undry Market, we can decide Wren's fate. That was what he said. And now I know what decision he will come to.

"Do not forget your place." She pokes me in the side. "You're not his servant. You're a queen."

"No longer," I remind her.

"Always," she says.

But my thoughts are on Oak, on the power I have over Lady Nore, and on how my death might be worth Madoc's life.

"I don't understand—why did she send those creatures against us if Oak was doing as she asked?"

Bogdana grins. "The message was sent to the High Queen, not to Oak. By the time the prince began his quest, Lady Nore had become frustrated, waiting. You need to wake up to the danger you're in."

"You mean from someone other than you?" I ask.

"I am going to tell you a story," Bogdana says, ignoring my words. "Would that I could say more, but certain constraints on me prevent it."

I blink at her, but I find it hard to concentrate on what she's saying, when her accusations toward Oak hang heavily in the air.

"It's a fairy tale of sorts," the storm hag begins. "Once upon a time, there was a queen who desperately wanted a child. She was the third bride of a king who'd murdered the two before her when they failed to conceive, so she knew her fate if she could not give him an heir. His need for a child was different than that of most monarchs in fairy tales—he planned for his issue to be his means of betraying the High Court—but his desire was as acute as any stemming from family feeling. And so the queen consulted alchemists, diviners, and witches. Being magical herself, she wove spells and brought she and her husband together on propitious nights, on a bed spread with herbs. And yet no child quickened in the queen's womb."

No one had ever spoken to me of my birth before, nor of the danger Lady Nore had been in from Lord Jarel. I had heard none of this, and my skin prickles all over with the premonition that whatever comes next, I won't like it.

Bogdana points a clawed finger at me. Behind her in the sky, I see a strike of lightning. "In time, they sought out a wise old hag. And she told them that she could give them the child that they'd wanted, but that they would have to do exactly what she said. They promised her any reward, and she only smiled, for her memory was long."

"What did you—" I start, but she holds up her finger in warning, and I close my mouth on the question.

"The wise old hag told them to gather up snow and form it into the shape of a daughter.

"They did this. The girl they made was delicate in form, with eyes of stone, and lips of frozen rose petals, and the sharply pointed ears of their people. When they finished sculpting her, they smiled at each other, captivated by her beauty.

"The hag smiled, too, for other reasons."

This seems like a bad jest. I am not made of snow. I am not some being who was sculpted just as Lord Jarel and Lady Nore wished. I never captivated them with my beauty.

And yet, Bogdana is telling me this story for a reason. *Sluagh.* Is that what I am? A soul given a body, one of the half-dead Folk that wail outside houses or promise doom in mirrors.

"*Now we must give her life,* the hag told them. *For this, she needs a drop of blood, for she is to be your child. Second, she needs my magic.*

"The first was easy to supply. The king and queen pricked their fingers and let their blood stain the snow.

"The second was easy for them as well because I gave it willingly.

When my breath blew across the girl, the spark of life lit within her, and they could see her eyelashes twitch, her tresses shiver. The child began to move. Her little limbs were slender and nearly as pale a blue as the reflection of the sky on the snow she'd been made from. Her hair, a deeper blue, like the flowers that grew nearby. Her eyes, that of the lichen that clung to rocks. Her lips, the red of that fresh-spilled blood.

"*You will be our daughter*, the king and queen told her. *And you will give us Elfhame.*

"But when the girl opened her mouth and spoke for the first time, they were afraid of the thing that they had made."

I shake my head. "That can't be true. That can't be how I was born."

I don't want to be a *creature*, shaped by their hands and quickened with their blood. Something made like a doll, from snow and sticks. An assemblage of parts, stranger even than the sluagh.

"Why tell me this now?" I ask her, trying to keep my voice even. "Why tell me this at all?"

"Because I need you," says Bogdana. "Lady Nore is not the only one who can seize power. There is myself as well. Myself, to whom you owe your life far more than you owe it to her. Forsake the others. Come with me, and we can take everything for ourselves."

I think of the Thistlewitch and the tale she told of Mab and Mellith's heart. Could *Bogdana* have been the hag who slaughtered her own daughter? Perhaps it is only that I heard the story days before, but Lady Nore must have been told about the bones from *someone* who remembered what had happened, who knew their true value.

And if Bogdana was that hag, then her belief that I owe her my life puts me in greater danger than ever. She murdered her own child, and even though it was by accident, I can only imagine what she'd be willing to do to something like me.

My ability to command Lady Nore is more curse than blessing. Anyone who wants Mab's bones will find me the easiest means to get them.

"You spoke of constraints," I say. "What are they?"

The storm hag gives me a fierce look. "For one, I may not harm that Greenbriar boy, nor any of the line."

I shiver. That would explain why she fled at the sight of him. Why she sent lightning only at Tiernan. And it would be the sort of curse that Mab might have put on the hag who'd intended the murder of her daughter.

I must keep my wild thoughts in check. "Is this story of my origins what you came to tell me that night on my unfamily's lawn?"

She gives me a crooked, frightening smile. "I came to warn you that Prince Oak was coming so that you could avoid him."

"Not about Lady Nore's stick creatures?" I demand.

Bogdana snorts. "Those, I thought you could handle on your own. Perhaps they'd wake you up to what you could be."

More likely, they would have shot me through with arrows, or the stick spiders would have ripped me apart. "You've told me your story. I listened. Now I am going to go. That was our agreement."

"Are you certain?" Her eyes are hard, and she asks the question with such weight in her voice that I am certain there will be consequences for my answer.

I nod, feeling as though that is safer than speaking. Then I begin to turn away.

"You know, the girl saw me."

I freeze. "What girl?"

Her smile is sly. "The mortal one whose house you creep around."

"Bex?" I was so sure she was asleep in bed. She must have been terrified to see a monster on her lawn.

"When the prince started waving his little toothpick sword, I doubled back. I thought I'd seen her face in the window. But she was outside."

I can barely breathe.

"She didn't scream. She's a brave girl." The storm hag seems to enjoy drawing out this moment. "Said she was looking for you."

"For me?"

"I told her that last I saw, you were in the company of a prince, and that he had taken you prisoner. She wanted to help, of course. But mortals will make a muddle of most anything, don't you find?"

"What did you do?" My voice is almost all breath.

"Gave her some advice, is all," says Bogdana, stepping into the shadows of the trees. "And now I am giving you some. Get away from that Greenbriar boy before it's too late. And when I see you again, you'd best do what I ask. Or I can snuff out that spark I put inside you. And snuff out your little unfamily, too, while you watch."

I am shaking all over. "Don't you dare touch—"

At that moment, Tiernan steps through the branches. "Traitor!" he shouts at me. "I caught you."

CHAPTER
11

Tiernan looks across the clearing at me, his sword drawn. I take a step back, unsure if I ought to race off into the night.

Bogdana has disappeared into the woods, leaving behind only the distant hiss of rain.

I shake my head vehemently, holding up my hands in warding. "You're wrong. Bogdana surprised me. I ran from her again, but she said she wanted to talk...."

He peers into the forest, as if expecting to find the storm hag still lurking there. "It seems obvious you were conspiring with her."

My mind is reeling, thinking of how puzzled Tiernan was when Oak suggested we part ways. Thinking of how clever it was to let me believe I was on this quest of my own free will.

I recall Tiernan tethering me in the motel. Barely speaking with me. Now I can guess the reason. He'd always considered me a sacrifice, something to look away from, something to which one ought not become attached. I shake my head. What defense can I give, when telling the truth would expose their deception?

"She warned me about continuing north," I say. "And she thought I should help her instead of Oak. But I never agreed to it."

He frowns, perhaps realizing all the things he would be unable to deny. Together we walk back to the camp. I pick up new wood as I go.

And as awful as it is to think about Oak handing me over, everything in me shies away from the story of my making. Am I no more than the sticks I carry and a little magic? Am I like a ragwort steed, something with only the appearance of life?

I feel sick and scared.

When we arrive back at the camp, Tiernan sets about moving the fire out from beneath the lean-to so it doesn't set the whole thing ablaze once the sticks dry out. To keep my hands busy, I weave branches together and knot them with more pieces of my dress to create a mat for our dwelling. Everything is still wet, droplets falling from trees with every gust of wind, causing the fire to smoke and sputter. I try not to think about anything but what I am doing.

Eventually, the heat dries things out enough for Tiernan to stretch out on my dampish mat, kick off his soaked and muddy boots, and warm his wet feet by the fire. "What did she offer you for your help?"

I reach out my hand to the fire. Since I was formed of snow, I wonder if I will melt. I hold my fingers close enough to burn, but all that happens when I snatch them back is that the tips are reddened and they sting.

"Stop that," Tiernan says.

I look over at him. "Bogdana's offer was to not murder me and my family."

"That had to be tempting," he says.

"I'd prefer greater politeness than I've gotten from anyone who wants to use me for my power," I tell him, knowing that what he wants to use me for is very different.

I think Tiernan hears a secret in my voice. But he cannot possibly guess what I have to hide. He cannot know what I am, nor why the storm hag believes I owe her. And if he wonders whether she told me that I am meant to be Madoc's ransom, he will try to convince himself otherwise. If he didn't like looking into my face knowing I was a sacrifice, how much worse would it be to look at me if I knew as well?

I am under no illusions that Bogdana would make for an easy ally, either. Too easily I can picture Bex confronting the storm hag, standing on her lawn in the moonlight. She must have felt dizzy with terror, the way I did when I first saw one of the Folk.

And yet Bex would not have been nearly afraid enough. I think about the phone in my pocket, now wishing that I could steal away and charge it, call her, warn her.

I stand and reach for Tiernan's cloak. He gives me a sharp look.

"You should hang it to dry," I say.

He undoes the clasp and lets me take it. I walk a short way to drape it over a branch, my fingers skirting over the cloth, looking for the strands of my hair he took. Such fine things, so easy to hide. Easy to lose, too, I hope, but I do not find them.

Oak's whistling alerts us to his return. His hair is dry, and he's wearing fresh clothes—jeans that are a little too short in the ankle, along with a cable-knit sweater the color of clotted cream. Over one shoulder he has the straps of a hiker's backpack. Perching on the other is the owl-faced hob.

The creature eyes me with evident dislike and makes a low, whistling animal noise, then flies off to a high branch.

Oak dumps the pack beside the fire. "The town would be lovely during the day, I think, although it lacked something by night. There was a vegetarian place called the Church of Seitan and a farm stand that sold peaches by the bushel. Both closed. A nearby bus station, where various entertainments could be gotten in trade. Sadly, nothing I was in the market for."

I glance up at the moon, visible since the storm cleared off. We began flying on the ragwort horses at dusk, so it must be well past midnight now.

Oak unpacks, taking out and unfolding two tarps. On them, he places an assortment of groceries and a pile of mortal clothes. Nothing has tags, and one of the tarps has a small tear in it. He's brought back a half-eaten rotisserie chicken in a plastic container. Peaches, despite his saying the stand was closed. Bread, nuts, and figs packed in a crumpled plastic bag from a hardware store. A gallon of fresh water, too, which he offers first to Tiernan. The knight takes a grateful swig from what ought to have been a milk jug, according to the sticker on the side.

"Where did you get all this?" I ask, because it obviously wasn't from the shelves of any store. My voice comes out with more edge than I intended.

Oak gives me a mischievous smile. "I met the family at the farm stand, and they were enormously generous to a stranger caught in a storm on a windy night. Let me take a shower. Even blow-dry my hair."

"You vain devil," Tiernan says with a snort.

"That's me," Oak affirmed. He slides the strap of his own bag over his head and sets it down not too far from the fire. But not with the communal offerings from the backpack, either. That bag is where he must keep the bridle. "I persuaded the family to let me have a few things from their garage and refrigerator. Nothing they'll miss."

A shiver goes through me at the thought of him glamouring that family, or making them love him. I imagine a mother and father and child in the kitchen of their home, caught in a dream. A chubby toddler crying in a high chair while they brought the prince food and clothes, the baby's cries seeming to come from farther and farther away.

"Did you hurt them?" I ask.

He looks at me, surprised. "Of course not."

But then, he might have a very limited idea of what *hurting them* meant. I shake my head to clear it of my own imaginings. I have no reason to think he did anything to them, just because he is planning to do something to me.

Oak reaches into the pile and pushes a black sweater, leggings, and new socks toward me. "Hopefully they'll fit well enough for travel."

Oak must see the suspicion I feel writ in my features.

"When we return from the north," he promises, hand to his heart in an exaggerated way that lets me know he considers this a silly vow rather than a solemn one, "they will wake to find their shoes filled with fine, fat rubies. They can use them to buy new leggings and another roast chicken."

"How will they sell *rubies*?" I ask him. "Why not leave them something more practical?"

He rolls his eyes. "As a prince of Faerie, I flatly refuse to leave cash. It's inelegant."

Tiernan shakes his head at both of us, then pokes at the foodstuffs, selecting a handful of nuts.

"Gift cards are worse," Oak says when I do not respond. "I would bring shame on the entire Greenbriar line if I left a gift card."

At that, I can't help smiling a little, despite my heavy heart. "You're ridiculous."

Hours ago, I would have thought he was generous, to joke with me after what happened at the Court of Moths. But that was before I knew he was going to trade me for his father, as though I were one of those gift cards.

I pick at a wing of the chicken, pulling off the skin, then meat, then crunching the bird's bones. A jagged bit cuts the inside of my mouth, but I keep eating. If my mouth is full, I will not speak.

When I am done, I take the clothes that Oak brought back for me and duck behind a tree to change. My beautiful new dress is coated in mud, not to mention ripped up all along the hem. Already well on its way to being worse than my last one. My skin feels clammy as I pull it off.

It has been many years since I wore mortal clothes like these. As a child, I was often in leggings and shirts, with sparkly sneakers and rainbow laces. My younger self would have delighted in having naturally colorful hair.

As I pull the sweater over my head, I hear Tiernan speaking quickly under his breath to Oak. He must be telling him about spotting Bogdana with me.

As I return to our lean-to with the weight of suspicion on my shoulders, with the schemes of Lady Nore and Bogdana and Oak winding around me, I realize that I cannot wait for fate to come to me.

I must leave them now, before they discover what I know. Before the moment when Oak admits to himself that he plans to give me to Lady Nore. Before he realizes that everything will be easier if I am bridled. Before I go mad, waiting for the inevitable blow to fall and hoping that I find a way to avoid it when it does.

Better to go north on my own from here and kill my mother, the one who shaped me from snow and filled my heart with hate. Only then will I be safe from her and all those who would use my power over her, no matter their reasons. I am a solitary creature, fated to be one and better as one. Forgetting that is what got me into trouble.

Once I realize the path I must take, I feel lighter than I have since Bogdana caught me in the woods. I can enjoy the sweet stickiness of the peach nectar, the slight plastic flavor of the water.

Tiernan gives a sigh. "Suppose we *do* go through the Stone Forest," he says. "Despite the deep pits that lead to oubliettes, the trees that move to make you lose your way, the ice spiders that wrap their prey in frozen gossamer, the mad king, and the curse. Then what? We don't have Hyacinthe to get us inside the Ice Needle Citadel."

"It's supposed to be very beautiful, the Citadel," Oak says. "Is it beautiful, Wren?"

When the light went through the ice of the castle, it made rainbows that danced along its cold halls. You could almost see through the walls, as though the whole place was one large, cloudy window. When I was brought to it for the first time, I thought it was like living inside a sparkling diamond.

"It's not," I say. "It's an ugly place."

Tiernan looks surprised. I am sure he is, since, if he stole Hyacinthe from Lady Nore, he knows exactly what the Citadel looks like.

But when I think of it, what I recall is grotesque. Making people betray themselves was Lady Nore's favorite sport, and one in which she was very skilled. Tricking her supplicants and prisoners into sacrificing that which they cared most about. Breaking their own instruments. Their own fingers. The necks of those they loved best.

Everything died in the Ice Citadel, but hope died first.

Laugh, child, Lady Nore commanded, not long before our trip to Elfhame. I do not remember what she wanted me to laugh at, although I am sure it was something awful.

But by then I had retreated so far inside myself that I don't think she was certain I'd even heard her. She slapped me and I bit her, ripping open the skin of her hand. That was the first moment I thought I saw a flicker of fear in her face.

That is the place I need to return to, that cold place where nothing can reach me. Where I can do anything.

"For now," Oak says, "let's concern ourselves with getting to Undry Market. I don't think we can risk ragwort again, even if we could find another patch. We're going to have to go on foot."

"I'll leave first," the knight says. "And start arranging for the boat. You take a different route to confuse our trail."

Somewhere on Tiernan's person—or in his pack—are strands of my hair. But even if I found them, can I be sure they don't have more? Can I be certain there isn't one stuck on the cloak Oak draped over my shoulders? Can I be sure Oak didn't pilfer another when he was brushing my hair?

My gaze goes to the prince's bag. I wouldn't need to care about the strands of hair if there was nothing that could be done with them.

If I snatched the bridle and ran, when I got to Lady Nore, I could be the one to make her wear it.

Oak sits by the fire, singing a song to himself that I catch only snatches of. Something about a pendulum and fabric that's starting to fray. The firelight limns his hair, turning the gold dark, the shadows making his features sharp and harsh.

He's the kind of beautiful that makes people want to smash things.

Tonight, while they sleep, I will steal the bridle. Hadn't Oak talked about a bus station, one that appeared to be open, no matter the hour? I will go there and begin my journey as a mortal might. I have Gwen's phone. I can use it to warn my unfamily of what's coming.

While I am thinking through this plan, Oak is telling Tiernan about a mermaid he knows, with hair the silver of the shine on waves. He thinks that if he could speak to her, she might be able to tell him more about what's going on in the Undersea.

Eventually, I curl up in my blanket, watching Tiernan cover the lean-to with Oak's burgled tarps. Then he climbs a tree, settling himself in its branches like a cradle.

"I'll take first watch," he volunteers gruffly.

"Titch can guard us for a few hours," says Oak, nodding to the owl-faced hob in the tree. It nods, its head rotating uncannily. "We could all use the rest."

I try to tamp down my rising panic. Surely Titch will be easier to get past than Tiernan would have been. But I had not counted on *anyone* standing watch. An oversight that makes me wonder what other obvious thing I have overlooked. What other foolish mistake is there to make?

Oak rolls himself up in his damp cloak. He looks at me as though
he wants to say something, but when I refuse to meet his gaze, he settles
down to sleep. I am glad. I am not as skilled at hiding my feelings as I
would like.

At first, I count the stars, starting in the east and then moving west.
It isn't easy, because I can't tell if I've counted some already and keep
going back and starting again. But it does while away time.

At last, I close my eyes, counting again, this time to a thousand.

When I get to 999, I sit up. The others appear asleep, the gentle
susurrations of their breaths even and deep. Above me, Titch's golden
eyes blink, staring into the dark.

I creep over to Oak's bag, lying beside his sword. The fire has
burned down to embers. Starlight shines on his features, smoothed out
in slumber.

Kneeling, I slide my finger into the sack, past a paperback book,
granola bars, candles, a scroll, and several more knives, until I feel
the smooth strap. My fingers tremble at the touch of the leather. The
enchantment on it seems to spark.

I tug the bridle out as gently and slowly as I am able.

Nearby, a fox calls. Frogs bellow at one another from the ferns.

I risk a look at the owl-faced hob, but it is still watching for danger
outside the camp. There is no reason, I tell myself, for it to believe that I
am doing anything more than rooting for a snack. I am no threat.

I don't have a bag like Oak's to hide the bridle in, but I do have a
scarf, and I wind it up in that and then tie it around my waist like a belt.
My heart is beating so fast that it seems as though it's skipping, like
stones across a pond.

I stand and take a step, so certain I am about to be caught that the anticipation makes me dizzy.

Two more steps, and the tree line is in sight.

That's when I hear Oak's voice behind me, thick with sleep. "Wren?"

I turn back, attempting not to panic, not to snarl and run. I can't let him see how afraid I am that he's caught me.

"You're awake," he says, sitting up.

"My mind keeps going around in loops," I say, keeping my voice low. That much is certainly true.

He beckons to me. Reluctantly, I come over and sit beside him. Leaning forward, he pokes the fire with a stick.

I can't help but see his face, soft from slumber, and remember what it was like to kiss him. When I recall the curve of Oak's mouth, I must force myself to think of the way it looks pulled into a sneer.

I don't want her. I remind myself of his words. And if there's any part of him that does, it's because I am, as Hyacinthe said, *a coin to be spent.*

I take a deep breath. "You're not really going to send me away, are you?"

"I should," he says. "This is a grievously foolhardy scheme."

I wonder if he believes the thought of being parted from him is what kept me awake. "I knew that from the first."

"I should never have gotten you into this," he says, self-loathing in his voice. Perhaps he is slipping a little, tired as he is. He cannot like what he plans to do. He is not that much of a monster.

"I can stop Lady Nore," I remind him.

He gives me a smile, a strange light in his eyes. "If we were capable of putting mistrust aside, we might be a formidable pair."

"We might," I say. "Were we sure of each other."

His hand touches my back lightly, making me shiver. "Do you know what I admire about you?"

Truly, I cannot imagine what he will say next.

"That you never stopped being angry," he tells me. "It can be brave to hate. Sometimes it's like hope."

I hadn't felt brave in the Court of Teeth. Or hopeful. I had felt only a clawing desperation, as though I was forever drowning in some vast sea, gulping seawater as I sank, and then just when I felt I was going to let myself drop beneath the waves, something would make me kick one more time. Maybe that thing was hate. Hating requires going on, even when you can no longer believe in any better future. But I am shocked that Oak, of all people, would know that.

"You will make an interesting High King," I tell him.

He looks alarmed. "I most definitely will *not*. The Folk adore Cardan, and they're terrified of my sister, two excellent things. I hope they rule Elfhame for a thousand years and then pass it down to one of a dozen offspring. No need for me to be involved."

"Honestly, you *don't* want to be the High King?" I ask, puzzled. It was all Lord Jarel and Lady Nore wanted, the entire focus of their ambition, the reason for my creation. It seemed almost an insult for him to shrink from it as though it was equivalent to eating an apple with a worm inside.

Even if I happened to agree with him.

"Cardan was smart not to want it before I slammed that crown on his head," Oak says, his mouth quirking at the memory, then flattening out again. "The desire to rule Elfhame ruined so many lives. Just being the heir is bad enough."

"What do you mean?" Watching him in the firelight, the sleep-mussed fall of gold curls against his cheeks and the curious intensity of his expression, I could almost believe he's telling me this because he wishes to be my friend, rather than knowing that the appearance of vulnerability is likely to make me drop my guard.

He stretches a little, like a cat. "Some people would prefer to see me on the throne, either because they think I'd be easier to manipulate or because they'd do anything not to be ruled by a mortal. They make no secret that were I to say the right word, they would pour poison in my ear and down my family's throats. Meanwhile, my sister Jude—I suspect she isn't having children to make it clear I will be next in line. She says not, but she's too good of a liar for me to know."

I picture the High Queen as she was in that final battle, blood flecked across her face. Chopping off the head of the serpent who'd once been her beloved, even if it doomed her side to failure, all to save a land that despised her.

Now, that was hate that was somehow also hope.

He laughs, surprising me. "I am grim tonight, am I not? Let me show you a trick."

I eye him suspiciously. But he only takes a quarter out of his pocket, then spins it on the edge of his finger.

I snort despite myself.

He tosses the coin up and catches it in the other hand, then opens both his palms. The coin is gone.

"Do you know where it is?" he asks.

"Magicked away into Faerieland?" I guess, but I am smiling.

With a grin, Oak reaches behind my ear, and I can feel the metal, warmed by his skin, against the side of my neck.

I am foolish for my delight, but I am delighted all the same.

"The Roach taught me that," he says, tucking the coin away. "I'm still practicing."

"I remember him," I say. "From your Court of Shadows."

Oak nods. "And before that, from the Court of Teeth. He wasn't just held there by himself, either."

The Bomb. I remember her, too. Lady Nore had called her Liliver. Considering how much the Court of Teeth corrupted, I can only admire their loyalty to each other. "They must have truly suffered."

Oak gives me an odd look. "As you did."

"We should try to sleep," I force myself to say. If I remain in his company any longer, I will *ask* if he intends to give me to Lady Nore. And then my plans will be discovered, and I, very likely, bridled.

He shakes his head, possibly at himself. "Of course. You're right."

I nod. *Yes. Go back to sleep, Oak. Please. Go to sleep before I change my mind about leaving.*

Though he means me harm, I will miss him. I will miss the way he moves through the world, as though nothing could be so terrible that he might not laugh at it.

I might even miss Tiernan's grumpiness.

I go back on my blankets and wait, counting to a thousand again. When I am certain the prince is asleep, I push myself up and walk steadily into the tree line. I do not look back to see if the owl eyes of the hob are on me. I must behave as though I am doing nothing of note, nothing wrong.

Once I am away from the camp and the hob gives no cry of alarm, I leave off caution and rush through the woods, then through the town, until I come to the bus station.

It takes me a full three minutes before my glamour is nearly good enough to allow me to pass for human. I touch my face and my teeth to be sure.

Then, taking a deep breath, I walk into the brightly lit station. It smells like gasoline and disinfectant. A few humans are sitting on metal benches, one with a garbage bag that seems to be stuffed full of clothes. A young couple with a single suitcase between them, whispering together. An elderly gentleman with a cane who has fallen asleep and may have already missed his bus.

According to the schedule, the next one is passing north and west, up toward Michigan. It's tricky to buy a ticket with glamoured money, because machines aren't unaware that you're feeding leaves into them, even if people are. Instead, I grab a receipt out of the trash and enchant it. It's only a rough approximation of a ticket, and I will have to glamour the driver to let me pass, but the role will be more convincing with something in my hand. My magic is wobbly enough to need all the help it can get.

When I look up, I see a man with dirty pants and an unkempt beard watching me. My heart speeds. Was he only noting that I'd been rooting around in the trash, or am I so unlucky as to run into one of the humans with True Sight? Or is he something else, something more?

I smile at him, and he flinches as though he can see the sharpness of my teeth. After that, he stops looking at me.

I plug Gwen's phone into the wall and wait.

I watch a girl kick a vending machine. A boy smokes a cigarette, pacing outside and talking to himself. An elderly man picks a penny off the floor.

Beside me, there is a sudden buzz. I look down and realize the screen of the phone has come back to life. I've missed ten calls while it was dead, none of them from numbers I know.

There are three texts from Gwen. The first reads: It's fucked to text my own phone, and even more because everything that happened seems like it can't be real, but I made it to my parents' house. That hot elf guy was kind of a dick bt he told me about his ex & the prince, and it sounds like your in trouble. Let me know your OK.

Below that there's a photo of her with the fiddler from the Court of Moths. They are draped over each other and smiling in the front seat of a car. The next message reads: MY BAE IS HERE. He says he woke up on the side of a hill. The last thing he remembers is someone who looked like a devil putting salt on his tongue. I don't know what you did, but THANK YOU THANK YOU THANK YOU.

And then: Are you OK? Please write to me so (a) I know you're good and (b) I didn't dream you.

I grin at the phone. Most of the people I broke curses for were as afraid of me as they were of the glaistig. It was strange to think that Gwen *liked* me. Fine, I had done something nice for her, but she still texted me as though we could be friends.

I text back: Hard to charge a phone in Faerieland. I made it to a bus station & am on my own. No princes. No knights. Glad you're okay and your boyfriend, too.

Then the smile fades off my face. Because I have to call home. I have to warn Bex.

I punch in the sequence of numbers from memory.

A man's voice picks up. My unfather. "Who is this?"

I watch the clock and the door, half-expecting Oak to come striding through and drag me back to the camp at sword's point. I remind myself that I have the bridle, and that even if he was looking for me, he'd have no reason to look here.

"Can I speak with Bex, please?" I ask, keeping my voice steady.

For a long moment, my unfather is quiet, and I think he's going to hang up. Then I hear him call for my unsister.

I bite my nails and watch the seconds tick by on the clock, watch the other people shuffle around the station.

She comes to the phone. "Yeah?"

"You have to listen to me," I tell her, keeping my voice low so that the whole bus station doesn't listen in. "You're in trouble."

She takes a sharp breath. "*Mom!*" she yells, then she sounds muffled, like she has her hand over the speaker. "She called back. No, it's *her.*"

I panic, worried that she's going to hang up. "Just hear me out. Before that monster comes for you."

Listen to *this* monster, not *that* one.

"Mom wants to talk."

I feel a little sick at the thought. "You. Just you. For now, at least. Please."

Her voice goes distant, as though she's speaking to someone other than me. "Wait. Yes, I'll tell her."

"Why did you go outside that night?" I ask.

There's a pause, footsteps, then I hear a door close. "Okay, I'm away from them."

I repeat my question, anxiety narrowing my focus to the gum on the floor, the smell of exhaust, the pinesap on my fingers, the sound of her sighs.

"I wanted to make sure you were okay," Bex says finally.

"You remember me?" I choke out.

"You lived with us for *seven years*," she says, accusation creeping into her voice. "After you went back to your birth family, we hoped we'd hear *something*. Mom used to cry on that made-up birthday she invented for you."

"She told me to leave." I growl out the words. I know it wasn't her fault, that she and Dad and Bex were glamoured. But how could I go back to them, make them face my monstrousness, allow them to reject me again? *"Dad kicked me."*

I look at the clock. It's nearly time for the bus to pull in.

Bex sounds angry. "That's not true."

I need to end this call. I pull the charging cord out of the wall and out of the base of the phone, then start to wind it up. Soon I will be on my way north. Soon I will be cold inside and out.

"You met the storm hag," I say. "You know that whatever story you heard can't be the whole of it. And you know that I was adopted, not a foster child any longer. I couldn't just up and return to my birth parents, nor could they come and take me away. Think about it, and the story falls apart. Because it's one that you were enchanted with to explain something unexplainable."

There's a silence from the other end, but I hear people in the background. I don't think the door is closed anymore.

"I thought you were a ghost the first time I spotted you," she says softly.

I feel foolish, thinking that no one saw me slipping in and out of the house. If you do anything for long enough, you're bound to be caught. "When?"

"About six months ago. I was up late reading, and I saw something moving outside. When I looked, it was like seeing your spirit, back from the dead. But then I thought you were in some kind of trouble. And I started to wait for you."

"And the milk," I say. "You left out milk."

"You aren't human, are you?" She whispers the words, as though she's embarrassed to say them aloud.

I think of my unmother's surprise at hearing my voice. "Did you tell—"

"No!" she interrupts me. "How was I supposed to? I wasn't even sure *what* I saw. And they're not happy with me right now."

I look at the clock. The bus should be here. For a heart-stopping moment, I think that I've missed it, that time has jumped while I've been speaking with Bex. But a quick glance around shows me that none of the people waiting have moved from their seats.

The bus is late, I tell myself. *It's coming. Just late.* But my heart keeps beating harder, and I shrink into myself, as though if I am still enough, anxiety will stop gnawing on my insides.

And if the bus is not the whole reason I feel the way that I do, it's enough of it.

"Listen," I say, my gaze going to the road, watching for headlights. "I don't know how long I have, but if Bogdana knows where you are, it's not safe. Fill your pockets with salt. Rowan berries will keep you from being glamoured by their magic. They hate cold-wrought iron. And they can't lie." I correct myself. "*We.* We can't lie."

"What are—"

I hear cloth rustling and my unmother's voice cutting off Bex. "Wren, I know you want to talk to your *sister*." She emphasizes the word as though I am about to deny it. "But I have something quick to say. If you're in some kind of trouble, we can help you. You just tell us what's going on. Bex made it sound like you were living on the streets."

I almost laugh at that. "I'm surviving."

"That's not enough." She gives an enormous shaky sigh. "But even if it were, I'd like to see you. I've wondered how you were doing. What you were doing. If you had enough to eat. If you were warm."

My eyes burn, but I can't imagine being there, in their living room, wearing my true face. I would horrify them. Maybe they wouldn't scream and shove me away at first, the way they did when they were enchanted, but it would quickly turn awful. I couldn't be the child that they had loved.

Not after everything that happened to me. Not after learning that I am made of sticks and snow.

Headlights swing into view. I am already moving by the time I hear the squeal of brakes.

"I never needed to be warm," I tell my unmother, my voice hard, full of the anger that has been gnawing at my insides for years.

"Wren," she says, stung.

I feel as though I am about to weep, and I am not even sure why.

"Tell Bex to remember the salt, the rowan, and the iron," I say, and hang up the phone, racing for the bus.

Only one person gets off, and then I get on, holding out my fake ticket to the driver and concentrating my magic on him. *Believe me*, I plead with all the force I possess. *Believe I have a ticket.*

He nods in a distracted fashion, and I flee to the back of the bus, still holding the phone. A few more people board, including the man who was watching me so strangely. My feelings are too tangled up for me to pay any of them much attention.

Once Lady Nore is dead, or perhaps wearing the bridle, maybe I will speak with Bex and my unmother and unfather again. Maybe, if I knew I could keep them safe from Bogdana. If I knew I could keep them safe from me.

Leaning my cheek against the glass, I slip my hand into the folds of the scarf, just to have the reassuring feel of the bridle's leather strap, to know I have a plan. I dig my fingers through the cloth, then reach around my body, scratching at my stomach, fresh panic flooding my chest.

The bridle isn't there.

Outside the window, Titch sits on the gutter of the bus station, blinking at me with golden eyes.

The bus begins to roll forward. I try to tell myself that I can still get away. That perhaps the bus will drive faster than the creature can fly. That Oak and Tiernan will not be able to follow.

That's when I hear a tire pop. The bus lurches to a stop, and I realize there is nowhere for me to go.

CHAPTER

12

As I walk back through the woods, I am furious with all the world, but especially myself.

Even though I knew Oak had played the entire Court of Moths false and gotten himself punched in the face twice to convince them he was a vain, useless courtier, had preened and drank a trough of wine to hide his swordsmanship. Even though Oak told me the Roach had taught him the trick with the coin, still I didn't consider that the goblin might also have taught Oak the far more practical skill of *stealing*.

The prince was careful to speak to me as if nothing at all was the matter, even as he lifted the bridle from around my waist. Worked it off with such deftness that I hadn't felt more than a single touch. Lulled by his conversation, I let myself believe I had fooled him at the very moment he was fooling me.

He was as deceptive as the rest of his family. More, maybe.

He never let down his guard with me, not once.

Too late, I understand what's terrifying about his charm. He seems entirely open when he is unknowable. Every smile is painted on, a mask.

Maybe I'm glad that you gave me an opportunity to be my worst self.

The campsite is as quiet as when I left it. Tiernan remains draped in the tree, making soft snoring sounds. Titch shadows me with shining eyes. I stare at Oak, half-hoping he will turn over and confront me, and half-dreading it.

As I pass him, I note that his breaths are even, though I bet he sleeps the way cats do, lightly. If I got too close, I bet he would spring up, ready to fight.

That is, if he's sleeping at all.

I creep over to my own blankets and flop onto them. Despair drags me down into dreams, where I am back in the snow, walking in circles.

When I wake, it is to the smell of buttered rolls and coffee from town. Oak and Tiernan are eating and talking quietly. I hear Tiernan laugh, and I wonder how much of what they are saying is about my escape attempt, if they find my failure hilarious.

Oak wears mortal clothes over his shining golden mail. It peeks out at his collar and cuffs. Tiernan wears his armor without any cover.

When the prince glances over at me, nothing changes in his expression. Maybe that's because, to him, nothing *has* changed. He'd never believed I was anything but a potential adversary or a potential sacrifice.

I bite my tongue until it bleeds.

He smiles, and finally I see the flicker of anger in his eyes. It's satisfying that he, who hides so much, can't hide that. He walks over and sits beside me. "You knew I was a trickster."

Then, before I can react, he presses a finger to his lips, glancing sideways at Tiernan. It takes me a moment to understand that he *hasn't* told the knight that I attempted to steal the bridle. What I don't understand is why.

Tiernan rises and throws water onto the fire, causing a cloud of steam to rise. The late afternoon is bright, the sky almost aggressively blue after the storm.

I stick a roll in my mouth and pack up the remains of my gown, transferring the knife Oak lent me to my boot.

Tiernan mutters something and then heads off into the woods.

"Where is he going?" I ask.

"To Undry Market, ahead of us, to negotiate for the boat. Tiernan believes if the goblins know who I am, they will ask for outlandish things. We will take another path and see if anything follows." He pauses. "You don't mind, do you?"

I get up and brush off my legs. When someone thwarted your attempt to rob them, made it clear you were *their* prisoner, and then asks you a question like that, it's not really a question.

We walk for a while in silence.

"Do you remember what I said about us being formidable, were we able to put mistrust aside?" he asks.

I nod reluctantly.

"I see we were not able," he reminds me. "Now what, Wren?"

I feel helpless, as though he's herding me around a chessboard to checkmate. "Why are you asking me this?"

He lets out a frustrated huff. "Fine, I will be plain. If you wanted to leave, why not go any other night?"

Another trap. "Why should I tell you anything, when you're the one with so many secrets?"

"Everyone has secrets," he says, although there is something like despair in his voice.

"Secrets about me," I clarify.

"You've betrayed me. You've stolen from me. You met with the storm hag, and then hours later you snatch a powerful magical object and run. Do I deserve no answers?"

"I wanted the bridle," I say. "So that you could never make me wear it."

He kicks up a tornado of leaves. "What cause have I ever given you to accuse me of that?"

I look sullenly away.

He says nothing, merely waiting for my reply. The silence stretches on, and I am surprised that I am the one who breaks first and fills it.

"Tiernan told me he'd use the bridle on me if I betrayed you again." I fix him with a glare.

Oak blinks in surprise and is quiet for a long moment. "He doesn't understand why you freed Hyacinthe and the others," he says finally. "He can't believe you did it because you wanted to help them. Folk do not do such things where we come from."

I kick a rock, hard.

"If you want to go, go," the prince tells me with an elaborate swish of his hand toward the trees around us.

I look into the woods but am not so foolish as to take his offer at face value. "Then why not just let me leave last night?"

Oak gives me a slightly guilty look. "Because I don't like being the fool who'd been tricked. I like games, but I hate to lose."

I blink at him in surprise. "What?"

He shrugs impatiently. "It's not my best quality," he says. "And besides, it seemed worthwhile to *ask* you if you were working with Bogdana."

"I'm not," I say, and when he gives me a long look, I say it in full. "I am neither working for nor with Lady Nore. I am not allied with Bogdana. I want to go north and keep Lady Nore from making more monsters. I even want to see your father freed."

"Then why leave?" This is the difficulty with Oak. He invites you to trust him, makes you feel silly for doubting, and then you find yourself in a bus station, discovering how thoroughly you've been played.

"Rather than be sent to Elfhame, I decided I would go north without you and face my mother alone." I wonder if I can get away with saying only that.

When he glances in my direction, his fox eyes are bright. "That's even more foolish than our current plan."

My stomach twists.

"I don't understand it," he says, scrubbing his hand over his face. "I feel as though I ought to be angry with you, but I admired what you did back at the Court of Moths. Even when it did, as you say, *inconvenience* me."

I grimace a little at my own words, but then the import of what he's saying sinks in. "*You*...admired *that*?"

"More than I'd like to admit." When he looks at me, I see that same intensity in his face that I remember from when he stood beside Queen Annet. "You cared about the mortal and the merrow and even Hyacinthe. You defied all of us and, as far as I can tell, got nothing in return."

I am not sure how to answer. "Did it weigh on you, keeping Hyacinthe prisoner?"

"He tried to kill the High King."

"What?" I recall Tiernan saying there'd been an incident.

Oak appears amused by the shock of my voice. "Once, my father said that conflicts seem as though they are between beliefs or desires. But more often conflicts are between rulers. Those that follow rulers can be perfectly nice, which is how you wind up with two perfectly nice people with daggers to each other's throats. Hyacinthe and I might have been friends, but for the part where we were set on opposite sides of a battlefield."

I think on that for a long moment, wondering if that's how he sees me as well. How it would be for him to discover that I am stitched together with magic, a manikin animated by a hag? Perhaps he would feel less guilty then.

I could take him at his word and attempt to leave. But he made no promises not to chase after me. Nor did he say he wouldn't make me wear the bridle.

I could slip away in Undry Market and find a place to hide. But I have no reason to believe that the Folk there would help me over their prince. Most likely they would give me up for a few coins.

Or I could try to get the truth out of him. "You like games," I tell him. "How about we play one?"

"What's the wager?"

"If I win," I say. "You answer my question. Without evasion."

Nothing about the way he looks at me suggests that he does not consider these to be large stakes. Still, he nods. "And what is the game?"

"You have the piece. Just as when we were children, let's see which of us throws better."

He nods again, taking it from his pocket. The peridot eyes glimmer. "And if I win?"

"What do you want?" I ask.

He studies me and I study him in return. No smile now can disguise the steel underneath. "You promise to dance with me so that our practice back in the Court of Moths won't be for nothing."

"Those are absurd stakes," I tell him, my cheeks hot.

"And yet they are mine," he says.

I nod quickly, unsettled. "Very well. You throw first."

We stop walking. He squats down and clears off the twigs and fallen leaves from a patch of grass. It feels like being children, like playing. It occurs to me that so many awful things in my life happened before that moment, and so many awful things in his life happened after.

The fox tumbles onto the ground, falling on its side. No points.

He looks over at me and raises his eyebrows.

I pick it up and throw, holding my breath. It falls on its side, too.

He reaches for it and I think he's going to throw again, but he sets the fox on its back, with its legs pointing up. "You win."

I shake my head, incredulous.

"You win," he says again, more firmly. "Ask."

Very well. If he is going to give me the game, I would be a fool not to take it. "Lady Nore asked for me in trade for Madoc, didn't she?" I brace myself for his answer, or for whatever he does in place of giving me one. "That's why you're really bringing me north."

His surprise is evident. "Is that what Bogdana told you?"

I nod.

He sighs. "No wonder you ran."

"Is it *true*?" I ask.

He frowns. "What did she say, exactly? So that I may answer without evasion."

"That Lady Nore offered to trade Madoc to the prince in exchange for *the very thing he is bringing north. A foolish girl.*"

"Well, it's accurate that Lady Nore offered to trade for what the storm hag *thinks* I am bringing north," Oak says. "Mellith's heart. That's what she asked for, and if I've managed to convince Bogdana that I have it, so much the better. Maybe Lady Nore will believe it as well. But what the storm hag told you—she meant to trick you with the way she put together those words."

I think over the tangle of what Bogdana said and what she didn't. Not simply *Lady Nore offered to trade Madoc for you.* If she'd been able to say that, she would have.

"So you *don't* have Mellith's heart and you're *not* going to give me— or it—to Lady Nore?" I need him to say the words.

He grins. "I am not planning on handing you over to anyone. Lady Nore did not ask for you in trade. As for Mellith's heart, I will show you what I intend when we reach the market. It's a nice bit of trickery, I think."

I stare into his fox eyes and feel relief so acute that I am dizzy with it.

I look up at the sky overhead, the intense blue that follows a storm, and let myself believe I am not in danger. Not right then. Not from him.

I pick up the gaming piece, and when he doesn't seem to notice or demand it back, I slip it into my pocket. Then we resume walking.

It's not far before a riot of colors shows through the trees. That must be Undry Market. In the wind, I hear the scrap of a song.

"What if," he says, mischief in his eyes, "in the interest of saving time, we pretend that we've played twice more and I won once, so you owe me a dance. But you won the second time, so if you have anything else to ask me, you may."

Those are teasing words, and I am suddenly in a teasing mood. "All right. Tell me about your girls, then."

He raises his eyebrows. *"Girls?"*

"Tiernan says there were two ladies in particular that you wanted to impress. Violet, I think. And Sibi. But he also says you fall in love a lot."

That surprises a laugh out of him, although he doesn't deny any of it. "There are certain expectations of a prince in Court."

"You cannot be serious," I say. "You feel *obliged* to be in love?"

"I told you—I am a courtier, versed in all the courtly arts." He's grinning as he says it, though, acknowledging the absurdity of the statement.

I find myself shaking my head and grinning, too. He's being ridiculous, but I am not sure *how* ridiculous.

"I do have a bad habit," he says. "Of falling in love. With great regularity and to spectacular effect. You see, it never goes well."

I wonder if this conversation makes him think of our kiss, but then, I was the one who kissed him. He'd only kissed back.

"As charming as you are, how can that be?" I say.

He laughs again. "That's what my sister Taryn always says. She tells me that I remind her of her late husband. Which makes some sense, since I would have been his half brother. But it's also alarming, because she's the one who murdered him."

Much as when he spoke about Madoc, it's strange how fond Oak can sound when he tells me a horrifying thing a member of his family has done. "Whom have you fallen in love with?" I ask.

"Well, there was you," the prince says. "When we were children."

"Me?" I ask incredulously.

"You didn't know?" He appears to be merry in the face of my astonishment. "Oh yes. Though you were a year my senior, and it was hopeless, I absolutely mooned over you. When you were gone from Court, I refused any food but tea and toast for a month."

I cannot help snorting over the sheer absurdity of his statement.

He puts a hand to my heart. "Ah, and now you laugh. It is my curse to adore cruel women."

He cannot expect me to believe he had real feelings. "Stop with your games."

"Very well," he says. "Shall we go to the next? Her name was Lara, a mortal at the school I attended when I lived with my eldest sister and her girlfriend. Sometimes Lara and I would climb up into the crook of one of the maple trees and share sandwiches. But she had a villainous friend, who implicated me in a piece of gossip—which resulted in Lara stabbing me with a lead pencil and breaking off our relationship."

"You *do* like cruel women," I say.

"Then there was Violet, a pixie. I wrote her terrible poetry about how I adored her. Unfortunately, *she* adored duels and would get into trouble so that I would have to fight for her honor. And even more unfortunately, neither my sister nor my father bothered to teach me how to sword fight for show."

I thought of the dead-eyed expression on his face before his bout with the ogre and Tiernan's angry words.

"That resulted in my accidentally killing a person she liked better than me."

"Oh," I say. "That is *three levels* of unfortunate."

"Then there was Sibi, who wanted to run away from Court with me, but as soon as we went, hated it and wept until I took her home. And Loana, a mermaid, who found my lack of a tail unbearable but tried to drown me anyway, because she found it equally unbearable that I would ever love another."

The way he tells these stories makes me recall how he's told me many painful things before. Some people laugh in the face of death. He laughs in the face of despair. "How old were you?"

"Fifteen, with the mermaid," he said. "And nearly three years later, I must surely be wiser."

"Surely," I say, wondering if he was. Wondering if I wanted him to be.

The threshold of Undry Market is announced by two trees leaning toward each other, their branches entangled. As we duck beneath, what had previously been scraps of song and spots of color lose their disguise and the entire panoply comes into view. Shops and stalls fill the clearing. The air is rich with perfumes, honey wines, and grilled fruits. We pass a tented area with lutes and harps, the vendor trying to call to us over the sound of one of his instruments recounting a terrible tale of how it was made.

As we walk, I see that the market stretches down to a rocky area near the shoreline, where a pier has been built out into the waves. A single ship bobs at the end of it. I wonder if that is what Tiernan is trying to buy from the goblins.

Then I am distracted by the hammering of smiths and a smattering of song. There is a forge not far from where we are standing, one with a display of swords in the front. And beside that, a maypole and a few dancers going around it, winding the ribbons. A stall selling cloaks in all the colors of the sky, from the first blush of dawn to deep as midnight and spangled with stars. A bakeshop hawking braided breads, their shining crusts decorated with herbs and flowers.

"Don't have gold?" calls an antlered shopkeeper. "Pay with a lock of hair, a year of your life, a dream you wish to never have again."

"Come!" calls another. "We have the finest jackets in a hundred leagues. Green as poison. Red as blood. Black as the heart of the King of Elfhame."

Oak stops to purchase cheese wrapped in wax paper, a half dozen apples, and two loaves of bread. He also gets us warmer clothes, along with hats and gloves. Rope, new packs, and a grappling hook, the tines of which fold down like the tentacles of a squid skimming through water.

We pass a fletcher, selling barrels of arrows with different feathers affixed to the ends. Crows and sparrows, even those from a wren. Pass a display of gowns in beetle-bright green, saffron, and pomegranate red. A stall with bouquets of drying herbs hanging upside down, beside seedpods. Then a bookseller, shelves of old tomes and empty, freshly bound books open to creamy pages waiting to be written in. One stall over, an alchemist displays a shelf of poisons, including poisoned ink. A row of oddly shaped skulls sits alongside them.

Oak pauses to purchase some explosives. "Just in case," he reassures me.

"Dear lady," says a faerie, coming toward us from a shop that sells jewels. He has the eyes of a snake and a forked tongue that darts out when he speaks. "This hairpin looks as though it were made for you."

It's beautiful, woven gold and silver in the shape of a bird, a single green bead in its mouth. Had it been in a display, my eyes would have passed over it as one of a dozen unobtainable things. But as he holds it out, I can't help imagining it as mine.

"I have no money and little to trade," I tell him regretfully, shaking my head.

The shopkeeper's gaze goes to Oak. I think he believes the prince is my lover.

Oak plays the part, reaching out his hand for the pin. "How much is it? And will you take silver, or must it be the last wish of my heart?"

"Silver is excellent." The shopkeeper smiles as Oak fishes through his bag for some coins.

Part of me wants to demur, but I let him buy it, and then I let him use it to pin back my hair. His fingers on my neck are warm. It's only when he lets go that I shiver.

He gives me a steady look. "I hope you're not about to tell me that you hate it and you were just being polite."

"I don't hate it," I say softly. "And I am not polite."

He laughs at that. "A delightful quality."

I admire the hairpin in every reflective surface we pass.

We cross a wide lawn where a puppet show is under way. Folk are gathered around a curtained box, watching an intricate paper cutout of a crow seem to fly above a mill. I spot a few human children and pause to wonder if they are changelings.

The crow puppet sweeps down to a painted papier-mâché tree. The hidden operator moves a pole, and the crow's beak opens and closes.

The bird sings:

Ca-caw, ca-caw,
My mother she killed me,

My father he ate me,
My sister gathered my bones,
And buried them beneath the apple tree.
Behold! I hatched as a young crow.
Ca-caw, ca-caw, how beautiful a bird am I.

I stop to watch. It turns out that the miller loves the song so much that he gives the crow a millstone in order to hear it again. And when the bird flies home, he drops the stone onto his stepmother's head and kills her.

The crowd is still clapping when I realize that Oak has gone on to the blacksmith shop. I arrive in time to see the bushy-eyebrowed smith returning from the back with what appears to be a metal-and-glass box, designed to display its contents. It is golden-footed and empty.

"What is that?" I ask as he carefully places it into his bag.

"A reliquary," he says. "Enchanted to keep whatever is inside forever preserved. It's much like the one that contained Mab's bones. I sent ahead Titch to commission it."

"And that's for—"

He signals me away from the shop. Together we walk toward the pier. "A deer heart," he says. "Because that's what I am going to bring Lady Nore. In a fancy reliquary, she won't know the difference for some amount of time, hopefully enough for us to be able to accomplish our goal and get you close to her."

"A deer heart?" I echo.

"That's what I am bringing north. A trick. Sleight of hand, like the coin."

I smile up at him, believing, for once, that we are on the same side.

When we come to the edge of the water, we find Tiernan still haggling with three goblins. One has golden hair and a pointy chin, the second has black hair and bushy eyebrows, and the third has very large ears and no hair on his head at all. The hairless one has a skin of wine and stares at me with the seriousness of the very drunk. He is passing his booze back and forth with a redheaded giant, who sits on the pier, dangling enormous feet in the sea.

The black-haired goblin holds up a silver-handled knife and tests its weight. "What else have you got?"

There is a small pile of treasure on a nearby boulder—a fat pearl, at least sixteen pieces of gold, and a stone that might be an emerald.

"You overestimate the value of what you're selling," says Tiernan.

The drunk goblin laughs uproariously.

In the water is a boat carved in the shape of a cormorant. At the front, the long curve of its neck makes it appear rampant, and the wings rise on either side, protecting those resting in the hull. It's beautifully made, and if I squint, I can see that it's also magical.

"Ahhhh," says the golden-haired goblin to Oak as we approach. "You must explain to your friend here that he cannot purchase one of our finest crafts with a few trinkets."

Tiernan is obviously frustrated. "We've come to a price, but I'm a little short of it, that's all. Now that you're here, we can make up the difference and go."

Whatever his reason for believing he would be better at negotiation than Oak, he's mistaken. It's not in his nature to dress up the truth, or slither around it.

The golden-haired goblin looks at us expectantly. "We would like the remainder of our payment now, please."

Oak reaches into his bag and pulls out several more gold coins, as well as a handful of silver ones. "Is this enough?"

"We'll have your rings," says the golden-haired goblin, pointing at the three encircling Oak's fingers.

I am not sure if they have any significance, but I suppose they mustn't since Oak heaves a sigh and starts to twist them off. Not only that, but he places his circlet beside them. Surely a crown is enough payment.

The golden-haired goblin shakes his head.

I see the shift of the prince's smile. Honey-tongued. "Mayhap your boat is too beautiful for our needs. We need seaworthy and little more."

Two of the goblins exchange glances. "Our craft is as seaworthy as they come," says the black-haired one.

"And yet, one might weep to see such a beautiful vessel as this battling the elements." Oak's expression turns thoughtful. "Perhaps you have something less fine you could sell us."

At this the black-haired goblin sniffs, offended. "We do not make ugly things."

"No, no," Oak says, acting as if he's disappointed. "Of course not."

I twig his game. "Maybe we should seek a boat elsewhere," I suggest.

Tiernan looks like he wants to strangle us. I can't decide if he's not sure what Oak is about or only skeptical that it will work.

The golden-haired goblin watches Oak. "You truly have nothing more to trade? I can hardly believe it, handsome travelers like yourselves. What's that in her hair?"

Oak frowns as I remove it from my braids. Regretfully, I set it down on the pile with the rest of our treasures. I tell myself that it doesn't matter. It would have been useless anyway, where we're going.

The bushy-browed goblin snorts, picking up the hairpin and turning it over. "Very well. If this assortment of baubles is all you can give us, I suppose we will take pity on you and make the trade. Your rings, the knife, the pearl, the coins, the emerald that's in no way the size of a duck egg, the circlet, and the hairpin. For these, we'll sell you the boat."

Smiling, Oak walks forward to shake the goblin's hand and seal the bargain.

Tiernan hops down into the sea craft, motioning for me to throw him down my bag. He looks relieved that the negotiations are finally over and we can get moving.

The drunk giant lumbers to his feet, fixing the prince with an accusatory stare. "Look at what he's wearing beneath his clothes. Armor of gold," he grunts. "We'll have that, too. Tell him!"

"We've agreed to a price," Tiernan warns.

Oak's hand goes to his sword hilt, and I see something wild in his eyes. "I don't want to fight," he says, and I am sure part of him means that.

"You meant to cheat us," the giant shouts.

Frantically, I kneel and begin to unknot the rope binding the boat to the dock. It is wet and pulled tight, with some magic on it besides.

"Rangi," one of the goblins says to the giant. "We've made a deal."

The giant is very drunk, though, too drunk to bother with further negotiations. He grabs for the prince, who jumps back, out of reach. Tiernan shouts a warning, although I am not sure to which of them. The prince's expression has turned cold and blank.

Finally, I get the knot loose and the boat begins to drift free of the moorings.

I grab for Oak's shoulder, and he looks at me with empty eyes. For a moment, I don't think he knows me at all.

"Can you swim?" I ask.

He nods once, as though coming out of a dream. A moment later, he lunges.

Not to stab the giant, as I expect. Or me. He grabs my hairpin. Then, turning, he races for the water.

"Thieves!" yells a goblin as we jump off the side of the pier together.

I land with a splash and a yelp about two feet from the boat. I go under, sinking until my feet hit the mud, then kick off toward the surface.

When I bob up through the waves, I see the prince holding on to the wing of the carved cormorant. He reaches out his hand.

I paddle toward him, spitting out muddy water.

Behind us, the goblins are shouting. Tiernan ignores them as he hauls me up onto the deck. Then he reaches for Oak.

Enraged, the giant jumps down and begins to wade through the waves.

The prince stumbles to the mast and unfurls a cloth sail. As soon as it goes up—despite the afternoon not being all that windy—it billows and then fills. Whatever magic speeds us out to sea cannot seem to be called back by the goblins. In moments, we are well out of the giant's reach.

I lick salt off my top lip. Tiernan takes the tiller, steering us away from the shoreline. With a whistling noise, Titch comes flying out of the market, circling once before settling on the mast.

It is not long before we are out of sight of the pier.

Oak walks to the prow, wrapping himself in a cloak. Staring into the sea.

I remember the voyage to the isles of Elfhame on a much larger boat. I was kept below for most of the trip but brought up once or twice to breathe the salty sea air and listen to the calls of gulls.

If you marry the boy, Lady Nore told me, *you can't carve out his heart right away. I know how bloodthirsty you are, but you'll have to be patient.* And she laughed a little.

I nodded, trying to look as though I was bloodthirsty, and that I could be patient. Wanting anything that would let me sit a little longer in the sun.

I wasn't looking forward to murdering a boy I had never met, but by then I hadn't thought much of it, either. If that was what she wanted me to do and it would spare me pain, I'd do it.

It's hard to believe how swiftly I became unrecognizable to myself.

I wonder how Oak sees himself when he's about to fight. And then I wonder how he sees himself after.

"Wren," Tiernan says, pulling me out of those thoughts. "What can you tell me about where we're going?"

I cast my mind further through that painful blur of time. "The Citadel has three towers and three entrances, if you count the aerial one." I sketch them with a wet finger on the wood of the hull.

Tiernan frowns.

"What?" I ask. "I know the place as well as Hyacinthe."

"I was only wondering over the aerial entrance," Tiernan says carefully. "I don't think I've heard that before."

I nod. "I mean, it's not a proper *door.* There's an arched opening in one of the towers, and flying things come in through it."

"Like birds," he says. "Hyacinthe might have mentioned that was what he used."

"There were guards at all the gates but that one," I say. "Mostly huldufólk then. Maybe stick creatures now."

Tiernan nods encouragingly, and I go on. "The foundation and the first level of the Citadel are all black rock. The walls beyond that are ice, translucent in some places—often closer to transparent—and opaque in others. It's hard to be certain there will be anywhere to hide where your shadow won't give you away," I say, knowing this fact all too well. "The prisons are in the black rock part."

Tiernan fishes a piece of lead from his pocket. "Here, see what you can draw with this."

I sketch out the garrison gate and the courtyard in the center of the Citadel in dull marks on the wood deck.

I know the Citadel, know where Lady Nore sleeps, know her throne room and banquet hall. Hyacinthe might have been better suited to explain its current defenses, but I know the number of steps to the top of every spire. I know every corner that a child could hide in, every place she could be dragged out from.

"If I could get into her chambers, I could command her," I say. "Lady Nore won't have many guards with her there."

What Lady Nore will have, though, is ferocity, ambition, and no hesitation about spilling an abundance of blood. She and Lord Jarel hated weakness as if it were a disease that could be caught.

I imagine the bridle sinking into Lady Nore's skin. My satisfaction at her horror. The moment before she realizes the trap is sprung, when she still wears her arrogance like armor, and the way her face will change as panic sets in.

Perhaps I am more like them than I would care to believe, to find the image pleasing.

At that upsetting thought, I rise and go to the prow of the boat, where Oak sits, wrapped in a sodden cloak.

Wet locks of hair kiss Oak's cheeks and are plastered to his throat and the small spikes of his horns. His lips look as blue as mine. "You should put on dry clothes," he tells me.

"Take your own advice, prince."

He looks down at himself, as though surprised to find himself half-frozen. Then he looks over at me. "I have something for you."

I put out my hand, expecting him to return my hairpin, but it's the bridle that he places in my palm.

"Why?" I ask, staring.

"One of us has to hold on to it. Let it be you," he says. "Just come to the Citadel by our side, and try to believe, whatever happens, whatever I say or do or have done, that my intention is for us to all survive this. For us to win."

I want to trust him. I want to trust him so much.

My hand closes over the leather straps. "Of course I'm coming to the Citadel."

His eyes meet mine. "Good."

I let myself relax into the moment, into friendship. "Now what about my hairpin?"

He grins and hands it over. I smooth my thumb over the silver bird, then use it to pull back *his* hair, instead of mine. As my fingers skim over his neck, threading through the silk of his locks, he shudders from something I do not think is cold. I am suddenly too aware of the physicality of him, his long legs and the curve of his mouth, the hollow of his throat and the sharp point of his ears, where earrings once hung. Of the hairs hanging loose from my pin, falling across one light brown horn to rest on his cheekbone.

When his eyes meet mine, desire, as keen as any blade, bends the air between us. The moment slows. I want to bite his lip. To feel the heat of his skin. To slide my hands beneath his armor and trace the map of his scars.

The owl-faced hob takes off from the mast, startling us. I stand up too quickly, jolted into awareness of where I am. I have to grab the wooden wings of the cormorant to keep from pitching into the sea.

Tiernan is perhaps twenty feet away, his gaze on the horizon, but my cheeks heat as though he can read my thoughts.

"Wren?" Oak is looking at me strangely.

I head to the cockpit, ducking under the boom as I go. But even with distance between us, the longing to touch him persists.

I can only be glad Oak does not follow me but heads below to put on dry clothes. Later, when he makes his way to the stern, he wordlessly takes the tiller from Tiernan.

The faerie boat, blown by unseen winds, flies across the sea. We catch sight of mortal schooners and tankers, pleasure barges, and fishing skiffs. Heading north, we skim the edge of the Eastern Seaboard, passing Maine on one side and the isles of Elfhame on the other. Then we sail farther north, through the Gulf of St. Lawrence to the Labrador Sea.

Everything ought to be as it was before, except it isn't. Whenever my hand brushes Oak's as he passes me a piece of bread or a skin of water, I can't help but notice. When we sleep in shifts, one of us left to navigate by the stars, I am drawn to watching his face, as though through his dreams, I will learn his secrets.

Something is very wrong with me.

On the third day, as we eat, I turn to throw an apple core into the sea and notice sharks circling the boat. Their fins cut smoothly through the swells. This close to the surface of the water, even their long, pale bodies are visible.

I suck in a breath.

Oak puts a hand up to shade his eyes from the sun just as a mermaid surfaces. Her hair is as silvery as the shine on the waves.

"Loana," he says with a smile that looks only slightly forced. I remember her name. She is one of the girls he fell in love with, the one who wanted to drown him.

I glance at Tiernan, who is gripping the hilt of his sword, though it is still sheathed. I do not think a blade is going to be particularly useful here.

"You sent for me and I came, Prince Oak. And lucky that I did, for the Undersea has challengers on all sides as Queen Orlagh weakens, each of them looking for an edge. Soon I may be your only friend beneath the waves."

"The treaty with the land still stands," Oak reminds her.

"For now, beautiful one." Her hair floats around her in a silver halo. Her eyes are the bright blue of chipped beach glass. Her tail surfaces lazily behind her, slapping the water before slipping beneath it again. "It is said that Nicasia intends to have a contest and marry the winning challenger."

"Ah," says Oak carefully. "Fun?"

"Or perhaps she will call on the treaty." A shark swims to the mermaid, and she strokes its side. I stare in fascination. The jaws of the beast look as though they could bite the boat in half. "And once she has all the contestants in one place, let the land destroy them."

"Alas," says Oak. "The land is trying to remedy its own problems. Which is why I sought your help. We would like to be concealed as we travel over the seas so that we may arrive onshore undetected."

"You could travel more swiftly beneath them." Her tone is all temptation.

"Nonetheless," he says.

Her expression turns into a pout. "Very well, if that's all you will have of me. I shall do as you ask for the price of a kiss."

"Oak—" Tiernan begins, a warning in his voice.

I take a step closer to the prince, who is going down on his knees on the hull.

"Easy enough," Oak says, but there is something in his face that cuts against those words. "And no hardship."

I spot a rope attached to the mast. As the prince speaks, I push the end in Oak's direction with my foot.

He does not look down when it hits his thigh. He loops it around one arm stealthily as he bends toward Loana.

She reached up with her webbed fingers, cupping the back of his head. Pressing her lips to his. They must be colder than the sea, colder than mine. His eyes almost close, lashes dipping low. Her tongue is in his mouth. Her grip on him tightens.

I hate watching, but I cannot look away.

Then she yanks him toward her sharply, thrashing with her tail. The rope goes taut, the only thing keeping him from being pulled into the sea.

He scrambles backward onto the boat, breathing hard. His shirt is wet with sea spray. His lips are flushed from her kiss.

"Come with me beneath the waves," she calls to him. "Drown with me in delight."

He laughs a little shakily. "A compelling offer, but I must see my quest to its conclusion."

"Then I will hasten to help you get it done," she says, diving down and away. The sharks follow, disappearing into the depths. I can see the shimmer of a mist just at the edges of my vision.

"I hope it was worth nearly being dragged down to the bottom of the sea," Tiernan says, shaking his head.

"We're concealed from Bogdana and Lady Nore," Oak says, but does not look either of us in the eye.

At nightfall we sail past floating chunks of ice, landing on a wind-swept beach just short of the Hudson Strait. Oak pulls the sea craft high onto the black rocks. Tiernan secures a rope to keep it there when the tide comes in. They do not ask me to help, and I do not volunteer.

Above us, a waning moon shines down on my homecoming.

I recall the words from the puppet show, when the crow sang for his millstone. *Ca-caw, ca-caw. How beautiful a bird am I.*

CHAPTER
13

Winds rake over the mountains, sinking into the valley with an eerie whistling sound. The late-afternoon sun shines off Oak's golden hair, almost as bright as the snow.

Thick cloaks hang heavily over our backs. Titch huddles in the cowl at the prince's neck, occasionally peering out to scowl at me.

Snow is seldom still. It swirls and blinds. It clings to everything, glimmering and glittering, and when a gust comes, it turns into a white fog.

And it stings. First like needles, then like razors. Tiny particles of ice chafe the cheeks, and even when they settle, they hide pitfalls. I take too heavy a step and plunge down, one of my legs sinking deep and the other thigh bending painfully on the ice shelf.

Oak leans down to give me his hand, then hauls me up. "My lady," he says, as though handing me into a carriage. I feel the pressure of his fingers through both our gloves.

"I'm fine," I tell him.

"Of course you are," he agrees.

I resume walking, ignoring a slight limp.

The Stone Forest looms in front of us, perhaps twenty miles off and stretching far enough in both directions that it is hard to see how we could get around it. Tall pine trees, their bark all of silvery gray. They grow out of the snow-covered plain, rising up like a vast wall.

As we move along, we come to a stake in the ground, on which a troll's head has been mounted. The wooden shaft lists to one side, as though from the force of the wind, and the entire top is black with dried fluid. The troll's eyes are open, staring into nothing with cloudy, fogged-over irises. Its lashes are white with frost.

Written on the stake are the words: *My blood was spilled for the glory of the Kings of Stone who rule from beneath the world, but my body belongs to the Queen of Snow.*

I stare at the head, the rough-cut flesh at the neck and the splinter of bone visible just beneath. Then I look ahead into the snow-covered expanse, dotted with curiously similar shapes. Now that I know they are not fallen branches or slender trees, I see there are a half dozen at least, with a grouping of three in one spot and the others spread out.

As I am wondering what they mean, the thing opens its mouth and speaks.

"In the name of our queen," it creaks out in a whispery, horrible voice, "welcome."

I step back in surprise, slip, and land on my ass. As I scramble to get up, Tiernan draws his sword and slices the head in two. Half the skull falls into the snow, scattering frozen clumps of blood large enough to look like rubies.

The thing's lips still move, though, bidding us welcome again and again.

Oak raises his eyebrows. "I think we ought to assume that our presence is no longer secret."

Tiernan looks out at the half dozen similar shapes. He nods once, wipes his sword against his pants, and sheathes it again. "It's not far to the cave. There will be furs waiting for us and wood for a fire. We can plan from there."

"When did you provision all of that?" I ask.

"When I came here for Hyacinthe," Tiernan says. "Although we weren't the first to use it. There were already some old supplies, from the time when the Court of Teeth and Madoc's falcons made camp nearby."

As we trudge on, I consider Tiernan's answer.

I hadn't really thought about the *timing* of Hyacinthe's abduction before. I'd known that he was in Elfhame for long enough to try to murder Cardan and get put in the bridle. That had to have predated Madoc being kidnapped.

But Hyacinthe being in Elfhame when the general was taken seems odd, coincidental. Had he helped Lady Nore? Had he known it would happen and said nothing? Has Tiernan more reason to feel betrayed than I knew?

The third head we pass is one of the Gentry. His eyes are black drops, his skin bleached by blood loss. The same message about the Kings of Stone that was on the troll's stake is written on this one.

Oak reaches out to touch the frozen cheek of the faerie. He closes the eyes.

"Did you know him?" I ask.

He hesitates. "He was a general. Lihorn. One of the cursed falcons.

He used to come to my father's house when I was young, to drink and talk strategy."

Mercifully, this head does not speak.

Oak shivers beneath his cloak. Tiernan is doing little better. The heavy wool of their wrappings offers them some protection from the freezing temperatures, but not enough.

The sun turns the ice scarlet and gold as we begin making our way up the side of a mountain. It's a craggy climb. We heave ourselves over rocks, trying not to slip. I find it hard going, difficult enough that I am silent with concentration. Oak clambers behind me, his hooves slippery on the ice. Tiernan's training keeps his steps light, but his labored breathing gives away the effort of it. The air grows colder the darker the sky becomes. Oak's breath steams as Tiernan shivers. The cold burns through the fabric of their gloves to stiffen their fingers, making them clumsy. I am unaffected, except perhaps a bit more alive, a bit more awake.

Gusts of wind whip sharp needles of ice against our cheeks. We edge along, barely able to see the path forward among the scrubby trees, rocky outcrops, and icicles.

The thought comes to me, unbidden, that I am looking at what I was made from. Snow and sticks. Sticks and snow. Not a real girl. A paper doll of a child, to play with, then rip up and throw away.

I was meant for the purpose of betraying the High Court. Never to survive past that. If I am the cause of Lady Nore's fall, it will give me all the more pleasure for her never having anticipated it.

The cave entrance is wide and low, its ceiling a pocked sheet of ice. I duck my head as I enter. The owl-faced hob darts from the prince's cowl, flying into the darkness.

Oak digs out a stub of candle from his bag. He places four around the room and lights them. Their leaping flames send shadows in every direction.

A confusion of supplies is piled in the back: shaggy bear pelts, boxes, a small chest, and stacks of wood that have been here long enough to be covered in a thin layer of frost.

"Interesting stuff," Oak says, walking over to the chest and knocking the side lightly with his hoof. "Did you open any of it when last you were here?"

Tiernan shakes his head. "I was in a bit of a rush."

He would have been with Hyacinthe—still a bird, before Oak removed the curse. Had he been caught then, caged? Had he ridden on Tiernan's shoulder, sure he was being saved? Or had he gone, knowing he would help Lady Nore abduct Madoc? I frown over that, since I recall him telling me how loyal he'd been.

Oak is peering at the lock on the chest. "Once, the Bomb told me a story about poisonous spiders kept inside a trunk. When the thief opened it, he was bitten all over. Died badly. I believe she was trying to dissuade me from stealing sweets."

Tiernan kicks the stack of wood with one snow-covered boot. The logs tumble out of formation. "I am going to make a fire."

I lift a fur and turn it inside out, brushing my hand over the lining to check for rot or bugs. There's nothing. No discoloration, either, as there might be from poison. The only odor it contains is the faint smell of the smoke used to tan the hide.

A few uniforms from the long-disbanded army are in a gray woolen heap. I shake them out and assess them while Oak tries to pry apart the rusty chest. "There *probably* aren't any spiders," he says when I look in his direction.

Inside is a waxed wheel of cheese and ancient rolls, along with a skin of slushy wine. He appears disappointed.

Again, I find myself studying his face. The curve of his smiling mouth and the hard line of his jaw. What he wants me to see and what he wants to hide. After a moment, I turn away, heading to the front of the cave, where Tiernan is striking an ancient flint against the side of his sword, hoping to get a spark.

I wonder how much it bothers him to be back here, alone.

"How long were you with Hyacinthe?" I ask, pulling out my twice-soaked matchbook and handing it over, though it might be useless.

Tiernan sighs. "We met the summer before King Eldred abdicated, at a late-night revel—not a Court one, the informal kind. I was still hoping to be chosen for a knight."

I frown, not sure what he means. "Aren't you a knight?"

Tiernan grins, as amused as I've ever seen him. "Me? No. I was trained for it but never got the chance."

I glance at Oak, more confused than ever. I don't know a lot about the process, but I was fairly sure it involved some member of a royal family tapping you on the shoulder with a sword. Surely, this mission alone was cause for that.

"I joined the Court of Shadows," he says, answering the question I don't ask.

"You're a spy?" I think my mouth might be hanging open.

"Who else would my sister choose for a guard?" Oak interjects from the back. "She has a great fondness for spies who wanted to be knights, since she was one herself."

"I wasn't then, though. I was young and hopeful and a little drunk." He smiles at the memory. "Hyacinthe was standing half in shadow, and he asked me if I knew anything about prophecies. I think he was *very* drunk.

"We got lost together in a hedge maze and spoke of the great deeds we planned on doing, like the knights of old. I thought his quest for revenge was impossibly romantic." His mouth twists, as though it hurts for him to remember that version of himself, or a Hyacinthe who hadn't yet chosen vengeance over him.

The fire catches.

"And here you are, doing great deeds," I say.

He half smiles. "Sometimes life gives us the terrible gift of our own wishes come true."

Oak has peeled the wax from the cheese in the chest. He sits beside us, chewing a piece of it and grimacing.

"It's *aged*," the prince says, as though that might be cause to recommend it despite the taste.

I rifle through his bag for a granola bar and eat that instead.

"Tell her the rest," Oak says.

At Tiernan's frown, the prince grins. "Yes, I've heard the tale before. *Many times.* But Wren has not."

"What Oak wants me to tell you, I suppose, is that Hyacinthe and I spent the better part of two years together, before he left with Madoc's army. We made the sorts of promises lovers make." There's a stiffness to his speech. Tiernan seems to be the sort of person who, the more deeply he feels a thing, the harder it is for him to talk about—although apparently he's told plenty to Oak. "But when Hyacinthe wanted me to commit treason with him, I couldn't.

"His revenge ought to be done, I thought. Prince Dain was dead. The High King did seem a bit of a fop, but no worse than Eldred. He disagreed. We had a big row, Sin declared me a coward, and I didn't see him for another year."

Sin? I force myself not to grin at the nickname he'd managed to keep quiet until now.

"Yeah, when he came back to kill you," Oak says, then turns to me. "Hyacinthe would have been traveling with the Court of Teeth, like the rest of Madoc's army. And would have fought in the Battle of the Serpent. *Against* Tiernan."

"We didn't see each other," Tiernan clarifies. "No less fight. Not until after."

I think about myself, under Oak's bed. I wonder if that's what he's thinking about, too.

Tiernan goes on. "In the prisons. I was part of the Court of Shadows by then, and they let me visit him. We talked, and I thought—well, I didn't know what would happen, or whether there would be any mercy, but I promised that if he was going to be put to death, I would save him. Even if it meant betraying Elfhame after all.

"In the end, though, all he had to do was repent. And he wouldn't so much as do that." Tiernan puts his head in his hands.

"He was proud," Oak says. "And angry."

"Was I supposed to be less proud?" Tiernan demands.

Oak turns to me. "So here's where falcon Hyacinthe goes to Tiernan, who could have fed him and in a year had him back, but..."

He refused him.

"I regretted it," Tiernan said. "So, when I heard he'd gone to the Citadel, I came here and retrieved Hyacinthe. Brought him to Elfhame. Persuaded Oak to break his curse. Whereupon I got my thanks when he tried to kill the High King."

"No good deed goes unpunished, isn't that what they say?" Oak breaks off another piece of the horrible cheese and attempts to spear it onto something to melt over the fire.

"He worried about you," I tell Tiernan. "Hyacinthe, I mean."

He looks over warily. "In what way?"

"He believes you've been ensorcelled by Oak."

Tiernan sniffs, annoyed.

Oak laughs, but it sounds more forced than delighted. After a moment, he speaks again. "You know, until this trip, I thought I liked the cold. One can dress extravagantly when there's no risk of sweating— brocades, gold trims, hats. But I am reevaluating."

I can tell that Tiernan is grateful to have the attention off him. Oak's silly words, his smile, all dare me to play along.

I roll my eyes.

He grins. "*You* have an understated elegance, so no need to worry about weather."

When it is time to sleep, Tiernan and Oak wrap themselves in bearskins. Oak drapes one over my shoulders. I say nothing to indicate that I don't need it, that I am never too cold. When we lie down by the fire, he watches me. The light dances in his eyes.

"Come here," he says, beckoning with a hand.

I am not sure I know the me who moves, who shifts so that I am resting my head against his shoulder. The me who feels his breath against my hair and the pressure of his splayed fingers at the small of my back. His feet tangle with mine, my toes brushing against the fur just above his hooves. My fingers are resting against his stomach, and I cannot help feeling the hard planes of him, the muscles and the scars. When I move my hand, his breath catches.

We both go still. Tiernan, close to the fire, turns in his sleep.

In the firelight, the prince's amber eyes are molten gold.

I am aware of my skin in a way I have never been before, of the slight movements of my limbs, of the rise and fall of my chest. I can hear the beat of his heart against my cheek. I feel as though I am shouting *kiss me* with every restless shift of my body. But his does not, and I am too much of a coward to do more than lie there and yearn until my eyes drift closed at last.

When I wake in the afternoon, it is to Tiernan dragging in the body of a deer. He butchers it quickly, and he and I eat charred venison for breakfast.

Oak washes the heart clean of blood and puts it into the reliquary while still warm. Once it's secured, the prince fiddles with the lock, setting it carefully shut and adjusting something inside to keep it that way.

Then we set off again, the prince and Tiernan wrapping bear fur over their cloaks for greater warmth. The Stone Forest is ahead of us, light shining off the trees where ice encases their branches.

"We can't go in there," I say. "The trolls must be working with Lady Nore."

"Given what we saw yesterday, I must admit you were right to suggest we circle around this stretch of woods," Oak says, staring into the trees and frowning.

Tiernan gives a half smile. "I congratulate you on this wise decision."

We veer off to the east, skirting the edge of the forest. Even from this distance, it appears remarkable. Trees of ice grow blue fruits the size of peaches, encased in a frozen crust. Some have fallen and split open like candy apples. Their scent is that of honey and spice and sap. The leaves of the trees give off a haunting sound not unlike wind chimes when the air blows through the branches.

The longer we walk, the more we realize we cannot get away from the Stone Forest. Sometimes it seems as though the woods itself moves. Twice, I looked up and found myself surrounded by trees. The drag of the magic reminds me of the undertow on a beach: a strip of calm, dark water that seems innocuous but, once it has you, pulls you far from land.

We walk throughout the day, fighting to stay beyond the edges of the forest. We do not stop to eat but, fearing to be caught by the woods, walk while chewing supplies from our packs. At nightfall, our march is interrupted by something moving toward us through the snow.

Stick creatures, enormous and terrible, huge spiders made of brambles and branches. Monstrous things with gaping mouths, their bodies of burned and blackened bark, their teeth of stone and ice. Mortal body parts visibly part of them, as though someone took apart people like they were dolls and glued them back together in awful shapes.

"Make for the forest," Tiernan says, resignation in his voice. His gaze goes to me and then to Oak. "Now."

"But—" the prince begins.

"We're not mounted," Tiernan reminds him. "We have no chance on foot, unless we can get to someplace with cover. Let's hope your mad plan was the right one after all."

And then we stop fighting the forest and plunge into it.

We race past an enormous black boulder, then beneath a tree that makes a tinkling sound as the icicles threaten to fall. When I look over my shoulder, I am horrified to see the stick creatures lumbering toward us, faster than I expected.

"Here," Oak says, beside a fallen tree half-covered in snow. "We hide. Wren, get as far underneath as you can. If they don't see us, perhaps we can trick them into passing us by."

Tiernan kneels, putting his sword in the snow beside him and motions for me to come. I crouch in the hollow beneath the tree, looking up at the spangled sky and the bright scythe of a moon.

And the falcon, soaring across it.

"They have eyes in the air," I say.

Puzzled, Oak follows my gaze, then he understands. "*Tiernan*," he whispers, voice harsh.

Tiernan rolls to his feet and takes off running in the direction of the creatures, just as the bird screeches. "Get her away from here," he calls back to the prince.

A moment later, a rain of ice arrows flies from the trees.

The shaft of one slams into the earth beside my feet, tripping me. I stop so short that I fall in the snow.

Oak hauls me up. He's swearing, a streak of filthy words and phrases running into one another, some in mortal languages and some not.

The monstrous creatures are closing in. The nearer they get, the more clearly I can see the roots writhing through their bodies, the bits of skin and unblinking eyes, the great fang-like stone teeth.

"Keep going," he tells me, and whirls around, drawing his blade. "We're almost to the Citadel. If anyone can stop her, it's you."

"I can't—" I start.

His eyes meet mine. "Go!"

I run, but not far before I draw my borrowed knife and duck behind a tree. If I do not have Oak's skill, at least I have ferocity on my side. I will stab anything I can, and if something gets close enough, I will bite out whatever seems most like a throat.

My plan is immediately cut short. When I step out, an arrow skims over my leg, taking skin with it. A twisted creature with a bow lumbers toward me, notching another arrow. Aiming for my head.

Only to have its weapon cut in half as Oak strikes from the side, slashing through the bow and into the stick thing's stomach. Its mouth opens once, but no sound comes out as Oak pivots and beheads it. The creature goes down in a shower of dirt, berries, and blood that scatter across the snow.

Oak's face is still, but the frenzy of battle is back in his eyes. I think of his father, the redcap, whom he plans to rescue, and of how the prince must have been trained. I wonder if he has ever dipped a cap in someone's blood.

More of the stick creatures come at him, with their claws and fangs and stolen flesh, their shining ice arrows and black-stained blades.

Oak might be a great swordsman, but it seems impossible that any one person could hold them all off. Nonetheless, he looks prepared to try.

His gaze darts to me. "Hide," he mouths.

I scramble behind the black boulder and suck in a breath. The Stone Forest is so full of magic that even that is dizzying. A pulse of enchantment echoes off the trees and branches, ferns and rocks. I had heard the stories, but it was another thing to be inside it, to feel it surround me. *The whole forest is cursed.*

Before I can stop it, I am drawn into the spell. I can feel stone all around, and pressure, and thoughts that flow like honey.

Let me be flesh again. Me. Me. Two voices boom, loud enough to cause me to cover my ears, even though I hear the words only in my mind. Their raw power feels like touching a live wire. This boulder was once a troll king, turned to rock by the sun, and its twin is somewhere deeper in the forest. Their curse has grown, expanding to encompass the entire Stone Forest. I can smell it in the pine and the split blue fruit, so potent that I cannot understand how I could have not known before.

Anticipation whispers through the trees, like an indrawn breath. Urging me on.

I reach into the root of the enchantment, knotted tightly through everything around me. It started with the original curse of all trolls, to be turned to stone in the sunlight. As the magic has weakened, the trolls in Elfhame turn back to flesh at nightfall, but this curse is from a time when the magic was stronger, when stone was forever.

That curse grew outward, feeding on the magic of the troll kings. Nourished by their anger at being trapped, now their curse imprisoned their people and their people's descendants.

I can feel the magic trying to bind me into it, to pull me into its heart the way the woods tried to envelop us. I feel as though I am being buried alive. Digging through dirt, ripping apart the hairy roots that attempt to encircle my limbs like snakes. But even as I pull myself free, the curse on the Stone Forest itself remains as sure as iron.

But now that I have its attention, perhaps I can give the magic another target.

There are invaders, I whisper in my mind, imagining the stick creatures as clearly as I am able. *They will take your people from you.*

I feel the strands of magic curl away from me with a sigh. And then the earth itself cracks, the force of it enough to throw me back. I open my eyes to see a fissure splitting along the ground, wider than a giant's mouth.

A few minutes later, Oak stumbles out from between two trees, frost-covered ferns crackling beneath his steps. A wind blows through the branches to his left, sending a scattering of bladelike pieces of ice plummeting into the snow. The prince is bleeding from a cut on his shoulder, and both the bear fur and his cloak are gone.

I push myself to my feet. My hands are scratched raw, and my knee is bruised. The wound where the arrow grazed my leg is throbbing.

"What happened?" I ask.

A bellow comes from the forest.

"This place," he says, giving the crack in the ground a wide berth. "Some of them fell into the earth as it opened. I cut a few apart. But there are still more. We have to keep moving."

He reaches for my hand.

I take his, and together, we dart between trees. "Have you seen Tiernan?"

"Not yet." I admire how thoroughly he is not letting himself think of any other possibility.

The prince stops suddenly. In the clearing ahead, an enormous spider creature of sticks and earth is shambling toward us.

"Come on," I say, but he lets go of my hand. "What are you doing?"

"There's only the one," he tells me, holding his needle-thin blade aloft.

The spider is enormous, half as tall as one of the trees. It looms over us. One is more than enough. "Oak!"

As he rushes at it, I cannot help thinking of what Tiernan said, about how Oak wanted to be a ship that rocks broke against.

The spider lunges, with snapping fangs that appear to be made from broken femurs. It comes down on the prince, who rolls beneath it, slicing upward with his sword. Dirt rains down on him. It swipes with a thorn-tipped leg.

My heart is beating so hard that it hurts.

Oak climbs up, *into* the creature. Into the weaving of branch and bone, as though it were a piece of playground equipment.

The spider flips onto its back, the thorns on its legs tearing at its own chest. It's ripping out its own insides to get to him. Oak strikes out with his sword, hacking at it. Pieces shred off. It thrashes and bites at the air as it pulls itself apart. Finally, what remains of it goes still.

Oak climbs out of the husk, scratches all down his arms. He grins, but before I can say anything, there is a sound behind me. I whirl as three tall trolls step out from between the trees.

They have light green skin, golden eyes, and arrows tipped in bronze pointing directly at my chest. "You brought those monsters from the Citadel here," one says.

"They followed us," I sputter.

They wear armor of heavy cloth, stitched with a pattern of sworls like the map to a hedge maze or a fingerprint. "Come with us and meet our speaker," says the tallest of them. "She will decide what to do with you."

"It's kind to invite a pair of strangers back to your village," says Oak, walking to us, somehow misrepresenting their intention without actually lying. "But we've lost a friend in your woods and wouldn't want to go anywhere without him."

The tallest troll looks as though he is on the verge of turning his request into an order. Then, from the darkness, a knife catches the moonlight as it is placed to the base of the shortest troll's neck.

"Let's point those weapons elsewhere," Tiernan says.

The tallest troll's eyes narrow, and he lowers his bow. So does the other. The third, knife to his throat, doesn't move.

"You seem to have found your friend," the troll says.

Oak gives him a slow, considering smile. "And are therefore left without a reason not to partake in your hospitality."

The troll camp is set in a large clearing, where buildings of stone and clay have been constructed around a massive bonfire. Sparks fly up from it, then fall as black rain, smudging whatever they touch.

The houses are cleverly and artistically made. The stucco-like clay has been sculpted into shapes—spirals and trees and faces, all in the same pale mud color, decorate the dwellings. High up on the walls, circles of mostly green and amber glass have been inset, creating the effect of stained glass windows. I draw closer and see that they are parts of bottles, and spot a few in brilliant blues and crimsons.

The scale of everything is intimidating. As tall as Oak is, the trolls are at least a head taller. Most are well over eight feet, with bodies that are green or the gray of the stone they become.

We're greeted by a troll woman, large and heavy of limb, who introduces herself as Gorga, the speaker of the village. She has an axe strapped to her back and her hair in braids tipped with silver clasps. She wears a skirt of leather, with slits up the sides for easy movement.

"You're hurt," she says, taking in our bedraggled appearance. "And cold. Stay the day with us, and we will provision you and guide you to your destination safely next nightfall."

That sounds like an offer entirely too good to be true.

Oak meets her eyes with great sincerity. "Your generosity appears boundless. But perhaps I could prevail upon you to tell me more about this place. And yourself."

"Perhaps," she says, looking pleased. "Share a cup of strong tea with me. I will give you some good black bread and honey."

I glance over at Tiernan. He gives me a half smile and a shake of his head, inviting me into his amusement at Oak playing the courtier. "Let's get something hot to eat and sit by the fire," he says, clapping me on my shoulder. "He doesn't need us."

We walk together, me limping a bit. A few young trolls bring us cups made of stone, heavy in my hands. They are full of a warm liquid that looks like tea but tastes like boiled bark. I sit on a rock near the firepit. The heat is such that the stones are warm.

I am on my second cup when Oak joins us, holding a honey sandwich that he takes apart to offer us each a slice. "The troll king, Hurclaw, is off courting, according to Gorga. She was rather cagey about who, exactly, he was intending to marry. She was also rather cagey about what would happen if we tried to leave."

"So we're prisoners?" I whisper.

He sighs. "We are indulging the fiction that we are not."

I take a bite of the sweetened black bread. Then I take two more, practically stuffing the thing in my face.

"For how long?" Tiernan asks.

Oak's smile is tight. "As short a time as possible. Let's all keep our eyes open. Meanwhile, Wren, maybe I can look at your leg."

"No need," I say, but he ignores me, rolling up the bottoms of my pants. There's blood, but it's truly not so bad. That doesn't stop him from asking for bandages and hot water.

Since I left the mortal world, no one cared for my wounds but me. The gentleness of his touch makes me feel too much, and I have to turn my face, lest he see.

An old troll man arrives carrying a wooden bucket full of water, sloshing over the lip when he moves. He has a patch over one eye and white hair in two long braids on either side of his head. In his ears, a half dozen gold hoops glitter.

"Let me take that," Oak says, getting up.

The troll man snorts. "You? You're little enough to take a bath in it, like a babe."

"Nonetheless," says the prince.

The old troll shrugs and sets the bucket down, indicating Oak should give it a try. He lifts it, surprising the troll.

"Put it on the fire to heat," he directs the prince. "It's for your lady."

Oak places it on the hook of the metal tripod over the flames.

The old man sits to watch it boil and takes out a roll of bandages from his bag, handing it over.

Oak kneels by my feet. He has dipped one of the bandages in the water and uses it to wipe off the blood and clean the cut. His fingers are warm as he wraps, and I try to concentrate on anything but the feel of his hands on my skin. "I worried you might have been poisoned back in the woods."

A troll child comes to sit next to Oak, saving me from having to answer. He shyly asks one question and then another; a second child comes over with more questions. Oak laughs as the kids compare the points of their ears with his, touch the small horns growing from his brow and the smooth keratin of his hooves.

"Grandfather," one of them says in a high, childish voice that belies his size. "Will you tell the prince a story?"

I was almost certain they knew who Oak was, but the confirmation does nothing to quiet my nerves.

"You want a story to pass the time, princeling?" the old troll man asks.

"I do love a tale," Oak says.

"Perhaps the story of the kings trapped in stone," I put in. "And the curse."

The troll man looks toward me, narrowing his eyes, then back toward the prince. "Is that truly what you want?"

He nods. The children's giggling has ceased, and I worry I have broken some taboo by asking.

He begins with no hesitation, however. "There are two versions of this story. In the first, the kings are fools. That's the story featured in songs we sang and plays we put on when I was a young man and given to laughter. When leaving the forest for longer than a handful of days seemed unimportant.

"They were supposed to be brothers, these troll kings. They shared power and riches peaceably for many years. Decked out in gold mined from deep in the earth, they had everything they wanted. That is, until they met a mortal boy, a goatherd, lithe of limb and with a face that ought to have been carved in marble. So comely that both the troll kings desired him above all others.

"He wasn't the sharpest knife in the drawer, but the pretty goatherd had a wise mother, and she told him that if he chose one of the brothers, the other would surely prefer him dead rather than see his brother have what he wanted. If the goatherd wanted to live, he had to be sure never to choose.

"And so, the goatherd and his mother came up with a clever plan. He offered his love to the troll king who could hurl the largest boulder. First one and then the other threw larger and larger rocks until they were exhausted and no one could tell who had won.

"Then the goatherd told them that whosoever could defeat the other in a game of wrestling would have his heart. And so the brothers fought each other all through the night, and when the sun came up, both were turned to stone, and the goatherd was free to give his love where he pleased."

I can imagine the funny play that might make, and how much it must annoy the cursed kings if they know about it. "What's the serious version?"

The old troll clears his throat, and there is a pride in his face that makes it clear that however he laughed over the first story in his youth, this is the tale he prefers. "It is similar in many respects. It still concerns two troll kings, but in this case, they were never brothers. They had always been enemies, engaged in a war that spanned many decades. After so much slaughter on both sides, they decided they would wager the war on a contest between the two of them. And so, they met on the field of battle and threw themselves at each other. They crashed back and forth, so evenly matched that as soon as one got a good blow in, the other would get the next. As morning came closer, there were cries from both sides to abandon the contest. But each troll knew that if he cried off, defeat would be his reward. And so, they held on to the last and became stone, locked in the embrace of battle.

"There is still one more variation. It is said that before they declared war on each other, they had been lovers whose passion for each other had turned to hatred, until their desire to best and possess the other was all-consuming." He smiles at me with crooked teeth.

I look over at Tiernan. He's staring at the fire as though he cannot help thinking of his own lover, now his enemy.

"You're a good storyteller," Oak says.

"I am *the* storyteller," says the old troll, as though the prince's praise is immensely inadequate. At that, he gets up and wanders off, taking most of the children with him.

"This forest is cursed," I whisper to Oak.

He frowns at me, probably thinking I mean it in the same vague way that everyone else has when they refer to the Stone Forest.

Tiernan rises, walking off. The story seems to have bothered him.

I hurry on speaking, words tripping over one another in my haste to get them out. "That's what the troll meant when he said *leaving the forest for longer than a day or two seemed unimportant.* Because there's something keeping them here."

"Then where's Hurclaw?" he asks.

I shake my head. "All I know is that if he isn't in the woods, then he must have found a way to stave off the consequences, at least temporarily. But I think that's why he wants to wake the old kings. Not because he's mad. Because it's the only way to end the curse."

Tiernan returns with bread and a soup of barley and onions. I see a few trolls skinning fallen reindeer and smell the cooking of freshly butchered meat. Music starts up, a rowdy tune.

There's a raucousness in the air that wasn't there before, the wild edge of revelry. The smiles of the trolls who look in our direction have a sharpness in them.

"We've been offered pallets for the night inside the speaker's home," says Oak carefully.

"That seems kind," I say.

"A fine way to put it," he says.

Tiernan is eating some of the reindeer meat, chewing on the bone. "We sneak out of here at first light," he says, his voice low. "That's when they can't follow lest they turn to stone."

We are interrupted by a handsome troll woman who comes over to the prince, laughing at how small he is and offering to braid his hair. Though it is not particularly long, he lets her, with a grin at me.

I remember his hands in my hair, combing out the tangles and braiding it, and feel a shiver all down my neck.

Just before dawn, the speaker arrives.

"Speaker Gorga," Oak says, rising. He has three little braids in the back, one coming undone.

"Let me conduct you to my home, where you can rest," she says. "Next nightfall, we will bring you safely across the snow to your destination."

"Generous," Oak says.

Tiernan glances around as we move through the village, alert to opportunities.

When we arrive at her house, she opens the door, beckoning us inside. A clay stove vents into the ceiling above and gives the place a cozy warmth. There's a pile of logs by the fire, and she adds more, causing the stove's embers to blaze up.

Then she waves us to a bed covered in furs of many sorts stitched together. I will have to hop to get up on it. "You may sleep in my bed tonight."

"That's *too* generous," Oak tells her.

"It is a small thing." She takes down a stoppered bottle and pours the contents into four little cups. "Now let us have a drink together before you rest."

She lifts her cup and throws it back.

I pick up mine. The herbal, almost licorice scent hits my senses. Sediment shifts in the bottom. I think of my fears that first night when Oak offered me tea. And I think about how easy it would be to put the poison at the bottoms of certain cups, instead of in a bottle, to make it appear we were all drinking the same thing.

I glance at the prince, wanting to give him a warning but unable to come up with a way to do so without Speaker Gorga noticing. Oak drinks his in a gulp and then reaches for mine, plucking it out of my fingers and drinking it, too.

"No!" I cry, but I am too late.

"Delicious," he announces, grabbing for Tiernan's. "Like mother's milk."

Even Speaker Gorga looks alarmed. If she had measured out the doses carefully, then the prince just drank three times what she'd calculated.

"Forgive my greed," Oak says.

"*My lord,*" Tiernan cautions, horror in his face.

"Perhaps you would like another round?" Speaker Gorga suggests uncertainly, holding up the half-full bottle.

"I might as well, and the others have yet to have a taste," the prince says.

She pours more into the cups. When I look into the depths, there is sediment, but significantly less. The poison, whatever it was, was already in the vessels. Prepared ahead of us even entering the room.

I take mine and tip it against my teeth, but do not drink. I make myself visibly swallow twice. Across the table, Oak has gotten Gorga's attention with some question about the fruits encased in ice, and so I am able to drop my hand beneath the table and surreptitiously pour out the contents onto my cloak.

I do not look down, and so I'm not sure if I've gotten away with it. Nor do I dare look at Tiernan to see if he has managed something similar.

"Why don't I leave the bottle?" Speaker Gorga asks, putting it down. "Let me know if there is anything else you require."

"What more could we ever want?" Oak muses.

With a small, tense smile, she rises and leaves.

For a moment, we sit just as we are. Then the prince stands, staggers, and falls to his knees. He begins to laugh.

"Throw it up," Tiernan says, clapping Oak's back.

The prince manages to make himself retch twice into a stone bowl before slumping down beside it. "Don't worry," he says, his amber eyes shining too brightly. Despite the cold, sweat has started on his forehead. "It's my poison."

"What have you done?" I ask him, my voice harsh. When he only smiles dreamily, I turn to Tiernan. "Why would he do that?"

The knight appears equally horrified. "Because he is madder than the troll king."

I open and close drawers, hoping to find an antidote. There's nothing that looks even vaguely promising. "What was it? What does he mean, *his poison*?"

Tiernan goes over to one of the cups, sniffs it, then shakes his head. "I don't know."

"I was born with blusher mushroom in my veins," the prince says, the words coming out slowly, as though his tongue is not quite his own. "It takes a great deal of it to affect me for long."

I recall what he said the night he'd been poisoned with deathsweet. *Alas, that it wasn't blusher mushroom.*

"How did you know what it was?" I demand, kneeling beside him, thinking of how recently he'd had another poison in his blood.

"I was desperate," he forces out. "I was just so afraid that one of you...that *you*..." His words trail off, and his eyes seem to be staring at nothing. His mouth moves a little, but not enough for sound to come out.

I watch the rise and fall of his chest. It is very slow, too slow. I press my fingers to his clammy forehead, despair making everything feel as though time is speeding and crawling all at once.

Just thinking requires pushing through a fog of dread. *He knows what he's doing,* I tell myself. *He's not a fool. He's not dying. He's not dead.*

Tiernan looks up at the shadows changing in the bottle glass high above us. A pinkish, soft light filters through, showing me the anguish on his face.

Dawn.

He tries the door. There's no visible lock, but it doesn't open. Barred. And there are, of course, no windows through which sunlight might strike Gorga and turn her to stone. He throws his whole weight against the door suddenly, but it doesn't budge.

"This is her house, not normally a prison, so whatever is keeping us inside has to have been moved for that purpose," I say, standing, numbly working through the possibilities as I speak. I recall the heaviness of the door, the thickness of the wood. "It swings outward. She's probably put something against it."

"Does it matter?" Tiernan snaps.

I frown. "I guess not, since we should just take off the hinges."

He stares at me for a moment and gives a panicked, despairing laugh. "I am not going to live it down, you being the one to come up with that."

There are many things I don't know, but I know a great deal about imprisonment.

Tiernan takes apart the hinges with a knife, making quick work of them, while I wrap Oak in a too-large woolen blanket. Giving in to temptation, I brush his bronze hair back from where it has fallen over one eye. At my touch, he gives a shiver.

See, I tell myself. *Not dead.*

"We won't be able to carry him far," I warn, although that must be obvious.

Tiernan has pried the door off to reveal a massive boulder blocking our way. It's more round than square, though, and there are gaps along the sides.

"You're small. Wriggle through and find something to put him on—a cart, a sleigh, anything. I'll try to move him," Tiernan tells me.

"I'll be quick," I say, and wedge myself into the gap between the boulder and the outer wall of the house. By climbing up a little and moving slowly, I manage to ease my way out.

It is strange to find the troll village so quiet as golden light spills over it. Since Gorga is the speaker, I assume that she has more than most of the others, so I figure I ought to start my search with her place. I creep around the back of her house. A small stone-and-clay outbuilding rests near the edge of the clearing. When I wedge open the door, I see a sled inside, and rope.

A sled. Exactly what we need for Oak.

He'll be fine, he'll wake in time to find his father, to be yelled at by Tiernan, and for me to . . .

The thoughts of what I will do after he wakes fade at the scent of rot in the air. The cold tamped it down, but it is definitely coming from something nearby. I move past the sled, deeper into the outbuilding. Whatever is decaying seems to be inside a chest in the back.

It's unlatched and opens easily when I push up the lid.

Inside are clothes, armor, and other supplies. Swords. Arrows. All of them stained with gore, blackened by time. Things worn by victims who have come through this forest before. My heart thunders, imagining my own clothes among them along with Oak's glittering golden mail. Then, gritting my teeth, I stick my hand inside and fish around until I come up with a tabard that looks like the sort worn by Madoc's soldiers. Possibly it belonged to Lihorn, whose head we found staked out on the snowy plain. I manage to find clothing that reminds me of what the huldufólk who used to serve Lady Nore wore, some of them blood-spattered.

My heart races at the evidence of what's happened to other travelers. I heap a few onto the sled and pull it back to the house. Tiernan is standing in the snow, Oak leaning against him as though he's passed out after a night of too much wine.

"We need to *go*," I whisper.

Using the clothes for padding, we strap him to the sled. Tiernan drags it behind us as we creep out of the troll encampment as quietly as we are able.

As we get closer to the tree line, I feel the curse try to steer me the wrong way, to make my steps turn back toward the forest's heart. But now that I am aware, the magic has a harder time putting my feet wrong. I cut in front of Tiernan so that he can follow me. Each step feels as though I am fighting through fog until we hit the very edge of the woods.

I look behind me to see Tiernan hesitate, confused. "Are we—"

Behind him, on the sled, Oak's body writhes against the ropes.

"It's this way." I reach for Tiernan's gloved hand and force myself to take it, to pull him along with me, though my legs feel leaden. I take another step. And another. As we hit the expanse of snow, my breaths come more easily. I release Tiernan's hand and squat, sucking in air.

On the sled, Oak has gone still again. "What was that?" he asks, shuddering. He looks back at the woods and then at me, as though he can't quite remember the last few minutes.

"The curse," I say. "The farther we are from the forest, the better. Come on."

We begin moving again. We walk through the morning, the sun shining off the snow.

An hour in, Oak begins to mutter to himself. We stop and check on him, but he seems disoriented.

"*My sister thinks that she's the only one who can take poison, but I am poison,*" he whispers, eyes half-closed, talking to himself. "*Poison in my blood. I poison everything I touch.*"

That's such a strange thing to hear him say. Everyone adores him.

And yet, I recall him running away at thirteen, sure so many things were his fault.

I frown over that as we trudge on, bits of ice catching in my hair and on my tongue.

"You're tough, you know that?" Tiernan tells me, his breath clouding in the air. "And quick-thinking."

Perhaps this is his way of thanking me for guiding him out of the woods.

"Not just some rabid animal, unworthy of being your companion on a quest?" I counter, still resentful over him tying my ankle to the motel bed.

He doesn't defend himself. "And not hideous, even. In case you wondered what I thought, which I am fairly sure you didn't."

"Why are you saying all this?" I ask, my voice low. I glance back at Oak, but he is staring at the sky, laughing a little to himself. "You can't possibly care what I look like."

"He talked about you," Tiernan says.

I feel like an animal after all, one that's been baited in its den. I both dread and desire him to keep talking. "What did he say?"

"That you didn't like him." He gives me an evaluating look. "I thought maybe you'd had a falling-out when you were younger. But I think you *do* like him. You just don't want him to know it."

The truth of that hurts. I grind my sharp teeth together.

"The prince is a flatterer. And a charmer. And a wormer around things," Tiernan informs me, entirely unnecessarily. "That makes it harder for him to be believed when he has something sincere to say. But no one would ever accuse me of being a flatterer, and he—"

He bites off the rest because, there, in the distance, rising out of the snow, is the Ice Needle Citadel.

One of the towers has fallen. The castle of cloudy ice, like some enormous piece of quartz, was once full of spires and points, but many of them have cracked and splintered. The jagged icicles that were once ornamentation have grown into elephantine structures that cover some of the windows and cascade down the sides. My breath stutters. I have seen this place so many times in my night terrors that, even half-demolished, I cannot help but feel like I am in another awful dream.

CHAPTER
14

Rays of sunlight strike the snow, melting an ice layer that freezes and re-forms every day. As I take a step, I feel the sheet break, a craquelure spreading from my feet.

This time, I do not fall. In that reflective, glittering brightness, though, it is hard to hide.

During our trudge toward the Citadel, Oak untied himself and crawled from the sled, declaring he was well enough, and then proved that his definition of "well enough" wasn't the same as "well," since he has spent the time since staggering along as though drunk.

Titch found us again, swooping low and settling on Tiernan's shoulder. The knight sent the hob off to scout ahead.

"Let's stop here," Tiernan says, and Oak collapses gratefully into the snow. "Wren has suggested we change clothes."

"I do appreciate your commitment to us looking our best," says the prince.

By now, I am used to Oak and do not think for a moment he doesn't understand the plan. I haul out the uniforms I stole from Gorga. For myself, with my bluish skin, I take the dress of one of the castle servants. Huldufólk, like Lady Nore, have gray skin and tails. My skin isn't quite right, and I have no tail, but its absence is hidden by the long skirts.

I wrap the bridle in a strip of cloth around my waist, then tie it on underneath the dress like a girdle. My knife goes into my pocket.

I change quickly. So does Oak, who shivers as he pulls rough woolen pants over his smooth linen ones. They hang low enough that his hooves look passably like boots when half-covered with snow. Tiernan shivers almost continuously as he pulls on the new uniform.

"You're still likely to be identified if anyone sees you close-up," I warn Oak.

He is the prince, after all, with hooves not unlike the former Prince Dain's.

"Which is why I should go in, not you," says Tiernan for what feels like the millionth time.

"Nonsense; if they catch me, they won't immediately put my head on a spike," Oak returns.

He's probably right. Still. "Yes, but they're *more likely* to catch you," I say.

"You ought to be on my side," he says, looking hurt. "I was poisoned."

"That's another good reason for me to go in your place," Tiernan puts in.

"Pragmatist," says Oak, as though it's a dirty word.

We get as close as we dare and then hollow out snow into a cavern to wait in until nightfall. Oak and Tiernan pull their hands and feet tight to their bodies, but the prince's lips still take on a bluish color.

I unclasp the cloak that I've been wearing and pass it to him.

He shakes his head. "Keep it. You'll freeze."

I push it at him. "I'm never cold."

He gives me an odd look, perhaps thinking of me lying with him by the fire, but must be too chilled to debate.

As they go over our plan one more time, I start to believe that this is possible. We get in, steal back Mab's remains, and leave with the general. If something goes wrong, I suppose we have the deer heart in the reliquary, but since Oak's bluff seems like a long shot, I hope we don't have to rely on it. Instead, I concentrate on remembering that I still have the power of command over Lady Nore.

And yet, as we approach the Citadel, I cannot help but recall being lost in this snow, weeping while tears froze on my cheeks. Just being here makes me feel like that monster child again, unloved and unlovable.

As night falls, Tiernan crawls out of our makeshift dwelling. "If you're going in, then at least let me be the one to go down and make sure all is how we expect it."

"You need not—" Oak begins, but Tiernan cuts him off with a glare.

"Wren ought to stay behind with the heart," Tiernan says. "If you're not planning on confronting Lady Nore, then it doesn't matter if Wren can command her, and Wren's no use to you in a fight."

"I could be useful in avoiding one," I remind him.

Oak does not seem moved by Tiernan's argument. "If she's willing to come, then she's coming."

Tiernan throws up his hands and storms off through the snow, obviously angry with both of us.

"I do think I may need you inside the Citadel," Oak tells me. "Although I wish that wasn't the case."

I am glad he wants me there, though I am no knight or spy. "Perhaps all three of us could go in," I venture.

"He needs to stay here, lest we get caught," Oak says. "He'll keep the heart with him and bargain for our return with it."

A moment later, Tiernan ducks his head back inside, the owl-faced hob on his shoulder. "You two can climb the side to the birdie entrance. Titch has been watching the patrol shifts, and they're sloppy. Makes it hard to know when they are going to happen, but there's a window of opportunity when they do."

Oak nods and pushes himself to his feet. "Very well, then," he says. "No time like the present."

"One more thing," Tiernan says. "There are trolls on the battlements, along with those stick creatures and some falcon soldiers."

"But I thought the trolls were trapped...," I begin, but trail off because there are so many possibilities. They could be trolls that do not come from the Stone Forest and are therefore not subject to its curse. But when I think about the heaps of clothing, and the mounted heads, I wonder if what we witnessed were the remains of sacrifices meant to appease the ancient troll kings to open the way from the forest.

My blood was spilled for the glory of the Kings of Stone who rule from beneath the world, but my body belongs to the Queen of Snow.

At that unsettling thought, I follow Tiernan and Oak out of our snow tunnel and into the frigid air.

We stay as low to the ground as we are able. In the dark, it's easier to approach the Citadel without drawing much attention to ourselves. At least until we see a great and horrible spiderlike construction of ice and stone, flesh and twig, lumbering through the night.

We hear a piercing scream, and I see that the spider has a huldu woman in its pincers. They are too far away for us to help her. A moment later, her screams cease and the stick-spider begins to feed.

"If that thing can eat," Oak says, "then it's truly *alive*. Not like one of Grimsen's ornamental creations with fluttering wings that move like clockwork. Not like that head on a spike, repeating the same message over and over. It hungers and thirsts and wants."

Like me.

Oh, I do not want to be here. I hate this place. I hate everything about it and everything it might teach me about myself.

Enormous braziers burn on either side of the Citadel gate. We wait in the snow until there is movement on the battlements.

Tiernan flips a knife in his hand. "I'll create a distraction at the garrison while you and the prince go up that wall."

This is my last chance to avoid returning to the place of my nightmares. All I have to do is tell Oak I changed my mind. Tiernan would be thrilled.

I think of Bogdana's words to me in the woods. *The prince is your enemy.*

I think about the feeling of Oak's breath against my neck, the way his fox eyes looked with the pupils gone wide and black. I think about how desperate he must be, to come all this way for his father, to gulp down poison, to risk his life on an uncertain scheme.

I think about the bridle wrapped around my waist, the one I tried to steal. The one he gave me to keep.

I have to trust him. Without me, we cannot command Lady Nore.

"We should go straight to the prisons," Oak says. "Get Madoc. Go from there."

"Better not," I tell him. "We don't know how hurt he's going to be, and we can move faster without him. If we get the reliquary, then we can free him and move him to the sled directly."

Oak hesitates. I can see the conflict between getting what he came here for and getting everything. "All right," he says finally.

"If you're not back by dawn," Tiernan says, "then you know where I will be with the reliquary." With that, he heads off through the snow.

"How exactly is he going to create a distraction?" I ask, attempting to walk with my head down, as though I am a servant who belongs to the Citadel and am returning from a dull errand—perhaps gathering crowberries. Attempting to behave as though Oak is a soldier walking me inside.

"Better not to ask," the prince says with a slight smile.

Up close, the outside of the Citadel is not a single piece of cloudy ice, but one composed of blocks, which have been melted smooth. Oak sticks his hand into his pack, and I recognize the grappling hook and rope from Undry Market.

He's eyeballing the spires, looking for the correct one.

"There," I whisper, pointing up.

The entrance, three stories above us, isn't visible when standing beneath it, as we are. It looks like an arch, the mirror of those that surround it.

"You ready?" he asks.

I'm not. When I think of Lady Nore, it's as though my mind becomes full of scribbles, blotchy and looping, scratching through all my other thoughts. I nod in answer, because I don't trust myself to speak when I have no ability to tell anything but the truth.

Oak throws the grappling hook. Built for ice, the sharp edge sticks in hard. "If I fall, you must promise not to laugh. I may still be a little bit poisoned."

I think of Tiernan and how exasperated he would be if he heard those words. I wonder exactly how much *a little bit* means. "Maybe I should be the one to go first."

"Nonsense," he says. "If you weren't behind me, then who would break my fall?" Then he grabs the rope, presses his feet to the side of the Citadel, and proceeds to walk himself up the wall.

I roll my eyes, grab hold, and follow far more slowly.

We stop at the edge of the tower, and he winds the rope and removes the hook, while I peer down into the chamber through the opening. I hear distant strains of music. That must come from the great hall, where the thrones sit, and where instruments strung with the dried guts of mortals, or ones inlaid with bits of their bones, had been played to the delight of the Court of Teeth. This sounds more like a lone musician, though, rather than the usual troupe.

As I look down, a servant rushes through, holding a tray filled with empty goblets that clatter together. Thankfully, they do not glance up.

I press my hand to my heart, grateful we weren't descending at that moment.

"This time you go first," Oak says, sinking the hook into new ice. "I'll cover you."

I think he means that if someone spots me, no matter if they are a servant or guard, he's going to kill them.

"They taught you a lot of things, your family," I say. The sleight of hand, the wall climbing, the swordsmanship.

"Not to die," he says. "That's what they attempted to teach me, anyway. How not to die."

Considering how often he throws himself directly into the path of danger, I do not think they taught him well enough. "What's the number of times that someone tried to assassinate you?"

He gives a one-shouldered shrug, his attention on the tableau below. "Hard to know, but I'd guess there were a few dozen attempts since my sister came to power."

That would be more than twice a year for every year since I met him. And that scar on his neck suggests that someone got very, very close.

I think of him as he was in the woods at thirteen, wanting to run away. Angry and afraid. I think of him lying on the sled this morning.

I poison everything I touch.

Every time I feel as though I know him, it seems there is another Oak underneath.

I shimmy down the rope, dropping when I am close enough to the ground not to hurt myself. My feet make a soft, echoing noise when they hit the floor, and I am struck by the nausea-inducing familiarity of the place. I spent not even two years here, and yet the very smell of the air makes me sick.

A massive bone chandelier hangs in the center of the room, candle wax dripping hot enough to melt indentations in the floor.

While the exterior of the Citadel is formed of giant slabs of clear, bright ice, some of the interior walls are enhanced by having things frozen inside the ice, resulting in something like wallpaper. Stones suspended, as though forever in midfall. Bones, picked clean, occasionally used to form sculptures. Roses, their petals forever preserved in their full flowering. This room's walls have two faerie women frozen inside them, preserved so that they never decayed into moss and stone, like the rest of the Folk. Two faerie women, dressed in finery, crowns on their heads.

The Hall of Queens.

I had never known that Lady Nore might have joined their number, if not for me. A fresh horror, on top of all the others.

I can't help feeling like a child again, with time seeming to dilate around me. Every hour, each day had felt endless, telescopic. The spaces were distorted in my memory, the halls shorter, the ceilings less high.

My wrists still show knots of skin where Lord Jarel pierced them to drive through the thin silver chains that leashed me. If I touch my cheeks, I can still feel, right underneath the bone, the marks of scars.

I do not realize how long I have been staring until Oak lands beside me, the clatter of his hooves louder than my soft-shod feet. He takes in the room, and me.

"Do you know the way from here?" he asks.

I give a quick nod and begin to move again.

One of the dangers of the Citadel is that the ice throughout varies in translucence, so there are places where movement is visible between rooms, or even through floors and ceilings. We could be semi-exposed at all times. Therefore, we must not crouch or attempt to hide. We must move in such a way that our faint outlines do not betray us.

I lead us into a hall, and then another. We pass a thin window of ice that looks out on the interior courtyard, and I glance through it. Oak pulls me back into shadow, and after a moment, I realize why.

Lady Nore stands outside, in front of sculptures of stick and snow. A line of ten, some in the shapes of men, some beasts, some creatures that are neither. Each one's mouth is filled with sharp, jagged icicle teeth. Each one has stones in place of eyes; a few have them pressed into sockets of flesh. I spot other horrible things: a foot, fingers, bits of hair.

From a bag, Lady Nore takes a little knife in the shape of a half moon. She slices her palm. Then she takes a pinch of bone gravel from a bag at her waist and smears it onto her bloody, open hand. One by one, she walks to the snow sculptures and presses those bits of bone, shining with wetness, into their mouths.

And one by one, they awaken.

They are like me. Whatever they are, they are *like me*.

And yet, these stick creatures seem like living puppets and little else. They stay in their neat rows, and when she orders them inside, they go obediently, as though they'd never had any other thought. But I do not understand why, if the magic of Mab's bones is animating these creatures, they are not conscious in the way that I am.

Although I may have been made from snow and sticks and blood, there is some difference that allows me to behave like a disobedient faerie daughter, when these creatures seem to make no choices at all.

But then I recall the spider hunting the servant and don't know what to suppose.

The sound of footsteps is the only warning before two guards turn the corner.

Oak puts his hands on my shoulders, pushing my back to the wall.

"*Pretend with me*," he whispers. And then he presses his mouth to mine.

A soldier kissing one of the serving girls. A bored ex-falcon attempting to amuse himself. Oak hiding our faces, giving us a reason to be overlooked. I understand the game.

This is no declaration of desire. And yet, I am rooted in place by the shocking heat of his mouth, the softness of his lips, the way one of his hands goes to the ice wall to brace himself and the other to my waist, and then to the hilt of my knife as they draw closer.

He doesn't want me. This doesn't mean he wants me. I repeat that over and over as I let him part my lips with his tongue. I run my hands up his back under his shirt, letting my nails trail over his skin.

I have been trained in all the arts of a courtier. Dancing and dueling, kissing and deceiving.

Still, I am gratified when he shudders, when the hand he was bracing with lifts to thread through my hair, to cup my head. My mouth slides over his jaw to his throat, then against his shoulder, where I press the points of my teeth. His body stiffens, his fingers gripping me harder, pulling me closer to him. When I bite down, he gasps.

"You there," says one of the soldiers, a troll. "Get to your post. If the lady hears of this—"

When Oak draws back, his lips are flushed red. His eyes look black beneath golden lashes. I see the marks from my teeth on his shoulder. He turns and drives a knife into the troll's stomach. The troll falls soundlessly as Oak turns to slash the other's throat.

Hot blood spatters the ice. Where it lands, steam rises and a constellation of pockmarks appear.

"Is there a room nearby?" the prince asks in a voice that shakes only a little. "For the bodies."

For a moment, I stare at him stupidly. I am reeling from the kiss, from the swiftness of the violence. I am not yet used to Oak's ability to kill without hesitation and then look chagrined about it, as though he did something in slightly poor taste. Spilled a rare vintage of wine, perhaps. Mismatched his trousers to his shirt.

Although I cannot be anything other than glad he killed them swiftly and soundlessly.

I lead him across the hall, into a strange little chamber for keeping supplies to clean and polish and provide for the needs of the Gentry in this part of the castle.

Inside, the frozen carcass of an elk hangs in one corner, slivers of meat cut off. On the opposite wall are wooden shelves, packed with linens, cups, glasses, and trays, as well as dried herbs that hang in bundles. Two barrels of wine sit on the ground, one opened, a ladle resting on the lip.

Oak drags both guards in. I grab up one of their cloaks and a tablecloth from the shelves to go back and mop up the blood.

As I do, I check to see if there are any translucent parts of ice through which anyone could have witnessed what happened. If they did, it would have appeared like a violent shadow play, and therefore not entirely unusual in the Citadel. Still, if someone was searching for us, it might be a problem.

I notice nothing to give us away, so I stash the soiled fabric back in the room. Oak has pushed the bodies into a corner and covered them with a cloth.

"Is there any blood on me?" he asks, patting down the front of his woolen shirt.

It was a fine spatter, and though it struck his clothes, the pattern is nearly invisible in the dark fabric. I find a little in his hair and wipe it off. Rub his cheek and just above the corner of his mouth.

He gives me a guilty smile, as though expecting me to take him to task for the kiss or the murders. I cannot guess which.

"We're almost to the stairs," I tell him.

On the landing, we spot two more guards on the opposite end of a long hall. They are too far to make out our faces, and I hope too far off to see anything inauthentic in our costumes. I keep my gaze straight ahead. Oak nods to one, and the guard nods in return.

"Brazen," I mutter under my breath, and the prince grins.

My hands are shaking.

We pass the library and the war room, then walk up another set of stairs. These spiral steeply for two floors until we come to Lady Nore's bedroom, at the very top of the leftmost tower.

Her door is tall and pointed at its apex. It is made of some black metal, frosted over with cold. The handle is a deer hoof.

I reach out my fingers, turn it. The door opens.

Lady Nore's bedroom is entirely new, the room washed in red. It takes me a moment to realize where the color is coming from. Viscera. The flayed-open bodies of Lady Nore's victims on display all around her, frozen inside the walls so that light could filter through them and give the room its odd, ruddy tint.

Oak sees it, too, eyes wide as he takes in the awful space. "Well, a reliquary full of bones can't be out of place among all this grotesque art."

I give him a grateful glance. Yes. That's right. All we need to do is find Mab's remains. Then we can escape with his father. And perhaps I will no longer feel trapped by the Citadel, no longer be frozen in my past, as though I were one of the bodies in the wall.

A large bed sits in the middle of the floor, the headboard and footboard of carved onyx in sharp, spear-like shapes. Over the cushions rests a coverlet of ermine. A brazier burns in one corner of the room, warming the air.

Opposite hangs a mirror with a black frame in the shape of intertwining snakes. Beneath that is a dressing table, with jewels and hairpins strewn across its surface. I find an inkpot and a golden comb in its drawers.

I expect everything here to be perfectly arranged, as it was in the memory of my childhood, but when I turn to Lady Nore's enormous wardrobe, built of ebony wood and inlaid with teeth from many beasts and beings, I see that several of her dresses lie on the floor. They are great, grand things in scarlet and shimmering silver, with droplets that appear like frozen tears. There are whole gowns of black swan feathers. But the closer I look, the more I notice the stains, the rips. They are as old as the broken towers of the castle.

The mess makes me suppose that Lady Nore readied herself quickly and without the help of servants. There is a desperation in all this that seems at odds with her sitting at the cusp of vast power.

Oak puts a hand on my arm. I startle.

"You all right?" he asks.

"When they first took me from the mortal world to the Court of Teeth, Lord Jarel and Lady Nore tried to be nice to me. They gave me good things to eat and dressed me in fancy dresses and told me that I was their princess and would be a beautiful and beloved queen," I tell him, the words slipping from my lips before I can call them back. I occupy myself with searching deeper in the closet so I don't have to see his face as I speak. "I cried constantly, ceaselessly. For a week, I wept and wept until they could bear it no more."

Oak is silent. Though he knew me as a child, he never knew me as *that* child, the one who still believed the world could be kind.

But then, he had sisters who were stolen. Perhaps they had cried, too.

"Lord Jarel and Lady Nore told their servants to enchant me to sleep, and the servants did. But it never lasted. I kept weeping."

He nods, just a little, as though more movement might break the spell of my speaking.

"Lord Jarel came to me with a beautiful glass dish in which there was flavored ice," I tell him. "When I took a bite, the flavor was inde-scribably delicious. It was as though I were eating dreams.

"*You will have this every day if you cease your crying*, he said.

"But I couldn't stop.

"Then he came to me with a necklace of diamonds, as cold and beautiful as ice. When I put it on, my eyes shone, my hair sparkled, and my skin shimmered as though glitter had been poured over it. I looked wondrously beautiful. But when he told me to stop crying, I couldn't.

"Then he became angry, and he told me that if I didn't stop, he would turn my tears to glass that would cut my cheeks. And that's what he did.

"But I cried until it was hard to tell the difference between tears and blood. And after that, I began to teach myself how to break their curses. They didn't like that.

"And so they told me I would be able to see the humans again—that's what they called them, *the humans*—in a year, for a visit, but only if I was good.

"I *tried*. I choked back tears. And on the wall beside my bed, I scratched the number of days in the ice.

"One night I returned to my room to find that the scratches weren't the way I remembered. I was sure it had been five months, but the scratches made it seem as though it had been only a little more than three.

"And that was when I realized I was never going home, but by then the tears wouldn't come, no matter how much I willed them. And I never cried again."

His eyes shine with horror. "I should never have asked you to come back here."

"Just don't leave me behind," I say, feeling immensely vulnerable. "That's what I want, for the game I won all those years ago."

"I promise you," he says. "If it is within my power, we leave together."

I nod. "We will find the reliquary and ruin her," I tell him. "And then I will never come back."

But as we open drawers and comb through Lady Nore's belongings, we find no bones, no magic.

"I don't think it's here," Oak says, looking up from a box he's poking through.

"She might keep it in the throne room," I venture. Even though we must go down steps again and slip past guards, I will be glad to be out of this terrible room.

"My father might know where it's kept," he says. "I know you don't think—"

"We can try the prisons," I say reluctantly.

As I turn to give the chamber one last look, I notice something strange about her bed. The base of it is ice, and I am sure there's something frozen *in* it. Not red but ivory and brown.

"Oak?" I say.

He turns, looking in the direction that I am. "Did you find something?"

"I'm not sure." I walk across the floor. Pushing back the covers, I see three victims frozen there. Not taken apart, like those in the walls. I cannot even tell how they died.

As I stare, one, impossibly, opens his eyes.

I shrink away, and as I do, his mouth parts and out comes a sound that is half moan and half song. Beside him, the other two awaken and begin to make the same noise, until it rises in a ghostly chorus.

Sounding an alarm.

Oak grabs my shoulder and pushes me out the door. "A trap," he says. "Go!"

I run down the stairs as fast as I am able, half-slipping, my hand bracing on the wall. The clatter of Oak's hooves is right behind me.

We make it to the second landing before ten guards appear— ex-falcons, huldufólk, nisser, and trolls. They fan out in a formation around us, weapons drawn. Oak's back presses against mine, and I hear the rattle of his thin blade pulling free from its sheath.

CHAPTER
15

Oak kills two trolls and a nisse before another of the trolls gets a knife to my throat.

"Halt," he calls, pressing the blade down hard enough to sting. "Or the girl dies."

For a moment, the prince's eyes are so blank that I don't know if he can hear the words. But then he falters, letting his blade sag. He looks as though it was a fight to come back to himself.

None of them get too close, even then. Blood still drips from that needle-thin blade of his. They'd have to step over the bodies of their comrades.

"Throw down your sword," one of the other soldiers calls to him.

"Vow she won't be harmed," Oak says, breathing hard. "Also me. I would like not to be harmed as well."

"If you don't drop that blade, I'll cut her throat and then yours," the troll threatens. "How's that for a promise?" He's so close to me that I can smell the leather of his armor, the oil on his knife, and the stink of dried blood. I can feel the heat of his breath. The arm across my neck is as solid as stone.

I try to think past my panic. My own knife is still in my hand, but the troll has gripped the wrist holding it.

I could bite his arm, though. My sharp teeth could rend even a troll's flesh. The shock of pain would either cause him to cut my throat or loosen his grip. But even if I was lucky, even if I could use that moment to slip out of his hands and run to Oak, what then? We'd never make it out of the Citadel. We would most likely never make it out of this hall.

The prince's sword dangles from his fingers, but he doesn't let it drop. "I was invited here and instructed to bring Mellith's living heart to your lady. I think she would be extremely disappointed to find you'd robbed her of her prize. Dead, I can hardly give it to her."

A shudder goes through me at the thought of Lady Nore getting what she wants, even though I know this is a game, a con, a hustle. Oak doesn't really have Mellith's heart. The danger lies in her seeing through his deception.

And it doesn't matter if it gets me into the room. All I need is to be able to talk.

Oak goes on. "You've almost caught us. You have to make only one small concession, and I will go with you, docile as a lamb."

"Throw down your blade, prince," says one of the ex-falcons. "And no harm will come to either of you by our hands while we escort you to the throne room. You can beg for Lady Nore's mercy and explain why, were you invited to the Citadel, we found you running from her bedchamber."

Oak lets the sword fall. It clatters to the floor.

One guard wrenches the knife out of my hand, while another takes a skein of rope and winds it between my lips, knotting it at the back of my head. As they push me along, I try to chew it apart, but though my teeth are sharp, I am bound well enough that we reach the throne room with the rope still in my mouth.

They have not bound the prince, but he walks surrounded by drawn blades. I cannot tell if that is meant as a sign of respect for his person or if they don't want to take their chances by getting too close.

All I know is that I must find a way to *speak*. Just a few words and I will have her.

The troll pushes me before Lady Nore so that I fall on my hands and knees.

She rises from her seat at a long, food-laden table. We have interrupted her banquet.

Lady Nore's white hair has been tied up on her head in a complicated arrangement of plaits, although a few have come down. Her gown is an opulent confection of black feathers and silver fabric that deepens to black at the floor. Ex-falcons crowd around her, formerly loyal soldiers to the Grand General of Elfhame, now hers to command.

When I look at her, I am filled with the same hate and fear that paralyzed me throughout my childhood.

And yet, there is fresh madness in her yellow eyes. She is not the same as she was when I saw her last. And disturbingly, I see myself in her. Resentful, and trapped, and full of thwarted desire. The worst parts of me, and all my worst potential.

New also are the two gray hands that she wears as a necklace. Horrifyingly, I see the fingers move as though alive, caressing the hollow of her throat. More horrifyingly, I suspect them to have once belonged to Lord Jarel.

Behind her, on a pillar of ice, is the cracked reliquary that must contain the bones and other remains of Mab. Strangely, tendrils, like roots, grow from the case, one with a bud on it, as though flowering.

On Lady Nore's left side sits a troll with a crown of beaten gold and a mantle of blue velvet stitched with silver scales. His clothing is leather, richly worked, with a pattern that reminds me of those we saw in the Stone Forest.

Hurclaw, who has somehow evaded the curse of the Stone Forest. Who has brought his people to help guard the Citadel. But why throw in his lot with Lady Nore? If what Oak got from Gorga was correct, Hurclaw is here to *court* her. If so, perhaps her power makes for a compelling dowry.

He and his trolls make up the majority of those seated, along with two huldufólk ladies, and Bogdana. She is in her usual ragged black robes, her hair as wild as ever. When she sees me, a strange gleam enters her eyes.

On the table before all of them are silver plates and goblets of ice filled with black wine from the night-blooming fruit of the duergar. Black radishes, soaked in vinegar and cut into thin slivers to show off their pale insides. Trays of snow drizzled with honey so that the honey freezes and can be lifted and eaten like a cracker. Jellied meat, with an uncomfortable resemblance to the walls of the Citadel with things frozen inside.

A single musician plucks at the strings of a harp.

Despite the feast, and the guards, and stick soldiers standing at attention along one wall, the room seems empty by comparison with what it was once like, when Lord Jarel was alive. There ought to have been tables filling the hall, with guests to make toasts. Cupbearers. Entertainers. A court shaped entirely to Lady Nore's whims. Have they all fled?

She looks past me, to Oak. "Heir to Elfhame, let's skip through the unpleasantness. Have you brought me Mellith's heart?"

Her guards are still tensed for the possibility of violence.

"I would hardly come here empty-handed with my father's life in the balance," Oak says. His gaze moves from the severed hands at her throat to the troll king.

I gnaw at the rope in my mouth, my desperation mounting. In a moment, she will ask him a question he cannot answer. I must speak. If I can speak, then I can still get us out of this.

But with Hurclaw's soldiers all around us, there is a new danger. If he guesses I can control her, he will order me shot.

"So you *do* have it?" says Lady Nore. "Unless you failed your quest, little prince."

My heart speeds. My sharp teeth are working through the rope, but I won't sever it in time to stop him from having to answer. This plan seemed risky, but now it seems doomed.

"Let me say it in full so you will not worry over being deceived," Oak says. *"I have brought Mellith's heart."*

I am stunned enough to stop chewing. The prince can't say that. His mouth shouldn't be able to form those words. He's one of the Folk. He cannot lie any more than the rest of us.

And yet, I saw the deer carcass cut open, watched him buy a reliquary from the smiths. I know it is no ancient heart he brought to the Citadel.

Try to believe, whatever happens, whatever I say or do or have done, that my intention is for us to all survive this. That's what he said to me on the boat. Was this what he meant? Was he willing to give away Mellith's heart if it meant we all lived?

If he *did*, and the deer heart was for the purpose of deceiving *me*, then he is about to hand over immense, terrible power to Lady Nore. The kind of power with which she could threaten Elfhame. With which she could carve up the mortal world that she despises.

And I have no way to stop him.

"Where is it, then?" Lady Nore asks, a snarl in her voice.

Oak does not flinch. "I may have it, but I am not so foolish as to have it on me."

Lady Nore scowls at him. "Hidden? To what purpose when you must hand it over to get your father?"

He shakes his head. "I would watch him leave, along with Wren, before I gave you anything."

She frowns, studying him. Her gaze flicks to me. Then she laughs. "I could quibble, but I can be magnanimous in my victory. How about I turn Madoc out of the prisons and into the snow right now? I hope he does well with cold, since I fear the clothing he is wearing is quite thin. And unfortunately, some of my creatures hunt the lands around the Citadel."

"That would be unfortunate, for all of us," Oak says. However firm he manages to keep his voice, he looks young, standing in front of her and Hurclaw. I worry that this is a game he cannot possibly win. "But I have an alternate proposal. Tomorrow night, my representative will meet us three leagues from here, near the rock formation. You will bring Madoc, me, and Wren. There, we can make the exchange."

"So long as you understand you won't be part of it, Greenbriar child. You are to remain here, in the Citadel, until I am done with you."

"And you're planning on doing what exactly? Making me a hostage to get some concession from my sister?"

"And not from the High King?" Lady Nore asks. She walks around the table, toward us.

Oak scowls, clearly confused. "If you like. Either one."

"They say that sister of yours has trapped him in some bargain." Lady Nore's words are light, but I can see that underneath it, nothing must have galled her as much as being outmaneuvered by a mortal. If anything other than the death of Lord Jarel has driven her mad, it's that. "Why else marry her? Why else do whatever she wants?"

"She's going to *want* to wear your skull for a hat," Oak warns. There is an uncomfortable shifting among the ex-falcons. Perhaps they are recalling their own choice to denounce her, their own punishment. "And Cardan is going to laugh and laugh when she does."

Lady Nore curls her lip. "Three things I need. Mab's bones, Mellith's heart, and Greenbriar blood. And here I am with two, and the third so close that I am able to taste it. Do not fail me, Prince of Elfhame, for if you do, your father will die and I will still get what I want."

Oak raises both eyebrows. However he actually feels, his ability to make himself seem unimpressed is immensely satisfying.

Lady Nore goes on, as though thrilled to have someone to whom she can deliver this speech. "Were it not for your father's weakness, we might have won the war against Elfhame. But I have a truer ally now and vast power. I am ready for revenge."

"King Hurclaw," Oak says, his gaze going toward the troll king. "I hope that Lady Nore hasn't promised you more than she can give."

A small smile quirks a corner of his mouth. "I do as well," he says in a deep voice.

Lady Nore scowls, then stands and walks to me. Oak's jaw tightens. His hand fists at his side.

"I suppose the prince thought that *you* could stop me." A terrible smile curls on her lips as she touches the frayed rope pressed between my teeth like a bit. "Little did he know what a sniveling creature you are."

I hiss, low in my throat.

To my surprise, she begins to loosen the cords I've been chewing. I part my lips the moment they fall away, desperate to speak. I am about to blurt out the stupidly unspecific *I command you to surrender.* But before I can get words out, she presses a petal into my mouth. I feel a twisting, worming sensation on my tongue. Whatever it is seems to move on its own, and I grit my jaw. The thing snakes around for another moment, then settles.

She lets go of the rope, smiling maliciously.

I shudder but finally can speak. I try to get the words out, but my tongue moves without my volition. "I renounce—" I begin to say before I slam my teeth down, trapping it painfully between them.

Lady Nore's awful smile grows. "Yes, my dear?"

Somehow she's woven a spell of control into the petal, no doubt plucked from the vine of the reliquary, where it grew impossibly from dry bones. If I try to speak, I will give up dominion over her.

I bite down harder on my tongue, to still it. It wriggles in my mouth like an animal.

"Bogdana told me how you lived," she says. "In your wretched little hut, at the edge of the mortal world, scavenging for scraps as though you were a rat."

I cannot reply, and so I do not.

There is a flicker of unease in Lady Nore's eyes. She glances toward Bogdana, but the storm hag is watching me from her place at the table, her expression unreadable.

"You dull little thing, open your mouth. I can give you what you most desire," Lady Nore snaps.

And what is that? I would ask were it safe for me to loosen my tongue. Instead, I keep it clamped between my teeth.

"I cannot make you human," she goes on. "But I can come very close."

I can't say part of me doesn't wish that were true. I think of the phone call, of how much easier it would be to slip into that old life if it didn't mean hiding or lying, if I didn't have to worry over them screaming at the sight of me.

She is still smiling as she walks to me and puts a finger against my chin. "I can put a glamour on you strong enough that not even the King of Elfhame is likely to see through it. I have the means to do that now, the power. I can make you forget the last nine years. You will return to the mortal world an empty vessel, free for them to project humanity on. They will decide that you were kidnapped, and whatever was done to you was so terrible that you blocked all memory of it. They won't press. And even if they do, what does it matter? You will believe every word you tell them."

I flinch away from her hand.

My greatest wish, the deepest desire of my heart. It infuriates me how well she knows me, and yet how she holds back every last mote of the comfort I so desperately crave.

Her yellow eyes study my face, trying to determine if I am hers yet.

"Are you thinking about the prince? Oh, do not suppose I don't know where you were when your own people died in the Battle of the Serpent. Hiding under that boy's bed."

My gaze is flat. I was a child, and I got away from her. I refuse to feel anything but glad about that. *He wanted me there*, I would say if I could speak. *We were friends. We are friends.*

But I can't help thinking about Mellith's heart, about what he told me in the boat.

... whatever I say or do or have done...

"Do you think he will protect you now? You're *useless*. The heir to Elfhame has no reason to spend any further time with an untutored savage of a girl. But think, you wouldn't have to remember him. You wouldn't even have to remember yourself."

"I'm not half as practical as you suppose," Oak says. "I like many useless things. I've been called useless myself from time to time."

Lady Nore doesn't turn her eyes from me, even when I give a little, unexpected laugh that almost makes me release my teeth's grip on my tongue. Lord Jarel's hands tighten on her shoulders as though in response to her mood. "His kindness will evaporate as soon as you need it. Now, child, will you take the bargain and trouble me no more? Or will you force me to deal with you more harshly?"

I imagine giving up. No more peering through windows, mourning the loss of a life that could never again be mine. No more hopeless desire. No more uncertain future. No more terror. Let her have Mellith's heart and Mab's bones. Let Elfhame rot and the Prince of Elfhame rot with it. Let her raze whatever parts of the mortal world she chooses. What would I care when I couldn't remember any of it?

I think of the Thistlewitch's words. *Nix Naught Nothing. That's what you are.* That's what I would be. I would be consigning everything I've been, all I've learned and done to meaninglessness. I would be accepting that I don't matter.

I spit in Lady Nore's face. The spatter is bright with my blood against her gray skin.

She curls her lip and raises her hand, but does not strike me. She stands there, shaking with fury. "You bite your tongue to spite me? Well, I will lesson you. Guard, cut it out of her mouth."

One of the huldufólk comes forward, taking hold of my arms. I kick and claw, fighting as I never have before.

"No!" Oak struggles, but two ex-falcons grab him. "If you hurt her, you can't expect me to just turn over—"

Lady Nore whirls toward him, pointing a finger. "Tell me where Mellith's heart is *this moment*, and I won't cut out her tongue."

Three more guards help subdue me. I twist against their grip.

Oak lunges for the troll nearest to him and grabs her sword, drawing it from the sheath. The prince is still surrounded, but now he is armed. A few huldufólk and nisser draw bows.

Hurclaw waves his hand. "Show the boy it is no use," he says.

"Come forward, my creations," says Lady Nore, and the soldiers of sticks and mud and flesh stride across the floor of the great hall. The guards step back, letting the creatures take their places.

"Seize him," says Lady Nore.

The stick soldiers rush at Oak without hesitation. He slashes one, cutting it in half, and then whirls to stab another. His sword sinks in deep to the branches of the thing's body. It continues to come forward, then twists aside, trying to wrench the sword out of Oak's hand with the force of its own movement, even as doing so is tearing it apart.

Oak pulls the blade free, but three more throw themselves on it so a fourth can grab him around the throat.

This time the guards bind his hands behind his back with a silver cord.

When he meets my eyes, his expression is anguished. He cannot help me.

I fight as they press me down to the floor. Bite when they try to pry open my mouth.

But it's all for nothing. Two soldiers hold my wrists, and a third hooks a barbed instrument through the end of my tongue. He pulls it taut.

Then a fourth begins slicing through it with a curved dagger.

The sharp, searing pain makes me want to cry out, but I cannot with my tongue nailed in place. My mouth goes from dry from being held open to full of blood. Flooded with it. Gagging. Drowning. I choke as they release me, the scream dying in my throat.

Scarlet flows over my chin. When I move, flecks of red fly.

The pain swallows me whole so that I barely can concentrate, but I know I am losing too much blood. It spills from between my lips, slicks my neck, stains the collar of my dress. This is going to kill me. I am going to die, here on the ice floor of the Citadel.

Lady Nore takes a slow walk around my crumpled body. She takes another small piece of bone from her bag and presses it against my lips, then past my teeth. I can feel the wound closing. "You might not think so, but this is for the best. As your mother and your sworn vassal, I must trust my own wisdom in the absence of direct orders."

Blood loss and shock have made me dizzy. I feel light-headed. I stagger to my feet and think very seriously about sitting back down. Think very seriously about collapsing.

Since she cannot lie, in some twisted way, Lady Nore must truly believe that what she wants is what I *ought* to want.

Still, I do not need a tongue for her to read the rage in my eyes.

Her lips turn up at the edges, and I see that she isn't so different from before. She doesn't want me dead, because once dead I can no longer suffer.

"The prince doesn't even know what you are," she says with a glance toward Oak. "Barely one of the Folk. Nothing but a manikin, little more than the stock left behind when a changeling is taken, a thing meant to wither and die."

Despite myself, my gaze goes to Oak. To see if he understands. But I cannot read anything but pity on his face.

I might be only sticks and snow and hag magic, but at least I did not come from her.

I am no one's child.

That makes me smile, showing red teeth.

"My lady," says King Hurclaw. "The sooner Prince Oak sees his father released, the sooner we will have what we want."

Lady Nore gives him a narrow-eyed look. I wonder if the troll king realizes how awful she can be, and if he isn't careful, how awful she will be to him.

But for now, she obediently waves at the guards. "One of you, lock her in the dungeon, wicked child that she is, that she may think on her choices. Prince Oak and I have much to discuss. Perhaps he will join us at the table."

One of the ex-falcons comes to stand behind me. "Move."

I begin to walk unsteadily toward the doors. The throb of my tongue in my mouth is horrible, but the bleeding has ebbed. I am still drinking saliva that tastes like pennies but no longer feeling as though I am drowning in it.

"I would say that you lost yourself along the way, but you lost yourself far before that," the storm hag tells me as I pass her. "Wake up, little bird."

I open my mouth, to remind her that what I've lost is my *tongue* and perhaps my hope.

She grimaces, and for a moment, a fresh wave of fear and dizziness passes over me. It must be very bad to make Bogdana wince.

"*Move,*" the guard repeats, shoving between my shoulder blades.

It's not until we make it to the hall that I glance behind me. Up into the purple eyes of Hyacinthe.

CHAPTER
16

For a moment, we just stare at each other.

"I told you it would be wise to send me here, and since you gave me no commands to contradict it, I came," Hyacinthe says, low, so only I can hear.

I cannot speak. Staggering a little, I lean against the wall. The pain is hard to think past, and I am not sure if he is on my side or not.

"Be glad I did," he says, swinging his spear toward me, the point inches from my throat. "Folk are watching. Move."

I turn my back on him and walk. He makes a show of shoving me into going faster, and I do not have to pretend to stumble.

Several times, I try to turn, to catch his eye, so I can read the intention there, but each time he pushes me so that I must resume walking.

"Is Tiernan with you?" he asks when we reach the prison gate.

Loyal, that's what Hyacinthe called himself. Loyal to Oak's father. Hopefully loyal to me. Maybe loyal to Tiernan, too, in a way. Hyacinthe didn't trust Oak's honey-tongued charm. Maybe he wants to save Tiernan from it.

I nod.

Together we march down the icy passageways, to the prisons. Dug down into the frozen ground, they stink of iron and wet stone. "He's the one with Mellith's heart?"

A dangerous question. Given Hyacinthe's dislike of Oak, I am not sure whether he would like to see Lady Nore get what she wants or not. Nor am I sure *what* exactly Tiernan has. Also I am finding it hard to concentrate with the pain in my mouth.

Since I can't figure out a way to communicate any of that, I shrug and gesture toward my lips.

He frowns, frustrated.

The cells are largely empty. When I lived in the Citadel, they were teeming with those who had displeased Lord Jarel and Lady Nore—bards who chose ballads that offended, presumptuous courtiers, servants who made errors large and small. But now, as understaffed as the castle is, there is only one other prisoner.

Madoc sits on a wooden bench, leaning against the stone wall, far from the bars, which stink of iron. His leg is bandaged in two places, hastily and poorly, as though he was the one who did it. There is a cloth over one of his eyes, a little blood seeping through the fabric. His green skin looks too pale in the flickering lamplight, and he's shivering. He's probably been uncomfortably cold for weeks.

Hyacinthe unlocks a cell beside the general's and ushers me inside. I enter, careful not to let my skin touch the iron bars.

"I will get you out of here," he whispers to me as I slip by him.

"When things are prepared, you will be given a key. Meet me in the alcove across from the great hall. I have a horse."

I look a question at him.

He sighs. "Yes, that creature. Damsel Fly. Despite her pretty name, she's fast and sure-footed."

And then he closes the door. I am grateful he didn't bother to search me, didn't discover the bridle banded around my waist, beneath my servant's uniform. I am not certain what he would do with it.

I head for a bench, a sudden feeling of light-headedness making me worry that I will fall before I get there. Though I am not still bleeding, I lost a lot of blood.

Hyacinthe's gaze flickers toward Madoc, and he looks pained. "Are you well, sir?"

"Well enough," the redcap says. "What happened here? She looks like she took a big bite out of someone."

I am surprised to find that makes me laugh. The sound comes out all wrong.

"Her tongue," Hyacinthe says, and Madoc nods as though he's seen that sort of thing before.

Although I knew Hyacinthe had been part of Madoc's army, I forgot that meant they might know each other. It is strange to hear them speaking like comrades, especially with one of them the jailer and the other in a cage.

As he departs, the redcap glances in my direction.

"Little queen," Madoc says with a crooked smile. Despite not sharing blood with Oak, the mischief in his expression is familiar. "All grown up and come to devour your maker. I can't say as I blame you."

I am fairly sure he's missing an eye. I remember the old general from the endless meetings and parties where I sat in the dirt or was tugged on a leash. I remember the calm of his manner and the hot wine he gave me, as well as the gleam of his teeth whenever there was blood.

Like now, when I spit on the ground rather than swallow what's in my mouth.

Hyacinthe says something else to Madoc, and I put my head down on my arms, sprawling over the bench. Another bout of dizziness hits me, and I close my eyes, expecting it to pass. Expecting to be able to sit up. But instead, I am pulled down into darkness.

When I come back to consciousness, it is to the sound of Oak's voice. "She's breathing steadily."

By the time I am able to focus, though, it is Madoc who is speaking, his voice a deep rumble. "You might be better served if she didn't wake. What happens when she discovers how you've deceived her? When she realizes her role in your plan?"

I try not to move, try not to let a twitch of muscle or a tightening of my body give away that I am conscious and listening.

Oak's voice is full of resignation. "She will have to decide how much she hates me."

"Kill her while you can," says the old general, softly. He sounds regretful but also resigned.

"That's your answer to everything," Oak says.

"And yours is to throw yourself into the mouth of the lion and hope it doesn't like your savor."

Oak says nothing for a long moment. I think about the way he took an arrow while grinning reassuringly, how he gulped down poison. How, back in Elfhame, he apparently draws out assassins by being an excellent target. Madoc's not wrong that Oak throws himself at things. In fact, I am not sure if Madoc realizes the extent of his rightness.

"I despair of you," says the redcap finally. "You have no instinct to take power, even when it is offering you its very throat to tear out."

"Enough," says Oak, as if this isn't the first time they've gone through this argument. "This—*all of it*—is your fault. Why couldn't you just have the patience to stay in exile? To resign yourself to your fate?"

"That's not my nature," the redcap says softly, as though Oak should have known better. "And I didn't know it would be you who came."

The prince gives a shuddering sigh. I hear rustling. "Let me look at those bandages."

"Stop fussing," says Madoc. "If pain bothered me, I went into the wrong trade."

There is a long silence, and I wonder if I should pretend to yawn or something else to indicate that I am waking.

"I'm never killing her," Oak says softly, so softly I almost don't hear.

"Then you better hope she doesn't kill you," the general replies.

I lie very still for a while after that. Eventually, I hear the shuffling of a servant and the clank of platters, and use that as an excuse to give an awkward moan and turn over.

Oak's hooves clatter against the floor, and then he's on his knees in front of me, all golden hair and fox eyes and worry.

"Wren," he breathes, reaching through the iron bars, even though they singe his wrists. His fingers run through my hair.

What happens when she discovers how you've deceived her? When she realizes her role in your plan?

If I hadn't overheard what he'd said to his father, I would never have believed he had a secret so terrible he thought I would hate him for it.

The servant girl places bowls in front of the cells, on the ground. Cruel, since the bowls are too big to fit between the bars, which means that one must put one's wrist against iron with every bite. Our dinner appears to be a pungent, oily soup that has barley in it and probably the meat of seabirds.

I shift myself into a sitting position.

"We're going to get out of this," Oak tells me. "I'll try to pick the lock if you loan me your hairpin."

I nod to show I understand and unclasp it.

His expression grows grave. "Wren—"

"Stop fussing at *her* now. She can't even complain over it." The redcap smiles in my direction, as though inviting me into laughing at his son.

Who he told to kill me.

The prince withdraws his hand from between the bars and turns away. He doesn't seem to notice the burn on his arm as he pushes himself to his feet.

What could he have done that's so awful? All I can think of is that he really does have Mellith's heart and that he really is planning on turning it over to Lady Nore.

"Hurclaw is a problem," Madoc says as he watches Oak bend the sharp end of my pin and slide it into the lock. "If it wasn't for his people,

I believe I could have escaped this place, perhaps even taken the Citadel. But Lady Nore has promised that she will soon be able to break the curse on the Stone Forest."

"Take the Citadel? That's quite a boast," Oak says, twisting the pin and frowning.

Madoc makes a snorting sound, then turns to me. "I am sure that Wren here wouldn't mind taking Lady Nore's castle and lands for herself."

I shake my head at the absurdity of the statement.

He raises his brows. "No? Still sitting at the table and waiting for permission to start eating?"

That's an uncomfortably accurate way of describing how I've lived my life.

"I was like that once," he tells me, his sharp lower incisors visible when he speaks. I know this conversation is an effort to assess an opponent and keep me off-balance. Still, the thought of him waiting for anyone's permission is ridiculous. He's the former Grand General of Elfhame and a redcap, delighting in bloodshed. He's probably eaten people. No, he's definitely eaten people.

I shake my head again. Oak looks over at us and frowns, as though his father talking with me makes him nervous.

Madoc grins. "No? I can hardly believe it myself, in truth. But I spent most of my life on campaigns, making war in Eldred's name. Did I enjoy my work? Certainly, but I also obeyed. I took what rewards I was given, and I was grateful for them. And what did I get for my trouble? My wife fell in love with someone else, someone who was there when I was gone."

His former wife, whom he murdered. The mother of his three girls. Somehow, I'd always assumed that she left him because she was afraid, not because she was lonely.

Madoc glances at Oak again before returning his attention to me. "I vowed I would use the strategy I studied for my own benefit. I would find a way to take all that I wanted, for myself and for my family. What a freeing thought it was to no longer believe I had to deserve something in order to get it."

He's right; that would be a shockingly freeing thought.

"Stop waiting," Madoc says. "Sink those pretty teeth into something."

I give him a sharp look, trying to decide if he is making fun of me. I lean down and write in the dirt and the crust of my own dried blood: *Monsters have teeth like mine.*

He grins as though I am finally getting his point. "That they do."

Oak turns away from the lock in frustration. "Father, what exactly do you think you're doing?"

"We were just *talking*, she and I," Madoc says.

"Don't listen to him." He shakes his head with an exasperated look at his father. "He's *full* of bad old-guy advice."

"Just because I'm bad," Madoc says with a grunt, "doesn't mean the advice is."

Oak rolls his eyes. I note he has a new bruise at the corner of his mouth and a wound on his brow that has caused blood to crust in his hair. I think of him fighting in the throne room, think of the pain when my tongue was cut out. Think of him watching.

I go to the bowl of soup, although I cannot stand to put anything into my mouth. Still, if I can get the dish into the cell, even if I tip out half the food, I can pass what's left to Oak and Madoc.

As I begin to tilt it, though, I see something metal in the soup. Setting the bowl down again, I stick my fingers into the oily liquid and feel around. I touch the solid weight of a key and remember Hyacinthe's words about getting me out of the Citadel.

Forcing myself not to look at Oak or Madoc, I palm the object. Then I tuck it away into my dress and retreat to the bench in the back of my cell. Oak has no luck with the lock. Neither of them seems inclined to eat the food.

I listen to them talk a bit more about Hurclaw, and how he argued with Lady Nore over some sacrifices that Madoc didn't quite understand, and what would become of the bodies. Oak looks toward me several times, as though he would like to speak with me but doesn't.

Eventually, Madoc suggests we rest, since tomorrow will be "a test of our ability to adapt to evolving plans," which puzzles me. I know that Tiernan will arrive at the proscribed meeting place, with whatever it is in that reliquary.

The old general lies down on the bench while Oak stretches himself out on the cold floor.

I wait until they're sleeping. I recall how he caught me in the woods and wait a very long time. But the prince is exhausted, and when I fit the key into my lock, he doesn't wake.

I shove the heavy door, and it opens easily, the iron stinging my hand. I slip out, then tuck the key in a corner of their cell so that they will find it if I don't return.

In the hall, I slip off my big boots. And then I walk, my bare feet quiet on the cold stone. The guard at the prison gate is sleeping, slumped over a chair. He must be used to having Madoc as his only charge.

Up the steps, rays of early-morning sunlight turn the castle into a prism, and every time the shadows change, I worry over being given away.

But no one comes. No one stops me. And I realize that this was my fate from the start. It wasn't going to be Oak who stopped Lady Nore. It was always supposed to be me.

I do not meet Hyacinthe. I head for the throne room. As I tiptoe into a corridor that looks on the great hall's double doors, I see they are closed and barred, with two stick soldiers standing at attention. I can think of no way to get past them. They do not sleep, nor do they seem alive enough to be tricked.

But no one knows the Citadel like I do.

There is another way into the great hall, a small pass-through tunnel from the kitchens where refuse is tucked away by servants—empty cups, platters, messes of every sort. The cooks and kitchen staff fish them out later to clean them. It is large enough for a child to hide in, and I hid in it often.

I move toward the kitchens. When I see guards passing, I duck into shadows and make myself unobtrusive. Although it has been a long time, I am well-practiced at being unnoticed, especially here of all places.

As I move, I have a strange dissonance of memory. I am walking through these halls as a child. I am walking through my unparents' house at night, moving like a ghost. That's what I've been for years. An unsister. An undaughter. An unperson. A girl with a hole for a life.

How appropriate to have my tongue cut out, when silence has been my refuge and my cage.

I creep down to the kitchens, on the first level of the Citadel. Their heat is what makes the prisons warm enough to survive. I would have thought the fires there, perpetually burning, would have melted the whole castle, but they do not. The base of the castle is stone, and what they do melt refreezes into a harder layer of ice.

I see a nisse boy, sleeping in the ashes before the fire, tucked into a blanket of sewn-together skins. I slip past him, past casks of wine. Past baskets of crowberries and piles of dried fish. Past jars of salted and pickled things and bowls of dough that are covered with wet towels, their yeast still rising.

I squeeze myself into the pass-through tunnel and begin to crawl. And although I am larger than I was the last time I was in it, I still fit. I slip by tipped-over wine goblets, dregs dried inside, and a few bones that must have fallen from a plate. I emerge at the other end, inside the empty throne room.

But as I push myself to my feet, I realize that I have failed again because the reliquary is gone.

I walk over to the place where it was, my heart beating hard, panic stealing my breath. I was foolish to come to Lady Nore's throne room alone; I was foolish to come to the Citadel at all.

There is a withered leaf on the ground, and beside it something that might be a pebble. I lift it between my fingers, feeling the sharp edge of it. It's what I hoped—a piece of bone.

The Thistlewitch said that with Mab's bones, great spells could be cast. That she had the force of creation within her. And although I have never been adept at magic, if Lady Nore could use Mab's power to create living beings from sticks and rock, if she could use it to control my tongue to make it speak the words she wanted to hear, then surely there is enough magic in this to allow me to grow my tongue back.

I put the withered leaf in my mouth first. Then I place the bone

on the cut root where my tongue used to be, close my eyes, and concentrate. Immediately, I feel as though my chest is being squeezed, as
though my ribs are cracking.

Something is wrong. Something is wrong with me.

I fall to my knees, palms pressed against the ice of the floor. Something seems to twist inside my chest, then split, like a fissure opening in
a glacier. The hard knot of my magic, the part of me that has felt in danger of unraveling when I push myself too hard, splits completely apart.

I gasp, because it *hurts*.

It hurts so much my mouth opens on a scream I cannot make. It
hurts so much that I black out.

For the second time in less than a single day, I wake on a cold floor. I've
been there long enough for frost to settle over my skin, sparkling along
my arms and stiffening my dress.

I push myself to my hands and knees. The remains of stick soldiers
are scattered around me, among berries and branches and chunks of
snow that might have once been stuck in their chests.

What could have happened here? My memories are tangled things,
like the stems growing from Mab's bones.

Kneeling and shaking with something that cannot be cold, I put my
hand against the ice beneath me, noting spiderweb patterns, as though
it were the shattered glass of a windshield, broken but not yet come
apart. Staggering across the throne room, I crawl to the tunnel.

There, I close my eyes again. When I open them, I am not sure if it
is moments later or hours. I feel leaden, sluggish.

With astonishment, I realize *my tongue is in my mouth.* It feels odd to have it there. Thick and heavy. I cannot decide if it is swollen or if I am just oddly conscious of it.

"I'm scared," I whisper to myself. Because it's true. Because I need to know if my tongue belongs to me and will say the things I mean it to. "I'm so tired. I'm so tired of being scared."

I recall Madoc and his advice. To sink my teeth into something. To take this castle and all of Lady Nore's lands for myself. To stop waiting for permission. To stop caring what others think or feel or want.

Idly, I imagine myself in control of the Ice Citadel. Lady Nore, not just beaten, but *gone.* Elfhame, glad of my service. So glad they are willing to name me the queen of these lands. And had I control of Mab's remains, if I could harness the power that Lady Nore has? Perhaps I would be someone his sisters might consider a fitting bride for Oak then, with a dowry like that.

The fantasy of buying my way into being acceptable to his sisters should make me resentful, but instead fills me with satisfaction. That even Vivienne, the eldest, who shuddered at the idea of my being bound to her precious brother, might desire me to sit at their table. Might see my sharp-toothed smile and smile in return.

And Oak...

He would think...

I catch myself before I build a sugary confection of a fantasy.

One in which, once again, I seek permission. Besides, I do not control the Citadel, no less Lady Nore.

Not yet.

I walk out the doors of the throne room and up winding ice steps toward the floors above. I hear voices just as I turn.

A patrol of two ex-falcons and a troll spots me. For a long moment, we stare at one another.

"How did you escape the dungeon?" one of them demands, forgetting I cannot speak.

I run, but they grab me. The chase is over fast. It's not as though I was really trying to get away.

Lady Nore is in her bedroom when I am brought before her. Three falcons—real birds, their curse as yet unbroken—sit on the serpent mirror above her dressing table and on the back of her chair.

My gaze goes to their hooked beaks and black eyes. All Lady Nore has been able to do for them is feed them and wait. But having broken Hyacinthe's binding, I wonder if I could break theirs. If I could, would they be loyal to me, as they are to her?

I wonder what it would be like, to never have to be alone.

"Sneaky little girl," says Lady Nore indulgently. She reaches out and twirls my hair around her finger. "This is how I remember you, stealing through my castle like a thief."

Poor Wren, I hope my expression conveys. *So sad. And her mouth hurts.*

Lady Nore sees only her simple daughter, sculpted from snow. A disappointment many times over.

Now that my tongue is regrown through the strange magic of Mab's bones, I could open my mouth and make her into my marionette, to dance when I pulled her strings.

And yet, instead I bow my head, knowing she will like that. Stalling for time. Once I begin, I will have to get everything exactly right.

"And quiet," she says, smiling at her own jest. "I remember that, too."

What I recall is the depth of my fear, the tide of it sweeping me away from myself. I hope I can mimic that expression and not show her what I actually feel—a rage that is as thick and sticky and sweet as honey.

I'm tired of being scared.

"Say nothing until I allow it," I tell her. My voice sounds strange, hoarse, the way it did when I first spoke with Oak.

Her eyes widen. Her lips part, but she cannot disobey me, not after the vow she made before the mortal High Queen.

"Unless I say otherwise, you will give no one an order without my express permission," I say. "When I ask you a question, you will answer it fully, holding back nothing that I might find interesting or useful— and leaving out any filler with which you might disguise those interesting or useful parts."

Her eyes shine with anger, but she can say nothing. I feel a cruel leap of delight at her impotence.

"You will not strike me, nor seek to cause me harm. You will not hurt anyone else, either, including yourself."

I wonder if she has ever been forced to swallow her words before. She looks as though she might choke on them.

"Now you may speak," I say.

"I suppose all children grow up. Even those made of snow and ice," she says, as though my control of her is nothing to be overly concerned with. But I see the panic she is trying to hide.

My heart beats hard, and my chest still hurts. My tongue still feels wrong, but so does the rest of me. She is not the only one panicking.

"Summon the two guards outside the door. Convey to them that they should bring Oak here." My voice shakes a little. I sound uncertain, which could prove fatal. "Tell them nothing else, and give no sign of distress."

Her expression grows strange, remote. "Very well. Guard!"

The two outside the door turn out to be former falcons. I recognize neither of them.

"Go to the prisons, and bring me the prince."

They bow and depart.

I have stood apart from the world for so long. That has made it hard for me to navigate being in it, but it has also made me an excellent observer.

I stare at Lady Nore for a moment, considering my next move.

"You may speak, if you wish," I tell her. "But do not raise your voice and, should anyone come into the room, cease talking."

I can see her considering not to say anything out of spite, but she breaks. "So, what do you mean to do with me now?" Around her neck, Lord Jarel's fingers scuttle.

"I haven't decided," I say.

She laughs, though it sounds forced. "I imagine not. You're not really a planner, are you? More of a creature of instinct. Mindless. Heedless. A little low cunning, perhaps, the way animals sometimes surprise you with their cleverness."

"How can you hate me so much?" I ask her, the question slipping out of my mouth before I can snatch it back.

"You should have been like us," says Lady Nore, her posture rigid. The words come easily, as though she has been thinking on them for a long time. "And instead, you are like *them*. To look at you is to see something so flawed it ought to be put out of its misery. Better to be dead, child, than to live as you do. Better to drown you like some runt of a litter."

I taste tears in the back of my throat. Not because I want her to love me, but because her words echo the worst thoughts of my heart.

I want to smash the mirrors and make her stick the pieces in her skin. I want to do something so awful that she regrets wishing I was anything like her.

"If I am so low," I say, my voice a growl, "then what are you, to be my vassal, and lower still?"

When the door opens, I turn toward it. I probably look furious.

I can see the confusion on Oak's face. He looks rumpled and must have been sleeping when they took him. He is brought into the room, wrists bound, by one of the ex-falcons.

"Wren?" he says.

In that moment, I realize I have already made a bad mistake. The guard stands there, waiting for orders, but Lady Nore can give him none. If I tell her what to say now, my power over her will be obvious— not to mention the restoration of my tongue—and the soldier will alert the others. But if I do nothing, and Lady Nore gives him no commands, it won't take him long to discern something is wrong.

The moment stretches as I try to come up with an answer. "You can go," Oak tells him. "I'll be fine here."

The former falcon makes a small bow and leaves the room, closing the door behind him. Lady Nore gasps, furious and shocked in equal measure.

My own surprise is just as great.

The prince looks at me guiltily. "I can imagine what you're thinking," he says, moving his wrist to cast off the silver binding. "But I had no idea what my father's plan was. I didn't even know he had a plan. And it turns out that it wasn't enough of one to win."

I recall Oak's words in the prisons. *This—all of it—is your fault. Why couldn't you just have the patience to stay in exile? To resign yourself to your fate?*

So Madoc had known he was going to be kidnapped—perhaps from Tiernan, who would have gotten it from Hyacinthe, or maybe even from Hyacinthe directly—and he'd let it happen. All so that he could recruit his own soldiers back to his side, take Lady Nore's Citadel, and impress Elfhame enough to let him back in.

The falcons had been loyal to him once, and so it made some sense—arrogant sense, but still sense—for Madoc to wager that weeks spent in the heart of the Citadel would allow him the time to win them over.

Hurclaw is a problem. If it wasn't for his people, I believe I could have escaped this place, perhaps even taken the Citadel.

Madoc hadn't planned on Hurclaw's trolls, which left the former falcons outnumbered. Not to mention the huldufólk and nisser.

And the monsters of stick and stone.

"And now?" I ask.

Oak's eyes widen satisfyingly at the sound of my voice. "How are you *speaking*?"

"I used a shard of Mab's bones," I tell him, and if I shiver a little at the memory, he cannot guess the reason.

"So you're saying that while my father and I were asleep, you found the reliquary—all by yourself—and then single-handedly subdued

Lady Nore?" He laughs. "You might have woken me. I could have done something, surely. Applauded at the right moments? Held your bag?"

I am flattered into a small smile.

"So," he asks, "what order ought I give the guards, now that you're in charge?"

Lady Nore sits rigidly, listening. Realizing, perhaps, that I do not need to have more than low animal cunning. All I need is an ally with a little ambition, one who will be a little kind.

Or, perhaps, realizing for the first time that she does not know me half so well as she thinks.

"Tiernan plans on meeting us still, correct?" I ask.

Oak nods. "It could be a way to get Hurclaw's people in one place and surround them. We'd have the element of surprise, and the stick creatures on our side."

I nod. "There's Bogdana to think of, too."

I push my feelings about what I overheard he and Madoc discuss aside and talk through possible plans. We go through them again and again. I command Lady Nore to have the guards fetch Oak's things for him. Send a message to Hyacinthe. Have servants bring me the sweet ice Lord Jarel used to give me, and send wine and meat pies to Madoc.

Then I send for Lady Nore's maidservants to help me get ready.

The door opens soon after to two huldufólk women, Doe and Fernwaif. Their tails swish. I remember them from my time here, sisters who had come to work for Lady Nore in recompense for some deed done by their parents.

They were kind, in their way. They did not prick me with pins just to see me bleed, as some of the others did. I am surprised by how sunken-eyed they look. Their clothing is worn at the hems and sleeves. I think of the briar-and-stick spiders hunting across the swells of snow and wonder how much worse it is to be in the Citadel now than it was then.

I choose a dress from Lady Nore's closet and sit on a fur-covered stool while Doe pulls it over my head. Fernwaif arranges my hair with combs of bone and onyx. Then Doe brushes my lips with the juice of berries to stain them red, and does the same to my cheeks. It happens in a blur.

Kill her while you can.

Oak and I have been playing games for a long time. This game, I have to win.

Outside, we meet more guards and Madoc, brought up from the prisons. I look for Hyacinthe, but he isn't there. I can only hope he received my note. A former falcon hands over a brace, hastily made from a branch. Madoc props it under his arm gratefully.

I see Lady Nore, mounting a reindeer, reliquary in her arms. Her hair, the color of dirty snow, blows in the wind. I see the gleam of greed in her yellow eyes, and the way Lord Jarel's grim gray hands tighten on her throat.

When I was here as a child, I was afraid all the time. I will not give in to that fear now.

We set off through the drifts. Oak maneuvers himself close to me. "Once this is over," he says, "there are some things I want to tell you. Some explanations I have to give."

"Like what?" I ask, keeping my voice low.

He looks away, toward the edge of the pine forest. "I let you believe—well, something that's untrue."

I think about the feeling of Oak's breath against my neck, the way his fox eyes looked with the pupils gone wide and black, the way it felt to bite his shoulder almost hard enough to break skin. "Tell me, then."

He shakes his head, looking pained, but so many of his expressions are masks that I can no longer tell what is real. "If I did, it would serve nothing but to clear my conscience and would put you in danger."

"Tell me anyway," I say.

But Oak only shakes his head again.

"Then let me tell *you* something," I say. "I know why you smile and jest and flatter, even when you don't need to. At first I thought it was to make people like you, then I thought it was to keep them off-balance. But it's more than that. You're worried they're scared of you."

Wariness comes into his face. "Why ever would they be?"

"Because you *terrify* yourself," I say. "Once you start killing, you don't want to stop. You like it. Your sister may have inherited your father's gift for strategy, but you're the one who got his bloodlust."

A muscle moves in his jaw. "And are you afraid of me?"

"Not because of that."

The intensity of his gaze is blistering.

It doesn't matter. It feels good to pierce his armor, but it doesn't change anything.

My greatest weakness has always been my desire for love. It is a yawning chasm within me, and the more that I reach for it, the more easily I am tricked. I am a walking bruise, an open sore. If Oak is masked, I am a face with all the skin ripped off. Over and over, I have told myself that I need to guard against my own yearnings, but that hasn't worked.

I must try something new.

As we trek across the snow, I am careful to walk lightly so that I can stay on top of the icy crust. But it still spider-webs with every step. My dress billows around me, caught by the cold wind. I realize that I am still barefoot.

Another girl might have frozen, but I am cold all the way through.

CHAPTER
17

A head of us, Lady Nore rides a shaggy reindeer. She is in a dress of
scarlet with a cloak of deeper red over it, long enough to cover the
back of the deer. The reliquary sits in her lap.

The troll king is mounted on an elk, its horns rising in an enormous
branching crown of spikes over its head. Its bridle is all green and gold.
He himself has coppery armor, beaten into that same strange pattern
again, as though each piece contains a maze.

I think of how Tiernan must have passed these last two days. At
first, hoping we would return, and then panicking as the night wore on.
By the time day dawned, he would have known he had to come with the
heart and play out Oak's scheme. He might have embroidered the plans
as he sat in the cold, angry with the prince and terrified for him. He had
no way to tell us.

And we had no way to tell him that Madoc had recruited so many
of the former falcons to his side.

Lady Nore swings down from her reindeer, her long scarlet cloak dragging through the snow like a shifting tide of blood.

"Take the storm hag," she orders, just as we planned. Just as she was commanded.

Stick soldiers grab for Bogdana. The ancient faerie sinks her nails into one of them. Lightning strikes in the distance, but she has no time to summon it closer. Her hands are caught by more stick creatures. The storm hag rips apart a stick man, but there are too many and all are armed with iron. Soon she is pressed down in the snow, iron manacles burning on her wrists.

"What is the reason for this betrayal?" Bogdana shouts at Lady Nore.

Lady Nore glances at me but does not answer.

The storm hag croaks. "Have I not done what you asked of me? Have I not conjured you a daughter from nothing? Have I not helped you make yourself great?"

"And what a daughter you have conjured," Lady Nore says, scorn in her voice.

Bogdana's eyes go to me, a new gleam in them. She sees something, I think, but is not yet sure what exactly she's seeing.

"And now, prince," Lady Nore says, returning to the plan. "Where is Mellith's heart?"

Oak is not armed, although the former falcon at his side carries the prince's sword where he can easily get it. And though his wrists appear to be tied, the cords are so loose that he can free himself whenever he wishes. The prince looks up at the moon. "My companion is supposed to be here presently."

I glance around at the assembled Folk. Part of me wants to give the signal now, to take command of Lady Nore's stick creatures and force the trolls into a surrender. But better for Tiernan to be in sight, to be sure he won't arrive at the wrong moment and jump into the fray, not knowing friend from foe.

I shift nervously, watching Lady Nore. Noting the hands of Lord Jarel around her neck, a reminder that if she could find comfort in something like that, her other actions may be impossible for me to anticipate. My gaze goes to King Hurclaw, tall and fierce-looking. For all the rumors of his madness, I understand his motives far better than hers. Still, the thirty trolls behind him are formidable.

"Perhaps you are used to your subjects biding at your pleasure, heir to Elfhame," Hurclaw says, "but we grow impatient."

"I am waiting just as you are," Oak reminds him.

Twenty minutes pass before Tiernan appears, walking over the snow, Titch on his shoulder. It feels far longer than that with Lady Nore glaring at me and Hurclaw grumbling. Madoc leans heavily on his stick and does not complain, although I worry he might collapse. At perhaps half a league off, Titch springs into the air, flapping wide wings.

The owl-faced hob circles once, then lands on Oak's arm and whispers in his ear.

"Well?" demands Hurclaw.

Oak turns to Lady Nore, as though she really is the one in charge. "Tiernan says that Madoc should begin walking toward him with a soldier, as a show of good faith. Tiernan will meet them."

"And the heart?" she inquires, and I bristle. My commands had to be more open-ended for her to perform in front of Hurclaw, but she's clever and will be looking for a loophole. I told her to behave like herself, but not to say or do anything that would give away that I had control over her. In this game of riddles and countermoves, I fear I have not been careful enough.

"He carries it in a case," Oak says. "He'll pass it to your soldier. Then Suren and I are to go to him."

Lady Nore nods. "Then make haste. Let the exchange begin."

Before, she said she wanted to keep Oak. Now she seems as if she's planning to release him. Will that seem strange to Hurclaw? Will he even notice? I slant a look at him, but there's no way to know his thoughts.

The hob takes to wing again, speeding over the snow toward Tiernan. "I have informed him you agreed to this plan," Oak says.

I doubt very much that's what he told Titch.

"With this heart, you can make the troll kings live again?" Hurclaw asks, narrowing his eyes at Tiernan and the case in his hands. "You can end the curse on my people?"

"So Bogdana told me, once, long ago," Lady Nore says with a glance toward the storm hag, whom the stick soldiers have hauled to her feet. "Though I sometimes wonder if she wanted it for her own reasons. But I remembered her story of the bones and the heart, remembered that they would be entombed beneath the Castle of Elfhame. And when the heart wasn't there, I knew that only a member of the royal family would be allowed to search through the tunnels extensively enough to find it—or to know if it had been deliberately moved. So I took Madoc and gave them a reason to look."

She nods at a former falcon, and he begins to help Madoc across the snow. I see the general lean toward him and say something. Their pace slows. We wait with the wind whistling around us and the hour growing later. Tiernan halts when he reaches Madoc and hands the case with the deer's heart inside to the soldier.

The soldier starts to walk back to us. Madoc and Tiernan remain, as though expecting that Oak and I will really be coming to join them in a moment.

Bogdana watches, amusement lifting a corner of her mouth despite the shackles she wears.

"What a delight it would have been," Lady Nore says in a tone of barely concealed malice. "To have had all that power and to have known it was Madoc's son who gave it to me."

The troll king looks at her, and I realize my mistake. I have instructed her to say nothing that will *give away* the power I have over her, but I failed to take into account that she could make airy, passive-aggressive statements implying a great deal.

"What does that mean?" Hurclaw asks.

"You ought to ask my daughter," she says with the sort of sweetness that is meant to cover the taste of rot.

His gaze goes to me. "I thought she had no tongue."

Lady Nore only smiles, and he nods to one of his Folk.

The troll soldier lifts a bow. He shoots before I can do more than raise my hand in warding.

The arrow slices through the pad of my thumb and strikes me in the side, slicing through flesh. The impact unbalances me. I hit the snow, falling to my hands and knees. I gasp for air, feeling the agony of trying to get a breath. I think one of my lungs was struck.

Scarlet stains my side. The snow is blooming red with it.

Oak starts to run toward me when the troll archers train their bows on the prince and Hurclaw calls for him to halt. The prince stops. I can see he has his sword, the restraints tying his hands are gone.

The former falcons are fanning out, and I see Hyacinthe weaving between them, moving in my direction.

This is all wrong.

"Prince," Hurclaw's voice booms. "Bring that heart to me, or I will fill you both full of arrows."

I want to call out, to order Lady Nore to command her troops to defend me, but I cannot seem to make the words come. This *hurts*.

It hurts like when—

The bone shard in my mouth—

My chest—

The ice spider-webbing under my fingers as I moved—

Oak glances at me with those trickster's eyes, panic in them. Then he inclines his head to the troll king. Walking to the former falcon, the prince takes the box with the heart from him.

And whispers something.

Hurclaw swings down from his mount.

Oak approaches him. They are close now, too close for arrows aimed at the prince not to strike their king.

Hurclaw lifts the latch with a flick of one clawed nail. A moment later the troll stumbles back, grabbing for his throat, where a needle-thin pin sticks out from his skin. The heart, dark and shriveled, falls into the snow. A deer heart, nothing more.

It was the case that mattered, the case that Oak commissioned from the blacksmith in Undry Market.

Once, the Bomb told me a story about poisonous spiders kept inside a chest. When the thief opened it, he was bitten all over.

The case was the trap.

I remember the care with which Oak set the lock, back in the cave. He must have been fitting a poisoned dart, ready to kill Lady Nore if all our other plans failed.

"Now!" shouts the soldier who'd been given the prince's whispered orders.

The falcons have made a careful circle behind the trolls. At the signal, they draw their weapons and rush in.

There is fighting all around me. Arrows and blades. Screams.

I push myself to my knees. *"Mother,"* I say, forcing it out.

That was the word meant to end the masquerade of control.

"All who follow me, you shall follow Suren's commands from this moment forward and forevermore," Lady Nore calls out, following my instructions exactly as she was supposed to, at least until she pitches her voice low. "If she can make any."

"Stop the trolls," I shout, pushing myself to my feet. When I cough, blood spatters my fingers.

"You are the one to order me captured, child?" Bogdana calls to me. "You?"

I snap off the end of the arrow, gritting my teeth against the pain. Freeing my other hand.

Hurclaw is trembling all over. Whatever the poison, it is acting fast.

"You played us false," the troll king says. "You never had Mellith's heart at all, did you?"

"He cannot lie," says Lady Nore, standing amid the carnage, watching it as though it is distant from her. "He told us he brought it north with him. He has it."

What happens when she discovers how you've deceived her? When she realizes her role in your plan?

"Call off your people," Oak tells Hurclaw. "Call them off, and I will give you the antidote."

"No!" The troll king lunges for Oak. They topple together onto the snow. Oak is skilled, but nowhere as strong as Hurclaw.

She will have to decide how much she hates me.

Oak, who abandoned looking for the heart after he went to the Thistlewitch. Who tried to send me away, who hadn't wanted to need me.

He'll steal your heart. Wasn't that what Bogdana said in the woods?

My mind drifts dizzily back to the feeling of something inside me unraveling.

To lying on the cold ice floor of the throne room. Memories flood me until it seems as though I am in two places at once.

I am another little girl, unwanted and afraid.

Hag child, a woman's voice says. *You will take Clovis's place in her bed tonight.*

The feel of heavy blankets, embroidered with stags and forests. Warm and soft. And then waking to agony, to breathlessness. To my mother looming over me, bloody knife in her hand. To the joy, the relief I felt before the feeling of betrayal so vast it consumes me.

My real mother. My beautiful mother. Bogdana.

I hear her voice. But she is not speaking to me now; she is talking to someone else, a long time ago. *I will make sure your heart beats in a new chest.*

I am terrified. I feel the agony of her nails reaching into my chest.

I blink, and it is as though I am seeing double, still half in that memory, half in the snow at the edge of night.

Mellith's heart is mine.

I ought to have known it since waking on the cold floor of the throne room. Since those dreams, which felt too real. Since the power sang through my veins, just waiting for me to reach for it.

I was afraid of magic from the first moment that Lady Nore and Lord Jarel stepped into my bedroom in the mortal world. And I couldn't stop being afraid of myself. Afraid of the monster I saw when I glimpsed my reflection in still pools, in windows.

But all I am is magic. Unmagic.

I am not nothing. I am what is beyond nothing. Annihilation.

I am the unraveler. I can pull apart magic with a thought.

An object flies from nearby. I have a moment to tell that it is made of bronze with a cork in one end before it explodes.

Flames scorch the ground. The wicker soldiers are on fire. Lady Nore screams.

I fall again. The heat on my face is scorching. My skirts are ablaze.

Tiernan is running through the snow toward Oak.

I struggle to my feet. And as I do, I see that though some of the stick creatures burn, it doesn't slow them. They fight on. A monstrous multilegged thing is ripping a troll apart, limb by limb, like a child taking apart a toy.

Hurclaw's body lies in the snow. It has gone very still.

Oak wipes dirt off his mouth with one arm and looks toward me as he gets up. I feel as though I am staring at him from very far away. There's a roaring in my ears. Now that the magic is loosed inside me, I do not think I can call it back.

And he knew. *He knew.* He'd known the whole time.

He used me like a coin in a trick. Used me so that he could say he brought Mellith's heart north, because it wasn't a lie.

I take a deep breath, pulling power toward me. The fire at the bottom of my dress goes out.

I close my eyes and focus my thoughts. When I open them, I let my power slice through enchantments. The stick things fall apart into a scattered field of blackened branches and twigs, forming a circle around me. The scent of smoke is still thick in the air.

"What have you done?" Lady Nore says, her voice coming out high.

The falcons and the trolls pause. Two run to their king and attempt to rouse him from where he lies.

Bogdana begins to cackle.

"Oak," Tiernan says, having made it to his friend's side. "What's happening to Wren?"

They're all watching me now.

Nix. Naught. Nothing. That's what you are. Nix Naught Nothing.

"Do you want to tell them, or should I?" I ask the prince.

"When did you—" he begins, but I cut him off before he can get the question out.

"When Lady Nore and Lord Jarel wanted a child to help their schemes, Bogdana tricked them." It is my turn to tell the fairy tale. "She made them a child of snow and sticks and droplets of blood, just as she told them she would. But she animated it with an ancient heart."

I recall enough of the Thistlewitch's story. I glance at Bogdana. "Mab cursed you. Is that right?"

The storm hag nods. "On my daughter's blood, that I should never harm any of Mab's line. Only Mellith could end my curse, but I could not give her new life without being asked to do so, nor could I speak of doing so without being questioned."

"You couldn't—this can't—" Lady Nore cannot bring herself to admit how deceived she was.

"Yes," I tell her. "I am what is left of Mellith. Me, whom you tortured and despised. Me, with more power than you've ever had. All of it at your fingertips. But you never bothered to look."

"Mellith. Mother's curse." Lady Nore spits the words at me. "That ought to have been your name from your making."

"Yes," I say. "I rather think you're right."

Tiernan tugs at Oak's shoulder, urging him to move. Madoc calls from across the snow. But the prince stands still, watching me.

Now I know the game he was playing, and who was the pawn. And flowing through me, I feel the endless power of nothingness, of negation.

"Will you trade Greenbriar blood for your own?" Lady Nore says. "You could have brought Elfhame to its knees. But I suppose it's me you want on my knees."

"I want you *dead*," I roar, and with no more than the force of that desire, she is spread apart on the snow. Taken apart. Unmade as surely and easily as a stick man.

I look at the red stain. At the storm hag, whose black eyes are glittering with satisfaction.

Horror chokes me. I hadn't meant to . . . I didn't think that would . . . I didn't know she would *die* just because I wished it. I didn't know I could do *that*.

The urge to shrink into myself, to hide from what I have done, is overwhelming. My shoulders hunch, my body curling in on itself. If

I was afraid of my anger before, now it has become something terrible beyond measure. Now that I can take all the pain I have ever felt and make everyone else feel it, too, I am not sure how to stop.

Hurclaw stirs. Either the poison wasn't meant to be lethal, or the dosage was for Lady Nore and is not enough to kill someone so much larger.

"Free Bogdana," I tell Hyacinthe. He does, removing the iron shackles from her wrists. His expression is wary, though. I wonder if he regrets his vow. I told him he would.

"Now take the antidote from Oak and give it to the troll king."

Hyacinthe stomps through the snow. The prince hands over a vial from his pocket without protest, his gaze still on me.

It takes a few moments for Hyacinthe to administer the liquid and a few more for Hurclaw to sit up.

I turn to the troll king as he staggers to his feet with the support of one of his subjects. "I can give you what she could not. I can break the curse."

He gives a grunt of assent.

"And in return, you will follow me."

Hurclaw, seeing the destruction around him, nods. "I await your orders, my lady."

"As for you three," I say, and look in the direction of Tiernan, Madoc, and Oak.

It is too late for them to run, and we all know it. No one can escape me now.

Go, I could tell him, and send him back to the safety of the isles of Elfhame, where he can return to being charming and beloved. A hero, even, bringing with him his father and the news of Lady Nore's demise. He could say he had an adventure.

Or I can keep him here, a hostage to force Elfhame to keep away. And mine.

Mine the only way I can ever trust, the only way I can be sure of.

"Heir to Elfhame," I say. "Get on your knees."

Prince Oak goes down smoothly, his long legs in the snow. Even bows his horned head, although I think he believes I am playing. He's not afraid. He thinks this is my revenge, to humiliate him a little. He thinks that, in a moment, all will be as it was.

"The others may go," I say. "The general, Tiernan, and any falcon who wishes to depart with them. Tell the High King and Queen that I have taken the Citadel in their name. Oak stays here."

"You can't keep him," warns Madoc.

Sink those pretty teeth into something.

I reach for the bridle, moved from around my waist when I dressed so that I might have it at hand. The leather is smooth in my fingers.

"Wren," Oak says, with the kindling of fear in his voice.

"There will be no more betrayals, prince," I tell him. He struggles at first, but when I whisper the word of command, he stops. The straps settle against his skin.

Madoc looks at me as though he would like to cut me to pieces. But he cannot.

"You don't need to do this," Oak tells me, softly. A lover's voice.

Bogdana grins from where she stands near the red stain of Lady Nore's remains. "And why not? Are you not the Greenbriar heir, the thief of her inheritance?"

"Don't be a fool," Tiernan says, ignoring the storm hag. He glances at the gathered soldiers, at the trolls, at everything he would have to fight if he tried to stop me, and narrows his eyes. "Jude might not have come for her father, but she will bring all the armies she can muster here to war with you for her brother. This can't be what you want."

I stare at him for a long moment. "Go," I say. "Before I change my mind."

"Best to do as she says." I can see Oak weigh his options and make the only real choice left to him. "Get my father back to Elfhame, or if Jude won't lift his exile, to somewhere else where he can recover. I told Wren I wouldn't leave without her."

Tiernan's gaze rests on the prince, then on me, then goes to Hyacinthe. He nods once, his expression grim, and turns away.

A few of the other knights and soldiers follow. Hyacinthe strides across the snow to my side.

"You may go with them, if you wish," I tell him. "With Madoc, and with Tiernan."

He watches as his former lover helps his former general across the snow. "Until my debt to you is paid, my place is here."

"Wren," Oak says, causing me to turn toward his voice. "I'm not your enemy."

A small smile turns up a corner of my mouth. I feel the sharpness of my teeth and roll my tongue over them. For the first time, I like the feeling.

CHAPTER

18

Bogdana leads the way to the Citadel. Hyacinthe walks by my side. When the servants bow, it is not out of mere courtesy. It comes from the same fear that caused them to make obeisances before Lady Nore and Lord Jarel.

Fear is not love, but it can appear much the same.

So too, power.

"Write to the High Court," urges Bogdana. "As its faithful servant, you've retrieved Mab's remains, ended the threat that Lady Nore presented, and set the former Grand General free. And then ask a boon—that you might remain here in her old castle and begin a Court of your own. That will be our first step. If your message gets there before Tiernan, the High Court could grant it all before they know better."

Bogdana goes on. "Tell them that the prince is with you, but sustained an injury. You will send him back to Elfhame once he is rested and ready."

Hyacinthe gives me a quick look, as though checking to see that I am the same person who so despised captivity as to help him escape from it.

I am not sure I am the same.

"Do not presume to give me orders," I tell the storm hag. "I may owe you my life, but I also owe you my death."

She steps back, chastened.

I will not make the same mistakes as Mellith.

"As soon as Tiernan and Madoc reach Elfhame, they will inform the High Court that we're keeping Oak prisoner," Hyacinthe says. "No matter what boon the High King and Queen have granted you, they'll demand his release."

"Perhaps a storm will delay their progress," I suggest, with a nod toward Bogdana. "Perhaps Madoc's injuries will require treatment. Many things can happen."

All around the hall, birds still perch. Soldiers doomed to feed on kindness. To kill nothing or be forever winged. I close my eyes. I can see the magic binding them. It is tightly coiled and weaves through their little feathered forms, tugging at their tiny hearts. It takes me a moment to find the knots, but when I do, the curses dissipate like cobwebs.

With ecstatic sighs and gasps, these falcons discover they are in their own faerie bodies once more.

"My queen," one says, over and over. "My queen."

Surely, I am easier to follow than Lady Nore.

I nod but cannot smile. Somehow as satisfied as I find myself with what I have done, it does not touch me. It is as though my heart is still locked away in a box, still buried underground.

I find myself inextricably drawn to the prisons. There, in his iron cage, I see Oak lying atop the furs I had sent down. He looks up at the ceiling, cloak pillowed beneath his head, and whistles a tune.

I recognize it as one of those we danced to back at Queen Annet's Court.

I do not shift from the shadows, but perhaps some small movement exposes me, because the prince turns toward where I am.

He squints, as though trying to make out my shape. "Wren?" he says. "Talk to me."

I don't reply. What would be the point? I know he will twist me around his finger with words. I know that if I give him half the chance, love-starved creature that I am, I will be under his spell again. With him, I am forever a night-blooming flower, attracted and repelled by the heat of the sun.

"Let me explain," he calls to me. "Let me *atone*."

I bite the tip of my tongue to keep myself from snapping at him. He meant to keep me ignorant. He tricked me. He lied with every smile. With every kiss. With the warmth in his eyes that should have been impossible to fake.

I'd known what he was capable of. Over and over, he'd shown me. And over and over, I believed there would be no more tricks. No more secrets.

Not anymore.

"You have good cause to be furious. But you couldn't have lied, had you known the truth. I was afraid you'd have to lie." He waits, and when I say nothing, rolls into a sitting position. "Wren?"

I can see the leather straps running across his cheeks. If he wears the bridle long enough, he'll have scars.

"Talk to me!" he shouts, standing and coming to the bars. I see the gold of his hair, the sharp line of his cheekbones, the glint of his fox eyes. "Wren! *Wren!*"

Coward that I am, I flee. My heart thundering, my hands shaking. But I can't pretend that I don't like the sound of him screaming my name.

ACKNOWLEDGMENTS

I am lucky to have had a bevy of encouragement and advice on this book.

I am grateful to all those who helped me along on the journey to the novel you have in your hands, particularly Dhonielle Clayton, Zoraida Córdova, Marie Rutkoski, and Kiersten White, who helped me kick around the outline of this book as we swam in a pool in the autumn. Even more so, I am grateful to Kelly Link, Cassandra Clare, Joshua Lewis, and Steve Berman, who helped me rip the manuscript apart and stitch it back together in winter (and several other times). And to Leigh Bardugo, Sarah Rees Brennan, Robin Wasserman, and Roshani Chokshi, who helped me rip it apart again in the summer.

Thank you also to the many people who gave me a kind word or a bit of necessary advice, and who I am going to kick myself for not including right here.

A massive thank-you to everyone at Little, Brown Books for Young Readers for returning to Elfhame with me. Thanks especially to my amazing editor, Alvina Ling, and to Ruqayyah Daud, who provided invaluable insight. Thank you to Nina Montoya, who gave me a different perspective. Thank you as well to Marisa Finkelstein, Virginia Lawther,

Emilie Polster, Savannah Kennelly, Bill Grace, Karina Granda, Cassie Malmo, Megan Tingley, Jackie Engel, Shawn Foster, Danielle Cantarella, and Victoria Stapleton, among others. And in the UK, thank you to Hot Key Books, particularly Jane Harris and Emma Matthewson.

Thank you to Joanna Volpe, Jordan Hill, Emily Berge-Thielmann, Pouya Shahbazian, Hilary Pecheone, and everyone at New Leaf Literary for making hard things easier. And to Joanna, Jordan, and Emily for going way above and beyond, reading through this book and giving me a bevy of critical (in both senses of the word) notes.

Thank you to Kathleen Jennings, for the wonderful and evocative illustrations.

And thank you, always and forever, to Theo and Sebastian Black, for keeping my heart safe.